TRAIN THROUGH TIME SERIES
BOOKS 1-3

BESS MCBRIDE

Train Through Time Series
Books 1-3

Compilation Copyright 2013 by Bess McBride

A Train Through Time © 2012 by Bess McBride
Together Forever Across Time © 2013 by Bess McBride
A Smile in Time © 2013 by Bess McBride

Contact information: BessMcBride@gmail.com

Cover Art by Tara West
Interior Formatting by Author E.M.S.

Published in the United States of America

ISBN-10: 1493714538
ISBN-13: 978-1493714537

BOOKS BY BESS MCBRIDE

Time Travel Romance

The Earl Finds a Bride
(Book One of the Fairy Tales Across Time series)

A Ship Through Time

The Highlander's Stronghold
(Book One of the Searching for a Highlander series)

My Laird's Castle
(Book One of the My Laird's Castle series)

My Laird's Love
(Book Two of the My Laird's Castle series)

My Laird's Heart
(Book Three of the My Laird's Castle series)

Caving in to You
(Book One of the Love in the Old West series)

A Home in Your Heart
(Book Two of the Love in the Old West series)

Forever Beside You in Time

Moonlight Wishes in Time
(Book One of the Moonlight Wishes in Time series)

Under an English Moon
(Book Two of the Moonlight Wishes in Time series)

Following You Through Time
(Book Three of the Moonlight Wishes in Time series)

A Train Through Time
(Book One of the Train Through Time series)

Together Forever Across Time
(Book Two of the Train Through Time series)

A Smile in Time
(Book Three of the Train Through Time series)

Finding You in Time
(Book Four of the Train Through Time series)

A Fall in Time
(Book Five of the Train Through Time series)

Train Through Time Series Boxed Set
(Books 1–3)

Across the Winds of Time

A Wedding Across the Winds of Time
(Novella)

Love of My Heart

Historical Romance

Anna and the Conductor

The Earl's Beloved Match
(Novella)

The Dishonest Duke

Short cozy mystery stories by Minnie Crockwell

Will Travel for Trouble Series
Trouble at Happy Trails (Book 1)

Trouble at Sunny Lake (Book 2)

Trouble at Glacier (Book 3)

Trouble at Hungry Horse (Book 4)

Trouble at Snake and Clearwater (Book 5)

Trouble in Florence (Book 6)

TRAIN THROUGH TIME SERIES

DEDICATION

To my loyal reader friends who let me know that they enjoy
the Train Through Time books and want the series to continue.

To the crews of commercial trains and the volunteers of vintage
steam trains who keep them running for our enjoyment and nostalgia.

The world would be a sadder place without passenger trains.

FOREWORD

Dear Reader,

Thank you for purchasing the *Train Through Time Series Boxed Set Books 1-3*. This boxed set is a collection of the three books in the *Train Through Time Series* which are *A Train Through Time, Together Forever Across Time* and *A Smile in Time*. All three titles are currently available for sale individually, however, the boxed set is discounted. The series will continue, and I am writing book four at the time of release of this boxed set.

Thank you for your support over the years, friends and readers. Because of your favorable comments, I continue to strive to write the best stories I can. You know I always enjoy hearing from you, so please feel free to contact me at BessMcBride@gmail.com and through my web site at www.BessMcBride.com.

Thanks for reading!
Bess

A Train Through Time

Bess McBride

PROLOGUE

"I'm not going to marry an eighteen-year-old girl, Grandmother." Robert turned away and strode to the bay window, where he stared down onto the city below.

"Robert, be reasonable. You need to marry sometime. Don't you want a wife? One young enough to give you children? Any one of your sister's friends would be quite suitable."

"I'm afraid not, Grandmother. I'm waiting."

"Waiting for what?" Mrs. Chamberlain demanded.

"The right one. She will come along. I know it."

"For goodness sake, Robert. Where will you find her? You never appear even to look."

Robert continued to stare out the window with his hands clasped behind his back. "I do not think I have met her yet, but I feel certain that I will know her when she does finally appear."

"Robert, what nonsense! You are usually so sensible in all matters, except when it comes to this subject. It seems my son's wife raised a silly romantic," the older woman muttered.

"Perhaps she did, Grandmother. Perhaps she did," he murmured with a soft smile.

"Give me great-grandchildren, Robert. I cannot live forever."

He turned away from the window and grinned at the frail-appearing, silver-haired woman resting on the green velvet settee.

"Yes, you will, Grandmother. You will outlive us all."

"Hmmpff." She looked away. "The house is quiet. We need children in it once again."

"Perhaps my sister can do the honors in a few years, Grandmother. All she lacks is a *suitable* husband." He consulted his pocket watch.

She eyed him with a piercing stare. "Have you become a confirmed bachelor, Robert? Has time passed you by, then?"

Robert laughed and bent to kiss his grandmother's pale cheek.

"I hope not, madam. I did not intend to remain a bachelor for the rest of my life."

"Then why do you wait? Give me a practical reason, none of your romantic musings."

He straightened and grinned. "I can only assure you once again that I wait for the *right* woman. I know it sounds foolish, but it is the truth." He turned toward the door. "I must go into the office to see to a few things before we leave tomorrow. I look forward to riding the train. I always do."

CHAPTER ONE

"Look at the mountain goats, Mom! Can you see them? Hurry, look!"

Ellie heard the boy's excited prattle from behind her seat and looked out the train window in time to catch sight of three white mountain goats perched precariously on a rock shelf on the craggy hills bordering the tracks. One brave goat nimbly jumped down to a lower ledge on the seemingly sheer cliff front. Ellie caught her breath and held it. The goat made a successful landing and immediately began nibbling on some tender morsel growing on the rock front.

"Did you see that, Mom? I can't believe it didn't fall. I wish we were coming here to Montana to visit, instead of going to Seattle."

A woman's voice murmured, "Shhh. Maybe we will, John. Maybe we will. Lay your head on the pillow and get some sleep. We'll be in Seattle in the morning, and then you can see Grandpa."

The view of the mountain goats receded into the dusky distance behind tall pine trees, and Ellie turned away from the window to stare down at the book in her lap, attempting once again to focus on the latest published papers on women's studies.

The voices behind her seat quieted, and she sighed. She agreed with the boy and wished she were coming to visit the magnificent Rocky Mountains instead of hurtling past to attend yet another boring seminar in Seattle.

"Women in the Pacific Northwest, Turn of the Century."

Ellie jumped slightly. Her elderly seatmate was a quiet gentleman who had spoken very little since she boarded the train in Chicago. His cultured voice startled her.

"That seems like rather heavy reading for a vacation." He favored her with a friendly smile.

Ellie glanced down at the book in her hand again, then up to his face with a sheepish grin.

"It isn't holding my interest, I'm afraid."

She studied him from under veiled lashes. Dark corduroy slacks flattered his charcoal turtleneck sweater. A silver watch adorned his left hand, which boasted a silver-colored wedding ring...the same silver that streaked his hair. Startlingly bright emerald green eyes met hers.

"Are you a student?"

She gave a quick shake of her head and nodded toward the book. "The teacher, I'm ashamed to say. I'm finding the book dull going. How can anyone take a vibrant era such as the turn of the century and make it so dull?" She shook her head and chuckled. "I'm doing some advance reading for a seminar I'm attending in Seattle."

She clamped her mouth shut, chatty soul that she was.

"Really? What kind of seminar?" He raised an elegant eyebrow.

She nodded toward the book again with a grin.

"Women's Studies, Turn of the Century America."

"So you teach women's studies?"

"Yes, at Chicago Community College."

"I see. How interesting."

"Not really," she demurred. "And what brings you onto the train today?" She eyed him with interest.

"Oh, I'm heading home. I've just been on a visit to my daughter and grandchildren in Washington, D.C."

The passing vista of snow-capped peaks atop rocky mountains dotted with evergreen trees caught her eye once again. The sun had set, and the mountains turned a hazy purple in the waning light. She sighed at the beauty of the scenery before her.

"It's beautiful here, isn't it?"

He looked past her out the window. "It is. One of the reasons I prefer to take the train."

She flashed him a quick grin. "Me, too. I love trains. I'd take them all the time if I could. They just don't have enough routes anymore," she ended on a wistful note.

"They certainly had more when I was a boy, that's for sure. My folks traveled everywhere by train in the thirties. My grandparents, too. They took us to Glacier National Park. But people have such busy lives today and no longer have time for the slower mode of travel." Green eyes twinkled as he gave her a whimsical smile.

Ellie nodded. "It's true. Every time I travel by train, I have to take extra time from work, but I do love it."

"So, why women's studies, may I ask?" He nodded toward the book in her lap.

Warmth tinged her cheeks. "Oh, I don't know. I've always found the subject interesting. Well, I would, of course. I'm a woman." She smiled crookedly. "I guess I'm what you would call a feminist. I don't really like the term, but you get the idea. I like the subject of women, their importance in history, their value in the world, and I want to pass that enthusiasm on to others, so I teach." She gave him a small self-deprecating smile. "I'm especially fascinated by women's lives at the turn of the century, but I'm finding this book a bit dry." She wiggled the book and wrinkled her nose.

"May I see it?" he asked.

She blinked and handed it to him.

He opened the cover and perused the index, stopping occasionally to smile.

"Corsets: Curves or Curses." He chuckled as he read the chapter heading aloud. "Well, that certainly doesn't sound dry." He handed the book back to her.

She grinned. "You should read the chapter titled "Hair: Halo or Hell on Earth." I can't believe women tortured their hair as much as they did in the name of fashion." Ellie virtually spat out the last word, then reined in her unruly tongue, though not before she saw the twinkle in her companion's eyes.

"Perhaps not all women in those days had your lovely brown hair." His appreciative glance brought a blush to her cheeks, and she tossed her head as if to shake off embarrassment.

"Thank you," she murmured, completely thrown off her feminist seat for a moment. She gave him a sideways glance. He appeared to be in his mid-eighties, but his full head of silver hair and bright green eyes left no doubt he'd once been a very handsome man—and still was, for that matter.

His eyes...

The twinkle continued, and for a moment, she had the craziest notion she'd seen those eyes before.

"Have we met? Have you been to Chicago? This may sound strange, but you seem familiar to me in some way."

"No, I don't think so. I've never gotten off the train in Chicago." He drew his brows together in a puzzled expression. "You know, I have to say you look familiar, as well. I wonder where we could have met."

Ellie shook her head slowly, searching his face for a clue. "I don't know. It's odd, isn't it?" She reached out a hand. "I'm sorry. I should have introduced myself. Ellie Standish." She grinned.

7

"Edward Richardson. It's nice to meet you." He gripped her hand in a surprisingly firm, warm clasp.

"And you," she murmured, reluctantly pulling her hand from his grasp, aware of an inexplicable desire to let it linger there a while.

Though handsome for a man his age, he had to be nearly fifty years her senior, and she found her blossoming attraction to him somewhat uncomfortable. Kyle would laugh, she thought, arrogantly unable to see that his fiancée might find other men attractive—even older men in their eighties. She dropped her eyes to the book in her lap, feeling slightly foolish and hoping she hadn't developed some sort of father fixation on her seat companion.

"Are you from Chicago?" Edward cocked his head to the side in a charming inquiry, eyes attentive with apparent interest.

"No, I've lived in many different places. I moved to Chicago to take the job at the college after I graduated from university."

"How do you like Chicago?"

"It's a big city," she sighed. "Fast paced. Probably too fast for me. It seems all I have time to do is go to work and come home, go to work and come home." She raised her eyes to his sympathetic face.

"I know what you mean. Washington, D.C. is hectic, as well. Although Seattle is a big town, I do find it a bit more relaxing. It has grown tremendously since I was a boy."

"Have you always lived in Seattle?"

"All my life, since 1921."

"I can't imagine living in one place that long," Ellie sighed wistfully, "but I often wonder what it would be like." She turned to look out the window as statuesque dark evergreens guarded the darkening hills above the moving train.

"Do you move a lot, Ellie?"

The intimate sound of her name on his gentle voice startled her. The question embarrassed her. It always did. She had no Romanian blood, as far she knew, but her gypsy soul would not sit quietly still...much to her regret.

"I do. I can't seem to stay in one place for long. I've been in Chicago for three years now, and I've got itchy feet. These little breaks to travel to seminars help ease the pain of trying to stay put." She gave the older man a quirky grin. "My fiancé, Kyle, is the only thing keeping me from dashing off in search of a new life, a new adventure."

"Your fiancé?" Edward's expressive eyebrows rose. "Congratulations. When are you planning to marry?"

Ellie's eyes flickered away from his before she replied airily. "Oh, we haven't set a date yet. I'm busy and so is he. He's an investment banker."

"How did you meet?"

She colored. "At a bar, of all places. I was out drinking with a few friends. He was there with friends." She shrugged carelessly. "What about you, Edward? Are you married?" Her eyes traveled to the gleaming silver band on his left hand.

His eyes followed hers. With his right hand, he gently caressed the band, the gesture suggesting love.

"I was. I feel like I still am." Green eyes met hers. "She passed away last year."

"Oh, Edward. I'm sorry."

"Thank you. It's been difficult." With a brief smile in her direction, Edward turned away to gaze out the window on the other side of the train.

Ellie surreptitiously studied his profile, open and friendly only a moment ago, now closed and somber. She didn't take his withdrawal personally. The working of his jaw revealed emotions he struggled to control. She still couldn't shake the familiar feeling she'd seen him before.

Forcing herself to turn away, she picked up her book again with a renewed earnest determination to make some headway in her reading. She stared at the words on the pages, each one blending into the next, unable to concentrate on the task at hand.

A glance from under her lashes to the left revealed Edward's eyes were closed. He appeared intent on sleep. She sighed and turned toward the window. Her pale face, softly highlighted by the overhead lights, reflected in the glass. The passing scenery faded into darkness with only an occasional twinkling light visible in the distance. She leaned her head against the cool glass and closed her eyes.

Drowsily, she wondered if Kyle were sleeping. For the last year, he'd adopted the habit of going to bed promptly at 10 p.m. and leaving the apartment by 7 a.m. to catch the El. Since she barely got home from class by 9 at night, she hardly saw him. Her absence to attend the seminar in Seattle would hardly be noticed in his busy world. It didn't matter. The first flush of love had long gone, leaving the makings of a long and boring marriage in its wake. But she was determined to follow through with the wedding, if and when she ever set a date. She was tired of moving, tired of being alone, tired of staring at an unknown future and ready to settle down—or ready to settle, at least.

CHAPTER TWO

An unfamiliar jolt of the train awakened Ellie. Her eyes flew open. For the most part, the train ride had been smooth, the huge silver giant effortlessly gliding along the tracks with few sounds other than an occasional whistle and no untoward movements.

Blearily, she looked out the window. Darkness had given way to dawn, and a soft rosy glow peeped through the tall evergreens which continued to grace the landscape. Softly misted mountains appeared in the distance. She glanced at her watch. Four more hours to Seattle.

With a crick in her neck, Ellie straightened and raised her arms above her head. She turned to ask Edward how he'd slept, but his seat was empty. In fact, something seemed to be wrong with his seat. She rubbed the sleep from her eyes and stared at it again. Something was definitely wrong. Where was the armrest she'd leaned on the night before? She ran a hand along the seat cushion, her eyes widening at the rich look and feel of the red velvet along the bench.

Bench? Had she wandered into another car in the night? Where was she?

A buzz of female voices from the rear penetrated her consciousness, and she craned her neck to see over the back of her seat, or rather, her bench. Six or seven young women lounged about on plush antique rattan furniture in various poses—some perched on the edge of their seats, prim and proper with clasped hands; others balanced teacups above saucers, while another young lady leaned over a pink velvet sofa and whispered to a blonde woman. An occasional tinkling laugh behind a discreet hand broke the steady hum of chatter.

Ellie blinked and stared at their clothing. Huge hats, festooned with feathers and flowers, towered above small heads supported by long delicate necks. As a group, the young women wore a similar style of clothing, with high-collared white lacy blouses. Some wore tailored dark jackets. Ellie's startled eyes traveled the length of their skirts—long, flowing garments in varying shades of dark colors that covered all but the tips of their shoes. The woman who stood had an impossibly tiny waist.

With a pounding heart and a dry mouth, Ellie slid down out of sight. What was going on? She backed into the corner of the bench with her face pressed against the velvet of the upholstered bench back. She strained to make out words but could hear only the lilting rhythm of the women's voices, broken by the timbre of an occasional male voice. She hadn't seen any men on first glance. Ellie rubbed her sweating palms on her denim skirt and dragged in an uneven breath. The rumbling of the train along the tracks proved she was still onboard, albeit the carriage rocked and swayed more than it had the night before. An unusual odor permeated the air—the pleasant smell of cooked food combined with...was it...coal?

Ellie chewed a corner of her lower lip nervously and pressed even more tightly into the corner of her seat, hoping to make herself invisible. She studied the carriage door just in front of her bench as it rattled with the motion of the train. Constructed of a large pane of antique leaded glass framed by dark varnished wood, the elegant door allowed as much light to stream in as possible, given the narrow confined space between cars. Lovely as it was, she hoped fervently the door wouldn't open to expose her presence to a newcomer entering the room. Fairly sure she'd unwittingly trespassed onto a first-class lounge, she wondered how on earth she'd managed to sleepwalk her way into a luxurious car that smacked of turn-of-the-century style.

The sound of a man's cheerful laughter caught her ear. Against her better judgment and free will, she slid up on one knee and peeked over the back of the seat to survey the scene behind her again. Her widened eyes homed in on the author of the husky laugh as he leaned against the leaded glass door at the back of the carriage. She gasped against the velvet upholstery of the seat back, mild hysteria robbing her of breath.

A dark head of well-groomed, thick, wavy chestnut hair crowned a handsome angular face. He smiled broadly at a woman seated in a chair nearby. The generous smile should have held her attention, but she couldn't take her eyes off his attire. A dark blue jacket hung carelessly open to reveal a gray vest over a white high-collared shirt. Matching dark blue trousers revealed long, lean legs that began at a slender waist and seemed to travel forever until they ended at the tips of highly polished black boots.

Mr. Debonair pulled a watch on a chain from a pocket in his vest and consulted it. With a charming smile which lit up his face, he leaned down to the young beauty at his side and spoke in a low voice. Ellie's ears perked at the woman's tinkling laugh. It seemed restrained, lacking gusto and spontaneity. She couldn't see the woman's face clearly in the back of the car.

Ellie lowered herself back into her seat, willing herself to miniaturize. She turned a speculative eye on the stylish door in front, presumably leading to the next car. The door looked as though it opened outward instead of sliding open as did the rest of the train's compartments. A brass handlebar preserved the glass from unruly fingerprints.

Ellie gathered her courage as she imagined a scene where she bolted through the door and escaped into the next carriage. If she acted quickly enough, the oddly dressed passengers would never see or hear anything except the sound of the door closing behind her. If the next car turned out to be first class, she would feign ignorance—which was true—and ask to be directed back to her seat in coach.

She lowered her feet to the carpeted floor and slid to the edge of her seat, no easy task on velvet. Just as she prepared to spring for the door, it opened wide, and she fell back against her seat. A strong smell of coal assaulted her nose before the door shut quietly behind the newcomer. A white-coated waiter of African descent precariously balanced china on a round silver serving tray with the palm of one hand while securing the door behind his back with the other.

Ellie scooted back into her corner, but the motion caught the waiter's eye as he took a step forward. He stared down at her, dark eyes widening at the sight of the stowaway.

"Ah, tea is here," a querulous female voice rung out. "Come, come, young man, bring it here. We've been waiting for quite some time for refreshment, and I must say I am quite parched."

Ellie hunched her head into her shoulders like a turtle and gave the startled young man an uneasy grin. With a plea in her eyes, she raised a finger to her lips and shook her head.

He hesitated and blinked at her, obviously debating what to do. Ellie mouthed the word "please" as she continued to shake her head.

"Young man." The impatient elderly female voice forced a decision on him. He furrowed his brow, gave a slight shake of his head and moved past the bench toward the open seating area of the car.

Ellie held her breath, wondering if anyone was going to come around the corner and demand her instant removal. She would be very happy to comply, she thought, as she eyed the door once again. She considered the wiser plan would be to exit in the waiter's wake. It seemed likely no one would follow the young man's progress out of the carriage.

"Ahh, there you are." The older woman seemed temporarily appeased by the arrival of her tea. Ellie didn't remember seeing any senior citizens on her quick survey of the passengers. "Yes, that's it. Two sugars will do. Thank you."

Ellie strained to hear the handsome man's voice, but the tinkle of teacups on saucers and the hum of muted voices drowned him out. She kept an eye on the aisle, preparing for a quick exit in the waiter's shadow.

Within moments, he returned to peer around the edge of her seat. She peeked up at him. His white cotton, brass-buttoned tunic jacket gleamed over a clean, ankle-length white apron which covered dark trousers. He gripped the now-empty tray tightly in both hands.

"Miss, what are you doing in here?" he hissed. "I don't think you're supposed to be here, are you?" He threw a quick glance over his shoulder.

Ellie hunched her shoulders and shook her head. She matched the hush of his whisper.

"I don't know what I'm doing here. I went to sleep in my seat last night and woke up here this morning. Seat 31B. Do you know where that is? Can I follow you back?"

Dark brown eyes blinked. "31B? I don't know where that seat is, miss. I've never heard of it. I think I'd better find the conductor and bring him to you."

"Oh, yes, that's a good idea. Please do. Actually, let me come with you. He'll figure out where my seat is. So, is this like some kind of reenactment thing?" Ellie moved to the edge of her seat to rise, her hand roaming the seat behind her in search of her purse. Oh, surely, she had her purse!

"Reenactment?" He raised his eyebrows and shook his head inquiringly.

"Yeah, you know, like Civil War reenactments. Where they all dress up in period costumes, act out historical scenarios?" She dropped her eyes to search the corners of her seat. Where was her purse?

"Steward, is anything wrong?"

The close proximity of the masculine voice startled her, and she jerked and twisted around to find Mr. Debonair standing at the end of the bench staring straight down at her.

The steward backed up toward the door with a subservient nod in the well-dressed man's direction. He clutched the tray to his chest.

"No, nothing's wrong, Mr. Chamberlain. This lady seems to be lost. I think she's from one of the other cars, you know, the immigrant cars. I don't know how she got in here. I'm gonna go get the conductor. He'll take her back where she belongs."

Ellie flung an astonished look in the steward's direction. *Immigrant?* What was he talking about?

"I see. Well, miss, how did you find your way to this car?"

Mr. Chamberlain came to stand in front of her. His green eyes ran up and down the length of her body with a frank appraising gaze, and Ellie took offense. She jumped up from her seat.

"Now just a minute there, Mr...uh...Chamberlain." She drew herself up to her entire five foot two inches and lifted her chin. "First off, you can drop that eyeing me up and down thing. It's very rude and typically male." An arch of one of his dark eyebrows did not deter her. "And another thing. Though this may be first class, it's not your train or your passenger car, and frankly, it's none of your business. So, if you don't mind, I'll just be off with the steward here."

The young steward gaped at her. He pressed himself into the thick glass door as if wishing he could disappear.

"Oh no, miss. You can't come with me," he whispered. "It's not safe."

Ellie twisted around to look behind her and caught a quick impression of the room in its entirety. Teacups stilled as the group of hat-festooned female heads looked up. She gritted her teeth, tightened her lips in a semblance of a smile, nodded in their direction and turned to face the steward.

"Oh, sure it is. I've traveled by train many times. So, let's go."

"Just a moment, miss." Ellie stilled at the sound of Mr. Chamberlain's velvety voice. She glanced over her shoulder, unwilling to give him the satisfaction of turning around to face him. Why should she?

"Yes, Mr. Chamberlain?"

He dipped his head to the side in a motion that cut into her anger with its charming boyishness. "I apologize, madam. You are quite right. No matter where your seat on this train, I did not have the right to stare at you so boldly. I would not have done so with any other woman in this carriage."

"Thank you," Ellie murmured with a regal nod in his direction which belied her inner turmoil. The man certainly was smooth. "And now, if you don't mind, I'm leaving." She turned toward the door. Seeing the steward still frozen in place with wide eyes, she pushed against the bar and opened the door to an unexpected blast of wind. Determined to leave with some semblance of huffy dignity, she hurriedly stepped out of the car, then reared back and faltered when she realized that the connector was covered only by some sort of canvas tarp, allowing a roaring wind to rush through the unsealed seams of the canvas. She stared at the uneven jostling between the two cars and wondered how she was going to manage to jump the crosswalk without losing her balance. With nothing to hold onto, Ellie braced herself against the wall, dizzy from the sight of the uneven dance of the connectors between the two cars and nauseated from the smell of coal and the increased rocking of the car on the platform. Her knees buckled.

A strong hand grasped her around the waist in a reassuring grip. Though she wore a bulky turtleneck sweater, the warmth of his hand seemed to sear her skin.

"Steady now, madam." Mr. Chamberlain decisively hauled her back into the carriage. His accomplice, the steward, shut the door behind them and posted himself as a sentry.

Ellie stared up at her handsome would-be rescuer as he lowered her back to the seat. He bent down to peer into her face.

"Are you well, madam? Though you stalked very prettily out of here, you seemed a bit shaky on the platform. I thought it best to bring you back inside." Twinkling green eyes belied the note of concern in his voice.

Ellie nodded, tongue-tied by his nearness. Her eyes locked on the cleft in his chin—a feature which gave his lean face a virile masculinity at odds with the fancy costume party she'd inadvertently crashed. His easy grin compelled an answering smile, and she clamped her lips together and fought against his obvious magnetism.

"Bobby, what is going on here? Who is this?"

Bobby's conversation partner, a young woman with golden hair swept up into a glorious Gibson-style hairdo, peered around the corner. She stared wide-eyed at a shrinking Ellie, who subconsciously raised a hand to tidy her own mop of curly brown hair, hopefully still tied back in a braid down her back.

Bobby straightened. "Nothing to worry about, Melinda. This unfortunate young woman strayed onto our car by accident, probably at the last stop. The steward was just about to locate the conductor for us." He turned to the young waiter still guarding the door. "What is your name, young man?"

"Samuel, sir." Samuel dipped his head. "But, no, sir, I didn't bring her here. No, sir. I found her sitting right there." He bobbed his head up and down.

Ellie cringed. Good gravy! What was the matter with the young fellow? He seemed so nervous. Did he think he'd lose his job? Surely, they had a union! She sprang to his defense.

"That's right. Samuel didn't—"

"Samuel, would you be so good as to find the conductor and bring him here?" Mr. Chamberlain glanced down at Ellie with a dancing light in his eyes. "Our guest still seems a bit shaken from the jostling between the cars, and I think she should take a cup of tea with us here."

"Bobby?" Melinda moved forward to stare at Ellie with frank curiosity. "Are you sure that's wise?" Her sweet smile took the sting from her words. "I mean...what if someone is looking for her...perhaps her...em...people from the other cars?"

Ellie rolled her eyes and struggled to rise, though it seemed that three people hovered in her confined space all of a sudden, making it almost impossible for her to get up unless someone moved. She sank back down.

"Listen, y'all." She felt compelled to drawl, though she'd never lived in the South in her life. "I'm just fine, and I can find the conductor on my own. I can't imagine how I wandered onto this car in the first place. I don't have any *people*." She tossed a quick glance at darling Melinda. "And I don't need your tea. I don't even like tea. So if you will just excuse me, I'll get out of your hair."

Melinda broke out into the laugh that Ellie recognized from moments before. Her laugh certainly seemed spontaneous, but she repressed it behind a graceful hand.

"Nonsense, madam," said Bobby. "You'll do no such thing. You cannot travel between the cars. I insist that you sit down at once, until I'm certain you feel better."

Ellie glared up at him. His six-foot frame might intimidate other women, but she had no doubt she could jump up and wriggle past him to escape through the door. If only she could cross to the other car. What kind of carnival train was she on, anyway?

"I'm perfectly fine, *Bobby*." The name hardly suited him. "Just a drop in my blood sugar, I'm sure. I probably just need to eat something."

Bobby inclined his head in a gesture that smacked faintly of arrogance. "My name is *Robert* Chamberlain, madam. *Robert*. Only my irrepressibly spoiled sister calls me Bobby...and always against my wishes."

"Whatever is the matter up there, Robert?" The quavering voice of the elderly woman seemed strong enough to reach the front of the car, though thankfully she did not appear, as well.

A faint hint of lavender wafted into Ellie's nose, and she twisted her neck upward to see several more young women peering over the top and around the corner of her bench. The large beribboned and feathered hats bumped into one another as they ogled her with curiosity.

Ellie hunched into her seat, her cheeks burning. She suddenly understood how animals felt in a zoo. Hopefully, these women wouldn't start petting her.

"It seems we have an unexpected guest, Grandmother." Robert favored Ellie with a considering gaze while he allowed his voice to carry to the rear of the train. "A woman lost her way on the train and found herself in our carriage by accident. She feels a bit unwell at the moment."

Ellie glared at him, her chaotic thoughts struggling to form choice responses.

"Well, bring her back here, Robert. Let me look at her. I'd be grateful for a new diversion."

Ellie's eyes widened and she opened her mouth to retort, but Robert managed to beat her to it.

"I doubt she considers herself a diversion, Grandmother, but with your permission, I will bring her back for a cup of tea to help settle her nerves."

Robert gave Melinda a look, and she immediately jumped into action. "All right, ladies, why don't we return to the lounge so Miss...er...the nice lady can come and have a cup of tea?" She skillfully shepherded the women away, to the increased sound of high-pitched questions.

"No, I don't know where she came from, ladies..." Melinda's voice trailed off as she moved away.

Ellie glanced back up at the two men staring at her. Robert nodded at Samuel, who gave Ellie a last sympathetic glance before pushing open the door to cross over to the next car. She would have followed, but Robert managed to block her way without really seeming to do so. He casually leaned against the doorjamb in a relaxed fashion but with a presence reminiscent of a stonewall.

She slumped, sudden exhaustion overcoming her desire for flight.

CHAPTER THREE

"May I help you up?" Robert moved away from the door and extended a hand to help her rise. Ellie stared at the well-groomed hand for a moment before she reluctantly took hold.

"I'm just waiting for the conductor. That's all. *Then* I'll be on my way."

"Certainly, Miss...em..." He extended his arm for her to take, but she pretended not to see as she glanced down and brushed imaginary wrinkles from her skirt. Out of the corner of her eye, she caught his wry expression and half smile as he dropped the supportive arm to his side.

"Ellie," she murmured. "Ellie Standish."

"Miss Standish." With an elegant wave of his hand, he indicated she should precede him toward the back of the car.

"Mr. Chamberlain," she acknowledged with a nod as she moved past him with a straight back. Her moment of dignity vanished when she tripped on the unexpectedly plush red and gold oriental carpeting underfoot.

Robert's hand shot out to take her arm and steady her. With a burning face, she righted herself, nodded thanks and pulled her arm from his warm grasp. She moved into the center of the room where the occupants of the lounge alternately stood or sat. An elderly woman in a dark, high-necked, Victorian-style silk dress presided on a red velvet-cushioned rattan loveseat. She signaled Ellie forward.

"Come, girl. Sit here." With an incline of the large, dark beribboned hat on her head, she indicated Ellie should sit in the single chair beside her own.

Ellie paused, unwilling to be spoken to in such a high-handed way, and equally unwilling to offend a senior citizen...especially a woman who apparently thought she had some sort of regal power. Acutely aware she was the center of attention as she hovered in the middle of the room, Ellie swallowed her pride, moved quickly to the luxurious chair and sat down.

Robert returned to his original position at the back door to lean against it with crossed arms. Ellie watched several pairs of admiring female eyes follow his progress and she understood their message. He presented a dashing figure—straight out of some Victorian romance in his well-tailored and immaculate dark blue coat and trousers.

"So, what is this I hear about you stowing away on our carriage, young lady?"

Ellie's bemused eyes flew to the older woman's arrogant face. She appeared to be in her late seventies, though her costume made it difficult to guess an accurate age. Sharp blue eyes appraised Ellie steadily.

"Listen, Mrs. Chamberlain, is it?" The older woman tipped her head in a slight nod. "Well, listen, Mrs. Chamberlain. I'm not a *stowaway* per se. I'm not sure how I came to be in *your carriage*, but as I've told your grandson over there, I'm more than happy to be on my merry way."

Ellie looked across the room to see Melinda's eyes widen with apprehension. Let the girl worry. She had no intention of being bullied any more by these strange characters. She returned her challenging gaze to Mrs. Chamberlain's face. Two red spots appeared on the older woman's cheeks. The smell of coal must have blurred Ellie's common sense because she didn't quit there.

"I didn't really know people had railway *carriages* of their own these days. But if you have leased this one, then I'm sorry to have stumbled onto it. As I said, I'm ready to skedaddle, but *Bobby* here kept me from leaving with Samuel."

"Samuel?" Mrs. Chamberlain wrinkled her forehead with an eye toward Robert.

"The steward," Robert murmured from his position along the wall.

"The steward? What does he have to do with all of this?"

"Nothing. He just happened to see me in the seat up there." Ellie jerked her head in the direction of the front of the car. "He seems very worried, by the way. You aren't going to try to get him in trouble, are you? Like report him? Because he didn't do anything."

"Good gracious! What is she talking about? Robert? Melinda, pour the woman some tea, will you, dear?"

Melinda sprang into action and picked up an empty teacup and saucer from the table in front of the loveseat on the opposite wall.

A rustle of skirts and quiet murmurs left a befuddled Ellie with a quick impression that all of the other women resumed their seats. Only a lone dark-haired woman in a white shirtwaist blouse and dark brown skirt remained standing near Robert.

"Samuel will be fine, Miss Standish." Robert surveyed her with continuing amusement. Even from this distance, emerald sparks lit up his eyes.

"Standish, you say?" Mrs. Chamberlain turned crinkled eyes back to Ellie, who tore her gaze away from Robert once again. "That's a fine old name in American history. Are you related? How is it that you come to be traveling in the immigrant section, then?"

Ellie reached up to rub her temples. A headache seemed imminent.

"I don't think I'm related to Miles Standish, if that's what you mean. If I am, it's probably through some illegitimate offspring or something. And I don't know what you mean by *immigrant* section. Are you talking about a coach section? Trains don't have class systems anymore. Thank goodness!"

Ellie rattled on, only slightly aware of several gasps from the other side of the room. She turned toward the unusually silent young women and noticed that several of them stared down at the carpeting with rosy cheeks.

"Young woman, we do not speak that way in public. I can see that you probably are indeed from the working class. Please refrain from any further unsavory comments while in my carriage."

Melinda rose and crossed the room with Ellie's tea, the delicate cup rattling in the saucer. Ellie looked up to see the young blonde biting her lower lip and shaking her head ever so slightly as she met Ellie's eyes. Ellie reached for the cup, forgetting she didn't want the tea.

With a cautious look in her grandmother's direction, Melinda swished her way back to her seat.

Ellie stared down into her cup and took a deep breath.

"I'm sorry, Mrs. Chamberlain. I didn't mean to offend you. I just don't know what you mean by an *immigrant* section."

"That is not the offense to which I referred, Miss Standish."

Robert interceded, a hint of laughter in his voice. "I believe my grandmother referred to the...suggestion that Miles Standish might have had an...indiscretion. Isn't that so, Grandmother?"

"Robert, that sort of talk does not bode well for you, either."

Ellie stared at two deep dimples in Robert's angular cheeks. Although seemingly a domineering, arrogant man—much like his grandmother—the whimsical dimples warmed his face and made her heart flutter. The teacup rattled in the saucer as her hand trembled. She lowered the cup to the teak occasional table beside her seat.

"Um, do y'all have any bottled water, by chance?" she asked.

Heads turned toward one another.

"Bottled water?" Melinda murmured.

"Yeah, you know, just some water. I've got the worst headache."

Melinda half rose, her sympathetic face filled with concern.

"Sit down, Melinda, there's a good girl," Mrs. Chamberlain said. "Miss Standish, I don't think we have anything such as *bottled* water. Would you care for a lemonade instead? When the steward comes back, he can fetch one for you."

Ellie rubbed her temples once again. "No, no, thank you, Mrs. Chamberlain. By then, the conductor will have come to get me, and I can get back to my seat and my purse and get something for my headache."

"I see." The older woman nodded. "Drink some tea. The hot water will help clear your headache."

Ellie gave her a quick smile and nodded. Would the conductor ever come? She picked up the delicate pink-and-gold-decorated porcelain teacup again and swallowed the hot liquid. It did feel pleasant in her dry mouth.

"Miss Standish. If you're not in the immigrant section...and forgive us for assuming so, are you in tourist class?" Melinda spoke from across the room. "I've seen that carriage before...once."

"I think there is some confusion as to what carriage Miss Standish was on, and I do not think she feels up to resolving the matter at the moment. Perhaps we should let her sip her tea in comfort for a few minutes before we assail her with more questions."

Ellie turned toward the voice of the dark-haired female who stood next to Robert. A beautiful woman who appeared to be in her late thirties, she stood almost as tall as Robert. Her slender build showed off her costume to great advantage. She regarded Ellie with dark-lashed, warm brown eyes and a pleasant curve of her full lips.

"A friend of the family, Mrs. Constance Green." Robert made the introduction with familiarity. Ellie's heart skipped a beat. When he looked at Constance, his grin took on an affectionate twist.

Constance nodded in greeting but did not move forward. Ellie studied the heightened color on the beauty's face, her feminine instincts telling her that Constance was interested in Robert. She bit back a small sigh of disappointment. She wasn't surprised. The man certainly was handsome!

Ellie nodded gratefully to Constance and took another sip of the surprisingly brisk tea.

"I really don't know what's taking the conductor so long to get here.

I'm sure he'll get me back to my car and my seat, and I can get out of your hair. You must have things you want to do."

"I doubt if the conductor will arrive before our next stop, at Wenatchee," Robert offered. "Unless he was in the dining carriage next door, Samuel will not be able to contact him until he can make his way to the carriages further down."

"Yes, I'm sure that's quite true, Grandson. You'll just have to settle in for a bit, Miss Standish. We won't reach Wenatchee for another hour yet."

"An hour?" Ellie looked from Robert to his grandmother. "Really? Well, why can't Samuel just call the conductor? I really should make my way next door to find out what's going on." She attempted to rise but Mrs. Chamberlain laid a restraining hand on her arm for just a brief second before removing it.

"No, Miss Standish. That is not possible. It is not safe." Mrs. Chamberlain's words reawakened a vivid picture of the funhouse connection between the trains. Never one for such carnival rides, Ellie didn't know if she would make the crossing in one piece. She slumped back into her chair and picked up her tea to toss off the last dregs. Uncomfortably aware that the women on the other side of the room continued to stare at her, she set her cup down, lowered her eyes and busily picked at a loose thread on her skirt.

"Miss Standish, forgive me, but I was wondering. What material is your skirt? I haven't seen one like that before."

A younger woman about Melinda's age gazed at Ellie with an earnest expression. Her blue hat with decorative netting contrasted wonderfully with golden chestnut hair.

Ellie suspected she'd fallen into a wormhole. What kind of a question was that?

"Denim. You know? A jeans skirt?" She hunched her shoulders self-consciously as she looked down at her ankle-length skirt. "I know they're a bit old-fashioned, but I like them. They're comfortable for traveling."

Melinda giggled. "There, Amy, I told you it was called denim...like serge. A sturdy fabric used by dockworkers and such." She turned to Ellie. "Did you make the skirt yourself, Miss Standish? I have never seen this material in a skirt before."

Ellie stared at the characters before her with narrowed eyes. Was this some elaborate hoax?

"No, I bought it, Melinda. Just like you can buy denim skirts in your local department store." The gig was up! Ellie crossed her arms and leaned back in her seat. She avoided looking at Robert, knowing he would continue the charade.

"I must say, you all are certainly deep in character. Is this some sort of Victorian reenactment I've wandered into?" She scanned the eyes of the women across the room, daring them to continue the lie.

"Reenactment?" Amy's young forehead wrinkled. "I beg your pardon?"

"Oh, please, ladies and gentleman. You know, like a Civil War reenactment or a Mountain Man rendezvous." She continued to avoid Robert's eyes, though she was acutely aware he watched her. "I'm just exhausted and confused enough to believe in all this. You've had your fun, though. Are you a period piece ensemble on tour? Oh, wait, I know! One of those mystery dinner theater groups!" Ellie clapped her hands, thankful to have found an explanation for her bizarre companions. She ignored the lack of affirmative response. "Well, y'all have done a wonderful job. I almost... I gotta tell you...I almost thought for a moment...that I'd stepped back in time. Good job!"

"Miss Standish, what are you babbling about?" Mrs. Chamberlain turned toward her grandson. "Robert, I do not think she is well. Come see if she has a fever. No, on second thought, do not. She might carry some sort of contagious disease."

Ellie shook her head warningly at Robert, but he dutifully crossed the carriage and put a hand to her forehead. His touch tingled. She jumped back into her seat and swatted at his hand.

"That's enough, thank you, Robert. I'm just fine. All right, you guys, so how 'bout that bottled water? Can I have some now?"

"She has no fever, Grandmother, though it appears her hazel eyes are flashing fire." With a playful grin, he chuckled and ran a finger lightly across her cheek before he moved away.

Ellie jumped up in agitation. "All right, y'all. I'll admit that I'm going to have a hard time getting to the next car. I'm petrified to cross that itty bitty thing between us, but I'm ready to head out." She ignored the well-acted stunned expressions on their faces and turned to head toward the door. A sudden thought struck her, and she rotated to face the group. "You know, I teach women's studies. The turn of the century is one of my areas of interest. What a coincidence that I should meet you all, eh? Too funny!" She dipped a quick curtsey in deference to the theme. "Thanks for the tea, and thanks for the show. It's been great."

Ellie spun away and made a beeline for the door before anyone tried to stop her. She slid the heavy door open and stepped out onto the narrow connector between the two cars. Dragging the door shut behind her, she hesitated on the landing as she stared wide-eyed at the precarious, wildly moving floor between the two cars. Wind rushed through the connector—wind and the dense smell of coal. She moved forward with a tentative step, preparing herself for a balancing act extraordinaire as she crossed the rocking corridor. That there was no way she could fall to her death on the tracks below did nothing to ease her fear of heights and fast moving, rocking trains.

She heard the door open behind her but refused to turn around. If anything, the sound gave her the impetus to jump across the uneven connection in a single motion. She steadied herself on the opposite landing.

"Well, Miss Standish, I see you made it across safely. I was worried about you." Robert raised his voice to make himself heard above the rumbling on the tracks and the whistling of the wind.

She turned to face him. With legs apart, he stood with effortless balance...of course.

"Oh, I'm fine, thank you very much." It seemed obvious her words faded on the wind, because he frowned and gave his head a slight shake.

She cupped one hand to her mouth to shout. "Yes, I'm fine, thank you. See ya!" Ellie turned away and stopped short with surprise. Facing yet another old-fashioned wooden door, she reached for the brass handle. The hairs on the back of her neck tingled. She knew he watched her. An unexpected sway of the carriage threw her off balance again, and she staggered against the closed door.

As she attempted to right herself on the lurching train, she saw Robert nimbly step across the connector. He grasped her hand and reached around her waist with the other to brace her body against his as another round of rocking overtook the train.

He spoke near her ear. "Here, now. I have you," he said soothingly. "You really should have asked for help, Miss Standish. I don't think you have your train legs yet."

Unnerved by the unexpected thrill that shot through her at his touch, she attempted to pull away. With a sigh, Robert kept firm hold on her and reached for the door.

"All right, madam. If you insist. By all means, let us see if we can find the conductor in the dining carriage." He pulled open the door and released her. Ellie stumbled through the entrance and entered another nightmare. White linen tablecloths with vases of flowers brightened dining tables hosting yet more people in Victorian dress. Several African-American stewards moved through the length of the car, ably balancing plates of food on large round trays. The ornate décor of the dining car matched the lounge car with the glow of highly varnished wood walls and ceiling, brass fittings and red/orange oriental carpeting.

Though the rocking motion of the car eased once they were out of the connector, Ellie leaned against the nearest wall for support. She turned to stare at Robert as he entered and quietly shut the door.

"Are you kidding? This is huge," she said.

Robert cocked his head with a puzzled look. With a glance over her head, he surveyed the room and nodded.

"It is a rather large dining car, isn't it? We usually take our meal in our carriage."

Ellie shook her head. "No, I mean your group. This Victorian thing. The train. I assume you all hooked your cars up to the train at some point, because I didn't see them when we left. How do you all do this? It must cost quite a bit."

With a slight shrug of his elegant shoulders, he searched her face with an expression not unlike a laboratory researcher studying his specimen. His lips twitched. "You say the strangest things, Miss Standish. I am not sure what you are asking."

She shot him a dark look and stomped her foot...just a bit. "Oh, stop this silly act, *Bobby*. Y'all are driving me nuts. I feel like I've landed in a madhouse."

Apparently unimpressed by her righteous rage, he chuckled and murmured in a low voice. "I am beginning to feel the same way, Miss Standish."

"Mr. Chamberlain, can I help you?" A tall man who appeared to be in his early forties approached—his wheel hat, dark suit and bow tie marking him as a conductor. A thick dark mustache dominated his pale face. Blue eyes flickered to Ellie and then back to Robert. He moved with a balanced stride undeterred by the rocking of the train, coming to a halt in front of Ellie and Robert, his manner deferential but quietly authoritative.

"Yes, Conductor, Miss—"

"I can speak for myself. Listen, Mr...?" With no encouragement from the conductor, she gulped and hurried on. "Listen, sir, somehow I've gotten myself onto this section of the train by accident. I don't know what happened. I went to sleep last night and when I woke up..." She paused, catching his perplexed eyes sliding toward Robert. "Excuse me, could you look at me and not Mr. Chamberlain, please? *I'm* talking." Ellie tilted her head back and eyed both tall men with irritation and a certain amount of trepidation as they exchanged a glance.

What if she stood on tiptoe?

"Miss Standish. If you would allow me, perhaps I could explain to—"

"No, thanks, Robert. I've got this covered." She tossed the words over her shoulder and turned back to the conductor. "If you would just listen to me for a moment." She swallowed hard, her courage failing. Why did the man continue to look over her head to Robert? "What I'm trying to say is I'm in seat 31B. That's where I went to sleep last night. This morning, I woke up on his carriage." She jerked her head in Robert's direction. "I don't know how or why—and believe me, I *will* be seeing a doctor about this when I get back—but for right now, I'd just like to get back to my seat, get my purse and get myself organized." She gulped air and waited expectantly.

The conductor stared at her with troubled eyes and a grave expression.

"Miss Standish, I am not sure what has occurred here. We do not in fact have a seat 31B." Could you be mistaken about the number?" She caught his veiled glance at her clothing. "Could you perhaps be traveling in tourist class or—forgive me—in immigrant class?"

CHAPTER FOUR

Although the dining car seemed warm, in fact too warm, Ellie broke out into a cold sweat. Her knees buckled slightly, and she would have slid to the floor had Robert not caught her elbow. She turned to him with a beseeching look.

"Robert, help me. Please don't continue to do this." She turned back to the conductor. "Are you part of this thing, as well?"

He raised a thick, dark eyebrow. "Thing, Miss Standish?"

She sighed and rubbed her forehead. What a nightmare!

"This period piece you all are doing." She heard the exhaustion in her voice.

"Miss Standish, please let me lead you to a table. I think you need something to eat or drink." Robert slid his hand from her elbow to the small of her back and guided her forward. The conductor stood to the side to let them pass.

"Conductor, if you will allow us a few minutes..."

"Certainly, Mr. Chamberlain. Take as much time as you need." He pulled a large golden watch from his coat pocket and flicked it open. "We reach Wenatchee in forty minutes."

Ellie watched in bemusement. Robert propelled her forward like a small child. About a dozen men and women occupied most of the tables in the dining car—all of them in period costume of the late Victorian/early Edwardian era, the women in lovely high-collar lace shirtwaist blouses and decorative hats, the men in suits with vests, many of them sporting large mustaches. Ellie felt their stares as she and Robert moved through the car. She had obviously crashed someone's private Victorian party, but the wide-eyed look of astonishment on several faces seemed unduly...astonished.

They neared a small table at the opposite end of the car, and Robert pulled out a chair for her. She sank into it gratefully, her knees continuing to buckle in an unpredictable way. At least Robert didn't have one of the ubiquitous mustaches!

"You know," she said with a shaky smile as she watched Robert take the chair across the table, "maybe I do need a little something to eat. I'm pretty sure my blood sugar must be dropping. I just can't seem to get my knees to stop wobbling."

His green eyes surveyed her with compassion. "Yes, I did wonder if you weren't feeling well. Tell me, Miss Standish, are you in the medical profession? A nurse, perhaps?"

Busily scanning the elegant white linen-covered table for something edible such as crackers, she looked up at his words.

"No, why do you ask?"

"I just thought perhaps your references to blood sugar suggest a knowledge of medicine."

She chuckled and leaned back in her chair, surprisingly more relaxed now that she was out of public view.

"Oh, *Bobby*. How long are you going to continue this charade? You guys are a hoot! And if I weren't so tired or confused, I could appreciate it. But as it is, I'm starved and I'm exhausted."

To her satisfaction, he winced. "My dear Miss Standish, please do not call me by that childish name." He turned to signal for a steward. Samuel seemed to materialize out of nowhere.

"Samuel. There you are. We thought we had lost you."

"I'm sorry, Mr. Chamberlain. The conductor came when you did. I didn't have a chance to talk to him."

Ellie watched the exchange with interest. Robert certainly had a way about him, a sort of friendly yet distant lord-of-the-manor confidence that she found both irritating and intriguing. Of course, it was a performance, but still...

"We would like a menu, Samuel. Miss Standish needs some nourishment."

"How about you, Mr. Chamberlain?" Samuel instantly whipped out a paper menu from a mysterious location behind his back and laid it in front of Ellie.

"Nothing for me, Samuel. We just had dinner, as you know."

Ellie raised her eyes from the rather intriguing menu to see Robert watching her while he spoke to Samuel. She blushed at his direct gaze. Samuel melted away.

"Y-you're not eating?" she stammered. "Listen, I can eat by myself.

You don't have to wait with me." She threw him a bright grin, as toothy as she could make it. "I'll just have a quick snack, snag that conductor and find my car."

"It is no trouble, Miss Standish. I think I should wait with you, to see if you feel unwell again."

Her face flamed again, and she dropped her eyes to the menu. As with most things that day, the menu proved to be another facet of her continuing nightmare in Victorian land.

"Does this really say *boiled leg of mutton*? Boy, you guys really went all out on this. I don't even know anyone who eats boiled leg of mutton. The prices are great, though." Ellie glanced up at Robert and pointed to the menu. "Seventy-five cents for the food." She shook her head and chuckled. "I can't imagine how they swung that price."

"I eat boiled leg of mutton, Miss Standish. Now, you know someone who does."

A quick glance revealed he maintained a straight face...and a handsome one, at that. He leaned back in his chair, his posture relaxed, green eyes watching her with amused interest. Ellie couldn't help but be flattered. Kyle never looked at her like that. She couldn't really understand why Robert did. She knew she looked a frump, but it hadn't mattered.

"Cute, Robert, really cute," Ellie chuckled. She set the menu aside. "Listen, I'm not all that hungry. I just need a snack. I think I'll just have some cheese and crackers. You know, a little protein."

Robert's lips twitched and he crinkled his brow.

"Protein?"

"Yes, you know. Protein. Cheese."

He nodded. "Ah, cheese. Are you sure you wouldn't like to have something more to eat? Some soup, perhaps, something hot?"

She shook her head. "No, that will be enough." She craned her neck to see down the length of the car, aware some of the other diners continued to throw curious glances in their direction...especially the women. "Now, where did Samuel go?"

Without turning around, Robert raised his hand, and Samuel appeared. Ellie's eyes widened. How did he do that?

"Hey, Samuel. Okay, could I have some of this Edam cheese and some crackers?" She pointed to the menu.

Samuel's eyes widened, and he threw an inquiring look at Robert.

Ellie put a stop to that. She waved her hand. "Yoohoo, Samuel! Over here. Pay attention to me. This is *my* order. I'm paying for it—or I will when I find my purse."

"Yes, ma'am." Samuel dipped his head and hurried away. She followed his retreating back, perplexed by his actions. Then she brought her eyes back to Robert who watched her with a puzzled frown.

"You could be kinder to him, Miss Standish. He is only doing his job."

She glanced at Robert in surprise. *Her?* Was he serious? He wasn't laughing.

"I *am* kind to him. In fact, I feel kind of sorry for him that he has to play this weird subservient role in your program here."

"Program?" He cocked a dark eyebrow in her direction.

"Well, whatever you want to call it. I'm just tired of everyone looking at you when I talk to them. It's really very odd. Makes me feel like I'm living in the Dark Ages."

A corner of his mouth lifted slowly. "The Dark Ages?" His smile broadened. "Surely not, Miss Standish. It is the turn of the century. We are much more advanced and civilized than the *Dark Ages.*"

"Oh yeah, the turn of the century. I forgot," she murmured with a sigh. Ellie planted her elbows on the table and rested her chin on her palms. She steeled herself to meet his eyes with a steady gaze.

"Okay, Robert, I'll play along. What year is it?"

Robert's amused gaze, which had fixed on her elbows on the table, returned to her face with a glint. "1901, Miss Standish. As I said, the turn of the century. And a fine year it is proving to be."

She sniffed and shook her head with a wry twist of her lips. "Mmmhmmm. Okay. And who is the President?"

His smile widened to an amused grin. He reached for a glass of water delivered by Samuel and took a deliberate sip before answering.

"William McKinley. And since we are *playing* at questions, I believe it must be my turn, Miss Standish."

Ellie narrowed her eyes and regarded him for a moment before crossing her arms and leaning back into her chair with a half smile.

"Okay, go ahead."

"What is your first name?" The sparkle in his green eyes robbed her of breath for a moment. Her heart bumped against her chest.

"Ellie," she murmured, suddenly shy at the unexpectedly intimate quality of such an ordinary question.

"Ellie," he repeated. The well-known name sounded suddenly fresh and desirable on his lips. "And does that stand for Eleanor?"

She inhaled deeply to bring oxygen back to her deprived brain, and she hugged herself tightly.

"No, just Ellie. It's just a name my hippie-dippy parents decided to give me."

"Hippie-dippy?" He shook his head with a wry smile. "And what part of the country are you from, Ellie? May I call you Ellie?"

"Oh yeah, sure." She was distracted by a sudden memory of the man who had sat next to her on the train yesterday with a similar question. Was it only yesterday? She remembered the color of his eyes. Green.

"Ellie?" Robert repeated his question with an inquiring arch of an eyebrow. She met his questioning eyes...the same green.

She shook off the odd coincidence. "I'm sorry. What was the question?"

"Where are you from?"

"Oh, Chicago. Well, no, not really. I mean I live in Chicago now. I've moved around a lot, though."

"I see. I have been to Chicago several times. Some of your expressions stupefy me. I do not believe I have heard them in Chicago, either. What do you mean by hippie-dippy parents?"

"Oh, so you're saying you haven't heard that expression, either, Robert?" She studied his face through narrowed eyes. His face registered genuine curiosity. Was it possible? "Well, maybe you haven't. I'll give you that. But you have heard of hippies, right? The late sixties and early seventies? San Francisco? Woodstock?"

She watched various expressions cross his face, the most prominent being a look of confusion. "Well, certainly I've heard of San Francisco. In fact, I've been there. The sixties and seventies? The reconstruction era?"

She almost laughed, but she wouldn't give him the satisfaction.

"Robert, you have an American accent, but are you actually *from* the United States? Everyone knows about hippies...flower children." The train took a sudden lurch, and water sloshed from Ellie's glass. She was surprised the whole glass hadn't jumped off the table by now, with the uneven movements of the old-fashioned carriages.

He quirked a quizzical eyebrow in her direction.

"Well, unless you are referring to children who carry flowers in a wedding procession, I have no earthly idea what you are talking about. Please instruct me."

She opened her mouth to retort, but Samuel appeared with a silver tray. He set an elegant porcelain plate before Ellie with slices of Edam cheese and saltine crackers.

"Oh, thank you, thank you, Samuel. I'm starving."

Samuel nodded, threw a last glance at Robert and moved away.

Ellie sliced several small sections off the small block and laid them on the crackers.

"Are you sure you don't want some?"

"No, thank you. I am fine."

She bit into her snack and paused, her teeth seemingly hitting solid rock. With a self-conscious glance in Robert's direction, she pulled the food from the edge of her mouth and examined the cracker. While it looked like a saltine, she could see now that the small white square was thicker than what she was used to. With another flushed look in Robert's direction, she bit into the cracker again. It gave way this time, and she ground it in her mouth. With one bite of the hard cracker swallowed, she eyed the rest with misgiving. She reached for her water to help the food make its way to its final destination.

"Wow, those crackers are really hard." Hungry and unwilling to fight the food, she popped a slice of the salty cheese into her mouth.

"They used to be called hardtack," Robert said. "Haven't you ever eaten them before?"

"Hardtack?" She eyed the crackers again with suspicious eyes. "Hardtack? Are you serious? No wonder. I've never had hardtack before." Ellie picked up another cracker and attempted to nibble the edges.

"Don't they have hardtack in Chicago?"

"Not that I'm aware of. At least not in this century."

"How interesting." He lowered his eyes for a moment while he ran his finger around the rim of his water glass.

"Tell me, Ellie. Are you married?"

Ellie almost choked on the dry cracker and grabbed another gulp of water.

"Er, no, I'm not." She bit her lip. She hesitated to say the words *But I'm engaged*, and she didn't know why.

"No Mr. Standish?" Robert asked with a sparkle in his eye.

Ellie blushed. "No Mr. Standish," she said. "How about you, Robert? Are you married?"

"No, I am currently not so fortunate."

Ellie chuckled at his odd speech pattern. "Never been married?"

"If I had ever been married, Ellie, I would still be wedded...to the same woman."

Her heart caught in her throat. He stared at her with a steady gaze, a half-smile playing on his lips. His words seemed so certain, so confident, so...permanent.

She cleared her throat. "Well, certainly. Of course. I just...well, you know, a lot of people are divorced these days. You never know. I...uh...I didn't mean to be rude."

"I did not take offense." His smile widened to a grin.

"I intend to marry only once, and I have not yet found the woman who could put up with me for the rest of her life." The twinkle returned to his eyes, but Ellie had no doubt about his firm stance.

"Mr. Chamberlain, Miss Standish." The conductor towered over the table, his wide stance preventing any need to brace himself against the rocking of the train. "Is this a good time for me to interrupt? The train will be pulling into Wenatchee in a few minutes. I think we need to figure out how we can help Miss Standish at that time."

Robert glanced up at him and turned to Ellie. "Do you feel better, Ellie? Have you eaten enough?"

Ellie nodded, having eaten only three slices of cheese. "Yes, I'm fine. I'll be glad to get back to my seat. I could use a nap." She gave Robert a small smile, hoping he wouldn't see the lie in her eyes—a lie that took her by surprise.

"Good. That is settled, then. I must return to my carriage to check on the ladies. They will be worried about my extended absence by now. It seems as if Mr...?"

"Bingham, sir."

"It appears as if Mr. Bingham is going to assist you in whatever way you need." Robert gave her an encouraging smile, and turned to the conductor, who stood by silently.

"You will let me know if Miss Standish needs any further assistance, of course. My family and I are more than happy to see to anything she needs should her seat...go missing."

Ellie rose slowly from the table and smiled with a slight shake of her head.

"You know, Robert, I'm beginning to think I woke up in another dimension...in a time warp. You're good, I'll give you that. I'll find my seat, if Mr. Bingham here points out the way."

She put out a hand. Robert looked at it for a moment, and then took it in his own warm grasp. She caught her breath.

"Thank you for everything, Robert. Again, it's been fun." Ellie reluctantly pulled her hand from his.

Robert tipped an invisible hat in her direction.

"As you say, Ellie, it has been fun. I will see you again." He turned away and strode down the length of the dining car, leaving Ellie to stare in his wake, temporarily robbed of breath, a delightful tingling in her hand.

"Miss Standish?"

She turned bemused eyes up to the solemn face of the tall conductor.

"Yes, Mr. Bingham?"

"Shall we?" He indicated a doorway at the nearest end of the train.

"Oh, but I have to pay for my meal." Her face burned. "Except I have to find my purse first."

"Of course. We can see to that shortly."

"Oh, okay." Ellie staggered and grabbed the table as the train lurched to a stop. Mr. Bingham reached out to steady her.

"Thanks."

He pulled his watch out of his pocket and studied it for a moment. "It seems we have arrived. We should be here for thirty minutes. I think I'd better take you down to the tourist cars to see if you recognize your seat."

"Oh, great!" Ellie said.

"I wonder if you could wait here for me until I return. Now that we have arrived, I have one or two duties to attend to in the station and then I can return for you. I shouldn't be more than a few moments at the most."

Ellie scanned the room, now empty of diners. Stewards moved about, cleaning tables and setting out new dinnerware.

"Can't I wait outside the car? I could use some fresh air and it looks like they're pretty busy cleaning up in here."

He barely glanced at the busy stewards. "I don't think it would be wise for me to leave you alone outside. It would be better if you were to wait in here."

She shrugged and sank back into her seat, wondering if he worried she would disappear without paying her bill or providing proof of her train fare. With a tip of his wheel cap, he consulted his watch again and hurried out the door.

Ellie strained to see out the windows, but dust impeded her view. She glanced at the stewards again, who paused occasionally to stare at her. Feeling as if she'd worn out her welcome, she jumped up and pushed open the door with the intention of waiting for the conductor outside, no matter what his wishes.

She stepped out onto the landing and was immediately assaulted by the thick smell of coal. To her surprise, the car appeared to connect to another historical carriage. How many of them were there?

A peek through the glass of the door to the left revealed a dusty field of harvested corn. She turned to the right and opened the door, gingerly descending the sturdy iron stairs down to gravel. The train depot caught her eye first—a small old-fashioned wooden structure with a boardwalk in front. Several people rested on benches or milled about stretching their legs.

She shook her head with a sigh. For the most part, they also wore Victorian era costumes, mostly as she had seen in the dining car, but a few men leaning against the walls of the station sported ragged felt hats, western-style flannel shirts, and thick dungarees that seemed the worse for wear. With a deepening sense of the surreal, she noticed a tall man, obviously Native American, with unkempt long dark hair, wearing a ragged flannel shirt and dark, baggy trousers. He was standing at the edge of the platform with a short, stout woman half hidden by the grubby blanket that covered her frame, a baby's face peeping out from her arms. The man raised his hand occasionally, bringing it to his mouth in a universal gesture requesting food. Everyone generally ignored the family.

An overwhelming atmosphere of dry dust permeated the air, and Ellie sneezed vigorously. Nothing at the minuscule station seemed remotely modern. The weathered wood and grimy windows of the building gave way to the warped boardwalk that led across a dirt road toward the gravel around the train tracks. She moved away from the train to investigate further. As she did so, she looked to her right and saw Robert on the ground assisting the ladies of his party down the steps of their carriage. He seemed not to see her, and that was fine with Ellie.

What she saw next took her breath away...perhaps even her sanity. She turned around to see twenty or so old-fashioned carriages just like hers, stretching away toward the front of the train. Gone were the modern gleaming silver cars like she'd boarded in Chicago. Every single car seemed to have come straight out of a vintage railroad photograph.

Ellie's knees started shaking as she stood in the middle of the tracks staring helplessly at the train. She broke out into a cold sweat; her mouth tasted of a nasty mixture of pungent coal, dry dust and bitter bile. A wave of nausea overtook her, and she turned toward the station to beg someone to save her from the nightmare. No sounds came from her frozen throat. The station blurred and grew suddenly dark.

CHAPTER FIVE

"Ellie. Ellie." A familiar masculine voice penetrated her consciousness. She rubbed her face against the warm hand touching her cheek.

"Miss Standish, wake up." Not Miss Standish again, she thought with confused dismay. Heavy eyelids refused to open, and she stopped fighting them for a moment as she listened to the hazy murmur of the voices in her dream.

"Robert, come away. Give the girl some air. Is there a physician on this infernal train?"

"No, Grandmother. I have already made inquiries."

"Do you think she is malnourished, Robert? She seemed so strange, so confused...almost delirious."

"No, Melinda, I do not think she is malnourished. She certainly looks well fed."

Ellie forced her eyes open to find Robert's concerned green eyes close to her face as he bent over her.

"Is that a fat joke?" Her parched throat thickened her voice.

Robert startled and blinked. "Ellie...Miss Standish, are you all right?" He withdrew his hand and straightened slowly. "A *fat* joke? Good gravy! Certainly not!"

Melinda hovered behind him, her smooth white brow knitted above troubled blue eyes. Ellie tried to sit up.

"Stay there, Miss Standish, until we are sure you are feeling better," Robert said.

"I'm fine, Robert. I need to sit up. I feel queasy."

"Very well, madam. Here." Robert helped her into a sitting position. She recognized her original bench seat, which was fortunately long enough for her to recline on. Amy and several of the other young women peered around the corner with anxious faces. Mrs. Chamberlain sat on the bench opposite and stared at her with a frown.

"Here, Robert, a glass of water."

"Excellent, Melinda. Thank you." He handed the glass to Ellie, who took a drink. She wrinkled her nose at the metallic taste but obediently drank a few sips. Anything to rid her mouth and throat of the dust.

The dust...

She looked up at Robert. "How did I get back on board?" A sudden lurch of the carriage jerked her toward reality, and she realized the train had been rumbling along the tracks since she'd been conscious. She bolted upright and gasped. "The train is moving, isn't it?"

"Robert picked you up off the ground like a limp rag doll and brought you back onto the train," Mrs. Chamberlain said. "You've been unconscious...or asleep, for some time." The older woman folded pale hands on the black silk of her lap and surveyed Ellie with sharp blue eyes.

"We pulled out of Wenatchee almost a half hour ago, Ellie." The quiet sympathy in Robert's voice threatened to break down her reserves. "I'm sorry we were not able to locate your seat. We thought it best to bring you back on board."

Ellie stared at him with wide eyes. His well-groomed clothes... So vintage. So new! She looked past him to Mrs. Chamberlain. Impossible to think she could ever have worn a polyester leisure suit. And Melinda? A short, frisky platinum blonde color and cut to her gorgeous hair?

Never!

"Ellie?"

Robert's insistent voice brought her back to a nightmare come true. The train...her seat. Where did they go? She returned her stricken gaze to his face. The kindly inquisitive tilt of his head as he looked at her broke the floodgates.

"I-I'm lost. I don't know where I am," she wailed before she burst into tears. She pulled her knees to her chest and buried her face in her hands. She hadn't known terror like this since she was a child waking up from a nightmare. Her mother would come to her then, sit on the bed beside her and tell her it was only a bad dream...that it would go away. And it always did...then.

But her mother didn't come this time. Robert did.

"Don't cry, Ellie," Robert spoke soothingly near her ear. "I am going to help you find your way home, wherever that is. Don't cry. Everything is going to be all right."

He'd lowered himself to one knee and leaned against the bench beside her. She turned a water-stained face to him, wishing he would take her in his arms as her mother once had.

"I hope you *can* help me, Robert. I'm done pretending I have a clue. I'm so confused. I don't know where my seat is anymore. I don't know where I am."

"What is she going on about, Robert?" Mrs. Chamberlain asked. "Ellie— Is that her name? Ellie, what do you mean, you are lost? Melinda, give her that blanket there to cover her legs. No well-bred woman sits that way."

In a daze, Ellie watched Melinda spring into action and pick up a dark blue wool blanket which she carefully spread over Ellie's hunched legs beneath her long skirt.

"Give her some time, Grandmother. She seems to have had quite a shock. This is hardly the time to worry about proper behavior."

"Hmmppfff. I have had a shock or two in my time, Robert, and I never forgot my manners."

Luckily, Ellie's view of Mrs. Chamberlain was blocked by Robert's face...his handsome face.

"Grandmother, why don't you and Melinda return to the observation lounge? I would like to talk to Miss Standish in private." Robert kept a searching gaze on Ellie's face while he spoke over his shoulder.

"Well, I hope you are able to make some sense of what she says," Mrs. Chamberlain said in a querulous voice. "Mind you keep that blanket on her. She probably needs the warmth."

Robert rose to his full height and extended his arm to the older woman to help her rise. She peered around him one more time to examine Ellie before he led her to Melinda, who took her arm and retreated to the rear of the car. A swell of female voices greeted their return, and then settled into a hum of questions and answers.

Robert turned back to Ellie, allowing his gaze to rest momentarily on the open bench beside her before he tightened his lips and moved to take a seat on the opposite bench. Ellie would have welcomed his nearness— in fact, she craved his very real presence in a world gone mad.

"You can sit here, Robert."

"I think you might feel more safe if I keep some distance from you, Ellie. My presence seems to disturb you, and I think you have had enough of a shock."

"Oh." Her face burned, and she pulled the soft woolen blanket toward her cheeks. She threw him a quick glance before she lowered her eyes to study the threads of the blanket.

"Ellie." The gravity in his quiet voice terrified her. She didn't want him to talk. Anything he had to say would be bad news. She was certain of it.

"Yes?" She raised reluctant eyes to his face. A muscle flexed in his jaw. His dark-lashed eyes watched her with a mixture of curiosity and concern. She burst into babble.

"I know you think I'm crazy, Robert. I can't even find my train, the one I boarded yesterday in Chicago. You know, the bright shining modern train that we all know and love. That one?"

He watched her patiently, his legs crossed, hands clasped in his lap.

Ellie hardly stopped for breath before she began again with an unladylike snort. "Of course, I think you guys are a bit whacked out myself. Or at least, I did...until I discovered I'd lost my train. It's not possible for me to fall asleep and wake up on another train...especially a vintage one."

She paused for a gulp of air. Robert tilted his head in that charming way, a hint of a smile on his face.

"I mean it's really not possible, unless I'm still dreaming. And I could be dreaming, Robert. Don't think I haven't thought about that. For all I know, I could be having a conversation with a dream. Do you know what I mean?

She ended on a winded note with a quick glance in Robert's direction. To her surprise, instead of responding, he rose and walked into the observation lounge, returning in seconds with a newspaper in his hands. He laid the paper on his bench and sat back down.

"Ellie." He began again in that same serious note that boded no good for her. "What year is it?"

Ellie's eyebrows shot up. She didn't know what she had expected, but that question wasn't it. She told him the current date.

Robert's eye's widened for a second and then narrowed. It seemed as if he held his breath for a moment and then released it with a hiss. Propping his arms on his knees, he leaned forward intently as if to say something. Then he straightened abruptly and his eyes fell to the paper at his side.

Ellie watched his dark bent head nervously. What was he thinking?

With a slight shake of his head and a sigh, he picked up the paper and stared hard at it, passing it from one hand to the other.

"I don't think so, Ellie."

"You don't think what?"

"I wonder if you could be ill, as Melinda suggested. Have you been eating well? Had a recent illness, a bout with fever?"

Ellie kept her eye on the hands that handled the paper. What was it about that paper that worried him so much? She shook her head.

"No, I don't think so. I haven't been sick."

He opened the newspaper and handed it to her. She pulled her hands out from under the blanket and took it with an uncertain look in his direction. At first glance, the paper resembled a local free weekly such as one might find at the entrance to the grocery store. The uneven print caught her eye, garish and old-fashioned, as if it had been typed on a manual typewriter. The bright, bold title caught her eye: *The Seattle Weekly*. Vivid headlines read "MOUNT BAKER PUFFS AGAIN."

Ellie glanced at Robert curiously. He gave her an encouraging nod.

"What do you want me to look at?" She turned a page. The paper felt coarse, unlike the smooth newsprint from her local Chicago newspaper.

"The date, Ellie. Look at the date."

Ellie returned to the front page and searched above the oversized headlines for the date. She found it in the middle, the print italicized and difficult to read.

April 20, 1901. She mouthed the words silently. Nineteen hundred and one. That would be about right for their costume period. The late Victorian/early Edwardian era. The year of Queen Victoria's death.

She turned to Robert, who had moved to the edge of his seat.

"Do you see the date, Ellie?"

"Yes, April 20, 1901." She held up the paper and smiled wanly. "I assume this is part of your reenactment."

"Ellie, this is no reenactment. We do not prance about in Napoleonic costumes pretending to relive glorious days of the past." He pushed himself back against his bench and crossed his arms, directing a frank stare in her direction.

"So, what are you trying to say?" Ellie swallowed hard. Black dots swam before her eyes.

"I think you know what I'm trying to say. I believe you are being deliberately obtuse."

"I am not. I haven't got the faintest idea what you're talking about," she retorted hotly. Of course she did, but the reality just seemed too bizarre to comprehend.

Robert tightened his lips and eyed her speculatively. He leaned forward again.

"Have you ever read H. G. Wells?"

"Yes. Don't even try that, Robert." Ellie shook her head, a warning note in her voice.

"Have you read his book called *The Time Machine?*"

"Read it, watched the movie, loved it." She stared at Robert with narrowed eyes. She wasn't going to allow what would surely follow.

"I don't know about this *moovee* you mention, but you've read about his concept of time travel, then?"

"It's fiction, Robert. Time travel doesn't exist, as far as we know. Not even in the twenty-first century."

"That is my point, Ellie. This is not the twenty-first century. It is April 25, 1901." He crossed his arms again and regarded her with a strange light in his green eyes. "Now, either you *are* delirious as Melinda suggested, or..." He left his sentence hanging as he eyed her with concern.

"Or I've traveled back in time?" She clapped a hand over her mouth to stifle a hysterical giggle. "Are those my only options?"

"Do you have an explanation for your appearance here...in your strange costume? Where is this seat you say you have lost?"

"*My* costume!" Ellie almost shrieked. She ran her eyes up and down his handsome figure. "How about I fell asleep and somehow accidentally walked off my own train in the middle of the night, crossed the tracks and climbed into your historical party here?" Ellie stared at him, trying to hide the fright she knew must be showing on her face.

Robert's lips twitched. "Ellie," he murmured. "Do you really think that's likely?"

"There's a third alternative, Robert. One that makes more and more sense, now that I think about it."

"And what is that, my dear Miss Standish?"

"Well, Mr. Chamberlain, the other alternative is that this is all just a dream." She dropped the edge of the blanket and raised her hands expansively to encompass the train.

Robert's eyes crinkled when he laughed, and he shook his head patiently. "That is not possible, Ellie. It is simply impossible. I am real. I am no dream."

Having found an answer she could live with, Ellie prepared to defend it like a faithful follower. She relaxed her grip on her knees and rested her head against the high back of the velvet bench with a self-satisfied nod.

"How would you know this isn't a dream?"

"Well, I'm certain I would know. How could I not know?" Robert's steady gaze faltered. He stared down at the ground for a brief second before returning his gaze to Ellie's face. His voice was grave. He shook his head again.

"No, this is not a dream, Ellie."

Ellie gave him a serene smile. All was right with the world at last.

"You would never know, Robert. Besides, this is *my* dream, but I'll tell you what I'm prepared to do." She pushed the blanket away, swung her legs over the edge of the seat and leaned forward. "I'm prepared to let you choreograph the dream, as it seems you've already been doing. I'll just sit back and let the dream take its course. How about that?"

She crossed her arms and leaned back against the seat once again, watching him from under veiled lashes. A myriad of emotions crossed his face—surprise, disbelief, a flash of something soft she did not recognize, and finally amusement.

Robert drew in breath to speak, and then closed his mouth. He turned away to stare at nothing in particular for just a moment. When he returned his gaze to her face, the twinkle sparkled in his eyes.

"So, you are saying that you are putting yourself in my hands in this dream of yours. Is that correct, Miss Standish?"

Suddenly full of the confidence only a dream could give her, she gave him a half-smile and a benign nod.

"Yes, Mr. Chamberlain, do with me what you will." Ellie grinned, suddenly emboldened. "Within reason, of course."

Robert's dark eyebrows shot up for a moment before he responded.

"Excellent. I am prepared for the challenge of...choreographing your dream, as you say. Since your *dream* has left you with no seat at your disposal and no visible income, you will come to my house, where my grandmother and sister reside, to stay with us until you *wake up*."

Ellie wasn't sure about the nature of dreams, but this one seemed to be taking a turn for the better. She took a deep breath.

"Sure, Robert. That sounds fine. I warn you, though. If you turn into some sort of murderer or monster, I'll do my best to wake up."

Robert's green eyes softened. "I am no monster, Ellie. I promise you that."

Ellie reached out to shake his hand. Robert stared at her hand for a moment and took it in his own. She gave it a good tug.

"Deal!" she said.

"Deal," he murmured, making no move to release her hand. She pulled away from his warmth reluctantly and leaned back against her seat.

"So, what's the plan?" she asked with interest.

Robert threw back his head and laughed—a hearty, happy sound that charmed her with its utter masculinity.

"You certainly are an enigma, Ellie. I think I had better let the ladies know you will be staying with us. There will be some concerns from

Grandmother, no doubt. I suspect Melinda will be delighted to have such...an unusual houseguest.

Ellie grinned.

"I'm looking forward to the stay, Robert. I always did want to know what life was like at the turn of the century."

"You promise to be quite an adventure, my dear Miss Standish." The sparkling challenge in Robert's eyes shook her bravado for a moment, but she recovered.

He rose slowly and gazed down at her briefly.

"Just remember, Ellie. It is my belief that you have traveled back in time, although I do not know why."

Ellie stared into the emerald depths of his eyes, afraid to lose herself in them.

"And *I* think this is all just a dream, Robert. One that could end at any moment."

His eyes darkened, and he reached down to trace the line of her left cheek with his index finger before straightening.

"Let us hope not...not too soon." He cleared his throat and ran a finger along the inside of his high collar. "I think you had better wait here until the questions are out of the way. You might find my grandmother... outspoken." He grinned.

"I noticed," Ellie murmured with a twitch of her lips. He chuckled and moved away.

Ellie pulled her feet back up onto the seat and stretched out with the blanket, suddenly weary. Did people feel tired in dreams? Did they sleep? That seemed redundant. Had she ever even boarded the train in Chicago? When did the dream begin? She swallowed hard against a sudden knot in her throat. When would it end?

Please, not too soon, she thought drowsily. Not too soon.

CHAPTER SIX

"Ellie? Ellie, wake up." A gentle hand shook Ellie's shoulder. She awakened to her dream. Robert bent over her, his face close to hers. Melinda hovered behind, trying to peer over his shoulder.

"Robert, you're still here," Ellie murmured. "I feel like I'm dreaming within a dream." She rubbed her eyes and attempted to sit up. He threw a quick glance over his shoulder at Melinda and put a cautionary finger to his lips.

"And you are still here as well, Miss Standish. Melinda and my grandmother are looking forward to your visit with us."

Ellie's eyes shot open, and she focused on the warning message in Robert's eyes.

"Oh, my visit. Yes, thank you very much." Uncertain what he had told them, she faltered. "I-I look forward to staying with your family." She exchanged a quick conspiratorial glance with Robert who nodded and straightened.

"Well, we were wondering if you wanted to have a light supper with us. It will be served here in the observation car." Robert pulled out a lovely gold watch from a pocket in his gray vest. "We will arrive in Seattle in approximately two hours, at 11:30 p.m."

Her stomach growled at the thought of food, and she bobbed her head enthusiastically.

"Yes, I'd love to eat. How long have I been asleep?"

"About five hours, Miss Standish. You must have been exhausted." Melinda had finally managed to get around Robert to peer at Ellie.

Ellie's eyes flew to Robert's face.

"Five hours? I-I'm lucky I managed to wake up at all. Why aren't we in Seattle yet? How long is the trip from Wenatchee?"

Robert gave a short laugh, which did not reach his eyes.

"I wasn't certain if you *were* going to wake up. You seemed dead to the world. The journey is nine hours."

"He has been very worried, Miss Standish," Melinda offered. "He has been back here about twenty times, checking on you as you continued to sleep. We told him you probably just needed some rest and to leave you alone, but Robert insisted he must check your breathing."

Ellie's face flamed and she found it hard to meet Robert's eyes.

"Shall we dine then, Miss Standish?" He held out an elegant arm, and Ellie rose to take it self-consciously. He led her toward the back of the carriage with Melinda following closely behind.

Soft lights now glowed overhead in brass and tulip chandeliers and cast a golden radiance over the teak walls and red velvet furnishings. Shades, pulled low against the night sky, lent the carriage an intimate atmosphere.

The women turned curious eyes on Ellie once again, and she gave them a pleasant smile and sank into the chair Robert indicated. She did not miss the speculative eyes that studied both Robert and her, but she chose to ignore them.

Several of the younger women had removed their hats, revealing hairstyles similar to Melinda's—the upswept Gibson—albeit with a few limp, dangling curls and wayward wisps from the long traveling day. Ellie put a hand to her own curly brown hair to see how much of it had escaped her braid. Some tendrils hung around her face, and she stuck them behind her ears, though they instantly popped forward once again.

Samuel served from a tray of odd-looking food. Ellie thought she recognized slices of roast beef and ham, but the rest of the food was unfamiliar to her.

Robert took a vacant seat across the room next to his grandmother, who eyed Ellie with an inscrutable expression. Luckily, Samuel distracted her attention by handing the older woman a plate.

Samuel crossed the room to approach Ellie.

"What would you like to eat, miss?" He stood aside to let her study the food on the large silver tray in the middle of the room.

Ellie shook her head with dismay.

"Gosh, I don't know. So much meat. Do you have anything that isn't meat?"

Samuel's eyes widened. "Pardon, miss?"

"I'm a vegetarian." Ellie wrinkled her nose and gave Samuel a sheepish grin. "You know, I don't eat meat? Do you have a baked potato or something?"

"Robert, do go over and see what you can do to help Miss Standish. She seems to be having trouble communicating." Mrs. Chamberlain's voice rang out, bringing all eyes back to Ellie...again.

Robert rose and crossed the narrow space between them.

"Is something wrong, Samuel?"

"Sir, I'm afraid...I don't know what she wants."

Samuel's eyes flickered nervously. Ellie hated to make him ill at ease. If she had truly awakened at the turn of the century...before the civil rights movement and lack of union representation, his subservient behavior made a great deal of sense. The man was afraid of losing his job at the whim of a cantankerous passenger.

"It's no problem, Robert. I'm afraid I'm giving Samuel a hard time. I don't eat meat, so I'm trying to figure out how I'm going to avoid starving to death while I'm here."

Robert blinked and drew his brows together. He turned to Samuel.

"Please wait on my sister and her guests, Samuel. I must consult with Miss Standish for a moment."

He held out his arm for Ellie, and she sighed and rose to take it, knowing all eyes continued to stare at her. Robert led her a few feet away, out of hearing, toward the front of the carriage.

"A vegetarian, is it?" The irresistible twitch of his lips returned, and Ellie stared helplessly at the deep dimples in his cheeks.

She nodded mutely.

"Well, since this is your *dream*, can't you just change that? I fear you'll become very hungry if you don't eat."

Ellie shook her head. "No, I don't think I can change it. Besides, we decided that you would *choreograph* the dream." She crossed her arms. "I'm just along for the ride."

He fixed her with a challenging eye.

"Very well, then. I command you to eat meat."

Ellie shook her head with exasperation and suppressed a gurgle of laughter.

"Ummm...no, Robert. I don't respond to commands, and I'm not going to eat meat...not even in my dream. Then it would become a nightmare."

He tightened his lips and leaned close to her face.

"So, I am to be the director of this dream, but am powerless, is that correct?"

Ellie smirked. "Well, I don't know how it's going to work, Robert. This *is* the first time I've been in this situation. I'm pretty sure *I'm* not in control of the dream, or I'd be lying on a sunny beach somewhere in a tropical paradise.

"Alone?" He quirked a teasing eyebrow.

"Most definitely not!" She waggled her brows suggestively.

Robert threw back his head and laughed, and Ellie responded with some nervous giggles of her own. She refused to turn around, knowing everyone was watching. When would they stop staring?

"If I could control the dream, Robert, I'd make everyone stop staring at me." She wiped tears of laughter from her eyes.

He caught his breath and looked past her to the room beyond.

"I'm afraid they will be watching for a while. Most of these young ladies are friends of Melinda. We took a trip to Spokane to celebrate her eighteenth birthday—a long and arduous journey which I'm not likely to repeat any time soon."

Ellie glanced over her shoulder. Most of the women had returned their attention to their food. She caught Constance staring at her...at Robert.

"Well, Ellie, what do you eat?"

"I think I'll just have some bread and cheese for now. I can't bear to see the worry in Samuel's eyes."

Robert nodded. "The working classes are at the whim and mercy of their employers. The system is changing, but it will take time. You and I must have a long discussion about the future. In the meantime, let us return to find some food for you to eat. I must remember to instruct our cook to prepare dishes of vegetables for you."

"Thanks, Robert. I hate to be so much trouble, but I can't seem to avoid it."

"Trouble, indeed," Robert laughed softly. "I think I can manage to cope."

Ellie glanced at him in confusion for a moment before she turned away. She faltered when she felt his hand on the small of her back. If she were really in control of the dream, she and Robert would... She quashed the thought.

Kyle, she remembered with a wince. Her dreams would never hurt him. He would never know.

****

Dinner over and most of the women dozing in their chairs, Robert stared at the fascinating creature that was Ellie. She rested her shining brown head of hair against the velvet drapes in the corner of the observation carriage, her feet crossed at the ankles in front of her like a child, her full-lipped mouth slightly parted, dark lashes against her pale cheeks.

He had no doubt that Ellie had magically descended on them for a reason, and he hoped he was that reason. That she'd given herself over to him in need was a sign, and he was honored to have the care of the strange woman who had traveled through time. Though Ellie believed she was in a dream, Robert knew different. Ellie had come for him. She was the woman for whom he'd waited all these years.

He turned to look at his grandmother, who gently snored next to him. He hated to shock the older woman, and he hoped her heart could survive the news, but he was determined to have Ellie for his own—if she stayed. He did not yet understand how she had ended up in his time, but he fervently hoped she would stay. He couldn't wait to discover what wondrous things she would reveal about life in the twenty-first century.

When she had fainted and fallen to the ground at the train depot, his heart had seized and he'd raced to her side, picking her up tenderly and brushing the dust from her soft brown hair. He had brushed off Mr. Bingham's entreaties to leave her to the care of the stationmaster. Impossible. He might never have seen her again. Ellie was no *immigrant* in the original sense of the word. She came from another place, that seemed certain, but that place was the future, and she had come to him.

He tilted his head and regarded her with a frown. She did not seem to realize that yet. How would he convince her?

He blinked and felt warmth rush to his face when he realized Ellie had opened her eyes to catch him staring at her. She straightened in her chair and flashed him a shaky smile.

Poor girl! So lost. He knew an overwhelming desire to cross the carriage and settle into a chair beside her, to hold her hand and study the hazel mix of her eyes. But there was no chair nearby, and he understood the need to move slowly. He did not want to frighten her away...back in time...or back into her dream.

"She is an interesting woman, isn't she, Robert?" Constance, apparently having followed his eyes, whispered next to him.

He turned to her with a start and looked back at Ellie, who studiously smoothed wrinkles from her skirt.

"Yes, she is, Constance. Poor thing. She seems so lost. I feel compelled to assist."

"Why, Robert, if I may ask? She *is* a stranger. What drove you to bring her back to the carriage when the conductor offered to see to her?"

Robert dragged his eyes from Ellie. Her nonchalant fussing with her skirt suggested she knew she was the subject of discussion. He looked at Constance. "I cannot explain it. I thought she would be safer with us. I do not think she is from the *immigrant* car, nor do I think she is mentally unstable. I intend to bring her to the house and see if she recovers her..."

"Wits?" Constance smiled.

"Constance," Robert reproved. He bit his tongue against an acerbic retort. "Recovers her bearings."

"Oh, I see," she murmured. "Take care, Robert."

Robert turned startled eyes to her. "Care of what, Constance?"

"Yourself." She smiled, but her eyes were veiled.

"Nonsense, Constance." He grinned, hoping to throw her off the scent. Was he that obvious?

****

The train pulled into Seattle's Union Station at midnight. Having slept for the final two hours of the journey, Melinda and her friends quickly tidied their hair and donned their hats, jackets and shawls.

Robert stood and helped his grandmother to her feet. He signaled for Melanie to assist the exhausted and pale woman while he crossed the room and bent his head near Ellie.

"Just follow me."

Ellie nodded, fascinated by the hustle and bustle accompanying the arrival of the train. As Robert moved away to supervise their disembarkation in an orderly fashion, she caught Constance's eye again from across the room. For the past few hours, Ellie had been acutely aware of the dark-haired beauty sitting next to Robert, conversing with him in low tones...much to her chagrin. The intimacy of their conversation suggested a close relationship.

Had Robert forgotten to mention that he had a girlfriend, a lady love or whatever they called them in 1901? Had she bothered to ask? Could she awaken from this dream if it became unbearable?

"Ladies, shall we?" Robert took the lead and descended the steps, followed by his grandmother and Melinda, whom he assisted. The young women followed, and Constance brought up the rear. Ellie lingered a moment to study the Victorian carriage one last time, committing its details to memory. Constance paused at the door.

"Miss Standish, are you coming?"

Ellie turned bemused eyes on her. "Yes, I am. I'm right behind you."

Constance gave Ellie a friendly smile and descended the steps. Ellie hesitated at the top of the stairs for a moment, gripping the handrail tightly. The last time she'd stepped off this train, she had passed out. What would happen this time?

Robert's hand reached for hers.

"Come with me, Ellie. Stay close. I have a lot of women to see to, and I cannot lose you."

Ellie's heart jumped to her throat at his words. She took the last step and fell into line with the women of his group. Robert gave her hand a quick squeeze before he let it go and moved to the front of the group to direct the unloading of luggage and the arrival of carriages.

Carriages? Ellie's eyes, nose and ears widened to the sensory overload of Seattle at the turn of the century. The smell of coal permeated the thick air of the bustling train station. The overheated locomotive hissed as leftover steam billowed onto the tracks. Conductors strode briskly along the wooden platform, barking out orders to porters who unloaded baggage and reloaded it onto wagons behind depressed-looking mules whose heads hung low. Several carriages awaited the exhausted arrivals, with restless horses that pawed the dirt road and whinnied.

"Melinda, please take Grandmother and Ellie to our carriage. You see Jimmy just over there?" He nodded in the direction of a large, black, hooded carriage. "I need to see your friends to their carriages. I trust you said your goodbyes?"

Melinda hadn't, it seemed, for the young women gathered around her with squeals of gratitude and coos of promised visits in the coming days. Ellie stood to the side, watching everything as if she were in a dream—which of course she was, she reminded herself. Finally, Robert was able to hand his grandmother off to Melinda and escort the rest of the young women to several waiting carriages. Further loud squeals of delight from inside the carriages proclaimed the welcome of waiting family members.

"What a wonderful birthday party!" Melinda sighed, tucking her arm into her grandmother's.

"Come along, Melinda," Mrs. Chamberlain said. "Let's make our way to the carriage. I have been standing too long on these old legs. Miss Standish, if you please."

Ellie obediently moved forward in their wake, but she hesitated when she saw Constance standing alone under an ornate gas streetlamp. Ellie was just about to see if Constance needed a ride when she saw Robert move toward the dark-haired beauty. He bent his head, now covered with a dashing derby, near hers, and she laughed brightly. Ellie cringed as Constance laid one dark-gloved hand on Robert's arm and accompanied him toward a waiting carriage. Was he going to take her home?

"Miss Standish, are you coming?" Ellie barely heard Melinda's polite inquiry as she watched the handsome couple through narrowed eyes. If this was a dream, then she might be able to wish Constance somewhere else. Nothing dreadful...just gone.

Ellie squeezed her eyes shut and wished. Go away, Constance. Go away on a vacation to a wonderful spa or something and meet some nice man. Ellie's eyes shot open at the sound of the soft thud of horses' hooves and jingling harnesses.

"Miss Standish, do you intend to stand out there all night?" Mrs. Chamberlain called out from the interior of the carriage. "What on earth are you doing?"

Ellie opened her mouth to answer but stilled as she watched Robert materialize out of the darkness and walk toward her, his hand outstretched in her direction.

She put her hand in his and tilted her head back to search his eyes. His dimples deepened with his grin.

"Why haven't you climbed aboard the carriage? Won't my grandmother let you on?"

"Nonsense, Robert. The girl has been standing there gawking at who knows what."

Robert handed Ellie up into the carriage. She marveled at the sturdiness of the iron steps and soft comfort of the velvet seat as she slid in to sit across from Melinda and her grandmother. Robert climbed in beside her, ducking low to avoid hitting his hat on the carriage roof. The driver raised the steps, and within moments the carriage pulled forward with a jerk, to the sound of snorting horses and creaking wheels.

Ellie turned to glance out of the window and saw the "immigrant class," finally released from their cars, shuffling along the boardwalk. For the most part, they seemed poor and downtrodden. No bright white shirtwaists or clean silk skirts for the women. No well-tailored dark suits and highly polished shoes for the men. Many of the women covered themselves and their children with thick shawls, while the men wore various styles of ill-fitting thick coats. The travelers looked exhausted as they trudged along, dragging suitcases and hauling bulging cloth sacks. The once-helpful porters stood by and leaned on walls, offering no assistance to the tired mass.

Ellie watched with a frown as some people moved toward large open-air wagons while others made their way down the street on foot, tired children clinging to skirts and huddling close. The group seemed strangely hushed; only the occasional fretful cry of a baby broke the loud silence. She watched and wondered about their lives until she could see them no more.

In general, Seattle seemed much quieter at night in 1901 than in modern day. It bore little resemblance to the bustling city she'd enjoyed visiting on occasion. No bright streetlights shone down from above to show the way, no traffic signals blinked orange in the intersections, no testy car horns blared.

"Robert, now that we are alone and you have had time to think, I was wondering what your plans for Miss...Standish are?" Mrs. Chamberlain's narrowed gaze studied them.

Ellie dragged her eyes and ears away from the eerily dark and silent city to look at Robert. He glanced at her with a reassuring smile.

"I'm not sure, Grandmother. I think that is something Miss Standish and I will discuss at a more convenient time...and certainly in private."

"I see," his grandmother said in an icy tone. "And what am I to make of that?"

"Mrs. Chamberlain, I'm just staying for—"

"No need, Ellie. Grandmother welcomes you as our guest...as *my* guest. Forgive her. She is tired from the journey, I suspect."

Ellie squirmed as she watched and heard the conflict between the two. By the soft yellow light of the interior coach lamp, Ellie saw Mrs. Chamberlain study her grandson for a moment with an unreadable expression. The older woman closed her eyes for a brief second and ran a hand lightly across her pale forehead. When she opened her eyes, she inclined her head in Robert's direction.

"Of course, you are right, Robert. I apologize if I seem rude, Miss Standish. I am weary, and I have forgotten my manners. Naturally, any guest of Robert's is welcome in his home."

"Well, *I* certainly look forward to your visit, Miss Standish...Ellie. May I call you Ellie?" Melinda leaned forward, seemingly full of energy even at this late hour.

"Uh...sure, Melinda. Thank you."

"Wonderful!"

Ellie grinned at Melinda's infectious goodwill. Before she could respond to Mrs. Chamberlain, the older woman closed her eyes and leaned her head back, to all intents and purposes unavailable for communication.

She looked up at Robert beside her to find him watching her with half-closed eyes.

"Are you tired?" she asked. The rocking of the carriage made her eyes heavy, as well.

"I am, a little. It's been a long journey. Two days to Spokane and two days to return."

"Two days? Of course, that seems correct, but I can't imagine." She glanced at Melinda, now settling in to doze next to her grandmother, and lowered her voice, cupping her mouth.

"It's only about seven hours by train now."

Robert's eyebrows shot up. "It does not seem possible." He shook his head slowly.

Ellie had an almost overwhelming urge to take off his derby and lower his sleepy-looking head to her lap, but she managed to resist the compulsion. Not only would she shock Melinda and Mrs. Chamberlain with such a bold move, a struggle might possibly ensue if Robert bucked her plans and decided to remain upright. She stifled a chuckle at the image of the awkward moment.

"What makes you laugh, Ellie?" Her heart fluttered at the intimate note in his voice. She blushed at the thought of telling him why she laughed.

"I can't say, Mr. Chamberlain." She took a deep breath and turned to stare out the window into the darkness, but his warm, strong fingers guided her chin back toward him. He tilted her face towards his, forcing her to meet his eyes. He quirked an eyebrow in her direction, laughter peeping out from his dark-lashed eyes.

"Can't or won't, my dear Miss Standish?"

Ellie forgot to breathe for a moment...or two. Stars swam before her eyes. Was this what they called starry-eyed?

She inhaled deeply, dragging much needed oxygen into her lungs. No, she couldn't possibly tell him her thoughts.

"Won't, Mr. Chamberlain. Won't." She gently pulled his hand from her chin, resisted a compelling urge to bring the hand to her lips, and leaned her head back to close her eyes and give her overworked, racing heart a much-needed rest.

"We are not done yet, Ellie. You may sleep now, but we are not done, you and I." She knew he leaned close to whisper—close enough to bring goose bumps to her arms and strange stirrings to other body parts—but she kept her eyes firmly shut, though she couldn't prevent a quick grin in response.

The steady thud of the horses' hooves and regular rocking of the carriage lulled her into drowsiness, with the warm, intimate feel of Robert's breath lingering against her ear. Who knew Victorian men could be so...so...sensual? On that thought, Ellie slipped off the precipice...in more ways than one.

CHAPTER SEVEN

It seemed like only moments had passed before she felt Robert shaking her.

"Ellie, we're here. Wake up."

Ellie opened her eyes to find her face pressed against Robert's chest, his arm around her shoulders. She gasped and pulled herself from his arms into a stiffly upright position, with a wary glance in Mrs. Chamberlain's direction.

Robert leaned near. "It is all right, Ellie. They are both asleep, but I must wake them now. I...enjoyed the short nap."

Ellie shook her head and bopped him lightly on the arm.

"You shouldn't have let me sleep like that. I don't know what your grandmother would have said," she hissed.

Robert grinned unabashedly. "We will never know."

The driver came around to open the carriage door. Ellie tried to see over Robert's shoulder but could not. He reached over to touch his sister's arm.

"Melinda, wake up. We're home at last." Melinda roused with a sleepy smile and turned to wake her grandmother.

Robert stepped down from the carriage and held out a hand to Ellie. She laid her hand in his and climbed down the stairs. As he turned to help the other women, Ellie moved away to stare at the house up on the hill. It was an old Queen Anne-style house, but it looked almost new as best she could see from the porch lights. She still couldn't grasp the concept. What she'd previously considered old-fashioned, antique, historical—was now new, modern, state-of-the-art!

Lights spilled out from the three-story house onto the street below. The door stood open and an older man in a dark suit hurried down the steep steps. Ellie's eyebrows shot up and she counted the brick steps as best she could at night—all thirty of them. She turned around to watch Mrs. Chamberlain being handed down from the carriage.

How did the woman do it?

The older man bounded down the last step with a puff, threw a curious glance in Ellie's direction, and moved toward Mrs. Chamberlain while Robert helped Melinda down from the carriage.

"Mrs. Chamberlain, Mr. Chamberlain, Miss Melinda. It's so nice to have you home."

"Thank you, Roger. We are exhausted," Robert replied. Roger offered Mrs. Chamberlain a solicitous arm, and turned to head back up the stairs. A sleepy Melinda lifted her skirts to begin what promised to be a long climb and followed her grandmother.

Robert turned to offer his arm to Ellie.

"Shall we?"

"Oh, Robert, I'll be hanging onto your arm for dear life by the time we get to the top. You don't want me dragging you down."

Robert laughed. "You say the strangest things, Ellie. Of course I want you *dragging* me down. Why else would I offer you my arm?"

She took it reluctantly, hoping against all odds that she wouldn't embarrass herself by huffing and puffing all the way up the steep stairs.

"Robert, do you walk up these stairs every day? How does your grandmother do it?"

He chuckled. "No, I most certainly do not. Some construction is being done to the back of the house, and the carriage is not able to discharge us there at the moment." He heaved a sigh. "So, for now, we must climb the stairs. I expect work to be completed by the end of next week."

Ellie alternated between watching her step and staring up at the house. The dark sky prevented her from determining its color or features, but the twenty or so well-lit windows in her immediate view indicated the house was immense.

"Umm...Robert?"

"Yes, Ellie."

"I don't think I asked. What exactly do you do for a living? I suppose I could just as well have ended up in the...umm...immigrant car in my dream."

Robert threw back his head and laughed, that wonderfully joyous sound she had come to crave. Melinda turned around and smiled.

"Ellie, Ellie. You make me laugh like I have not laughed in years." He pressed her arm closer to his side.

Ellie had all she could do not to start gasping for air at the effects of his nearness and the steepness of the ascent. She tried to drag in air between her teeth as quietly as possible.

"I am a banker...as was my father before me. This was my parents' house. They left it to me."

"Not to Melinda?"

He gave her a curious look. "No, not to Melinda. She has money in trust, which I manage, but daughters do not usually inherit property."

Ellie studied the back of the young woman ahead of her and shook her head.

"Of course. I knew that. How archaic!" she muttered.

"How so, Ellie?"

"I just want you to know that in my time women have as many legal rights as men. So, hang on to your derby, Robert, because the times they are a-changing." She turned a firm, challenging eye on him, to which he responded with a dimpled grin.

"I cannot wait to hear about all the changes, my dear Miss Standish, and I look forward to their challenge as well as to that light in your eyes."

Ellie's face flamed, and she turned her face forward. Mrs. Chamberlain's slow progress halted them halfway up the stairs.

"You really need to get that construction done," Ellie muttered, as an excuse to inhale deeply.

"Yes, I know. I will press the crew tomorrow. This should have been finished while we were gone."

"You said the house had been left to you. Have your parents passed away, Robert?"

He gave her a brief nod. "Yes, they both contracted pneumonia five years ago and died within days of each other. Melinda was only thirteen."

"Oh, Robert, I'm so sorry!"

He laid a warm hand on hers as she clung to his arm. "Thank you. It is one of the diseases that I hope has been eradicated in your time. Has it, Ellie?"

Ellie bit her lip and sighed, though short of breath.

"No, I'm afraid not, Robert. More people survive pneumonia than they used to, but I'm afraid people do still die from it."

He sighed. "I am sorry to hear that. And your family, Ellie? What of them? Will they miss you? Did you leave anyone behind?"

Kyle's face flashed before her eyes, and she wondered if she were lightheaded from the climb.

"No, no one, Robert," she lied. "I left no one behind. My parents passed away several years ago in an accident, and I'm an only child. Of course, as you know, I think I'm dreaming, so I'm likely to wake up at any time." She fervently hoped not, not yet.

They neared the top. Robert pulled her up the last two steps and turned to face her.

"If you *are* dreaming, Ellie, then I hope you do not wake up in the near future. But if you have traveled back in time, then you have come for a reason, and we must discover what that is. I have my suspicions."

Ellie shook her head and smiled but said nothing. It would be interesting to travel in time, but she'd never heard of anyone who actually had in reality—and she, Ellie, would hardly be the first person to do so. More likely, that would be some physicist or somebody with a government black-ops program.

They followed Mrs. Chamberlain, Melinda and Roger through the front door and into a large, circular foyer crowned by a massive, sparkling chandelier which hung down the length of a round staircase leading to the second and third stories. The chandelier's light illuminated the foyer's pale cream paint and reflected off the highly varnished parquet oak floors.

An older woman in a plain, dark gray dress stepped forward.

"Thank you, Mr. White. I'll take Mrs. Chamberlain from here." She took the frail-looking older woman by the arm and began to ascend the stairs.

"Thank you, Mrs. White," Robert said. A married couple Ellie thought. "I'll see about organizing some tea. Would you care for some refreshment before you retire, Mr. Chamberlain?"

Robert removed his hat and laid it on the magnificent oval teak table in the middle of the foyer. He turned to Melinda with an inquiring look.

"Nothing for me, thank you, Robert, Mr. White. I think I will just go up to bed." She followed the two older women up the stairs.

Robert intercepted the butler's curious stare at Ellie. "Yes, Roger, I would like some tea. Two cups, please. Could you ask Sarah to prepare a guest bedroom for Miss Standish, please? She will be staying with us for a period of time."

Ellie winced as the butler studied her clothing for a brief moment before responding.

"Certainly, sir. Where will you take your tea?"

"The study, I think, Roger. When you and Sarah are finished, you can retire. I apologize for keeping everyone awake so late tonight. The train schedule is unforgiving."

Roger nodded. "Think nothing of it, Mr. Chamberlain." He moved away, leaving Ellie standing alone in the foyer with Robert.

She dropped her eyes to the floor with the thought that in a romantic movie, alone at last, she and Robert would now be rushing into each other's arms. If this were a dream, why wasn't that occurring? What kind of rip-off dream was this, anyway? She choked on a slightly hysterical giggle.

"Ellie?" Robert's voice penetrated her rambling inner dialogue.

She looked up to see him gesturing toward a large, closed, paneled door.

"Would you care to join me in the study while your room is being prepared?"

"Oh, sure," she murmured with a barely suppressed chuckle and moved toward the door.

Robert followed and reached from behind to open the door. A shiver ran up her spine as she moved past him.

"You're giggling again, Ellie. I suppose you still won't tell me why."

With shaking shoulders, she turned her head from side to side. "I can't, Robert. I'd be too embarrassed."

"Embarrassed? You? Surely not." He gave an exaggerated sigh and grinned. "Very well. I'll be patient. You will tell me one day."

Ellie entered a massive room remarkable for its dark wood paneling. Long green velvet curtains framed highly polished shelves housing hundreds of hardback books. Several elegant brown velvet chairs rested on an immense golden oriental carpet and faced a massive brick fireplace. A large wooden desk occupied one third of the room.

Ellie dropped into one of the chairs indicated by Robert, finding it surprisingly soft and comfortable. She felt instantly at home and settled into the chair.

"Oh, Robert, this room is beautiful, absolutely beautiful," she breathed as she stared at the carved teak mantelpiece and eye-catching gilded mirror above it.

Robert lowered himself into the chair opposite hers. He surveyed the room thoughtfully.

"Thank you. I'm glad you like it. The house was built by my father, but I decorated this room last year."

"Well, you did a fine job. It is truly wonderful."

He smiled. "You may use it when you like. Grandmother and Melinda do not like the room. They think it is too dark, and they prefer the parlor."

"Well, thank you. I will."

Robert consulted his pocket watch. "It is past one o'clock in the morning. You must be tired."

Ellie grinned. "I am, though I'm not sure what time it is in *my* time. For all I know, I could be getting plenty of rest right now while I sleep."

He narrowed his eyes and fixed her with an exasperated smile.

"Time," he murmured as he crossed his legs and laced his fingers together.

"Dream," Ellie chuckled teasingly.

Roger entered with a tea tray which he set down on a mahogany table between them.

"Cream and sugar, Miss Standish?"

"No, thanks, Roger." Ellie took her steaming cup and admired the delicate gold leaf embossing small roses on the fine white porcelain.

"Thank you, Roger," Robert said. "I will see you in the morning. Not too early, mind you. I'll leave for the office at ten."

"Good night, sir, Miss Standish." Roger closed the door quietly behind him.

Ellie again dropped her eyes to her cup.

"You know, Robert, we have huge mugs to drink tea from now...like your shaving mugs. You do have a shaving mug, don't you?"

"Tea from shaving mugs?" He lifted a skeptical eyebrow. "I cannot imagine. Yes, I have a shaving mug. How did you know?"

"I don't know if you remember, but the Victorian era is one of my areas of interest. I have studied it quite a bit, especially women's rights."

He took a sip of tea and eyed her over the rim of the cup. "Ah, yes, women's rights. Melinda...inheritance. Shall I be hearing about that often from you in the future?" A sly grin goaded Ellie.

"You most certainly will, Mr. Chamberlain. If this isn't a dream and I've traveled back in time—as you believe—then that might very well be my reason for being here."

"*That* being what, Miss Standish?" A playful light in his green eyes threatened to make her laugh, but she refused.

"*That* being to educate you and your ilk on the notion that women are equal to men."

"My *ilk*, Miss Standish? My *ilk?*" he murmured with a twitch of his lips.

Ellie pumped her eyebrows comically. "You like that, eh, Mr. Chamberlain? I'm just trying to remember some old-fashioned words and use them...in honor of my visit to your time." She inclined her head graciously in his direction.

Robert sputtered his tea and set the cup and saucer down with a clatter. He leaned forward, rested his elbows on his knees and buried his face in his hands. Ellie watched his shaking shoulders with apprehension. Did she make him mad?

He dropped his hands to reveal his face convulsed with laughter.

"Oh, my dear Miss Standish! How is my century going to cope with you? How will *I* cope with you?" He shook his head in mock despair.

"As a true Victorian gentleman, Mr. Standish. Unfortunately, as a true Victorian gentleman," Ellie murmured partially under her breath as she longed to throw herself onto his lap and run her fingers through the chestnut waves of his shining hair. Her dream rapidly promised to turn into an epic of unrequited passion and bittersweet yearning.

****

Robert leapt out of bed the next morning and rang the bell for his valet. He could not wait to begin the day, to see Ellie once again, to listen to her strange expressions and watch the charmingly rosy color flow and ebb in her face.

With a knock on the door, his long-time valet, Charles, entered the room, an older gentleman who had been in service with Robert's father. He crossed over to open the curtains.

"You are up bright and early, sir."

Robert paced the room like a caged tiger. He rubbed his hands together briskly.

"Yes, I am, Charles. I could not sleep but merely waited for the sun to come up." Robert crossed to the window and stared out over the city as Charles laid out his clothing. "And the sun has certainly come up. Isn't it a beautiful day?"

He turned from the window to catch Charles' startled look.

"Yes, I know what you are thinking, my good man. What has possessed me, eh?"

Charles pressed his thin lips together and handed Robert his trousers.

"No, sir, I would not presume."

Robert glanced up quickly and grinned.

"Of course you would presume, Charles. You would never tell me, that is all."

"As you like, sir," Charles stoically handed Robert his undershirt.

Robert slipped the soft cotton undershirt on and paused for a moment as if listening. He put a finger to his lips.

"Do you hear anything in the hall, Charles? Is anyone else awake?" Robert crossed to the door and pulled it open, peeking out into the empty hallway. He sighed and closed it quietly.

"We have a guest, you know, Charles. A woman. Her name is Miss Ellie Standish."

"Yes, sir, I heard," Charles responded as he handed Robert a freshly starched white linen shirt.

"Yes, you probably have. She is from Chicago. She will be a guest with us for a while. For some time, I hope."

"Indeed, sir. How fortunate."

Robert paused and looked over at Charles. "Charles, I know you too well. What is it?"

Charles hesitated, then handed his employer a charcoal blue vest.

"Nothing, sir. We heard about Miss Standish's arrival this morning. She sounds like a lovely young woman."

Robert shrugged on his jacket.

"Yes, lovely. Yes, she certainly is lovely. Indeed. I think I will leave work early today and take Miss Standish on a tour of the city. Does that sound like something that might be of interest to a woman, Charles?

Charles dropped the tie he was handing Robert and bent to pick it up. His face was impassive as he held it out. Robert eyed him narrowly. How did the man manage to hide all emotion? Robert hoped he *had* startled the long-time servant, but other than dropping the tie, Charles had betrayed no surprise at Robert's unexpected scheme.

"Certainly, sir. A wonderful idea! So, you will leave work early?"

"Yes, Charles. I will. I will stop by the bank and see if anything pressing requires my attention, and then I will return." Robert drew in a deep breath. "It really is a beautiful day!"

****

Sunlight peeped through the thick curtains of Ellie's bedroom to tease her eyes open. She stretched like a cat from the tip of her head to the last little toe, every muscle stiff and sore as if she had indeed traveled back in time and aged a hundred years. She clasped her hands behind her head and studied the room.

The mattress had proven surprisingly soft and comfortable. She didn't know what sort of material filled it, and she didn't want to know. Her pillow felt like down and feathers, and her vegetarian soul cringed at the thought. Well-ironed, white linen sheets caressed her skin...all of her skin. Without a change of clothes, she'd slept naked. And she had dreamed of Robert...a dream within a dream. A heated blush spread throughout her body, and she pulled the quilt up to her chin. In the dream, Robert had discarded his true Victorian gentleman persona and...

Ellie blocked the thought, heaved a sigh and turned onto her side. Green velvet curtains failed to keep tiny streams of light from spilling into the room. The maid, Sarah, had put her in a whimsically circular room with a four-poster bed and what some might have called antique Queen Anne furniture. Ellie had examined the room and its furnishings thoroughly before she hopped into the massive bed the previous night. The highly polished furniture shone brightly, without nicks and dings, and smelled of freshly cut wood. A cedar chest at the foot of the bed lent a wonderful scent to the room. The antique furniture was, in fact, new.

With no idea of the time, Ellie reluctantly crawled out of bed and found her clothes. She gingerly pressed them to her nose and grimaced. Her clothes were ripe from traveling. She slid into the skirt and sweater, wishing she had something fresh to wear, though she drew the line at a corseted gown. Perhaps a nice loose gingham dress, such as she'd seen photos of pioneer women wearing.

She opened the door and peeked out into the hallway. What time was it? She used her cell phone to tell time, but that was in her purse, somewhere on the train. The modern silver train. She slid out the door and surveyed the darkened hallway. Which way to go?

Trying to retrace last night's exhausted steps following Sarah to the room, Ellie turned to the left. She shuffled quietly along the oriental runner until she reached the grand staircase. Sounds from downstairs reached her ears—a feminine voice, perhaps Mrs. White, or a younger voice. Sarah?

Running her hands lovingly along the gleaming wooden banister, Ellie crept down the stairs. Ornately framed portraits and landscapes decorated the rounded walls of the staircase. Her apprehension grew as she neared the first floor. What would she find in the light of day?

She came to a stop at the bottom of the stairs and listened for the sounds of activity. The wonderful smell of cooked food made her mouth water, and she followed her nose. She crossed the hall and entered a formal dining room such as she'd seen only in photographs of Victorian homes. White lace curtains diffused and softened the bright light from outside. A long mahogany dining table sported a white linen and lace runner underneath a festive arrangement of flowers in the center. The room was empty.

She moved through the room in the direction of the delicious smell and the sound of voices. To her right she saw another room, a circular room painted a soft buttercup yellow. A large round table presided in the center of the circle, and seated opposite the door was Robert, looking rested and refreshed, reading a newspaper. His wet hair gleamed in the sunlight flooding the room. When he looked up, her heart melted at the sight of his cheerful grin.

"Ellie! You're awake! Good morning. Here, come sit down with me. We'll have breakfast together." He jumped up and pulled out a chair next to his.

Ellie hesitated.

"What's wrong?" He cocked his head to the side.

"I...uh...haven't had a shower, and my clothes are...um...travel stained." She gulped. "Maybe I should just sit on the other side. You know...away."

Robert grinned, the charming cleft in his chin deepening.

"Nonsense," he murmured. "Come sit here. I cannot imagine that you would ever smell... That is...not be fresh as a daisy," he finished triumphantly though his face took on a bronze tinge.

Ellie chuckled. "Okay. Don't say I didn't warn you." She slid into the chair next to his.

"I apologize," he said with a sigh as he returned to his seat. "I should have instructed Sarah to show you to the washroom in case you wanted to bathe this morning. Mrs. White will see to it after breakfast." He eyed her speculatively. "You do need some clothes, though. As interesting as yours are, they will only bring uninvited attention. You will need to have something in the current fashion...from this time."

Ellie grinned and shook her head. "Robert, you are such a science fiction fan. What am I going to do with you?"

"Well, I do not rightly know, Ellie. Whatever you like, I suppose. I am at your disposal." He pressed his lips together in a failing effort to stifle a grin, and his green eyes danced.

Sarah, a gangly young girl who appeared to be in her late teens, rushed into the room.

"Oh, Miss Standish, I didn't know you were awake. Mrs. White said I was supposed to show you the washroom as soon as you woke, but I didn't know you were up and about." Her panicked brown eyes flickered from Robert to Ellie and back.

"No need to worry, Sarah. Miss Standish will bathe after breakfast. Could you please bring out some tea and breakfast for her?"

Sarah bobbed. "Right away, sir. Right away." She turned to leave.

"Wait, Sarah!" Ellie called to her escaping back. "Please don't bring anything with meat. I-I'm not sure what you have in there for breakfast, but anything without meat will be fine."

Sarah turned back with an open mouth and a wrinkled brow. "Without meat?" she asked incredulously.

Ellie glanced at Robert for help, only to see him watching the exchange with amusement. He remained mute but gave her an encouraging nod.

She turned back to Sarah.

"Yes, you know, potatoes or eggs. I eat eggs...without the yolk, that is. Or toast! Toast would be just fine."

"I don't know, Miss Standish. I'll have to tell Cook. She'll know what to do." With a last nervous glance in Robert's direction, Sarah fled the room.

"Thank you very much for all the help, Robert." Ellie quirked a wry eyebrow in his direction.

"I thought you handled it yourself beautifully, Ellie. How could I have assisted you any better?" He raised his hands in a mock helpless gesture. She sniffed and crossed her arms.

"Eggs without the yolk?" Robert asked. "What is this about?"

"Cholesterol, you know?" Ellie said. "I'm watching my cholesterol. My dad had high cholesterol, and it can be a genetically inherited trait."

"Cholesterol? I take it this is derived from fat."

She nodded. "Well, I'm no nutritionist, but yes, most of it comes from fat."

"We will have to discuss your menu with Cook. That means no lard, I suppose?

Ellie huffed and shook her head. "Animal fat."

"Cheese?" His smile was rapidly turning into a sly smirk.

"You know I eat cheese. I would like to believe that the milk is humanely obtained."

Robert dropped his smile, and his expression turned grave for a moment.

"I do not know if your visit to the turn of the century is going to make you happy, Ellie. There are many things here that are not necessarily humane or safe or healthy."

Ellie blushed. She was as happy as a clam...in his presence.

"I'm quite content, Robert. Thank you."

He laid a warm hand over hers. "I hope you are, Ellie. I fervently hope that you are."

Ellie's eyes flew to his, and she stilled at the intensity in them. She dropped her gaze and pulled her hand from his, afraid she might lose herself in the depths of his eyes and never come back up for air.

"So, you were saying about clothes?" she said unsteadily.

He leaned back and took a sip of tea. "For today, I think you should borrow some clothing. Would you prefer to borrow from Melinda or from my grandmother? You are all of similar size." The laughter sprang back into his eyes.

Ellie gave him a severe look, but she couldn't repress a chuckle.

"Melinda, please."

"I will ask her before I leave. I must go in to the office this morning. We will see about buying some clothing for you."

"I couldn't, Robert. That's too much trouble and expense. I'm just a stranger—and one who might be simply passing through, at that. Please don't spend any money on me."

"You are no stranger to me, Ellie. I may have met you only yesterday, but I know you. I do not believe you are simply *passing through*." Though he didn't move, Ellie felt as if he whispered in her ear. A smile lingered on his face, but his eyes grew dark and solemn.

At his words, Ellie turned startled eyes on him, but was distracted by Sarah's return with another cup of tea and a plate of food which she placed in front of Ellie with a slight clatter.

"Here, miss. This is everything Cook had ready for breakfast without meat." She dashed out quickly.

Ellie's eyes widened at the sight of the extensive quantity of food heaped on the delicate china plate. A large mound of fried potatoes, two pancakes, four pieces of toast and an oversized, glazed, cinnamon roll all begged for attention.

Ellie gasped. "I can't possibly eat all this."

Robert gave a hearty laugh. "I see Mrs. Smith, our cook, is in rare form today." He leaned forward to study her plate. "She never gives me that much."

"Well, here, have some," Ellie murmured although she had already dug into the potatoes. "This is delicious. My compliments to Mrs. Smith," she mumbled on a bite of toast.

"I will be sure to pass those along to her."

Ellie noticed he stared at her mouth, and she lifted her napkin to her face.

"Do I have crumbs on my face?"

"No, I'm just watching you." He leaned forward conspiratorially. "I was just wondering how they eat in the twenty-first century, but I can see that nothing has changed."

Ellie colored, certain that she did indeed have crumbs on her face. She slowed her pace to an occasional nibble.

"I wonder, Robert..." She hesitated. Such an awkward question.

"Yes, Ellie?" Robert swallowed the last of his tea and checked his watch.

"Who is Constance Green?" Ellie studiously examined the piece of toast in her hand. "Are you and she...?"

"Are we what?" His half smile told her he was being deliberately obtuse.

"You know. Are you...uh...dating?"

"Dating?" His dark eyebrows flew up. "Do you mean are we courting?"

Ellie couldn't remember. Didn't they use the word dating in 1901?

She nodded, her toast suddenly one of the most fascinating objects in the room.

"Yes, courting."

"Why do you ask, Ellie?"

She gave him an exasperated look. The gleam in his eyes matched the dimples in his cheeks.

"Just wondering, Robert. Just wondering." Ellie shrugged with seeming indifference and raised knife and fork to attack a helpless pancake.

"Constance is an old family friend. Her husband was a friend of mine from college."

"Oh. So she's married." Relief flooded through her, and she turned to him with a grin.

He shook his head. "No, Constance is a widow. Her husband died several years ago."

Ellie's spirits drooped again, and she leaned back into her chair and stared at the festive centerpiece of colorful Asiatic lilies. She gave him a speculative look from under her lashes.

"Why aren't you married, Robert?"

Robert burst out laughing. Ellie blushed and glared at him. When he caught his breath, he murmured, "Ellie, that's not the sort of question we usually ask in polite society."

"Well, in *my* world, we don't really ask strangers such things either, but since I'm not sure how long I'll be here, I thought I'd bypass the niceties."

He held up a hand. "Don't remind me, madam. You are just *passing through*, I believe."

"That's right, mister. *Just passing through.* So, why aren't you married?"

He regarded her with amusement for a moment before answering.

"It's hard to say, Ellie. I've never asked anyone to marry me. I suppose that would be a fine answer."

"Why not?" she drilled. She studied his face over her cup of tea.

He gave her a harried look and ran a finger around the edge of his collar.

"Well, it's difficult to say. I-I have not found someone...suitable."

Her eyebrows shot up. "Suitable?"

"Em... Yes, suitable."

"Really?" She eyed him with skepticism.

"Yes, really."

"And what does suitable mean?"

His cheeks bronzed and he shook his head with a weak smile. "I am not quite certain, Ellie. The word sounded...suitable."

"So, you're *not* waiting for someone suitable."

"No, most likely not."

"Then what are you waiting for?" What a stubborn man!

He adjusted his tie and consulted his watch once again.

"Why are you asking me this, Ellie?" His eyes begged for mercy, but Ellie could not relent.

"I don't know, Robert. I suppose because you won't really say. Now, I'm curious, and I can't seem to let it go." She chuckled. "It's awful of me, isn't it?"

"Yes," he murmured. "It is. You are merciless." His lips curved in a faint smile. With another check of his watch, he stood up and rested a hand on Ellie's shoulder. She fought the urge to rub her face against his warmth like a kitten.

"I must go. I will be back in a few hours. I hope to take you on a tour of the city this afternoon. Would that be acceptable to you? I will speak to Melinda before I leave about some...suitable clothing for you."

"Thank you. That sounds wonderful. The tour and the clothing."

"Good. We'll make an afternoon of it. I look forward to it as well."

Her shoulder felt suddenly chilled when he lifted his hand. Watching him cross the room, Ellie admired his tall, lean form in the dark suit and the way his well-trimmed hair kissed the edge of his collar.

He paused at the door and turned slowly, his cheeks still high with color. His gaze flickered beyond her to the window and then back to her face.

"I suppose I have not married because I have never fallen in love before." With a sheepish smile, he turned and left the room.

CHAPTER EIGHT

"What do you think about this?" Melinda held up a dark blue silk skirt. "It goes with this little bolero jacket." She tossed them on the bed and dragged another outfit from the wardrobe. "Wait. I think this would suit you nicely!" She held up a rose-colored wool skirt and jacket and draped them against Ellie. "This is the one! Do you like it? Put it on. We shall see if it fits."

Ellie envied Melinda her youthful enthusiasm. Had she herself ever been that bubbly as a young woman? She thought back over her years of study, long hours in the library with her head stuck between the pages of a book while other girls fell in love and went on dates.

"Come on, Ellie. If you are shy, I can turn my back."

"Thanks, Melinda, if you wouldn't mind."

Melinda, not yet dressed for the day but decidedly attractive in a pale peach and white tea gown, drifted away to sit in a lovely blue brocade chair. She turned her head away.

"Wait, what about a blouse? Don't I need a blouse?" Ellie asked.

Melinda jumped up. "How silly of me. I forgot. Of course you do." She crossed over to her wardrobe and pulled out a white ruffled creation from a large selection of similar white blouses.

"Here," she said as she handed the white batiste blouse to Ellie and sped back to her chair to turn her head toward the wall once again.

Ellie laid the clothing out on the bed and kept a wary eye on Melinda. She'd hated physical education classes for the very same reason—changing in front of other girls. Melinda kept her head firmly turned away.

"I do not hear anything, Ellie. Are you changing? You cannot want me to get a crick in my neck, do you?"

"I'm hurrying...if I can...figure out...how to get this..." Ellie pulled her bulky turtleneck sweater up and over her head and dropped her skirt. She rolled her eyes as she surveyed her undergarments. Why couldn't she have been blessed with an overnight bag for her dream...or travel...just a small carryall with an extra pair of underwear, a clean, crisp bra, a toothbrush and some deodorant.

Ellie stepped into the soft rose wool skirt and pulled it up, dismayed at the tight fit over her hips. She suspected she'd have to sit very carefully in order to prevent the seams from ripping. She grabbed the blouse and tussled with the small buttons and extra unidentified material. Ellie tried to remember photos she had seen of the fashions of the time. The extra fabric had to be some sort of bow or tie for the neckline. She slipped into the soft blouse and pushed her arms through the long sleeves which were narrow along the lower arms and wrists but puffed to gigantic proportions at the shoulders and upper arms.

Ellie giggled. She couldn't possibly wear this in public.

"Are you dressed, Ellie?"

She choked back a gurgle of laughter. "Not yet. One more minute." Ellie reached to zip up the skirt but it stuck. No amount of tugging would free it.

"Can you come help me, Melinda? I'm stuck."

Melinda turned and jumped up. She began to laugh, this time without hiding it behind her hand. As frustrated as Ellie was, she responded to the infectious tinkling sound with a grin.

"Oh, Ellie, you look a fright. Let me see." Melinda turned Ellie to face her and surveyed her critically. "Well, you must tie the bow of course. What is wrong with the skirt?" She reached for it and tugged. It did not budge.

"Oh, dear, Ellie. I am afraid it does not fit. Are you wearing a corset?" Melinda's cheeks took on a pink tinge.

Ellie's eyebrows shot up. "A corset? Certainly not!"

Melinda nodded sagely and stepped back. "Well, I am afraid the skirt will not fit without a corset. It was designed to be worn with a smaller waist. *I* cannot wear it without a corset. We had better find one for you."

"No," Ellie squeaked, bringing Melinda to an abrupt halt as she headed for the wardrobe. "I-I can't wear a corset!"

Melinda turned slowly, tilted her head and regarded Ellie with wide blue eyes. "Why ever not, Ellie? All proper ladies wear corsets. Even grandmother."

Ellie wanted to sink into a chair, but the tightness of the skirt prevented it. She bit her tongue against her first instinct to rant about the sexism of squeezing a female form into a binding corset as she studied Melinda's innocent face. It seemed obvious that women perpetuated their own fashion crimes...especially among the upper classes.

"I-I don't think I can squeeze into one."

Melinda's eyes widened. "Are you saying you have never worn a corset, Ellie? How is that possible?"

Ellie bit her lip. "Umm...we just don't wear corsets where I come from, Melinda."

"Really?" Her eyes almost popped.

"Really." Ellie nodded.

"Well, that is just not possible here. You must wear one, certainly if you want to get into any of my clothes. They are *all* designed to be worn with a corset." She moved toward her wardrobe. "And you want to go out in the carriage and see the city today with Robert, don't you?"

The thought of spending more time in Robert's company clinched the deal. Ellie suspected Melinda might have great success selling used cars.

"All right," Ellie sighed. "Then I think I'm going to need...umm..."

"You will need a chemise and a corset cover and several petticoats." The fashion crisis averted, Melinda bustled around importantly, pulling white garments from drawers. "I had better summon my maid, Alice, to help." She handed Ellie the soft white underclothing and crossed the room to pull on a small cord hidden near the curtains.

Ellie stared at the pile of clothing in her hand, uppermost of which was a dauntingly heavy and stiff corset with deceptively soft and feminine pink ribbons.

"How am I going to wear all this underneath, when I can't even squeeze into the skirt as it is?"

Melinda crossed her arms and regarded Ellie with a matronly expression.

"You will manage. We all manage."

A tap on the door heralded the arrival of a petite maid dressed in the ubiquitous plain gray servant's dress. Ellie eyed her with suspicion. It seemed obvious that the tiny, freckle-faced, redheaded maid had never had to wear a corset in her life.

"Yes, miss?"

"Alice, could you please help Miss Standish into these garments? I am going downstairs to have some tea and breakfast while you dress." She moved toward the door. "Oh, and could you dress her hair? An upsweep. You know what to do, Alice."

Alice bobbed at the closing door and turned to Ellie. Ellie held up a hand to ward her off. "Wait, Alice. Just a minute. I can get into the...um...undergarments by myself. Could you just turn around for a minute while I put them on?"

"Yes, miss." Alice's brown eyes popped, but she rotated and faced the wall.

Ellie managed first to extricate herself from the tight clothing and then slipped out of her bra and underwear, promising to give them a good washing in the bathroom sink when she returned to her room.

She sorted through the undergarments and pulled out something that remotely resembled pictures of a chemise. She shook the simple white linen garment out and slipped it over her head. Conscious of a draft on her nether regions, she grabbed a pair of drawers and slipped them on, knowing she would never be able to return these intimate garments to Melinda. But one look at the clothing spilling from Melinda's wardrobe suggested she would hardly miss a few things.

With still more white lacy undergarments in her hand, Ellie drew a blank.

"Okay, Alice, I'm lost. What is this thing?"

Alice turned and blinked. She moved forward hesitantly.

"Why, it's a corset cover, miss. It goes over the corset."

"So, what do I put on next?"

"The corset, miss. I can help you with that."

If Alice had questions, as her wide-eyed look suggested, she was too polite to ask.

"If you would raise your arms, miss."

Alice took the beribboned corset and wrapped it around Ellie's waist. Ellie instinctively sucked her stomach in and straightened.

"I'm just going to tighten it now," Alice murmured.

As Ellie felt the corset begin to mold to her body, she noticed her upper torso pushed forward while her rear bent backward. Something was seriously wrong. She couldn't breathe.

"Wait, Alice, wait." Ellie took a shallow breath and murmured. "Is this thing on straight? I'm practically bent over."

"Yes, miss, that's the way it is supposed to look. It's an S-bend corset. All the ladies wear them."

Ellie twisted her neck to quirk an eyebrow at Alice.

"I don't think you have one on, do you, Alice?"

Alice's face turned pink. "Me? Oh no, miss. The servants don't wear them." She began to pull again. "Actually, I think only the wealthy ladies wear them."

"You must be kidding. Why, for Pete's sake?"

"Why...to look beautiful, ma'am. With small waists and rounded... Well, you know what I mean. I wish I could wear one. They're so pretty."

Ellie grunted. "I can't breathe. Can you loosen it?"

"No, miss. This is as loose as I can make it. You will get used to it. Miss Melinda used to cry when she first started wearing her corsets, but she doesn't any more. Are you ready for the petticoats?"

"I feel like a pigeon. My chest is sticking out." Ellie tried desperately to straighten but the corset kept her bent. "Petticoats? There's more than one?"

"Yes, miss."

Alice helped her step into not one but two white linen petticoats adorned with lace and light blue ribbons. Ellie thought it a shame no one would ever see the beautiful undergarments.

Finally, Alice helped her into the original rose-colored tailored skirt, which now magically zipped up all the way. Alice grabbed the blouse and slipped it over Ellie's shoulders. She buttoned the blouse, tucked it inside the waistband of the skirt and tied a decorative bow at the neck.

"Should we do your hair before we put the jacket on? Do you have shoes, miss?"

Unable to bend her ribcage to see her feet, Ellie stuck out a bare toe.

"Oh, dear. You need shoes, stockings and garters. Let me see if Miss Melinda has anything. You may have the same size feet." Alice moved away to the magic cupboard and pulled out a pair of silk stockings and a set of little black boots.

"You'd better have a seat here, and I'll put these on. I'm sorry, miss. I should have helped you put these on earlier. We're going about this backward." She busied herself pulling up the stockings and sliding garter belts up to Ellie's thighs.

Ellie's face flamed at the intimacy. "That's all right, Alice. It was my fault. I put on the undergarments out of sequence, I think."

Alice tied the boots and stood back. Ellie held out a helpless hand. Alice grinned and pulled her up.

"There, now. You look lovely, ma'am. How do you feel?" She pulled Ellie toward a white-painted dressing table crowned by a charming oval mirror. Ellie sank onto the small blue velvet stool, doing her best to sit as straight as an S-bend corset would allow.

"I'm miserable, Alice, but thank you for all your hard work."

"It will get easier, miss," Alice murmured. "Don't you worry. Women dress this way every day." She undid Ellie's braid and began to brush her long hair with a silver-backed brush in long, soothing strokes. Ellie had a quick recollection of her mother brushing her hair in just that way before bedtime.

A knock on the door brought Melinda back into the room. Ellie looked at her in the mirror, gaining a new respect for the uncorseted tea gown she wore.

"You look beautiful, Ellie, absolutely beautiful." She flitted across the room and pulled a small, rose velvet chair next to Ellie. "How do you feel?"

Ellie gave her a wry smile. "As I mentioned to Alice here...miserable. I can't believe you wear all these clothes every day."

Melinda sighed. "I know." She brightened. "Still, it certainly displays your tiny waist to perfection."

Ellie tried to glance down at her so-called "tiny waist," but Alice had a mass of hair in her hand which prevented any movement.

"Mmmmm, thank you."

"Tell me about Chicago, Ellie. That is where you come from, isn't it? How is it they do not wear corsets in Chicago? I thought it a truly modern city...much like Seattle."

Ellie tried to regress a hundred years.

"Oh, I'm sure they do, Melinda. I-I don't wear them, but I think many women do."

"Hmmm...only the working class does not have to wear..." In the mirror, Ellie saw Melinda bite her lip and blush. "Well, never mind. I know so little about you. Are you married? Do you have family? Where are they? Do they miss you?"

Ellie concentrated on remembering the sequence of questions in the bubbly barrage.

"Wait, let me see. No, I don't have family, my parents passed away several years ago. I'm not married yet, and I doubt if my fiancé misses me—" Ellie froze, her heart in her throat. Maybe Melinda missed it. She didn't.

"Your fiancé? Are you to be married then?" Melinda's blue eyes popped and she clapped her hands. "How exciting! What is his name? When?"

Ellie swallowed hard and wondered if she could ask for Melinda's confidence. To what end? Melinda would only wonder why Ellie wanted to hide her engagement.

"Oh, Melinda, I shouldn't have mentioned that. It's not a big thing...really. I don't know when." She sniffed. "Maybe never. Forget I ever said anything."

Melinda stuck out a pink lower lip and eyed Ellie with concern.

"Not a big thing," she repeated in the tone of someone savoring an unfamiliar expression. She nodded. "I take it you do not wish to discuss it, then. I understand. It is a private matter. I apologize for prying." Melinda jumped up in a restless movement. "Still though, I would love to be engaged." She twirled around the room with her arms wide. "Parties and balls and dinners and breakfasts...plus a handsome man at my side. Wouldn't it be wonderful?"

Ellie watched her with a stirring of affection. An engagement would come soon if Melinda had anything to say about it.

Alice was working miracles into what Ellie recognized as a Gibson hairdo—a glorious upswept style guaranteed to make any woman look tall and elegant.

"So, you want to be married," she murmured.

Melinda stopped dancing and plopped down on the chair once again with a whiff of lavender. "I do not know that I want to be married *yet*, but I would love to be engaged. That would be exciting. Some of my friends want to marry so they can be free to set up their own homes, but Robert lets me do as I please, and I do not feel restricted here. I would like to be in love though." Her voice trailed away on a sigh.

Ellie couldn't help herself and matched Melinda's contagious sigh, the memory of a pair of green eyes tugging at her heart. "I know what you mean."

Melinda's sharp ears turned toward Ellie. "But you are already engaged." She bit her lower lip. "I apologize, Ellie. I am such a busybody." She jumped up and glided toward her wardrobe. "Hurry, Alice. I have to dress for Amy's tea party this afternoon."

"Yes, miss."

"I didn't know you were going out," Ellie said. "So, you're not coming on the tour, then?"

"Oh no, that is just you and Robert. Grandmother feels unwell, and I have the party to attend."

"Oh."

Melinda misunderstood. "I would invite you to accompany me, but you had the previous engagement with Robert. You will have an enjoyable time, Ellie. Robert is a wonderful man, kind and gentle. There is no need to be afraid of him."

"I don't doubt it," Ellie said with a blissful sigh.

Alice stuck a sprig of small silk roses and baby's breath into the crown of Ellie's hair. Freed from the maid's ministrations, Ellie turned to watch Melinda. She chewed on her lip for a moment and drew in a deep breath.

"Melinda, why hasn't Robert married before now?"

Melinda rummaged through her undergarment drawers, tossing aside one petticoat after another.

"What?" she asked distractedly. "Robert? I do not know why he has not found a wife, really. I tease him about being a confirmed bachelor all the time. He is in his late 30s, you know. Quite old." She grinned and continued ransacking her wardrobe.

Ellie held out her hand to Alice with beseeching eyes. Alice grinned and pulled her upright. She almost toppled over and leaned on Alice while she regained her balance.

Melinda continued. "Although that may change soon. Constance has her eye on him, you know."

"I didn't know," Ellie murmured with a pain in her chest. The corset...too tight.

"Yes. She has not said anything to me directly, but I have seen the way she looks at Robert...ever since her husband died."

"Really?"

"Grandmother thinks she is too old for Robert. She says that Robert needs to look for a young woman who can give him children. I think Constance is the same age as Robert."

Ellie felt faint. Her thirty-fifth birthday had come and gone.

"But Constance can still have children in her thirties." Ellie knew she defended herself.

"Yes, but Grandmother still thinks she is too old for Robert. She wants Robert to marry someone in her early twenties. Something about healthy children. I do not know what she means exactly."

Melinda finally found a few garments that pleased her and tossed them on the bed.

"Are you feeling well, Ellie? You look positively green. Is the corset too tight?" Melinda moved toward her and raised a motherly hand to Ellie's forehead.

"I'm fine. It is tight, but Alice says it's as loose as it can be. I'll be fine."

"Well, you look absolutely stunning."

Ellie shrugged on the matching rose bolero jacket and surveyed herself in the mirror. Her face did look pale, but she had to admit she looked very...Victorian. Her ash-brown hair shone from Alice's brushing, and the upswept style suited Ellie's oval face. The clothing, although miserably uncomfortable, gave her an elegant height she'd never known in all her vertically challenged years. She preened.

"Thank you. I do look quite regal, if I may say so."

Melinda laughed and turned away. "I must hurry to dress as well. Robert should be here soon. I will see you this evening at dinner."

Ellie's best intentions to sashay to the door were hampered by the corset and the boots which covered her feet somewhere far below her skirts. She managed a stilted prance until she got through the door.

She leaned on the wall to catch her breath and eyed the round staircase which once seemed so charming but now loomed terrifyingly as a death-defying stunt. The bedroom door flew open, and Melinda erupted into the hallway.

"Wait, Ellie. You forgot your hat. No well-bred lady goes outside without a hat."

"A hat? On this fabulous hairdo?"

Melinda laughed and dragged her back inside. From the nether regions of the mysterious wardrobe, Alice brought out a large, black, velvet hat trimmed with rose-colored ribbons.

"Sit down, Ellie. Alice cannot put it on your head if you do not sit down."

Ellie eyed the stool, remembering she had to be levered off it. She sighed.

Alice perched the dark hat atop Ellie's hairdo at an angle which dipped toward her right eye. Ellie rolled her eyes. She couldn't see anything but the brim of the hat above her nose. In the mirror, she saw Alice approach with a long pearl-tipped hatpin that she stuck into the hat and through the bun on top of her hair.

Melinda hovered. "There now. You look ravishing. Off you go."

Ellie put a tentative hand to the creation on her head to see if it would move with her...or against her. It stayed in place. She twisted her neck gingerly to eye Alice, who grinned and pulled her upright.

Once outside the door, Ellie again paused to lean a hand against the wall. As if matters had not already been treacherous with the unfamiliar boots, the corset, her bizarre posture and the heavy hairdo, now she needed to contend with a heavy, oversized, albeit beautiful, hat which threatened to throw her off balance.

She moved to the head of the stairs and gripped the railing. Tilting her head back as best she could to counterbalance her weight, she stepped down gingerly, feeling her way down the stairs one step at a time since she could not look down to see her feet. Halfway down the interminable descent, the front door of the foyer opened and Robert came into view. He looked up, and his eyes widened. Ellie heard his quick intake of breath. She paused for a moment and gulped, hoping she wouldn't disgrace herself with a tumble down the stairs. His lips curved into a slow smile, and Ellie's knees wobbled in response.

"Ellie, you look absolutely beautiful." He moved to take the steps two at a time arriving to hold out his arm.

"May I?"

Ellie nodded mutely, and gratefully took his arm. Once they reached the bottom step, Robert stood back and surveyed her once again. Ellie's face burned, and she attempted to take a deep breath.

"I knew you were beautiful, Ellie, but I had no idea how charming you would look in *my time*." He grinned.

"Thank you, Robert, but I have to tell you *your time* is killing me." She grimaced. "There is absolutely no question of my eating or drinking while I am in this costume."

His eyes ran up and down her body rakishly. "Yes, I can see that you are much more...restricted than you were in your other clothing."

She laid a hand on the table for support.

"I'll say."

"Shall we?" He took her arm and led her outside.

Ellie paused on the elegant wraparound porch and stared at the city below. No skyscrapers towered above this turn-of-the-century city of rolling greenery and sparkling blue lakes. A light haze of pollution hung in the moist air, settling over the panoramic vista. From the landmarks, she recognized their location. The Chamberlains lived on Queen Anne Hill, so named for the number of homes built at the end of the nineteenth century in the Queen Anne style of architecture.

"What are you thinking?" Robert murmured as they descended the stairs.

"Oh, gosh, lots of things! How different the city looks, how much pollution already hangs in the air, yet how beautiful it still is."

"It is a beautiful city, isn't it? You will have to tell me about this...pollution some time. I would be interested to hear of that."

Despite Ellie's unfamiliarity with the mechanics of her voluminous clothing and her inability to see her feet, their descent of the stairs was quicker today than the ascent the night before, and Robert handed Ellie up into the carriage. She put out a protective hand to guard her hat while trying to hoist her skirts up with the other, and she wondered how women got anything done in this century, hampered as they were by their clothing. She remembered reading, though, that while upper-class women were restricted in their movements and probably could do little significant manual labor, they did contribute heavily with time and energy to charitable works.

Robert climbed in beside her, and the carriage moved off. Ellie sat awkwardly forward not only because the bend of the corset required it but also because the wide brim of her hat needed extra room. She tried to turn toward Robert but hit him in the face accidentally.

"Oops, sorry. I'm trying to get used to this thing."

He laughed. "I'm sure you are. Women have taken to wearing larger and larger hats recently. I suspect it has very little to do with keeping their heads warm and more to do with outshining each other."

"You're probably right, Robert. And believe me, that will not change by the twenty-first century."

He laughed with his endearingly unique male resonance and touched her hand briefly. Ellie had enough trouble gasping for air in her corset without having her breath stolen by his charm.

Robert proved to be a wonderfully insightful tour guide. Giving in to her requests to see specific sites, he took her down to a vendor's market, the forerunner of the modern Pike's Place Market, she realized. As they wandered the covered stalls, she described how it would look...as well as she could remember, having only been to the market once before. She asked to go down to the waterfront, but he vetoed that as being too rough a neighborhood for a lady.

"It's quite trendy now, you know, with restaurants and musicians and lots and lots of tourists," she murmured with a sigh.

"Trendy? What does that mean?"

Ellie loved stumping the normally confident man with strange terms. The confusion on his face gave him such a vulnerable look.

"Popular."

"Ah! Popular." He nodded. "Trendy," he repeated to himself.

"I wanted to get a closer look at the clipper ships in the bay. We don't have those anymore, or if we do, they're very rare. Historic."

"You can see the ships in the bay from any window in the front of the house. They are much more attractive from a distance. They boast quite a heavy stench close up."

"Really?" She sighed.

He gave her a sympathetic look. "Would you like to have some lunch at a park? I had Mrs. Smith put a picnic together for us."

She turned to him with a pleased smile. "Aw, Robert, that would be wonderful! Yes, let's go to the park."

A half hour later, the driver pulled into a lovely park on a beautiful blue lake. Robert helped Ellie down while the driver unloaded several baskets from the coach. After spending the last several hours clutching at her skirts to keep them from the dirt roads common to the turn of the century, Ellie was pleased to see a wooden promenade skirting the lake. Small boats took passengers out onto the calm water to lull the day away in the rare sunshine of the often rainy Pacific Northwest.

Ellie hesitated, unsure of what to do, but Robert took her hand in his arm.

"Shall we walk for a while?" he asked.

Ellie watched the couples and families strolling along the lake's edge, and she hesitated.

"I don't know, Robert. Teeter-tottering around in this outfit in the vendor's market was one thing. It was too crowded for anyone to notice anything, but these people are strolling like professionals. I mean, they're *really* promenading."

Robert laughed, and she tilted her head back at an angle to glare.

"Oh, Ellie, you make me laugh with your odd sayings. Promenading, indeed. Of course, they are. It *is* a promenade."

He turned to the driver, a silent young man with dark hair and a mustache.

"Jimmy, lay our things out over there, please." He nodded in the direction of a picnic area dotted with several black wrought iron tables and chairs. "We will return shortly."

He looked down at her and gave her hand a firm squeeze.

"Shall we, madam?"

He didn't wait for an answer but moved out, his pace slow to accommodate Ellie's unsure steps. Ellie kept her eyes on the boardwalk for several reasons—one was to watch her footing.

"Ellie, my dear, lift your head. No one will notice anything unusual about you except that you are a beautiful woman." He peered around the corner of her hat. "Although quite fetching, that hat is extremely inconvenient. I cannot see your face."

She tilted her head and turned toward him, knowing her cheeks must be as rosy as her dress.

"There you are," he murmured softly with a dancing light in his eyes.

"Mr. Chamberlain, I believe you are flirting with me." She used her hat to shield her embarrassed face. The large black, rose-ribboned concoction actually had some value after all.

He paused for a moment, standing stock still so that she had to rotate, since he still held her arm. She ended up facing him. He dipped his head and looked into her eyes with a playful grin.

"Why, Miss Standish, I do believe I am." He reached up with his free hand and softly touched the line of her cheek. Ellie's blush deepened. She longed to rub against his hand but resisted once again.

"Robert. Miss Standish."

Ellie turned quickly, almost knocking herself off balance.

Constance stood in front of them on the promenade, an odd expression on her face. She was accompanied by a younger blonde woman dressed like Constance in a dark blue, tailor-made silk skirt with a white blouse.

CHAPTER NINE

"Constance. How are you today? I did not expect to see you up and about so early after our late arrival." Robert dipped his hat in her direction.

Ellie nodded a greeting, but ran a quick hand up to steady her hat. She did not miss Constance's frank, appraising stare.

"I promised my niece, Amanda, that I would bring her to the park today. Amanda, you remember Mr. Chamberlain. And this is Miss Standish."

Ellie greeted the young girl, who watched her aunt with adoration.

"Miss Standish, you look quite...stunning today." Constance's voice held some reserve.

Ellie ducked her head. "Thank you, Constance. You also look very beautiful."

Constance had the grace to blush. She put a hand to her large, dark blue, netted hat.

"Well, thank you. I could murmur *this old thing*, but in fact, it is new."

"Are we still expecting you for supper tonight, Constance."

Ellie flinched for just a moment, and Robert tightened his arm.

"Yes, Robert, I am still planning to come. Seven p.m., correct?"

Robert nodded with a practiced smile. "Yes, seven it is." He tipped his hat to her. "Well, if you will excuse us, Constance, we must move on. I am doing a poor job of showing Ellie the city."

"Are you new to Seattle then, Miss Standish?" Constance fixed Ellie with dark eyes, an almost imperceptible narrowing the only sign of strong emotion.

Ellie blinked. "Please call me Ellie. Yes, I am new. I've never been here before." It seemed better to lie than to dream something else up.

"Well, you have a fine tour guide in Robert." Constance relaxed her face and nodded. "Please excuse us. I will see you this evening, Robert."

She moved away with Amanda, and Ellie resisted the urge to turn around and watch her graceful gait. She was fairly sure she could learn a lot from Constance about the art of feminine elegance in this era.

She moved on with Robert, wincing as they passed an occasional fellow stroller who nodded, tipped his hat or dipped her head and murmured "Good day, Mr. Chamberlain."

"Robert, I didn't realize we would see so many people who know you. What will they think?"

He greeted another couple who nodded at him.

"About what, Ellie?"

"About me, I guess. I really feel like I'm sticking out. Like they can tell."

"Tell what?" He paused and turned to her. "What can they tell?"

"Well, that I'm..." She ducked her head, but he raised her chin with a gentle index finger, forcing her to meet his green-eyed gaze.

"You're...?"

"Different, odd, out of place," she muttered.

"That's what I love about you, Ellie. You *are* different...from any woman I've ever met." He tapped the tip of her nose and resumed walking.

She trod on in a daze. Had he just said *love*? As *in love*?

"Come, I am famished," Robert said. "Shall we have our luncheon now?" He led the way over to the picnic Jimmy had set up. A large, white, linen tablecloth covered the small, round, wrought iron table. Robert pulled out a matching, black-painted, wrought iron chair and lowered her into it. Jimmy had set out several simple white porcelain plates and plain silverware along with linen napkins.

"Let's see what Cook has prepared for us."

He brought out a plate of roasted chicken, a bowl of potato salad, a packet of cheese, bread, several slices of chocolate cake, bananas, two apples, raisins and almonds. Ellie eyed the large hamper with amazement. It seemed bottomless, like some magician's hat. The food just kept coming.

"Is there anything here that you can eat? I see that there are some things without meat, but will it be enough to satisfy your hunger?"

"I doubt if I can eat anything while I'm wearing this corset, but yes, there is plenty of food." She ran a hand along her narrow waist.

Robert paused and stared at her waist with a frown.

"You look to be in pain, Ellie. You must do away with that silly thing. I don't know why women wear them anyway."

Ellie raised an amused eyebrow. "Well, in my case, I can't get into Melinda's clothes without them."

"We should have a seamstress come by tomorrow. She can adjust a few things. Please do not wear that thing again. I do not like to see you so miserable. I want you to be happy here."

"I don't think I'll be able to wear it again. I'm fairly sure I've cracked a rib...or two." She grinned, wondering about the improbability of discussing her underwear with a man she'd met only the day before...in the late Victorian/early Edwardian era.

"Ummm...Robert? Don't you think it's strange that we are discussing my...underwear?"

He ladled some potato salad onto her plate and flashed his dimples. A bronze tinge touched his cheeks.

"Actually, yes, I do, Ellie. Very odd! In fact, I cannot say that I have ever had a discussion with a woman about her...em...undergarments."

Ellie saw an opening and went for it with an arched eyebrow in his direction. "Not once, Robert?"

While Robert busily searched the basket for wine and glasses, Ellie watched with glee as his hands stilled. He turned to her with a decidedly bright red face.

"I...em... Well, that is..." He scanned a mysterious spot over her shoulder in the distance.

"Oh, Robert, you should see your face." Ellie broke out into a rib-clutching laugh, the more so because her clothes did not allow for expansion. "It's priceless. No need to answer, Mr. Chamberlain. I would assume at your age that you are no...uh...saint."

"Ellie," he reprimanded, his color still high. "I hardly think this is an appropriate subject for discussion." He tossed back the entire goblet of wine he'd just poured.

She patted his hand, loving him all the more for his charming vulnerability. "Don't worry, Robert. I won't bring it up again. Unless you do."

His color receded, and he reached for a slice of bread with an unsteady hand.

"Thank you," he murmured, busily making a sandwich as if it were the most challenging task he had faced to date.

The imp on Ellie's shoulder goaded her.

"But you will tell me some time, won't you?" she prodded. "Whether you've been a saint or not, that is?"

She gurgled with laughter when he dropped his sandwich.

"Ellie, I really must insist you stop this line of questioning. It is not seemly."

"I know," she said with a quirked brow and a mischievous grin as she bit into an apple. Undaunted, she continued to chuckle. "I'm from the twenty-first century, you know, Robert. Things are different now."

"Now or then?" he muttered while he tried to pick up the pieces of his bedraggled sandwich.

"Then."

"I see. Well, I'm sure it must be very...adventurous in your time, Ellie. We are not so bold at this time."

"*We* are. Besides, I thought you said you *loved* that about me—that I'm so different. Remember? Just a few moments ago?"

He tossed back another glass of wine and eyed her with a raised brow. "Really, was it only a few moments ago?"

She nodded, forgetting the weight of her hat.

"Mmmm-hmmm."

"And what about you, Ellie?"

Busily adjusting her hat, which seemed in danger of sliding off her head and taking her hair with it, Ellie lost track of the thread of the conversation.

"What about me?"

Robert rested his arms on the table and leaned forward. "Are you a...a saint?"

As his words sunk in, she stopped fidgeting and stared at him. Color flooded her face. She could honestly say she had never expected proper Robert to tease her back along the same lines. His eyes glittered, and his smile sported a rakish tilt to the corner.

She thought fast and hard. The wrong answer might turn this turn-of-the-century man from her.

"In your time? No, I wouldn't be considered a saint. But in my time? I might as well be."

Nonplussed, Robert sat back against his chair and toyed with his empty glass.

"What does that mean?"

Ellie grinned. "Maybe I'll tell you someday, Mr. Chamberlain. This food is wonderful." She bit into her food with apparent gusto and said no more. She felt Robert's intent gaze but kept her eyes on the plate in front of her until she saw out of the corner of her eye that he picked up his own food and began to eat.

****

Robert returned to his room from the washroom and sat down to allow Charles to comb his hair and trim the ends.

"How was your outing today, sir?"

Robert looked at the older man in the mirror. He caught sight of his own reflection. For pity's sake, his cheeks were as pink as a girl's. He ran a quick hand along his jaw with a rueful smile and cleared his throat.

"Wonderful, Charles. I had a very pleasant time."

"I am glad to hear it, Mr. Chamberlain. You certainly deserve to take some time from work."

"Yes, it was really very pleasant to walk about during the middle of the day. I don't do it enough. As you see, my face took some sun today."

The comb in Charles' hand stilled for a moment. Robert narrowed his eyes, grinned and dared the older man to say something.

"Yes, sir, of course."

"Oh, Charles, you know I am teasing. Behold me blushing like a child."

"Blushing, sir? I would not have known it was a blush."

Robert jumped up and pulled his dark blue velvet bathrobe closely about him.

"Yes, I had a wonderful time. Pick out some clothing that suits me well, Charles. I want to look very handsome this evening."

"Mr. Chamberlain, you always look handsome."

Robert's face reddened once again. "Good gravy, it seems even you can make me blush. Have I no self-control?"

"As much as you need, sir. I am certain of that."

With a sigh, Robert shrugged out of his robe and slipped on his undergarments.

"I hope you are right, Charles. I am not as certain of that as you."

He continued to dress in silence as he contemplated the night ahead. Would Ellie dance with him? Would he do her justice or fall all over her feet in an effort to impress her? She had looked quite stunning today in her lovely rose suit, albeit a bit uncomfortable. What would she look like tonight? What did her hair look like down around her shoulders? He longed to find out, but it seemed unlikely that would happen tonight.

****

At 6:30 p.m. Melinda and Alice were still trying to stuff Ellie into an evening dress of dark blue silk.

"Ellie, you really must wear the corset."

"No, Melinda, please don't make me wear that thing again. My ribs are bruised. Robert said I didn't have to."

Melinda froze. "Robert?" She peered into Ellie's face. "What does he have to do with this? Do not tell me you discussed your...undergarments with him!"

Ellie colored and grinned sheepishly. "Yes?"

"Ellie, you are such a strange creature. Sometimes, it is as if you are from another world. We do not discuss those matters with men, and it is really none of their business."

"Well, then why do we wear these things? If men don't care, why do I have to torture myself in a corset?"

Melinda grimaced and tugged some more on Ellie's dress. "I have no earthly idea. Alice, why do we wear those silly things?"

Alice's eyes bulged. "Oh, miss, I wouldn't know." She giggled. "I don't even own one."

"Lucky you," Ellie whispered under her breath as she sucked in her stomach to see the dress finally snap into place around her curves. She tested it gingerly by walking across the room. The silk material rustled delightfully, and she felt like a princess going to a ball. Alice had redone her hair to leave a few curls falling to her shoulders. A sprig of glass crystals peeked out from the crown of her hair.

Melinda followed Ellie to the mirror and made some minor adjustments to the off-shoulder gown with its heart-shaped bodice. She stood next to Ellie and surveyed her own golden taffeta dress, similar in style but uniquely flattering to her particular blonde coloring.

"We look very stylish tonight, I must say."

"Yes, we do, don't we?" Ellie murmured. "Is your grandmother coming down to dinner?"

"Yes. We are having quite a few guests tonight, as a matter of fact."

Ellie turned to stare, open-mouthed. "What? Like a dinner party? I thought this was just your family and Constance."

"Oh, no. We have had this planned for some time. I am surprised Robert did not explain. There is to be dancing afterward."

"Dancing?" Ellie choked. She held up a hand as if to ward off an invisible terror. "Melinda, *I* don't know how to dance. I'll just head to bed early. No wonder Robert didn't mention this. He knew I would take off," she muttered.

"What do you mean *take off?*" Melinda leaned into the mirror and smoothed back a wisp of hair.

"Leave. Depart."

Melinda turned to Ellie with a waggling finger.

"Well, you are not *taking off* then. You are staying for the evening. We should have great fun. Some of my friends are coming, and there is one young man...James." She blushed. "It will be great fun."

Ellie eyed her skeptically. She tried to smile, but one or both sides of her lips failed to cooperate beyond a slight grimace.

"Are you ready? We should go downstairs."

"As ready as I'll ever be." Ellie tried to take a deep breath but failed.

The air seemed thin. "Good night, Alice. Thank you."

"Oh, good night, miss. I've laid out a nightgown for this evening, and a tea gown for the morning."

"Thank you, and thank you so much, Melinda, for loaning me your clothes."

"You are welcome, Ellie. I am happy to see you wear them. I have grown too tall for them."

Ellie hovered in Melinda's shadow as they descended the stairs. She followed Melinda as the younger woman lifted her chin and sailed into the drawing room, where some guests already waited. Ellie found an inconspicuous spot by the wall while she watched Melinda, the first of the family to arrive, work the crowd by welcoming the guests, cooing over beautiful gowns and shaking men's hands. Already quite the accomplished hostess at her young age, she appeared to be in her element.

"You look as bashful as I feel, madam." Ellie jumped when a warm, masculine voice spoke near her ear. She turned to find an attractive sandy-haired, mustached man of medium height smiling at her. He executed a small bow.

"How do you do? My name is Stephen Sadler."

"Ellie Standish," she murmured.

"It is a pleasure to meet you, Miss Standish." He nodded toward the group with a small sigh. "I do not know why I allow my sister to bring me to these gatherings. I am usually uncomfortable in large crowds." He nodded his head in the direction of one of Melinda's friends, a young blonde woman in a pale blue gown.

Ellie turned to him with relief. "Me, too. I'm only here because I'm staying with the family."

Stephen regarded her with sympathetic blue eyes and a pleasant smile.

"I see. And will you be visiting for a while?"

Ellie scanned the room briefly and shook her head.

"I don't know. I really don't know."

"Are you new to Seattle, Miss Standish?"

"Please call me Ellie." She turned back to him. A handsome man who appeared to be in his early thirties, Stephen wore a dark blue suit with a pale yellow waistcoat over a well-starched white shirt.

"Yes, I am new." Ellie paused. Had she told someone else she was new to Seattle, or that she wasn't? She had to remember to keep the lies straight.

Unsure of what to talk about, she settled for watching Melinda work her way toward a tall, handsome young man with curly brown hair, who had eyes only for the vision in gold. He blushed when Melinda drew near, and Ellie noticed that Melinda's cheeks took on a rosy hue, as well.

"And where are you visiting from, Ellie?"

"Chicago," she murmured without thinking.

"Chicago! I know it well. My grandfather lives there. I visit there often. Perhaps I have met your family?"

Ellie turned back toward Stephen. "Uh...no, I don't think so. I'm an orphan."

"Oh, dear. I *am* sorry to hear that."

Unexpected tears sprang to her eyes...either at the sincere note in his voice or the fact she'd used the word *orphan* to describe herself. Or maybe she was just homesick and wanted the comfort of her own bed and her own clothes. She'd never had a dream go on this long or continue in such a sequential, story-like fashion.

"Ellie? Miss Standish? Forgive me. Did I say something wrong?" Stephen bent near to peer into her eyes. He took one of her hands in a gentle grasp and shook his head. "I can be very tactless. I'm sorry."

She dashed at her eyes and swallowed hard. "Oh, no, you didn't say anything wrong. I don't know what that was. Silly me." She gave him a watery smile.

"I do apologize." He continued to hold her hand and study her face with his soft, sky-blue eyes.

"Please don't worry, Stephen. Whatever that temporary aberration was, it wasn't your fault."

"Sadler. Perhaps you should let my guest have her hand back. You have held onto it long enough."

CHAPTER TEN

A tight-lipped Robert stood in front of them in a deceptively relaxed posture, his hands behind his back, but Ellie felt the tension in his body even at a distance of three feet.

Stephen looked at Robert for a moment, then to Ellie. He smiled at her and unhurriedly patted her hand before letting it go.

"Robert, how nice to see you." Stephen gazed passively at the taut man in front of him.

"Stephen," Robert nodded briefly. "Miss Standish, I believe it is just about time to go in to supper. Are you ready?"

Ellie looked from Robert to Stephen and back again. The situation felt surreal. They weren't...surely they weren't staring daggers at each other? Stephen's soft blue eyes grew hard. Robert eyed him narrowly.

"Okay, sure, let's eat." Ellie decided it was time for some good old-fashioned twenty-first-century lingo.

She caught Stephen's startled look as she moved away on Robert's arm.

"What was that about, mister?" she muttered between clenched teeth and a tight smile.

"I would like to know the same thing, madam. Tears in your eyes and some chivalrous handholding? If something troubles you, perhaps I may be of assistance." Robert nodded his head graciously at the guests as they started to file out of the room in Melinda's wake. Mrs. Chamberlain walked on the arm of a tall silver-haired gentleman who bent his head to hear the older woman.

"It was nothing. But your behavior was embarrassing. For Pete's sake, the man was just holding my hand," she hissed.

"Yes, madam, I noticed. If I did not know better, I would think you must have known Mr. Sadler for some time." His whisper seemed loud to Ellie's ears.

"What is that supposed to mean?" Ellie asked. "And lower your voice, please. People can hear you."

"It means exactly the way it sounds. Crying on a man's shoulder and holding hands is usually reserved for someone you have known for months...someone who is courting you, at least in *this* century." He cleared his throat. They moved through the foyer and toward the back of the hall into the fabulous dining room, now glistening with sparkling china, crystal stemware and elegant silverware. Harvest gold velvet curtains were drawn against the night, and candles cast a warm, festive glow over the table.

"Don't be such a fuddy-duddy, Robert." She pulled her hand out of his arm, leaving him to lead the way to her seat. He waved away a staff member and pulled out her chair, bending low near her ear to whisper.

"What on earth is a fuddy-duddy, woman?"

"You are!" she flung over her shoulder. She turned away and plastered a pleasant smile on her face. Robert moved away to take his seat at the head of the table with a grim look. Melinda sat next to her grandmother, who presided at the opposite end of the table from Robert.

Over the top of a lovely white rose centerpiece, Ellie saw Constance for the first time that evening, across the table. She looked years younger in an off-the-shoulder satin gown of emerald green, which suited her complexion...and matched the color of Robert's eyes. Constance caught Ellie's eye and nodded with a small smile. Ellie saw her look to Robert and then back at Ellie again. She gave the dark-haired beauty a toothy grin and dropped her gaze to fiddle with her linen napkin. When she raised her eyes again, Constance was deep in conversation with the attractive silver-haired gentleman who'd escorted Mrs. Chamberlain in to dinner.

"Well, this is most fortunate, Ellie. How could I have been so lucky?"

Ellie turned toward her right to see Stephen sliding into the chair next to her. She smiled in relief. Now she wouldn't have to try to converse with a stranger.

"Oh, I'm glad you're sitting here, Stephen."

"Why, thank you, Ellie. I am flattered."

She blushed. "Oh, you know what I mean. It's just that I don't know anyone here, and I've already met you, so..."

Stephen chuckled and nodded. "Just so. I feel exactly the same way."

Ellie found herself in the difficult position of either having to lock her eyes on Stephen or occasionally glance past him down the table to see

Robert watching her with narrowed eyes and a deepened cleft in his chin as he frowned.

"Ummm... So what do you do, Stephen, for a living?"

"My family has some holdings in Seattle, so I am blessed such that I do not have to work. I teach history at the University on occasion."

Previously distracted by Robert's continued glares, Ellie did lock eyes on Stephen at that.

"Really? *I* teach college too."

Stephen's eyes widened, and he sat back to study her. "You, Ellie? A college professor?"

"Well, I'm not a professor. Adjunct faculty, actually."

"I did not know women..." He left the sentence hanging. "Chicago has certainly taken some unusual steps in their educational system."

Ellie knew she'd made a mistake, given women's roles at the turn of the century, but she tried to bluster through.

"How so, Stephen?"

"Well, I...em...I have never heard of a female teaching at the college level."

"Oh, really?" Ellie moved into her drawl. "But you make it sound farfetched. An improbability."

He blushed. "Oh, no, far be it from me to judge. No, I think it is an excellent idea."

Ellie couldn't keep her eyes from Robert. He had turned away to speak to an older woman at his side.

"Do you teach home economics, then?"

Ellie narrowed her eyes and regarded him. He was growing less attractive by the moment.

"No, like you, I teach history. Women's studies."

"Women's studies? I have never heard of such a class. What would a class like that entail? What sort of material might you cover?"

Ellie sighed. She had to give the man a break. He was just another turn-of-the-century kind of guy.

"Women, Stephen," she spoke patiently. "We study women. The contribution of women in history and society."

"Oh," he murmured with the grace to blush. "Forgive me, Ellie, I did not mean to sound boorish. It is just that I have never heard of such a curriculum."

"I'm sure a lot of people haven't. It's fairly new." Ellie snuck another look at Robert, who had downed his second glass of wine, by her count. Good gravy, was the man an alcoholic? He met her eyes over the rim of her glass, his narrowed gaze cool and distant.

She dropped her eyes and welcomed the arrival of the first course.

Course after course arrived. Cook had prepared a few things especially for Ellie, and she soon found herself full of food, in part due to the tightness of the dress. Stephen spoke of benign matters such as Seattle and the university; she listened with half an ear while she watched Robert. Occasionally, she turned and caught glimpses of Constance, apparently deep in conversation with her silver-haired neighbor.

While Stephen was occupied with his companion to the right, Ellie looked down the table at Mrs. Chamberlain, who caught her eye and gave her a reserved nod. Seated next to Mrs. Chamberlain was a terrified-looking James. He wore the look of a trapped animal as he stared at Melinda across the table to her grandmother's right.

In between courses, Ellie found time to greet the young girl on her left, who seemed as shy as Ellie felt. They smiled at one another in recognition and left the conversation at that, relaxed and silent as they surveyed the room or picked at their food.

When the twelve-course dinner ended, the guests returned to the drawing room, where chairs and tables had been rearranged to allow for dancing. A trio of string players was warming up in a corner of the room.

Stephen had offered Ellie his arm following dinner and now led her to a seat near the wall.

"Oh, I couldn't sit. I'd better stand. I ate too much," she murmured as she patted her stomach. She kept a watchful eye out for Robert, who had not yet entered the room.

Out of the corner of her eye, Ellie saw Stephen blink in surprise at her comments. She realized with a twinge of guilt that she needed to make more of an attempt to conform to the customs of the day, especially simple ones in etiquette and language. She was sufficiently well read on the era to avoid making huge mistakes, but some mischievous part of her insisted on acting as if she were in the twenty-first century. For now, only Robert knew of her origins—what little they both knew.

"Sorry. I'm a bit outspoken," she murmured.

"Not at all," Stephen said gallantly. "I find your forthrightness quite refreshing."

Ellie dragged her eyes from a search for Robert long enough to meet Stephen's sincere gaze. He certainly was a nice man, she thought wistfully. Seemingly uncomplicated and honest. Relaxing. Safe.

Robert entered the room at that moment accompanying the older woman with whom he'd been seated. Ellie watched with admiration as he bent his dark head toward the woman, who literally batted her eyelashes at her handsome escort.

She sighed and bit her lip with a pang of remorse. She had treated him poorly before dinner, forgetting that she took of his generosity by staying in his home, eating his food and wearing his sister's clothing.

Still, wasn't it all just a dream, she wondered? Did she need to worry about the niceties? About pretending to be from this era? What did it matter, if she was going to disappear soon anyway? Time travel, indeed! Didn't there have to be a catalyst, some angst, or at least a machine to facilitate such a journey?

Robert seated the woman on a green velvet settee across the room, next to his grandmother, then lifted his head and met Ellie's eyes for a brief moment. Her heart began to pound in her throat, and she wondered if he could see the surprise in her eyes as she realized she'd fallen in love. She tried to smile, but her lips refused to do more than lift at one corner. Robert turned away and made his way over to the musicians.

"Ellie, did you hear me?"

Ellie came back to reality at the sound of Stephen's voice. She turned to him in a daze.

"I'm sorry. What?"

"I asked if you would like to dance. The musicians appear to have warmed up, and the music should begin momentarily. I do not normally dance, but I would be pleased if you would honor me."

His face finally came into focus as she let go of a green-eyed image. "What? Dance?" She turned toward the musicians who indeed were rubbing bows across willing strings. "Oh, Stephen, I don't know how. I can't."

Stephen took her hand in his warm, reassuring grasp and tucked it into his arm.

"Neither one of us does, so we will just muddle as best we can out there." He led her away from the wall and toward the center of the room. Ellie looked around in a panic, the blur of faces seeming to stare only at her. Melinda arrived to join them with an extremely tall James. A young, redheaded man led her friend Amy onto the floor.

Ellie had visions of standing in the middle of the floor, completely ignorant of the steps to some intricate quadrille while onlookers stared and whispered. As the music began in earnest, Stephen opened his arms as any twenty-first century man might, and Ellie went into them. He began to move her around the floor in a modified waltz suitable for the size of the room. For all his protestations, Stephen danced with a smooth, elegant style, and Ellie relaxed into his arms.

Over his shoulder, she saw a grim-faced Robert lead a glowing Constance onto the floor. He glanced at Ellie once without expression and looked away. She dropped her eyes to Stephen's shoulder, hating the jealousy that hit her with a wave of nausea. She'd only met Robert two days ago—if they'd really ever met at all. She was engaged to Kyle. Robert would have a life of his own—without her. She reminded herself as she had reminded Robert. She was just passing through. It seemed quite likely that she would wake up in the morning—or in an hour—and Robert would be the fleeting whisper of a dream she couldn't remember in the light of day.

"You are making me look like a very accomplished dancer, Ellie." Ellie looked up to see Stephen smiling. She'd almost forgotten where she was.

"Yes, we do dance well together, don't we, Stephen? I didn't know what everyone was dancing these days."

"I take it you have not been out in public much lately, then?"

She peeked over his shoulder to watch Robert and Constance. *They* danced well together, with an ease of familiarity. It seemed likely they had danced before.

"Ellie?"

She returned her preoccupied gaze to Stephen's kind eyes.

"Yes? No. I mean, no, I don't usually dance, so... I don't know how you managed to get me out here." She smiled at him weakly.

"By sheer force, Ellie. I manhandled you out here, but it is working very nicely, I think."

She managed to return his grin but found her eyes straying toward Robert once again.

The dance ended, and Stephen returned Ellie to her position by the wall, apparently intent on remaining by her side, for which she was grateful. He nodded to acquaintances and introduced Ellie, giving her more insight on who they were once they'd moved on. A lively dance ensued, and Ellie watched the younger people frolic on the floor. Robert remained glued to Constance's side, his head bent to hear her every word, an occasional smile lighting his face.

Ellie continued to feel sick to her stomach, with an ache near her chest. She suspected it might be heartburn...or something.

"Stephen, you'll have to forgive me. I'm really not feeling well. I think I'm going to have to go upstairs."

He turned to her with concern. "Ellie, I am sorry to hear that. Is there anything I can do? Should I call someone? Melinda, perhaps?"

She shook her head vehemently. She just wanted to sneak out and disappear.

"No, no, thank you. It was very nice to meet you. I hope I see you again soon."

Stephen caught her hand as she turned away. "And you, Ellie. I hope to see you again soon." In a surprise move, he brought her hand to his lips and pressed a kiss on the back.

Ellie caught her breath at the bold move and dipped into a teensy curtsy with downcast eyes before she moved out of the room. Her plan to hurry up the stairs was thwarted by having to drag her gown with her, but she made it to her room in good time. Unwilling to call Alice to help her get out of the dress, Ellie dropped onto the bed face first. Whatever she'd been holding in released itself, because she promptly burst into tears and sobbed into the quilt.

A firm knock on her door penetrated her consciousness, and she clamped her mouth shut and held her breath, hoping whoever it was would go away. Another knock followed. Ellie sighed. It was probably Melinda or Alice come to check on her. She tussled and struggled with her voluminous gown and unyielding corset to throw herself off the bed and move toward the door, opening it at last to find Robert with his hand raised, ready to knock again.

"Is everything all right? Are you ill?" The concern in his voice threatened to send her off into another crying spell.

Ellie dashed a hand across her face, hoping he couldn't see her tears in the muted light of the hall.

"No, I'm fine. I must have eaten something that disagreed with me. I-I apologize for leaving without saying anything."

"Well, apparently you thought it important enough to advise Mr. Sadler of your poor health." His eyes hardened as he gazed at her.

"What?" she mumbled, confused and miserably unhappy. What had happened to the carefree man she'd met only two days ago?

"I am afraid I found it necessary to ask your constant companion, Mr. Sadler, where you had gone, and he was so kind as to tell me that you felt ill."

"Oh." She shook her head and rolled her eyes. "I said I was sorry, Robert. I didn't think anyone would miss me. You seemed...occupied."

"Well, you thought wrong. Do you need a physician?" He clasped his hands behind his back and searched her face.

She shook her head. "No, I'm fine. You should probably return to your guests. I'm sure Constance would like to see you." She hated her snide remark.

"Yes, I am sure she would," he said without a blink. Ellie's heart sank. "Very well, then. I shall leave you to rest. I will send Alice up to help you."

"No, thank you, Robert. I hate to bother your employees at night. I can undress by myself."

"If you could, you would be out of that dress by now. I was not unaware of how uncomfortable you looked this evening."

"Me?" She looked at him in surprise. "Actually, the dress is quite comfortable now that I am used to it."

"Oh! I thought you looked...unhappy." His eyes softened, and his tight mouth relaxed for a moment.

"I-I'm fine. I do apologize for being so rude to you earlier. I must seem very ungrateful, after all you have done for me."

He shook his head firmly. "There is no need to apologize. I was rude, as well. I was not myself. If you will not have Alice, is there anything I can do for you?"

Ellie thought about asking him to take her in his arms and lay with her for the rest of the night...or even for the rest of her life. Then she recovered her sanity.

"Noooo. Well, yes, actually, there is." She swallowed hard. He would turn her down flat.

"What is it?

"I wonder if you could... umm...unzip this dress. After that, I'll be fine, really. It's just I can't reach." Having asked the question, Ellie wished the earth would swallow her up. The shocked expression on Robert's face humiliated her. She hadn't exactly asked the man to make love to her...as she really wanted.

"Oh, I-I'm sorry," she said hastily. "I can see you're shocked. Never mind, I can do this. I'll be fine. Forget I asked." Ellie grabbed the door to shut it, but he put out his hand to block it.

"No, no, that is fine. I am not shocked. At least, I do not think I am. Turn around."

Ellie obediently turned. Nothing happened for a long, long moment, and she looked over her shoulder.

"Is everything all right? Can you see the zipper?"

He cleared his throat, but when he spoke, it sounded husky.

"Em...yes. Just a moment."

Ellie felt his hand flat against her back as he used his other to unzip the dress. The zipper seemed overly long because it took him a long time to lower it. She grabbed the front of the dress to keep it on. Her neck and back tingled to his touch. If he would just press his body against her, she would be the happiest woman in the world. She almost willed it, but he cleared his throat once again and moved away. She could tell by the sudden coolness on her back. She stepped behind the door and turned, peeking out from the side.

"Thank you. I appreciate it. I'll see you in the morning."

Robert stared hard at her, his hand still in midair. He seemed at a loss for a moment. He dropped his hand and cleared his throat once again.

"Yes, yes, of course. You are welcome. Good night, then."

"Good night," she murmured, closing the door on the man she wanted above all others. Unwilling to let him go, she pressed her face against the wood, listening for his footsteps. A full minute passed before she heard his soft step on the carpet as he moved down the hall toward the stairs.

With a sigh, she turned away from the door and crossed to the bed. She wriggled out of the dress and petticoats and slipped the soft white linen nightgown over her head. Alice had laid out a matching robe, but Ellie tossed that onto the chair before she climbed into the bed. She burrowed into the covers and pressed her face into a pillow.

Her chest still ached, and she realized it wasn't heartburn. She now knew where the word heartache came from. It really did hurt. The deeper she fell under the Victorian man's spell, the more awkward things became. If this was a dream, why couldn't she control its outcome? Was he in love with Constance? Would he marry her someday? Why couldn't she awaken when it became too painful?

She closed her eyes and willed sleep to come, but it took its sweet time arriving.

****

Ellie opened her eyes to a sliver of gray light coming through the curtains. She turned over and looked at her clock. 5:57 a.m. The alarm would go off in a few minutes. She stared at it again drowsily, aware of an intense feeling of sadness. Her dreams! She must have been dreaming. Ellie squeezed her eyes shut in an effort to recall the dream, to locate the source of the strange grief that ached in her throat. A sense of loss, green eyes, a warm hand on her back. The elusive memory escaped her, and she sighed. She pushed a button on the clock to turn it off and turned over.

Kyle faced her, snoring lightly, his blonde hair ruffled like a little boy's mop. She studied his face. Perennially young, it seemed as if he would never age. At thirty-five, he had no wrinkles, no sun damage, no worry lines. She sighed softly. He hardly ever worried. Life seemed to happen around him but not to him. She wondered how they'd ever managed to stay together, given her inability to control her emotions, and his inability to emote. Inability or unwillingness—she never knew.

His blue eyes drifted open, and he stared at her for a moment.

"Good morning," she murmured.

"Morning," he said as he turned over, leaving Ellie to stare at the back of his tousled head. She'd hoped for a good-morning kiss, at the least, though that was not their custom. In fact, Kyle had just done what he did every morning—turn over and go back to sleep for a few minutes while she dressed.

She wished he would look intently into her eyes just once, but she couldn't remember him ever looking intently at anything other than the newspaper. She sighed and crawled out of bed to head for the shower. Fifteen minutes later, she gently shook his shoulder to wake him. Moving to her closet, she dragged out the nearest sweater and skirt and slipped the one over her shoulders and the other over her hips. She paused as she stared at the zipper, a memory tugging at her subconscious, along with the oddest thought that getting dressed had been particularly easy this morning.

Kyle rolled out of bed and stepped into the shower. Ellie made her way into the kitchen and turned on the coffeepot. Kyle liked to have his coffee ready when he woke. She poured herself a cup of orange juice and looked at her watch. No time to drink it. She'd have to fly out of the apartment to catch the El to the college. She grabbed her purse and headed for the door.

"See ya, Kyle."

"Wait, Ellie." Kyle rushed into the living room, still wet from his shower, a towel wrapped around his waist. Ellie turned back in surprise. "Wait," he murmured as he dashed back into the bedroom. He emerged in a moment, wearing a robe.

"I have to go, Kyle. Can this wait?"

"No. No, Ellie, it can't. I've been waiting for a while now."

Ellie stared at him, normally such a calm man, now nervously clanking in the kitchen for a coffee cup. She held her bag and waited.

"Sit down," he mumbled as he moved toward the breakfast table.

"Ummm...okay." She pulled out a seat and perched on the edge. "What's going on?"

Kyle stared down into his cup for a moment and then glanced at her across the table. His eyes flickered around the room; he couldn't seem to keep them steady. He resumed his study of his coffee.

"Kyle? I have to go." Ellie was going to miss the train, and she would be late. It didn't really matter. She didn't have an early class, but she did have papers to read and grade.

"I know. I know. Wait just a minute." He put up a hand and took a deep breath. "Ellie, I don't know how to say this to you, but...I-I'm moving out."

Ellie dropped her purse. "What?"

"I've met someone. I'm sorry. I hate to do this to you. We've been together so long."

"But how? I thought we were going to..."

"I know. I know." He couldn't keep his eyes on her face. "I know we were going to get married, but we've never set a date. *You* never set a date."

"*Me*? What about you?" Confusion more than anything reigned supreme in Ellie's mind. She assumed the shock of the moment trumped everything and that misery and grief would soon follow, but for now she just felt confused.

"Okay," he raised a pacifying hand. "Neither one of us set a date." He finally managed to meet her eyes. "Doesn't that tell you something?"

She shook her head and remained silent. He was right. She'd felt more of a sense of loss when she'd awakened from her dreams.

"I-I don't know what to say. Are you in love with her?"

Kyle blinked for a moment and nodded sheepishly. "Yeah, I think I am. Maybe. I don't know." He raised a hand to his forehead and rubbed it. Then his eyes flickered back to her face again.

"I always loved you, Ellie. You have to know that."

Ellie smiled weakly. "I know, Kyle. I know. I loved you, too."

They looked at each other blankly for a few moments. It seemed they'd said all they could. She rose once again, trying to remember what her morning routine was. Go out the door, catch the El, go to work. "I still love you," she murmured in a daze.

Kyle moved toward her, unexpectedly pulling her into his arms in an unusual gesture of affection.

"I still love you, too, Ellie. I'm sorry." He pressed her face against his chest. He smelled of soap, his scent familiar, recognizable.

She pulled away, tears in her eyes. "When? When are you leaving?"

He hung his head for a moment before he looked up.

"Today. I'll be gone before you get home."

Ellie caught her breath. "So soon? I-I didn't know it would be so soon. Why?"

"I think it's best, Ellie."

"Are you...are you going to move in with her?" Ellie knew she shouldn't ask but she couldn't help herself. The future looked bleak. While their relationship lacked spontaneity and romance, he had been her companion—the man she'd expected to marry until a few short moments ago.

Kyle studied the carpet for a moment. "Ellie, I don't think you want to know."

She bit her lip and turned away in humiliation. "You're right. I don't want to know." She hurried toward the door before the tears fell onto her face. "I have to go."

"Ellie," he called, but she did not turn back.

CHAPTER ELEVEN

Ellie woke up in the dark—disoriented, confused. She turned to look at her clock but couldn't see the bright blue numbers. She rolled over onto her other side and put out a hand. The rest of the bed was empty and cold. No Kyle.

He was gone!

A sliver of light peeped under the door, and she crawled out of bed to make her way toward the faint glow. She pulled open the door and peeked out. A soft light from a wall sconce kept the darkness of the hallway at bay. She was back in the Queen Anne house again. But in what era? What if she'd slipped back into the dream in another time? What if Robert no longer lived? Had she dreamt about Kyle? Was she dreaming now? The alternative—time travel—was just not possible.

Ellie turned back and grabbed her robe from the chair. She tiptoed into the hallway and shut the door behind her with a small click, unwilling to wake Melinda just down the hall...if she was still there.

Ellie made her way to the staircase, gripped the banister tightly, and followed it down, one careful step at a time. The darkened foyer revealed nothing. A round table stood in the middle...as it had. She ran her hand along the sleek wood, but couldn't tell if the table was the same.

The first floor lay in darkness except for a sliver of light under the study door. She moved toward it and rested her ear against the wood, listening for sounds. The last thing she wanted was to wake up in the house with a complete set of strangers. Ellie found the handle, eased open the door and peeked in.

A small lamp on an occasional table provided the only light in the room. Robert slumped in one of the easy chairs—jacket and tie discarded, his normally well-groomed hair disheveled, an empty wineglass in his hand. A bottle of wine sat on the carpet at his feet. The scene, though at odds with the controlled man she thought she knew, brought her an intense feeling of relief. She had not lost him forever. Not yet.

"Robert," she whispered, unsure if he slept.

His eyes flew open, and he turned in her direction.

He struggled to rise.

"Ellie, what are you doing here? Are you ill?"

He moved toward her, his hand outstretched. In the soft light of the room, she found courage and reached for his hand.

"No, I feel all right. I had a dream. I thought I had returned to my own time. Or maybe I'm dreaming now. I was so scared I wouldn't see you again." Ellie's voice broke as she looked up into his haggard face.

Robert pulled her into his arms and buried his face in her neck, holding her tightly to him. Taken completely by surprise, she froze for a moment. His breath against her neck made her knees weak. She tilted her head back to look at him for a moment. Was he drunk? This was so unlike the seemingly proper turn-of-the-century man she'd met.

Robert stared down into her face with troubled eyes. He cupped her face in his hands and bent his head to kiss her. At the first warm touch of his lips on hers, he slid his arms around her once again and held her as if he would never let her go.

Delirious with the unexpected pleasure of his spontaneous kiss, Ellie wrapped her arms around his neck and rose up on tiptoe in an effort to mold herself to his body. She kissed him with abandon...without reserve. The past, present and future came together in a passionate crescendo as she moved against him. She felt him respond to her, pulling her tighter and tighter against him until she couldn't breathe. His hands roamed her back until his hand caught in her hair.

Then he stilled suddenly and put Ellie from him. Unable to stop herself, she reached for him again, but he placed gentle hands on her shoulders. In the soft light of the study, she saw that his eyes traveled the length of her body as no well-bred Victorian man should allow. She blushed. What was he thinking? That she had no morals, no self-control?

"Ellie, we cannot." His breathing was ragged. "I cannot tell you how much I want you, but I will not take advantage of you."

"Yes, you can." Ellie heard the words she wanted. He wanted her. She moved toward him again. With a groan, he pulled her to him. Still, he held back. With one hand under her chin, he raised her face to his. He gazed into her eyes and shook his head.

"No, this is not right. I am drunk. I have had the most difficult night.

You are a guest in my house with few resources. I will not compromise you."

Ellie grinned. He'd gone Victorian on her. She couldn't believe he'd actually said *compromise*. How cute!

"Robert, I forgive you for being drunk. You are no less appealing to me. I choose to come to you willingly. You could never *compromise* me. I'm a twenty-first-century woman. We don't get *compromised* anymore."

Still, he held back, refusing to do more than hold her against him and bury his face in her hair.

"We did not have an opportunity to dance this evening," he murmured in her ear.

Ellie tilted her head back to look at him. "Were you going to dance with me tonight? I couldn't tell."

Even in the soft light, she could see the deep dimples above his grin. "Of course I was going to dance with you...if Sadler could be persuaded to leave your side for a moment."

Ellie snorted. "You mean if you could tear yourself away from Constance long enough."

He pulled her against him more tightly. She struggled to breathe but relished the moment.

"Nonsense. Let's dance."

Ellie looked around the fully furnished and carpeted study.

"Here? Now?"

"Yes, here and now." Robert kept hold of her with one hand and raised his other arm. Ellie slid her hand into his palm. He stepped out and began to move her around the room in a graceful waltz. She followed him effortlessly, prancing around the room in her bare feet on the carpet, two or three steps to his every one. Though no music accompanied their dance, a symphony played in Ellie's head. She began to hum a tune as Robert twirled her around the furniture. As she laughed and responded to his charming grin, she felt heady, carefree, romantic and very much in love. The dreamy dance ended when Ellie stubbed her toe on a leg of the desk.

"Ouch," she mumbled, grabbing her foot and hopping.

"Oh, my dear, I am so sorry," Robert chuckled. He led her over to his chair and pulled her down onto his lap. He held her while they examined the toe together under the lamp, but no bones appeared to be broken. When she tried to rise, he held her against him.

"Well, don't you think this is a bit compromising?" She arched an eyebrow but snuggled into his arms.

He grinned. "Yes, I do, but I cannot help myself." He raised her hand and brought it to her lips.

A book on the small table, next to his wineglass, caught her eye. She peered at it closely.

"You're reading the H. G. Wells book, Robert."

He stared at it for a moment. "Yes."

"Is that a coincidence? Did you conjure me up with a time machine?"

Robert failed to respond to her joke. He eased her off his lap and jumped up to pace the room restlessly. Ellie knew a moment of desolation. She hugged herself. Robert noticed and took both her hands.

"I am looking for answers," he murmured as he pulled her into his arms again.

"Answers to what, Robert? What?"

"To tell me how to keep you here. How to keep you with me." His husky voice tore at her heart. "I-I have written a letter to Mr. Wells to discuss some of his thoughts on time travel. I do not expect a response for weeks, but I hope he will give me some encouragement."

Ellie leaned back to stare at him. "Robert, you didn't tell him about me, did you?"

He laughed without humor. "Do you think I am mad, woman? No, no, I did not discuss your...ah...arrival with him. I asked if he believed time travel was possible, and that if one traveled in time, could the traveler stay in the time or would they have to return." He cleared his throat. "I asked other things, but that was the gist of the letter."

Ellie touched the side of his face tenderly. "Robert, I didn't come in a machine, other than the train. It's not the same thing."

He pulled away from her to pace the room once again. "I know, I know. But perhaps Mr. Wells used the machine with literary license. Perhaps it was just an acceptable metaphor for something we do not yet understand."

Ellie watched him as he wandered the room, restlessly placing one hand on his hip and the other to the back of his neck or alternatively clasping both hands behind his back. The man seemed possessed with finding an answer to something she thought she already knew. It was a dream. And in the dream, he was in pain...because of her. The happy-go-lucky, charming, suave man had evolved into a grim-faced, unhappy and morose man seized by doubts and confused by a phenomenon neither of them understood.

She sank into a chair and watched him stalk about the room.

"Robert, come here. Please sit down," she called. He stopped pacing and returned to the chair beside her.

"What is it, my love?"

Her heart soared at the endearment, but she tightened her lips against the romantic aura his words evoked. He'd known her for only a couple of days. How could he be in love? She ignored the fact that she herself had fallen fast and hard.

"I can't stand to see you like this, Robert. You look miserable. If this is my doing, then I need to fix it."

Robert reached for her hand and brought it to his lips, turning it over to kiss the inside of her wrist. His mouth felt warm and delicious on the tender, exposed skin. Against the responding stirrings in her body, Ellie held fast to her thoughts.

"Do you hear me, Robert? I need to fix it."

"And how would you do that, Ellie?" he murmured as he kept her hand in his. "Can you guarantee me that you will not disappear? Can you promise me that the future will not snatch you away again? Can you assure me that I am not some poor sap in a dream of your making?"

She shook her head mutely.

Robert rose from his chair and pulled her back into his arms.

"I cannot bear to lose you, Ellie, not now that I have found you. I have waited so long for you. I do not care whether this is a dream or if you have traveled through time to come to me. I do not want you to wake up one morning and forget me. I do not want you to disappear."

Ellie shivered at his words, though her heart craved the love he so eloquently expressed. His fear and pain seemed genuine, and she knew she must make a decision. It could not go on. But for now...just for now...she would forget the future.

"Stay with me then, Robert. Don't let me go to sleep. I'm terrified that I'll wake up and you'll be gone...that I'll be taken from you."

He whispered against her hair. "Hush, my love. I will stay with you. I will not let you go." He lowered himself into the chair and pulled her down into his arms, cradling her on his lap like a child. "I have waited all my life to fall in love. I will not lose you now."

They stayed together for hours, without words, without movement. Ellie rested her face on his chest and listened to the rhythm of his heart. How could such a strong, steady heartbeat belong to a shadowy figure in a dream? She fell asleep toward dawn.

****

Robert did not sleep. Sleep was an impossibility with Ellie in his arms. While she slept, he studied her face and her body, longing to trace a line from her eyes to her lips with his fingers. He barely suppressed the urge to caress the soft curves of her thinly dressed figure. It was all he could do not to stroke the sleek curls of the dark hair that dangled over his arm.

But he did not want to awaken her, and he chose to do nothing but watch her—committing her face to memory—in case the worst came to pass. He drew in a deep breath and released it, gritting his teeth as he contemplated losing her. He was determined that would not happen this night. He would not let it. He would hold Ellie against him until dawn, securely in his arms. She would not slip away from him through time or in a dream. Not on this night.

****

Ellie made her way to her room early in the morning, after Robert kissed her and told her he had to go work.

She looked around her room and wished things could have been different, but they weren't. Robert's safe and secure life had turned upside down. He was miserable and uncertain of the future, and it was her fault. She would take action.

She found paper and pen—not a ballpoint but the old kind, with metal nib and ink—in the drawer of the nightstand, and she wrote out a note. When Alice came to help her dress, she gave her the note and asked her to have it delivered immediately. Alice left with the letter, and Ellie waited in her room. She couldn't face the rest of the house. Melinda would probably sleep in, and Mrs. Chamberlain always took breakfast in her room.

Two hours passed, and still Ellie heard nothing. She tried to think of mom's apple pie and the boy next door while she waited for a response. What if an answer never came? What if she had exposed her plans only to have them betrayed?

Alice tapped on the door.

"Mrs. Green is here to see you, ma'am."

Ellie jumped up. Constance! She hurried out the door and down the stairs, tripping occasionally on the green skirt Alice had managed to squeeze her into earlier that morning.

Alice followed her down and opened the door to the parlor. Ellie slid in and shut the door behind her quietly.

Constance stood at the window, gazing down on the view of the city below. Her dark blue tailor-made silk suit and jacket showed her slim figure off to perfection, the netted hat giving her a regal bearing that Ellie knew she could never hope to achieve.

"Constance, thank you for coming. May I offer you some tea?" Some well-trained servant had thoughtfully placed a tea tray on the mahogany table in front of the sofa.

"No, thank you, Ellie. Your note sounded urgent. Is everything all right? How can I help?"

Now that Constance had arrived, Ellie's grand scheme suddenly looked foolish.

"If you don't mind, I think I'll just have a cup. Are you sure?"

Constance looked at her curiously and acquiesced. They sipped tea for a few minutes while Ellie composed her chaotic thoughts.

"I need your help, Constance."

"Yes, so you said in your note."

Ellie's face burned. She had to be insane asking a stranger for help.

"I'm sorry to trouble you, but I don't know many people here."

Constance tilted her head. "You know Robert."

"Yes, well, that's just it. This is about Robert."

Out of the corner of her eye, Ellie saw Constance stiffen.

"I see," she murmured.

"Oh, no, it's not what you think, Constance. You see, I need to *leave* the house. Then I'll be out of your hair and out of Robert's hair."

"*My* hair. Whatever do you mean, Ellie?" Two bright spots of color shown on Constance's pale skin.

Ellie turned a frank look on her. "You know what I mean, Constance. It's obvious that you have a crush on Robert...that is...that you care for him. That's what I mean by *out of your hair*."

Constance dropped her cup onto her saucer and put the cup down. "I-I...well, I... Is it that obvious?" she murmured.

"It is to me. I share the same problem as you."

"You are saying that you too...care for him?"

Ellie drew in a deep breath and released it. She nodded. "Yes, I do. I think I'm in love. So you see, we are both in the same boat."

From the shocked look on Constance's face, Ellie thought the dark-haired beauty was going to jump up and stalk out of the room, but she tightened her lips and stayed in place, her eyebrows raised in inquiry.

"Ellie, I do not know why you are here or where you really came from. I must speak frankly. I wish that you were not here. Since you first appeared, Robert has hardly spoken two words to me. I thought he and I were close friends. In fact, I hoped..." She picked up her tea again and studied the inside of the cup.

"You hoped that he would ask you to marry him?" Ellie knew she took a chance with the woman's good graces, which she really needed at the moment.

Constance threw Ellie a self-conscious look and nodded.

"Yes," she said quietly. "I did."

Ellie stared down at the light blue oriental carpeting, fighting an unexpected blast from her own jealous furnace. Constance hadn't revealed anything Ellie didn't already know, but to hear her say it aloud was painful. She took a deep breath.

"Well, you might still get your chance. As I mentioned, I need to leave the house, and it should be in such a way that Robert knows I'm okay but doesn't know where I am."

"Why?" Constance asked bluntly. She narrowed her eyes and watched Ellie's face closely.

Ellie colored. "I-I have outstayed my welcome. Robert and his family have been very kind to me, but I can't live off their generosity forever. The truth is...I-I'm not staying in Seattle. I will be leaving soon, though I'm not sure when. I-I'm just waiting on a letter from my parents. They'll send word when they are settled in their new house and I can return home." Ellie could hardly keep up with her convoluted lie, but she did the best she could with little sleep and a heart that ached.

"I see," said Constance though her puzzled face showed that she clearly did not.

"I know it doesn't make sense right now. So difficult to explain. My parents. Such odd creatures, really." Ellie babbled on till she was out of breath.

"And how can I help you, Ellie?"

"I need to find a boarding house. I have a piece of jewelry that I need help selling so I can pay for my room."

Constance drew in a deep breath and stared into the distance.

"This sounds so irregular, Ellie. Are you sure? Have you ever been to a rooming house?"

"No, but I've read about them. I was hoping you could find a suitable one, perhaps one for working women." A small smile broke through. "If I have to stay here long, I'll have to go to work, so..."

"Work? What could you do?"

"I can teach, Constance. I am a teacher by profession."

"Really? How interesting. Yes, now that you mention it, I do recall a boarding house for professional women. My next-door neighbor has a sister who runs such a house. I will make inquiries right away. When do you need to leave?"

Ellie swallowed hard. "Today, right now."

Constance turned to stare. "Ellie, that is impossible. What has happened to make you run from this house? Are you in trouble? Did Robert—" Her soft face hardened, and her eyes flashed unexpectedly.

"No, no, nothing like that, Constance." Ellie's face flamed. "I simply need to leave. I hope you understand. If you are as hopelessly in love with Robert as I am, you'll understand."

108

To Ellie's surprise, Constance shook her head. "In this situation, I do not understand. I enjoy Robert's company very much, but I have not been *hopelessly in love* since my husband died." She paused and stared into the distance with a small smile. "I loved him like no other." She returned her gaze to Ellie. "I care for Robert a great deal. He was very kind to me when my husband died, but I am not madly in love with him."

"Oh," Ellie murmured, momentarily stumped. How was that possible? Who wouldn't be madly in love with a charming, arrogant, kind, rash, affectionate, debonair man with laughing eyes like Robert?

"I did hope to marry again some day, and Robert would make a very suitable husband, but..." She quirked a wry eyebrow in Ellie's direction. "I think his interests lie elsewhere."

Ellie swallowed hard. Another wave of color heated her cheeks. "Well, not with me, that's for sure. We hardly know each other. And as I said, I'm going to be leaving at some time in the near future. I don't think it would be right to continue to live off his largesse, as it were."

"I understand. From what I know of Robert, he does need a woman who is willing to stay with him. It is a shame that you cannot move to Seattle permanently."

Ellie bit her lips. "Oh, well, you know. My duty lies with my parents. They need me."

"I understand." Constance rose. "Well, I have much to do if I am to find you rooms before the end of the day. What is the jewelry that you will be selling? I do not think you will need the money today, but you might need some pin money by tomorrow if you are to be on your own."

Ellie pulled a ribbon out from beneath the high lace collar of her shirtwaist blouse and showed Constance the white-gold diamond engagement ring dangling from it. Bought too large for her finger, Kyle hadn't gotten around to having it resized, so she'd worn it around her neck.

Constance gasped, wide-eyed. "Oh, my word. I have never seen such a beautiful ring. It must be worth a fortune."

Ellie chuckled. "Not really, but I hope I can get a reasonable amount for it."

"It almost looks like... Is that an engagement ring, Ellie?"

Ellie grimaced. "It was."

"I had no idea."

"It's over."

"Oh!" Constance replied. "I am sorry to hear that. Well, we can take it to a pawnshop tomorrow. For now, I must hurry. If I am able to obtain a room for you, I will send a note to you with the address. I will meet you there."

Ellie reached to hug the taller woman. "Thank you, Constance. Thank you! I can't tell you how much I appreciate this."

"Of course, Ellie. I will have the carriage wait for you when I send the note." She left the room like a woman with a mission, and Ellie felt infinitely better than she had all morning.

She returned to her room and waited for news. While she waited, she considered her situation. She could not possibly take Melinda's clothing, and yet she really couldn't walk around unnoticed in her oversized sweater, denim skirt and clogs. In addition, she had to say goodbye to Melinda and Mrs. Chamberlain...and Robert.

Ellie sat down and pulled out paper and the irritating pen that dripped blotches of ink all over her letters. She penned a thank-you note to Mrs. Chamberlain, a more sincere and affectionate note to Melinda telling her she would have to borrow at least one set of clothes until she could obtain her own, and a final note to Robert—that broke her heart and set her to sobbing—with words that seemed trite and contrived.

How could she tell him she was leaving because she was in love? How could she explain she thought it best to remove herself from his existence now, while he was merely infatuated with the thought of a time traveler and before they grew closer? Before she disappeared back to the waking world or her own time? How could she say he needed to get on with a life based in reality—as did she?

Her reasons for leaving seemed foolish when written down, but she was as sure as she'd ever been in her life that she had to go. She loved him too much to have him wake up one morning to find her gone. Ellie squashed the inconvenient thought that, if all went as planned, he would simply come home that day and find her gone.

After several false starts and crumpled pieces of paper, she finally decided on the best approach to make him forget about her. She told him she was engaged.

She left the letters on the dressing table, knowing one of the maids would find them later. Noon had come and gone. A carriage pulled up, and Ellie peeked out the window, expecting to see a messenger with a note. She panicked when she saw Robert descending. Having made her decision to go, she could not face him. He might come looking for her. She ran to the door and locked it. How would she get out of the house without his knowledge? He would surely hear a carriage arrive.

Ellie pressed her head against the door and waited. She heard footsteps in the hallway. They paused at her door for a moment. She felt sure he would hear the pounding of her heart through the thick wood. She held her breath. An eternity seemed to pass in a few moments, and then he moved on down the hall to his own room.

Ellie tiptoed away from the door and peeked outside the window. She had no choice. She would have to make a run for it when the carriage came. Hopefully, the messenger would have good news. Otherwise, she'd look quite the fool jumping into a carriage only to be tossed right back out onto the street.

An hour passed. She heard Melinda's voice in the hallway, a whispered conversation with Alice, and then silence as Melinda descended the stairs. Ellie crept back to the window again. Melinda and her grandmother climbed into the carriage. She wondered where they were going. Perhaps to someone's house for tea. Ellie thanked her lucky stars for having the foresight to tell Alice that she had a headache and wanted to sleep.

Ellie bundled her clothes together and continued to wait. She heard the thud of horse's hooves and the jingle of a carriage's livery. She looked down again. A strange carriage. A short man stepped down from his seat beside the driver, an envelope in his hand.

This was it! Ellie grabbed her things, pulled open the door and dashed down the stairs. She reached the front door before the messenger knocked and startled him by swinging open the door, grabbing the note and flying toward the stairs.

"Come on, let's go! I'll read it on the way."

The surprised messenger hurried down the stairs in her wake, handed her up into the carriage and jumped up beside the driver. The carriage started forward with a jerk.

Ellie opened the note. Constance wrote that she'd had success and had instructed the driver to deliver Ellie to a particular address where she would meet her.

"Ellie!" She heard a shout behind the carriage. She peered through the window and looked back at the house. Robert stood at the bottom of the steps staring after the carriage. He waved his arms over his head to signal her. "Ellie, wait! Where are you going?" The carriage drove on, his shouts unheeded by all but the sobbing passenger inside.

****

Robert watched the carriage distance itself from him. He was certain Ellie had seen him. Where was she going? And in whose carriage? Why didn't she stop when he called?

If he'd had his druthers, he would have jumped into his own carriage to follow, but his grandmother and Melinda had taken it for the afternoon, leaving him stranded. He could certainly send someone to hire a private conveyance, but he would have no idea where Ellie had gone.

With a last look at the settling dust where the carriage had disappeared down the road, Robert turned back toward the stairs. He looked up at the house. Perhaps Melinda's maid, Alice, would know where Ellie had gone. He took the stairs two at a time, hoping against hope that Stephen Sadler had not come by to pick her up for an outing. Would Ellie go with another man? An inexplicable sense of impending trouble drove him at full speed into the house.

His heart raced as he grabbed the banister and hauled himself up the stairs to the second floor.

"Alice?" he called. "Alice?"

The tiny redhead popped her head out of Melinda's room, several piles of clothing in her hand. Her eyes widened when she saw him. Suddenly winded, he bent double and struggled to catch his breath for a moment.

"Yes, Mr. Chamberlain? Are you all right?"

Robert nodded and swallowed hard. He straightened. "Yes, yes. Thanks. Do you know where Miss Standish has gone, Alice?"

"Miss Standish, sir?" Alice stared at him.

"Yes, Alice, Miss Standish. She just left in a carriage. Did she say where she was going?"

Alice shook her wide-eyed head. "No, sir. I didn't know she had left the house. She told me to say she had a headache and wished to stay in her room."

Robert dropped his head and shook it, turning away with slumped shoulders. Perhaps she would return soon. He had no need to worry, either about her safety or her possible disappearance. He suspected that if the worst came to pass—if she indeed returned to her own time—it would occur as fast as her appearance, through whatever portal she had arrived. And he would know.

"Is there anything else, Mr. Chamberlain?"

"No, thank you, Alice," he called over his shoulder as he eyed Ellie's door. He moved slowly toward the door and laid a hand against it. It wasn't proper, but he simply could not resist. He wanted to smell her scent, to reassure himself that she had not vanished as suddenly as she came.

He pushed open the door and slid into the room. The bed was made, the room tidy. He crossed to the bed and ran his fingers across the pillow where her head had rested. He imagined her beautiful hair flowing across the pillow as she lay next to him. Would she lie next to him one day? Would his dreams come true?

Robert turned to leave the room and noticed several envelopes lying on the desk. His own name handwritten on the top envelope caught his attention, and he grabbed the white square and ripped it open. With a sinking heart, he read:

Dear Robert,

Thank you for everything you have given me over the last few days. I cannot tell you how grateful I am for your kind assistance on the train and the hospitality of your home.

I must go, Robert. I have made arrangements to stay elsewhere in the city, and I do not want you to try to find me. This is best for both of us. I cannot bear to hurt your feelings, and I am afraid I might if I stay with you any longer.

There is no graceful way to say this, so I will just blurt it out. I am engaged, Robert, to a man in Chicago, a man from my time. When I wake up from this wonderful dream, he will be there beside me, and I owe him my loyalty.

Please forgive me for running away like this. I could not look into your eyes and speak without stuttering.

Take care, Robert.

Ellie

Robert crushed the letter to his forehead and sagged onto the desk chair. He could not think straight. Pain seared through his chest. He could not breathe. Where had she gone? Why had she run from him? Engaged? Had he misread the sparkle in her eyes when she looked at him?

He lowered his fist and pressed open the letter once again, angry that he had crushed it. If the small white missive were all he had left of Ellie, he planned to treasure it. He straightened his shoulders and lifted his head. This was not over! He jumped up!

"Alice," he roared.

Alice came running down the hall and into the room. Her brown eyes threatened to pop out of her head.

"Mr. Chamberlain, what is it? What's wrong?"

"Tell me everything you know about Miss Standish's activities today."

CHAPTER TWELVE

After a tearful journey that seemed to last forever, the carriage delivered Ellie to an older Victorian house in downtown Seattle. She stepped out to meet Constance, who waited on the steps of the house.

"Constance! I can't thank you enough for everything you've done."

"I am happy to help, Ellie, though your puffy face tells me that this decision has been difficult for you."

Ellie nodded but did not trust herself to talk.

"Come inside. Mrs. McGuire runs this rooming house. It is for ladies only. They will be sitting down to supper soon. Are you hungry?"

Ellie followed Constance up the wooden steps to a lovely, narrow, rose-colored, three-story house. Mrs. McGuire, a plump, gray-haired, motherly sort, met them at the door.

"Welcome, Miss Standish. It is a pleasure to have you. Please step into the parlor. May I offer you some tea? Dinner will be ready within the hour."

Constance answered for her. "Yes, please, let's have some tea, Mrs. McGuire. I think Miss Standish could use some refreshment." Ellie demurred, but Constance insisted.

Mrs. McGuire showed them into a comfortable room at the front of the house and left them alone while she fetched the tea. The soft rose and blue colors of the room served to soothe Ellie's jangled nerves. Lace curtains at the tall bay windows muted the light. Ellie sank onto the velvet rose sofa and took off her hat to ease the aching in her head. She closed her eyes and rubbed her temples.

"Does your head hurt?" Constance asked solicitously as she sat down beside Ellie on the couch.

Ellie opened her eyes and smiled wanly. "Yes."

"Some nice hot tea will do you a world of good."

At that moment, Mrs. McGuire returned with a silver tea service and set it down on the cherry wood table in front of the sofa.

"I would love to sit and take tea with you ladies, but I must return to the kitchen, or I am likely to burn tonight's dinner." The plump woman beamed and left the room.

Constance poured some tea and gave Ellie a cup.

"You look very tired."

"I am. I hardly slept last night, and Robert arrived back at the house before I left."

"Yes?" Constance tilted her head inquiringly.

"I had left him a note. I wanted to leave before he came home. So, when the carriage came, I ran out the door." Ellie remembered her flight and giggled nervously, a sound that seemed inappropriate. She certainly didn't feel like laughing.

"You left without telling him? Why, Ellie?"

"I have my reasons, Constance. Please believe me. It was extremely difficult. Promise me you won't tell him where I am...although I suspect he won't want to know after the ungrateful way I left the house."

"Oh, Ellie. I am so sorry."

Ellie looked at her former competition. "Just treat him well, Constance. I know you will."

Constance reddened and stood abruptly to walk to the window. "Ellie, I-I don't know what to say. The truth is...after today, I do not think I want to marry Robert anymore. I think he is quite taken with you, and I do not want a man who is in love with someone else."

At any other time, Ellie would have loved to hear those words, but she had burnt her bridges. There was no going back.

"I don't think he'll fancy himself in love with me after he reads my letter, Constance. I told him I was engaged."

Constance turned from the window. She raised her eyebrows. "But I thought you said that was over. You are selling the ring."

"It is over...as far as I can tell. But that is what Robert needed to hear."

Constance approached and laid a gentle hand on her shoulder. "I cannot pretend to understand what is going on here, Ellie, but I trust you know what you are doing." She sighed. "Let's go up and see your room."

Constance led the way upstairs to the second floor, where she opened a door on the right. The room was small but cozy. A small twin bed with a bright yellow coverlet rested against one wall. A highly polished mahogany dresser with oval mirror, a well-varnished night table with white glass lamp, and a small, rose velvet chair completed the furnishings.

"The washroom is down the hall. Mrs. McGuire will explain the house rules. I think they are standard. No cooking in the rooms, no men beyond the parlor, no overnight guests. That sort of thing."

Ellie shrugged. She knew she was in the Dark Ages, and the light was only getting dimmer. When would she wake up from this dream? It held no pleasure or excitement for her any longer.

Constance wished her a good evening and said she would pick her up the following day to take the ring to a jeweler. Ellie fought the urge to beg her to stay, hating how clingy and dependent she'd become. That she was penniless and alone, without friends and family, a hundred years before her time, did nothing to make her feel better about her character flaws.

Though Ellie longed for nothing more than to curl up into a ball on her bed and go to sleep, she dragged herself downstairs at the sound of the dinner bell, thinking it better to avoid creating undue interest and suspicion. She longed for her credit card so she could book a cruise and run away to the Caribbean. In fact, she wondered where her purse was at the moment. Next to her bed in Chicago? On a train to Seattle a hundred years from now? Clutched in her lap while she rode the El and cried about the loss of a fiancé?

Mrs. McGuire had set a lovely table, with white linen, decorative porcelain dinnerware and a centerpiece of bright yellow chrysanthemums. Three other women sat at the table, all younger than Ellie. They wore conventional clothing of white shirtwaist blouses and tailored skirts. Their hairstyles were all similar, upswept Gibsons in various designs depending on the shape and texture of their hair.

They stared at Ellie in surprise for just a moment before smiling and welcoming her to the house. Mrs. McGuire made the introductions to Miss Samantha Stevens, Miss Martha Brown, and Miss Dorothy Simmons. Ellie shook hands with each of them and sat down in the indicated seat opposite Mrs. McGuire.

The young women were not much older than Melinda, and the conversation was lively. Ellie felt a sharp pang of regret. She would miss Melinda's bubbly personality. Samantha taught school, Martha worked as a typist at the newspaper, and Dorothy clerked in a bank. They asked Ellie questions about her stay in Seattle and her future plans, and Ellie fielded the answers as best she could. Certain her lies were growing more distorted with each embellishment and that she risked exposure, she hoped she would soon wake up or return to her own time—whichever the case might be. The latter still seemed farfetched. Wouldn't she know if she had traveled in time? Wouldn't she feel tired? Different? Older? Younger?

As depressed as she was, dinner proved to be a soothing gathering of women. The food was delicious, though Ellie had a frustrating moment when she had to explain once again that she didn't eat meat.

"Why not?" Dorothy asked, her fork in midair.

Ellie looked around the table at the sea of eyes that watched her curiously. The young women looked so similar in their white shirtwaist blouses and dark skirts. Only their hair color and body frames were different. Martha wore small round glasses on her pale face.

"I-I'm an animal lover, you see." Ellie gave a helpless shrug and bit into a delicious homemade biscuit, hoping they would take her answer at face value.

"Really?" Samantha, a petite blonde, murmured. "I love animals too, but..."

"What do you eat, then?" Dorothy asked with a napkin to her rosy face.

How could she tell them about the varied inventory of delicious vegetarian foods available in stores in the twenty-first century? She thought fast.

"Well, I eat a lot of vegetables, of course. I do eat cheese and eggs. Those are just like meat, really."

"Oh." Samantha nodded sagely. "Yes, I can see. There really must be quite a bit to eat besides meat."

"As you see, ladies, she has some potatoes and carrots on her plate, as well as having a glass of milk. She really has plenty to eat." Martha, future investigative reporter, pushed her glasses back up to the bridge of her nose.

"All right, girls, let's not badger Miss Standish any longer. Eat your dinner," Mrs. McGuire urged with a kindly look in Ellie's direction. "I'll prepare something additional for you tomorrow, Miss Standish."

"Oh, you don't have to go to any trouble for me, Mrs. McGuire. I choose not to eat meat. I don't expect anyone to put themselves out because of my choice. And please call me Ellie."

"May we all call you Ellie?" Samantha asked, with a scrunched-up button nose.

"Yes, please." Ellie felt like she was back in the classroom, calling on students who waved their hands in the air with questions.

"Wonderful," Dorothy murmured as she resumed eating.

While the girls continued their conversation regarding the day's events and the latest sighting of an attractive eligible bachelor, Ellie munched her food and listened with half an ear as she wondered what Robert was doing at the moment. She tried to imagine how he had handled her ungracious departure and wondered what he thought of her now. Hopefully, he would put her in the past as a temporary aberration in his world and move on, although Constance had indicated she might not be willing to consider him as a potential husband any longer.

Ellie bit her lip. She hoped she hadn't done any irreparable damage to Robert's life. Constance and he suited each other well, though it seemed likely that if Constance had not already fallen madly in love with him, she would not be doing so in the future. And perhaps mad, passionate love did not suit Robert. Ellie had seen Robert in the throes of infatuation. He'd become moody, aggressive, and unhappy—quite unlike the confident, witty, debonair man she'd met on the train. She hardly took his crush on her as a sign of true love, having never been one to incite such passion in men. She thought it more likely his fascination stemmed from his notion that she had traveled back in time. What man didn't like a good science fiction story...even at the turn of the century?

"Well, I am sure my boss will not say. He was absent from work for a few days and has been preoccupied since his return." Dorothy's words penetrated Ellie's distracted musings.

Ellie returned her focus to her current setting. The table for six was set with white linen and dishes of simple white porcelain. The dining room was much smaller than that in the Chamberlain home, but all the more cozy because of its reduced size. A well-polished mahogany china cabinet matched the sideboard, and both stood out impressively against pale blue walls. Sheer white lace curtains hung at the windows. Ellie studied as much detail as possible, hoping to store the memories away for when she returned to her own time...or woke up. This first-hand experience in the late Victorian/early Edwardian era could only help to inform her teachings.

Dinner ended on a festive note, and they all helped Mrs. McGuire clear the table and wash the dishes. When cleanup was done, Ellie professed herself exhausted after the long day and skipped the house's customary after-dinner tea in the parlor. She climbed the well-varnished wooden stairs to the second floor. After a brief stop in the washroom to wash her face and hands, Ellie returned to her room, shed her clothes, took down her hair and climbed into bed. She'd left any extra clothing belonging to Melinda at the house and would need to purchase a few things tomorrow once she'd sold the ring—that is unless she finally woke up in her lonely apartment.

Ellie surveyed the room in the dark, noting how the moon came through the large window and cast silver beams across the walls. And she willed herself to sleep and to wake up from her Victorian dream. She'd had enough of the past. Her present didn't look very promising, if indeed Kyle had cancelled the wedding, but she didn't think life would hurt as much as it did here at the turn of the century.

****

Morning brought Constance in the carriage. Ellie climbed into the conveyance and off they went in a cloud of dust...literally.

"Ellie, I must say, you have created quite the maelstrom at the Chamberlain house."

Ellie caught her breath. Though Constance smiled, her eyes were quite serious.

"What do you mean?"

"When I arrived home last night, I had a message from Robert waiting for me. He wanted to know if I had assisted you in leaving, where you were, and if you were safe."

"Oh, Constance. I'm so sorry to have involved you. How did he know? Did you reply to the note?"

"I am not sure how he knew. Alice did meet me at the door when I came to visit you in the morning. Perhaps he questioned the servants." She paused and sighed. "At any rate, I did not have time to send a note around this morning before he appeared on my doorstep, only an hour ago, with the same questions." She smiled. "I would say he *demanded* the answers, but he is far too well bred to be so rude."

Ellie turned to stare out the window. The carriage rumbled along dirt roads as they passed a bevy of lovely Victorian homes which appeared startlingly new.

"I don't know what to say." Shame kept her from meeting Constance's eyes.

"Well, Ellie, I think one thing is certain. You made quite an impression on Robert, one he is not likely to forget as soon as you think. I knew that from the first moment he introduced you on the train."

Ellie turned startled eyes to Constance. "I-I hoped he would accept my thanks, take the engagement at face value, and let me go."

Constance gave her head a slight shake and grimaced. "He might still. I assured him that you were safe, but I refused to tell him where you were. He asked me about your plans to be married, and I confirmed that I knew you had been engaged. While I did not lie to him directly, I think he believes the engagement is ongoing." Constance bit her lip and looked at Ellie. "He seems to be very infatuated with you, Ellie. He has never looked at me like that once. Are you sure you are doing the right thing?"

Ellie sighed and brushed away an escaping tear with the back of her hand. "No, Constance, I'm not sure about anything, except that my time here is limited, and I cannot stay. I thought I should leave before we fell in love. Well, before I fell in love, I should say."

"It may be too late. He is already in love, Ellie."

Ellie turned stricken eyes on Constance. "Oh, Constance, surely not! It has only been a few days! If he is infatuated, I think it is only a fascination with someone from...uh...another place, from Chicago."

Constance burst out into a surprisingly rich, husky laugh. "Chicago? Robert is well traveled. He has been to Chicago many times! No, I do not think that is it. I think it is probably you. You are quite unique, Ellie."

"Not in my own world," Ellie muttered with a red face. Her theory did sound silly without being able to explain "Chicago" meant a hundred years into the future.

"I beg your pardon?"

"Nothing. I was just thinking aloud." She patted Constance's hand. "Thank you for not telling him where I was. Hopefully, he'll just assume I'm engaged and move on."

"Perhaps," Constance murmured. The carriage came to a halt in front of a jeweler's shop, and Ellie followed Constance into the elegant establishment. Constance, an unexpected fairy godmother in disguise, expertly negotiated a hefty sum for the ring, and they sailed out of the store with enough money to buy Ellie a few clothes, some necessities, and room and board for at least a year should she need. Ellie convinced Constance that her luggage had been lost on the train, and it was under this assumption that Constance took her to a series of ready-to-wear stores to buy some tailored suits, dresses and undergarments.

With bags and hatboxes in hand, they hopped aboard the carriage once again and stopped to refresh themselves and rest in a teashop in downtown Seattle. Ellie followed Constance into the small shop on the first floor of a three-story brick building on a busy main street.

Ellie had lost her bearings and had no earthly idea where she was in the city. The streets looked completely different with hard-packed dirt instead of asphalt. Street signs seemed to be in short supply, and the absence of traffic lights stumped her. Without the view from the elevated interstate which passed through the modern city, without the Space Needle or the gleaming skyscrapers with their glass windows, Ellie couldn't even figure out where she was in relation to the waterfront of Elliott Bay. Her world had suddenly become much smaller, consisting of a few dirt roads, forests of pine trees, a neighborhood of similar

Victorian houses and the shopping and business district in which they currently drank tea.

A young waiter in white coat and black slacks seated them at a small round table, took their order and left. Ellie ordered the same items as Constance, tea and a scone—neither of which she particularly craved but both sounding like something a turn-of-the-century woman might order.

"Where are we, Constance? I can't seem to get my bearings." Ellie adjusted her hat, wondering if she would ever learn to ignore it as some of her fellow female tea drinkers did.

"We're on Second Avenue. I thought you had not been to Seattle before, Ellie." Constance eyed Ellie inquisitively as she laid her napkin across her lap.

Ellie colored. "No, I haven't. I was just wondering where we were in relation to the rest of the city, to the bay, that's all."

"Ah." Constance nodded in understanding. "I do not really know to tell you the truth. I leave that up to my driver."

Tea arrived in a plain porcelain teapot with matching white cups, along with scones on a simple white plate. Constance poured.

"I was surprised to find so much ready-to-wear clothing in the store. I thought..." *Careful, Ellie.* "I thought we might have to visit a dressmaker."

Constance took a sip of tea and smiled. "This *is* the twentieth century, Ellie. We have a great many more modern conveniences than we did a decade ago. When I think of the fashions back then! Parting our hair in the middle? Those uncomfortable bustles and large crinolines? Do you remember? I am so grateful those days are gone. I love these sleek, modern styles." She ran a hand down the sleeve of her emerald green tailored silk jacket, the picture of elegance.

Ellie's eyes crinkled, and she wanted to burst out laughing, but she pressed her lips together. To Constance, this clothing *was* the height of fashion, and Ellie had to admit it was much more stylish than her bulky turtleneck sweater and denim skirt and clogs, now safely stowed away in her dresser at the rooming house.

Ellie murmured her assent. She gazed out the window at the busy street. Carriages and wagons passed to and fro, kicking up dust in their wake.

"Oh, dear," Constance murmured almost under her breath. She stiffened and stared out the window.

Ellie followed her eyes. "What is it?"

"Oh, dear. I had hoped. Well, this was the only teashop near the stores. I-I hoped..."

"What, Constance? Is something wrong?"

Constance turned to Ellie, a disconcerted look in her eyes. Her apologetic smile put Ellie on the edge of her seat.

Constance nodded in the direction of the window. "I did not tell you before, because I thought he would not...that is I did not know he was at work today." She looked back at the window. "That is Robert's bank across the street, and his carriage has just arrived."

Ellie's eyes darted to the window and she froze, her heart thumping in her throat. Robert descended from the carriage and strode rapidly inside a large brick building with the name "Washington Bank" over the door. From this distance, she could see nothing more than that he was dressed well—as always—and that his stride seemed purposeful and determined—as always. However, the sight of him renewed the ache in her heart. Such a handsome man! But a much more vulnerable man than she had previously thought. Underneath that confident exterior lurked a man who longed for love, and he deserved a real live woman...not a figment of his imagination...or hers.

"Can we go, Constance? I'm afraid he'll reach his office and see us leaving from a window."

"Yes, certainly, of course. I am very sorry about this, Ellie. I should have had the driver find another shop." She rose from the table.

Ellie rose on shaking knees and held onto the back of her chair. "No, no, that's not your fault. But to see him so soon..." She wondered if her face was as pale as it felt. "I had hoped to be settled before I saw him next...if ever."

Constance moved toward the door, and Ellie followed her outside. Ellie cringed when she saw that their carriage was down the road about a block. She felt exposed and vulnerable to the three-story building across the street with seemingly hundreds of windows, and she turned her back to the street to hide her face. She heard the clop of the horses' hooves nearing, though the carriage's progress seemed unbearably slow.

"The carriage is here, Ellie. Get in." Ellie turned and climbed in, and Constance followed. The carriage started forward, and with a sigh of relief, Ellie peeked out to study the building where Robert worked. She gasped when she saw Robert standing on the sidewalk staring after their carriage, and she ducked her head back in to press back into the corner of her seat.

"He saw us, Constance. Oh, I can't believe I had to stick my head out the window." Ellie felt perfectly awful, her eyes threatened to release a torrent of tears.

"Are you sure? Ellie, I cannot tell you how sorry I am. What a silly decision on my part."

"Yes, I'm sure he saw. He was standing in front of the bank watching the carriage."

Constance peered out the window.

"I do not see him, Ellie."

Ellie took another chance and stuck her head out the window again to look behind. Robert no longer stood on the sidewalk, but his carriage was in motion, and it moved in their direction!

CHAPTER THIRTEEN

Ellie pulled her head back in, banging her hat on the edge of the door. With wild eyes, she turned to Constance. "He's right behind us! I-I think he's following us. Can the driver speed up?" Visions of old western movies with masked desperados chasing racing stagecoaches as they careened wildly out of control popped into her mind.

Constance stared at Ellie with round eyes and shook her head slowly. "Speed up? Do you mean go faster?"

Ellie gave her a fervent nod.

"We cannot go faster, Ellie. This is a city street. Robert is a gentleman. He would not follow us to the boarding house. That would be quite irregular for a man of his upbringing and stature."

Ellie eyed her skeptically, remembering the only boyfriend she'd had in her teen years—a romance lasting one whole week, and how she'd followed him one night to another girl's house. Had things really changed that much in a hundred years?

"Are you sure, Constance?"

Constance nodded firmly. "Yes. If Robert really wants to talk to you, I am sure he will contact me, and I will let you know. Remember, he thinks you are engaged. I do not see Robert as the sort of man who would interfere with such a promise."

It was all Ellie could do not to peek outside the carriage again, but she resisted the compelling urge. Not to mention her head hurt where her hatpin must have pulled out hair when she'd smacked her hat on the carriage window.

The ride back to the rooming house seemed to take forever, and in between bouts of overwhelming anxiety, Ellie tried to understand the origin of her fear. Was she afraid to face Robert, to reaffirm that she was indeed engaged and not available? Lies, all lies. Was she afraid that with one look into his emerald green eyes she would fly into his arms and beg him to take her back? True. Was she afraid that he just wanted to have one last conversation with her, to tell her he despised her? All of the above were correct.

At long last, the carriage pulled up to the sweetly painted Victorian house fronted by rose bushes in riotous bloom, and Constance stepped out. Ellie kept her head inside but peeked through the window. She saw no other conveyances on the quiet, tree-lined street.

"Well, of all the nerve!" Constance muttered as she stared down the street.

"What?" Ellie froze, bent over awkwardly as she prepared to descend from the carriage.

"Wait right there. I am going to have a word with him."

Ellie swallowed hard. Was it Robert? Her back began to hurt from the unnatural posture. Should she sit down or get out of the carriage? She couldn't stand in her current ridiculous position any longer.

She cautiously stepped down and saw Robert's carriage pulled up near some neighboring houses. He wasn't visible, but Constance stood at the foot of his carriage seemingly in a heated discussion as she pointed to her own carriage and vehemently shook her head.

Unsure of what to do, Ellie threw one look at Robert's driver, who watched Constance curiously, and then made a mad dash for the front door of the house. She closed the heavy teak door behind her and turned to peer out of the lovely leaded glass. Robert had now descended from his carriage, and he pointed to the house.

"Ellie! How was your day?"

Ellie whirled around to see Mrs. McGuire emerging from the kitchen, wiping her hands on a white apron.

"Oh, wonderful. We managed to do a lot of shopping." She twisted around to look out the door once again.

"Where are your bags? Are they out in the carriage? Shall I help you carry them in?"

"No!" Ellie almost shrieked. She blushed at the startled look on Mrs. McGuire's face. "No, thank you. Mrs. Green will help me with them. She is just talking to someone right now."

Mrs. McGuire moved to the door to peer out. "Oh, I see. Is that...? Is that Mr. Robert Chamberlain?" she exclaimed. "Why, yes, it is! How wonderful! I think I'll just go and say hello."

Before Ellie knew what was happening, Mrs. McGuire had pulled open the door and stepped onto the porch to wave at Robert. Ellie slumped against the nearest wall. Had the world suddenly gone mad? How could Mrs. McGuire possibly know Robert?

She peered out again to see Mrs. McGuire approach the carriage. Robert and Constance turned, and then Robert shook Mrs. McGuire's hand with his ready smile and a slight dip of his handsome head. Even from this distance Ellie could see that Mrs. McGuire was under his thrall. Wasn't everybody? Ellie fumed.

In unison, all three turned toward the house. Ellie panicked. Robert was going to come in. What should she do? She eyed the staircase, wondering if she could drag her skirts up to the second floor in time to avoid a meeting. Without further thought, she grabbed a handful of material, bunched it up around her knees and took two steps.

"Ellie...Miss Standish. Mr. Chamberlain and Mrs. Green are staying to tea. Won't you join us?" Mrs. McGuire sang out to her retreating back.

Ellie dropped her skirts and turned around on the stairs. She grasped the banister with a cold, clammy palm. Mrs. McGuire beamed, Constance eyed her with a mixture of apprehension and apology, and Robert watched her with a small enigmatic smile.

"Well, I was just about to—"

"Yes, Miss Standish, please join us," Robert said smoothly. "You might not know, Mrs. McGuire, but Miss Standish is already a friend of my family." He turned on the charm and flashed his captivating boyish dimples at Mrs. McGuire.

The older woman turned to Robert with rosy cheeks. "No, I did not know that. Though why would I? Ellie, Mr. Chamberlain is my banker. He helped me keep my house when my husband died. Please come down to tea, my dear."

Ellie could do nothing but return to the ground floor. Mrs. McGuire showed them to the parlor with promises to return momentarily with refreshment.

Robert paused at the door and allowed Constance and Ellie to enter ahead of him. Constance seated herself on the lovely rose sofa. Ellie dropped down beside her, keeping her eyes on the dark blue and old rose oriental carpet, though she watched Robert in her peripheral vision. He walked over to the window and gazed out onto the street with his hands clasped behind his back. Ellie threw Constance a quick inquiring look, but Constance gave her head a small shake and an almost imperceptible shrug of her elegant shoulders.

Robert returned to stand by the fireplace. Out of the corner of her eye, Ellie watched him lean one arm on the mantle and stare down into the empty hearth. She fixed her eyes back on the carpeting, willing Mrs. McGuire to return as soon as possible.

"Well, ladies, I find myself at a loss for words." A small mirthless chuckle followed Robert's words.

Ellie's eyes flew to his face. His eyes were those of a stranger, his smile polished but flat. He looked at Ellie without expression and then to Constance.

Ellie slid her eyes to Constance who stared at Robert with narrowed eyes and pink spots on her cheeks.

"Now, see here, Robert—" Constance began.

The door opened, and Mrs. McGuire entered with the tea service. Robert sprang forward to close the door behind her.

"Well, here we are. Isn't this cozy?" the effervescent little woman asked as she set the tray down on the small coffee table in front of the sofa.

Ellie didn't particularly think so, and Constance looked like she wished herself elsewhere. Robert's face reanimated at Mrs. McGuire's arrival.

She poured four cups of tea, handed them out with sugars or cream as her guests desired and seated herself in a high-backed, dark blue velvet chair. Robert took the seat beside her and across from the sofa. Ellie kept her eyes on her tea, seemingly intent on divining her future in the bottom of the cup.

"Well!" the happy hostess murmured. "Seattle is such a small world. Who could suspect we would all know each other?"

Ellie's eyes flew to Robert, though he beamed at Mrs. McGuire. Who knew, indeed?

"I must say, Mrs. McGuire, that it was with some surprise that I found both Mrs. Green and Miss Standish here today. I just happened along the street and saw them descending from the carriage in front of your lovely home...and now here I am, having tea with a bevy of beautiful women. How fortunate can one man be?"

Mrs. McGuire tittered and blushed, while Ellie dropped her jaw at Robert's blatant lie and flirtatious lines. She slid a look toward Constance whose lips twitched as she watched Robert.

"Oh, for goodness' sake, Mr. Chamberlain, I am sure you must not include me in your bevy." Mrs. McGuire delicately raised a small linen napkin to her face.

"Oh, but I do, Mrs. McGuire."

Ellie gulped her tea and relaxed into her seat to watch Robert at his finest. Perhaps the two of them would chat the entire time, and she could escape without a word.

"Ellie, how do you come to know Mr. Chamberlain and his family? Do you bank with him?"

Her eyes flew to Robert who turned to watch her with the same half smile she could not interpret.

"Um...I...uh...met them on the train."

"Oh, really! How nice!" Mrs. McGuire took a sip of tea. "I must tell you that when Mr. McGuire passed on, he left me in quite a pickle with the house. It was not paid for, and he left little insurance, so Mr. Chamberlain suggested I turn the house into a boarding establishment. He made all the arrangements for the bank to accept payments from the profits of the house. I consider him a most trusted financial advisor...and a dear friend." She beamed and reached over to pat his hand as it rested on his knee.

Robert had the grace to blush.

"It was my pleasure, Mrs. McGuire. I must say you are doing a remarkable job."

"Thank you." She eyed him with a twist of her lips. "Although I should note that this is the first time Mr. Chamberlain has had time to accept my invitation to tea. He works very hard and has little time for socializing."

Robert cast a quick, enigmatic glance at Ellie before he looked away to take a sip of tea.

"Yes, that is true, Mrs. McGuire," Constance chimed in with an amused note in her voice. "In all the years I have known Robert, I do not think he has taken more than an hour or two at lunch. Now, I have seen him on several outings over the last few days. How nice of you to join us today, Robert." She smiled innocently.

"Well, as I mentioned, I was in the neighborhood and...ah—"

"Yes, you did mention that. And what brings you to this neighborhood, Mr. Chamberlain?" Ellie surprised herself most of all when she spoke. She hoped to tease him as Constance had, to watch the adorable color on his grave face.

Robert's eyes narrowed and he turned in her direction, staring hard at her. "Well, the truth is, Miss Standish, I thought I saw an old friend of mine with whom I had a misunderstanding. I heard that he became engaged recently, and I wanted to congratulate him and tell him we must let bygones be bygones." High color stained his cheeks and he tightened his lips. "But alas, I could not catch up to him. Now, perhaps I will never get a chance to talk to him again."

Tears sprang to Ellie's eyes, and she ran a hand over her face as if she had a headache. From the side, she saw Constance throw a mortified glance her way.

"I miss my friend," Robert added in a quiet note.

"Oh, my dear Mr. Chamberlain, what a sad story. Is there no hope of reconciliation? Do you know where he lives? Can you drop him a note?"

Robert shook his head. "No, Mrs. McGuire, I do not know where he lives. I am afraid there is no hope of reconciliation. It seems he is lost to me forever."

Ellie couldn't hold back a sob, and she jumped up. "Excuse me. I have such a headache." She stumbled toward the exit, but Robert jumped up to open the door for her. He turned his back to the room and brushed tender fingers against the side of her face as she passed.

"Ellie."

She heard him whisper her name, but she turned away as she grabbed her skirts and flew up the stairs to her room. Heedless of the pain, she dragged off her hat, threw herself on the bed and buried her face in her pillow, sobbing and sobbing like she had never cried before. Within ten minutes, a small tap on the door heralded the arrival of Constance. She came in at Ellie's response and sat down on the edge of the bed. Ellie wiped her face on the back of her sleeve and turned on her side, pulling her knees up in a modified fetal position.

"Ellie, do you really have a headache? I am so sorry you feel poorly."

Ellie nodded, wishing for nothing more than the over-the-counter pain reliever sitting in her medicine cabinet at home.

Constance peered sympathetically at Ellie's face. "You have been crying. Robert's story was quite a ploy to make you feel bad, was it not?"

Ellie rubbed her head against the pillow and nodded. "I guess I deserve it. I should have had the courage to tell him in person that I was leaving, but I wasn't sure if I could leave once I saw him."

"I understand," Constance murmured. "Robert and the driver brought in your bags. They are downstairs."

"Is he gone?" Ellie sniffed.

Constance nodded. "Yes. He made his excuses as soon as you left."

"Mrs. McGuire really loves him, doesn't she?"

"Many people do. He is known to be a very generous and kind man."

Ellie pushed herself up into a sitting position. She held her pillow to her chest and rested her face against it.

"Why hasn't he married before now, Constance?"

Constance blushed. "I do not know. You know, of course, that I hoped he would ask me after my husband died. But that did not happen, and I know now it never will."

Ellie nuzzled the edge of her pillow.

"He told me that he hadn't found a woman who could put up with him yet, and then he said he had never fallen in love." She looked at Constance. "How is it possible to be in one's thirties and never have fallen in love?" At her words, she saw Kyle's face. Had she ever really been in love with him?

Constance stared out the window above Ellie's bed. "I do not know. I fell in love at eighteen with the most wonderful young man...my husband." She sighed. "Robert works a great deal. He has always worked hard to support his family. His parents died when Melinda was young, and he took over parental duties. I do not think he ever had many opportunities to gad about town as a young bachelor might."

"But the train trip. He seemed so relaxed. And all those young women?"

Constance scoffed. "Girls! I know for certain that Robert is not interested in young girls. Those are Melinda's friends, and while his grandmother would prefer he choose someone that young for...em...the purposes of bearing a large, healthy family, he is not attracted to young, simpering girls."

"Are you certain you and he...?" It galled Ellie to ask, but if she had to give him up to someone, she preferred it be Constance.

Constance flushed and shook her head. No, I am certain I am not the woman for him. At any rate, I have met someone who seems interested in me."

Ellie dropped her pillow. "Who?" she asked with wide eyes.

"A certain Mr. Malcolm Stidwell. Perhaps you met him? At the dinner party the other night?" Constance took on a girlish coyness that brought a sparkle to her dark eyes.

Ellie grinned. "The handsome man with the silver hair."

"Yes, silver hair."

Ellie leaned forward to give Constance an unexpected hug. "Oh, good for you, Constance!"

"Well, we will see. I do not know how we will get along, but I am to go to the park with him tomorrow."

"Fabulous!" Ellie leaned back and surveyed Constance, whose cheeks burned bright.

"As you say, fabulous!" Constance eyed Ellie thoughtfully. "Ellie, you should come with us. Please say you will."

"Oh, Constance, I can't. I mean...it's your first date. How would that look? You don't want me there."

Constance laughed. "Oh, yes, I do. First date, indeed! I would much prefer it if I had a female companion there. Please come. You cannot stay cooped up in this house all day."

"Are you sure, Constance?" Ellie wrinkled her nose uncertainly.

Constance gave her a firm nod. "Yes, I am sure. I would be grateful if you could...facilitate my first...date as you say...with Malcolm. I fear I shall be too tongue-tied to say a word."

"All right, then. I owe you a lot. I'll come."

"Wonderful!" Constance rose and turned toward the door. "We will pick you up tomorrow at noon."

"Tomorrow," Ellie echoed as she watched Constance leave the room. She closed her eyes and willed herself to sleep, but its merciful oblivion eluded her.

Mrs. McGuire popped her head in shortly to see how Ellie fared and to inquire about her desires for dinner. Feeling extremely guilty about running out on the hospitable woman's tea party as she had, Ellie agreed to come down to dinner.

Dinner with the girls was a panacea for any depressed woman. Their lively chatter, occasional bickering and genuine friendship left no room for miserable faces at the table. Mrs. McGuire ran the boarding house much like her personality—bubbly, energetic, full of warmth and love.

"Dorothy, did you know that Mr. Chamberlain was here today?" Mrs. McGuire grinned and cast a sly glance in Ellie's direction.

Dorothy's eyes widened. "Oh, my goodness, really?" She drew her brows together for a quick moment. "Did I do something wrong?"

Ellie watched the exchange with confusion. What were they talking about? Did Dorothy know the man, too? Was there one woman on the planet who had not yet met that aggravating man?

"No, dear, he did not say anything about you. He said he was in the neighborhood and came for tea. Miss Standish...Ellie knows him, as well." Mrs. McGuire nodded in Ellie's direction. "This is such a small world!"

Ellie held her fork in midair. What?

All three girls turned curious eyes on Ellie.

Dorothy cocked her head in inquiry. "Do you know Mr. Chamberlain, Ellie?"

Ellie stuffed food in her mouth and nodded—now unable to discuss the matter since her mouth was full.

"Oh." Dorothy turned an inquiring look on Mrs. McGuire.

"She met him on the train to Seattle." Mrs. McGuire happily supplied the details.

"Really?" Dorothy continued to eye Ellie with a curious stare.

Ellie nodded and attacked her plate for another large mouthful of food.

131

"That would be when he took his sister and her friends to Spokane for her birthday," Dorothy said.

Ellie looked up in surprise.

"Mr. Chamberlain is my employer. He is the head of the bank where I work. Mrs. McGuire recommended me to him, and he hired me as a clerk."

Ellie's cheeks burned, and she chewed her food with a nod.

"Well, perhaps you know, then, Ellie. He has hardly been at the bank lately, and people are wondering where he has been." Dorothy bit her lip. "I mean he is *always* at the bank. Every single day. The first person in to work and the last to leave. But for the last few days, he has only been in the bank for a few hours. Today, he dashed out of the bank as soon as he got there, and he never returned."

Ellie froze and threw a glance at Mrs. McGuire.

"Well, that is very interesting, Dorothy," Mrs. McGuire said. "Of course, you know he stopped by here for tea, but he said he was just in the neighborhood looking for an old friend."

"Do not misunderstand," Dorothy said earnestly. "I do not wish to gossip, but some people in the bank are talking about his unusual behavior."

Ellie's face burned.

"Dorothy, dear, are you sure this is not Mr. Chamberlain's private life and best not discussed at the dinner table?" Mrs. McGuire regarded her with a kind smile but her eyes brooked no argument.

"Yes, Mrs. McGuire." Dorothy smiled sheepishly and returned to her food.

"Oh, please tell us what they have been saying at the bank, Dorothy. Now, you have us all agog to hear," Samantha piped up, seconded by Martha.

Dorothy glanced at Mrs. McGuire, who looked as if she, too, couldn't wait to hear the story.

Ellie wondered if she could just crawl under the table and die, but first, she had to hear the gossip.

"Well," Mrs. McGuire drew the word out, "if it is nothing disrespectful, I might like to hear."

"Oh no! It is rather curious, in fact. The other clerks say that he has fallen in love!" Dorothy delivered the sentence as if she'd dropped a bomb and waited for the fallout.

Samantha and Martha stared for a moment, then resumed eating, the matter of Mr. Chamberlain's love life obviously not of great importance. Ellie swallowed hard, a dry piece of bread lodged in her throat threatening to choke her. She grabbed for her glass of water and gulped. Mrs. McGuire threw her a quick glance.

"Really?" the older woman murmured. "How do they know such a personal detail?"

Dorothy warmed to her audience. "Well, another clerk's mother said they saw him at the park the other day with a woman...and that he appeared quite infatuated with her. I have never heard of Mr. Chamberlain doing anything so frivolous as to stroll about the park in the middle of the day. I think that is very significant." Dorothy quirked an eyebrow.

Ellie didn't miss Mrs. McGuire's quick glance in her direction, but she smiled and resumed eating, though she felt slightly nauseous.

"That does sound promising. Well, if he has finally met someone, I am happy for him. I began to think he was a confirmed bachelor." With a last lingering look at Ellie, Mrs. McGuire returned to her food.

"We all did," Dorothy murmured. "I hoped he was waiting for me." She grinned unexpectedly and dug into her food with bright pink cheeks.

"Oh, he is too old for you, silly!" Samantha and Martha giggled and poked her teasingly in the ribs, and Dorothy snickered along with them. Ellie knew how the young girl felt. Robert was hard to resist. She averted her eyes from Mrs. McGuire, who'd already given her several curious looks during the conversation.

The following day, Ellie dressed in her new clothing, a white shirtwaist with a soft lace collar and a conservative, tailored suit in dark chocolate brown. She surveyed herself in the small oval mirror. The color flattered her brown eyes. She loved the lace at the sleeves and the way the skirt fell away from her hips to the floor. The fitted jacket trailed down to her knees like a brown tuxedo, and she wondered how comfortable it would be when she had to sit down. She'd done her hair as best she could in an upswept Gibson and perched a matching brown velvet hat with harvest gold ribbons on her head. She twirled and preened in front of the mirror, very satisfied with her first Victorian era purchase.

Ellie went downstairs and told Mrs. McGuire she was going to the park with Constance for the afternoon. Mrs. McGuire looked up distractedly from the stove, smiled and wished her an enjoyable outing. A carriage pulled up outside at noon, and Constance and Malcolm Stidwell presented themselves at the door. On closer inspection, she saw that the silver-haired gentleman had eyes of a peaceful sky blue and his smile held a note of gentle humor.

"Miss Standish, it is very nice to meet you at last. I am afraid we were not introduced the other night at the dinner party."

Ellie stuck out her hand. He blinked and took it in his own.

"Mr. Stidwell, thank you for taking me along on your outing. I hope I'm not in the way."

"Not at all, Miss Standish. We are happy to have you along, isn't that so, Constance?"

"Yes, Malcolm. I was very pleased when Ellie accepted my invitation."

"Shall we, ladies?" Malcolm indicated the waiting carriage. Ellie climbed in first, followed by Constance and then Malcolm, who sat on the opposite seat. He kept up a pleasant running commentary on the city as they made their way to the park. The carriage dropped them off in the same location as before when she'd come with Robert, and she tried to block the memory from her mind. Unsuccessful, she settled for blocking Robert from her mind—just for the day.

Malcolm held out both arms, and Constance took one while Ellie reluctantly took the other. They promenaded along the boardwalk by the lake, and Ellie kept silent while the other two chatted. She allowed the tall Malcolm to guide them as she strolled mechanically, lost in memories of handsome dimples and dark-lashed green eyes.

"Isn't that right, Ellie?" Constance's voice broke through.

Ellie returned to the present. "I'm sorry. What?"

Malcolm laughed. "She has been daydreaming, I see. A penny for your thoughts, Ellie."

She tossed him a quick grin. "Oh, that's way too much money for one of my scatterbrained thoughts."

"Malcolm, Constance, Miss Standish," a familiar male voice hailed them. "How do you do? May I join you for a moment?"

"Robert! How nice to see you out of the bank! What brings you out on such a fine day?" Malcolm nodded jovially.

Robert eyed a stunned Ellie for a moment. "The same as you, I expect, Malcolm. Warm sunshine and pleasant company."

Malcolm laughed. "Well, as you can see, I have my hands full with pleasant company. Ellie, would you care to walk with Robert?"

CHAPTER FOURTEEN

Ellie gritted her teeth and smiled up at the innocent Malcolm. Other than causing a scene, she had little choice except to release Malcolm's arm and take the one that Robert proffered. They fell into step behind Malcolm and Constance, who threw a quick glance over her shoulder to meet Ellie's stricken eyes.

Ellie attempted to stay close to Malcolm and Constance, thereby avoiding an intimate conversation, but Robert thwarted those plans by lagging a few steps behind them. With her hand tucked in his arm, there was little she could do.

"It is nice to see you, Ellie."

Ellie locked her eyes on Malcolm's back. "Thank you, Robert. It is nice to see you," she replied mechanically.

"How is your head today?"

She blinked and looked up at him. His eyes almost caught hers in a lock, but she dropped her gaze quickly. "My head? Oh, yes, my headache. That's fine, thank you."

"I am glad."

"How is it that you are at the park today, Robert?"

"Oh, I stopped by the boarding house...to see Mrs. McGuire...and she informed me that you and Constance had come to the park with a man," he replied airily. "I thought it a fine day for an outing myself. I was pleased to see that Malcolm was taking good care of you two."

Ellie tipped her head to raise a skeptical eye in his direction, but she remained mute.

He dropped the airy note, and his voice grew quiet. "I must say I was surprised to read of your engagement, Ellie. I wonder that you did not share the news with me when we first met."

Ellie faltered for a moment. Robert steadied her and she recovered.

"I-I...it didn't come up. It didn't seem important at the time." She avoided eye contact.

Robert gave a short mirthless laugh. "Not important? How is that possible?"

"When should I have told you, Robert? The moment I met you? When I realized I was lost on a hundred-year-old train with no money and no phone? When you took me into your home? When..." She couldn't say anymore.

"When I kissed you...and you returned the kiss?" Robert squeezed her hand against his arm. Her heart rolled over. Against her will, she welcomed the warmth of his body. "That would have been an opportune moment to tell me, Ellie."

"I know. I'm sorry, Robert. You're right." She peeked up at him to see that now it was he who stared straight ahead.

"Tell me about this...fiancé of yours. He is from your time, is he not? You have not gone and engaged yourself to Mr. Sadler already, have you?"

"Robert!" She almost chuckled. She didn't want to talk about Kyle. He seemed like a lifetime ago...unless she woke up with him next to her in bed tomorrow morning. "I don't want to talk about him. He doesn't seem to belong to this time," she murmured, forgetting whom she was talking to for a moment.

Robert paused and turned her to face him. "You are right, Ellie. He does not belong to this time. He belongs to a past life. You are here now—in my time—with me."

She stared at the disarming cleft in his chin, unwilling to meet his eyes, to drown in them and throw herself into his arms. She needed to stay strong.

"Robert, it's time we woke up. Both of us. There is no past life, no other time. This is just a dream, and a very bittersweet one at that." She finally met his eyes and fought against the love he allowed her to see. "What if we wake up tomorrow, and I am home alone in my bed, and you are here alone in yours? Then what? What is the point of falling in love in a dream? To wake to a painful, lonely reality?" Her voice cracked, and she was only vaguely aware that Malcolm and Constance had paused to look back at them but had moved on again.

Robert grabbed her hands in his, uncaring of who saw.

"I love you, Ellie. I do not care if it is a dream or whether you have come to me from the future. I love you, and leaving me is not going to change that."

Ellie longed for nothing more than to move into his embrace and bury herself against his chest. In a perfect dream, she could have done just that. Why couldn't she just throw caution to the winds and give in? She couldn't remember her reasons for leaving. What were they? They had seemed valid and necessary at the time.

She pulled her hands from his and walked on. He caught up to her and tucked her hand under his arm once again.

She glanced up at him, grief forcing a confession from her. "I miss you, Robert. You are the only person who truly knows me here, the only one who knows where I come from."

"All the more reason to return to me, Ellie." His voice was husky.

"If I knew why I was here... If I knew that I wouldn't suddenly wake up one morning in my time, and be unable to recapture the dream to get back to you... If I knew for certain that I had traveled in time and would not return..." She stopped and turned to him. "What makes you think I won't simply disappear? Do you want to risk that?"

Robert nodded grimly. "I would risk anything for you, Ellie, for the way I feel when I am with you." He gave her an ironic smile. "And perhaps you have forgotten. You did *simply disappear* from my home."

She grimaced and shook her head. "You're infatuated with a creature of your imagination, a character from a science fiction novel who travels back in time." She dropped her head. "That's not me. I'm just a regular woman who has hardly ever incited a great passion in any man. In fact, I never have." She looked up at him with a rueful smile.

"Miss Standish, Robert! How do you do?" Ellie turned a startled face toward Stephen Sadler. She smiled weakly and cast a quick glance at Robert hoping he would behave. He gave Stephen a brief nod, but Ellie saw a flash in his narrowed eyes.

"Sadler, how do you do?"

"I am well, thank you, Robert. It is a fine day at the park, isn't it? How have you been, Ellie?" Ellie saw the blue of his eyes harden for a moment in response to Robert's curt greeting.

"Fine, thank you, Stephen." Ellie stood between the two men who exchanged unspoken words, and she wondered if there was a shortage of women in Seattle at the moment. Or was her dream prepared to indulge her in every possible fantasy, including the jealousy of two very handsome Victorian men?

"Ah, there you are, Ellie! We are about to have a late lunch. Good day, Stephen. Won't you join us, gentlemen?" The irrepressible Malcolm arrived with Constance in tow to make matters worse.

"Certainly, I would love to," Stephen murmured.

"My pleasure," Robert responded, taking up Ellie's hand once again. Constance cast her a sympathetic look, but Ellie was sure she saw the other woman's lips twitch ever so slightly.

The group sashayed off the boardwalk and toward the picnic area. Malcolm's driver had laid out a sumptuous feast on a linen-covered table, much as Robert had supplied two days ago. Ellie found herself seated between Robert and Stephen and across from a twinkling Malcolm and apologetic Constance.

Malcolm served food while Constance, Robert and Stephen chatted about innocuous matters such as the weather. Ellie kept her lips sealed as she surveyed the faces of the people at her table. Was it possible that she actually sat in the company of three men and a woman from the turn of the century? In her time, they would all be dead long ago. She shuddered for a moment. The thought was too horrible to contemplate.

"Ellie, you look cold. Would you like my jacket?" Robert spoke low near her ear.

"Oh, I'm fine," she murmured.

Stephen beat him to it by whipping off his outer coat and settling it on her shoulders.

"There you are, Ellie."

"Oh, thank you. Thank you very much."

Ellie stared hard at Constance who watched the exchange of glances between the men with wide eyes and a lift at the corner of her mouth.

"You were telling me about your engagement a few moments ago, Ellie. When is the happy day?" Ellie turned a startled eye to Robert who threw Stephen a challenging glance over Ellie's head. She shot Constance a harried glance. Malcolm raised his eyebrows.

"Many felicitations, Ellie," Malcolm murmured.

"Ellie. I did not know," Stephen's voice rose an octave. "Is it true? Are you engaged?" He turned a frank, disappointed face to Ellie.

"I-I...uh...why yes, I was...I am...I think."

"Yes, Ellie is engaged. She told me so herself...to a young man back in Chicago," Constance offered helpfully, unaware that to Robert and Ellie, "Chicago" meant something other than just a city.

"Yes, Chicago. That is true, isn't it, Ellie?" Robert reaffirmed in a low voice.

She turned to him for a moment. His eyes glittered as he stared at her.

"Umm...yes...Chicago."

"And when will the marriage take place, Ellie?" Stephen's somber eyes met hers.

"Oh,...uh...soon...that is...um...when I return."

"I see," Stephen murmured. "I must extend my congratulations. How fortunate for you."

"Yes, very fortunate indeed." Robert chimed in with a narrowed gaze at Stephen.

"And what does your affianced do, Ellie?" Stephen ignored Robert. Ellie swallowed hard.

"He's a-an...investment banker."

"A banker?" Robert snapped. At his harsh tone, Ellie jerked her head in his direction.

"How interesting." He eyed her with a curious glint.

"What exactly does an investment banker do, Ellie?" Malcolm had no idea how much further he dug Ellie's hole by pursuing the subject.

"He manages investments for clients. You know, stocks and bonds?" She couldn't remember. Did stocks and bonds exist at this time? Surely they did. The stock market crash would occur in thirty years.

"Ahh," Malcolm nodded. "Yes, of course. I was not familiar with that term."

Ellie discovered she could tilt her head slightly and dip her hat in Robert's direction to block him from her line of sight, and she promptly did so. She looked over at Constance, who pressed her twitching lips together and raised a linen napkin to her mouth. By tipping her hat, Ellie exposed herself to Stephen more, but he didn't seem to be a problem.

Stephen gave her a regretful smile. There was nothing she could do, short of jumping up and announcing she was a fraud but return his smile and resume eating.

"And how long has your betrothed been an investment banker, Ellie?" Robert asked.

Ellie acquiesced to good manners and turned her head slightly to allow him to see her face. He looked irritated with her ploy to avoid him, and she bit back a smile.

"About five years, I think." She tilted her hat once again.

"I see. I must say, Ellie, that is quite a fetching hat you are wearing. It certainly shades your face well...from the sun."

"Thank you," she murmured on a gurgle, with a raised eyebrow in Constance's direction. "I just bought it yesterday."

"Yes, you will remember I saw you and Constance shopping. Is this part of your trousseau?" he needled.

The man was impossible! Trousseau, indeed! Was she living in some gothic novel?

"Yes," she said shortly.

Stephen leaned in to speak in a low voice. "Well, it is lovely, Ellie. It matches your eyes perfectly. Your future husband is a very lucky man."

Ellie blushed. "Thank you, Stephen."

A small commotion occurred on her right, and she turned ever so slightly to see Robert pick up his chair and move it to his right, toward Constance. All eyes turned to him, and he smiled pleasantly at the group and sat back down. She watched a muscle in his jaw working and wondered how pleasant he really felt at the moment. He'd moved into Ellie's line of sight, and she could no longer avoid meeting his eyes short of laying her head flat on the table.

"The sun...was in my eyes," Robert looked skyward.

No one commented on the fact that the day had grown cloudy as Pacific Northwest days often did.

He turned bright green eyes on Ellie who dropped her own gaze to her plate.

"And will we have the good fortune to meet your fiancé, Ellie? Will he visit Seattle in the near future?"

Ellie's head shot up. She couldn't remember where she was in her sequence of lies, so she took a chance.

"No," she replied evenly, fed up with the harassing line of questioning. "He will remain in Chicago. I'll be returning shortly."

"No, Ellie! When?" Constance's mournful note tugged at Ellie's heart. She was echoed by an equally saddened Stephen and Malcolm who joined in the chorus of "no." But it seemed Robert was finally silenced! His tightened lips and angry glare gave Ellie a small measure of satisfaction...or so she thought. She swallowed a lump in her throat the size of an apple.

She had to continue. "Soon, I'm afraid. I'm not sure exactly when, but it will be soon. My parents should send word any day now."

"I hoped you would stay longer," Constance murmured. Ellie watched Malcolm reach over to pat Constance's hand. "How can you face that long train trip again so soon, Ellie? Are you sure you cannot stay for a while?"

Ellie avoided Robert's eyes.

"Well, as you know, I lost all my things on the train, so I am just waiting for my parents to send money for my fare." Did that sound plausible, she wondered? "I must return to Chicago, where my fiancé is waiting for me."

Ellie's uneasy eyes passed over Robert's face. His jaw relaxed and his eyes softened. A gentle smile played on his lips.

"I am afraid this is the first I am hearing of this. Did you lose your luggage on the train?" Stephen turned to her with interest.

"I did not hear, either, Ellie. What happened?" Malcolm asked.

Ellie panicked for a moment. She couldn't remember what happened exactly. Involuntarily, she turned to Robert.

He came to the rescue. "Ellie's tickets, money and luggage were misplaced on the train, and I—my family and I, that is—had the good fortune to take her into our home until she could secure funds and other accommodations." He blithely ignored Ellie and Constance's startled looks.

"Ellie, how awful for you," Stephen said sympathetically. "Have they found your things yet?"

Ellie tore her eyes away from a complacent Robert and shook her head.

"No, I am afraid not."

"And how are you managing...that is...do you need...?" Stephen hesitated delicately. "May I offer some financial assistance in your time of trouble?"

"Well, of course...goes without saying." Malcolm cleared his throat. "Certainly, Ellie, if you need anything, I would be more than happy to help."

Ellie's face burned. She felt like a homeless beggar stomping her feet over a heated grate with a cup held out to passersby.

"No, I'm fine. I-I...uh...sold something, and I have enough money to cover my needs. I'm fine, thank you." She didn't miss the sharp look Robert gave her, but she kept her eyes on Malcolm and Stephen. Stephen nodded understanding and discreetly returned to his food. Constance looked mortified for Ellie.

"And what brought you to Seattle, Ellie? I am afraid I did not hear?" Malcolm seemed to have no idea that Ellie wished the earth would swallow her up.

She coughed on a sip of water and put her napkin to her lips before scanning the seemingly hundreds of eyes turned in her direction. Had she said?

"Umm...I...uh..." Ellie drew a blank. Was it possible for her to stand up and just start screaming? She would feel much, much better, though she wasn't certain where she would end up. Bedlam? Where was Bedlam, anyway? Probably England.

"Apparently, Ellie was on her way to Wenatchee to visit a favorite aunt. She fainted just as she descended the train. Unaware Wenatchee was her destination, we brought her back to our carriage, resulting in an unintentional kidnapping as we dragged her to Seattle...thereby stranding her here." Robert shook his head with a glance at Constance. "Isn't that correct, Constance?"

Constance nodded slowly, her brow furrowed, confusion clouding her lovely eyes. "Yes, I do believe that is what transpired, though I did not know Wenatchee was her final destination. Is that so, Ellie?"

Ellie bit her lip and nodded, refusing to look at Robert. Although he'd rescued her once again, she thought his talent and ease with lying far surpassed her own abilities.

"Yes, that's about it." She pressed her napkin to her lips once again. "Well, Malcolm, I must say this has been a very pleasant meal. Thank you."

Ellie successfully moved the conversation away from herself, and Constance picked up the thread and moved into talk of the mundane.

The picnic ended within the hour, and Malcolm, Constance and Ellie said goodbye to Robert and Stephen as they made their way to Malcolm's carriage. Ellie remained silent on the ride home, exhausted from being under the interrogatory spotlight so long at lunch. She was fairly sure she'd managed to cross a few lies, though she couldn't remember which, and she hoped no one had noticed.

****

"Robert, surely you are not serious!"

Robert stared out the window of the parlor with his hands clasped behind his back.

"Oh, I most certainly am, Grandmother."

"But why this woman? There are so many others who are more...suitable."

Robert glanced at his grandmother over his shoulder for a brief second with a wry smile. Then he turned away again to continue scanning the city below. It was as if he viewed it with new eyes.

"Suitable. Yes, what a word! I used that term myself once." His shoulders shook at the memory. "I sounded quite foolish."

"Well, I think it is an admirable word," Mrs. Chamberlain said in a huff.

Robert turned away from his survey of the city with a sigh. What was Ellie doing now, at this moment? He looked at his watch. He really needed to go in to the office. He'd been far too lax about his duties over the past few days. Robert sat on a green velvet chair and faced his grandmother.

"I am sure the word has its uses, Grandmother, but I cannot think of a single one right now."

She pursed her lips and narrowed her eyes.

"The woman ran away from you, from this house."

Robert smiled with a faraway look in his eyes. "Yes, she did, didn't she?"

"Robert, stop that daydreaming and pay attention."

"Yes, Grandmother?" He continued to smile, finding it extremely hard to draw his face into an attentive, grave expression.

"It seems quite likely she does not want to marry you, or she would not have left. And at any rate, there is no point to these romantic notions of yours. She is engaged to someone else." Mrs. Chamberlain sniffed and regarded her grandson with a raised brow.

"Yes, she does say so, does she not?" Robert flicked an imaginary speck of dust from his dark blue trousers. When he raised his head, he continued to smile.

Mrs. Chamberlain leaned forward. "Robert, did you hear me? Engaged! She is to marry another. Surely, you would not interfere in the betrothal promises of a woman, would you?"

Robert met her eyes but didn't really seem to see her.

"Certainly not, Grandmother."

"Well then?" she pressed with exasperation.

"I think Ellie overstated the case. I feel certain she is not as betrothed as she describes."

"*Not as betrothed as she describes*? What foolish nonsense is that? Either one is engaged or one is not, young man!"

"Yes, I see what you mean. It does sound strange," he murmured with a bemused smile and another glance at his watch. Robert rose and bent over his grandmother to place a kiss on her cheek. "I must go in to the office today."

Mrs. Chamberlain clutched his hand and stared up at him.

"Robert, I don't wish to be unkind, but she is too...old...especially to begin a family."

Robert's smile broadened into a grin. He patted his grandmother reassuringly on the shoulder. "Old!" he repeated with a chuckle. "You have no idea, Grandmother. You have no idea." With shaking shoulders and a muffled laugh, he turned to leave the room.

CHAPTER FIFTEEN

Ellie had just finished a small lunch with Mrs. McGuire when a knock on the door of the boarding house announced the arrival of Melinda and Mrs. Chamberlain. Melinda fell into Ellie's arms.

"Oh, Ellie, I am so glad to see you. Robert finally told us where you were last night. I was certain he knew where you were, but he said you needed time to yourself and that we must not badger you."

"I'm so glad to see you, Melinda! And Mrs. Chamberlain, how are you?"

"I would be better if I could sit down, my dear. Is there a parlor? Could I have a cup of tea?" She surveyed the foyer with an air of vague disapproval.

Mrs. McGuire, who'd been hovering in the background, rushed forward. "Yes, of course, right this way." She led the way into the parlor and settled Mrs. Chamberlain and Melinda on the sofa. Ellie followed with a sense of dread. For Melinda to visit her was one thing, a pleasant surprise, but Mrs. Chamberlain's presence seemed ominous.

"I'll just run and get some tea," Mrs. McGuire murmured as she plumped a throw pillow and set it on the sofa next to the older woman.

Ellie threw her a grateful glance.

"I have never been to a rooming house before. It is quite lovely." Melinda studied the sunny room with interest. Her light blue velvet hat and matching wool suit brought out the morning glory blue of her eyes. Mrs. Chamberlain wore her usual conservative dark colors and hat.

"It is, isn't it? I've never stayed in a boarding house before, either. It's a lot of fun. There are three other young women staying here. Dinner is always lively."

Melinda sighed. "It sounds wonderful...lively dinners that is. Our house is quiet."

"There is nothing wrong with a dignified house, Melinda." Mrs. Chamberlain tapped her granddaughter's hand.

Melinda raised her eyes toward the ceiling for a moment, out of her grandmother's line of sight, and Ellie chewed on her lips.

"That is an unattractive habit, Ellie. Do not mutilate your lips so. They will thin and vanish soon enough. Perhaps sooner in your case."

Ellie's eyes widened to match Melinda's. "I beg your pardon, Mrs. Chamberlain? Are you referring to my age?" She wasn't sure whether to laugh or cry.

Mrs. Chamberlain raised an eyebrow in Ellie's direction. "Of course I am. Youth and beauty are fleeting. You have very little of one and plenty of the other, but you must take care to preserve your complexion. Stay out of the sun, moisturize your face frequently, and do not make excessive facial expressions which will cause wrinkles. Smiling brings many lines to the mouth and eyes. You should attempt a more serene tilt of the lips rather than the toothy grin such as you favor us with at the moment."

Against her will and better judgment, Ellie burst out laughing.

"Oh, my goodness, Mrs. Chamberlain, I thought you were serious for a moment."

Melinda watched the exchange between them with confusion. She smiled hesitantly at first, but sobered as soon as her grandmother spoke.

"I *am* serious, Miss Standish. My grandson is determined to ask you to marry him, and I cannot have my grandson's new wife looking older than half the ladies in town."

Ellie gasped and stared at the older woman. Melinda echoed the gasp, and her shocked eyes flew from her grandmother's stern face to Ellie's surprised one.

Just then the door opened and Mrs. McGuire sailed in with the tea. Ellie looked at her for a second and snapped her mouth shut. She thought she would kill for a drink at the moment, a nice stiff concoction of some mind-numbing liquor. Or maybe just an effervescent, mouth-tingling, brain-freezing, carbonated soda pop. Anything but tea, which always seemed to bring insanity in its wake.

Mrs. McGuire poured and passed out cups and saucers. Ellie received her tea with a shaking hand.

"Well, I will leave you to visit, then. I have dinner to see to." The door shut behind Mrs. McGuire, and the noise began.

"Look, Mrs. Chamberlain—"

"But, Grandmother, she is already engaged to—"

"I hardly know Rob—"

"They only met a few—"

"I have no intention—"

"Grandmama, how do you know—"

"Enough, girls!" Mrs. Chamberlain held up a hand.

Ellie stared open-mouthed, but Melinda knew to clamp her lips shut.

"Now, just a min—" Ellie began hotly.

"Miss Standish. Please drink your tea and let me finish."

Ellie's eyes took in both women, and she obediently raised her tea to her lips and stared at Mrs. Chamberlain over the edge of the cup.

The older woman sighed. "I have talked to my grandson until I am blue in the face, and the boy seems set on his course. That you ran from his house in secrecy with a trifling excuse has done nothing to deter him. I have told him that you would not have hidden from him if you returned his love, but he will not listen. Melinda told me of your engagement, and I rallied with that information, but it seems he already knew of your betrothal and feels it lacks substance. The young man I once knew as a sensible, honorable gentleman seems to have vanished before my eyes, and I have you to blame, Miss Standish. The least you could do for me is stop that unbecoming biting of your lips as you again do now."

Ellie pressed her lips together and took another unladylike gulp of tea. Mrs. Chamberlain, two bright spots of red on her cheeks, did likewise. Melinda opened her mouth to speak and closed it. She reached for her tea and drank. The women eyed each other with mixed emotions.

Ellie lowered her cup and took a deep breath. "I'm sorry about Robert, Mrs. Chamberlain. I think he is infatuated with a stranger. I personally do not believe he could have fallen in love in just a few days. I left the house because I knew I would be returning to Chicago fairly soon, and I could see that he was..."

"Falling in love?" Melinda offered helpfully.

Ellie shook her head, her cheeks burned. "For lack of a better term, yes. I thought it would help. I didn't mean to disappear like I did. Well, I did mean to, but I didn't mean to be disrespectful to you or hurtful to Melinda. I just didn't have the courage to face Robert." She bowed her head. "I am a coward."

"And the engagement?" Mrs. Chamberlain asked.

Ellie hesitated, no longer clear on her thoughts. "The engagement is cancelled."

Mrs. Chamberlain let out a hiss. Melinda put down her tea and clapped her hands with delight.

"Does Robert know?" she breathed.

Ellie shook her head. "I do not want him to know. I think it best he still believe I am engaged."

"But why?" Melinda's voice rose an octave.

"Because I still have to return to Chicago...to my life back there. I cannot stay here."

"Are you certain? Why can't you stay in Seattle?"

Melinda asked with a dejected slump of her shoulders.

"Yes, I'm sure. I have responsibilities back there...my parents."

Melinda opened her mouth, but Mrs. Chamberlain interceded. "That is enough, Melinda. Do not press her any further. Ellie has explained herself sufficiently on the matter. It really is none of our concern."

Ellie shot the older woman a grateful look, but the older woman refused to meet her eyes and looked away toward the cold fireplace.

"Well, you must do as you think best, Ellie. I am sure my grandson will recover. As you say, it has only been a few days since you met."

"Exactly," Ellie murmured with a lump in her throat.

"Although time has little meaning in matters of the heart. It may surprise you to know that Mr. Chamberlain asked me to marry him the first night we met, and I said yes." Robert's grandmother met Ellie's startled eyes with her own bright blue gaze.

"Grandmama, I did not know that!" Melinda turned an appraising stare on her grandmother.

Ellie blinked. Was the older woman trying to tell her something? Didn't Mrs. Chamberlain want her to leave? To leave Robert?

"How wonderful for you!" Ellie murmured.

Mrs. Chamberlain's cheeks turned pink. "Yes, it was quite romantic really." Ellie watched her quick and unexpected smile droop. "I confess to being quite crotchety since he passed away ten years ago. I miss him a great deal."

"Oh, Grandmama." Melinda slid over next to her grandmother and kissed her cheek. "I am sorry."

"Yes, well, no need to crowd me on the sofa, child." She shooed Melinda, who moved over a few inches again, no small feat in her long skirts and corset.

"Well, then." Mrs. Chamberlain cleared her throat. "You will not reconsider having my grandson, is that correct, Ellie?"

Ellie couldn't bear the finality of the statement. Of course, she would consider him. She was head over heels in love with the man. And who wouldn't die to have such a handsome man pursue her so relentlessly? Or pursue the fantasy of a science fiction character, that is.

Ellie gave her head a slight shake.

"You have nothing to worry about from me, Mrs. Chamberlain."

"Oh, Ellie," Melinda mourned. Tears sprang to Ellie's eyes, and she gritted her teeth and stared straight ahead.

Mrs. Chamberlain rose. "I am not worried about you, Ellie, though if you do change your mind and marry Robert, you had better waste no time in having children."

"Grandmother!" Melinda giggled. "I cannot believe you—"

Ellie dashed the back of her hand to her eyes. "I'm not *that* old, Mrs. Chamberlain."

The older woman snorted and headed for the door. Melinda stopped to give Ellie a brief hug before following her grandmother out of the parlor. Mrs. McGuire bustled out from the kitchen to bid the guests farewell and then returned to her baking after ascertaining that Ellie planned to take a walk through the neighborhood.

Ellie climbed the stairs to her room and grabbed her jacket and hat. She jammed it on her head, wondering if the burning spots on her cheeks would ever fade back to their normal color. This adventure of hers kept her in a heightened emotional state of perpetual embarrassment, it seemed. She needed to get outside in the fresh air to think about things and make some plans.

Ellie stepped out of the house and looked up and down the street in every sense of the expression. The street was on an incline, as most things in hilly Seattle seemed to be. In need of a good workout, Ellie turned to the right to climb up the steep road.

As she walked and studied the "old" Victorian houses in their new condition, she wondered how best to extricate herself from the current problems. Though she had plenty of money for the moment, it would not last forever. Should she find a job teaching? Could she move to another town where Robert would never find her? Both possibilities seemed daunting in this particular day and age. One thing she'd noticed was a lack of the anonymity she knew in her own time. Everybody knew everyone's business here. She lifted her skirts over muddy patches on the walk and smiled. The modern expression seemed out of place.

The image of a train popped unbidden into her head, and she swore she could almost feel the rocking motion and hear the whistles blowing. Was that a message? Should she get back on a train for Chicago? Would that somehow return her to where she needed to be, where she was supposed to be? If Robert was right, and she had traveled through time, would that take her back to her own century? Did she want to return to her lonely existence?

Kyle was gone. That seemed clear. And if he wasn't gone, he would have to go, because she could never have fallen in love with Robert so readily, so completely, if she and Kyle had ever had a hope of a successful relationship.

What if by some miracle she stayed? Could she survive in the early 1900s with virtually no women's rights, no financial means of her own, no airplanes, no television, no modern medicine? Did she even have the choice to stay?

Ellie looked up from the sidewalk to nod at a couple who strolled by. A carriage rolled down the street, while she could hear the horses' hooves of another carriage or wagon laboring up the hill behind her.

She shook her head. Ellie felt sure she couldn't stay. Be it a dream or some odd shift in a space-time continuum, she was going to wake up in her own bed soon, and all this would be gone. She sighed and paused to survey her surroundings with the colorful Victorian houses, lush gardens and tall evergreen trees. Turning around to capture the vista of the city which spread out below, she shrieked as she bumped directly into Robert's chest. She thrust her hands against him.

"Good gravy, what are you doing here? You scared me half to death."

Robert reached out to steady her, immaculate as always in a well-fitting gray suit and charcoal blue-gray vest.

"I am sorry. I did not mean to startle you. I meant to call out when I neared, but you turned so suddenly."

She eyed him narrowly and looked past him to see his carriage standing by, Jimmy staring discreetly off into the distance. "Why aren't you at work? Don't you ever go to work? I heard you were a workaholic."

He reared back and stiffened. "A workaholic? You mean drinking? I do not overindulge. Well, except for the other night."

Ellie giggled. "No, *work*aholic...someone who works all the time. Dorothy told me you work all the time."

"Dorothy, eh? I had forgotten she resides at Mrs. McGuire's boarding house. Yes, I have been known to work a great many hours. It has been my habit of many years."

"Why are you here, Robert? Your grandmother came to see me this morning."

He sighed. "Yes, I know. I was afraid of that, and I wondered how you managed."

"I managed very well, thank you." Ellie fiddled with her skirt. "She had some interesting information for me."

Robert tightened his lips and turned away momentarily. "I hoped she would not mention our talk. She told you, then?"

"Told me what, Robert?" Ellie closed her eyes for a moment. Would he actually say the words?

"That I intended to ask you to marry me," Robert murmured in a tender voice.

Ellie opened her eyes and looked into his sparkling green eyes, hating to extinguish the light. "I am engaged, Robert."

"No, you are not, Ellie."

Color flooded Ellie's face. "I most certainly am," she retorted. He couldn't possibly have seen his grandmother or Melinda in the last few minutes, could he? How could she have expected them to keep a secret?

"Then what is this?" Robert held her engagement ring in the palm of his hand.

Ellie gasped and fell back a step. "Where did you get that?"

"The pawn shop on Second Avenue, near the teashop where I saw you and Constance. It did not take much to deduce you had...ah...sold your *something* there." He looked down at the ring. "This is your engagement ring, isn't? What sort of betrothed woman sells her ring?"

"The sort who needs money," she snapped. "Did you pay the jeweler for that? I must owe you a fortune."

"You do not owe me anything. I will take it out in trade when we are married." His eyes danced merrily, and Ellie had all she could do not to fall into his arms.

"Your grandmother thinks I am too old," she muttered self-consciously.

"I love older women," he murmured, a seductive note creeping into his voice. He reached for her hand, but she snatched it away.

"I am leaving, Robert. I told you I cannot control this...this phenomenon. I'll be gone before you know it."

"Ah, yes, back to your parents in Chicago. You told me you were an orphan. Another fabrication, Ellie?"

She blinked and stared at him. "Oh dear, I did say that, didn't I? That's actually the truth. My parents are both dead." She quirked an eyebrow. "You certainly have quite the way with lies yourself, don't you? Wenatchee? On my way to visit a favorite aunt?"

Robert grinned. "I was only trying to help you out in an awkward situation...and very successfully, I might add."

Ellie chuckled. "Yes, very successfully. Thank you."

"Come, Ellie, come with me in the carriage. Let's drive around the city. I will take you to the waterfront this time, if you like." His dimples were irresistible.

Ellie hesitated. Under the hypnotic gaze of Robert's eyes, all her reasons for running from him seemed insubstantial and wispy. Why had she left, anyway?

With a smile, she put her hand in his, and he lifted her up into the carriage. Ellie put her fears aside for the afternoon as Robert set out to entertain and enthrall her with the sights and sounds of the city. He could have simply read a newspaper and she would have sat at his feet equally captivated by his charm. She kept her eyes on him as he described the city he loved, pointing out various lakes, parks, buildings and mountains. The afternoon passed all too quickly.

Robert left Ellie at her door just before dinner with a chaste kiss to her cheek, given that several pairs of feminine eyes peeked through the glass to observe them.

"I will come for you tomorrow, Ellie, in the morning." Robert turned and walked away. Ellie stared after him. *Come for her?* What did that mean, exactly? Were they going somewhere? Obviously Robert had not seen the latest horror films. "Come for you" meant something totally different to someone in a darkened theater clutching a bag of popcorn with an unsteady hand.

She entered the house and joined the women for another lively dinner, fielding questions as best she could about her morning visitors as reported by Mrs. McGuire, and about her afternoon outing. She studied the girls with affection. Was this the rest of her life? No matter how many times she said she was leaving or how many times she said she would wake up, she remained in the year 1901. Would she marry Robert? Was that even possible? Of course, he hadn't asked her. And children? Could she bear to have children, never knowing if she would wake up to lose them or leave them in time? Ellie shuddered. No, she could not bear that.

After dinner, she dragged herself up the stairs for bed, wishing for a moment that she had the solace of television to block her chaotic thoughts. As she undressed and climbed into bed, she wondered whether Robert was thinking of her as she now thought of him. She turned on her side to look out the window and gaze at the bright white moon, high in the sky. Her eyelids drooped and she slept.

****

Bright sunlight slipped through Ellie's half-closed eyelids. She turned over on her side to avoid the light. Her clock said 6:00 a.m. Clock? Ellie jerked and sat up. She was back in her bed in Chicago, the modern furnishings in the room all too sickeningly familiar.

"Honey, are you awake?" Kyle poked his head in from the bathroom, his blonde hair freshly washed and uncombed, a white towel draped

151

loosely around his waist. Ellie had a sudden, wistful thought that she would never see Robert with a towel around his waist. Was it possible? Was her dream over?

Kyle moved toward the bed and bent to kiss her lips. "Good morning, Ellie. I think you overslept this morning." He sat down on the edge of the bed and took her hand in his own.

Ellie stared at him in mute silence. Wasn't he gone? Hadn't he moved out? When had he returned?

"Kyle. I-I thought you left."

He looked at the clock and then back to her. "Nope, not me. I don't leave till 6:30. You know that." He patted her hand and stood up to return to the bathroom. He returned with a cup of coffee. "Made my own coffee this morning. Are you proud of me?"

Ellie nodded and pulled her knees up to her chest. "I mean I thought you moved out."

Kyle turned a startled face to her. "What? What are you talking about?"

"I... Didn't you tell me that you were leaving? That you'd met someone? Was that a dream?"

Kyle eyed her like she'd lost her mind. And she had, there was no doubt of it. Where was Robert? He always seemed to understand her insanity. He wasn't the dream, was he? Surely *this* was the dream! Ellie felt a searing knife-like pain in her chest. She was afraid she knew the answer.

"Wow, that *was* some dream! Yeah, I left, but I came back, remember?"

"I thought..." Ellie grabbed a pillow and clutched it to her aching chest.

"Come to think of it, you *were* dreaming last night. A lot. You kicked a lot and talked and moaned and all sorts of things. I have to admit I finally moved to the couch to get some sleep." He jumped up and headed back to the bathroom.

Ellie bit back a sob. "What did I say?" she asked his retreating back.

"Oh, I don't know," he yelled from the bathroom. "Hard to make some of it out. Let's see. I heard Seattle, train, Victorian and a few names...Roger or Robert. You must have had quite the trip to Seattle last week."

"Last week?" she croaked.

He poked his head back out and stared at her. "Yeah, last week, remember? Seattle, the conference? The one you just got back from?"

Ellie rubbed her eyes with the palms of her hands. Real life had suddenly become a nightmare.

"Are you okay? Got a headache?" Kyle removed his towel and moved toward his closet to grab some clothes. Ellie looked up. She would never see Robert without clothes, would she? They would never live together. It was all a dream. She remembered waking up from dreams in the past and trying to recapture the moment. It never happened.

"No," she muttered. Ellie watched Kyle dressing, realizing with an aching finality that she could never marry him. He had never entranced her as Robert had with a look from his green eyes or a flash of his dimples. She suspected no living man ever could. Were she and Kyle even engaged any more? The idea seemed suddenly so foreign to her.

"Kyle?" she hesitated.

He turned from the closet. "Yes, Ellie?"

"I-I don't think I can marry you." She winced as she watched him. His reaction was unexpected in its lack of reaction. He turned away to pull on his trousers.

"I know, honey. You don't have to remind me. We talked about that already. You said after I came back that you weren't going to be able to marry me, and I told you that was okay. I'm obviously not the most faithful guy in the world, am I?" He gave her a sheepish grin and turned to the mirror to knot his tie.

"I'm sorry, Kyle." What she really longed to do was go back to sleep and find Robert.

He turned around and crossed over to the bed, bending to kiss the top of her head. "It's okay, Ellie. We've been through all this." He picked up her hand and studied it.

"Where's your ring? Did you put it away?"

Ellie stared at her hand. Had there been a ring? Really?

"I-I don't know. Didn't I give it back to you?"

Kyle shook his head and returned to the closet to grab his jacket. "Nope. I told you to keep it. I mean you've had it for what...two years now? It's definitely yours."

Ellie stared at her left hand. Where was the ring?

Kyle turned at the door and waved. "Better get up, Ellie. You're already late. I'll see you tonight."

As soon as the front door shut, Ellie jumped up and ran to her jewelry box. She rummaged through it, looking for her ring, but the shining diamond did not materialize from the clutter of costume jewelry. She retraced her steps and climbed back into bed, closing her eyes tight and burying her head under the covers. She tried deep breathing and counting sheep, but sleep eluded her. She pressed the pillow over her head and willed herself to sleep, to slip back into her dream, but the real world maintained its choking hold on her. She turned over. Hot tears poured from her eyes and ran down the sides of her face.

Please, please, please let me go back to sleep! Robert, you said you would come for me. Please come for me!

An hour passed and still her inability to sleep kept the man of her dreams from her. Ellie pulled herself up in bed and sobbed into her hands. How could life hand her a magical romance and then take him away? She dragged herself out of bed and paced the apartment, pulling shades down to darken the rooms. She flopped into an easy chair and squeezed her eyes shut. She jumped up in seconds and went into the bathroom to search the cabinets for sleeping pills. There were none, of course. Sleep had never before been an issue.

Robert! Can you hear me? Robert!

Ellie returned to the bedroom and lay down on the floor, resting her burning face against the carpet, rubbing her face against the roughness. She thought she must be going insane. The world had gone quiet. Only the rumble of the El disturbed the dead silence.

The El! The train! Was it possible? Ellie jumped up and flew to the living room to flick on a lamp. She grabbed the phone book and phone and dialed the number for the train station, waiting with bated breath through an endless, painful series of recorded telephonic menus while she sought for her answer.

At one point, she banged the phone against the arm of her easy chair while she begged the recorded tinny voice on the other end to treat her like a human being. She had *real* questions, and she needed *real* answers. At last, the proper menu monotoned its arrival, and she waited forever to hear the information she wanted. With a quick glance at her watch, she jumped into some jeans, a sweater and tennis shoes, grabbed the cash from the cookie jar and flew down the stairs. Ellie had no idea where her purse and cell phone were, but she had no time to look for them. If she'd lost them in a dream, then where were they?

Ellie ran down the street for the El and raced onto the next train. She refused a seat as she paced from pole to pole waiting for the subway to reach the train station. She wanted to scream at the constant stops and starts, but she bit her lip and willed the El to move faster...if that were possible.

They arrived at the train station, and Ellie jumped off the El and ran into the station. She hustled through the throngs of people and popped up to the ticket window, thanking her lucky stars she'd found one without a line. She paid for her ticket and ran down the concourse as she headed for the train that would leave in five minutes. Where was the gate?

Where was the gate? Ellie's chest ached as she gasped for air. She felt lightheaded, as if she might pass out. Anxiety robbed her of oxygen. She stepped outside onto the platform and beheld her dear, beloved, gleaming silver train. There it was! The train that would take her once again to Seattle! Ellie knew it was a long shot, but it was all she had. She couldn't sleep. Perhaps Robert hadn't been a dream!

CHAPTER SIXTEEN

Ellie waved her ticket in the conductor's face and sped past him to hop aboard the train.

"31B, 31B," she muttered as if possessed while she hurriedly scanned the seat numbers. "Where is it?"

"Aha!" she exclaimed to no one in particular when she located the seat she wanted. Luckily for someone else, it was empty, because Ellie had every intention of sitting in that seat. She slid into it and nestled against the window, hoping for a miracle.

Nothing happened. She squeezed her eyes shut and waited.

Still nothing. Ellie tried to regulate her erratic breathing. Her heart paused and skipped beats like Morse code. She willed herself to calm down.

"Not yet. Just wait," she murmured to herself. Passengers continued to board the train, and Ellie tapped her foot impatiently, hoping to see the last of them onboard and safely stowed in their seats so the train could leave.

Finally, the train began its stealthy movement, so unlike the jerking and whistle-blowing fanfare of the Victorian train in her dreams. She pressed her head against the cool glass and watched as the train tracks of Chicago fell away into the distance. Once they were out of the city, the train picked up its pace and Ellie closed her eyes, waiting for sleep.

Nothing happened. No sleep. No time travel. A single hot tear slid down Ellie's face and she brushed it away. She wouldn't give up hope. There was still time. Reluctant though she was to leave her seat in case *it* happened, she had to use the bathroom. She hurried down the stairs and washed up, returning to her seat within minutes. As she settled in once again, Ellie wondered, had that been the moment? Had she missed the "window" by going to the bathroom?

The hours passed slowly as the train made its way through Wisconsin. By the time they reached Minnesota, she knew Kyle would be home from work and wondering where she was. She'd left no note for him. He might assume she'd stayed late at work. She often did. In fact, she realized she herself had been a workaholic—grading papers, preparing lectures, working on articles for publication. Just like Robert. The last week...or last night...had been one of the most restful of her life in terms of leisure time, though the stress of falling in love had been incredibly tense.

Ellie took a break from her vigil around eight that night and went down to the snack bar for a bite to eat. She returned to her seat with a sandwich and a surprisingly unexpected cup of tea and stared out the window at the passing lights. The tea wasn't nearly as tasty as that which she'd shared with Robert, but she had somehow grown fond of the ubiquitous beverage.

She closed her eyes as the train rolled out of St. Paul, Minnesota, and drowsed with her head lolling back and forth in the corner of her seat. She dreamed of a handsome silver-haired man with green eyes who visited his children in Washington, D.C. She awoke with a start and looked around. It was dark, but the rumbling sound of the tracks and a loud whistle revealed she was still on the train. What time was it? Where was her cell phone? Her purse?

She reached out to the empty seat next to her. The sterile roughness indicated a polyester blend, not luxurious velvet. She squeezed her eyes shut against the burning tears, but they slid down her cheeks. She didn't bother to wipe them in the dark. Who would see?

She turned a miserable face to the window. Her grand idea to recreate the trip on the train was an abysmal failure. She was still here, on a modern train in her own time. Robert did not smile at her or take her hand under his arm. Melinda didn't ogle her in curiosity. Mrs. Chamberlain didn't disapprove. By Grand Forks, North Dakota, Ellie was numb. Nothing mattered. She thought she might as well get off the train, but she lacked the energy to do even that. She'd already paid the fare to Seattle, and she found it easier to sit in misery than to get off the train and call Kyle to send her money for a return trip home.

When the sun came up over North Dakota, Ellie stared at the Great Plains as the train rolled through wheat fields brightened to gold by the first rays of dawn. She blinked at the beauty of nature, and her spirits lifted...a little. The dark night had passed, and although Robert had not come for her, she felt better in the light of a new day.

"How are you doing, miss? Do you need anything?" The tall, young conductor leaned over to check her ticket. "Seattle, huh? Visiting family there?"

"Ummm...yes," Ellie murmured with a yawn. She stretched and wished her silver-haired gentlemen had joined her on this trip. She recalled dreaming about him the night before. What was his name? Edward? His eyes...so green...like Robert's.

The young conductor in wheel hat, dark blue jacket and vest consulted his wristwatch. "Well, the snack bar opens in a half hour, at 6 a.m. We reach Minot, North Dakota at 8:54 a.m. You can get off the train and stretch your legs there, if you like."

"Thank you," Ellie murmured. Did she want to stretch her legs in Minot, North Dakota? She had no earthly idea. On a modern train, she could stretch her legs by virtually running from car to car. Since the conductor had given her the idea, she stood at that moment and worked out the kinks in her knees. Another cup of tea and some breakfast might be in order.

Ellie spent the day wandering from car to car, studying the people on board. She wondered about their lives, who they visited, who they loved, whether they'd left anyone behind or were on their way to meet their true love. She hung around in the lounge car and stared out the panoramic floor-to-ceiling windows at the rolling fields of eastern Montana, a continuation of the Great Plains of North Dakota. She counted her money. Dangerously low on funds, she grabbed an inexpensive snack for lunch. She would be lucky to make it to Seattle before she ran out of money. Once there, she would call Kyle to book a hotel room for her and reserve her return fare...by airplane. She had no idea how she would explain her mad dash on the train, but she resolved to worry about that another time.

By evening, she dozed in her seat once again as they crossed into the Rocky Mountains.

"Mom, look, look! Up there! Look at those mountain goats!"

Ellie's eyes popped open at the young boy's shout from the seat behind. She peered out the window, and craned her neck to see three mountain goats hugging the side of a steep hill above the tracks. Well, to her, they seemed to be "hugging" the mountainside. She suspected that, for mountain goats, they merely lazed about as a sunbather might do at a beach.

"Aw, Mom, why can't we stay here in Montana? I want to go to the Park."

The conductor strolled down the aisle intoning the next stop. "Essex, Montana. Essex, Montana. Glacier National Park." He didn't shout. He didn't have to. The modern train muted much of the rumbling along the tracks.

A woman's voice shushed the boy. "Quiet, Patrick. You'll wake the other passengers. Maybe we will go to the Park one day. Get some sleep now. We'll be in Seattle in the morning, and Grandma will be there to meet us."

The view of the mountain goats receded into the blue-gray dusk behind tall pine trees, and Ellie leaned her forehead against the cool window with her eyes closed. For a moment, she thought that it had actually happened. She'd traveled back in time! Young Patrick's voice sounded exactly like the little boy she'd heard just last week on the train...before she met her seat companion, Edward...and before she fell asleep to awaken to Robert.

But a quick glance around the darkening car revealed she was still on the same train—a comfortable but sterile silver snake that silently wound its way across the United States. She hugged herself and stared out of the window, willing the light to stay with her a little longer to keep the long, dark night at bay. By breakfast, they would be nearing Seattle, and the trip would end. Her hopes of finding Robert would end.

Had Robert ever really lived? Or had he been a figment of her imagination? The aching sense of loss in her throat and chest seemed too real and painful to suffer over a mystical dream lover. She remembered the day she'd imagined Robert, Constance, Stephen and Malcolm dead and buried a hundred years later. The memory still made her shudder. Perhaps she could go to the library in Seattle and see if any of them had ever really existed.

Perhaps find their graves? Was it possible?

Ellie brushed away the tears from her eyes with the back of her hands. She turned her face away from the aisle as a tall man approached. In the moment before she looked away, something about the waves of his dark hair caught her attention. She gasped and swung her head back in his direction.

The tall man glanced down at her, nodded pleasantly and passed.

It wasn't Robert! How could it be? She shook her head and pressed a hand to her racing heart. What was she thinking?

Ellie closed her eyes once again and dozed fitfully. During the night, she heard the conductor's monotone as he passed through the car with a quiet, "Spokane, Washington. Spokane, Washington." She pulled up her legs, hunched her shoulders and pressed tighter into her corner.

"Wenatchee, Washington, five minutes. Wenatchee, Washington."

Ellie pried open one eye to the faint rosy light of dawn. Her ears pricked. Wenatchee?

This was it! This had to be the moment. If she were ever going to find Robert, this had to be it! She jumped up from her seat, stumbling against the back of the seat in front of her. She had to get off at this stop. This is where Robert would be. She bent down to look out the window. Tall pine trees hugged the train tracks. Streaks of daylight broke through the openings in the forest. This had to be right.

The train slid into a smooth halt, and Ellie tripped down the stairs. She hopped off the train and surveyed the area around the concrete platform. Up and down the length of the gleaming train, other passengers descended to stretch their legs. Something was wrong. Nothing looked as it should.

She turned to the young conductor who stood by the door of the car. "Excuse me. Is this Wenatchee?" The modern concrete platform, paved parking lot and steel and glass station bore little resemblance to the old wooden station surrounded by dirt.

"Yes, ma'am." He pointed to the sign over the station which read "Wenatchee" in glaringly huge letters. Ellie stared at it for a moment, and her exhausted knees wobbled. Then Wenatchee wasn't the answer! Robert did not appear. He didn't stride up to her and take her hand in his. He didn't fold her in his arms.

Ellie's feet began to move with a will of their own, and she headed toward the train station. A large round station clock read 5:35 a.m. She pushed open the glass and steel door and stepped into the deserted lobby. Modern acrylic benches in a multitude of colors decorated the room. No one waited for her. The lobby was desolate.

This had been her last hope! Gone!

A bout of dizziness and a wave of nausea overtook her. Her knees buckled and she fell against one of the benches. She gave in to a strange urge and laid her head down for just a moment, hoping the world would soon right itself. But the world continued to slide, and Ellie slipped into unconsciousness.

"Miss. Miss, are you all right? Did you fall asleep?"

Ellie woke up to gentle prodding of her shoulder by a kindly, bespectacled, gray-haired man sporting a train conductor's uniform. She tried to raise her aching head but slumped for a moment.

"I-I'm fine. I'm okay. What time is it?" she asked assuming only a few moments had passed.

"It's 5:45 a.m., Miss. The station is closed. How did you get in here?"

Ellie met the older man's kind blue eyes and looked behind him to see weathered wooden walls and a dusty floor. The varnished pine bench under her legs bore no resemblance to the acrylic bench onto which she'd slumped. Her heart began to pound.

This was it! She'd done it!

The loud whistle of the train brought her to her feet.

She rushed past the startled stationmaster and pushed open the wooden door, careening to a halt. The train no longer stood in front of the station. A puff of black smoke was all that remained of the gleaming black vintage train as it barreled out of the station on its way to Seattle.

"Wait!" Ellie screamed as she ran across the dusty wooden platform toward the empty tracks. She stopped for a moment and bent over, bracing her hands on her knees to draw in a deep breath.

"Wait!" she screamed even louder. "Wait for me!" Her throat burned, but she kept screaming. "Robert! Wait for me! Please don't leave me! Robert! Come back for me!"

"Ellie, wake up!" Strong arms enveloped her.

CHAPTER SEVENTEEN

"Ellie, wake up!"

She awoke with a start, tears streaming down her cheeks, and burrowed her face into Robert's neck. He held her against him and kissed the top of her head as he rubbed her back in long soothing strokes.

"Another dream, my love?"

Ellie nodded, rubbing against his warm skin.

"Were you running for the train again, sweeting?" Ellie calmed to the rumble of his voice in his chest.

"Again," she murmured. She drew a deep breath to calm her racing heart. "I still haven't caught it," she said with a watery chuckle.

Robert's low laugh bounced her face on his chest, and she craned her neck to look at him. He bent his head and kissed her lips in a slow, lingering caress, pulling her closer to him, molding her body against his as they lay together. He lifted his head and studied her face with warm green eyes.

"Maybe the dreams will end someday, my love. I hope so."

She buried her face against him again. "I hope so too," she mumbled. "I don't think they're good for the baby."

Robert slid his hand down to her rounded stomach. "The baby will be fine, Ellie. She has been a hundred years in the making. She must be strong, don't you think?"

Ellie chuckled at Robert's logic. "Yes, dear. I think *he* will be very strong." She leaned up on one elbow and stared into her husband's soft, dark-lashed eyes. "I love you, Robert. I cannot tell you how much I love you."

"And you are the only woman I have ever loved, Ellie. I waited for you a long time." He stared at her as he reached to brush the tangled curly brown hair from her face. "I hope the baby looks like you. I hope she has your hair."

Ellie grinned. "Well, your grandmother just hopes I have a baby with two arms and two legs. You know she thinks I'm too old."

Robert smiled and his eyes twinkled. "If only she knew *how* old. Almost one hundred and fifty years, I would say." He snorted. "You look remarkable for your age, Mrs. Chamberlain."

She gave him a playful smack on his shoulder.

"Thank you, Mr. Chamberlain."

His face grew serious. "Thank you, Ellie, for marrying me and having our child. Thank you for coming back in time for me."

Ellie wrinkled her nose. "You know I still don't believe in time travel, Robert, though it appears likely that this isn't a dream. No one could possibly dream up a man like you...the love we've shared...the nights." Her face burned at the light in his eyes. She looked down on her rounded belly. "And the baby we created together."

"This is no dream, my love. Though Mr. Wells wrote back to tell me he thought I had taken his book a little too seriously, *I* know you heard my loneliness and came through time for me."

She pressed her lips against the adorable cleft in his chin and tilted her head to study his face.

"I can't imagine how a handsome man like you could ever be lonely, Robert."

His eyes narrowed seductively. "Well, it took you forever to come to me. I waited and waited, though I understand you had quite a long journey."

Ellie laughed, and the baby in her stomach moved in response. She lay back and reached for Robert's hand to place it on her stomach. He rolled over on his elbow and looked down into her face. His green eyes sparkled, reminding her of another set of eyes.

"Robert. Do you think it's possible that I could have met my grandchildren in the future? There was a man on the train..." She let her voice trail off as Robert began to kiss the corner of her mouth.

****

Edward awoke to the voice of the conductor.

"Wenatchee, Washington. Wenatchee, Washington."

He rubbed his eyes and turned to look at his seatmate. She was gone. He checked his watch. 5:45 a.m. The hour was early. Muted light broke through a few cracks in the curtains. Maybe she'd gone to the restroom.

He stood to stretch his legs with a fervent wish that he could get a cup of tea at this early hour, but the snack bar would not open for another fifteen minutes. He eased himself back into his seat and waited for the young woman...Ellie...to reappear. Maybe she would like to join him. There was something about her that intrigued him. He wasn't certain what it was. The color of her hair, the hazel of her eyes, the tilt of her lips as she smiled?

Edward studied her empty seat for a moment and suddenly he stiffened.

Ellie! Good gravy! That was his grandmother's first name! How had he not remembered that? The name was not that common. He'd always just thought of her as "Grandma." He shook his head with a bemused smile. What a coincidence.

He turned to the window and watched the first rays of dawn streaking through the tall pine trees of his home state. Memories flooded in as he recalled his youth, playing at his grandparents' house on the hill...the house he still owned. He smiled as he remembered his grandmother's odd mode of dress for gardening—an old skirt she fondly referred to as her "jeans skirt" and the open-backed shoes she'd called "clogs," as if she were some Dutch woman. How odd that both styles had recently come back into fashion. The cyclical nature of fashion!

He and his older sister had adored spending time with their eccentric grandmother and doting grandfather. No one else had grandparents quite like them, but all their playmates envied them the big house with nooks and crannies suitable for playing hide-and-seek and a sloping lawn that turned into a wonderful sled hill on rare snow days. Grandma Ellie had always been the first to acquire any new gadgets on the market—the first car, the first radio, the newest kitchen appliances. She and Grandpa had taken them on their first train trip to Glacier National Park, where she'd shown them mountain goats and old historical trains like the one where she had met Grandpa.

Great Aunt Constance had often said that he looked just like a younger version of his grandfather. Uncle Malcolm agreed. He always agreed when Aunt Constance spoke. She and Great Aunt Melinda often speculated whether he would grow to be as tall as the handsome silver-haired man he'd worshiped. And he had. Edward stretched out his legs.

Grandma Ellie used to make him blush whenever she bent down and peered into his eyes. He was never quite sure what she was looking for, but she always smiled, kissed his forehead and told him he was the "spitting image of Grandpa and would some day grow to become a handsome old gentleman."

Edward smiled at the memories. Grandma Ellie had always been ahead of her time, full of new ideas, controversial thoughts and strange colloquialisms...for the time. He remembered whispers from other parents behind covered hands, but his grandparents shook their heads and kept laughing.

He looked at his watch again. 6:00 a.m. The snack bar was open, and still the young woman had not returned. Neither did he see any of her possessions. He stood and scanned the boarding passes above the seats. Only his pass remained. She said she was going to Seattle. Where had she gone? Had she ever even been on the train?

He shook his head and smiled. He moved down the car toward the snack bar. Maybe she had just been a dream.

TOGETHER FOREVER ACROSS TIME

BESS MCBRIDE

PROLOGUE

"A beautiful wedding," Stephen said as he bent over the bride's hand and kissed it. "Please accept my felicitations, Ellie. Robert." He executed a small bow in front of the beaming couple—Ellie, vivacious, petite and chestnut-haired; and Robert, graver and much taller with well-groomed dark hair.

"Thank you, Stephen!" Ellie Standish Chamberlain said as she held onto her husband's arm. "I'm so glad you could come."

"Thank you, Stephen," Robert said. He took Stephen's proffered hand with a broad smile. Stephen noted Robert had finally dropped his belligerent attitude toward him. After all, Ellie was *his* bride now, not Stephen's. This moment had not come as a surprise to Stephen. He had seen the way Ellie and Robert looked at each other during their unusual courtship, even when they appeared to be at odds with each other. Ellie—unconventional and different from any woman he had ever known, and Robert more like himself, conservative and a traditionalist of the old school. Although lately, Robert had changed due clearly to Ellie's influence. He seemed...happy.

Ellie and Robert turned to receive their next guests, and Stephen moved through the line, nodding to acquaintances as he made his way through the crowded reception hall in search of something strong to drink. With a last regretful look over his shoulder toward the beautiful and happy bride, he squared his shoulders, picked up a glass of champagne and surveyed the room.

Filled to capacity with gaily-dressed people, he recognized many faces of his acquaintance. Not unusual as he and Robert Chamberlain traveled in the same social circles.

"Mr. Sadler!" A matron in a dark blue silk gown with a young blonde

169

woman in tow swished to a stop in front of him. "How nice to see you here. The wedding was simply lovely, was it not?"

"Mrs. Cornish, Miss Cornish," Stephen bowed. "It was indeed. Mr. and Mrs. Chamberlain make a fine couple. I wish them a happy marriage."

"As do we, Mr. Sadler," Mrs. Cornish said. "Hannah was just saying how much she admired Mrs. Chamberlain's dress."

Stephen nodded in the blushing girl's direction. He knew what Mrs. Cornish was about, and he had hoped to avoid her machinations. Miss Hannah Cornish was a fine young woman, a very pretty girl, but Stephen did not see in her the spark that he had once seen in Ellie—in fact, still saw in Ellie although she now belonged to another.

He had no need to turn and follow their eyes toward Ellie. He knew how beautiful she looked on her wedding day.

"Yes, it is indeed a beautiful dress." Stephen bowed again and prepared to make his excuses in an attempt to preempt what he knew would soon come, but he was too late.

"Mr. Sadler, I wondered if you might like to stop by for tea this week," Mrs. Cornish said. "Hannah has a history book that she particularly hopes to have you examine and perhaps explain a few passages to her."

Stephen pitied poor Hannah. Whether the young woman liked him or not, he might never know. Her cheeks flamed at her mother's blatant attempts at matchmaking, but she said nothing, keeping her eyes downcast on her clasped hands. Although he taught an occasional history course at the university, he hardly thought young Hannah interested in his opinion on a history book.

Stephen searched for an excuse and was saved by the timely arrival of Mr. and Mrs. Stidwell.

"Stephen," Constance murmured. She held out her hand, and Stephen bowed over it.

"Well, what do you think, Sadler?" Malcolm Stidwell said. "More festivities! What a year this has been. First, our marriage," he nodded toward his wife, "and then Ellie and Robert." He paused to bow to Mrs. Cornish and Miss Cornish. "Who is next?" he said in a jovial tone.

All eyes turned on Stephen, most particularly those of Mrs. Cornish, and he coughed and gulped his champagne.

"Malcolm!" his wife remonstrated. "You are embarrassing Mr. Sadler." She gave her husband an affectionate smile. "Forgive us, Mr. Sadler. My husband only teases." Her eyes darted to the continually blushing Miss Hannah Cornish and her mother, and she favored Stephen with a sympathetic smile.

Her sympathy galvanized Stephen, and he thought it high time he moved on before the entire group had him married off.

"If you will excuse me, Mrs. Cornish, Miss Cornish. I must take my leave. Thank you for your invitation, but I am away from town for the next week. Perhaps when I return." He bowed toward the group in general. "Constance, Malcolm, a pleasure," he said. He set his glass on the serving table and made his way out of the reception hall. There was really no reason to remain. He felt particularly unsociable that day, due in large part to the sight of Ellie married. Resigned, he was. Happy, he would never be.

CHAPTER ONE

"Wenatchee! Fifteen minutes," the train conductor announced over the loudspeaker.

Dani slipped out of her clogs and pulled her feet up under her as she gazed out the large windows of the observation car, her crochet needle and afghan square resting in her lap. The golden light of dawn highlighted the last of the prairies as the train worked its way toward the snow-capped Cascade Mountains of Central Washington. The clock on the wall said 5:20 a.m. She hadn't been able to sleep and had settled into the relatively empty observation car to stretch her legs and watch the sun come up.

"No matter how many times I take this trip, I never tire of seeing the plains," she said to the elderly man sitting in the next seat. "I love evergreens, don't get me wrong, but sometimes you really *can't* see the forest for the trees." She smiled.

"I know what you mean," he said. "It's like being in a tunnel, isn't it, when the trees are so close, you can't see anything."

"That's *exactly* what I mean," Dani said. She offered him her hand.

"My name is Dani Douglas."

"Edward Richardson," he took her proffered hand in a gentle shake. "Where are you traveling to?" She blinked under the unexpected emerald light in his green eyes. Bright for an older man, she thought. Silver hair framed a handsome face.

"It's nice to meet you, Edward. I'm heading back home to Seattle. I've just been visiting my mother in Whitefish, Montana. How about you?"

"I live in Seattle, too. I just spent a week in Washington, D.C. with my grandkids."

"Oh, how nice!" Dani said. "Where do you live in Seattle?"

"Queen Anne Hill, in an old house that belonged to my grandparents."

"Ohhhh! Queen Anne Hill." Dani wagged her eyebrows. "Well, that must be a very *nice* 'old house' I'm thinking." She gave him a knowing grin.

Edward smiled. "It is. My family took good care of it. And whereabouts do you live in Seattle?"

"Oh, nothing so glamorous. I live in a condo in the University District." She propped her chin on her fist and turned toward him, crocheting forgotten on her lap. "So, tell me about your house. When was it built? How large is it?"

Edward laughed. "Ah! I take it you like the old Queen Anne architecture."

Dani nodded. "Oh, yes," she breathed. "I've often wondered what it would be like to live in one of the turn-of-the-century houses." She shook her head. "Then again, I don't know. I love looking at them, but I'm a pretty modern gal. I like my *new stuff*."

"Perhaps you will come visit one day," Edward said.

"Oh, shoot, Edward! I wasn't angling for an invitation to your house!" Dani's cheeks heated. "It's not safe to invite strangers to your home."

"Oh, I think you look pretty safe, my dear."

"Well, maybe I'll take you up on that sometime." Of course, Dani had no intention of intruding on the man's home. "Though I'm not sure what your wife will say." She grinned and nodded toward the silver wedding ring on his left hand, the one he toyed with occasionally.

"I am a widower," Edward said. "My wife passed away some years ago."

"Oh, dear. I'm sorry, Edward, I really am." Dani bit her lip. "Yes, of course, I'd love to come see your house. I'd be honored."

"Good," Edward said. He pulled out a small memo pad and tore out a piece of paper. "This is the address, and my phone number. I don't have one of those modern cellular phones, but I have an answering machine!"

"Thank you, Edward! I'll call." Dani, tucking the slip of paper into her purse, sensed the conversation was ending, and she was right.

Edward, a tall man, raised himself gingerly from his seat. "I think I'd better return to my seat for a short nap before breakfast."

Dani rose as if to help him but he waved her off kindly.

"Thank you. Maybe I'll see you later," Edward said. "Perhaps at breakfast?"

"That sounds great!" Dani said. "It's a date. Eight o'clock?"

He nodded and walked slowly toward the next car.

Dani watched his tentative steps and speculated he was in his late eighties. But he still had his faculties about him. And those eyes...

She stifled a yawn and picked up her crocheting once again, wondering if she wasn't going to need a short nap herself as soon as the train left Wenatchee.

****

After stretching his legs, Stephen climbed aboard the train and entered the observation carriage. Their stop at Wenatchee had been of short duration, for which he was grateful. The journey from Chicago seemed particularly long this time, though he could not say why. He seated himself in a sturdy wicker chair at the desk in the library of the carriage and opened a newspaper.

"Ouch!"

Stephen startled at the sound. He had thought himself the only passenger in the carriage. The dark green velvet curtains had been drawn against the night, and the globes of the electric lights shone softly.

"What the heck?" The voice was unmistakably female.

Stephen rose from his seat and peered around the curtained panel into the observation carriage beyond.

A young woman held onto the back of a seat bench, her lower limbs braced wide as if she were a sailor on a ship. Those limbs, Stephen noted with widened eyes, were encased in trousers—extremely snug-fitting trousers. Her feet were encased in colorful socks, but she wore no shoes. Her hair—a lively shade of red—hung about her shoulders unbound in a wild untamed fashion, much like that of a young girl.

"Madam, may I be of assistance?" he said.

She stiffened and attempted to straighten, but another lurch of the train threw her off balance, and she toppled over onto the floor.

Stephen ran forward to grasp her hands, cold and clammy as they were.

"Here, please allow me to assist you." He pulled her up and settled her onto the bench. Such a tiny thing, the top of her head came only to his shoulder.

"Who are *you*?" she demanded.

"Stephen Sadler, at your service, Madam." He gave her a small bow, trying without much success to avert his gaze from the sight of her limbs. "And may I ask your name?"

"Dani," she said with a frown on her pale brow. She seemed quite preoccupied with searching the carriage as if she had never seen it before.

"Miss or Mrs. Dani...?"

She returned her attention to him. Eyes the color of light green crystal regarded him, surveying the length of his body. She narrowed her gaze as if she found him peculiar.

Stephen stiffened, and clasped his hands behind his back. He had certainly never been assessed by a lady before in such a bold fashion. It was not *he* who was peculiar.

"Douglas. Dani Douglas," she said. "Where am I?"

"May I sit, Miss Douglas?" Stephen asked, indicating the bench beside her.

She nodded and lowered her eyes to stare at the bench as he sat. He watched her run her hands along the red velvet of the seat as if she explored the material.

Grateful to be out of her critical purview of his person, he set his newspaper down beside him and clasped his hands in his lap.

"We have just left Wenatchee, Miss Douglas. Is it Miss?"

"Wenatchee..." she murmured in a bemused tone. He waited, but she said no more.

"Yes, Wenatchee. Were you sleeping during the stop? Please forgive me, Miss Douglas. I thought I was alone in the carriage. I was reading the newspaper over there." He nodded his head in the direction of the library portion of the carriage separated only by a half screen above the desks. "I would not have entered the carriage had I known you were resting in here."

"I was in the observation car." She continued to appear bemused, and he wondered at her origins.

"Yes, you *are* in the observation carriage." He waited.

"No, not *this* car," she said. "I wonder if I'm hallucinating."

"I cannot say, Miss Douglas," Stephen said. "What is it you think you are seeing that is not there?"

"This car. The velvet bench. The wood paneling. The globed lights. The carpet." She nodded toward the red floral carpet. "You." She regarded him with a furrowed brow.

"Me, Miss Douglas?" Stephen shook his head with a kindly concerned smile. "I am not a hallucination, I can assure you of that." He leaned forward, resting his hands on his knees. "Is there someone I can call for you? A family member? A traveling companion? The steward?" He chose his words carefully. "You seem...confused."

Miss Douglas tilted her head sideways and eyed him. "That's an understatement." Without warning, she jumped up. Startled, he rose hastily.

"I think I'll just head back to my seat." She hurried to the carriage door and pulled it open. A rush of wind and a strong smell of coal sent her reeling backwards, and she lost her footing again, falling to the floor. Stephen jumped forward to close the door before coming to her aid. The woman really did need assistance. Where was the steward?

"I should have warned you that we have picked up speed, and the train is jostling a bit." He half carried her back to the bench. She seemed disoriented. "Miss Douglas? Perhaps a glass of water? I am not sure why the buffet is not open. There should be a steward here serving tea at the least, although the hour is late." Stephen poured her a glass of water from a nearby jug and offered it to her.

She took the glass as if in a trance and drank from it, scrunching her nose and peering into the glass before handing it back to him. He replaced it on the table with the thought that she certainly had the oddest behaviors.

"Look," she began. "I really don't know what's going on here. This isn't the observation car. At least not the one I was in. And this doesn't look anything like the train I'm supposed to be on."

"I beg your pardon?" Stephen was at a complete loss.

"We don't use coal in our trains anymore, Stephen. And I definitely smelled coal."

Stephen blinked at her ready use of his first name, but he quite enjoyed the sound. It had a familiarity he was not used to.

"May I ask where you are from, Miss Douglas?"

"Originally Montana," she replied almost mechanically, again studying the interior of the carriage with a bewildered expression. "But I live in Seattle now."

"Ah! That explains it!" Stephen said before he could bite back the words.

Miss Douglas quirked an eyebrow and returned her gaze to him. "Explains what? Because if there's something that explains anything, I'd like to hear it."

"Forgive me. I shouldn't have said anything. But it explains your particular form of address, your ease with societal rules."

"Societal rules? What on earth are you talking about?"

"Well, your...mode of attire, for example!" he offered. His cheeks heated, and he cleared his throat.

She followed his eyes to her legs.

"My jeans? So, you think I wear jeans because I'm from Montana?"

Stephen, who had actually thought just that, hastily amended his words at the look on her face.

"No, certainly not. Well, perhaps. Well, you might be a cowgirl for all that I know." Stephen thought he neared the mark. Yes, a woman from a Western ranch, that was it!

"A cowgirl!" She laughed, a high-pitched sound that lacked amusement. "This is nuts! I think I should ask you where *you're* from, Stephen. If you tell me the turn-of-the-century, I'll believe you. Your own...uh...*mode of attire* seems a little bit outdated."

Stephen stiffened and surveyed his dark suit, newly delivered from the tailor only two weeks prior to his trip to Chicago.

"I beg your pardon," he said. "My suit is most certainly not outdated. It is quite new, I assure you."

"Well, Stephen, I don't know what to say. You might want to rethink your tailor."

"*Rethink* my tailor! What unusual expressions you have, Miss Douglas."

"For Pete's sake, just call me Dani." She eyed him narrowly. "Let me see that newspaper, will you?"

Stephen handed it to her. She flattened it and stared at the front cover. Her face paled even more so than normal, and she squinted to study it more carefully.

"What is it, Miss Douglas? Which article has captured your attention?"

She lowered the newspaper and stared at him with that irksome assessing glance again as she surveyed him. She really was the most brazen woman!

"Miss Douglas. Really, I must insist—"

"I'm reading the date, Stephen. The date of the newspaper. It says September 15, 1901."

"Yes?"

"1901, Stephen," she repeated. "*1901.* The turn-of-the-century."

"Yes, Miss Douglas. That is correct."

"I must be dreaming...or this train is traveling backward in time."

"Miss Douglas, you really do say the most extraordinary things. I fail to understand your meaning. This is not a dream."

"When I got on the train, it was September 17, 2012."

CHAPTER TWO

"*2012?*" Stephen stumbled over the date. "Impossible," he said with a shake of his head.

"I know," Dani murmured.

"You are suggesting you have traveled in time, Miss Douglas. Time travel is simply not possible."

"I know," Dani repeated.

"So, it is not even possible in *your* time," Stephen said.

"What do you mean, *my* time? If you don't believe in time travel, then why are you asking about *my* time?"

Stephen acknowledged his mistake. "What I meant to say was...the time you *think* you are from."

"You know, Stephen, if I thought I could just walk out that door, I would," Dani said with narrowed eyes. "But I'm pretty sure if I try, I'll either fall off the train...or jump."

"Oh, come, Miss Douglas. Surely not *jump.* I understand you are at present confused about the date, but that seems too drastic an act."

"Well, what would you do if you woke up on a train a hundred and ten years in the future?"

Stephen pondered the question for a moment before responding.

"I cannot imagine such a thing," he said quietly. "Would *you* be there?" He smiled unexpectedly, the expression lighting up his sky-blue eyes. Dani blinked. She studied his face for a moment as she hadn't before. Handsome would describe him perfectly. Well-cut sandy blonde hair framed a strong face and firm chin. His mouth, partially hidden by a thick blonde mustache, appeared to be generous and full. She could see his hair had a tendency to wave away from a widow's peak which he appeared to take great pains to control, and she wondered what it would look like if left to its own desires. Gorgeous, she imagined.

"Me?" Dani blinked. "I'm sorry. What was the question?"

Stephen shook his head and dropped his eyes for a moment. "It was nothing, a foolish comment." He rose to pace the floor. "The question should be, what can we do to assist you, Miss Douglas?"

Dani shrugged her shoulders. "I have no idea. I guess I'll just wait till the train gets to Seattle and see if things *change* then. I'm probably dreaming anyway, so maybe I'll just wake up, and this will be all over."

Stephen paused for a moment and bent near her bench. He picked up her crocheting and handed it to her.

"Does this belong to you, Miss Douglas?"

"Yes, it does! See? I *was* in the observation car, because I was crocheting. And I met a nice older gentleman, and we were going to have breakfast together. Do you see my purse anywhere? I really need that!" She stood to search the floor then dropped to her knees to look underneath the bench.

"Miss Douglas! Whatever are you doing?" Stephen's voice cracked. "Please allow me. You should not be crawling about on the floor this way."

Dani looked over her shoulder to where he stood.

"What? Why not?" She stilled at the shocked look on his face. "Oh, gosh, yes. *1901.* The only women crawling around on their knees are maids and inmates scrubbing floors, right?" Her purse was nowhere to be found. She rotated to a sitting position, pulled her knees to her chest and wrapped her arms around her legs.

"I can't *be* here, Stephen. I have a job. I have a mother who is sick. I *really* can't be here. Please tell me this isn't happening." Moisture blurred her vision, and she dashed at her eyes.

Stephen lowered himself to the floor beside her and took her hands in his.

"Please do not cry, Miss Douglas. We shall see this right, I promise you. As you say, when we arrive in Seattle, I am sure all will be made clear."

"You don't sound very sure about that, Stephen," she said on a strangled chuckle. She pulled her hands from his gently, though she wasn't quite sure that's what she really wanted to do. In a world turned suddenly upside down, the warmth of his hands felt very real. She thought she saw a look of regret pass over his face.

The sound of the carriage door swinging open startled her, and the strong smell of coal burst through the door, along with a woman and a man.

Stephen scrambled up, and threw Dani a harried look. In one fluid motion, he lifted her onto the seat, shed his jacket and threw it down over her legs. Instinctively, maybe picking up on a vibe of Stephen's, she tucked the coat around her legs and ankles.

The couple held onto their hats in the gust of wind which followed them in before the man managed to push the door shut.

If Dani ever had a doubt about the year, it was laid to rest by the woman's *costume.* She sported a large straw hat which defied description, festooned as it was with satin roses, leaves and feathers and perched atop a faded brunette pompadour coiffure. A cameo adorned the high-neck collar of the white lace blouse peeping out from a tailored jacket of forest green cotton. A matching bell-shaped skirt, which ended just above the top of her black boots, completed her ensemble. Her posture seemed a bit awkward as her chest protruded to the front while her back curved emphasizing her backside, reminding Dani of a pigeon. Scoliosis?

"Goodness!" the woman said as she came up short at the site of Stephen and Dani. "What a struggle to reach the observation carriage. The conductor noted it would be arduous crossing the carriages while the train was in motion, but I must have my way!" She breezily moved forward into the carriage. "My husband will agree, I know."

"Yes, dear," the tall, slender man agreed with a faint smile. He removed his derby and ran a hand across his thinning gray hair to smooth it back.

"I so wanted to see the library and observation carriage before we reached Seattle," the woman said. She moved forward to offer her gloved hand to Dani who took it with alarm and a quick look in Stephen's direction.

"How do you do? My name is Lucinda Davies, and this my husband, Gerald."

Dani opened her mouth but nothing came out—an unusual situation for her.

"Stephen Sadler, Madam, at your service." He made one of those charming little bows of his. "My...wife, Mrs. Dani—Danielle Sadler." His cheeks bronzed but he pressed on. "Delighted to make your acquaintance."

"Thank you, Mr. Sadler. May we join you?" Lucinda didn't wait for an answer but took a seat next to Dani, whose throat had closed.

Wife! Dani almost choked. Couldn't he have thought of something else? Sister, maybe cousin? Why not just friend? Or did the era require him to show some valid reason why the two of them were skulking about in an empty car at night?

"Is there tea?" Lucinda asked looking around.

"No, Madam," Stephen replied. "I am afraid there is not. I have not seen a steward since I came into the carriage."

Lucinda was having none of that. "Gerald, be a dear and run back to the next carriage and fetch a steward to bring us tea. Mrs. Sadler looks as if she could use a good strong cup." She seated herself on the bench next to Dani, her posture impeccable.

"Oh, I'm fine—" Dani began but Stephen cut her off. Gerald obediently stood, donned his hat again, and went for the steward. The distinctive swoosh of coal-infused wind followed his departure.

"Thank you, Mrs. Davies. I wanted to fetch a steward myself but did not wish to leave my wife alone. She is not feeling well. I believe she has a sore throat, and must rest her voice."

Stephen took a seat across from them with an innocent-looking smile directed toward Dani. She narrowed her eyes at him but said nothing. He was right. It was best she keep her mouth shut, though he was obviously too much of a gentleman to say so.

"Oh, you poor dear," Mrs. Davies cooed. "A hot toddy is what you want! Mr. Sadler, please be so good as to seek out Gerald and ask him to order a hot toddy for your wife. Some tea, lemon, honey and brandy should put her right!"

At this, Dani opened her mouth. "Oh, no, I don't—"

"I do not think—" Stephen looked from Lucinda to Dani uncertainly.

"Nonsense. She will be right as rain. Go now! I shall take care of your wife."

No matter how much Dani begged him with her eyes to stay, even she realized he was powerless under Lucinda's force.

"Then, of course I will go. Thank you, Mrs. Davies."

Stephen bent near Dani's face. He pressed warm lips against her cheek and whispered, "Say nothing." He pulled the jacket further up her lap by an inch to remind her not to expose her legs then he turned for the door. Dani put a hand to her cheek. The tickle of his mustache remained. He smelled quite wonderful, his aftershave or cologne some sort of combination of citrus and spice.

"What a handsome man," Lucinda exclaimed as she followed Dani's eyes. "You are a very lucky woman."

Dani put a hand to her throat and nodded. Stephen wasn't far off the mark. Her throat did hurt from the lump in it.

"We cannot very well sit here and say nothing, Mrs. Sadler, so since you must rest your voice, I shall ask you a few friendly questions, and you must nod yes or no."

Dani's eyes widened.

"Do you and your husband live in Seattle?"

Dani nodded.

"My husband and I do as well. And how long have you been married? Just hold up fingers." Lucinda appeared to be enjoying herself.

Dani's eyes darted to the door, but no hope came. She held up two fingers, wondering how she was going to pass her answers on to Stephen in case Lucinda decided to quiz him as well.

"Two years?" Dani blinked. "Two months?" Another blink. "Two weeks? Oh, you are still newlyweds!" Lucinda exclaimed without waiting for a response. "Gerald and I have been married for thirty years now. Thirty years!" She shook her head in apparent disbelief. Dani noted the massive hatpin secured the hat to Lucinda's head and prevented it from falling off when she shook her head.

"Is Mr. Sadler in business?" Lucinda pressed on.

Dani blinked. She had no idea what Stephen did for a living. None. Besides, what was she supposed to do even if she knew? Pantomime? She coughed then coughed again.

"Oh, my dear, I am so sorry. I must not press you," Lucinda said as she adjusted her seat to move slightly further away on the bench. "I do hope they hurry with the tea." Lucinda looked toward the door.

As if Lucinda willed it, the door opened on Stephen and Gerald. Stephen queried Dani with his eyes, and she gave him a slight shrug. She wasn't sure he would understand her message. She herself didn't understand what she was trying to convey except to say she'd survived her time alone with the older woman.

"The steward is returning. The conductor stated the young man had stepped away from the carriage and should have been here to serve from the buffet." Stephen nodded toward an area near the middle of the carriage where a serving station had been set up. Dani hadn't noticed it before. On looking over her shoulder, she also noted the car had another exit, and she wondered if she could escape through that door...from whatever she had fallen into.

She had to chance using her voice.

"Are there anymore stops between Wenatchee and Seattle?" she eked out in a hoarse voice.

"Oh, dear, I do not know," Lucinda said before Stephen could answer. Stephen gave Dani a sharp look, and she eyed him with her best look of innocence. Gerald took a seat and picked up Stephen's newspaper to read, seemingly unconcerned with the conversation.

"No, my dear," Stephen replied. "There are no stops until we reach

Seattle. Why do you ask?" Dark sandy brows narrowed over his blue eyes.

She shook her head and coughed.

"The poor girl, Mr. Sadler. We shouldn't tax her anymore, I think," Lucinda murmured. "Ah! Here is our steward!"

A white-coated steward arrived, and hurried past them to the buffet with apologies for having left the car unattended. Within minutes, he served tea and some sort of biscuits.

"And a hot toddy? Gerald, did you mention that?"

Gerald looked up from the newspaper and nodded. "Yes, dear."

"Yes, ma'am," the steward stated. He handed Dani a cup of tea. Even before she took a sip, she could smell the rum in it. Drinking seemed to be a really bad idea at the moment, but what was she to do?

"Drink up, dear," Lucinda said, watching her. Dani shot Stephen a pointed look from out of the corner of her eye, and she took a sip. The hot liquid did indeed feel good as it slid down her throat, and Dani thought she might actually have developed a sore throat. Maybe it was just the smell of coal. The combination of sweet honey and sour lemon delighted her, but it was the tasty rum that made her finish off her cup in a few swallows. She set the cup down on a side table with a look of regret and raised her eyes, unaware that she'd had an audience.

Stephen looked taken aback.

Lucinda grinned. "There's a good girl. Steward! Another hot toddy for Mrs. Sadler, please. And I think I will have one myself. To ward off any possible illnesses." She winked. "Traveling, you know. So wearing on the body."

Dani returned her grin. The woman really was quite the character. So she and Lucinda would get tipsy together. Why not? Maybe things would make more sense. Dani quirked a mischievous eyebrow toward Stephen who couldn't hide his look of alarm. The man was an absolute heartbreaker with his gorgeous wavy hair, warm smile and crystal blue eyes, but he seemed to be a bit tightly wound. He could use a hot toddy—or two—himself.

Besides, she thought, this couldn't last forever. It had to be some sort of temporary aberration, maybe a dream, probably not longer than the length of any time travel movie she had ever seen. About two hours?

She attempted to slow her intake to a sip on the second hot toddy, but failed. Two more hours of hot toddies, and she'd be singing karaoke.

****

As expected, within two hours, and several more hot toddies with Lucinda, Dani was well on her way to being drunk, much to Stephen's consternation, or so she suspected. Her vision seemed distorted, and she couldn't focus on his face. She was aware he had come to sit beside her...right beside her. She felt the occasional elbow nudge, and she shut her mouth on cue.

"So, Lucinda, I just love your dress. Love it!" she mumbled. "Is that off the rack or...?"

"No, dear, I know ready-to-wear clothing is quite the thing now, but I prefer to have my clothing tailor made. And who is your tailor?"

Dani opened her mouth to say something nonsensical but Stephen interjected.

"My wife does not at present have a tailor in Seattle but will be using Baker and Sons Tailors, Mrs. Davies. Have you heard of them?"

"Oh, yes," she trilled. Dani thought the toddies might have gone to her head as well. "Yes, fine tailors. I must try them someday. Perhaps we could go together, Danielle?"

"Sure," Dani pumped her head. "Sounds good." Nodding had not been a good idea. Her head started spinning, and she attempted to rise.

Stephen put a restraining hand on her thigh. As lightheaded as she was, she didn't miss the intimate movement, and she looked up at him in inquiry. A muscle worked in his jaw, and he stared hard at her, allowing his eyes to travel to her lap. Dani looked down. Ah, yes! The jeans.

She looked toward Gerald who dozed in the opposite bench, his head resting on the seat back. She gave Lucinda a crooked smile.

"Excuse me," Dani whispered. "I just have to speak to my husband for a second."

"Of course," Lucinda answered with a yawn. "I think I may follow my husband's lead and rest my eyes for a little bit." She pulled the hatpin from her hat, removed the hat, and leaned her head back against the seat.

Dani turned toward Stephen and whispered. "Stephen, I have to go to the bathroom. Do you all have bathrooms on the train?" She noted he had hastily pulled his hand from her lap.

Stephen spoke between his teeth. "I was afraid of this. Yes, there is a ladies toilet midway. But your trousers. They will elicit comment."

"I have to go, Stephen," she moaned. "They won't see me."

Stephen looked toward the couple opposite. Both seemed to be snoozing.

"Very well," he said. "I will follow you closely in a vain attempt to block anyone from seeing you."

Dani chuckled. "Not *into* the bathroom, right? You'll wait for me outside?"

Stephen's cheeks bronzed. Dani was surprised she hadn't noticed the surprisingly rugged stubble of darker blonde hair on his cheeks and chin. The look was unexpected for such a well-groomed man. He must have been traveling for some time.

"That was not my intention, Miss Douglas." He didn't respond in the indignant tone she expected but with a wry smile. She wondered irreverently if he was married—to anyone besides her that was.

With a barely concealed smile, she put his coat aside and attempted to stand, but her legs wobbled. Stephen hastened to assist her, and she fell against him.

"Ooops, sorry," she whispered to his chest. "I'm a sloppy drunk." She looked up at him from under her lashes. "But I'm not sick any more." At that, a paroxysm of giggles hit her, and Stephen half guided her and half pulled her toward the rear of the compartment.

"Here you are, Miss Douglas," he said as he delivered her to a door marked *Ladies Toilet.* He steadied her as he pulled open the door and ushered her in.

Though Dani's thought processes were a bit hazy, she noted that the bathroom was quite large and clean. On her way out, she eyed herself in the mirror. Auburn hair having gone wild and her light-blue long-sleeved shirt a wrinkled mess, she tried to smooth both down. With a view toward looking more presentable, she rummaged in her jeans pocket for an ever-present rubber band and tied her hair up into a ponytail somewhere at the back of her head—she hoped. So difficult to see straight.

"I thought I might have to rescue you," Stephen said dryly when she emerged. "Your hair, while quite beautiful, is very wild, isn't it? I see you have made efforts to bring it under control."

Dani leaned against the wall for balance while the train rocked. She put a hand to her hair.

"Does it look dumb?" she asked. "If I'm really in 1901, most women are wearing their hair up, aren't they? Lucinda is."

Stephen nodded with a sigh. "That they are. I take it you are able to wear your hair down in *your* time."

Dani chuckled. "*My* time. That sounds so funny when you say it. But yes, we can wear it any which way we want. Even purple if we want."

Stephen surveyed her for a moment and looked toward the front of the compartment.

"Shall we brave this again? I can walk in front of you."

"You know, Stephen, *I'm* not the one who is ashamed of my jeans. I'm quite comfortable in them, and I don't mind if Lucinda sees them one little bit."

"Yes, I can see that," Stephen said with a quirked eyebrow. "However, the scandal would be long lasting. I may not have met Mrs. Davies until today, but I am not unaware of who she is. I could not place the name when they first introduced themselves as I was understandably distracted." His eyes dropped to her legs again before returning to her face. "But I remembered too late. She is a socialite, well known in Seattle, and her reach is far. *I* do not wish to immerse myself in such notoriety, nor do I wish you to become the fodder for gossip."

Dani, her head swimming along with the movement of the train, grasped his jacket lapels and shook them.

"Then why, for Pete's sake, did you say I was your wife? How are you going to get out of that? Divorce? Murder?" She giggled foolishly. "You could have said I was your cousin or something."

"Miss Douglas, please try to control your chortling. It would not be acceptable for you to travel alone with me as my *cousin*. No one would believe that charade."

The train shifted again, and Dani, her hands still on his lapels, jerked for balance, bringing his face close to hers. Their eyes locked, and Stephen covered her hands with his own.

"*No* one, Miss Douglas, would believe you are anything to me other than a woman who has captured my imagination...much as you have my coat."

CHAPTER THREE

"Mr. Sadler, we must return to our seats to collect our things," Lucinda whispered a few hours later as the train arrived at the outskirts of Seattle. Dani slept, her head tucked into a corner of the bench. "Please take my card and ask Mrs. Sadler to call on me. I quite enjoyed our time together." She smiled and urged her husband out the carriage door.

Stephen looked down at Dani's sleeping form. Luckily, Mr. and Mrs. Davies had slept most of the way, and he had not had to further dissemble, lie, prevaricate and generally make things much worse than they were already.

Why he had said Dani was his wife was beyond him, and he regretted his foolish action—not that she was not beautiful and desirable, but it seemed impossible that he should return to town after a two-week absence with a wife in tow. Especially a wife who was as unusual as Dani.

Time travel. Was it possible? In looking at her, he thought it might just be. Nothing about her smacked of the present. Her hair was untamed, her clothes were at once manly and yet quite alluring, her skin appeared almost luminescent against her red hair. He had never seen anything like it, and he longed to run his fingers across her cheek, but resisted. Her speech? Not from this time or place, that seemed certain. A cowgirl? It was possible. Although he taught history, his forte was European history, and he was not well educated about the American West. Perhaps he could consult with a few colleagues, discreetly of course, but just to inquire as to possible mannerisms and colloquialisms of a woman from Montana.

He looked at Dani. What was he going to do with her? Especially now that he had *married* her.

The train jolted as it switched tracks, and the whistle blew. From the window, he saw the lights of Seattle. They would arrive at the train depot within minutes.

"Are we here?" Dani bolted upright. She rubbed her eyes, looked around in confusion, cast his coat aside and flew to the window. "Your time or my time? Come onnnn, Seattle!" She squinted out the window. "I can't tell yet. It's so dark."

Stephen shook his head, having forgotten that she seemed a bit unhinged at times. Perhaps she hadn't traveled in time so much as she had lost her faculties. The latter option seemed more plausible. He sighed and rose to join her at the window.

"It does not appear to be any darker than normal. It is very late at night." Stephen consulted his watch. "Eleven o'clock."

Dani turned to him with stricken eyes. "This doesn't look right. There should be a lot more lights, even at this hour."

The train slowed further and then stopped. Stephen steadied her as she swayed with the motion, and he tried to imagine what she might be seeing if this were his first time arriving in Seattle by train. The depot boasted a few lights. The surrounding buildings were darkened on the first-floor shops and the apartments above. A few carriages and carts stood by, including his own, but generally, the entire scene was subdued given the lateness of the hour.

"This isn't right. This isn't King Street Station." Dani's voice held a hint of hysteria, and Stephen longed to comfort her, but he did not know how. While she slept, he had considered what was to be done with her, and he spoke.

"Miss Douglas, please do not distress yourself. I hear the alarm in your voice. If there is truly no one to meet you here in Seattle, if in fact, this is not your *time*, then you shall come to my house. My housekeeper will see to you. You need have no fear from me. In the morning, we shall discuss what is to be done."

She turned to him. "No! This can't be happening! I just want my car."

Before he knew what she was about, Dani had run to the back door, pulled it open and escaped through it. He followed hastily and was in time to see her take the steps from the observation carriage platform two at a time. She jumped to the ground and paused to scan the area.

"Miss Douglas," he called while trying to keep his voice low so as not arouse suspicion. "Come back. Where are you going?" He clambered down after her.

Dani seemed not to hear him. She turned one way then turned another. The nearby carriage horses whinnied. She stared at them.

Stephen finally reached her and caught her arm in his.

"Miss Douglas, my carriage is just over there." He nodded toward one of the carriages. "Please let me help you in."

Her body shook uncontrollably.

"Stephen, I can't *be* here," she repeated herself. "I'm supposed to go back and see my mother in two weeks. She's having surgery. I *have* to go home."

Stephen's heart melted at the forlorn note in her voice, and he longed to fold her into his arms to comfort her, to ease the tremoring he felt in her arm. Out of the corner of his eye, he saw Mr. and Mrs. Davies descending from the train several carriages away. Should they see her dressed as she was, he could not imagine how much more difficult her life would become.

"Miss Douglas! I insist you come with me at once. We can do nothing here in the street at this moment." He urged her in the direction of his carriage, and to his surprise, she came willingly. He dared not leave her to recover their things from the train lest she attempt to run away into the darkness again, and he spoke to his driver.

"Samuel, please gather my luggage. If you could step aboard the observation carriage, please retrieve my hat, my coat and some sort of knitted thing that Miss—Mrs. Sadler dropped on the floor. Also, there was a needle with it. I shall await you here in the carriage with Mrs. Sadler. Then home." He handed Miss Douglas in and climbed into the carriage.

Samuel, a short elderly man, tipped his cap, shut the door without comment or expression and hurried over to the train. Stephen appreciated the man's loyalty. To announce a wife without warning must surely have piqued the man's curiosity, but he was too well trained to show it. His parents had been fortunate in their driver, as was he to have Samuel's continued loyalty.

Stephen eyed Dani with concern. She had slid to the far side of the carriage to peer into the night and watch the activities. She rested her elbow on the side of the coach and chewed on her clenched fist. Her eyes were wide in her pale face, and he could see the occasional tremor pass through her body.

"What can I do for you, Miss Douglas?" he asked quietly.

Dani did not turn to him but merely shook her head. "I don't know. I don't know."

There seemed nothing to say at the moment so he remained silent, not daring to touch her or offer comfort. Her rigid posture suggested she wanted nothing to do with him...or anyone else for that matter.

Samuel returned in good time and handed Stephen the items he requested. While the older man loaded luggage onto the rear of the carriage, Stephen handed Dani her knitting.

She clutched it and pressed it to her face. "Thank you," she said in a muffled voice. "Thank you. You have no idea how much this means to me right now...and it's just a silly bit of crocheting."

"It is a pretty piece."

"It's just a granny square for an afghan blanket, but what it does mean is that I am me. I *did* exist. I *do* exist." She lowered the square. "I know I'm not explaining it very well. But you know what I mean."

Stephen did not have the slightest idea what she meant, but if it made her happy, then he was content.

"You refer to the possibility of time travel?"

She nodded. "I have to find a way back. I just have to."

Stephen knew a moment's despondency at her words. Just then, the carriage moved forward.

Dani looked out the window. "I'm riding in a carriage. At just about midnight. I don't feel like Cinderella. But I sure could use a fairy godmother right about now."

Stephen could think of only one woman who could fit the bill, who could possibly understand Dani—a woman who shared some of the same characteristics and mannerisms.

He resolved to send a note to Ellie Standish Chamberlain in the morning to see if she could help. And to discover why it was that Miss Douglas reminded him so much of Mrs. Chamberlain.

****

Stephen tapped on Dani's door the next morning. The previous night had been eventful with directing his housekeeper, Mrs. Oakley, to organize a room for Dani along with some refreshment. Fortunately, his sister had been abed, and so knew nothing of Dani's arrival. He was unsure of her response.

The first order of business this morning was to see Dani suitably attired. He had already sent the note to Ellie asking for her help. He suspected she would come without question.

"Who is it?" Dani whispered from the other side of the door. He had instructed her to let no one in other than himself or Mrs. Oakley. The less people saw her clothing, the less damage to her reputation he would have to repair.

"May I come in?" Of course, the request was improper, however, it was very necessary at the moment.

She opened the door a crack, and he slipped in.

"My apologies, Miss Douglas. This is entirely unacceptable for me to present myself at your door, but we must put the niceties behind us at the moment."

She nodded. "I know it's different in your time."

"Is it?" he asked distracted. Her hair was even more unruly than the day before though she'd made some attempt to capture it on her head. She looked bright-eyed this morning, perhaps too wide eyed, but her wits seemed to have returned.

"Yes. You mentioned that you were going to ask a woman for help. Did you manage to contact her?"

"I sent a note around. I am sure she will come. She shares some of your mannerisms, and I wonder now about her."

Dani sat down on the blue velvet couch in front of the fireplace. Mrs. Oakley had placed her in one of the guest rooms of his home on Queen Anne Hill.

"Do you think she's a time traveler?" Her cheeks brightened with a rosy hue. She was beautiful, and his heart thudded in his chest. He swallowed hard.

"I do not know, but I begin to wonder. At any rate, I have asked her to bring a few things for you to wear until we can see you properly dressed. You and she appear to be of the same size." His cheeks bronzed. "My sister is taller, but I dared not creep into her room last night to steal a few articles of clothing. There is no telling what I might have grabbed. She does not know of your arrival yet."

"My arrival," Dani snorted, a most unladylike noise. "You know I appreciate everything you're doing for me, Stephen, but this seems a bit excessive for a stranger, don't you think? Why didn't you just leave me at the train station?"

"Because I am a gentleman, Miss Douglas," he said with a rueful smile. "That would have been an ungentlemanly act." And because he simply could not imagine letting her disappear from his life forever, he thought to himself.

"I see," she smiled. She looked around the room with interest. "Ummm...I'm starving. Those two biscuits your housekeeper gave me last night are long gone. Do you all eat breakfast?"

"Mrs. Oakley is bringing you a tray. I think it best you stay in here until Ellie arrives."

"Okay," she said in a reasonable tone. It was that tone which concerned him.

"Okay, yes?"

"Sure."

Reassured, Stephen seated himself opposite her.

"You mentioned *a job* and your mother last night. What sort of job did you refer to?"

"Well, I'm a librarian."

"Ah! A lover of books."

Dani nodded.

"And your mother?"

Dani drew in a sharp breath, and he regretted raising the issue. Tears pooled in her eyes again.

"I can't leave my mom. She's going to have surgery for breast cancer in two weeks. I need to get back there."

"Cancer? Oh, Miss Douglas, my condolences." Steven bronzed at the graphic description of her mother's anatomy, but he said nothing.

Dani jumped up to pace restlessly. "I don't need your condolences, Stephen. I need to get home." Stephen rose to stand by the fireplace and watch her. What could he do? He could not be so selfish as to wish her to stay if her mother were ill. How could he help her return?

A soft knock on the door caught his attention. He crossed to the door and opened it a crack. Mrs. Oakley stood there with Ellie behind her, a satchel in her hand.

"Thank you, Mrs. Oakley. Could you bring some breakfast for Miss Douglas and tea for Mrs. Chamberlain?"

"Certainly, Mr. Sadler." The tall, lean woman nodded and glided away leaving Stephen once again grateful he had such loyal servants.

"Stephen," Ellie said. "Your note was pretty cryptic, but I'm here...with some clothes." She nodded toward the satchel.

Stephen pulled her inside and bent to kiss her cheek. "Ellie, thank goodness, you are here. I could not explain as much as I wished or I would have been writing all night."

He pulled her forward into the room.

"This is Miss Danielle Douglas. Miss Douglas, this is a friend of mine, Mrs. Ellie Chamberlain."

Ellie took one look at Dani. "Oh, crap," she said. "It's happened again, hasn't it?"

Stephen drew in a quick breath at the vulgarity, but relaxed as he saw Dani's eyes widen. Something passed between the two women—a recognition, and he understood he was in the fortunate position of witnessing it.

"Oh, my gosh, you too?" Dani said. She surveyed Ellie from head to foot in an overly familiar fashion. "I would never have believed it."

Ellie shot Stephen a quick look, and sighed. "Stephen doesn't know. This is a surprise for him."

Dani looked at him. "You mean he didn't know you..."

Ellie shook her head. "No, we've been very careful not to let on. I didn't know what would happen."

Stephen noticed that Ellie put a hand to her stomach, but he hesitated to say anything to spoil the revelations that would surely follow.

"Let's sit down," Ellie said. "I'm as shaken as Stephen looks."

Ellie took Dani's hand and guided her to the sofa. Stephen opted to retake his position at the fireplace. He surveyed the women—so different, and yet so much alike.

Ellie raised her eyes to him with a sheepish expression. "So, now you know, Stephen. I have to warn you. No one else knows. No one."

"Not even Robert?"

"Oh, yes, Robert knows. But that's it."

"This certainly explains much about you, Ellie," Stephen smiled gently. "Your forthrightness, your speech pattern, your appearance seemingly from thin air."

"I'm sure it does," she said dryly. Stephen noticed that Dani kept a tight grasp on Ellie's hand.

"We need assistance, Ellie," he said. "I cannot take Dani to a tailor without proper clothing to get there. She cannot even go downstairs for breakfast because I am not certain of my sister's reaction to her—at least to her attire."

"Say no more, Stephen, I know what to do, but you'll have to leave. What are your plans for her?"

"Wait a minute, you two. He can't have plans for me. I have to get back." Dani clutched Ellie's hand. "Ellie, you must know how to get back. Please tell me you do."

Ellie threw a quizzical glance at Stephen who had stiffened.

"Oh, Dani, I don't know what to say to you. I don't know if there's a way back. I didn't know if I was dreaming or awake half the time. I never wanted to try to get back because...well, I fell in love." She looked from Dani to Stephen. "Where did you come from?"

"The train from Chicago," Stephen replied. "She simply appeared in the observation carriage, stating she seemed to be in the wrong place. She seemed very lost and thought she was from the future."

Ellie nodded. "Same thing happened to me. Had you been sleeping before you 'appeared' in the observation carriage?"

Dani nodded. "Yeah, I think I'd fallen asleep."

"That seems to be the key. Don't tell me. Somewhere around Wenatchee?"

"That's it!" Dani said. "I remember the train had just left Wenatchee."

"It seems to play a big part in it. I'm not sure what it means. What year did you come from?"

Dani told her.

"Oh, me too!" Ellie exclaimed.

Mrs. Oakley returned with tea and food for Dani. She left quietly.

Ellie rose and retrieved her satchel.

"Well, you'd better get scootin', Stephen, so we can at least get her dressed while she's still here. Thank goodness I've figured out how to do hair by now so we won't need a maid. I also brought a dinner dress and an extra set of underthings and stockings."

Stephen turned for the door, but hesitated. He looked from Ellie to Dani. "Ellie, did you never *want* to return?"

She threw Dani a quick look. "I thought I did...for a moment...when things were going badly, but I fell in love with Robert the moment I met him. I never really wanted to be without him." Her cheeks reddened, and she patted her stomach once again. "And now? No way. I'm with the man I love more than anyone else in the world—in this time or my old time, and I'm going to have his child."

CHAPTER FOUR

As soon as Stephen left, congratulations having been extended for the coming baby, Dani turned to Ellie who rummaged in her bag. "Have you known him long?"

"Stephen? Probably as long as I've known anyone here. I met him soon after I arrived. He was very kind to me." She pulled some clothing out of the bag. "Better take off those jeans."

"Ellie, I can see that you found the love of your life here in the past, but I have to get back. Not only do I have a job, but my mom is ill. She's having breast surgery in two weeks for cancer."

Ellie paused and turned to her. "Oh, Dani! I'm so sorry. I can see the urgency to return. Can you tell me about it?"

While Ellie helped her into a chemise, stockings and several petticoats, Dani explained about her mother's illness, her quiet life in Seattle, and her job.

"No husband, no boyfriend?" Ellie asked. She twisted Dani this way and that way assessingly.

"No, work keeps me busy, and then when I get home, I'm too tired to worry about not having a love life. Sometimes, on my days off though, I wish I had someone." She looked down at her clothing—a poofy white lace blouse that made her chest look bigger than it already was. A long periwinkle-blue embroidered skirt of silk fell away from her hips into a bell shape at her feet. She ran a finger around the high-necked frothy collar. "What the heck is all this?" she asked, apprehensively eyeing a jacket of matching blue silk and a pair of boots in Ellie's hands. "There's more?"

"Consider yourself lucky *I'm* dressing you. When I first got here, they tried stuffing me into a corset, something that makes your chest and butt stick out in opposite directions. I said no way. Just give me bigger dresses!"

"Oh, I think I saw a woman on the train wearing something like that. She walked like a pigeon."

"That's the one!" Ellie eyed her curiously. "So you met someone else on the train...from this time? And what did they make of your clothes?"

"I think her name was Lucinda Davies, and her husband was Gerald. They never saw my clothing because Stephen threw his jacket over my lap the minute they showed up in the observation car, and he wouldn't let me get up after that." Dani chuckled at the memory.

"Stephen didn't want me to talk either, you know, in case they thought my particular brand of English was odd, so he told her I was ill. Lucinda, it seems, is a believer in hot toddies, so she insisted I have a few, and she joined me." Dani's chuckle evolved into laughter, and she bent over to ease her aching sides as best she could in the tight skirt. Ellie's face crinkled as she joined her.

"The rum went right to my head. You should have seen Stephen's face! He was panicked."

"I can imagine," Ellie said on a laugh. "Poor Stephen! He's a pretty serious guy. This whole thing must be quite a shock to him." Her laughter subsided. "I've met Lucinda Davies by the way. You'll want to be careful around her. She's gets around pretty well, has a lot of friends and enjoys a good gossip. I'm not saying she's a bad person or would harm you in any way, but if she figured you out—figured us out—there could be a lot of questions."

Dani stopped laughing. "Oh, Ellie, I wouldn't want to do anything to hurt you here. I'll behave," she said. "Besides, I don't think I'll be here that long. At least I hope I'm not." She bit her lip and turned away to look toward the breakfast laid out. "I'm starved! Let's eat and brainstorm how I can get back home."

On Dani's second cup of tea, a soft knock sounded at the door. Dani rose to go to the door but tripped on the skirts pooled at her feet. She cried out as she hit the carpet with her elbow. The door burst open and Stephen rushed in.

"What has happened?"

Ellie, having dropped to her knees to help Dani, looked up. "She just fell, Stephen. She'll be all right. The hazards of the early twentieth century, I'm afraid." She turned back to Dani who had risen awkwardly to her knees. "This won't last forever though. Skirts will get shorter."

Ellie attempted to rise and fell back, her own skirts tangled in her legs. "Stephen, please help. Now, we're both stuck."

Dani and Ellie looked at each other and broke out into another round of laughter, as Stephen helped each one rise to their feet. He looked between the two and smiled broadly.

"I can see that you two will become fast friends," he said.

Dani laid a hand on Ellie's arm. "Oh, I am sure we would, but you all know I can't stay." She almost wished the words unsaid as Stephen's smile faded. Even Ellie sighed.

"No, I don't think you can. Your mom." Ellie turned to Stephen. "I think we need to get Robert. Between the four of us, we should be able to figure out how to get Dani home."

"Yes, of course," Stephen said quietly with a nod. "You and he would be the persons most qualified to help Miss Douglas...to return home. We shall send a note to him at once."

"Speaking of which, Stephen, I think Dani should probably come and stay at my house. It would just be easier for her there, don't you think? What about your sister? Has she met Dani yet?"

Dani's heart melted at the wounded look on Stephen's face before he managed to mask it. A muscle twitched in his jaw, and he seemed to take a deep breath. He bowed his head.

"Yes, of course, that is the most sensible plan for her at the moment. You can guide her and comfort her in a way that I cannot." He lifted his chin. "Susan is still abed, I think, and she has not yet met Miss Douglas."

A knock on the door startled them, and they looked from one to the other. Stephen moved to the door, and Dani ran her hands along her skirts to press out any wrinkles.

Mrs. Oakley entered and spoke in hushed tones to Stephen at the door, but Dani heard the conversation.

"A Mrs. Lucinda Davies is downstairs in the parlor, Mr. Sadler. She says she has come to call on *Mrs.* Sadler?" The normally unflappable housekeeper threw a curious glance in Dani's direction.

Stephen braced one hand on his hip and ran the other through his hair. "I was afraid of this," he muttered. "Thank you, Mrs. Oakley. Please tell Mrs. Davies we will be down at once." The housekeeper nodded and slipped out of the room.

"*Mrs.* Sadler?" Ellie squeaked. "Oh, Stephen, you didn't..."

"Yes, he did, Ellie," Dani said with a smirk on her face, her arms akimbo. "Oh, yes, he did." She eyed Stephen with a raised eyebrow. "Now what, Stephen?"

"I can hardly say we have divorced in the last twelve hours," he said with a twitch of his lips. "I believe we must face the music."

"Well, she can't go down right now! I have to do her hair," Ellie said.

She pulled Dani over to the dressing table and settled her there before running to her satchel for a hairbrush. "Five minutes, Stephen. Stall her for five minutes."

"I could say she is unwell?" Stephen offered.

"That sounds like a good plan!" Dani said as Ellie mercilessly yanked through her hair. "Gosh, woman, take it easy, will you?"

"Sorry, Dani," Ellie said. "No, let's get it over with. She'll just come back. Go on, Stephen. We'll be right down. Maybe you can tell Mrs. Davies about the wedding while you wait!" Ellie shook her head with a wry smile.

"It was the best I could do at a moment's notice, ladies!" Stephen protested as he moved toward the door.

"I know, Stephen, I know," Ellie muttered. "I'll send a note over to Robert. I think he's still at home. It's a good thing we live so close by."

Dani gave Stephen a reassuring smile through the mirror as he paused at the doorway to look at her. He nodded, returned the smile and left.

Five minutes later, Ellie and Dani descended the stairs with Dani grabbing at her skirts with one hand and adjusting her hair with the other. Ellie had pulled Dani's hair on top of her head and wrapped the mass of it into a chignon which felt dangerously close to falling down, but a poke or two with an exploratory finger revealed it stayed intact.

"How do you walk in these dresses?"

"You'll learn. No choice," Ellie said as they reached the foyer at the bottom of the stairs. A man in a cutaway coat stood by a large wooden door and opened it.

"Mrs. Sadler. Mrs. Chamberlain, this way please."

Dani froze at the name. How was Stephen going to get out of this? She wasn't too concerned about herself because she believed that she would leave all this behind, but she worried about Stephen when she was gone. He had really gone out on a limb to protect her.

Ellie grabbed her arm and guided her into the drawing room. At first glance, Dani was dazzled by the myriad of color in the room. Soft green embellished wallpaper adorned all the walls. Sofas and chairs in various shades of green and rose velvet surrounded a fireplace of white marble near which Stephen stood. A delicate gold filigree chandelier crowned the room. Velvet drapes of moss green framed a large picture window which looked out over the city below.

"Ellie!" Lucinda cried as she rose to kiss Ellie on the cheek. "Stephen told me you were here. How nice to see you!" She turned to Dani. "You look as if you have recovered nicely from the journey and your illness, Danielle. As I said, hot toddies! The cure for all."

She seated herself and patted the sofa beside her. Dani sat next to her and Ellie sat beside Dani. Mrs. Oakley accompanied a young maid who brought a tea service.

"I do hope you do not mind that I called so early, Danielle. I did not have a chance to say goodbye to you last night."

"Oh, no, that's fine," Dani said with a quick glance toward Stephen. She had no idea if the hour was fine or not but Lucinda was already there, so the point was moot.

"I also wanted to offer my felicitations on your marriage again!" Lucinda said with a broad smile. "My daughter, Evelyn, who is acquainted with your sister, advised me only this morning at breakfast that she thought you were unmarried. She seemed taken aback when I mentioned there was a Mrs. Sadler. In fact, she was quite distressed." Lucinda wagged a finger at Stephen. "I am not at all sure she did not have her eye on you herself."

To say that everyone looked at everyone did not describe the varying expressions which traveled around the room. Dani looked finally toward Stephen whose high cheekbones bronzed at Lucinda's last words. The thought that Stephen was probably in high demand as a handsome, single man disturbed her.

She surprised herself by speaking up. "Yes, it *was* sudden. We met in Chicago, and it was love at first sight." She flushed and bit her lip, aghast at her comments. She had no idea what scenario Stephen would have chosen for his "marriage." She threw him a quick look from under her lashes. He regarded her with a soft smile. Good! She hadn't blown it.

"Yes, that is correct, Mrs. Davies. We met in Chicago. A whirlwind romance."

"How romantic!" Lucinda beamed. "I shall have to confirm to Evelyn that you are no longer eligible. Pity me the task. I fear there will be tears."

"Who is no longer eligible?" A slender blonde girl of about eighteen entered the room in a swish of pink silk and lace. She nodded in the general direction of the room and crossed to her brother's side, linking her arm in his. She raised her face for a kiss.

"Welcome back, Stephen," she said. "Mrs. Chamberlain, how are you?"

"I'm good, Susan, and how are you?"

"I am as well as could be, thank you, Mrs. Chamberlain." Dani had no idea what to make of that cryptic statement, but Ellie didn't seem to worry too much about it.

"Susan, let me present Mrs. Lucinda Davies. I believe you are acquainted with her daughter, Evelyn?" Stephen made the introductions.

Susan nodded her head in the older woman's direction, but her eyes locked on Dani. "And?"

Dani's eyes flew to Stephen. The situation had deteriorated rapidly. How was he going to lie to his sister—especially one who seemed overtly protective? Dani didn't miss the firm grip Susan had on her brother. She wished she could disappear back to her time at that very moment.

"Susan, may I present my wife, Danielle."

Susan's eyes widened.

"Oh, goodness. This *is* new then if your sister did not yet know!" Lucinda crowed.

Dani cringed when Susan turned sky-blue eyes on her. She stared hard at Dani for a moment and seemed to take a deep breath.

"So, someone has finally caught you, dear brother," she murmured.

"Now, just a min—!" Dani couldn't hold back, but Ellie grabbed her arm and shook her head. Lucinda's attention was on the brother and sister.

"Yes, she has, sister," he replied with a firm chin. "Or rather, I should say, I had the privilege of catching her." The smile on his face did not match his eyes, and his expression seemed a bit forbidding. Dani wondered if anyone else saw it.

Susan seemed to get his message because she turned to Dani. "Welcome to the family, Danielle. Please accept my congratulations."

Ellie pulled her hand back, and Dani let go of the breath she had been holding. How awkward this must have been for Stephen to force his sister to accept her.

"Thank you, Susan. It is so nice to meet you," Dani said inadequately. She rose as Susan approached to kiss her cheek. She met Stephen's eyes over Susan's shoulder but his expression revealed nothing save for the fixed smile which did not match his eyes. She felt distanced from him for the first time since she'd met him, and she didn't like the feeling.

As if the room wasn't already brimming with people, a tall, dark-haired man was shown in by the butler.

Ellie jumped up. "Robert! Look who is here. Mrs. Davies!"

Robert paused at her words, took in the room at a glance, and turned to Lucinda.

"Mrs. Davies, how nice to see you again." He turned to greet everyone in the room, his eyes pausing on Dani. She thought she saw a glimmer of interest in them but couldn't decipher the expression. She wondered if he could tell she was from the twenty-first century just by looking at her, or had Ellie said something in the note she sent him before they came downstairs.

"Robert, this is my wife, Mrs. Danielle Douglas Sadler."

Robert bowed over her hand, and Dani thought she saw what Ellie had fallen in love with.

"Please accept my congratulations, Stephen. Mrs. Sadler. It seems only a few months ago that you said those words to Ellie and I." He smiled, his clean-shaven face revealing straight white teeth.

"Yes, I remember," Stephen acknowledged.

"All very exciting, don't you think, Robert?" Lucinda chimed in. "All these Seattle men falling in love with women from Chicago! Just like you and Ellie!"

Robert smiled faintly. "Ah, yes. Chicago," he murmured.

He moved to the mantle to lean on it as Stephen did. Dani studied the men, one so dark, the other so fair. They dressed alike in well-tailored dark suits, white shirts with stiff collars and ties under vests of different shades. Such stylish men, she thought. Why didn't men in her day dress that way anymore?

Susan had taken a seat across from the sofa and poured tea for herself and others. Dani suspected the job of pouring tea was hers now but she had no idea what to do, and Susan seemed quite at home hostessing. No need to usurp the girl's position in the house. Stephen would somehow find a way to explain Dani's disappearance when she left—she hoped for his sake.

General conversation continued for another half hour until Lucinda rose stating she had to leave.

"Remember, Danielle, we spoke of making an outing to your tailor." She bent to kiss Dani's cheek. "Would tomorrow be convenient?"

"Oh, dear," Ellie interjected. "I had already made arrangements to take Mrs. Sadler to my tailor tomorrow, Mrs. Davies. Would you care to accompany us? And you, Susan?"

Dani turned to Stephen for his unspoken opinion. He gave an imperceptible nod.

"Why, yes, Ellie," Lucinda said. "That sounds lovely!" They settled on a time in the morning.

"Wonderful! I shall see you then." Lucinda sailed out of the room in her indomitable way, leaving a silent void behind her. Dani had the impression that questions were on the tip of everyone's tongue but no one dare say anything because of Susan who continued to sit and sip her tea thoughtfully.

Robert and Ellie exchanged glances. Dani threw Stephen an inquiring look. He shrugged his shoulders lightly. Everyone turned to look at Susan, the white elephant in the room, the only one who didn't know something was going on.

"I know something is not quite as it seems here," Susan suddenly said. "I am not a child. I would be most appreciative if you would all explain it." She set down her teacup and faced them directly. "I think even Mr. and Mrs. Chamberlain must know more than I do."

Dani, after her initial shock, burst out laughing. Ellie joined her.

"Geez, Stephen, she doesn't miss much!" Dani sputtered. "I think you'd better tell her about *me*." She sobered with the emphasis on *me*. Susan didn't need to know about Ellie.

Stephen sighed and moved to take a seat near Susan, and Robert joined the women on the sofa.

"I should have known I could not fool you," Stephen said.

"Yes, you should have," Susan said with pursed lips. "I have been watching out for you for years, and I am sure you would have told me ahead of time if you were planning to marry."

"Perhaps not, my dear," Stephen said with a look in Dani's direction. The expression in his eyes—an unexpectedly intimate look—brought a blush to her face.

"At any rate, Miss Douglas and I are *not* married. I met Miss Douglas on the train from Chicago, and she needed my assistance, so I brought her here. And Ellie came to help this morning."

"That's probably not going to be enough, Stephen," Dani said watching Susan's sharp eyes.

"I know," he murmured, "but I have not actually put the matter to words before. I am at a loss."

"What difficulties had befallen Miss Douglas?" Susan asked.

"She...em...had lost her way, her luggage, funds."

Susan turned to Dani. "Miss Douglas, forgive me for being so inquisitive, but it seems my brother holds some reservations regarding your privacy. Would you be so good as to tell me why he has introduced you as his wife?"

"Oh, well, that..." Dani grinned. "We met Lucinda—Mrs. Davies—on the train, and Stephen thought he ought to introduce me as some sort of relative."

"And why would he need to do that?"

"We were in the observation carriage alone together, and I sought to protect Miss Douglas's reputation."

"How chivalrous of you," Susan said in a dry tone. "I am hopeful you will explain how Miss Douglas came to be alone with you in the observation carriage?" She turned to Dani. "Were you traveling alone, Miss Douglas?"

"Yes. Yes, I was," she said almost defiantly. The child was incredibly persistent and astute. She really thought she ought to put a stop to the inquisition, but she didn't have the heart to be cruel to the young girl.

"Stephen," Dani pleaded. "Just tell her."

Robert and Ellie, having remained silent throughout the conversation, exchanged glances of amusement.

"Yes, well, Miss Douglas simply appeared in the observation carriage. Out of thin air."

Susan's cheeks flushed and her eyes, so like her brother's, narrowed. "Out of thin air?"

"Yes, that is exactly right. Out of thin air." He looked to Dani. "I cannot do this."

"Do you want to, Stephen?" Dani asked. "We don't have to."

"Yes, I think it is necessary, but I worry about the effect on her."

"Stephen! Miss Douglas! I am right here," Susan almost shrieked.

Dani sighed and took a deep breath. "I've traveled to your time from the twenty-first century, about one-hundred ten years into the future." She held up a quick hand at Susan's protest. "Don't worry, I'm not staying, but there it is. We don't know how it happened, but I'm going to try to return to my own time. Your brother is just trying to help me out."

Susan opened and shut her mouth—several times—as she stared at Dani. She was speechless, a state which Dani suspected Susan didn't often fall into.

Dani turned to Stephen. He had that set look on his face whenever she mentioned returning. She supposed he thought it wasn't possible and didn't want her to be crushed, but Dani had to believe she could do it.

"My word!" Susan said.

The next hour was spent in explaining what they knew...or suspected. Dani managed to keep Ellie's own time travel out of the discussion, and she acknowledged Ellie's grateful look.

Ellie and Robert rose to return home. Dani, Stephen and Susan rose to bid them farewell.

"I don't think you'll be coming to stay with me now, Dani," Ellie said. "Not if you're *married* to Stephen."

"Of course not. She shall stay here. We can take care of her," Susan said, her overprotective maternal drive having apparently expanded to encompass not only her brother but also her new *honorary* sister-in-law.

Ellie chuckled. "Yes, I believe you will. I'll see all tomorrow. Call me... Well, send me a message if you need anything, Dani. I've got a phone but I can't figure out how to work it yet!"

She gave Dani a hug and left with her husband.

"I wonder if we should have the wedding reception here or in a hall downtown," Susan mused.

Dani and Stephen swung toward her.

"What?"

CHAPTER FIVE

"Well, we cannot have you just recently married and simply ignore the event, Stephen," Susan said. "People will talk."

"Oh, Susan, I don't think—" Dani began.

Susan held up an imperious hand. "Do not worry. I will plan the entire event. I think we should have it here, Stephen. We never host any gala events here. I shall procure the advice of Mrs. Chamberlain on organization of the event. Though like you, brother, I believe she is not overly fond of festivities. Perhaps Mrs. Davies might be of assistance." Susan's pale cheeks glowed as she marched around the room thinking aloud. Stephen did not have the heart to tell her no. She had been ill for the past few months with an infection of the lungs, and this was the first time in a very long while he had seen her enthusiastic about anything.

"I think we must allow Susan to have her moment, Miss Douglas. I do not think she will be thwarted on this." Stephen tilted his head and smiled at Dani.

"*Mrs. Sadler*, Stephen," Susan interjected. "It is *Mrs. Sadler*! It will not do for you to call her Miss Douglas in public."

Dani blinked then laughed. "She's really into this, isn't she?" she said as Susan hastened over to the desk and pulled out pen and paper.

Stephen laughed as he watched his sister. "If by 'into it,' you mean zealous, then yes, Susan has been known to pursue various causes and interests with unbridled passion. She is like our mother in that way."

"Where are your parents, Stephen?"

"They both passed away from a flu that devastated the city some years ago. Susan herself has been ill with an infection of the lung, and I have been worried about her."

"Oh, I didn't know." Dani looked at her. "She seems to be on the mend."

"Yes, I hope so," he said. He looked at Dani for a moment as if he wanted to ask her something but stopped.

"No, Stephen, we still have the flu, but less people die from it. Was that your question?"

Stephen smiled and nodded. "You seem to know me well, Miss Douglas, for such a short acquaintanceship. Please do not tell me that mind reading is a normal event in your time."

Dani grinned. "No, I don't think so. Some people can do it, I think, but not me."

"I am hesitant to ask questions regarding the future. I think there might be things I do not wish to know."

Dani tilted her head and nodded. "I can understand that. Let me know if you have any questions. Otherwise, I'll try not to share too much information with you."

"The revelations over the past twenty-four hours have been astonishing. I had no idea Ellie Chamberlain had come from the future. And to think that Robert knew." Stephen shook his head.

Dani eyed him curiously. "Did you have a crush on her? Do you?"

"A crush?" Stephen asked. His cheeks bronzed, and he rubbed his chin. "You do ask the most intimate questions, do you not, Miss Douglas?"

"Mrs. Sadler," she said with a chuckle, her cheeks a rosy red. "You don't think your wife should know if you're infatuated with another woman?" She nervously laced and unlaced her fingers, and Stephen thought he saw something in her eyes that was not entirely laughter. His heart sped up for a moment.

"I liked Ellie very much when I first met her, but she was already very much in love with Robert even by then—I suspect from the moment they met, though I was not there."

"Oh!" Dani said. She turned to look toward Susan who continued her list writing from the looks of the growing pile of scribbled paper on the desk.

"I hate to hurt her, but I have to find a way to get home, Stephen. I don't think I can wait for a party. My mother is due to have surgery for two weeks, thirteen days now, I guess, but I need to be there before she goes in. I promised I would be back. I can't wait until the last minute. I have to go as soon as possible."

She kept her eyes on Susan while she spoke but turned back to him on the last sentence. Stephen had clenched and unclenched his jaw while she spoke, leaving an ache in its wake. Of course he had to help her. At once! Not in a week, not even in several days. At once.

"What would you like me to do?"

"I think I need to take the train back to Wenatchee. I'm not sure if I need to fall asleep, but I'm willing to try."

Her light green eyes entreated him, and his heart swelled. She needed him. It seemed clear. She asked for his help.

"Of course we will leave tomorrow. I will tell Susan we will be away for a few days, and that she must continue making arrangements for the reception."

"No!" Dani spoke sharply. "No, you don't need to go. I was asking you to pay for my ticket."

Stephen stiffened. "No!" he said harshly, surprising himself with his vehemence. "You will *not* travel alone. It is not safe. I brought you here, and it pleases me to return you to where you came from." Dani's eyes widened with a stricken expression. Aghast at his severe tone, Stephen pressed his lips together. He had never spoken to a woman before in such a manner. And yet he did not yield.

"Tomorrow," he muttered. "I will make the arrangements today." He strode from the room, crossed the foyer and entered his library, slamming the door behind him. He poured a measure of brandy and threw himself into a chair only to rise precipitously again to pace the floor.

If she wanted to return then he would facilitate it, if that were within his power. Of course her mother was ill. Of course Dani needed to return to her own time. That she had no intention of returning to 1901 seemed clear, even were it within her power. Were he in the same situation, he was not sure he would return either.

He tossed back his drink, poured another and resumed pacing once again.

There was nothing for her in his time. She left no doubt she found the era backward, different, distasteful, he fumed. He thought back to her words. Well, perhaps she had not exactly used terms such as backward or distasteful, but the implication was the same.

Money, indeed! He cared not for the money. He had ample funds. Traveling alone? Had she not learned anything? She could not simply board a train on her own and be treated with any measure of civility. She would most certainly be seated in the third class carriage, perhaps even the immigrant carriage. Silly woman! Had she learned nothing in her time here? He looked at his pocket watch and calculated she had been in his time a grand total of eighteen hours. Eighteen hours. He stopped pacing and slumped in his chair.

No, of course she had not learned anything. She had hardly been there very long, not even a full day. His anger spent for the moment, Stephen crossed the room to his desk and penned a note. He rang for a footman and handed him the note and some money. He returned to his chair, leaned his head back and brooded, an unnatural state for him, and one he was not enjoying.

A knock on the door thirty minutes later brought the butler to announce that Mr. Robert Chamberlain asked to see him. Stephen, surprised, jumped up.

"Yes, of course, show him in," he said as he straightened his vest and adjusted his tie.

Robert entered and offered his hand.

"Forgive the intrusion, but Ellie thought it best if I were to return to speak to you, man-to-man I think she said." He smiled broadly.

Stephen, never quite comfortable in his presence, smiled briefly. He shook Robert's hand and offered him a drink which Robert accepted. They sat and faced each other. Stephen waited.

"The past is behind us now, Stephen," Robert said. "Let us be at peace. I apologize for treating you poorly in the matter of Ellie. But you see, I was very much in love and quite jealous."

Stephen raised his eyebrows at Robert's frank words. He thought he heard Ellie's influence. Like Dani, she often spoke her mind without regard for convention or restraint. Robert seemed different somehow since he met Ellie—more candid, less disciplined, more expressive.

"Yes, your feelings for Ellie were obvious," Stephen said with a faint smile. "I accept your apology."

"Good," Robert said. He hesitated, and Stephen wondered about his real purpose for being there.

"Ellie felt you might have some...em...questions regarding Miss Douglas's origins, perhaps even regarding Ellie herself since your discovery this morning. She thought I might be able to provide some insight from a 'turn-of-the-century' man's perspective—her phraseology, not mine." Robert smiled and cleared his throat. "Normally, I would not presume to interfere in an acquaintance's personal affairs, but Ellie and I have kept this secret for months, and frankly we welcome a trusted ally. We wish to be of service to you and Miss Douglas in any way possible." He tossed back his drink and declined another.

Stephen spoke slowly. "Although I am pleased to be considered an ally in this matter, I cannot say that I am happy to be part of this...surreal fantasy." He could not keep the bitterness from his voice.

Robert raised his eyebrows. "Forgive me. Ellie imagined there was something between you and Miss Douglas, some sort of warmth." He cleared his throat again.

"Ellie thought wrong. I am simply assisting Miss Douglas to return to her time, nothing more. On that score, I may well seek your advice. However, I must make it clear that I did not ask for her presence in my life, I did not seek it, and I will consider myself well rid of her when the time comes and she returns to her home."

Stephen rose abruptly from his seat and began to pace, aware that Robert watched him with surprise but hardly caring.

"I do not know how you managed when you discovered that your wife was from the future. I simply cannot imagine. One moment, your life is steady, uneventful, perhaps a bit empty, but set on a true course of logic and sanity. Then, one day, a person appears—a woman—and your world is turned upside down with no way to know which way is up or which way is down."

"Do you refer to me or yourself, Stephen?" Robert asked quietly.

Stephen barely heard him. "Do you know how many matrons thrust their eligible young daughters at me? How many simpering looks I must endure every time I attend a function?" He ignored Robert's knowing nod of understanding. "I do not flatter myself that it is for my winsome personality or my rugged manly looks. It is for money. Always for money."

Robert nodded.

"And so I have not yet married. I have not yet found the woman whose soul speaks to me, whose words warm my heart, whose smile brightens my day." Stephen paused, and stared out the window. "And then Miss Douglas appears, unbidden, unwanted, and I cannot think straight, I cannot control my temper and I cannot make her stay." He turned back toward Robert and slumped into his chair, spent.

When Stephen spoke again, his voice was quiet. "I apologize, Robert. How silly of me to go on like some besotted romantic fool. I hardly know the woman."

"It may not surprise you to know that I understand your struggles, Stephen. You will remember I too was sought after as an eligible bachelor for much the same reasons as you. I too longed for a woman who touched my heart, but I was not expecting that woman to be from the future. I loved Ellie from the first moment I saw her, and I also feared I could not keep her, that she would return to her own time—whether she wanted to or not."

"In my case, I was fortunate that Ellie chose to stay with me, that Ellie was *able* to stay with me. In this we differ though, and I cannot imagine how you must feel right now, Stephen. Ellie has told me that Miss Douglas's mother is ill, and that she must return to her own time to be with her."

Stephen nodded heavily. "Yes, she wishes to leave at once. My plan at present is to take the train east tomorrow to see if she can somehow re-create the events and reverse the process to return home."

"Tomorrow! That soon?"

"Yes, as soon as possible. That is her wish."

"Good gravy, man. I am sorry," Robert said.

"Do you think it is possible to return her to the twenty-first century?" Stephen asked.

Robert shook his head. "I do not know. Ellie and I have not dared taken the train since, for fear of losing her to the future." He looked toward the door. "Where is Miss Douglas now?"

Stephen gave a short laugh. "Probably making her way to the train depot on foot. I am afraid I was short with her about her adamant desire to leave at the earliest opportunity."

"Do not blame yourself, Stephen. I have never known you to be mean spirited, so I assume this is a temporary aberration. Women can do that to you." Robert smiled.

"I hope it *is* temporary," Stephen said with a crooked grin. "I am not used to such strong emotions, and I find them exhausting—exhilarating but exhausting."

Robert checked his pocket watch and rose. "That sounds like love, Stephen. Go patch things up with Miss Douglas, take her to dinner. Perhaps if her mother's health improves, she will consent to return—if she can."

Stephen rose. "But you said Ellie had never tried to return. Is it not then likely that if Miss Douglas returns, she will not be able to come back again?"

"I think the phenomenon is extremely unpredictable, Stephen, and we cannot know what will happen. I am sorry."

****

At about that moment, Dani marched down the road toward where she thought the train depot might be. She stumbled over her skirts occasionally, and Ellie's loaner boots hurt like the dickens, but she was heading to the train depot. *Take that, Stephen Sadler!*

She'd left a note for him and one for Susan to prevent them from worrying. She suspected Susan would fret, and she didn't want to hurt the young girl who was so enthusiastic about planning a wedding reception. So, she told her she had gone to visit Ellie. Susan wouldn't know Dani had no idea where Ellie lived but knew it was nearby. Stephen? She'd told him the truth—that she was mad, walking off steam, and heading to the train depot to check on departure times.

By her fuzzy calculations from the night before, given her confusion and disorientation, she deduced that if she were on Queen Anne Hill, and the train depot somewhere along the waterfront on modern day Alaskan Way, then she probably only had a three-mile walk. Not too far at all. And just right for an angry woman.

What she hadn't calculated on when she left Stephen's elegant mansion on a hill was that there were no sidewalks of note, the roads were dirt or more aptly mud given a probable early morning shower, and that Queen Anne Hill was much steeper in 1901 than it was in present day.

She had assumed that if she headed straight down Queen Anne Avenue, she would run right up to Elliot Bay and find the train depot somewhere along the waterfront further south. It had sounded easy when she'd stormed out of the house in a huff a half hour prior.

Her visions of sauntering down to the pier while waving at fellow strolling pedestrians went by the wayside as she negotiated mud puddles and saw no other people on her way down the steep hill. Seattle in 1901 was somewhat civilized, she could tell by the brick buildings of the city center barely visible through a haze of pollution and chimney smoke, but the city lacked the finesse and polish that would come later in the twentieth century.

She neared the bottom of the hill just as rain began to fall. She had no umbrella, and no hat. She turned to look back at the hill, unwilling to climb back up until she'd found the train depot.

Dani grabbed her skirts and hurried down the muddy road paralleling the waterfront. A sign marked it as Railroad Avenue. She didn't remember seeing the road in modern day Seattle. She'd lowered her head to keep rain from her eyes, with the odd thought that she had finally run into other people in the form of carriages sloshing down the wet road, their large wheels throwing up mud.

A particularly large chunk of mud hit her in the face, and she cried out and stopped to wipe her face with her sleeve. She surveyed the clothing Ellie had lent her with guilt, thinking the shoes, stockings and skirts were ruined by the mud.

Dani looked around to orient herself but could see no familiar landmarks. The rain came down faster, and she clutched her skirts again and ran down the road.

She spied a two-story building on the right and beyond it, a steam locomotive. The train depot! She turned onto the property, past wagons and carts to hurry toward the entrance to the building nearest the railroad tracks. A large shed roof covered an outdoor waiting area which was empty. She attempted to run under the overhead but found herself mired in the mud, thicker and dense in the ruts where carriages probably awaited passengers and supplies on a regular basis.

"Crap!" she yelled as she bent over to free her feet.

"Your language, woman!" Stephen shouted behind her through the driving rain. "Here, let me!"

"Oh, Stephen! I'm so glad you're here. I'm so stuck! Where did you come from?" Dani cried out.

"From the house, silly! Where else?"

Dani looked at Stephen, his beautiful well-tailored clothing muddied as he kneeled to free her feet. She couldn't bear to leave him. How could she leave him? But how could she stay?

"You know, Stephen, I think I love you." Dani couldn't hold the words back. Even to her ears, they seemed ludicrous, hasty, impossible. Maybe she was just grateful he had rescued her from a city much rougher than she remembered. Maybe she just loved him with all her heart.

"What?" Stephen stilled and looked up at her. Her feet were still stuck, and the thick clay-like mud encased his hands.

"I said I think I love you, but will you please not stop until my feet are free?" Dani reached a hand to his back for support as she threatened to topple over.

Stephen's face shone, even in the pelting rain, and he returned to work on her feet. "I think I love you too, Dani!" he muttered, struggling to scrape the mud from around her ankles.

Dani heard his words and thought she could float though her feet were trapped. Stephen freed her feet, picked her up in his arms and carried her over to the wooden platform beneath the shed roof of the waiting area.

He set her down on her feet, and ignoring their public surroundings, kept her in his arms and kissed her. Dani wrapped her arms around his neck and pulled him close.

"Sir, is there anything I can do?" Stephen's driver ran under the overhang. Stephen broke away and let Dani go. She plopped down onto a bench, her skirts heavy with mud and rain, and her emotions in turmoil. She stared at the train on the tracks and absently ran her fingers across her lips while Stephen spoke to his driver.

"Well, Miss Douglas," Stephen said, taking a seat beside her, his driver having entered the train depot. "We are a fine pair."

And indeed, he looked worse than a chimney sweep, his hands and trousers muddied, wet hair plastered to his face, the rest of his clothing soaked.

"Where is your hat, Miss Douglas?" he asked. He reached a tender hand to brush her soaking wet hair from her face. Dani's bun had slipped down to her neck.

"I didn't wear a hat," she said in a bemused tone. The tender touch of his hand threatened to bring her to tears. Well, closer than she was already.

"All ladies wear hats, my dear," he said softly. "It keeps the sun from their faces and the rain from their eyes."

Dani turned to him with a watery grin, partly from rain, partly from unshed tears. "Very funny." She wanted nothing more than to bury herself in his arms.

"My driver has gone to find a towel to dry your face. You were probably not aware, my dear, but I had sent the driver here earlier to purchase our tickets for tomorrow. The train leaves at seven. You had only to ask."

"I know," Dani said with a grimace. "I was mad. I wanted to take a walk, and this seemed like a good place to walk to."

Stephen shook his head, his fingers toying with a tendril at the nape of her neck.

"I think not. It is too dangerous for a lady to walk about alone. My heart almost stopped when I read your note."

"What are we going to do, Stephen?" Tears finally spilled over and down her face, lost in the moisture from the rain.

"I do not know, my love."

"Here, Sir!" Samuel, the driver, arrived with two clean linen towels. They wiped their faces and hands.

Stephen rose and helped Dani up. She thought he might pull her into his arms again, but he looked beyond her to several people who had come out of the station to stand on the platform.

He picked her up in his arms again and carried her over to where the carriage waited. Stowing her safely aboard, he climbed in after her and wrapped his arms around her as the carriage rocked and rolled while the driver maneuvered the wheels through the mud of the train depot yard and out onto the road.

"Where was that train going?" Dani asked, looking out the window back toward the depot.

"To Portland, I think, but not back toward Montana...or Chicago. That train leaves tomorrow. So, we have tonight together."

Dani, still wrapped in his embrace, nuzzled his neck. "Come with me, Stephen," she whispered, the idea just forming. "Come back with me."

CHAPTER SIX

Stephen stiffened for a moment, and pulled away to look at Dani, but he didn't let her go.

"You mean to your time? Forever?"

Dani, knowing she probably just asked the impossible, nodded.

"I cannot," Stephen shook his head. He turned to stare out the window. The rain seemed to be easing. "I cannot leave Susan."

Dani pulled away and buried her face in her hands.

"Oh, Stephen, I'm so sorry! I forgot about Susan. How stupid of me to suggest that! I'm so sorry."

Stephen pulled her hands from her face and bent to kiss her lips again.

"Do not be sorry, Dani. Were it not for Susan, I might just consider it. Perhaps I might have asked Robert and Ellie to see to my estate such that it was still intact in your time. But I cannot leave Susan behind, and I cannot force her to come with me."

"I know, of course you can't." Dani shook her head. "How could I have fallen in love in one day? What is it about you?" She smiled tenderly.

"I have asked myself the same question over and over. How can I love you when I do not even know you?"

Dani pressed herself back into his arms and laid her face against his chest.

"You know me, Stephen. You may not know what music I listen to or what books I like to read or whether I sleep on my side or my back, but you know me."

"Yes, you are right. I feel I do know you, enough to know that I love you, and my love for you will only grow."

"It might not grow if I'm gone, Stephen." Dani hated to point out the obvious.

Stephen turned his head away again.

"Do not remind me. We still have tonight." He sighed and seemed to pull his shoulders back. He turned to her with a forced grin. "You have yet to tell me how you have come to fall in love with me in only a day. Am I so charming?"

Dani beamed. "Yes, you are, Mr. Sadler. You are just about adorable."

Stephen's cheeks bronzed and he coughed.

"Adorable? I am not a puppy, Madam."

"Yes, you are. You're adorable like a puppy, and charming, and such a gentleman, and loving, and tender, and caring, and very handsome, and quite, quite unique. I've never met anyone like you," Dani finished. She took his face in her hands and kissed him. Dani suspected he was shocked by her boldness, but she couldn't hold back.

"And you are a brazen woman, Miss Douglas," Stephen said on a laugh as she let him up for air. "But I quite enjoy it."

On their arrival at the mansion, Susan hurried outside to greet them as they climbed out of the carriage. Dani sympathized with the driver who would no doubt have to clean the carriage inside and out.

"What has happened to you? Stephen, you rushed out of the house so fast, I did not hear where you were going, but I assumed it had to do with Miss Douglas." She stared at them aghast. "I thought you went to visit Mrs. Chamberlain, Miss Douglas. Surely, her garden is not so poorly cared for that a walk rendered you thus."

Dani laughed at Susan's quip.

"No, I...uh...I got caught in the rain and fell in a mud puddle on my way to her house, I'm afraid. Your brother was kind enough to fish me out, but as you can see..." She gestured to Stephen's mud-caked clothing.

"I also took a tumble," he finished with a broad smile. "We are a sight, the pair of us. Let us wash and change clothing then I shall take you all to dinner at the Hotel Seattle."

"Me?" Susan asked with an incredulous look on her pale face. "But you have not let me leave the house in a month."

"I think you are well enough for some festivities, my dear." Despite Susan's protests, Stephen wrapped a muddied arm around her shoulders and Dani's shoulders and shepherded them inside.

Twenty minutes later, Dani stepped into the steaming water of the white porcelain claw foot bathtub in the bathroom adjacent to her room. A young Irish maid named Bridget had brought a wrapper of Susan's and collected Dani's muddy clothing to launder. She fervently hoped the clothing survived without stain to be returned to Ellie.

Dani scrubbed her hair with a lavender-scented soap, and marveled that they actually had hot and cold running water in 1901. A shower had been too much to ask for, she knew, and she managed to wash her hair and scrub the mud off her body. She luxuriated in the deep tub with the thought that maybe life at the turn of the century wouldn't be as hard as she had originally thought. The fact that the man she loved lived in this century and not hers certainly made it much more attractive.

She stepped out of the tub, dried herself with a large towel and slipped into Susan's pink embroidered silk wrapper—far more luxurious than her own fuzzy robe at home. Bridget had laid out the extra evening dress Ellie brought and shoes borrowed from Susan who fortunately shared the same shoe size. Bridget offered to return to help her dress but Dani self-consciously declined.

A check of the clock on the mantle revealed she had about thirty minutes before they were due to leave. Dani eyed the orange silk and cream lace dress Ellie had provided, no doubt not realizing that Dani was a redhead. She hoped she could figure out how to get it on as she'd been distracted when Ellie helped her dress earlier and hadn't paid attention. Maybe it had been a bad idea to send Bridget away.

Twenty-eight minutes later, huffing and puffing from her exertions with her hair, Dani lowered her hands and twisted this way and that in the mirror. The dress was on, though she wasn't sure everything was as buttoned and zipped as it needed to be. Her stockings were up, garters in place, and Susan's shoes were on her feet albeit pinching her toes. Her hair was wrapped, twisted and stuck on top of her head with the stickpin Ellie had provided earlier.

A soft knock on her door caught her attention, and she opened the door hesitantly.

Susan stood outside looking charming and ethereal in a pale blue dinner dress of a similar style to Dani's. She held a sprig of white silk roses in her hand.

"May I come in?"

Dani stood back. "Yes, please! Maybe you can tell me if I've got my clothes on right." She grinned. "I should have taken Bridget's offer to help."

Susan smiled. "I cannot imagine how you dressed yourself without assistance. Let me see."

Dani twisted and turned, watching Susan's expression over her shoulder. Apparently, she passed muster because Susan's eyebrow didn't quirk as Dani had seen it done before.

"You have done well. Here is one button that is undone." Susan buttoned the top button at the back of her dress. "Did you do your hair?"

Dani raised a self-conscious hand. "Yes? No?"

"It will do," Susan said, her own smooth hair perfectly coiffed. "You must have difficulty restraining all that hair," she noted with a smile.

"I could have used some creme rinse, that's for sure," Dani said.

"Creme rinse?"

"You know, a hair conditioner? To keep my hair from flying around like it does?"

"Oh, yes, I use an olive oil on occasion," Susan said. "I shall ask Bridget to bring you some for your use the next time you wash your hair." She displayed the sprig of roses in her hand. "Would you like to wear this in your hair? I have one similar in mine."

And indeed, she did have a tiny sprig of baby blue silk roses tucked into her chignon.

"Yes, please. Could you put it in my hair? I wouldn't know how."

Dani turned, and Susan inserted the sprig into her bun.

"There," Susan said in a motherly tone. "You look very pretty." Her cheeks reddened.

"Thank you!" Dani leaned in to give her a hug. Susan stiffened at first but relaxed into it. "We'd better go," Dani said. "Your brother will be waiting."

They descended the stairs together. Stephen awaited them at the bottom, dashing in a black dinner jacket with tails over a black silk vest with a white tie and stiff shirt collar. He held a top hat in his hand. He looked so dashing that Dani thought her heart stopped for a moment when she saw him.

He blinked when he saw them, and his welcoming smile broadened. "Two of the loveliest ladies I should ever hope to behold," he murmured as they reached the bottom step. Susan blushed and swatted playfully at him. He met Dani's eyes over Susan's head, a light shining through them. Dani took a deep breath, again wondering how she could leave.

"I have hired a carriage for this evening as our carriage is not at present in any condition to transport us," he smiled. He donned his top hat and led the way to the door.

"Wait! I don't have a hat," Dani said. She turned to Susan. "Aren't you wearing one?"

Susan shook her head and furrowed her brow. "No, not at night. It is not necessary."

Dani turned to Stephen who shrugged with a sheepish grin.

"How does one ever know when things are done around here?" she asked as she followed Susan out the door. "When to wear a hat? When to change clothes? When to bow, when to curtsey?"

"You will learn, Miss Douglas. It will come," Susan said, climbing into the carriage with her brother's help. "And we tend not to curtsey anymore unless we are meeting royalty. We are not expecting any royalty in Seattle in the near future, I think."

Stephen laughed as he handed Dani into the carriage.

Within twenty minutes, the carriage arrived in an area downtown which Dani recognized as Pioneer Square. The sound of a hard surface under the carriage wheels caught her attention.

"Oh, so *now* the roads are cobblestoned?" She turned to Stephen.

"Yes, they are here in the city and Pioneer Place. But the rest of the roads, including our own are only graded."

"Well, they'll be paved soon enough," she said. "You'll be happy about that."

"With what material?" he asked. "Cobblestone pavers? Brick pavers?"

"Oh, geez, I don't know. Asphalt?"

"And what is asphalt? No, tell me later, we have arrived."

The carriage stopped in front of a beautiful red brick five-story building—one of those triangular structures that large cities often built in the flatiron block at the corner of two perpendicular roads. Gold-colored lettering at the top of the building read 1890 and further lettering above a large awning proclaimed it the Hotel Seattle.

As Dani descended the carriage, she stared at the building and then turned to survey the Square or Place, as Stephen called it, to orient herself. Gone were the cars and pedestrian walkways over asphalt roads, gone were the glorious trees that decorated the downtown area. In their place were cobblestone streets embedded with trolley car tracks teeming with pedestrians and carriages, massively tall electric power poles and an overhead network of wires for the trolley cars.

She remembered this corner. A parking garage half buried under the street and resembling the bow of a ship sinking below the waves now presided where the beautiful Hotel Seattle stood. She'd had no idea such a wonderful building once stood at the apex of the intersection. She turned to Stephen to tell him but bit the words back. Maybe this was what he meant when he asked her not to share too much of the future with him.

They climbed the steps and entered the hotel. Dani blinked at the dazzling display of red carpets, marble Ionic columns, soft-globed lighting, and gilt-edged furniture of velvet and marble. Emerald green ferns abounded in pots throughout the lobby. Men in coattails and women in a colorful array of silk fabrics milled about or worked their way toward the restaurant.

Dani clutched Stephen's arm tightly with the thought that he probably shouldn't have brought her into public like this. What if someone "detected" her? What if they figured out she wasn't from their time? Certain she stuck out like a sore thumb, she hesitated.

"Be brave, dearest. You are safe with me," Stephen bent to whisper near her ear. She gave him a shaky smile. It was as if he could read her mind. There was no doubt he knew her well.

"There you all are!" Ellie said as she came toward Dani with her arms outstretched. Dani hugged her back, a little more tightly than was necessary. Robert followed.

"Stephen sent a note over to our house and asked us to join you," Ellie whispered before she let Dani go. "He thought you might be uneasy in public."

"He's right. I didn't realize how nervous I was until we ran into all these people." Dani spoke in a low voice as Robert greeted Stephen and Susan.

Ellie laughed. "Don't *I* know it! It gets easier though. They'll never know. Would *you* believe it if it hadn't happened to you?"

Dani shook her head.

"Shall we?" Stephen said.

They entered the restaurant, a beautifully dark-wood paneled room with round tables festooned with white linens and fresh-cut flowers in crystal vases. The maitre d' led them toward a table.

To Dani's surprise, various people hailed both Stephen and Robert as they moved through the aisles. Having never seen him in a large gathering, she hadn't realized Stephen knew so many people. He was forced to stop at a table when a matron stopped him. Susan paused beside him to greet a younger woman at the table. Robert had stopped to shake hands with an elderly gentleman at the table.

Ellie, on the heels of the maitre d', didn't stop but forged her way to the table with Dani in tow.

"I still don't know very many people," she said in a low voice out of the maitre d's hearing. "I've only been here about five months myself." She slid into the seat pulled out by the maitre d' and Dani took the seat beside her.

"Don't you ever want to go home? I know Stephen asked, but I'm curious too." Dani threw a furtive look over her shoulder and kept her voice low.

Ellie shook her head. "Even if I thought I could, I wouldn't. My world is right here...with Robert. I'm perfectly happy here with him."

"But what about...you know...medical care? What about the birth?"

Dani hated to ask the question, but she was driven to hear Ellie's answer.

"Well, sure, I'd like a nice clean hospital with lots of anesthesia to kill the pain. The hospital here looks pretty clean, but I'm having the baby at home. As far as the anesthesia goes, I'll just hang onto to Robert's hand—bite it if I have to," she grinned. "He promised me he'll be there, which is very unusual for a man who grew up in the nineteenth century." Ellie looked toward Robert and Stephen who approached the table.

"What about trying to take him forward in time?" Dani whispered.

Ellie's eyes widened and she gave her head a quick shake, but was prevented from replying by the arrival of the men and Susan.

Dinner was a lively affair with Ellie and Robert teasing each other, and Susan, grateful to be out of the house, exhibiting her dry sense of humor. Stephen, to Dani's surprise, shared the same sense of humor. She'd only seen flashes of it until now, not surprising given the circumstances. Dani almost forgot her surroundings for a moment and relaxed in their care. For it was certain that she was cared for by these people. She imagined what she felt for both Ellie and Susan was a bond of sisterhood, for different reasons, though she'd never had any siblings. Robert knew her secret. And Stephen—well, Stephen loved her.

They had just begun dessert when Lucinda and Gerald Davies sailed past with a young woman in tow.

"How lovely to see you again this evening!" Lucinda sang out, a vision in purple silk and black feathers in her hair. "Had I known you were coming out tonight, I should have suggested we make a party of it." She turned to her husband. "Gerald, you remember Mrs. Danielle Sadler, of course, from the train?"

The slender man nodded, and shook hands with the men.

"This is my daughter, Evelyn, Mrs. Sadler. Evelyn, Mrs. Danielle Sadler."

Robert and Stephen rose. Dani moved as if to stand up to meet the young woman, but Stephen stayed her with a hand on her shoulder.

"How nice to meet you, Mrs. Sadler," the young brunette said in a voice that suggested anything but. She threw Stephen a quick glance, a blush staining her cheeks. "Congratulations on your marriage, Mr. Sadler."

"Marriage? You, Sadler?" A gentleman at the next table called out. He jumped up to shake Stephen's hand. "I hadn't heard," the older man said. "Did you hear that, Mother? Sadler here has gone and gotten married! Well, when did this happen? Introduce us."

Dani cringed. What had Stephen's small white lie gotten him into? Or her?

Robert seated himself, a twitch of his lips betraying his amusement. Ellie coughed and put her napkin to her mouth. Susan beamed at Evelyn Davies, seemingly aware of, and tickled by the other girl's unhappiness. There must be some history there, Dani thought.

"Good evening, Mr. and Mrs. Davies. Thank you, Miss Davies. Yes, Mr. Brown, I did recently marry." Stephen turned to Dani. "This is my wife, Mrs. Danielle Sadler."

Though her knees shook, Dani tried standing up again, but Stephen kept a hand on her shoulder. Wasn't anyone supposed to stand up when introduced?

"Congratulations, Mrs. Sadler," the elderly man said. His wife remained seated but nodded and smiled. He resumed his seat, and Stephen turned toward Mrs. Davies.

"I am so glad we were able to see you tonight, Mrs. Davies. Mrs. Sadler and I are called away tomorrow, and she will not be able to participate in the planned events tomorrow."

Dani had forgotten. She looked at Ellie, who seemed not surprised. Somehow, she knew.

"I'm afraid I shall have to cancel as well, Mrs. Davies. My sole intent was to take Mrs. Sadler shopping but that will have to be delayed now," Ellie said, always quick on her feet.

"Oh, dear, I was so looking forward to our day tomorrow," Lucinda said to Dani and Ellie. "Perhaps next week then. Do you intend to be gone for long?" She addressed Dani and Stephen with a curious glint.

Evelyn looked completely bored with the conversation, and Gerald stood passively by.

"Not long, a week, perhaps," Steven said.

"Well, we shall reschedule when you return. Send a note to me. Come along, Evelyn, Gerald, I am famished."

Stephen almost slid down in his seat.

"Oh, Stephen. You have put yourself in a very difficult situation," Ellie chuckled behind her napkin.

"But he did it to protect me," Dani said. She turned to Stephen. "I just don't know what you're going to say when—"

"Let us not concern ourselves with that this evening," he said with a sideways glance in Susan's direction.

Dani pressed her lips together. That was right. Susan didn't know she was returning to her own time but thought they were going away for a few days.

"In honor of which, I have some things in our carriage for you to wear on your trip," Ellie said with a careful look in Susan's direction.

"Since you won't have time to go shopping before you leave."

Dani grinned, tears forming in her eyes. She wiped at them with the back of her hand. She was going to miss Ellie terribly. It occurred to Dani that she might discover what became of Ellie, Robert, and their children when she returned. And Stephen and Susan. But they would be dead—" She couldn't finish the thought. She would *not* finish the thought. The people before her would live forever in her heart. She was reminded of the older man she met on the train. Edward? His green eyes...like Robert's.

"Sadler! Where have you been?"

Not again, Dani thought, as she looked up at a very handsome, raven-haired man of Stephen's age. He greeted Robert by name as well.

"Rory!" Stephen rose and embraced the man. "How long has it been?" he said with a broad smile.

"Too many years." Rory sported an arresting pair of blue eyes and a broad sardonic smile. "Not since college, I think." He stared at the party with interest.

"My manners," Stephen said. "You know Robert, of course. His wife, Mrs. Ellie Chamberlain. Susan, all grown up." He turned to Dani. "And my...wife, Mrs. Danielle Sadler."

"Your wife?" One dark eyebrow rose. "Never say! Mrs. Sadler, how delighted I am to meet you." Rory bent over her hand and kissed the back of it. "I had no idea you were married, Stephen, and certainly not to such a beauty."

"That's quite enough, Rory. Thank you." Stephen retrieved Dani's hand from Rory's.

"This is an old college friend of mine, Harold O'Rourke."

"Delighted to meet you all. I have just returned to town from several years in Ireland, so I am trying to reacquaint myself with everyone." He looked across the room to where several people at a table waved to him. "My party awaits me. Forgive me. Call on me, Sadler. You know my address. It has not changed." He strode away, a tall, lithe man brimming with energy.

"I really had no idea I had been so reclusive," Stephen said. "So many people are about tonight, and everyone wishes to visit."

"You have been staying home to take care of me, Stephen, but now that I am well, you must start going out. And Danielle must go with you."

Stephen looked at Susan, startled, and coughed. "Yes, of course." He rubbed his chin. The waiter brought the bill, and Stephen took care of it with protestations from Robert and Ellie.

"Nonsense. I enjoyed the company," Stephen said. "And I know Miss Doug—Danielle did."

They rose and followed Ellie and Robert to their carriage where Ellie handed Stephen the same satchel she had brought over that morning.

"Here, she'll need these for the train," Ellie said. Dani stood by helplessly, unable to say everything she wanted to Ellie in Susan's presence. Stephen, intuitive as always, took Susan over to their carriage.

Ellie threw her arms around Dani, while Robert turned away.

"I'm going to miss you so much," Ellie said, her voice breaking. Dani broke down into tears and clung to Ellie.

"Me too. I'm so sorry. I hate to leave, but I know you have Robert, and soon you'll have your baby. But I still hate to leave. And I hate to leave Susan...and Stephen. This is breaking my heart."

"Shhhh," Ellie said. "It's all right. This is what you need to do. Part of me wishes it doesn't work—your attempt to return. I know that's selfish. But I really do wish you well, and I hope your mom recovers."

Dani lifted her head and rubbed her nose. "If I can come back, I will, Ellie. Wouldn't it be great if I could just run back and forth? At least until my mom... Well, while she's still alive?"

"Yeah," Ellie said. She let Dani go. "Take care."

"Goodbye, Robert. It was so nice to meet you," Dani said. "Watch over Stephen. He means a great deal to me."

"As you do to Stephen, Dani. Safe journey."

Dani crossed the street to where Stephen waited for her by the carriage with a handkerchief. She grabbed it and wiped at the tears streaming from her eyes. What she really longed to do was bury herself in Stephen's arms and listen to him tell her everything would be all right. But under Susan's eye, that didn't seem quite the thing to do.

The ride back to the house on Queen Anne Hill was uneventful. Susan dozed. Ellie and Robert's carriage preceded them up Queen Anne Hill. Stephen pointed their house out as they passed, and Dani waved one more time from the passing carriage to Ellie and Robert as they stepped down from the carriage in front of their home. She thought they waved back, but it was dark and she wasn't sure. The house, built on a hill, was stunningly elegant, the lights from the porch and house pouring onto the street below.

On arriving at Stephen's own beautiful Queen Anne house, Susan, yawning, bade them goodnight.

Dani stood uncertainly, unwilling to walk away from Stephen on her last night with him. He had said earlier "We still have tonight." Did he mean...? Stephen watched his sister climbed the stairs then turned to take Dani by the hand and lead her into the library, where he seated her in one of the large easy chairs in front of the unlit fireplace.

"Would you like some tea? A drink?" he smiled softly. "A hot toddy?"

Dani smiled, nervously lacing her fingers. "Maybe a drink?"

Stephen poured them each a brandy and settled into the chair beside her. Neither of them spoke for a moment. Stephen stared at the cold fireplace.

Dani had so much to say, yet nothing really seemed adequate. What do you say to someone whom you love but might never see again? She committed Stephen's face to memory—the beautiful golden waves of his hair, the square cut of his chin, his tender mouth now unsmiling.

"I'm terrified that I'll never see you again," Dani said with a catch in her voice making speech difficult. She fought back another bout of tears.

Stephen jerked his head toward her. He set his drink down, rose and came to kneel before her at her knees. As he took her hands in his, tears spilled down her face. She clung to his hands.

"Stephen, when I return to my time, you will be dead." She bit back her sobs. It sounded horrible and insensitive to verbalize but she needed to say the words. "I can't bear it. I just can't bear to live in a world where you don't."

Stephen stood and pulled her into his arms. She sobbed against his chest. "What am I going to do?" she cried. "What am I going to do?"

"Hush, now, my love," he murmured against her hair. "Hush now. It is only natural. We must all pass."

"No, not you! Not you. Not Susan, not Ellie, not Robert, not even Lucinda." Her sobs continued.

"We will all have lived full lives, dearest. Do not fret."

She pulled back from him for a moment. Yes, he would live a full life, wouldn't he? He would marry, have children. Maybe one day...one crazy day, she could locate his descendents and meet them.

"I know what you are thinking, Dani. I feel I know you well. I can see the softening in your face. You are thinking that I will marry another, aren't you?" He brought her back to him in a tight embrace. "I cannot think of it. I cannot imagine the moment. I have waited for you for so long."

Dani looked up into his face.

"But why me?"

"I do not know why you," he smiled gently. He ran a thumb across her cheeks to wipe away tears. "I only know that I longed for someone...for a woman who captured my imagination, my heart...as you have. Within an hour of meeting you, I no longer felt that longing. And I knew you were the one."

"Oh, Stephen," Dani buried her face against him again. "I love you," she sobbed.

"I love you, too, Dani. With all my heart."

He lifted her chin and bent his head to kiss her, his lips warm and tender. She clung to him with all her might, wishing that life could have been different.

He lifted his head and smiled crookedly. "I am truly going to miss you, my love."

A knock on the door startled them. Stephen sighed, pulled away and said, "Enter."

Mrs. Oakley entered, her hands wringing, her face distraught.

"Mr. Sadler, it's Miss Susan. She's burning with fever. Oh, Mr. Sadler, I'm so afraid her lung infection has returned."

CHAPTER SEVEN

Stephen raced up the stairs to Susan's room. She lay curled on her side, shivering, coughing as she had during her illness. He touched her forehead. As Mrs. Oakley said, it burned.

Dani ran in behind him and came to the bedside, her breathing rapid. She took several deep breaths to calm herself and bent to touch Susan's forehead.

"I am so sorry, Stephen. I feel so cold...and hot." Susan said in a raspy voice. "I must have overdone it. I am sure this will pass." If determination could rid one of illness, Stephen thought his sister might be able to cure herself, but he had learned over the past several months that it was not enough.

"There now, dear. Mrs. Oakley sent Samuel for the doctor," he told Susan. She fell into another paroxysm of coughing, and he turned to pour a glass of water for her.

To his surprise, Dani climbed onto the bed and pulled Susan into a sitting position into her arms.

"Get me some cool water and a cloth, Stephen."

Of course, why had he not thought of that? He had lost his wits. To bring the fever down.

As if she had heard Dani, Mrs. Oakley brought in a bowl of water and linen. She moistened a cloth and handed it to Dani who laid it on Susan's forehead. Silently, she reached for another wet cloth, and Mrs. Oakley provided it. She bathed Susan's face and neck.

"There, there," Dani soothed as Susan began coughing again. "Breathe deep through your nose. That's it. Just breathe if you can."

Stephen stood by helplessly watching, his heart in his throat. Susan had come near death with her lung infection. Mrs. Oakley left to await the doctor.

"It is not tuberculosis," he said quietly, moving to sit on the edge of the bed. "It is called chronic bronchitis. There is no cure for it. She has had several bouts over the last few years, and they seem to grow worse. She almost died last time. I should not have allowed her to go out tonight. It was too much."

"Please don't blame yourself, Stephen. She wanted to go, and she had a lovely time. You don't know that she wouldn't have gotten ill staying right here. It's probably the pollution in the air anyway." She handed him one of the cloths and he rinsed it with cool water and handed it back to her. Susan's coughing eased, and she seemed to doze for a moment.

"She breathes easier," he said with hope.

"That's because she's sitting up," Dani whispered. "It's easier to breathe that way. Just prop pillows behind her in the future when she's coughing like this. And she could probably use some steaming water to loosen the phlegm. She could put her head over a bowl of steaming water or maybe even the bathtub." Dani's brow furrowed. "Gosh, I wish I had some stuff with me. Medication to bring the fever down. Antibiotics."

"Bronchitis is curable in my time, Stephen. Maybe not permanently, and she might have recurrences, but she can get antibiotics to help with the infection." Dani continued to bathe Susan's face and neck.

Stephen sighed. "I have heard of antibiotics. The doctor brings pills, but they are not effective."

"Ours are."

"Would that you could take her with you," he said bitterly.

"I wish I could," Dani said in a mournful tone as she brushed Susan's hair from her face. "I would, you know. I would take her right now if she weren't so sick. But I can't wait for her to get better. I have to get back to my mom. I have no idea how much time has passed since I've been gone." Her voice broke, and he knew she feared the worst.

He took her hand in his. "I understand your fears, my love. I can only hope that you are able to get back to your mother in time, and that she recovers from her illness."

Dani gave his hand a squeeze and smiled faintly. "Now, go wash your hands with soap and water. Bronchitis can be contagious. We don't need both of you getting sick."

Stephen tilted his head and regarded her. "I was not aware of that!"

"Which—washing hands or contagious?"

"That bronchitis was contagious," he said. "Clean hands are always important."

Dani chuckled at his boyish observation. "Yes, bronchitis can be contagious, so it's best to practice good hygiene."

Stephen rose. "Of course." He crossed to where a basin of water and soap stood on a dresser. "What about you?"

"I have a lot of immunities built up. I'll be fine," she said.

A knock on the door brought Mrs. Oakley with Dr. Sterling whose home was fortunately nearby. The doctor gave Dani a curious look but hurried toward Susan's side. He felt her forehead and listened to her chest with his stethoscope.

Dani removed herself from the bed and moved to stand beside Stephen while the doctor examined Susan. A long-time family physician, the tall lanky silver-haired doctor knew Susan's condition well. He had tried many treatments over the years but none had permanently cured her, and she relapsed several times a year.

Stephen waited anxiously, incredibly touched when Dani took his hand in hers. He clung to her hand as if her small fingers could somehow make his sister well, and he suspected she could if she had the proper medicines from her time. How he wished she could take Susan with her. How he wished *he* could go with her. But he had never heard of anyone traveling through time before, and suspected the phenomenon was not available in his time. It occurred to him that they were still not sure Dani could return to her own era.

The doctor turned to him. "This episode is not as bad as the last. I will leave you some pills. Keep her warm when she is cold and cool when she is hot. She is perspiring so the fever has already broken."

"Thank you, Dr. Sterling," Stephen said. "Is there nothing else we can do? A more permanent cure? Some new medication perhaps?"

Dr. Sterling shook his head. "Not yet. We await a more effective treatment but at present, there is nothing else."

Stephen caught him looking at Dani.

"Oh, I'm sorry, Doctor. My wife, Mrs. Danielle Sadler."

"Mrs. Sadler, how do you do?" The doctor nodded but did not take her hand. She didn't blame him.

"I'm well, thank you, Doctor."

"There is one thing you could do, Stephen, to help your sister. Take her away from the city. There is too much smoke and congestion in the air. It cannot be good for her poor lungs."

Stephen blinked and looked at Dani. "Where do you suggest I take her, Dr. Sterling? What area would be more beneficial to her?"

"I am not sure, Stephen, but somewhere else, somewhere far away from the city. The country? An island? Someplace that has clean air and uses little coal." Dr. Sterling sighed. "I will return tomorrow to see how she does. Someone should stay with her tonight."

Mrs. Oakley escorted him from the room, and Dani and Stephen looked at each other.

"Wherever could he mean? Shall I take her to a Pacific island?"

"Or you could bring her to me," Dani smiled teasingly as she moved into his arms. Susan still slept. "And you could come with her. Then we'd get my mom after her surgery, and we'd all go off to Hawaii."

"Hawaii?" Stephen kissed the top of her head. Her hair smelled wonderfully sweet. "How very exotic. Have you been?"

Dani nodded, her face pressed against his chest. "It's only a five-hour flight from here."

"Flight?" He had so much to learn. What was a "flight?" A journey? Something similar to the movement of a bird?

"Big machines that fly in the sky and carry people to their destinations."

"My word!" Stephen murmured. He had a vision of the paper dragons one saw in Seattle's Chinatown, but larger.

"I know," she whispered. She wrapped an arm around him and turned to look at Susan.

"You're not going to be able to go on the train with me tomorrow," she murmured. He felt a tremor run through her body. "And that's okay. I don't know how I could try to get back to my time if you were there anyway. How I would even want to?"

"I cannot let you go alone. How can I let you go at all?" He pulled her back into his arms, embracing her gently but with determination.

"I have to go, Stephen. We both know that." Her voice, resigned, almost fatalistic, belied her shaking hands.

His chest ached. "I know, sweeting. I know. Please come back to me...if you can."

"I will," she said. She hugged him fiercely, and his ribs ached from the motion. Strong little thing she was, he thought tenderly.

He hesitated to bring up his most fervent desire. "And if you cannot return, if you find yourself in Chicago in 1901? How will you feel then?"

She shook her head. "I can't think that way. I have to believe I can get back."

"But if you cannot, my dear, send word to me at once, and I will make arrangements for your return. In fact, I shall give you some money before I take you to the train tomorrow for any needs you might have."

She shook her head against his chest, and he kissed the top of her head once again.

"I must stay here with Susan tonight, Dani. I cannot ask Mrs. Oakley to do so. You should go to bed so you can be refreshed for your trip tomorrow."

Dani raised her face to his. Her eyes were luminous as she searched his face, looking for something he could not seem to give her. Reassurance? Hope?

"I'm staying with you."

He delighted in her answer but tried once more to do what was correct.

"No, you must get some sleep."

Dani took him by the hand and guided him toward the sofa in front of the bed. She urged him to sit and sat down beside him, nestling into his arms once again. Little had he known only a short day before that the woman he met on the train would fit so snugly against his body, that he would crave her touch, her warmth, her laugh. His life had changed forever, and he could not envision a future without her.

Mrs. Sadler. He loved to hear the sound of the words. He had not realized when he invented such a story that his wishful thinking would come to pass. He chuckled inwardly. No, perhaps that was not quite true. He could probably have said she was a cousin, and they could have survived the few days of notoriety that might have occurred. No, he wanted to say *Mrs. Danielle Sadler.* It had a lovely ring. *My wife.* Lovelier still.

Susan slept on, and Dani's breathing slowed and deepened. She had fallen asleep in his arms. Never in his life had a woman slept in his arms, and he wished above all else that she should stay there. What he thought he felt for Ellie could not compare to the intensity with which he loved Dani. It seemed ludicrous that the perfect woman for him should not be from his time, but that she should be from some distant future he could not envision. He was a historian, not a connoisseur of science fiction. His strength lie in what he understood from the past, not the future. And yet the future had deposited his heart's desire in his lap for a brief, ecstatic, painful, glorious moment.

I'll come back if I can. He clung to those words.

****

"Dani," Stephen whispered. "It is time to wake."

Dani jerked then bolted upright.

"Oh, my gosh. I fell asleep. How long did I sleep?" she asked, rubbing her eyes.

"All night long. The sun is coming up." Stephen nodded toward light filtering in through the windows.

Susan continued to sleep. He had risen several times during the night to check her temperature and listen to her breathing. Her fever had abated, and although her breathing sounded constricted, she seemed to rest comfortably. He had returned to the sofa and taken the sleeping Dani in his arms once again.

"How is she?" Dani whispered.

"The fever is gone. She rests well, though she still breathes with some difficulty. I believe the medicine the doctor gave her is working...this time. We were not so fortunate last time."

"I'm so glad," Dani said. She rose to approach the bed and lay a hand on Susan's forehead.

Stephen watched her with an ache in his heart. With every hour that passed taking them nearer to her departure, he wondered how he could bear to say goodbye to her.

She turned to look at him. "What time is it?"

He pulled out his pocket watch and looked at it. Soon. Restlessly, he rose to walk to the window which looked out over the city.

"It is five o'clock. The train leaves at seven."

"I'd better get ready," she said, almost in a mournful voice.

Nothing Stephen could say would make her stay, and he knew she must return to see to her mother. Yet he longed to plead with her, to beg her to stay. He bit his lower lip so hard he tasted blood.

"Say goodbye to her for me, Stephen," Dani said as she brushed Susan's hair from her forehead.

"What do you mean?" Susan said hoarsely, her eyes opening. "I thought you and Stephen were traveling together."

Dani stiffened and threw Stephen a startled look. He came to the bedside and sat down to take Susan's hand in his. Her skin was warm but not feverish.

"Susan, my dearest, how do you feel?"

"Better," she said in her raspy voice. She coughed. "What were you talking about?"

Dani looked to Stephen.

"Nothing for you to worry about now, dear. Dani is going on the journey we had planned, and I will stay here to take care of you."

Susan's eyes widened, and she snatched her hand away to push herself straighter on the pillows.

"Stephen! You cannot let her travel on the train alone. Where were you going anyway? You never actually said."

"I'll be fine, Susan," Dani soothed. She sat on the opposite side of the bed. "Really, I will. Remember, I've traveled by train many times by myself."

"But where are you going?"

Dani winced at the forlorn sound of Susan's voice. Stephen sighed. His young sister had already lost so much. She had become quite attached to Dani in a very short time. Perhaps he should have married before now...if only to give Susan a mother of sorts.

He looked toward Dani. She met his eyes, and he knew a moment's gratitude that he had not married another.

"My mother has been sick, Susan. I need to go see her," Dani said softly.

"But you can't!" Susan almost shrieked but for the hoarseness of her voice. "How can you see her?"

"I don't know, Susan, but I have to try. We didn't want to tell you yesterday." Dani reached for Susan's hand as tears flowed down her face. Dani's eyes glittered with unshed tears.

"Susan, dear, this is difficult for Dani—both her mother's illness and her imminent departure. You and I must not attempt to reproach her or make her unhappier than she already is. I have been guilty of this too."

Dani smiled at him gently.

"I am sorry. I know it is wrong," Susan whispered. "But I do not want you to leave."

Dani brought Susan into her arms and embraced her, whispering soothing words in her ears as she cried. Stephen saw Dani's tears spill over. Dani abruptly kissed her cheek and hurried from the room, leaving Stephen and Susan to stare after her.

"Stephen, you cannot let her go alone. Please go with her. Mrs. Oakley can take care of me. If I were well enough, I would go with you!"

Stephen smiled tenderly. "My dear, if you were well, I wonder if we all would not go with her." He looked over his shoulder but the door had closed behind Dani. "Please bear in mind that we do not know if Dani can return to her time. We do not understand the mechanics of her arrival or of the concept of time travel itself. I will give her ample money to return here to Seattle if she cannot make the transition to her time, but I cannot leave you, Susan. Not while you are ill."

Susan nodded in a resigned fashion. "I understand. I worry about her traveling alone though."

"I worry less now that I know women travel alone in her time, but it is still not seemly."

"What about Mrs. Chamberlain? They seem to get on very well. Maybe she could go with her?" Susan gave her brother an assessing look.

Stephen stiffened. The child was very astute.

"No, Mrs. Chamberlain cannot travel as she is in the family way."

"That's it then," Susan said defeated. "No one else knows about Dani."

"No one," Stephen said.

****

They arrived at the train station with a half hour until departure time. Dani noted with relief that the train yard had been regraded, and she hitched up the skirts of the brown cotton traveling dress Ellie had loaned her and tiptoed over the still moist soil until she stepped onto the platform. She balanced the small straw hat Ellie had sent with the dress precariously on her hair, not holding out much hope for the stickpin holding it in place.

She had clung to Stephen's hand on the carriage ride from his home, but they remained silent, having nothing left to say. He wanted her to stay, she had to go; she wanted him to go with her and he might have considered coming but for Susan's illness...which Susan would survive in Dani's time.

And all of this was a big "if" she could get home. She had no firm idea how it might work. Dani had stuffed the now-cleaned clothing she'd worn the day before into a small satchel Stephen had given her...just in case. She was unwilling to dwell on any further thoughts in that area in case they somehow inadvertently hexed her plan to return home.

The train was in station—steam hissing, smoke billowing, conductors, stewards and porters busily about the business of loading passengers, luggage and supplies. Stephen handed Dani her ticket, some money and something else. From his coat pocket, he withdrew her small afghan square and crocheting needle and held them out.

Dani took them wordlessly, unable to speak over the ache in her throat. If she said one word, she would start bawling. She glanced around to see people boarding the train—women and children hugged, men shook hands, but she didn't see any men and women embracing. Dared she kiss Stephen goodbye...yet again? Would he be shocked?

Stephen settled the matter by taking her in his arms and kissing her deeply and thoroughly, almost as if willing her to stay by promises of nights of passion and days of tenderness.

Dani came up for air with a watery chuckle. "You don't have to convince me in one kiss what a wonderful life I might have with you, Stephen. I already know that."

"I just do not want you to forget," Stephen said in a husky voice. He clenched his jaw, and Dani knew he struggled for control.

"I will never forget you. Never!" She pulled off her hat and clung to him, pressing her face against his chest. His heartbeat raced. "I'm going

233

to try to come back, Stephen. But if somehow I can't, don't wait for me. Find someone."

"I already have," he said.

"I'm going to get on the train now," Dani said, "before I change my mind. Don't wait to wave me off. Just go." Her chest ached with unbearable pain, and she could only drag in shallow breaths. The possible loss of her mother or the almost certain loss of Stephen were choices no one should have to make.

Stephen shook his head. "I cannot do that."

"Please go, Stephen," her voice broke. "I don't want my last memory of you to be standing on the platform waving goodbye."

"Oh, Dani," he sighed heavily. "You ask too much of me."

He bent his head and kissed her hungrily before turning away and striding toward the carriage.

Dani froze, staring after him. The last memory she would have of him was walking away from her, which seemed a hundred times worse than watching him wave goodbye from the platform. He jumped into the carriage without a backward glance, and Samuel set the carriage in motion.

Dani turned away, blinded by tears. She dashed at her eyes, trying to focus on the train. She moved toward the train on leaden legs. The conductor nodded his cap.

"Which way is the observation car?" she muttered, her watery eyes on the ground.

"The observation and library carriage, Madam? Two carriages down. I suggest you board the carriage directly down there."

With a glance over her shoulder, she walked toward the observation car. Stephen did not stand on the platform to wave at her. He had done as she asked. He had left. Even now, the carriage probably inched its way toward Queen Anne Hill.

She entered the observation carriage and took up the same seat she'd sat in before, when she first met Stephen. Obviously, her best chance of getting back was to re-create the same set of events...without Stephen's presence though.

Unlike her first experience in an almost empty observation carriage, the carriage hosted about ten other passengers, perhaps due to the earliness of the day. Several people were already ensconced in various seats throughout the carriage, some in the library, some in the observation car. A steward, already on duty, asked her if she wished anything. She came very close to asking for a hot toddy but opted for a cup of tea.

"Right away, Madam."

While mulling over various ways her travel to the future might occur, Dani studied her fellow passengers in the observation portion of the carriage. Several middle-aged couples visited with each other as if they traveled together. The women dressed in sensible-looking dark traveling dresses with white blouses, and the men in dark neutral-colored suits and conservative ties. Two older women chatted excitedly with frequent gestures out the window, suggesting they didn't ride the train very often.

The steward returned with her cup of tea.

Around the edge of the divider between the observation portion of the carriage and the library, Dani saw several pairs of crossed legs housed in male trousers. One of the men rose and entered the observation section as if in search of something to the rear of the carriage.

On seeing Dani, he paused and tilted his head inquiringly.

"Mrs. Sadler! How nice to see you again. Is Stephen with you?"

Rory O'Rourke, the handsome dark-haired friend of Stephen's, turned to scan the room.

Dani cursed inwardly. How, if she knew almost no one in 1901, could she run into one of the few people she had met? She almost jumped up, but remembered the pressure of Stephen's hand on her shoulder at dinner. She supposed she was expected to remain seated.

"Mr. O'Rourke!" she murmured. "No, Stephen is not." She swallowed hard. No, Stephen was not with her.

He blinked his blue eyes, and quirked a dark eyebrow.

"Surely, you do not travel alone, Mrs. Sadler?"

Dani pressed her lips together.

"Well, yes, actually. Stephen was going to come with me, but Susan was ill...so he had to stay."

"I am so sorry to hear that. Perhaps I might step in as a companion until you reach your destination, Mrs. Sadler. It is what I would wish Stephen to do if my wife were in such a situation."

"Oh, no need to do that, Mr. O'Rourke." How on earth was she going to attempt to "travel," however that defined itself, under his watchful eye?

"Please call me Rory. May I?" he gestured to the seat bench.

"Yes, of course," she replied. She studied him as he settled into a seat and hailed the steward. Such a handsome man, charming and animated. "Are you married, Rory?"

"No, no, not me," he smiled. "I simply meant that *if* I were married and *if* my wife were forced to travel alone, I would welcome the companionship of Stephen or other friends on her behalf."

The steward brought her tea, and Rory placed an order.

"Stephen didn't want me to go alone, but I have to visit my mother in Montana." She felt the need to defend Stephen. "Susan was very ill, and she needed her brother there."

"Yes, of course, I understand." He eyed her with interest. "You say you are from Montana?"

"Well, originally, yes."

"I have spent time there but do not remember meeting any women as delightful as you. Even at our meeting last night, I noted you were pleasantly original...even in your speech."

Dani eyed him narrowly, suspecting he was probably reacting to her mannerisms rather than her universal appeal to all men.

"Are you flirting with me, Rory? A married woman?"

He blinked and laughed outright. "I suppose I am," he said sheepishly. "It is a bad habit of long standing. Forgive me. My flirtatious attentions are not often so boldly pointed out."

"I don't think Stephen would like you flirting with me," she said with a smile. He seemed harmless.

"No, he would not," Stephen said, standing before them.

CHAPTER EIGHT

Dani jumped up. "Stephen! What—"

"Rory, what do you think you are doing?" Stephen stood over him, his eyes narrowed and angry.

Rory stood. "It is nothing, Stephen. I overstepped my bounds and made my apologies to Mrs. Sadler."

"Stephen, what—" Dani tried again. The train began to move, dropping her back into her seat. Stephen balanced himself on the edge of the bench as he stared at Rory.

"What are you doing on the train, Rory?"

"I might ask you the same question, Stephen. Mrs. Sadler stated you were not traveling with her." Rory appeared relaxed, but a telltale muscle twitched in his jaw.

"Which does not give you permission to harass my wife."

"Stephen! He wasn't—" Dani grabbed Stephen's lapel and gave it a quick tug. "Sit down. People are staring. Rory didn't do anything. He offered to keep me company until I got to Whitefish, that's all."

"I am truly sorry, Stephen," Rory said with a sincere expression. "Mrs. Sadler and I had agreed that my behavior was improper before you arrived."

Stephen sat down, and Rory retook his seat. The steward, who had stood by apprehensively with Rory's coffee, served it quickly and moved on. The two men eyed each other steadily for a few moments—visually exchanging whatever communication was necessary to clear the air.

"Thank you, Rory," Stephen conceded, appearing slightly mollified, but not entirely. "I had not thought to be able to travel with *my wife* today but found I could not let her travel alone after all. My sister has been unwell, but my housekeeper will care for her."

"I am sorry to hear of Susan's illness. Please give her my best," Rory said with a frown.

"Of course," Stephen nodded. He threw Dani a sideways glance, but she kept her mouth shut for the moment, at least in front of Rory.

"I believe you two must have things to discuss, and I think I will just leave you alone for a while and find a newspaper to read," Rory said, astutely observing Stephen's reticence to speak.

"Thank you, Rory," Dani said. Rory nodded, rose and walked away toward the library.

"What are you doing here, Stephen?" Dani whispered. "What about Susan?"

"I could not let you travel alone. I simply could not, although I discover that my old friend, Rory, has offered to stand in my stead." He shook his head and looked over his shoulder to where Rory had taken a seat in the library.

"He was being kind, Stephen, really. I think he's just a bit of a flirt, but he wasn't hitting on me, I don't think."

"Hitting on you?" Stephen gave her a wry smile. "I am sure I understand the meaning of the expression, but I cannot say I have heard flirting described as such. The expression has a very violent connotation."

Dani smiled tenderly, her heart swelling at the sight of his face. "What about Susan?"

"I sent Samuel back to the house with a note for Mrs. Oakley and Susan. I had thought to have Ellie check on her, but as she is with child, I decided against it. Susan urged me to accompany you. She will not be upset that I could not force myself to abandon you."

Dani grabbed his hand. She resisted the urge to bring it to her lips, assuming those around them would be shocked.

"I cannot imagine you ever abandoning me, Stephen. Not ever."

He touched her face lightly with his free hand. "Not ever," he repeated.

"So, what's the plan?" she asked.

He looked taken aback. "Plan? I do not know. I thought *you* had a plan. We did not really talk about it. You seemed reluctant to discuss the matter of your return short of adamantly insisting that you needed to go home."

Dani colored. "I know. I'm sorry. It's easier for me not to think about the consequences, but to just do it. Otherwise, I won't be able to."

"I understand, my love, truly I do." Unabashed, Stephen brought her hand to his lips.

Dani took a deep breath. "Both Ellie and I seemed to travel through time near the Wenatchee station, but she's not sure she ever returned to our time. She thinks they might have been dreams." Dani kept her voice low in case they were overheard.

"She said she had fallen asleep in her seat and woke up in Robert's private carriage. She didn't mention the observation car, so I'm not sure that's a significant factor, but I'm not taking any chances. I'm staying here. When I traveled, I started out in the observation car, although ours looks very different from yours."

"What do you see as the most significant factor?"

She shook her head. "I don't know. Wenatchee? Sleeping? I'd fallen asleep too. At least, I yawned, and then it seemed like I was here. There was this wonderful old fella on the train. We'd talked a bit. He had an old Victorian house in Seattle that had belonged to his family for generations. He invited me to visit it." She smiled. Such a gracious man he'd been, tall with green eyes.

"Do you think his presence is significant?" Stephen raised his eyebrows.

Dani shook her head. "No, I don't think so. I don't see how. Ellie never mentioned him, and I never asked. There was something very old-fashioned about him though. Beautiful green eyes."

"Should I be jealous?" Stephen asked with a smile. "Perhaps of his ancestors? If his family had been in Seattle for generations, they must surely be there now."

"Silly!" Dani grinned and squeezed his hand. "I imagine they are though. Isn't that strange?"

Stephen consulted his pocket watch. "We reach Wenatchee in five and a half hours."

"Five and a half hours! Gosh, that's slow."

"Is it?" Stephen spoke in a bemused tone, his eyes on her face. Dani blushed under his loving regard. "It seems too short."

She sighed, and settled in beside him as near as she dared given the public setting. Over the next few hours, they drank tea, laughed about hot toddies, chatted with Rory who returned for a visit, and ate lunch.

Dani reached for Stephen's pocket watch. The time had flown all too quickly. They would arrive in Wenatchee in approximately thirty minutes. She stared at him with wide eyes.

"I think I need to sleep, Stephen. I don't know if I can return while I'm wide awake."

He drew in a deep breath. "I had procured a sleeping compartment for you in the possible eventuality that you might not be successful. Would you like to go there now to sleep?"

Dani shook her head. "No, I don't think so. I'd better stay here in the observation car. How can I possibly go to sleep while you're here?"

"You managed last night," he said, smiling.

She responded to his smile. "I did, didn't I? I must have been exhausted, because all I really want to do when I'm with you is bury myself in your arms and enjoy the moment." She didn't hold back. There was no time to be bashful.

Stephen's face bronzed charmingly. "I feel the same about you, my love."

"Wenatchee, twenty minutes." A conductor passed through announcing their imminent arrival.

"Hold me now, Stephen." Dani threw a quick glance over her shoulder toward the nearby passengers. She gathered the satchel in her lap. "Hold me now so I can sleep."

Stephen didn't hesitate but pulled her into his arms. Her face rested against his chest, and she closed her eyes, giving herself up to the warmth of his body.

"There, there, my love," he whispered. "Sleep. I will watch over you." He kissed the top of her head.

His heart thumped loudly against her ear. A tear slid down Dani's face, and she wrapped her arms around him as if she could take him with her.

"I love you, Stephen."

"I love you too, Dani, with all my heart."

****

"Whitefish, Montana, twenty minutes."

Dani opened her eyes to the sound of the conductor's voice. Her face pressed against something warm, something dark blue. She jerked her head. The seat! The sun shone through the large window onto the train seat, warming it against her skin. For a moment she thought it was Stephen's vest.

"Stephen?" Dani bolted upright in her seat and looked around the modern observation car of the gleaming steel train. She was back! Back in her own time. And Stephen wasn't with her. She was alone.

A searing pain tore through her chest, and she doubled over sobbing. Stephen. Stephen. His name repeated itself again and again in her consciousness. He was gone. It was as if he was dead.

She blocked the thought that he was dead in her time as too horrible to contemplate.

"Ma'am? Are you all right?" The conductor, a young man in a crisp dark blue suit, paused at her seat, his face a picture of concern.

"I'm fine," she gasped. "I'm fine. Just had to say goodbye to someone. I'm fine."

"I'm sorry," he said with a click of his tongue. "That's always tough."

Dani pressed her hand against her mouth and nodded, wishing he would go away. She wanted to wail, she wanted to scream, she wanted to keen like some medieval woman who had lost her man. But even in the conductor's absence, she wouldn't be able to give in to the anguish that tore at her heart. Though the observation car was fairly empty at the moment, there were a few passengers in it, and they watched her with round eyes.

"Well, if there's anything I can do, let me know," the conductor said. He eyed her skirt curiously and moved on.

Dani looked down at her lap. She wore the dress Ellie had given her. Still. The straw hat was not in sight. She remembered taking it off to rest against Stephen. The satchel rested at her feet, as if it had fallen from her lap. It hadn't been a dream. It had been real. She had traveled in time. Stephen had been real, not a figment of her imagination.

She hugged her waist, her dress—as if in some way she also hugged Stephen, never to lose him. She had always known Stephen couldn't come with her. There hadn't been any question. Susan needed him. And yet to fall asleep in his arms and wake up alone had been a shock. She didn't understand the mechanism that allowed her to travel through time but kept Stephen in the past. Did it depend on desire? Need? As Dani needed to get back home, she did, but since Stephen needed to stay with Susan, he did?

Dani, her eyes still flooded with tears, tried to focus on the terrain through the large windows of the observation car. Somehow, Wenatchee had come and gone, and she'd slept all the way through to Whitefish. Thick pine trees bordered the track like a tunnel on both sides, signaling their approach to Whitefish, a lovely little resort town tucked away in the Rocky Mountains near Glacier National Park.

"At last, you are awake, my love!" Stephen whispered as he slid into the seat next to her. Dani gasped and jerked her head toward him as if he was a ghost. His eyes were bright, his smile broad, his expression filled with excitement.

"Stephen?" she said hoarsely. "Are you real?" She touched his arm tentatively.

Stephen grabbed her hand and pulled it to his lips.

"Did I frighten you, dearest? Yes, I am real. I am here with you." He looked over his shoulder toward the other passengers. "Can I pull you into my arms in your time? I do not know your customs yet." He kept his voice low.

Dani launched herself at him. "Oh, Stephen," she cried. She kissed his cheeks, his forehead, his mouth, his chin and back to his mouth again. "You're here! You're here."

Stephen laughed at the onslaught but did not push her away. He held her against him.

"I see public kissing is permissible in your time. Excellent! I am all for it." He pulled her face to his, and kissed her deeply as if he would never let her go. He lifted his head and regarded her tenderly.

"I could not wake you, but I saw that you breathed. I decided to let you rest, and I traveled the length of this train. What a marvelous bit of engineering! Wonderful accommodations! A smooth ride. This observation carriage leaves nothing to be desired. The washrooms are superb, albeit a bit small for my taste."

Dani eyed him with wonder. If he ever looked handsome in his own time, something about his golden hair, the crystal blueness of his eyes, the excitement and energy emanating from him made him that much more striking. She thought she must be the luckiest woman in the world—for just a moment.

"What about Susan? You have to try to get back to her."

His expression grew grave. "Yes, I do. I cannot stay here with you for long, no more than a few days. But I do want to meet your mother and see how she is doing."

Dani clutched his hand and stared out the window. The train slowed.

"I hope I'm not too late. I wonder what day it is."

"I asked the conductor, ignoring his strange expression regarding my clothing. It is the same day as it is in my time. So, it would appear only a little over a day has passed since you left."

Dani sighed with relief.

"Do you think you can get back on your own?" she asked. "I hate to say it, but both of us have taken our respective trains many times and not traveled through time. How will you know if you can get back?"

"We will not know until I try. I know that you cannot come with me, my love, as your mother needs you, but I must try."

"I wonder what Rory thought when we disappeared."

"I cannot imagine," Stephen said. "I do not know if we simply vanished, or faded as an apparition might."

The train slowed further, and Whitefish came into view.

Dani clutched Stephen's hand.

"We're here," she said. The implications of Stephen's arrival in her time now dawned on her. It would not be as simple as showing up in his time. There were issues of identification and citizenship status. They wore period costume. An astute policeman might observe them closely and ask for ID. What would Stephen show? Did he have identification? A passport from 1901?

She hoped they could manage for a few days. If Stephen had planned to stay forever, however, that would present an entirely new set of complications involving his date of birth, Social Security, a driver's license. She shook her head and resolved to take things one step at a time.

"I wonder what my mother will say about you," she said with a smile.

"I will be frank. I am a bit nervous about meeting her." Stephen gave a boyish shrug of his shoulders.

"She'll love you, I'm sure of it," Dani said. "Just like I do."

She kissed Stephen one more time, and rose to pull him up as the train came to a stop in front of the station.

"Let's do this," she grinned.

He grabbed her satchel and checked the seats. "My hat and yours seem to have disappeared. I shall look like a vagabond without my hat. Perhaps I could purchase one."

"You don't need a hat in my time, Stephen." Dani eyed his golden hair appreciatively. "No sense hiding that beautiful head of hair of yours."

Stephen blushed. "Beautiful indeed, woman."

Dani ignored the stares from fellow passengers as she and Stephen descended the train. He arrested on viewing the station.

"My word!" he said, enrapt. "What lovely architecture."

"It is, isn't it?" She tugged on Stephen's arm to get his attention. "Listen, dear, I've been trying to figure out what to do. My purse is lost, completely lost in time. I imagine it's at the King Street Station in Seattle, but I don't know. I have no money, no phone, so I can't call my mother to come get us. I usually get a rental car when I travel here by train, but I can't do that either. So, we'll have to get a taxi, and have him wait while I get some money from my mom. If she's home. Gosh, there's so much to do. My debit cards, a phone..."

Dani stopped at the confused look on Stephen's face.

"Oh, I'm sorry. You probably have no idea what I'm talking about."

He gave a small laugh. "I understand only a small portion of what you said, but if there is a concern with money, I have funds."

Dani, aware of constant stares around them at their attire, chewed on her lip.

"Your money is from the turn of the century, Stephen. It would definitely raise questions. I don't even know if we can use it. I'll bet a taxi driver would hesitate to take it."

Stephen furrowed his brow. "Why ever not?"

"Well, it would be like you trying to use money from the Civil War era."

"Ah, I see. Most of that currency is in private collections and museums now. What do you suggest?"

"Well, if my mother isn't home, we could try to use twenty dollars of your money to see if the taxi driver will take it when we get to my mother's house. I hate to do that though. I'm sure your money is actually worth more than the face value at any rate."

"Twenty dollars?" Stephen coughed. "For local transportation? I cannot imagine such a thing." He pulled his wallet from his jacket and pulled out a bank note.

Dani grinned. "Everything costs more now, dear, but we make more, too." She examined the money he handed her. "Oh, gosh, Stephen, this is quite a bit different from the money we use now. I think we should save this for an antique money dealer...if there is one around."

"Antique?" Stephen rubbed his chin and chuckled. "So, I am an antique now?"

Dani grinned. "I love antiques. Lots of people do. They have good bones, good structure." She reached on tiptoe to kiss him.

Stephen laughed.

Dani grabbed his hand and led him toward a taxi stand. "Hopefully my mother will be home, and I can just borrow the money from her for the moment."

Twenty minutes later, they pulled down a long paved drive and to the front of a large A-frame pine log cabin backed by evergreen trees.

"Please wait here while I get the money," she told the driver. She pulled a bemused Stephen from the vehicle. He had remained silent on the drive but clutched her hand as the taxi flew down the highway.

Dani trotted up to the front door and knocked on it. Her mother came to the door.

"Dani! What are you doing back here? I thought you weren't coming until right before the surgery."

Margaret Douglas, an older version of Dani, with silvering red hair, stopped and looked them up and down.

"What on earth are you wearing?" she laughed. "Is there a Victorian festival in town I don't know about?"

Dani, holding Stephen's hand, felt him stiffen.

"I'll explain in a minute. I lost my purse, Mom, and I need to pay the taxi. Neither one of us has any money. Can you loan me twenty bucks?"

Her mother narrowed her eyes and stared hard at Stephen for a moment.

"Come inside. I'll get my purse."

"No, we'd better wait here in case the driver thinks I'm trying to stiff him."

Margaret turned away.

"Dani," Stephen whispered. "She thinks I am a man without means. One who preys on women. I saw it in her eyes."

"Yup, I think you're right, Stephen. I'm not sure what I'm going to tell her, but I'll clear that right up."

Her mother returned with a twenty-dollar bill, and Dani ran down to the taxi to pay him. She returned to find her mother glaring at Stephen, and Stephen meeting her expression with a charmingly innocent smile. How could her mother resist that?

Dani grabbed Stephen's hand again.

"Mom, this is Stephen Sadler. Stephen, my mom, Margaret Douglas, or Maggie."

"Mrs. Douglas, I am honored to meet you. I have heard so much about you."

Dani's mother blinked. "Well, uh, thank you. It's nice to meet you as well. Come inside, you two."

They followed Maggie into the house, a comfortably furnished home with walls of highly varnished pine logs. Bright furniture livened the place, an open loft with an iron railing presided on the second floor. Her mother, widowed and retired from nursing, had moved to her new house a few years after Dani had relocated to Seattle for college and then stayed for work. Other than her current bout with cancer, she had been healthy and happy in her small community. Dani worried that she lived alone, but her mother had been on her own since Dani's father died when she was twelve. She had several close friends with whom she spent the majority of her time.

"Can I get you something? Some tea?"

Stephen looked to Dani, who nodded. "That would be great, Mom. In fact, I'll come help." Dani turned to follow her mother into the kitchen, throwing a reassuring look over her shoulder toward Stephen who stood with his hands laced behind his back gazing at the view of the mountains from the large floor-to-ceiling windows.

Maggie paused as they entered the kitchen."Okay, Dani, just what is going on? Why do you have some guy in tow who doesn't have a penny to his name? And what happened to your purse? Did something happen on the train on the way back?"

"Put the kettle on. I'll answer your questions."

Dani perched on a stool at the breakfast bar and thought quickly as her mother set the kettle onto boil.

"Well, I'd like to tell you that I traveled through time and ended up in Seattle at the turn of the twentieth century, but I guess you won't believe that?"

Her mother braced her hands on the opposite side of the breakfast bar, one eyebrow raised.

"Not likely." She waited.

Dani smiled. "And that Stephen was born in the nineteenth century, and I fell in love with him there?"

Her mother's other eyebrow quirked.

"You've only been gone two days. That's a lot of story for two days."

Dani sighed and thought fast. "No? Okay, you're right about the reenacting. I never told you about it before. Stephen and I were on our way to...Havre, Montana, for a Victorian/Edwardian festival, but I lost my purse. He didn't have his wallet on him because, well, the pockets of his costume weren't that big, so I had his wallet in my purse. I don't know whether it got stolen or I just can't find it. Anyway, since the train passed through Whitefish again, I thought we'd better jump off here and see what I could do. You know, get some temporary ID or access to my bank. Something."

Her mother's forehead creased. "You know, I think I like the time travel story better. It seems more simple."

"Okay," Dani grinned. "Have it your way."

The teakettle hissed and screeched, and Maggie turned toward it. Dani wiped the perspiration from her upper lip, and leaned back on her stool to look into the living room for Stephen. He was peering at the monitor of her mother's laptop computer on a small desk in the corner. The screensaver scrolled through images of nearby Glacier National Park.

Maggie poured the tea into mugs, and Dani grabbed Stephen's cup as well as her own. They returned to the living room.

"A Victorian festival in Havre, huh?" Maggie said to Stephen who swung around, startled. "Havre?" She looked toward Dani. "I can't imagine that small town having anything like a Victorian festival. Maybe a rodeo. Whose idea was this anyway?"

"Mine," Dani said blithely. "I've always been into reenacting the Victorian and Edwardian eras. Love it." She turned her back to her mother and handed Stephen his mug with a pointed look. Stephen nodded with a brief smile, and studied the mug in his hand with interest.

"Tea," she said. "A *mug* of tea." She emphasized the words for him, hating treating him like a child but knowing she must if he was to learn fast.

"Thank you, Mrs. Douglas. It looks delicious." Stephen took a sip and beamed. "Yes, quite good. I must take some home with me, if possible."

Maggie tilted her head and regarded him. "It's just generic store bought. I'm sure you have some in Seattle."

"Ah, yes," he replied with another hasty sip.

Maggie gestured for them to sit. Stephen waited until the women sat.

"So, how long have you been doing this reenacting thing?" Dani knew from her mother's tone that she still suspected something, but she hadn't believed the truth. Dani smiled. Her poor mother.

"Have you heard anything about your surgery since I left?"

Maggie turned a quick eye on Stephen who studied the graphic design on the side of the cup depicting a moose from Glacier National Park. His cheeks bronzed.

"He knows, Mom. I tell Stephen everything."

Stephen remained silent, continuing his perusal of his cup.

"Well, as a matter of fact, yes. They've moved the surgery up. To tomorrow."

Dani set her mug down on the wooden coffee table with a thump and a splash. Stephen looked up.

"Mom! How long have you known that? Did you know when I was here?"

"No, actually, they just called me yesterday afternoon and asked if I wanted to move surgery up. That *never* happens. They had a cancellation. So, I thought I'd go for it. I didn't call you because I thought I'd wait until it was over. You'd just left, and I didn't want you to have to drive all the way back...or take the train. You must need to get back to work."

"Do I look like I'm working, Mom?" Dani said. "Well, at any rate, I didn't have my cell phone, but I can't believe you weren't going to call me and tell me."

"Sarah and Jean are coming over, and they're going to stay with me."

Maggie and her childhood friends were like sisters, always there for each other, probably a significant reason why her mother never felt the need to marry again. Life with her mom had been like living with three single lively aunts full of giggles, local gossip, sympathetic ears, and the nurturing of three women who more than made up for Dani's lack of siblings or other family. Both her parents had been only children.

"Still, I wanted to be here." Dani picked up her tea and looked toward Stephen. He smiled gently at her, reassuringly, and she felt immeasurably better just knowing he was there. "Well, I'm glad we ended up back here then. We'll stay for your surgery, and I'll stay for your recovery. Stephen needs to get back."

"The house will be full, honey, with Sarah and Jean practically moving in as they threaten to do. I don't know where you'd stay."

"I can stay at a motel."

Maggie shook her head. "I hate to think of you doing that. I'm going to be fine, I just know it. The doctor said he can't say for sure until he operates, but he thinks with the surgery and oral chemotherapy for a couple of years, my chances are good."

Dani bit her lips, willing herself not to cry. It seemed she had cried so much over the last few days, always about a fear of loss. Now, the two people she loved most in the world were in one room together...at least for the moment. She swallowed her tears. She had nothing to cry about.

"I love you both, you know that? I'm so glad you're both here," she said on a watery chuckle. Maggie's eyes widened and she looked at Stephen. Stephen drew in a sharp breath but favored her with a tender smile, his blue eyes, so like his sister's, soft. An image of Susan's piquant small face came to her.

"Mom, what do you know about chronic bronchitis? Is it treatable with antibiotics?" Dani turned toward Stephen. "My mom was a nurse."

Stephen's eyes sharpened, and he waited for Maggie's response.

"Why? Who has chronic bronchitis?"

"Oh, just a friend. She lives in a city where they still burn a lot of coal and wood-burning fires. I was just wondering if that could be her problem. She's only eighteen."

"Where on earth does she live? Sounds like the dark ages."

Stephen coughed. "Quite," he said.

"I can't remember. Some little town. I only know her from the reenacting." Dani amazed herself with her newly discovered skill of lying. She'd never been able to lie to her mother, or Sarah or Jean as a teenager. They'd caught her out every time.

"Well, you're right. It's often brought about by environmental conditions and smoking. Acute bronchitis is often viral, and there isn't much that can be done about that."

"But if she doesn't smoke, and she gets ill a couple times a year, then it's chronic, right?"

"Yes, I would think so. Do they treat it with antibiotics? That would be best just to make sure an infection doesn't set in."

Dani looked at Stephen who clenched his teeth. She recognized the muscle twitch in his jaw.

"I'm not sure," she said. "Is there an over-the-counter antibiotic available?"

Maggie shook her head. "No, not legally. It has to be prescribed by a doctor. And anything illegal like you might get over the Internet wouldn't be safe."

Dani sighed and shot Stephen a sympathetic look. He looked away toward the window, his face pensive.

"Well, listen, how about I cook dinner?" Dani said. "You should probably get to bed early tonight. So should we. It was a long train ride."

"Are you...both...planning on staying here?" Maggie quirked an eyebrow.

Stephen rose quickly. "No, I could not impose."

"Yes, we are, Mom. I hope you don't mind. Stephen can take the day bed in the office."

"That's fine," Maggie shrugged. "What's for dinner? I can't eat past eight o'clock. Surgery, you know."

"Spaghetti?"

"Sounds great," Maggie said. "I'm just going to go call Sarah and Jean. I'll be back down in a few. Do you want to change, honey?"

Dani looked down at her dress and then at Stephen. "No, I'm good for now."

Her mother climbed the open stairway and went into one of the rooms in the loft area.

Stephen crossed the room quickly.

"I cannot stay here. It really would not be proper, Dani. Is there some sort of hotel I might stay at?"

"No." She reached up to kiss him quickly, and he froze, his eyes on the loft above. "I mean yes, there are hotels, but you're staying here. Relax, dear, we won't be sleeping together."

Stephen stiffened, but his lips twitched. "Danielle Douglas Sadler! Behave!"

Dani grinned and pulled him in for another kiss.

"Sadler?" her mother said, halfway down the stairs, her round-eyed expression showing shock. "Did you get married?"

CHAPTER NINE

"Mom! You scared me!" Dani squeaked. "I thought you went upstairs."

"I forgot my cell phone." She descended the rest of the stairs. "Did you get married without telling me?"

Dani chuckled. "No, Mom, not yet."

"Yet? Are you engaged?" Maggie stared at Stephen, her eyes surveying him from head to foot. "I don't mean to be rude, but you've never even mentioned Stephen before.

"Well, it's been a whirlwind romance," Dani said. She held onto Stephen's hand.

"Mrs. Douglas, I apologize for not requesting your permission to court Danielle...that is, Miss Douglas."

Dani chuckled as her handsome love tried hard to say the right thing in a world he didn't understand.

"That's okay, Stephen. Mom wouldn't expect that. She's just surprised because I never mentioned you before. In fact, I've never brought a guy home before."

"No, you haven't," Maggie murmured.

Stephen cleared his throat and bowed his head. "I am honored to be the first."

"So, are you engaged or not? I still don't understand," Maggie said.

Dani looked up at Stephen, with the certainty that she could never love anyone as much as she did him, even if they couldn't stay together forever.

"Yes, I am," she replied. "At least I think I am."

"You are engaged to me," Stephen said firmly. He possessively pulled her hand into the crook of his arm, and Dani relished the feeling of belonging to him.

She turned to her mother. "We're engaged."

Maggie shook her head. "Honestly, if I didn't know any better, I'd think you two just got engaged in front of my face. I'm going upstairs to call the girls. I'm not sure what they're going to make of this." She grabbed her cell phone from a table and turned away to climb the stairs again.

Dani watched her enter her room and turned to face Stephen with shaking hands.

"We're engaged and we don't even live in the same century," she said, keeping her voice low. "That's going to take some planning."

Stephen smiled and pulled both of her hands to his lips.

"I no longer believe it is an impossibility."

Dani cocked her head, gave him a wistful smile and turned to drag him into the kitchen. She pulled out a stool for him.

"Why don't you sit here while I cook?" She kissed him and turned away to find pots and pans.

"Your mother does not have servants?" he asked with interest.

"No, we're hopelessly middle class. Hardly rich enough to afford servants. Not even a maid." Dani tossed a grin over her shoulder as she gathered the ingredients.

"And what is it that you prepare?"

"Spaghetti? You've heard of spaghetti, right?"

"Ah! Yes. I have eaten spaghetti in Italy."

Dani paused to look at him. "Italy?" Not by plane, that was for sure.

"Yes, I quite enjoyed Italy. Beautiful country. I toured Europe one summer during college. In fact, Rory and I traveled together."

She resumed preparations. "By boat?"

"Yes, the passage took about six days, very fast."

Dani bit her lip against reporting six-hour flights to Europe. There had been too much shock for one day.

"Tell me about your father, Dani. I do not hear you speak of him."

Dani hunched her shoulders. "He died when I was twelve. I loved him very much. I still miss him." She turned to face Stephen and drew in a deep breath. "He was an old-fashioned guy. A little bit like you, I suppose." She tilted her head to look at him. "Not in looks but he had the same sorts of values that you do, maybe even the same courtesies. Odd, I hadn't really remembered that."

"He sounds like a fine man, Dani."

"He was. He died of lung cancer. Never even smoked a day in his life. Everybody gets cancer in my family, it seems."

"I am so sorry," Stephen said.

"Thank you," she said turning to stir the pasta. "He was a train conductor here in Whitefish. I got to ride the train with him when I was old enough to sit by myself while he worked. That's why I still take the train occasionally. I love it!" She threw a smile over her shoulder before returning to the stove.

"He loved my mom very much. Even as a child, I could see that. And she loved him. Never even dated another man after he died. But she hasn't been lonely. I once asked her why she didn't date. It seems like Dad was her one true love, and that was that."

"As you are to me," Stephen said softly.

****

Dani turned to him, her cheeks bright, her eyes luminous. In one hand, she held a wooden spoon bright red with sauce, in the other a glass jar of the sauce. He longed to take her into his arms but thought better of it given the imminent return of her mother.

"You should probably kiss me if you're going to say things like that," she said. She set down the spoon and jar and came around the counter toward him.

Stephen pulled her into his arms and kissed her in such a way as to leave no doubt that she would be his one true love.

He released her breathless and smiling, and he cupped her face in his hand.

"I've never been in love before," she said quietly. "Not like this. Not ever. I don't even know what to say or do."

"Nor I," said Stephen. "I have waited for you all my life, though I did not know it was you. I feel like a nervous schoolboy."

"Me too," Dani said. "Well, like a schoolgirl, anyway." She chuckled and turned her head to kiss the palm of his hand. "I don't know how this can work, I don't even know if it can, but I'm willing to try. The time traveling is the difficult part. Everything else with you is...easy." She ran her fingers along the side of his face.

"We have hurdles to overcome, that is certain. Whether we can travel through time at will is certainly the most important factor, you are right. If we can resolve that, I too believe everything else will be very simple...as long as we are together."

The sound of water boiling over onto the stove caught her attention, and she dashed over to turn down the burner.

"What on earth are you two talking about?"

Mrs. Douglas stood just inside the door of the kitchen, almost sagging against the frame. She clutched a small metal object in her left hand.

"Mom!" Dani said. "Why are you creeping around the house like this?" She turned off the stove and sprang forward to assist her mother.

"Creeping? I told you I'd be back downstairs. I'll tell you what's creepy. What I just heard."

Stephen opened his mouth to speak, but thought better of it. Dani knew her mother best, and he was not at all certain he might not precipitate an unfortunate fainting spell for the poor woman whose face had grown pale. That she was already ill alarmed him further.

"Come here, Mom, sit down," Dani said. "You look white as a ghost."

Stephen jumped to pull a chair out for her at a small round table in a corner of the large kitchen. Mrs. Douglas sank into the chair but not before favoring him with a look of suspicion. Dani sat down opposite her. Stephen returned to his position by the counter and laced his hands behind his back as he waited.

Dani reached for her mother's free hand and held it. Mrs. Douglas continued to clutch the small metal object in her other hand.

"Mom, what can I say to make this better?"

"Can you get me a glass of water? I feel kind of lightheaded."

Before Dani could rise, Stephen moved quickly into the kitchen.

"Glasses in the third cupboard, top left. Just use the tap water," Dani said, returning her attention to her mother.

"When I said I preferred your time traveling story, I was just kidding," her mother said in a shaky voice. "I'd really rather you were just wearing a costume."

"Gosh, Mom. I really didn't mean to bring all this on you when you're sick. I don't suppose you can just ignore this, and we can talk about it another time...when you're better?"

Stephen delivered the water as ordered. It would have been his preference to serve it with a crystal glass and bottled water instead of an odd orange plastic cup and water from the sink, but he assumed things had changed a great deal in the previous century.

Mrs. Douglas shook her head and took a drink. "No, I'd better hear it now. In case you disappear or something." She looked from Dani to Stephen, again with a suspicious expression. He gave her what he hoped was a reassuring smile, but she did not look reassured. He did not blame her. The timing of this revelation could not have been worse.

The small metal object on the table trilled with the sound of birds, startling him.

"I'd better take this," Mrs. Douglas said. "It's Sarah."

"Don't say anything," Dani whispered as Mrs. Douglas picked up the instrument and positioned it next to her ear.

"Hey, there," Mrs. Douglas spoke as if to Dani, but Dani sat back in her chair eyeing him with some alarm. He could only try to reassure her with his eyes. Susan had survived the revelation of their secret. Robert had survived the revelation of Ellie's secret. He himself had survived the discovery of Dani's time traveling, and he knew that although shocked, one's heart did not stop at the surprise though it felt as if it must.

"No, I'm fine. Yeah, Dani came back. Uh huh, she'll be here for the surgery, but then I don't know." Mrs. Douglas appeared to listen to the metal device in between speaking, almost as if it were a telephone such as he had in his home.

Dani waggled her eyebrows at her mother, and Stephen bit back a smile, thinking she must have been a very precocious child.

"I'll see you tomorrow." Mrs. Douglas pushed something on the miniature telephone, as Stephen now assumed it was, and set it down on the counter. He eyed it with interest wondering how the instrument worked without cords, wires or electricity.

"That was Sarah calling me back. She didn't answer earlier. So, what's going on?" She looked toward Stephen. "You should probably sit down. I'm not sure what to think about you, but having you hover above us like that is making me very nervous."

"My apologies," Stephen said. He took a seat next to Dani. "How can we help?" he asked.

"We should probably tell her," Dani said. "It's not like she didn't hear us."

For the next half hour, Dani explained what she understood about her time travel, with Stephen interjecting a few observations or comments. He understood that his presence was of interest to Dani's mother, and he patiently endured her rather merciless scrutiny of his person.

"Mom, will you stop staring at Stephen! He's got two arms, two legs, a couple of feet and a beautiful head of sandy hair. He's just like you and me, only older." Dani grinned. Stephen returned her smile, wondering that she could jest at the shock in her mother's face, but her humor had some effect as Mrs. Douglas's face lightened.

"Oh, I'm sorry. I can't help but stare. We always wonder what men and women were like in the old days, but to see one..." Seemingly unable to help herself, she studied Stephen again, and he coughed behind his hand and re-crossed his legs.

"Yes, of course," he murmured inconsequentially.

"Well, dinner got cold," Dani said. "I'd better warm it up again. Are you ready to eat?"

"I couldn't eat a thing right now," her mother murmured.

Dani sat down heavily and reached for her mother's hand. "Oh, Mom, I'm so sorry to confuse you like this. You need to eat. You'll be starving by tomorrow night."

"Okay, just a bit. It's getting close to fasting time." She did not move but continued to cast sideways glances at Stephen.

Stephen thought he had never quite tasted Italian cuisine such as Dani served, but it had a certain flavor that appealed. Along with Mrs. Douglas, his appetite suffered as well. He had not cared to worry Dani, but he was concerned for Susan and for the repercussions of his absence. Susan was a sensible girl, and were he not able to return to his own time, she would do reasonably well if in good health. He had left his estate in good order, and she stood to inherit the bulk.

But it was her health that worried him. If they could but procure these antibiotics Dani and her mother spoke of, perhaps Susan might be cured, or at least better situated for a speedy recovery the next time she fell ill. There was always the possibility he could return and attempt to bring his sister forward in time for treatment. Were that to fail, however, were he not able to return to Dani's time, he would lose her forever. And he did not think he could face that.

He smiled politely throughout the meal and responded when spoken to, but he was distracted as he contemplated how Dani and he could live out their lives together...in the same century. He did not think she would risk saying goodbye to her mother possibly forever and returning to his time, nor did he think she would enjoy living in his time, not when she clearly had the most modern and convenient amenities such as he witnessed at the moment. The ice box that hummed, the stove that lit without a match, the small box above the oven which heated sauce within minutes, the small portable telephone, the warmth of the house in the absence of clanging radiators—how could he ask her to give up all the comforts to which she was accustomed?

As if she could read his thoughts, Dani smiled at him and nodded her head. His heart rolled over at the affection in her eyes.

"Are you staying here?" Mrs. Douglas asked suddenly.

"Yes, I thought I mentioned that. Stephen can sleep on the couch."

"No, I mean *are you staying here...*in this time? Are you going back to the past?" Mrs. Douglas pressed her lips together. Moisture pooled in the older woman's eyes. Stephen's throat tightened at her expression.

"We don't know, Mom," Dani said softly. "It's possible that I could travel back and forth. Stephen can't stay. He has an eighteen-year-old sister who needs him. She's the one that's sick with bronchitis, and they don't have the right antibiotics for her."

"I can get those for you," her mother said. "I still have connections. My doctor will give me anything."

Stephen sat up straighter.

"Really?" Dani breathed. She turned to Stephen. "Did you hear that?"

"Mrs. Douglas, I could not impose...but I will, for my sister's sake. Thank you!" Stephen took her hand in his and placed a kiss on the back.

"Oh my!" Mrs. Douglas said, her cheeks red. "He really *is* old fashioned, isn't he?" She laughed for the first time that day, a charming sound much like Dani's laugh.

"Thanks for cooking, Dani," Mrs. Douglas rose, and Stephen stood. She gave him an odd look. "I'm going to go upstairs and get ready for bed. If you don't mind, Stephen, I'd like to borrow my daughter for a few minutes."

"Certainly, Mrs. Douglas." Stephen bowed his head.

Dani squeezed his hand as she passed him and went upstairs with her mother. Stephen surveyed the table and wondered how the dishes would be cleared. Surely, Dani did not wash the dishes herself, did she? No servants? Such a hard life she and her mother must lead.

****

Dani's mother settled onto the large king-size bed in her room. Dani, as she had done many times over the years, crawled onto the bed to lie next to her.

"I can't tell you how bad I feel about laying all this on you right now," Dani said. "But I had to get back here, and it's a good thing I did."

Her mother looked at her. "I'm glad you managed to get back." She rubbed her forehead. "I still can't believe we're talking about time travel though."

"I know! I couldn't either, but it didn't really feel like a dream either. I'm not the only one either. There's this gal, Ellie? She traveled back about six months ago. Now, she's married with a baby on the way, happy as a clam."

"Do you think there are more?" Maggie asked, her brow furrowed.

"I imagine there are, Mom, but I don't know. Don't look so worried. They're not aliens." Dani chuckled, but she hated to see the concern on her mother's face. She sobered quickly.

"Mom, I'm not real sure what to do. There's a chance that if I return with Stephen, I may not be able to get back. Maybe we can't get back at all, and that would be devastating to Stephen's sister. She'd have enough money to live well, but she would be alone. Their parents died when she was younger."

She drew a deep breath.

"But I don't think I can say goodbye to you forever either." Her throat ached at the thought. "I know you have Sarah and Jean, and your life here, but..." Dani couldn't form words. She didn't know what to say.

"But you're my daughter, and I don't want to lose you," her mother finished. A tear slid down her face, and Dani froze.

What had she been thinking? That she could happily return to 1901 and live out her life with Stephen? Leaving her mother? Forcing her to lose her only child? Possibly forever? No! She couldn't do it. Not right now.

Dani wiped the tear from her mother's face with a trembling hand. She thought about Stephen waiting for her downstairs, and she struggled for air, quietly attempting to drag in a ragged breath. Pain coursed through her body, originating from somewhere near her chest...her heart. She would stay in the present. Stephen would return without her.

"I'm sorry. I don't know why I'm bawling like a baby," her mother said with a shaky laugh.

"Because you're sick and scared, and then I've brought all this bizarreness to you at the worst possible time. Don't worry about anything, Mom. I'm staying here. I'm not going anywhere."

"You're right, Dani. I *am* scared. I'm scared of the surgery, and terrified that the treatment won't work." She wiped at her eyes with an embarrassed smile. "I know I'm supposed to be used to this, being a nurse and everything, but it doesn't seem to help at the moment."

Dani squeezed her mother's hand. "I can only imagine, Mom. I wish you didn't have to go through this."

"Thanks, honey. I know." She rubbed at her eyes. "I think I'm going to see if I can get some sleep now. Why don't you go downstairs and see what your historical gentleman is doing?"

Dani managed a crooked smile. She kissed her mother on the cheek.

"Sleep tight. I'll see you in the morning."

"Good night, hon," her mother said. "Shut the door behind you, will you?"

Dani returned downstairs to find Stephen in the kitchen, jacket off, his sleeves rolled back, washing the dinner dishes by hand. Handsome in a dark vest, he looked like a pin-up poster some woman might hang in her bedroom of a Victorian man.

He smiled broadly at her arrival, and she wrapped her arms around his waist, ignoring his wet and soapy hands.

"You did dishes," she said in wonder. "I can't believe you did dishes."

"Nor can I," he said with a laugh. "But I persevere." He kissed the top of her head, and managed to pick up a dishtowel to wipe his hands. Once dried, he wrapped his arms around her and leaned back to look into her face.

"Is everything well, my love? Your mother?"

Dani pressed her head against his chest and nodded. Then she shook her head.

"She's fine, just tired. She's scared too."

"Yes, she must be. This sort of surgery is not done in my time, as you can imagine. I hope for a successful outcome. Is it very dangerous?"

Dani shook her head. "The surgery? No, not really, but the disease is. There have been remarkable breakthroughs in curing many forms of cancer, but nothing is ever certain. She will probably have to take medicine following the surgery for a while." Dani didn't have the heart to explain chemotherapy to Stephen at the moment.

His embrace tightened. "I truly hope for the best for her, Dani."

"I know you do. You're such a good man. I love you so much." The last words came out on a sob.

"You are crying, my love," Stephen said softly. He lifted her chin to look at her face. Dani closed her eyes against the tenderness in his soft blue eyes. "You are not returning with me, are you?"

Dani shook her head, keeping her eyes closed, hoping he wouldn't drop his arms and walk away from her.

"I suspected as much. You cannot leave your mother during her illness."

Dani squeezed him tighter, tears rolling down her cheeks. She shook her head silently.

Stephen picked her up in his arms and carried her into the living room. He lowered himself to the sofa and settled Dani onto his lap where he held her, murmuring soothing words, while she quietly cried. Tears spent, Dani looked up at him.

"Isn't this a little risqué for you?" She gave him a crooked smile.

"It is," he chuckled, burying his face in her hair. "Quite improper, I assure you."

She sighed and laid her head back down.

"When will you leave?" she asked.

"Tomorrow night. I noted that the train leaves at 8:56 p.m. I will stay for your mother's surgery and then I will take the train back to Seattle."

Dani raised her head again to stare at him. "What if you don't manage to travel back, Stephen? What if you end up in Seattle in my time? That would be awful! I can't imagine you lost in that big city...the cars, the highways, the fast pace of everything."

"I may be out of my element, as you once were, Dani, but I am not a child. Should that occur, I would come back to be with you here. Or perhaps I might look for my house to see if it still exists, and lay myself at the mercy of the present owner." He smiled reassuringly. Dani wasn't reassured.

"I'm not sure, Stephen. There is a reason Ellie and I traveled to the past, and into the same year, but I don't know what it is. It can't just be random. Otherwise, the concept of time travel would be much better known and widely accepted. Most people don't believe it's possible. Wouldn't you have heard if someone from the past could have traveled forward in time and then returned? I mean, millions of people have slept on a train and not traveled through time." She sighed impatiently. "I'm not explaining this very well, I know, but what if you can't travel back in time without me. What if you only traveled because you were holding me at the time?"

"Believe me, I have pondered many of these possibilities, Dani, but I have no recourse. I must try to get back to Susan. I cannot abandon her, not if it is within my power to return. I am the only parent she has known for years."

"I know," Dani said. She buried her face in his neck, luxuriating in the smell of his skin, while she brainstormed. She popped her head up again.

"What if I go with you, and when we get to Wenatchee, you sleep while I stay awake. I'll hold your hand, and if you start to *disappear* or whatever it is we do, I'll let go. You travel, and I stay in this time." A surge of pain hit her chest again at her final words, but she took a deep breath and it passed, leaving an ache in its wake.

"Oh, my love," Stephen said, tightening his arms around her. "This seems such an intricate matter. I believe your theory is correct. I have taken the train to Chicago many times, and never experienced anything other than fatigue. It seems likely that you are the key—the cause of the time travel, at least for us. I cannot say why Ellie came from the future to our time.

"Well, what we both found was love." She kissed him tenderly. "Maybe when two people are meant to be together, no matter what century they live in, they will find each other. I knew I loved you almost from the first time I met you."

"And I you, sweeting. You are the love of my life," Stephen said. He buried his face in her hair and held on tightly, a shudder passing through his body. Dani didn't know whether it was from joy or pain. She suspected both.

****

The following day, Dani and Stephen waited at the hospital while her mother underwent surgery. Her mother's best friends, Sarah and Jean, both tall and slim middle-aged women, waited as well, eyeing Stephen with varying degrees of interest and curiosity. Dani introduced him but didn't go into detail about their relationship. They discussed her mother at length—her illness and recovery, which they noted they had under control. Dani knew her extended presence would only get in the way in the smaller house, and she resolved privately to return to Seattle in the near future. Her mother didn't want her to disappear forever, but she really didn't need Dani there to care for her on a daily basis either.

The doctor emerged to tell them that her mother's surgery had gone well, and that the tumor, smaller than expected, had been removed. He advised them he expected a full recovery with an excellent prognosis following chemotherapy.

Dani clung to Stephen's hand. She knew he didn't understand some of the medical terms, and in fact, invariably stiffened when the word *breast* was mentioned, but to his credit, he remained silent. The night had been long, and Dani was tired. Her mother, unable to sleep, had come downstairs several times in search of bottled water, and Dani had accompanied her back to her room and stayed with her until she fell asleep again.

Reassured by the doctor's prognosis, Dani popped in to see her mother in recovery with a smile on her face. Her mother, groggy, would be sent to her room, and Sarah and Jean had made plans to stay with her.

Feeling a bit like a fifth wheel as she had often in the past in the presence of the three best friends, she set about restoring the contents of her missing purse. Using her mother's car, she acquired money from a branch of her bank with a copy of her birth certificate, and stopped by the Department of Motor Vehicles to get a replacement license.

"Let's get you some clothes, Stephen. You look handsome, but miserable in the same clothes." Dani herself had changed into an old pair of jeans and a T-shirt from the spare clothing she kept at her mother's house, eliciting admiring glances from Stephen.

She pulled out of the Department of Motor Vehicles and headed to a nearby mall.

"I know this has been difficult for you, Stephen, especially the references to mom's...anatomy, but you've been so great." She smiled at him. Like an enthusiastic young boy, he fingered buttons on the car, his seatbelt, the door and window locks, and the radio, startling himself when music came on.

"It is my pleasure to provide what comfort I can to you, Dani," he said. "I can see that there have been many, many changes over the past century. Many," he emphasized as if he hadn't said it enough. He seemed remarkably resilient, much more so than Dani had felt when encountering his era.

"Sarah and Jean were quite taken with you," she said. "But who wouldn't be?"

Stephen's cheeks bronzed. "You flatter me too much, my love. As long as *you* are taken with me, I am happy."

Dani grinned. "Which reminds me, Sarah is going to drop the antibiotics for Susan off at the house after they leave the hospital. My mother called her last night, and Sarah picked them up from the pharmacy. Mom's friends were nurses too. Those three did everything together."

"Yes, they do seem very close to your mother," Stephen said. "Very protective."

Out of the corner of her eye, she saw Stephen study her face.

"You're wondering if I felt left out, aren't you?"

"How did you know?" he asked with a chuckle.

"The same way you knew how I felt. We just seem to know each other, don't we?" Dani said.

"That we do."

"Yes, actually, many times over the years I felt left out. I don't think my mom meant to do that, but..." Dani shrugged. "Neither Sarah nor Jean has kids, and they all had the same interests. Card games, crocheting, genealogy. I did get to crochet with them once in a while. But I had my own life too. You know, school, after-school activities, my own friends."

She threw him a quick look.

"I wish we could travel back and forth at will. That way she wouldn't lose a daughter, and we could stay together."

"Perhaps it is not an impossibility."

"I don't know," she murmured. "Ellie won't try it. She's afraid she won't be able to get back to Robert. And what if she had her child and couldn't get back to her child. That would be a nightmare."

"Yes, it would." Stephen turned to look out the window at the passing scenery. "I cannot imagine Ellie taking that risk. Nor can I imagine risking that with you."

Dani swallowed hard. "I should not have brought it up again. It only hurts us both."

Stephen cleared his throat and turned to smile at her.

"Let us enjoy our time together now."

CHAPTER TEN

A half hour later, Stephen emerged from a dressing room in jeans and a T-shirt, revealing a well-muscled chest and arms. Dani blinked. The jeans, a snug fit, curved over his backside and ran the length of his long legs. Her handsome and proper Victorian gentleman had transformed into a very sensuous and rugged cowboy.

"Oh, my goodness," she breathed. "Look at you."

Stephen blinked sheepishly. He looked down at the clothing. "Do you not think the trousers are a bit tight? And the shirt? Must it cling so to my torso?"

"Well, yes, the T-shirts normally cling, and no, I don't think the jeans are too tight. You're just used to wearing a coat and looser slacks." She sighed like a star-struck teenager. "We can get you something more loose if you want."

"Is my appearance pleasing to you?" he asked, his eyes flickering away from hers, almost shyly.

"Yes, Stephen Sadler, your appearance is most definitely pleasing to me."

"Then I shall wear the clothing. I enjoy the look in your eye." He grinned.

Unable to keep herself from touching him at every opportunity, she hopped off her bench and slid into his arms, the fit perfect. He kissed the tip of her nose.

"And footwear? I should like some shoes such as yours."

Dani looked down at her trainers. "Running shoes? I would have thought you more of a boot kind of guy. No cowboy boots?"

"In the absence of a horse or a cow, I suspect I should probably dress as you do." At the moment, a man walked by sporting a set of cowboy boots, and both Stephen and Dani eyed him pensively.

"Ya know? I think the sneakers will be just fine," Dani said with a laugh.

They emerged from the store a half hour later with Stephen dressed like a modern American male, carrying his suit and shoes in a shopping bag. The plastic bag itself seemed to fascinate him, and she delighted in his enthusiasm for her time.

They returned to the hospital to check on her mother, who slept. Sarah and Jean waited in her mother's room, silently reading magazines. Their eyes widened at the sight of Stephen in jeans and T-shirt, but they remained silent in the quiet hospital room. Dani grinned and waggled her eyebrows to which they responded with grins and expressions of approval. Her mother had agreed not to tell them about Stephen or the time travel. Stephen nodded politely in their direction and made a hasty retreat to await Dani in the hallway.

"What would you like to do now, Stephen?" Dani asked, linking her arm in his as they left the hospital.

"As long as I am with you, it does not matter."

"Have you ever been to Glacier National Park?"

"I saw a reference to it on the tea mug you served me last night. What is this park? What shall we see?"

"Gosh, that's right, it wasn't even established in your time." Dani climbed into the car, and watched him lovingly as he fumbled with his seatbelt. "Well, we can't see a lot of it today because the road through is closed for the winter, but there are rivers and waterfalls and hiking trails and beautiful flowers in bloom and bear and moose and, of course, glaciers."

"Lead on," Stephen said. "It sounds wonderful, much like our Mount Rainier."

"It *is* a lot like Mount Rainier."

Dani kept up a running commentary on the sights as they drove the forty-five minutes to the park. Dani stopped at Apgar Village and picked up a few sandwiches and some coffee for an impromptu picnic lunch. She drove out of the village and along Going-to-the-Sun Road to Avalanche Creek where the road was closed for the winter before it entered the alpine regions. Stephen's wonder at the beauty of the majestic glacier-covered mountains filled her with joy. They turned back and found a picnic spot at the edge of Lake McDonald, a ten-mile long, one-mile wide lake that mirrored the surrounding glaciated mountains and preened like a girl in a new dress.

Dani and Stephen got out of the car and took their lunch to the picnic bench.

"If you look across the lake, you can see a few cabins." Dani pointed to several cabins and A-frame homes perched on the side of the large rectangular glacial lake. "Those belong to the descendents of people who owned property before the land was incorporated into a national park."

"In about ten years, your time, the railroad will build lodges for visitors to stay at. The road we just traveled will be built in about thirty more years. If I can't come back to your time, Stephen, you'll have to come here...to bring your family here."

Stephen shook his head and grabbed her hand. "Do not speak that way. I cannot listen."

"I'm not saying this to upset you, Stephen, but I would regret it if there were things I didn't say when I had the chance. I'll come back to Glacier many times in the future. It's like a local park. And it would make me so happy to know that you had seen it in the early years when the park was being developed, and the beautiful chalets and lodges were being built...when they were fresh and new. It would make me so happy to know that you had been here, and that your loved ones had been here too."

Stephen sighed heavily. "My loved one is here, Dani. Now."

"But *if* we are parted, *if* we can't be together again, you *will* marry and have a family, Stephen." She turned earnest eyes on him. A muscle twitched in his jaw.

"You make it sound as if you can direct the course of my life, my love. You do not have that power. Whether I marry or not, or whether I have children or not depends entirely on you." He leaned in to kiss her.

"I understand that you have fears about our future, as have I. And I am willing to offer what comfort I can in that direction, but I will not, Dani, tolerate further discussion of my possible marriage to another woman. It simply will not occur."

Dani stiffened, a bit taken aback by the unexpected anger in his eyes.

"In the eventuality that the worst comes to pass, I am, however, willing to come back here, as you suggest, perhaps with Susan and her children, to watch the park develop as you wish."

"Then you do understand," Dani said, relaxing. "I just want to know that you're happy and living life to its fullest."

"And I want that for you, Dani, but I will have no way of knowing."

She shook her head. "Not unless I tuck a note into the hand of a sleeping passenger on the train, I guess."

Stephen jerked his head in her direction, and then burst out into laughter. Dani joined him, and the somber mood was lightened for the moment.

Lunch finished, they drove out of the park and returned to Whitefish. Dani stopped by to visit with her mother, who now sat up in bed sipping on some soup. Stephen waited in the lounge at Dani's request.

"I didn't think you'd want a stranger in here," Dani told her mother.

"Thanks, hon, but there are plenty of strangers wandering around in here. Why don't you bring him in?"

Dani called Stephen in from the waiting area, and he entered the room.

"How are you feeling, Mrs. Douglas?" he said.

Dani's mother blinked. "My gosh, what did you do to him? I wouldn't have recognized him."

Dani laughed and took Stephen's hand. "I know. Isn't he gorgeous? Either way!"

Stephen's face flamed. "Please, ladies, you are making me blush like a schoolboy."

Dani's mother smiled. "I'd laugh, but it hurts too much. Did you get the pills Sarah picked up?" She looked at Dani.

"No, we haven't been back to the house yet. Thank you so much, Mom. I'm so grateful."

"Now, make sure your sister doesn't have an allergic reaction to them, Stephen. Watch her closely. If her throat starts to swell or she breaks out in a rash, discontinue the pills immediately and call your doctor. In fact, I am not at all sure you should be dispensing these without the knowledge of your doctor."

"I am not sure of the consequences of bringing such advanced medication to his attention," Stephen replied. "As you can imagine, time travel is not a normal thing in my time."

"It isn't here, either. Still, make sure she's not taking the other antibiotic he prescribed. She shouldn't take both. And the instructions are on the bottles. I've given you enough for about six episodes of bronchitis. Hopefully, that will be enough. Poor thing. Is it very smoggy where you live?"

"Smoggy?" Stephen asked. He turned to Dani with an inquiring eye.

"A combination of smoke and fog, I think, but yes, Mom, there's plenty of pollution from chimney smoke and the use of coal."

"You ought to consider taking her out of the city."

"You are not the first person to say so, Mrs. Douglas. My physician recommended the same thing."

"I hope you think about it. Buy a place around here!" she grinned. "You can spend summers here at least...that is, if you don't have to work."

266

Stephen smiled. "I do not have to work, thank you, Mrs. Douglas, although I do enjoy teaching history at our local university." He looked at Dani. "Perhaps I shall purchase a summer place here as you suggest. It is truly spectacular, and I feel very at home here."

Dani reached for his hand. The nurse came in to check her mother's bandage, and they left. Sarah and Jean would soon return. Dani opted not to say anything to her mother about leaving but would leave Sarah a note at the house where she would surely stop by the following morning.

"Dinner? Are you hungry?" Dani asked. "It's getting late. I could make some sandwiches at the house."

"Famished," Stephen said.

They returned to the house, and Dani made sandwiches for them from cheeses and cold cuts in her mother's refrigerator. Sarah had left Susan's antibiotics on the kitchen counter. Following the impromptu dinner, Dani went upstairs to get the satchel. She left Ellie's clothing in there with the hope Stephen could return at least some of the borrowed clothing, and she brought the bag downstairs. She stowed the pills inside and gave Stephen the bag with a shaking hand.

"Some of Ellie's clothing is in there. Please return them to her for me."

"I will, my love. I think I had better put my suit on," Stephen said with a wry smile. "It would not do to arrive back in 1901 with my new modern clothing."

While Stephen changed, Dani stared out the window at the mountains, lost in thought, wondering what the next day would bring. Given the long days of early fall, the sun would not set until the approximate departure time of the train.

Stephen returned to the living room and came up behind her. He wrapped his arms around her, and she rested her head against his chest.

"I love you, Stephen. I will always love you, no matter what happens."

"And I will always love you, Dani." He buried his face in her hair. "Please come to me," he whispered. "When the time is right, please come. I do not think I can face the years without you."

She turned to face him. "I'll try," she said quietly. "I'll try." She had promised herself she wouldn't cry, but holding back the tears made her throat ache. "Are you ready?"

He nodded.

Dani wrote out the note for Sarah telling her that she had to return to Seattle but would be back the following day. It would cause comment, maybe a little bit of concern, but it was better than telling her mother outright what they planned. Dani couldn't worry her mother that she might get caught in whatever time travel process occurred and disappear.

Stephen took the clothing he bought that day, folded it carefully and put it in the satchel.

"Are you taking the new clothes?" Dani asked with a lift of her eyebrow.

"I am," he said firmly. "I will treasure them."

Dani wondered if the man could possibly touch her heart more than he already did.

They drove to the train station and entered the terminal to buy the tickets. Just in case something didn't occur by Wenatchee, Dani bought tickets for Seattle. They waited outside the station for the arrival of the train. Dani noted with amusement that passersby, especially women, eyed Stephen with interest. He didn't look particularly out of place, especially in the absence of his derby, but he was a very striking man in his jacket, vest and trousers, and she didn't blame the women for ogling him.

"Are you planning on wearing the jeans, T-shirt and tennis shoes at some point?" Dani asked with amusement.

"Will you don your dress at some point?"

"Yes, I will," Dani said. "I hadn't thought about it, but yes, I will. I may really join a Victorian/Edwardian reenactment group."

"There is no group for me to join," Stephen said with a pretend pout. "I shall just don the clothing and move about the house pretending I am a man of the twenty-first century. When do you think the clothing will come into fashion?"

"Hmmm...those jeans? Maybe about the 1950s. I don't know, Stephen. You'd better take care of yourself if you want to make it to the fifties." Dani realized what she had just said—almost predicted the span of his life—and she squeezed his hand.

"I'm sorry, Stephen. I don't even like the way that sounded. I don't want to think in those terms."

She heard the sound of the train whistle and the rumble of the cars on the track. "The train is here. I feel like crying, and I'm not even saying goodbye to you yet."

"We are still together for now, my love. Let us hold onto that."

The train pulled into the station, and they rose. Darkness had fallen, and the lights on the platform illuminated the gleaming silver of the train.

"We have to get onto the observation car." She pointed to the car, and they boarded the train at that entrance. They settled themselves into the same seats on which they'd arrived, luckily vacant, and Dani tucked herself into the crook of Stephen's arm, unwilling to be away from his warmth for even a moment.

"We're supposed to get into Wenatchee in seven and a half hours, at just about dawn with the time change," Dani said, looking at the car's digital clock on the wall. "We should have the observation car to ourselves, I would think. It's too dark to be able to see anything outside except for a few lights from towns and farms."

Dani was correct. Other than the occasional wandering passenger, no one else took a seat in the observation car. The conductor came by to check their tickets and moved on, dimming the overhead lights as he left the car.

"I think I have to stay awake, and you have to go to sleep sometime before we get to Wenatchee, Stephen. You could sleep now if you want."

"Not a chance, my love. I will stay awake with you as long as possible. I will not lose one minute of my time with you in slumber. I am still not certain how this can work. If we both need to be sleeping for the travel to occur, how will you know to let go?"

"I don't know, Stephen, but we've got to try. And if I accidentally travel back in time again, then I'll just take the next train east and do it all over again—this time, by myself." She smiled, but her heart wasn't in it.

They settled in to watch the darkness, their faces reflected on the glass windows from the soft overhead lighting. An occasional lonely light in the distance broke the blackness of the night. The rocking motion of the train and the warmth of Stephen's body were hard to resist, and Dani's eyelids drooped. She jerked several times when she realized she'd fallen asleep for a moment.

"You should sleep, Dani," Stephen said quietly. "I will wake you when the time approaches."

"I have to stay awake," she said with a grimace. "Not that I wouldn't rather just sleep in your arms forever, but..."

"That notion appeals to me as well," Stephen said with a chuckle. "Shall we stretch our legs?"

Dani clutched the seat edge. "I know nothing will probably happen until Wenatchee, if Ellie's experience and my experience are anything to go by, but I'm actually afraid to move from the seat."

Stephen rose, pried her fingers loose and pulled her up. "What is the worst that can happen, my love? That we arrive in Seattle in the present time? You have a home there, do you not? We shall have a roof over our heads, and most importantly, we shall still be together."

Dani wrapped her arms around him. "Together," she whispered. "I wish we could."

They strolled the car, even daring to venture into the two adjoining cars, but only for a few minutes before Dani panicked and demanded they return to the observation car. Stephen waxed enthusiastic about the amenities on the train. Dani appreciated the modernity of it, but thought she preferred the Victorian beauty of the older carriages. They retook their seats and talked of Susan, Dani's mother, and their lives. They mutually avoided discussion of the future.

The train barreled on through the night, stopping at several small towns along the way. A stop in the larger city of Spokane, Washington, brought Stephen to the car door.

"Shall we step off the train and stroll a bit? I would love to see Spokane in modern times."

Dani hovered at the door, hanging onto his arm. Only three and a half hours until Wenatchee.

"What if you step off the train and disappear? You know, travel in time? What if the train is the key, not me? What if—"

Stephen kissed her forehead. "Shhhh, Dani. Do not fret. The train may be an element, but it is not the key. Remember, I left the train at your home in Whitefish and did not *disappear*."

"Oh! You're right, of course," she said with a nervous laugh. "I'm getting anxious, saying dumb things."

"Not dumb, never dumb," he murmured. "Shall we? Remember, we are still together. Hold my hand."

Dani took his hand, and they descended the stairs. The train depot clock said 2:00 a.m. The city seemed quiet, and there wasn't much to see really.

"Come, let us go into the terminal to explore. I heard they are going to construct a large train station next year with an imposing clock tower." He led her by the hand, and they entered the terminal—a fairly sterile, ubiquitous building with nothing out of the ordinary to recommend it. Passengers waited in lines to board the train, most of them bleary eyed at the late hour.

Stephen paused and studied the terminal with less excitement than she had seen him show in the past.

"I think I know what you're talking about, Stephen, and I hate to say it, but that terminal must have come and gone. There is a clock tower now, but it's part of something called Riverfront Park. I think I remember seeing old pictures showing it as part of a large railroad station, but that wasn't here. They must have already torn down the building—which wasn't even built in your time yet."

Stephen shook his head. He gripped her hand tightly. "It is hard to conceive that buildings have been built and demolished in the years that lie between us, my love. I feel very old." He smiled, but the spark was gone from his eyes. "Let us return to the train."

They retook their seats and held onto each other as the train left Spokane and ventured out into the plains of Eastern Washington. The remaining hours to Wenatchee alternately flew by and dragged, depending on Dani's chaotic emotions. She tried hard not to doze, but her eyelids drooped once more.

"Don't let me sleep," she whispered as she snuggled against Stephen.

"I will wake you if you do."

"You have to sleep."

"Yes, I know," Stephen sighed.

****

"Wenatchee, thirty minutes," the conductor said on his way through the observation carriage. Stephen looked down at Dani's tousled redhead resting on his chest. The time approached, and he had no idea what would occur—if anything.

From the moment he had met her, they seemed destined to be together, his heart's desire. And yet, here they were on the train trying to find a way to part—something that neither one of them wanted.

Exhausted, he no longer seemed able to think clearly. He knew he should awaken Dani and sleep himself, but his exhaustion did not translate into drowsiness. Nervous energy hummed through his body.

"Dani," he whispered against the top of her hair. "Wake up, Dani."

Dani jerked awake and bolted upright to look at him with stricken eyes. She looked toward the clock and relaxed.

"I shouldn't have fallen asleep. I could have slept through the whole thing—if there is a *thing*."

"I did not have the heart to wake you. You look so tired."

"What about you, Stephen? You need to get to sleep. I know that's not a recipe for relaxing, but you *really* need to get to sleep." She grinned slightly. She put the satchel in his lap. "Hold onto that and don't let go. For Susan."

His fingers closed around the bag. "I will try to sleep, my love. I would not do this for any amount of money in the world except for Susan. I truly would not."

Dani kissed him, a long lingering kiss that only served to remove ideas of sleep from his head.

"Any more of that, my love, and I will not sleep a wink."

Dani smiled, and brought his head to her shoulder. She wrapped an arm around him. "Here, it's time for me to hold you."

271

Stephen stretched out his legs and closed his eyes, listening to the rhythmic, if rapid, beating of her heart as her chest rose and fell with her breath. He was so very tired.

He opened his eyes quickly.

"Remember to let go."

"I will," she said. "Shhhhh.... Sleep."

CHAPTER ELEVEN

Stephen opened his eyes to the red velvet-upholstered back of the bench. Beyond, the image of dark mahogany paneling and the soft yellow lighting of the globe sconces, accompanied by the sound of the train rumbling on the tracks, told him he had returned to his own time. His fingers clutched the satchel on the seat beside him.

He dreaded raising his head, knowing even without looking that Dani was not there. He could feel her absence, as if half his soul were missing. He straightened, swallowing against his desire to scream her name. Several passengers lounged in the observation car, sipping tea, visiting. Dani was not among them. Resisting the urge to dash through the car peering into faces and asking if they had seen Dani, he knew it was futile. Dani was where she needed to be, and he had returned to his own time.

"Would you care for anything, sir?" a steward, sporting a tray, asked.

Stephen tried to focus on his words.

"Sir? Would you like something?"

Stephen shook his head. "Where are we? What time is it?

"About an hour away from Seattle, Sir. It is 10 p.m."

"Thank you," Stephen said automatically. The velvet curtains of the observation car had been drawn against the night, and he could not see out.

He rose abruptly, and strode to the door of the connector, as if he could somehow walk off the train, but he paused, his hand on the door. Jumping off the train would solve nothing. Despite his grief, he could not forget the reason why he and Dani had parted. He needed to return to his sister, and Dani to her mother.

He pushed aside one of the curtains and stared into the black night. Not even an occasional light blinked in the distance, not in his time.

Electricity was not used so freely as it was in the future.

Stephen settled himself in the library, desirous of being alone, away from the prying eyes of the man and woman sitting in the observation car. He pressed a hand against his chest as if to massage the place where his heart ached. His arms felt barren and empty, his being incomplete. He picked up the newspaper listlessly, and tossed it aside again to stare morosely at the connector door. And so he passed the time until the train arrived in Seattle.

With no carriage awaiting him, he hailed a commercial conveyance. With money that once again served as proper currency, he paid the driver on arrival at his residence. Mrs. Oakley ran out of the house, and his heart thudded.

"What is it?" he asked tersely. The older woman's look of distress warned him the situation was dire. "Miss Susan?"

"She is well, Mr. Sadler," Mrs. Oakley said hurriedly. "What has happened? Is Mrs. Sadler with you?"

Stephen relaxed, but found himself resenting Mrs. Oakley's well-meaning questions.

"She stayed behind with her mother," he answered shortly. He strode past the housekeeper, partially aware of her taken aback expression at his abrupt response, but uncaring at the moment.

He ran up the stairs to Susan's room and knocked on the door. From the carriage, he had seen the light in her bedroom illuminate.

"Enter," she said. Stephen opened the door, and his sister flew into his arms.

"Stephen, I heard the carriage arriving and hoped I was not going to have to entertain visitors at this late hour. I am so glad it was you."

Stephen embraced her, and held her back to look at her. She wore a dressing gown over her nightgown.

"I would have rather hoped you were glad to see me, dearest." She looked well, her cheeks with a slight rose tinge. A huskiness remained in her throat, but he knew that was to be expected.

"You are back sooner than I expected. I thought you would be gone for several days."

"It has been several days, my dear."

"Not more than two. Where is Dani? Is she in her room? Can I see her?" Susan turned toward the door, but Stephen stilled her with a hand on her arm.

"She is not here, Susan. She—she needed to stay with her mother."

"Her mother?" Susan's face paled, and he wondered if he should have lied. "What do you mean her mother? Her mother is in the future!" Tears pooled in Susan's eyes as the realization of Stephen's words dawned on her.

She sat down heavily on the sofa.

"She has gone back to the future," she said dully.

"Yes, I am sorry, dearest." He sank down next to her to take her in his arms, but she stiffened. "You are angry with me."

Susan nodded silently, her body rigid as she fought tears. She had always resisted tears, though she had often had much to cry about in her young life with the loss of their parents, and her own bouts of ill health.

He sighed. "It is what she wished, Susan. Dani did not want to tell you she had to leave. You see, she was never meant to be here at all." Even Stephen did not believe his words. "Her mother is seriously ill, and Dani needed to be there with her."

"I do not blame Dani, but I do blame you," Susan said with her face averted. "I could have said goodbye to her. I could have arranged to correspond with her."

"Correspond with her? Whatever do you mean, dear? She cannot receive correspondence from us." Had the fever confused his sister?

"Yes, she can. I could have left notes in various places throughout the city in prearranged sites. I thought about this while you were gone. Perhaps some part of me knew that you would not embark on another journey only a day after your return. It really did not make sense."

"I know," he said in a gruff voice. "I am afraid I have botched this entire matter."

"Yes, you have," she said without mercy though she reached to pat his hand. "But I see that you are in a bad way, brother, and I will desist scolding you. Did you love her so very much?"

Stephen slumped back onto the sofa and nodded.

"I do. Very much."

"And is there no way?"

"I do not know. Even were her mother not ill, she does not wish to lose her only daughter. This *time travel* is a great deal different than traveling to Chicago. Dani chose to remain with her mother, perhaps indefinitely."

"Did you travel with her, Stephen?" Susan turned to him with rounded eyes of awe. "To the future?"

"Yes, I did. I did not mean to, dearest. I only meant to see her safely on her way, and then I planned to return here to you, but somehow, I was transported forward in time."

"Oh, Stephen! Tell me all about it!" She settled next to him on the sofa.

For the next half hour, Stephen attempted to describe the sights and sounds of the twenty-first century, or at least the limited portion he had seen. He described Montana, Glacier National Park which was not yet a park, motorized vehicles called cars and the streamlined steel train with the secure and safe connectors. He described Dani's mother, omitting details of her illness, and he spoke of Dani's desire that they return to the park one day.

"Oh, yes, we must go there! It sounds wonderful."

"Yes," Stephen said quietly, lost in memories.

Susan's hand covered his.

"I know you are thinking of Dani. If it is possible for you to go there, and for her to come here, can you not be together in some fashion?"

"Dani is the key to the travel. I have ridden the train many times to Chicago, and have never traveled anywhere but to Chicago. Without her, I cannot go forward in time. Only Dani can return here, if that is at all possible. We do not understand the mechanism of the travel and can only gamble on the outcome." He patted her hand. "At any rate, I cannot abandon you again."

She eyed him with a raised brow. "Stephen, I am not a child any longer. Someday soon, I hope I will marry." She blushed. Stephen swung his head to look at her. "No, no, I have not yet met a possible candidate, but someday I hope to. And when I marry, what will you do? Moon around the house saying that you cannot be with Dani because you cannot *abandon* me?"

He chuckled, surprised that he could. "Yes, my dear, I will moon about the house because I cannot abandon you. I shall be uncle to your children." He sobered. "The point is moot, my dear. Dani lives in the future, and I cannot reach her from here."

"You could if we left her notes where she could find them."

For a moment, Stephen's heart sped up, but then he tamped down his hopes.

"Even were we to put them somewhere she could find them in the next century, I cannot ask her to come back to me here. She cannot leave her mother."

"But you could ask her to return and take you back with her to the future."

"Live in the future?" Stephen eyed her narrowly. "Yes, I would live with Dani in the future if that were possible, but I do not think it is. I cannot simply stand around hoping you marry so I can run away to the future, nor can I discover a way to contact Dani. Though your scheme of correspondence has some merit, it is not certain that she will find any notes we leave her. I did not care to tell you how many buildings are destroyed between now and her time—even our favorite restaurant at the Hotel Seattle. I do not even know if this house continues to stand."

"There is another alternative."

"And what might that be, young lady?"

"That we attempt to contact Dani, to bring her back here for a short while, and that you take me with you to the future."

Stephen brought his sister into his arms, and tousled her hair as he used to do when she was younger.

"Stephen," she shrieked. "Stop! I have been unwell." She pushed against him in laughter. He knew she used that as an excuse, but he released her.

"The scenario grows ever more convoluted the longer I listen to you, child. Get some sleep. We will speak of this again another time."

"Soon," Susan said. "We will speak of this again soon."

"Good night, sister. Sleep well." Stephen left her room and crossed over to his room. His satchel sat on the floor next to his dresser. He opened it, and pulled the new clothing from it. Dani's eyes had glowed with admiration and something quite improper when he had worn the clothing, and he had reveled in her regard.

Where was the clothing she had left? He dashed out of his room and down the hall to the room she had occupied. There, on the bureau was her clothing, washed and folded—the jeans, T-shirt and strange little backless shoes that she had worn when he first saw her. He picked up the clothing and returned to his room with them. He set the shoes on the floor, and dropped onto his bed, cradling the clothing in his arms. Sleep descended quickly as he dreamed that he and Dani had never parted.

****

A knock on his door awakened Stephen, and he rubbed his eyes. He unwrapped his arms from Dani's clothing and set it aside.

"Enter," he called, swinging his legs over the edge of the bed.

"You have slept in a long time." Susan bounced into the room. "Make haste. It is time for us to write our notes and scatter them throughout the city for Dani."

Stephen rubbed his chin, whiskered beyond what was proper. "Susan, I did not yet agree to this scheme. It does not even seem plausible. Dani will have returned to her mother in Whitefish at once, as she did not tell her mother she was leaving. As fast as travel occurs in her time, and with the speed of the modern train, I do not think she would have spent the night in Seattle. She most likely would have bought another ticket and returned to Montana at once. I believe it is only a fifteen-hour journey in her time, and not the twenty-four hours it is in ours."

"Nevertheless, it will not hurt to try."

Stephen sighed. Frankly, the thought of writing love letters to Dani actually appealed to him—anything to feel as if he were still with her.

"Let me bathe, dress and have breakfast before we set out."

"And write the notes!" Susan waved a small stack of white envelopes in her hand. "I have prepared mine already, and I have shamelessly begged her to come back to us." She grinned.

"Susan, that is not fair to her. She is already so torn between her desire to stay and her mother's need to have her only child with her."

Susan, turning to leave, paused at the door, her smile fading. "I know, Stephen, I did not really beg her to come back to us, but I did let her know that we missed her terribly." She left the room, and Stephen rose from the bed and crossed to his desk. He pulled out pen and paper, and wrote, pausing occasionally to choose his words with care. He truly believed she would never see the letters, but like Susan, it made him feel better to speak to her.

****

Several hours later, just as he and Susan were about to set out, a messenger arrived with a note from Ellie asking him to call at his earliest convenience. He had sent a note around to her earlier in the morning advising her of his journey and to tell her that Dani had arrived in her time safely.

"We must stop by Mrs. Chamberlain's house, Susan."

"Excellent!" Susan said. "If Dani were to attempt to revisit any houses in Seattle in the future, she would go to ours and then to Mrs. Chamberlain's. We can include her in our scheme."

Stephen patted his sister's hand but said nothing to discourage her enthusiasm.

"Thank you for your note, Stephen," Ellie said on their arrival. "If I could figure out how to use this telephone, I would have called you. I thought about running over to your house, but Robert is at work, and you know...rules being what they are, I couldn't just drop in on the single guy. But I just had to see you for myself since your return." She ran her eyes up and down his person, much like Dani had done when they first met. He shuddered to think he had taken offense at the time, and would have given anything to see his own dear love eyeing him in such a way once again.

"And am I all here?"

"You are," Ellie grinned. She turned to Susan. "How are you feeling, Susan? I heard you'd been sick"

"I am well, thank you, Mrs. Chamberlain. We are embarking on an adventure this morning. Stephen and I are going to drop notes off for Dani throughout the city in the hopes that she might find them one day."

Ellie's eyes widened, and Stephen coughed behind his hand. He hoped Ellie would not be blunt in telling Susan that the scheme was farfetched.

"Well, you know, that's not a half bad idea!" Ellie surprised him by saying. "A lot of the buildings are torn down—"

Stephen threw a warning glance in Susan's direction. Susan still did not know about Ellie. Ellie caught the glance.

"I would think a lot of the buildings will be torn down in the future, but I would think Dani might stop by your house and my house, if nothing else. So, you must leave a note here. I suspect it will still be standing well into the future." She tapped a finger to her lip. "I wonder what other locations might be intact in a hundred and ten years where you leave notes so they wouldn't be destroyed by weather, and yet where Dani could possibly find them."

"Stone buildings?" Susan offered.

"Yes, I think so! Let's put together a list of stone buildings." She rose to get paper and pen from a small table in the sitting room. "I think I'll drop her a short note myself if you all don't mind."

Ellie and Susan wrote down several buildings that held promise. Ellie balked at several of Susan's suggestions including hotels other than the Hotel Seattle.

"Well, if you think so," she said. "Though I think some hotels might be torn down and renovated in the future. I heard the library burned down at the beginning of the year, so we can't put something there, otherwise, I think that would be an ideal place." When at last they had a short list of locations, Susan pronounced herself satisfied and ready to venture out.

"Where shall we put the notes for this house? I can't guarantee that my descendents would keep a letter like that, or that they'll own this house in Dani's time." Ellie asked. She looked to Stephen. "If I were to visit an old Victorian mansion which might still stand but has probably been refurbished and modernized on the inside, where would I find an old letter that has been protected from the elements? Which I didn't actually know was there? We can't very well bury the letters, not even in a tin box, because she wouldn't have a chance of seeing them."

Stephen had wondered the same thing about his house.

"We should go look for a place," Susan said. "Outside?"

"Wait!" Ellie trotted off, and Stephen and Susan looked at each other.

She returned quickly with several sheets of paraffin paper.

"Here, Stephen, wrap them in this wax paper. Maybe they'll last longer."

They left the sitting room and made their way out onto the porch. Stephen looked out onto the city, more aware now than before of the smoke and haze which often hung over the city as it did today.

"I would think the stone foundation might be the best place to protect something though the building above might be remodeled," Stephen murmured. He climbed down the stairs and stared at the house from the lawn, scrutinizing the foundation and the steps. Susan and Ellie followed.

"So, we're looking for a crack in the foundation, Stephen? To stick the letters in?" Ellie laughed. "That's worrisome."

He approached the house and pointed. "Here," he murmured. "Just by the stairs. The mortar has fallen out between these two large bricks. May I?" He pointed to a gap between two bricks on the side of the porch, not particularly visible to the public, but not hidden either.

Ellie nodded, her fingers tightly laced. "Oh, yes, please do! I'll make sure no one touches it while I still live in the house!"

Stephen removed his letter from his jacket pocket, took the notes Susan and Ellie proffered and wrapped them in the paraffin paper. He worked the remaining bits of mortar from between the two large bricks and tucked the small package inside. He stood back and examined the opening. Ellie and Susan joined him.

"It looks pretty safe there. I'm not sure if she would ever see it. She'd have to walk around the side of the house to see it," Ellie said. "Well, let's hope she does."

"Come inside and have some lemonade and tell me about your trip, Stephen. Then you all can finish your treasure hunt."

For the next half hour, Stephen described events as best he could understand to Ellie. Susan, sipping on her lemonade eyed them curiously.

"Mrs. Chamberlain," Susan interjected.

"Yes, Susan?" Ellie turned to her with an inquiring eye and a smile.

"You are from the same time as Dani." She stated it as a fact, not a question.

Ellie laughed and threw Stephen a rueful glance.

"I had hoped to hide that from you, Susan, but yes, I am."

"Why would you wish to hide that from me when I already know about Dani?"

"Susan, dear, do not be impolite," Stephen said firmly. "Mrs. Chamberlain does not have to explain herself to you."

"That's all right, Stephen. It would probably be easier for her to know." She turned to Susan. "With Dani gone, I'm the only person I know who has traveled from the future. Well, besides your brother here. If anyone other than us were to find out, I would hate to think what would happen to me, to Robert or my child. Even in my time, a *time traveler,* for lack of a better word, would be subjected to psychological tests, physical tests, ridicule and disbelief, maybe even a mental institution. So, I've kept it a secret. Your brother just found out about me when Dani came. He noticed we use the same colloquialisms and have a lot of the same mannerisms." She smiled at Stephen.

"Yes, you do," he murmured with affection.

"I understand," Susan said with a grave expression. "Your secret is safe with me."

"I know it is, Susan. You're very mature for your age."

"Thank you," Susan said with a blush.

"So, you probably realize that if I say it is best not to leave Dani notes in certain buildings, it's because I believe they are now gone...or will be gone."

Susan nodded, wide eyed. Stephen was not absolutely sure the events of the past week had not been too much for his young sister, notwithstanding her illness. She was so young, how could she understand the concept of *progress* in the form of destruction of many of the city's grand buildings?

Stephen rose. "We must go, Ellie, if we are to make our way around the city. Please give Robert my best."

"I will. He had pressing business at the bank today, otherwise he would have been here to greet you."

"I had forgotten! Dani sent back some of the clothes she borrowed. I will have them delivered to you tomorrow."

Ellie followed them to the door. "Keep them for now, Stephen. If she gets our mail, she may need them."

Stephen kissed her cheek. "I am grateful for your encouragement," he said quietly. "It eases me."

****

Later, the notes having been dropped at strategic locations throughout the city that Ellie felt might survive into the twenty-first century, Stephen and Susan returned to the house. Stephen removed his derby and dropped it on the hall table in the foyer.

"I think you need to lie down, Susan. I should not have had you running about the city so soon after your illness." Her face was pale.

"It was my idea, Stephen," she said, her voice raspier than in the morning. "But not for anything in the world would I have missed the sight of you skulking about buildings looking for crevices in which to hide the notes." Her face brightened with a mischievous smile.

Stephen chuckled. He had looked the fool, but Susan had enjoyed the spectacle, and it pleased him to hear her laugh.

"The chances of Dani finding any of those notes are slender, my dear."

"I know," she said, sobering, "but not of the notes at Mrs. Chamberlain's house or the ones you shall leave her here. Where will you put them?" She looked around the house. "Will you leave them in the house or outside?"

Stephen shook his head. "I do not know, dearest. I cannot say if this house will still stand in Dani's time, and if so, who might own it by then."

"It will remain in our family, Stephen, I am certain of that."

Stephen swallowed hard. "Then you shall have to convince your future husband to live in your house as it is likely I may not have children." He attempted a smile to soften his words but failed.

Susan narrowed her eyes. "Stephen Sadler! Stop speaking that way at once." She stomped her foot for emphasis. "Of course, you shall marry and have children."

Stephen tightened his jaw. He had revealed too much of his pain to his young sister who was still unwell. He needed to guard his tongue better.

"Of course, dear." He kissed her on the cheek. "Now, go rest."

Susan threw one more worried look in his direction before turning away to ascend the stairs, her step visibly fatigued.

Stephen eyed the remaining two notes in his hand from Susan and himself. It was not inconceivable that Dani, on her return to her own home in Seattle, might look for the house. Whether it continued to stand or not was not certain, but if it did, where might she find a letter addressed to her without knowing it existed?

CHAPTER TWELVE

Dani staggered off the train in Seattle at about 10:30. The morning sky was overcast as usual. Numb, she wandered aimlessly into the train station uncertain of her next move. Putting one foot in front of the other seemed to be the only thing she could manage. She remembered having some firm plans to hop off the train and purchase an immediate return trip to get back to Whitefish, but her feet didn't lead her to the ticket counter. She followed them to the parking lot in a vague search of her car. Had she even left it there so many years ago? Taken a taxi? She couldn't remember.

Since she'd lost Stephen, she'd had difficulty focusing, and she wondered if she'd lost her mind, perhaps had a breakdown, or even become delusional? Was this what insanity felt like?

She wandered further into the parking lot. She had no keys. She had nothing but the clothes she wore, her temporary ID and some money in her pocket. What good would it do to find her car, even had she left it there?

Dani turned around and retraced her circuitous steps back to the station, presenting herself at the customer service window. Yes, they had retrieved her purse. They verified her picture on her driver's license. A miracle it was not stolen, they said. She hardly cared. Were the keys in it? She rummaged through the bag. Keys.

When she left the building again, a heavy rain started to fall. Good. Why not? She found her car and climbed inside, settling herself into the driver's seat. Placing two hands on the steering wheel, she pressed her head against the wheel and alternately screamed and sobbed for the next half hour as rain pelted the hood of her car. Everything she could not beg for, curse about or shout over at the loss of Stephen on the train came out of her now in the privacy of her car. No one tapped on her window to ask what was wrong with the shrieking woman. The rain provided a cover for her noisy grief, though she barely cared.

No sooner had Stephen's breathing relaxed into a pattern of sleep, than his image had begun to fade in and out, and his body grown insubstantial. She herself had felt dizzy from swirling images of colors. Blackness had threatened to descend. Though her instincts had told her to hang onto Stephen, to wrap herself around him, she let him go. The image of the single tear slipping down her mother's face grew stronger, pushing the colors out of reach. When it was over, she sat there alone, and Stephen was gone.

While on the train, she had changed her mind several times—deciding to go with Stephen, then standing by her earlier decision to stay with her mother, and then again giving into her heart's desire to stay with him. It had only been a matter of timing—the swinging of the pendulum had fallen and the travel occurred when she felt the pull of her mother's grief as strong as she felt her need to remain with Stephen. And she had let go.

Spent, her throat raw from her shrieks and sobs, Dani rubbed her eyes and rested her head on the seatback, a vague plan forming in her mind. She would return to her mother's house tomorrow, but she would stay the night in Seattle, in her own condo. And at the immediate moment, she would see if she could find Stephen's house.

The rain had eased by the time Dani left the train station and headed north to Queen Anne Hill. With the advent of paved roads, traffic lights, housing congestion and overgrown trees, she struggled to find the road on which Stephen's house had been, and she directed a baleful glance at her phone—the GPS dead along with the battery. Once she found the street, she couldn't find a house that remotely resembled his, and she wondered with a sinking heart if his house had been demolished—Stephen's beautiful gabled Queen Anne-style mansion.

Out of the corner of her eye, Dani spotted the roofline of a house, the house itself mostly hidden by large trees. Something about the pitch of the roofline looked familiar, and she pulled the car over to peer down the driveway—the only clearing through which one could see the house.

She thought at first that she had found Stephen's house but soon realized that the roofline didn't show the turrets and gables of Stephen's house. Her heart raced as she realized that the front of the house, although repainted and modified, bore a strong resemblance to Ellie's house.

On shaking legs, Dani climbed out of her car and slowly walked up the driveway, intently studying the landscape and structure of the house to see if she recognized any details. She climbed the stairs and, with a shaking hand, knocked on the front door, or at least what she thought was the front door. The house was large, and for all she knew, the front could have been around the back. So many years had passed, though she'd seen the house only several days ago in 1901, and then only at night.

Dani clasped her trembling hands behind her back. What would she say if someone answered? She had no earthly idea. The address was etched into an old mailbox by the front door. It seemed familiar, yet she couldn't remember seeing an address prominently displayed at Ellie's house. It had only been known as the Chamberlain House, as Stephen's had been known as the Sadler House.

An image of the address written down on a card came to mind, but she couldn't remember where she'd seen the image. Her breaths were shallow and fast as she awaited a response to her knock. She knocked again, and tried the doorbell. No car sat in the driveway. Maybe no one was home.

Deflated, Dani turned to descend the brick steps. Several looked loose, and she stepped over them tentatively, thinking the owner should throw some new mortar on them. Pausing at the bottom of the stairs, Dani took a last look at the house. It looked so much like Ellie's, but she couldn't be sure. A thick hedge hid the foundation of the house, and too many large overgrown oak and maple trees, their leaves turning red for fall, hid the contours of the house.

She climbed back into her car, and with a last look toward the house, drove away. She tried to remember where Ellie's house had been in relation to Stephen's. Not more than a mile it seemed, but which way? As Dani rounded the corner, she noted that the back of the house she'd just stopped at descended down a heavily treed slope to another street. She traveled down that street for a few moments, but it ended abruptly, forcing her to turn left and drive back up the hill to yet another road. Having spent almost no time in Queen Anne Hill in the present time, Dani had no idea the roads were so narrow or tortuous. They certainly hadn't felt that way in Stephen's time.

Two miles down the road, she spotted what she'd been looking for—a witch's cap on a gabled roof. She slowed and parked across the street. There seemed to be no driveway on this house, not unusual for the old homes on Queen Anne Hill. Stephen's carriage had deposited them in front of the house before disappearing somewhere to the rear to park and unhitch the horses. She hadn't had time to figure out the process.

This house lacked the overgrown trees of the previous house, but the landscaping was much different than it had been in Stephen's time. In 1901, the landscaping had been sparser, less mature, less regimented than it was now. A few young trees had adorned the grass between the sidewalk and the road. Massive power poles had flanked the house. None of those were in evidence now.

The color of the house was different, lighter, the shingles probably having been replaced. Though sandwiched as it was now next to a narrow white Colonial mansion and a Tudor-style house which had not existed in 1901, Dani nevertheless recognized the house as Stephen's.

Her heart thudded, and she felt almost nauseous with excitement at the wild thought that if she were to walk up to the house and knock on the door, Mrs. Oakley might answer and tell her that Stephen was in his library.

She climbed out of the car, and on shaking legs, crossed the street to step onto the sidewalk. A small iron gate had been erected with a short fence and hedge serving to ensure bystanders didn't wander onto the lawn. Dani looked up at the long-paned decorative windows almost imaging Stephen watched and waited for her. Perhaps Susan would wave from a window.

The pain she thought she'd left behind at the train station resurfaced, and she struggled for air, her chest aching. At that very moment in time, as she stood on the sidewalk with her hand on the gate, the realization that Stephen and Susan were dead brought a wave of dizziness, and she gripped the gate with both hands. Despite her best efforts, tears spilled down her face, and she sagged against the gate on weakened legs.

The front door opened, and a woman called out.

"Can I help you? Are you all right?" A tall woman with gray hair came out to the gate and peered into Dani's face with startling bright green eyes. "Miss? Are you all right?"

Dani shook her head but could not speak.

"Should I call an ambulance?" The older woman, appearing to be in her late 80s, looked up and down the street. "Are you on foot?"

Dani could only shake her head. If she opened her mouth, she thought she might scream. Stephen was dead. Though he lived in the past—a wonderfully vibrant loving man—in her time, he was dead.

"Is that your car?" The woman asked. She indicated Dani's car across the street.

Dani nodded.

"Well, you're in no shape to drive. You don't look well. Why don't you come inside and I'll get you a glass of water?" She pulled open the gate, and Dani almost lost her footing so tightly did she still grip it.

"This gate wasn't here," Dani mumbled inconsequentially.

"What?" The woman paused and stared at her.

"This gate wasn't original to the house." Dani finally let go of the gate and attempted to straighten.

"That's right," the woman said. "It's only about fifteen years old. How did you know that? Come inside, it's starting to rain again." She pulled her cardigan tighter.

Dani followed her robotically through the front door and into the foyer. Even after all these years, the foyer was as beautiful as ever, almost unchanged.

"I'm Edwina Sutton, by the way. And you are?" Mrs. Sutton showed her into the parlor which faced the back of the house, just where it had always been. Dani stared out the window over the city of Seattle, the view much different than it had been.

"Dani Douglas," she stated mechanically. Bemused, she turned around to inspect the room further.

A young blonde woman came to the door, with a suspicious look in Dani's direction. "Is everything all right, Mrs. Sutton?"

"Yes, Tammy, thank you. Would you please get Miss Douglas a glass of water? Or would you like tea, Miss Douglas? It might help revive you."

Dani nodded wordlessly as she struggled for control.

Tammy left.

"My helper," Mrs. Sutton said with a wry smile. "My brother insisted I needed someone to watch over me, and my children and grandchildren agree. I'm lucky I get to stay in my own home."

"Please sit down," she said hurriedly as Dani weaved unsteadily. The furnishings had changed but the fireplace mantle, and the woodwork were the same. Dani sank into a forest green velvet easy chair.

"I was actually coming to knock on your door, Mrs. Sutton." Now that tea had been mentioned, Dani longed for a cup, her mouth suddenly dry.

"Oh, really? What can I do for you?" Green eyes, somehow oddly familiar, regarded her with interest.

"I used to know the family—that is..." Dani swallowed hard. She hadn't prepared anything. "I was interested in the family who owned this house back in 1901."

Mrs. Sutton nodded, again with interest. "Yes? And why did you want to know about them? Is it the house? It's a registered historic landmark, you know."

Dani shook her head. "No, I didn't know." Stephen would have been so pleased.

"Oh, I thought you knew. The Sadler House."

Dani gasped.

"Oh, my goodness, Miss Douglas! Whatever is the matter? I really think I should call you an ambulance." Mrs. Sutton stood, but Dani jumped up to put a staying hand on her arm.

"No, don't! I'm not sick. I've just been traveling all night, and I'm a little tired. I just didn't realize the house was still called Sadler House."

Mrs. Sutton retook her seat, now eyeing her as suspiciously as Tammy had.

"Well, many of these old houses retained the names of the owners. Before they had street addresses, you know?"

Dani did know.

Tammy entered, carrying a tea service. She set the tray down on an oval mahogany table that looked vaguely familiar, and she left.

Mrs. Sutton poured out tea.

"Is that table original to the house, Mrs. Sutton?"

She looked at the table. "Yes, I believe it is." She handed Dani a cup of tea. "I inherited it from my mother."

Dani's cup clattered in her saucer. She gulped some hot tea, soothing to her raw throat.

"Do you mean to say that some of the furniture stayed with the house?"

"Oh, yes, much of it has. What I don't have downstairs is either upstairs or in the attic." Mrs. Sutton eyed the table lovingly.

Dani thought again how happy Stephen would be to know that his things had remained intact. She thrust aside the thought that his wife would probably have been pleased as well.

"So, the furniture was sold intact with the house?"

Mrs. Sutton cocked her head. "Sold? This house has never been sold that I know of. It's been in my family since the late 1800s."

Dani jerked, spilling her tea on her T-shirt.

"Oh, dear, here's a napkin." Mrs. Sutton handed her one.

Dani searched her face, studying her features. Stephen's grandchild? Could she possibly be looking at Stephen's granddaughter?

"Are you...are you Stephen Sadler's granddaughter?"

"Stephen Sadler?" Mrs. Sutton laughed. "Oh, no, not Stephen Sadler. My grandmother was Susan Sadler Richardson. Stephen Sadler was her brother."

Dani could have cried to see Susan's descendent. She longed to throw herself upon the older woman and ask a million questions—about Susan, about Stephen. Relief that Susan had survived her illnesses and gone on to have a family filled Dani with joy and pride. And here was her granddaughter.

"I didn't know she'd married," Dani whispered. "I thought she was sickly."

"How could you possibly know that?" Mrs. Sutton said. "You're right. She was ill a lot, until she turned about eighteen according to my mother. Then she just started improving, and went on to get married and have children."

"And her brother?" Dani held her breath, her pulse pounding in her ears.

"I'm not sure. You should probably talk to my brother, Edward. He's the family historian. He lives about a mile away in the Chamberlain House. Have you heard of *that* house?"

Dani nodded silently. Everything was falling into place. Everyone she loved had existed. They had lived, and they had died, but their legacies lived on. She recognized the green eyes now.

"Are you both descended from Robert Chamberlain?"

"So you know about him too? Yes, Susan Sadler Richardson had several children and her son, my father, married one of Robert and Ellie Chamberlain's daughters. So, that's why we own both of the houses. I'm not sure where the original owner, Stephen Sadler, went or why Susan got the house, but..." Mrs. Sutton eyed her curiously. "You sure seem to know a lot about this family. Are you related to us in some way? We have cousins all over, I think."

"I don't think so," Dani said quietly. No, she wasn't related. She hadn't married Stephen, hadn't borne his children. She worried at the vague reference in Mrs. Sutton's voice to Stephen's whereabouts. He had married, hadn't he? Oh, please say that he hadn't waited for her forever.

"Well, listen, my brother printed out this big family outline from some kind of computer program he has about genealogy, and he gave it to me. Would you like to look at it?"

Dani fervently nodded, her eyes wide, her throat dry.

"It's just over here." Mrs. Sutton crossed the room to open the bottom drawer of a modern desk. She pulled out a manila folder and brought it to the coffee table. Dani jumped up and relocated the tea tray to another table.

Mrs. Sutton opened the folder and leafed through it. A plastic baggie filled with some old water-stained envelopes fell out, and she set the packet aside. She spread out the outline which appeared to be on several pieces of paper.

"Let's see. Here I am, and Edward."

"Edward Richardson?" Where had Dani heard that name? The man on the train? The old gentleman on the train? She turned to look at Mrs. Sutton again. The green eyes were the same. And he had invited her to visit his house on Queen Anne Hill—Robert and Ellie's house. Ellie would be so tickled to know Dani had met her grandson, that she had descendants. Dani was pleased to know that Ellie's pregnancy apparently went well.

Dani suddenly froze with a horrifying thought. She couldn't possibly look at the family history. It would show when people died...when Stephen died, or Ellie, or Susan. She couldn't bear to know when they died.

"Here! Here's my grandmother, and her brother."

Dani balked. She couldn't look at it.

"I think it's so sad to see the sum of peoples' lives on a piece of paper, don't you?" Dani said. "I'm so sorry I had you drag that out, but I think I would get depressed looking at the family history and knowing when people died."

Mrs. Sutton paused and looked at her. "Well, yes, I can see your point. Are you sure you're not related to the family? You look kind of familiar, but I can't think why."

"No, no relation," Dani said. She kept her eyes averted from the family history outline and focused on the baggy. "So, are those family letters?"

"Well, they're kind of interesting. They're letters that were discovered at both the Chamberlain house hidden inside a crevice in the brick steps, and at this house in one of the books in the library—an old history of Seattle. They were found a long, long time ago by my parents. My brother gave them to me to read not too long ago when he gave me this printed family history. I haven't read them yet, but he says they're from my grandmother Richardson, great-uncle Sadler, and grandmother Chamberlain. They're all addressed to some woman named Danielle Douglas." As soon as Mrs. Sutton had uttered the words, her eyes widened and she snatched the bag and opened it up. She pulled out the letters gingerly and laid them out face up on top of the family history sheets. On the outside of the envelopes was written *Miss Danielle Douglas.*

She turned to Dani with a stunned expression. Dani stared at the letters, her heart bursting with a complex combination of joy and grief.

"Is that you?" Mrs. Sutton shook her head. "Or I mean, is that an ancestor of yours?" She held one of the letters out.

Dani nodded. She could do nothing else. She couldn't tell Mrs. Sutton that the letters were addressed to her...in the hopes that she would find them when she returned to her own time.

"Yes," she whispered. "I had an ancestor named Danielle Douglas, a namesake, who knew the family back at the turn of the century. May I read them?" She reached for them with a shaking hand.

"I knew it! I'm certain we're related in some way!" the older woman said with glee. "Yes, here, read them. I'm just going to go call Edward and tell him."

Dani opened the first envelope gingerly. Faded and fragile with age, she pulled the letter out and read the thin sheet.

Dear Dani,

We miss you so much! Stephen is miserable without you. I know you had to go but please think about coming back when you can. I hope your mother is well.

Love, Susan

Tears streamed down Dani's face, and she kissed the sheet. A second envelope, this one not water stained, in the same handwriting held the same message. Mrs. Sutton had said they left letters at both homes.

She opened a third envelope, the handwriting different, more modern.

Hey, there!

If you're reading this, then you made it back. I wished we could have spent more time together while you were here. I can't tell you what a relief it was to have someone from the future here. No pressure, but if you decide you don't want to stay there, you're always welcome back here. You know, of course, that Stephen misses you. But if you decide to stay there, say hi to my grandkids for me. Just goes to show I got through the lack of anesthesia pretty well. I'm pretty sure I met my grandson, Edward, on the train before I traveled. Spitting image of Robert, or at least what Robert will look like when he's older.

Ellie

Dani kissed the sheet as well. She missed Ellie terribly, and she longed to tell her how well she'd done in creating descendents. Ellie had only written one note, if the handwriting was anything to go by.

Dani's heart was in her throat as she opened the first of the final two letters. The handwriting bore a distinctive flare.

My love

You have been gone less than a day, and yet I miss you more than I can say. I am sure you know that it took all of my strength for me to make the decision to return to my own time...and to leave you. I believe I know what it cost you to let go of me at the last moment. Your plan succeeded, and here I am, safe and sound in my own time, and missing you dreadfully, so much so I feel I can hardly breathe.

You must know that I longed to beg you to come back with me, but I could not. It would have been wrong of me to add to your burden. I hope that by the time you read this letter, if you find it, your mother's health will have improved.

I love you, Danielle Douglas, now and forever. My love for you will never die, not even with the passage of a hundred years. I believe I was meant to meet you, to fall in love with you, and to love you for the rest of my life...and the rest of yours.

I do not say this to add to your grief but to let you know that there will be no descendents from me. Do not look for them. I will not marry, Dani. I cannot imagine loving anyone as much as I do you.

I must end the note, dearest, as Susan is impatiently waiting for us to deliver our notes about the city, and I must write a few more in the hopes you will find them someday.

I will love you forever,
Stephen

Tears poured down Dani's face, and she reached for the other note blindly. The note was identical if a little more water-stained than the first.

Mrs. Sutton returned.

"My brother wasn't home, so I left a message for him." She stopped short. "Oh, my dear, what's wrong? Is it the letters?"

Dani nodded and reached for the tissue Mrs. Sutton proffered. "Love letters? From my ancestor to your ancestor, I think?"

Dani nodded again silently. Mrs. Sutton picked the letters up, and began to read them. Dani squirmed at the thought of a stranger reading Stephen's letter to her, but there was nothing she could do.

He had said he wouldn't marry. The knowledge tore at her heart, and she couldn't bear the pain. She couldn't do that to him! Dani suspected that Stephen had meant it when he wrote the note, but hopefully time would have softened his stance. She had to know!

"Mrs. Sutton?" Dani hesitated, wanting to know, yet afraid she would find out more than she needed to, including the date of his death.

"Yes? Oh, my, these letters are so sad. It seems your ancestor, Danielle Douglas, left? Do you know anything about that?"

Dani shook her head. "No, not really." She hated lying to the kind woman, Susan's granddaughter, but she could hardly tell her the truth.

"I was wondering," Dani started again, "does your family history outline tell you if Stephen Sadler was married?"

"Well, let me see." Mrs. Sutton picked up a sheet and scanned it then she picked up another.

Dani felt faint from holding her breath as the older woman scanned each sheet.

"Don't tell me the date of his death," Dani said. Mrs. Sutton looked up in surprise. "Oh, I'm just sentimental that way, hate to know when people die."

"Yes, of course. I feel the same way." Mrs. Sutton found the sheet she was looking for. "Here it is. Yes, he did marry, and had children." She offered the sheet to Dani, but Dani put out a hand to stop her at the same time she let out a deep sigh. So, Stephen had married after all. That was the way it should be.

Mrs. Sutton perused the sheet once again and let out a chuckle. "Do you want to know who he married?"

Dani shook her head fervently. "No, no, I don't!"

"It's your ancestor, Danielle Douglas! The one who left!"

CHAPTER THIRTEEN

Stephen awakened, focusing his eyes on the red velvet of the seat back. He had dreamed Dani had returned to him. Her mother had survived her illness, and Dani had made the decision to come back. Though the time traveling seemed dangerous at best, she had successfully traveled in time twice and he had once. It was possible they could do it again!

He straightened in the chair, the book on the table catching his eyes. He opened it as he had done some many times over the past two days to assure himself that the letters were still tucked inside, the tips of them peeking out over the top. He would have to let Susan know the notes were here so that she could watch out for the book. He surveyed the library once again. He would leave the house to Susan, and she could take ownership once she married.

Early dawn light filtered in through the velvet curtains. He checked his watch. Five o'clock. Restlessly, he stood and paced the room, feeling a bit like a caged lion. Inactivity wore at him. He needed to *do* something, anything to resolve his grief. He could not make Dani return, but surely there must be something he could do to come to terms with his loss. Wallowing in self-pity had its place, but that might come later. Had he done absolutely everything he could do to resolve the chasm between himself and Dani?

He thought of Dani probably now at home again in Whitefish, Montana, at least in her time. And the nearby park with its majestic peaks. Susan would enjoy such a sight. Susan, who needed fresh air.

He strode from the room and ran up the stairs to tap on Susan's door.

"Susan, dearest, wake up!"

"Enter," Susan said sleepily.

Stephen burst into her room and crossed the room to her wardrobe. He opened the doors, reached in for a portmanteau and grabbed a few of her dresses.

"What on earth are you doing, Stephen? Are we going somewhere?" Susan rubbed her eyes and raised herself on one elbow to watch him.

"Yes, we are going to visit Montana. You will like it there."

"Montana! Where Dani is from?" She sat bolt upright.

He turned and smiled. "Where Dani is from. The doctor said you must have fresh air, and so you shall. So will I."

An hour later saw them at the train station purchasing tickets to Montana.

"Good gravy, man, you are not heading out on another train trip again so soon? Where did you and Mrs. Sadler disappear to the other day? Did you return to your compartment? I looked up and you were gone."

Stephen turned to see Rory O'Rourke standing behind them, tickets in his hand. Rory nodded to Susan. Stephen's question was answered. Rory had not seen them *disappear* as he put it. Their secret was safe.

"I should ask you the same thing, Rory. What takes you on another journey so quickly?"

"Business interests in Spokane, Stephen. Business interests." He patted Stephen on the shoulder. "And where is Mrs. Sadler?" The tentative manner of his question reminded Stephen of his behavior on the two days prior.

"She is visiting her mother. We go to join her." Stephen ignored Susan's quick intake of breath.

"Excellent!" Rory murmured. "It is time to board, so I shall see you on the train?" He reached out a hand to Stephen, who took it in his own. He was no longer angry with Rory but still held reservations about his old friend. Rory flirted as easily as other men breathed, but that was no excuse for his behavior toward another man's wife—even if they hadn't really been married.

"On the train," Stephen murmured. Rory moved away.

Stephen took the tickets and his sister's arm and climbed aboard the observation car of the train.

"Stephen, are you trying to travel forward in time?" Susan whispered as they seated themselves on a bench. She cast a furtive glance around her shoulder.

Stephen patted her hand. "No, dear, we cannot travel in time without Dani. She and Ellie are the only ones we know about who have traveled in time. I managed to travel because I was with Dani."

"Oh!" Her face deflated. "I had thought..."

"That we might travel to the future to see Dani?" Stephen's heart leapt at the thought. "If only we could, Susan. If only we could."

"How long is the trip to Montana?"

"We should reach Kalispell in about twenty-four hours, which is why I negotiated heavily with the ticket agent to procure you a sleeping compartment."

"Oh! Such a long time," Susan said. "I think travel must be much faster in Dani's time."

"Yes, it is."

"Would you care for some tea, Sir? Miss?" The steward awaited their order. Stephen ordered tea, feeling as if he were in a strange dream of repeating everything all over again.

Rory entered the observation car, and with a wave in their direction, seated himself in the library with the newspaper, further cementing Stephen's impression of déjà vu. Rory had done the very same thing in just the same pose that last time he saw him.

Susan pulled a book from her purse and settled in to read. At liberty to devote himself to thoughts of his past trips with Dani, Stephen relaxed into his seat and surveyed the passing scenery as he awaited the train's approach to Wenatchee. He fully expected nothing to happen other than the train would continue on toward Kalispell with Susan and him on board, but one could always hope.

****

"Wenatchee, ten minutes," the conductor announced. Stephen jerked awake. He had been dozing and dreaming. Susan rested next to him, her hat removed, her eyes shut as she too dozed against the back of the bench.

Wenatchee! His heart thudded in his chest. What if... What if they indeed did travel forward in time? Was it possible? Was Dani really the key to the travel? Could it be love? The longing to be with someone no matter how far distant in time or space one was from their beloved.

He took Susan's hand gently in his own, hoping not to awaken her. She would surely wonder what he was about. But if they did slip through some sort of door to the future, he wanted to ensure that Susan came with him.

The train rumbled as loudly as his heart did. Rory had disappeared, perhaps to the rear of the car where they offered a barber service. An occasional voice could be heard above the sound of the train as fellow passengers readied themselves to step off the train, either with Wenatchee as a final destination or simply to stretch their legs.

Stephen had no intention of stepping off the train for any reason, but what he needed to do was go back to sleep. Whether Dani was the catalyst or not was unclear, but sleeping seemed to be an important element. He closed his eyes and willed himself back to sleep, his grasp on Susan's hand firm.

Some time later, he opened one eye to the sound of his name being uttered.

"Stephen! Stephen, wake up!" Susan shook his shoulder. "I think it is time for dinner."

Stephen straightened. The dark mahogany paneling of the carriage told him everything. They had not traveled in time. Bleakly, he pulled his watch from his vest. Five o'clock—approximately three hours past Wenatchee. It seemed that time travel was not possible for him alone. He had no way to read Dani without her presence.

"Stephen! What is wrong? You look so unhappy!"

"When Dani and I traveled, it was near Wenatchee. I must admit that I hoped..."

"That we could travel forward to see her? As I did?" Her mouth drooped.

Stephen nodded. "Even though I told you I did not believe we could, I still hoped." He gave his head a quick shake and scolded himself for making his sister unhappy. That had not been his intent.

****

They arrived in Kalispell in the late afternoon of the following day. Stephen had spent a restless night in the sleeping compartment, superstitiously concerned about his absence from the observation lounge, but one could not simply overnight in the lounge...at least not in his time. He felt closer to Dani in the observation carriage than in any other part of the train.

He checked in at the ticket office, and was disappointed to discover that a train station in Whitefish did not exist, at least not in his time.

"No, Sir, nothing like that. Are you trying to get over to Belton?" the ticket agent asked.

"Belton? No, I do not think so. I was trying to get transportation to Whitefish."

The agent, an older man with a large handlebar mustache, removed his cap and scratched his head. "Well, I don't know why you would want to go up to Whitefish, other than to go fishing. Seems like everyone is going to Belton these days. You can catch the coach to Lake McDonald from there.

"Lake McDonald?" Stephen stiffened. "Where is this Belton?"

"Well, it's little more than a train stop a few miles east of Lake

McDonald. It is a forest preserve now with some mining and homesteading. There's a leaflet on the wall there about the homesteading." The ticket agent pointed to a wooden board containing various notices. "Some folks say they are going to create some sort of national park there."

Stephen turned to read the leaflet, a notice from a land office company regarding homesteading and property for sale.

"May I have this copy?"

The ticket agent shrugged. "They will be by to put another one up in its place. Go ahead."

Stephen pocketed the flyer. "Two tickets to Belton for tomorrow morning!" He knew the place. Dani had called it the West Glacier train station. In her time, there had been a small hotel just across from the entrance to the National Park. He took the tickets and turned to smile at Susan, tucking her arm in his as they left the depot to hire a carriage.

"You will enjoy this," Stephen said. "I was able to see this wonderful park with Dani, and she made me promise to bring you back here. Of course, we will not be able to see as much of it as I could in Dani's time, but they will build a road through it, and I will bring you, your husband and your children here...as Dani requested."

"What a great adventure we are on," Susan said with color in her cheeks.

They spent the night in a nearby hotel and settled in for the night, arising early the next morning to take the train to Belton. On arrival, Stephen and Susan followed the ticket agent's instructions to hire a carriage to Lake McDonald.

"It is so ironic. I have not seen this place in my time, but in the future. A hotel in the style of a Swiss chalet will be built there." He pointed to a spot across from the simple train depot. "It is as if *I* am the time traveler now."

"I wish I could have seen it with you and Dani. Do you think Dani will know we have come here? We cannot very well leave notes for her all about the wilderness, can we?"

Stephen laughed and shook his head. "I think we must dispense with the notes for now." He sobered. "Yes, Dani will know we have come. I promised her, and you know I always keep my promises."

Susan nodded.

The carriage ride up a bumpy road, unlike the smooth black surface upon which Dani had driven, led them toward the serenely beautiful Lake McDonald.

Stephen felt quite at home in the preserve, as if Dani's essence was somewhere nearby. Her love for the park had shone in the sparkle of her eyes as she spoke, and he had determined then and there to purchase a summer home nearby. He fingered the flyer tucked safely in his pocket. It seemed as if some force guided him, given that the ticket agent had most conveniently mentioned the flyer. He vowed to contact the land agent as soon as possible.

Stephen looked at his sister who stared at the snow-capped mountains with rounded eyes and pink cheeks. She already looked better away from the smoke of Seattle. He imagined her bringing her children to the park for summer holidays.

****

Dani drove straight through back to Montana, arriving at her mother's house about ten hours after she left Seattle, close to midnight. Ten glorious hours of knowing she would see Stephen again no matter what. History had shown she would marry him, and she would have his children. The conversation with her mother would be painful, but she knew without a doubt that she and Stephen would be together.

A few lights in the living room were still on when Dani arrived, and she unlocked the front door with her keys and tiptoed in.

Her mother lay on the sofa in the living room, the television on but apparently muted. Dani peeped over the edge of the sofa to see her mother sleeping. She turned away to head for the kitchen for a glass of water, but her mother's voice stayed her.

"Dani? Is that you? Where *have* you been?"

"Yes, it's me." She came around to the front of the sofa and sat down on the large ottoman which served as a coffee table. Her mother, in a pink cotton robe, lay on her side, a bandage showing above the edge of her nightgown.

Dani took her mother's hand in her own.

"How are you feeling?"

"Sore," her mother grimaced, "but I'll live. The doctor says they got all of the tumor, and that everything looks promising. Just have to go through the chemotherapy."

Her mother tried to raise herself on one elbow but slumped back down. "Ouch!"

"Ohhhh, I'm sorry," Dani winced. "Where are Sarah and Jean?"

"Sarah is upstairs sleeping. Jean went home. She'll be back tomorrow. I couldn't sleep so I came downstairs to watch TV."

"I'm so sorry I had to leave, Mom—" Dani began.

"Where is Stephen?"

"Well, that's just the thing. He had to go home." Dani noticed she no longer felt the exquisite pain at the thought of Stephen's return to his own time. She knew she would see him again.

"Are you saying he...?" Words failed her.

Dani nodded, smiling. "Traveled back in time."

"I didn't know he could come and go as he pleased."

Dani shook her head. "He can't. I'm the only one who can travel back and forth apparently, so far."

"I just can't wrap my head around this, Dani."

Dani rubbed her mother's hand soothingly.

"I know. Believe me, I know."

"So, Stephen is gone? How do you feel about that? I thought the two of you were..." Her mother adjusted herself to raise her head and gaze at her daughter. "I thought you were in love with him. He certainly looked smitten with you."

Dani grinned widely.

"I *am* in love with him. And that's what I need to talk to you about."

"I think I know what's coming."

"Maybe, maybe not," Dani smiled. "The historical records show that Stephen and I get married."

Her mother stared at her in stunned silence, so long that Dani's smile drooped.

"Mom? Are you all right? I know this is an awful time with the surgery and all, but I thought you should know."

"When?"

"When?"

"What year do you get married?"

"I didn't wait to find out," Dani said. "I heard the information and then I hotfooted it over here."

"You're leaving, aren't you?"

"I am, Mom. I'm going to try to go back. He needs to stay there for now because of Susan."

Her mother pushed herself to an upright position.

"When are you going?"

"I'll wait until you've recovered from your surgery and chemotherapy. That will be in about six months, right?"

"That's what the doctor says."

"That's when I'll go, if you're in remission. That will give me some time to convert my money into something I can use in 1901, take a weekend to clear out my apartment, and let them know at work that I won't be back."

"So, you're willing to wait six months to see Stephen? Six months is a long time, honey. A lot can happen."

"I know," Dani said. "I know, but I don't think I can leave while you're still undergoing treatment. It would break my heart to leave you so soon."

"But you'll be back, won't you? At this point, I'm thinking about Stephen. As far as he knows, he's never going to see you again, right? And he can't come to you?"

Dani regarded her mother with love and a new respect. "No, when we parted, it was with the understanding that I wouldn't return."

"Because of me?"

Dani looked away. "Well, not really..."

"It *is* because of me, isn't it?"

Dani didn't respond.

"Do you honestly think, Dani, that I would have let anyone come between your father and me except for death? Even you?"

Dani stiffened.

"I love you dearly, Dani, but I loved your father just as much. Luckily, I never had to make that decision. I'm telling you though, no matter what the records show, you need to return to Stephen because if he's suffering the way I did when your dad passed away, it's agony. I wouldn't wish that on anyone. You've got the upper hand. You're the one who can travel, and you're the one who has seen some evidence of your marriage. He's got nothing but despair."

A tear slid down Dani's face. She knew Stephen probably suffered, but to hear her mother say the words so harshly made it seem so immediate.

"Mom, how can I leave?" She held her hands out in a supplicating gesture.

"By getting on the train." Her mother sighed. "Look, I know I put some pressure on you to stay the other day, but the fact that you can control how you travel..." she paused at Dani's shaking head, "the fact that you seem to be able to control when you travel, give or take, makes me feel much better. I know I'll see you again."

"Oh, Mom," Dani leaned forward to kiss her mother's cheek. She dared not embrace her given her recent surgery.

"I've given it a lot of thought over the past few days. Who knows? Maybe I'll pop into the past with you for a quick visit of the grandkids!"

Dani chuckled, and her mother joined her with a few choice words regarding the pain when she laughed. Dani laid her head on her mother's lap, and her mother stroked her hair.

"Go back tomorrow, honey. You probably won't need the money. Stephen sounds pretty affluent. Leave a message at work that you won't return. And Sarah and Jean can clean out your apartment, sell the furniture and bring the rest of your stuff here. It will be here when you come back to visit. It's no different than living in Seattle and visiting here twice a year."

"What if I manage to get there but can't get back, Mom? There are all kinds of what ifs. What if the train route changes? What if I can't sleep when I'm supposed to? What if I travel to another year?"

"I know it's not failsafe, Dani, but you have to try. Your future lies in the past. I don't know if it's possible to change the past, but I'd rather not find out. If the records show you marry Stephen, then you must go back. Tomorrow."

"Tomorrow," Dani agreed. "I'll return as soon as I can."

The following morning, Dani drove out to Glacier National Park, feeling closer to Stephen there than anywhere else. The air was brisk, the leaves bright orange and gold. New snow capped the mountains. She had packed a picnic lunch and returned to the spot at the edge of Lake McDonald where she and Stephen had eaten. The still lake mirrored the mountains and trees surrounding it.

She munched her sandwich and studied the few houses and cabins on the other side of the lake, wondering about the lucky people were who had owned land around the lake before Glacier had been made a park. For those fortunate few homesteaders or landowners, the homes remained theirs unless they sold them. Then the park had first rights to buy.

Stephen's words echoed in her ears. *In the eventuality that the worst comes to pass, I am, however, willing to come back here, as you suggest, perhaps with Susan and her children, to watch the park develop as you wish.*

Dani smiled, feeling almost as serene as the lake. She would accompany Stephen back to the park, she was sure of it. After all, they were to be married.

Dani returned to her mother's house and spent the rest of the day with her.

Although Sarah suspected something was up, she didn't ask, and Dani was grateful. Her mother would probably fill Sarah in soon enough, but Dani didn't think she could take one more *What? You traveled through time?* revelation. As far as Sarah knew, Dani was returning to Seattle to go back to work.

"It's almost time, Mom. I've got a little over an hour before the train leaves. I wanted to talk to you privately before I go," Dani said on entering her mother's room. Her mother lay propped up in bed reading a magazine. Sarah and Jean were downstairs washing dinner dishes with the intent of joining her mother in her bedroom later for a game of cards.

"I know," her mother said quietly. Dani settled herself on the bed next to her mother.

"It's not too late, Mom. I can stay." As much as Dani longed to see Stephen, she would have stayed. "You and I have talked about this like I'm just going back to Seattle, but I'm traveling back over a hundred years. It's a little bit different."

"Don't I know it!" her mother said with a hint of a smile. "I'm counting on the fact that you'll be able to travel back. Besides, you're taking me for a visit, remember? The more I thought about it, the more I liked the idea."

"You're serious, aren't you?"

"Dead serious. Besides, if I have grandchildren, I want to get to know them, but I don't want their molecules getting all screwed up in the process of time traveling, so I'll come back and see them."

Dani laughed. "Oh, Mom!" She sobered. "How will we coordinate that?"

"Well, I'll have to wait for you to come get me, so you'll be the one making contact. Didn't you say Stephen left you notes? You could do the same thing."

Dani thought quickly. "What isn't going to change in the last century? Everything is going to change. Everything. Notes would get lost. Why don't I just arrange to come back at the same time twice a year? You can leave my car here."

"Sounds good. And bring Stephen. I kind of liked him. Good choice."

Dani leaned in to hug her mother carefully. "Thanks, Mom. I do too."

"Now, tell me everything. I don't feel like we've had a single uninterrupted moment. I'm ready to listen."

For the next hour, Dani told her mother about life in 1901 as much as she understood, about Susan and Stephen, Ellie and Robert, and Edwina and Edward Richardson. She even described her encounters with Lucinda Davies and Rory O'Rourke.

Dani said a tearful goodbye to her mother and drove down to the train station and parked her car. She preferred to go alone, and she asked Sarah and Jean to pick up her car up at the terminal the following day. Dani packed a small bag with the clothes from Ellie, as she had no intention of showing up in 1901 again in jeans.

After purchasing her tickets, Dani boarded the train at the observation car. She was taken aback to find her favorite seat was taken by a young couple who cuddled, seemingly in a world of their own. Hoping they would soon leave, perhaps to get a late dinner, she sat near them. She picked up her afghan square and stared at it. The small piece of acrylic fiber had been through centuries of travel, still intact. Wherever she had gone, the small square had gone with her. She hadn't thought to ask Stephen or Ellie if yarn was readily available but assumed it was.

The train pulled out of the station a little before 9 p.m. and wasn't due to arrive in Wenatchee until 5:35 a.m. Dani thought about the last time she had taken the train only days before when she had let go of Stephen. Now, she was heading back to him, secure in the knowledge that they would be together.

Over the next few hours, Dani eyed the young couple intermittently, waiting for them to budge so she could nip into the seat she wanted. Not only did they not move, in fact, they seemed inclined to sleep in the seats as they dozed on each other's shoulders.

Dani suspected the seats weren't all that important to the traveling equation, but being naturally superstitious, she really wanted *her* seat. She looked at the fire alarm on the wall but thought better of it.

Midnight came and went, and Dani's eyes drooped. Tired, and desperate for sleep, she again willed the couple to rise, but they stayed put. What could she do short of asking them to move?

****

"Seattle, twenty minutes."

Dani opened her eyes to the sound of the conductor's voice as he passed, her head bent at an awkward angle over the chair next to her. Sunlight streamed in through the observation windows. The observation car had filled with travelers.

Dani stiffened and jerked upright. She still hung onto her bag, and still wore her jeans—as did several of the other people in the gleaming observation car with its modern blue and gray interior.

She hadn't traveled! She hadn't traveled! Dani's eyes flew to the seats where the young couple had sat. It was the seats! It wasn't just the train, or Wenatchee, or her... It was the seats! And the young couple still sat in them.

She jumped up from her seat, clutched her bag and pushed her way past several people to approach the couple. She hurried around to the front of the seats and positioned herself between the young couple and the observation windows.

The blonde woman and tousled-haired man looked at her in surprise.

"Do you know what you've done?" Dani just about shrieked. "Do you know? I should have asked you to move last night, but I was too polite. Oh, polite Dani, always trying to do the right thing. I should have just tapped you on the shoulder and asked you to move. That's *my* seat. In fact, they're both my seats. They mean everything in the world to me. Don't you get it?"

"Now, just a minute," the young man began, but Dani planted a hand on his chest and pushed him back into his seat. By now, she had an audience staring at her, but she didn't care.

"I'm a time traveler, you know? A time traveler? And I have to get back to 1901. Stephen is waiting for me. Well, no, he's not expecting me, but in a way I know he's waiting for me. You see, he would never believe that I would leave him forever. How could he? I can't. I love him so much."

"But I needed to be in those seats! Those seats! I've traveled back before, and I've come back, but each time I was in those seats. They're the key. He thinks I'm the key, but it's those seats!"

The young man attempted to speak, but Dani, tears streaming down her face, felt as if she'd lost her mind.

"And now I have to catch the train again going east, and then I have to catch it going west again. I'll be exhausted, and what if the next time they change the route of the train? What if they never go through Wenatchee again? What if Wenatchee means nothing in the time traveling equation? What if I can't get back to Stephen?"

She knew she was hysterical. The young blonde woman looked terrified, but no one tried to stop her.

"But you know? You sat in those seats all night, and you slept, and you guys didn't go anywhere. So, it isn't the seats! Or did you? Did you guys travel back in time? Did you?"

CHAPTER FOURTEEN

"Dani! Wake up! Dani!"

Dani opened her eyes to her mother's face, her hand shaking Dani's shoulder gently.

"Mom! I had the worst dream. I couldn't get back to Stephen. I rode the train over and over and still couldn't get back. Where am I?" Tears ran down the side of Dani's face.

"In your bed at home. You had a bad dream. I heard you hollering down the hall."

"Oh, Mom, am I still here? How do I get back to Stephen? How can I get back?" Dani turned over and sobbed into her pillow.

"Get back where, my love?" Stephen entered the room, wearing a ridiculous-looking apron over his T-shirt and jeans. Dani knew she was still dreaming. Why would he be wearing his T-shirt and jeans?

"I'm still dreaming, aren't I?"

"You deal with her, Stephen," her mother said with an exasperated smile. "She's always been a noisy dreamer. I'll go get the baby." She left the room, her skirt swishing about her ankles.

Stephen approached the bed, sat down and pulled Dani into his arms.

"I love you, Stephen. I love you. I'm so sorry I couldn't get back."

"Dani, Dani, you are not dreaming. You came back to me. I am here." And to prove it, he kissed her deeply and passionately. "Now, do you believe me?"

She leaned back and stared at him hard. The same sky blue eyes, the same beautiful golden-sandy colored hair, a bit of a golden beard growing on his face. She ran her hands along his muscled arms and up the T-shirt. He loved to wear this clothing, and still wore it often.

She let her eyes travel around the room, the walls made of pine logs, the ceiling pitched toward the peak of an A-frame. She loved this room. It was their bedroom, the bedroom in the new house.

"Oh, my gosh, what a dream," she whispered as she buried her face in Stephen's neck. "It was so vivid!"

"You were about due to have one, dear. Remember? You have them about once or twice a year when you return from picking up your mother. I do not like them, but you always seem to awaken from them and come to your senses fairly quickly."

"My senses!" Dani playfully punched Stephen. "Well, as mother would say, the time traveling is screwing all my molecules up."

"Yes, well, you have traveled back more than I thought you would to collect your mother."

Dani's mother appeared at the bedroom door. "Here's your daughter, wide awake and ready to see her mom. I'm just going to go down to the kitchen and see what Stephen left burning down there."

Dani grinned and took the baby, a tiny blonde with the same color of eyes as her father.

"Are you burning something in the kitchen, dear? Where did you get that ridiculous apron?"

"Your mother brought it as an anniversary gift for me. Do you think it unmans me?"

Dani eyed his handsome face, the strong jaw, the grizzled beard. She thought of the many nights of passion they had shared and the baby in her arms they had conceived.

"No, dear, I know it doesn't unman you."

He leaned over and kissed her thoroughly over the top of the baby's head.

"Come, get out of bed. Come and see the lake this morning."

He pulled her from bed, and Dani handed him the baby while she slipped into a loose blouse and some baggy trousers. She liked to be comfortable unless she was in public sporting the longer skirts.

"What time are Ellie, Robert and the kids supposed to be here?" she asked Stephen who bounced the baby.

"Soon, I think. They overnighted in Kalispell and will arrive by rented automobile this morning."

"We're going to be a full house," Dani said with a smile, reaching for the baby. "I love it!" They descended the stairs and stepped out onto the verandah facing Lake McDonald. Susan, her husband, William, and their toddler son, Luke, played at the edge of the lake.

"Mom!" A young boy came running out of the kitchen with a pancake in his hand. Crystal green eyes pleaded. "Can I go down to the lake and play before breakfast? Grandma gave me a pancake."

"Of course, honey. Make sure you stay where Aunt Susan can see you." She watched the almost five-year old hop down the stairs, his hair the same red as hers.

"You make wonderful children, my dear," Stephen said as he wrapped his arms around his wife and baby.

"Well, you had a hand in it, lover." She chuckled and turned to see Stephen blush. Even now, he wasn't completely used to her uninhibited speech.

She listened to the quiet on the lake. "This is the first year we haven't had construction workers hammering and sawing since you bought the place. I still remember the night I got back and Mrs. Oakley told me you and Susan had gone to Montana. It was all Ellie could do to hold me back from jumping the train again to find you." She nuzzled his neck and returned to watch her son skipping stones in the water. "I'm so glad Susan will be able to stay all summer. She looks so much better when she's here."

"When do you take your mother back, Dani?" Stephen asked. "You know I worry every time you go that I will not see you again, and you have the dreams soon after your return."

"Didn't I tell you? She's staying for a while this time. No definite plans to return, she says. Sarah and Jean are moving to Florida, and she's not sure she wants to stay if the girls move away. Mom says her health is good, and she likes it in 1906, says she feels very comfortable with this era, especially now that we have a car. She says she wants to join me in being part of the suffragette movement."

"Good!" Stephen said.

"Good that Mother is staying or good we're going to be activists for women's rights?" She peeped up at him with a laugh.

"Good for both." He leaned in to kiss her cheek. "Everything is perfect."

Dani looked up at him with affection. "It is, isn't it?" She leaned her head on his shoulder and watched a duck land on the lake and glide along, breaking the mirrored image of the mountains. "I can't imagine what my life would be like without you, Stephen."

"You do not have to, my love, for we will be together forever...in this life or in any other."

****

Edward waited patiently at the table in the dining car, having shooed the waiter away twice. He understood they wanted to move the service through quickly so they could seat the next group of passengers, but he wanted to give the young lady a little more time. Ladies were notorious for arriving fashionably late, he knew.

He suspected though that she wasn't coming, and he wondered if he'd dreamt the whole meeting up. Before his nap, he remembered being in the observation car and meeting the young woman, Dani, short for...? Danielle? The name seemed familiar.

Ah! He remembered now. His great uncle, Stephen, had been married to a Danielle. He remembered her now, best friends with his grandmother, Ellie. They had seemed like two peas in a pod, those two, always buying the latest gadgets as soon as they became available. When his grandparents, Ellie and Robert Chamberlain, had taken Edwina and him to Glacier National Park for the summer, they had stayed at his great uncle Stephen's large cabin fronting Lake McDonald. His other grandparents, Susan and William, and their family had joined them. It had been such a merry time with cookouts on the beach, pancake breakfasts made by Uncle Stephen, hiking and riding bicycles and marshmallow roasts.

Great Aunt Danielle and Grandma Ellie had both looked at him and commented what a handsome old gentleman he would become one day, just like his Grandpa Robert. Aunt Danielle told him to memorize the family because one day he would want to keep the family history. She had said, after all, someone needed to keep it. She had always had a soft spot for his sister, Edwina, but Edwina's memory wasn't as good as it used to be. She didn't remember much of the family history.

Edward snapped out of his reverie as the waiter asked him for the fourth time if he wished to order. He checked his watch. Eight o'clock had come and gone. It seemed likely the young woman wasn't coming. He ordered breakfast.

He supposed she wasn't going to stop by to see the house he had inherited from Grandma Ellie and Grandpa Robert either. Too bad! He thought she might have enjoyed it.

Breakfast was served quickly, and Edward dug in with an appetite. He picked up a few hash browns with his fork, and his hand stilled. What had been the name on those notes he'd found in the brick steps of his house and in the book in Edwina's house? It had seemed significant at the time. Danielle? Had they been addressed to his Great Aunt Danielle? What was her maiden name? He couldn't remember.

Probably no relation to the young lady he had met earlier. If she had ever really been there, that is. Maybe she had just been a dream. He seemed to have the strangest dreams when he rode the train.

A Smile in Time

Bess McBride

PROLOGUE

"Wenatchee, twenty minutes," the conductor announced in muted tones as he walked down the aisle.

Annie yawned and checked the time on her cell phone with bleary eyes. The hour was still early, barely five-fifteen.

She glanced at her sister, slumped into a corner of the adjoining seat, her blonde head buried in a small traveling pillow. Marie looked completely out of it, and no wonder. They'd been on the train for about thirty-eight consecutive hours since leaving Chicago. As much as she loved trains, Annie swore at the moment that she'd never take a cross-country train trip again—at least not sitting in coach. Next time—if there was a next time—she'd find a way to pay for a sleeper of some kind. Thank goodness she and Marie had plane tickets back to Chicago at the end of their Alaskan cruise.

"Hey, Marie, wake up." She poked her sister's arm. "Let's go see if they've got any coffee or anything."

Marie batted Annie's hand away and pressed her face deeper into her pillow.

"Are we there yet?" she said in a muffled, slightly whiny voice.

"Almost," Annie said with another yawn. One of the books she'd downloaded onto her phone before the trip caught her interest the previous night, and she had skipped sleep in favor of yet one more chapter. "Do you want to go get coffee or do you just want to sleep?"

"I'm coming," Marie mumbled, her eyelids still firmly shut. "I have to go to the bathroom anyway. What time is it?"

"Twenty minutes to Wenatchee. I heard it *die-rect* from the conductor himself."

Marie straightened with effort and dragged an ineffectual hand over her tousled hair. She eyed her sister with exasperation.

"And exactly what time is it when it's twenty minutes to Wenatch… Winatch…wherever?"

"Five-fifteen," Annie said. She looked at her phone again. "No, make that five-twenty! Gotta stay on schedule. Timing is everything on a train! It's the difference between catching the train or being left behind at the station, don'tcha know?"

"Gosh, you're irritating this early in the morning," Marie said with a yawn. "Let's go."

Annie grinned, slipped her feet into her running shoes and rose from the seat. She bent over to tie her laces while Marie untangled her legs from her blanket, stuck her feet in her flat shoes, and climbed out of the seat. They made their way to the back of the car and crossed the bobbing connection to enter the observation car. Annie, never a fan of the idea of traversing two train cars moving at high speeds, leapt across as if she could see the ground below—which she couldn't. The connector was well protected and enclosed, and she wasn't going to fall out of the train. But knowing something and feeling it were two completely different things.

On entering the observation lounge, Annie noted through the large picture windows that the sky was only just beginning to lighten to the hazy purple of pre-dawn. A few early morning observers lounged on seats facing the large windows—some sipping coffee and conversing, others reading newspapers.

Annie and Marie climbed down the steps in the observation car to the first level and used the restroom before entering the small snack bar where the attendant sold them two cups of coffee.

"Let's go back upstairs and grab a seat in the observation lounge before it gets too crowded," Annie said. "We can watch the sun come up."

"I'm never letting you talk me into taking a train again," Marie muttered as they retraced their steps to the second level. "I'm honestly too pooped to get on a cruise ship now. Probably won't do anything but sleep for the next seven days just to make up for not getting any sleep on the train."

"Yeah, I don't think this was one of my best ideas," Annie said as she slid into a seat facing the windows next to an elderly gentleman. Marie took the seat on Annie's other side. "It probably would have been better to fly. Or at least find the extra money for a sleeper."

"I'm flying from now on," Marie said. She blew on her coffee. "I'm glad we did it, but man, this was long."

Annie nodded and sipped her hot drink. Out of the corner of her eye, she noted the elderly gentleman to her left lowered his newspaper and looked at her. She met his bright green eyes and smiled politely.

"Long trip, eh? Where did you come from?" he asked in a smooth, melodious voice.

"Chicago," Annie said. "My sister, Marie, and I are headed to Seattle for an Alaskan cruise."

"That's a wonderful trip. I went on that cruise with my sister and daughter some years ago. You'll enjoy yourself."

"You've been on it?" Marie asked as she leaned forward to look at the man. "Oh, good! Could you tell us about it? My name is Marie St. John, by the way, and this is my sister, Annie." She reached out to shake his hand. Annie followed suit, noting the fragility of his light grip.

"Edward Chamberlain," he said. "Pleased to meet you. My daughter is traveling with me, but she's still asleep in her compartment. I am supposed to wake her up in a few minutes. This is the first time I've ever had a sleeping compartment. It's pretty relaxing I have to say. I've always ridden coach, but my daughter insisted on the sleeper. Something about my age." He quirked an eyebrow in their direction.

Annie smiled. His thinning white hair and pale, blue-veined skin did suggest advanced age, but he seemed quite alert.

"I wish we could have afforded a sleeping compartment," she murmured. "We've been living in our coach seats for the past thirty-six hours, and we're exhausted. Marie and I were just saying we should have flown to Seattle, but I've always loved trains, and I wanted to travel by train."

"I understand the feeling," Edward said. "I love them myself and travel by train as much as possible. It's getting a little harder these days." He smiled wryly. "So my daughter accompanied me this time." He checked his watch and looked past her to Marie. "I would love to tell you about the cruise, but as I mentioned, she asked me to wake her up. Could we meet at breakfast at about seven o'clock? We could discuss it then. My daughter could probably help add some information that I might forget."

Marie met Annie's eyes for confirmation and nodded. "That sounds great! We'll see you in the dining car at seven o'clock then."

"Good. See you then," Edward replied with a smile as he rose and shuffled off toward the end of the car.

Annie watched him with concern, poised to jump up if need be and help him through the connector to his compartment.

"I guess he's going to be all right," she said, watching him pass through the connecting door. "I'm tempted to go help him, but he seems to be doing okay."

"He looks kind of old, doesn't he, but he seems pretty steady on his feet," Marie noted. "I'm sure he'll be all right."

Annie sipped the last of her coffee as the train slowed.

"We must be getting into Wenatchee," she said. "It's still kind of dark outside. Are those mountains?" She studied the horizon.

Marie squinted. "I can't tell." She rose and tossed her cup into a nearby trash container. "Well, if it's all the same to you, I'm going to head back to my seat for some more shuteye until breakfast."

"I'll come with you. I don't think I slept a wink last night. Too much reading." Annie rose, disposed of her coffee cup and followed Marie toward their car. "That coffee isn't helping me wake up. Maybe I'll just take a little catnap with you. I'll set the alarm on my phone for about ten to seven."

They returned to their seats and burrowed in—Marie in her corner and Annie positioning her pillow on her sister's shoulder, a position they had adopted off and on since the beginning of the trip. Annie closed her eyes.

CHAPTER ONE

Rory set his newspaper down on the small table beside his bed and rose to turn off the lights. The new "compartment-observation" car in which he rode was much to his liking. Although the recently launched Oriental Limited lacked the library he had come to enjoy on previous trains, the new observation car offered four staterooms, and he had secured one and advised the steward he would stay the night and dispense with his sleeping compartment.

Earlier in the day, the steward had attended him with tea, reading material such as newspapers and the daily telegraphic bulletin, and he felt himself quite satisfied overall, especially in light of the especially large fifteen-seat observation room and the constant foot traffic and noise generated by the opening and closing of the door leading to the observation platform. While he enjoyed scenery as much as the next person, he abhorred the dirt and grit, which flew in the door every time it was opened.

However, most first-class passengers had returned to their sleeping compartments, and the only sound was the rhythmic rumbling of the train along the tracks. He had no idea whether the other three compartments were in use, but if so, the occupants seemed to be of the quiet sort.

A light sleeper, he knew he would awaken when the train stopped at Wenatchee, so he had waited until the train left the station and picked up speed before he folded his newspaper and settled in for a few hours of rest. He stretched his arms behind his head and closed his eyes, willing sleep to take hold of him.

A nearby crash startled him, and he shot up and listened carefully. Voices, presumably coming from the next compartment, caught his attention, and he reached for the lamp above his head to turn it on. Soft light filled the room. The voices, possibly female, continued, and with exasperation, he grabbed his dressing gown and threw it on over his pajamas. He pulled open the door of his compartment and peered out into the hallway. The car was silent save for the sibilant whispers coming from the next compartment. He was surprised that no one else in the remaining two compartments opened their door to raise an objection. Could they not hear the ruckus?

He rapped on the door sharply and stood back.

One voice squeaked, much like a mouse, and the room fell silent. Rory waited and listened for a few moments but could hear no further movement and no further commotion. Although fully prepared to express his displeasure at the late night carousing, the occupants had apparently taken his knock as notification and silenced themselves. Having achieved his goal with no further need to pursue the matter, Rory turned to return to his own compartment.

No sooner had he reached his room than the door of the other compartment opened, and a young woman stuck her head out into the hallway. He could not see her clearly in the darkness of the hall, but her voice marked her as a woman.

"Yes?" she said in a breathless voice.

Rory shoved his hands in the pockets of his dressing gown.

"I wondered if anyone in your compartment needed assistance?" he said, though he suspected not. "I heard a crash and then *loud* voices."

"Oh, sorry," she said, though her tone did not sound apologetic. "We bumped into something."

"I see," Rory said. "I will return to my own compartment to *sleep* then."

"Wait!" The squeak he had heard earlier. Definitely not a mouse.

"Yes, madam?"

"Where are we?"

Rory sighed. Now he was to be a conductor?

"We left Wenatchee twenty minutes ago."

"Wenatchee," she said without purpose.

She looked over her shoulder. "Just a minute! I'm trying to find out," she whispered to the person in the room behind her.

Rory, tired and in an unaccountably bad mood, waited.

"When do we get to Seattle? We *are* going to Seattle, right?" the woman asked.

"In a little over seven hours, madam, which is why we should all get some *sleep*." Apparently, the woman did not understand his emphasis.

"Seven hours? Are you sure? It's only supposed to be five hours from Wenatchee to Seattle!"

"Not in my experience, madam. This train is known for its speed—the reason I took it in the first place—and I have not heard of anything faster. Seven hours is excellent time!"

She shook her head. "This isn't possible," she muttered. "I don't know, Marie," she whispered over her shoulder.

The door opened wider, and another woman thrust her head through the door to survey him. Although the car was dark, Rory was certain he could see the whites of her widened eyes.

"What the...?" she breathed. "Who are *you*?"

Rory, feeling somewhat at a disadvantage standing about in his nightwear, introduced himself.

"Harold O'Rourke, Junior, madam, at your service. I apologize for my state of undress, but I heard a crash and loud voices and thought someone might be injured. If you ladies are well, I shall return to my room."

"Wait!" the first woman called out. "Harold! Don't leave us! I mean, wait—we need to ask you some questions."

Rory, in the act of turning toward his room, froze. No one called him Harold. He detested the name. That his father was a Harold O'Rourke did nothing to endear the name to him.

"*Rory*, madam, *please*. How may I be of assistance?"

"Can you help us turn on a light? We can't even see, and neither one of us knows what's going on."

"A light? In your compartment? Is it malfunctioning? I could certainly take a look at it if possible in the darkness." It seemed a small matter, and it did not appear as if a steward attended to the compartment-observation car at night. He wondered briefly now if the other compartments were occupied, as surely someone would have opened their door to discover the cause of the noise in the hallway.

The women stepped back to allow him to enter. The shades were drawn against any possible moonlight and the room was indeed dark. No wonder the ladies struggled to find their way around. He felt along the wall for the switch, and the lights came on—an overhead globed chandelier and two wall sconces.

He stiffened as he surveyed the two young women standing before him, barely aware that they eyed him with equal expressions of surprise.

One of the young women, the first one who had addressed him, wore black slacks that appeared to be molded to the curves of her body. The other wore shorts such as young children might, her long limbs bared. Both women sported short-sleeved, jersey-style shirts in bright colors.

With a lifelong appreciation of the female form, Rory could not find fault with their figures although their attire seemed very risqué. He considered himself well traveled, but he could not for the life of him speculate as to their country of origin based on their costumes. They spoke English with an American accent.

They looked at him and then at each other.

"There you are, ladies. The lights needed only to flip the switch," Rory said to break the onerous silence. "May I ask where you are from?"

The smaller of the two, the young lady who first addressed him, responded in a tentative voice.

"Ummm...Chicago?"

"Are you asking me?" Rory said in an attempt to lighten the palpable tension in the small compartment. He noted the bed had not been slept in.

"No, I'm just..." She turned to her sister. "We're just...ummm... confused. Is this the Empire Builder?"

Rory eyed the chestnut-haired woman with misgiving. Her pale brow wrinkled with apparent confusion and her eyes darted around the room as if she hadn't seen it before. Her companion, the blonde one called Marie, bore much the same expression but said nothing as she clasped and unclasped her hands.

Rory shook his head. "I have not heard of an Empire Builder. What is it?" He forced himself to speak with patience, although his inclination was to leave the two women to their confusion. Still, he could not in good conscience simply turn his back on them and say good night. Clearly, some untoward event had occurred to frighten these women.

"Can I assist you ladies further in some way? Forgive me for prying, but I feel I see apprehension on your faces, and I am reluctant to depart without ascertaining the cause of your concern."

"My gosh, Annie, what's going on?" Marie said. She grabbed Annie's hand.

"I have *no* idea," Annie said with a glance toward Marie. She turned back to Rory.

"The thing is, Rory, this isn't exactly where we're supposed to be." She surveyed the vermillion wood paneling and dropped her gaze to the plush-upholstered maroon bench and olive carpeting.

"I'm afraid I do not understand. Where should you be? Are you in the wrong compartment?"

Annie shook her head, her shoulder-length hair bouncing around in a ponytail.

"I don't think so. If anything, we're on the wrong car, but I don't remember leaving ours, and neither does my sister apparently."

"Were you in the tourist sleeper perhaps?"

The young women shook their heads in unison.

"No, we didn't have a sleeper," Marie responded.

"What car were you in?"

"I don't remember which car exactly, but it was coach."

"Ah! The day coach. Yes, I think I saw it when I boarded the train, but that is four cars away toward the front of the train. We are at the rear. And you do not remember leaving your car to come to the compartment-observation car?"

Annie shook her head, and Marie followed her example.

Rory thought quickly.

"It is late, ladies, and I do not think we can pass the sleeping cars and the dining car to return you to the day coach tonight. As this compartment appears to be vacant, I suggest you rest here until morning, at which time you can sort out your arrangements with the conductor." He had another thought. "However, that might not even be necessary as we arrive in Seattle at eight-fifteen. All you will need to do is collect your baggage and be on your way. Unless you left any personal belongings in the day coach?"

The sisters looked at one another again.

"I left my purse and my backpack in coach, and I don't see your purse anywhere either, Marie." Annie scanned the floor. "Did you say coach was four cars up? We'll have to get back there as soon as they open up the dining room and the sleeping cars because I have to get my stuff."

Stuff? Rory almost smiled. Her language belonged to that of the working classes. Not that he did not degenerate into slang himself on occasion—the hazards of traveling the world and living amongst a wide variety of people from other cultures and backgrounds.

"I think that is the wisest recourse. Do not concern yourselves, ladies. This will right itself in no time at all." Rory ended on a breezy note, hoping to reassure the women. "Good night." He turned and left the compartment, forbidding himself to turn around. He had no doubt the expressions on their faces—reminiscent of lost babes in the woods—would compel him to stay and render assistance, and he wished himself rid of the matter. He hardened his heart and entered his compartment, where he shrugged out of his dressing gown, turned off the lights and climbed back into bed.

Perversely, he noted the silence from next door was almost deafening, and he strained to hear any voices at all. Surely they did not just retire for the night without further discussion, did they? As bewildered as they had appeared? Of course, the walls of the compartments were sturdy and probably acted as an effective soundproof barrier under normal circumstances—that is, in the absence of shouting or furniture being overturned. What had made that crashing sound? He had forgotten to ask.

He took a deep breath and closed his eyes. The image of supple limbs encased in close-fitting dark trousers, as well as bare legs below a very short skirt, came unbidden, and he smiled in the darkness. Chicago? He had been to Chicago many times and had never seen women attired thus.

Something about Annie's speech reminded him of someone. He had not heard Marie speak enough to judge her accent, but the slang of Annie's speech tugged at his memory.

Dani Sadler? And Ellie Chamberlain? Both women used odd turns of phrase on occasion.

He had just returned from photographing the Flathead Forest Reserve and Lake McDonald in Montana for the *National and World Magazine*, and while there, he had stayed at the lakeside cabin of his college classmate, Stephen Sadler, and his wife, Danielle. Ellie Standish and her husband, Robert, had been visiting for a few weeks with their children as had Stephen's sister, Susan, and her family. Dani Sadler's mother had been there as well—another unusual woman, progressive in her sentiments.

A knock on the door startled him, and he rose from bed, slipped on his robe and flipped the light switch.

Annie stood on the other side of the door. Rory had all he could do to keep his eyes on her pale face and ignore her skimpy leg coverings, which resembled nothing so much as thick stockings...without a skirt. Her hair was now unbound, falling to just below her shoulders.

"Yes, Miss...?"

"St. John," she said. "Annie St. John. My sister is Marie."

"Delighted to meet you, Miss St. John. How may I be of assistance?"

"Well, I don't know exactly, but you're the only person on this car right now, and you say we can't go through to the other cars."

Rory shook his head. "No, I don't think it is possible. The dining car is usually locked at night, and you must go through that car to reach the first-class sleeper car. An attendant would probably be there."

"It doesn't make sense to have people flailing around here at the back of the train, and you can't contact anyone," Annie muttered. "Well, look, I didn't want to mention this to my sister because I might be way off base, but I was wondering if you could tell me the date?"

"Certainly," Rory said, unclear why the date must be of such great importance at midnight. "June 5, 1906."

"1906?" she whispered with a stricken face, clutching her throat as if she could not breathe. "This can't be happening. I-I…" she began.

Rory jumped forward to catch Annie as she slumped to the floor, but he lost his balance and used his body to cushion her fall. Winded, he rolled over and looked down at her. Cradling her head carefully in his arms, he called her name softly.

"Miss St. John! Miss St. John, can you hear me?" He laid a hand gently along her cheek and patted it. "Miss St. John."

Dark lashes lay against pale cheeks. He remembered her eyes as brown. Her hair—silky and wavy—fell across his arm and the carpet in wild abandon. Soft-looking lips parted slightly as she breathed. The skin of her face felt like satin to his touch, and he stilled his hand and let it rest against her face.

"Miss St. John," he murmured.

"What are you doing?" A shriek erupted from behind him, and Rory felt himself unceremoniously grabbed by the shoulders of his dressing gown. "Get off her! Get off her!"

Marie St. John screeched as she pulled against him with a strength he did not think women could possess.

"Miss St. John!" he shouted, attempting to free himself. "Let go! Please release me! Your sister's hair is caught up under my arm."

"Get off her, you creep! What do you think you're doing? Annie! Annie?"

Rory lifted Annie's head and removed his arm—no easy feat, as Marie pulled at him as if she would drag him away and bodily throw him from the train. In the midst of the chaos, he realized what she thought— that he had attempted to ravish her sister. Such an odd pair of women. Rather than take advantage of the sisters, he could not wait to see the last of them!

"Unhand me, woman!" Rory barked as he attempted to raise himself to a sitting position. "Your sister fainted in my arms, for goodness sake. I did not—" He stopped abruptly. One did not simply shout such things to young women.

Marie dropped to her knees beside her sister. Unlike Rory, she showed no tenderness, and she smacked her sister's cheek twice.

"Annie! Annie! Wake up!"

Rory stayed Marie's hand when she would hit her sister again.

"Miss St. John, I must protest. Stop slapping your sister in such a vigorous manner. I fear I see a lifetime of repressed sibling rivalry in your enthusiasm. She will come around in good time. She has simply had a shock."

"What shock?" Marie asked with narrowed eyes. "What did you do, Rory?" She surveyed Rory's person with suspicion, and he shook his head at her implication but was prevented from retorting by Annie's revival.

"What happened?" Annie said as she opened her eyes. She looked from one to the other with confusion, raising a hand to her cheek. "Did I faint?"

"Yes, Miss St. John, I am afraid you did," Rory said as he helped her to a sitting position. "Your sister was just...ah...attempting to revive you."

"He means I slapped your face...several times," Marie said. "What made you faint? Rory said you'd had a shock? What? More than we've already had?"

"You slapped me?" Annie said, rubbing her cheek once again. "You've been watching too many movies, I swear." She turned to Rory. "Please tell me you didn't slap me, too. I'd be lucky to have any teeth left if you did." She eyed his hands, now clasped in his lap.

"No, no, not I, Miss St. John," Rory said with a twitch of his lips. "My attempts to revive you, short-lived as they were, involved calling your name and placing a hand lightly upon your cheek. Your sister, however, came upon us at the moment and thought I was...em...abusing you. She was quite the tigress in your defense."

Marie sat back against the opposite wall of the narrow hallway facing both Rory and Annie. She crossed her arms.

"So, what was the shock?"

"Shock?" Annie asked with a quick glance in Rory's direction. Rory knew nothing about her, but even he could tell she stalled for time. He thought he saw a plea in her eyes, but he did not know what she required of him.

"Shock," Marie said.

"Ummm...shock, yeah, shock," Annie hedged.

"Perhaps the date?" Rory offered.

"What about the date, Rory?" Marie looked to Rory, but he deferred a response by turning to Annie.

Annie pulled her knees to her chest in a most unladylike fashion, and rested her elbows on her knees as she rubbed her eyes.

"Annie!" Marie urged.

"Give me a minute," Annie said. "I don't quite know how to say this."

Rory regarded both of them with interest. There was something so eccentric about the sisters—at once charming and yet unsettling.

"What?" Marie squeaked impatiently. "Just spit it out!"

"Oh, my gosh, Marie! Fine! I think we've traveled back in time." Annie shot a quick look toward Rory, who stiffened at her words.

"Traveled back in time?" Marie and Rory said in unison. "Impossible!" Rory said with a shake of his head. "Whatever can you mean?" He ignored all the signs that pointed toward some untoward event.

Marie was not so quick to denounce Annie's theory, he noted. She stared at her sister for a moment and then turned to survey the train.

"What year do you think it is?" she asked her sister in a small voice, which cracked on the last word.

Annie turned to Rory with an imploring look.

"I can't say it. You tell her!"

"Ladies, I do not pretend to understand what is happening here. It is almost as if you play a trick on me, but I do not know you and do not understand why I would be the target of such a practical joke." He could barely keep the exasperation from his voice. "The date is June 5, 1906. You are on the Oriental Limited on the way to Seattle."

"1906," Marie breathed.

"Don't faint," Annie warned her. Rory noted she favored her sister with a sympathetic smile.

"Ladies, I think I will return to my compartment. Perhaps I am short on sleep. Perhaps this is all just a bad dream," Rory muttered as he pushed himself off the floor.

"Wait!" Annie called out. She grasped his arm, forcing him to slide back down to the floor in an ignominious position. "You can't just leave us. Even if you don't think time travel is possible, and believe me, buddy, I definitely didn't think it was, you can't just leave us here. We need help. What if we get into Seattle and it's still 1906?"

"But of course it will be 1906 when we arrive," Rory almost snapped. These women were sorely testing his Irish mother's lessons in manners. But she had also taught him chivalry, and he forced himself to stay though his sole desire was to be done with the peculiar train trip and to be comfortably ensconced in his home in Seattle. "However, I will concede that something is amiss here. What may I do to assist you ladies?"

"At this point," Annie muttered in a voice similar to his, "I can't imagine what you couldn't do for us." She looked toward Marie, whose cheeks burned brightly. "*If* it really is 1906 Seattle, we don't have any money. Our purses are missing. We don't have anyplace to stay, and we don't know anybody in Seattle."

Rory did not hesitate. "I can offer you some funds and assist you in procuring a hotel for a week or so while you arrange your affairs or are able to contact others. Would that be helpful to you?"

"Oh, yes, thank you, Mr. O'Rourke, that would be great! I hate to ask since you're a stranger, but..." Annie shrugged her shoulders helplessly with a rueful expression. He noted irreverently that she used the usual formal term of address for him, whereas her sister used his first name in a more familiar, if inappropriate, manner given the length of their acquaintanceship.

"You are welcome. And now, ladies, I believe I will return to my compartment with your permission. We will arrive in Seattle in a few hours. I suggest you get what rest you can." He rose and stood over them, loath to leave them while they still sat unceremoniously on the floor like a pair of orphaned waifs.

"Come, ladies, I cannot leave you wallowing about on the cold floor." He reached down to help Annie stand and then Marie.

"Thank you," Annie said. Her sister nodded her thanks.

He watched as they entered their own compartment before entering his own. Annie's face of unease as she looked over her shoulder softened his heart...a little. Her expression suggested she thought he might withdraw his offer of aid and disappear in the night.

"I will see you shortly, Miss St. John. Do not worry." Rory hoped he sounded much more reassuring than he felt. Save for giving the young women some money and putting them up in a hotel room, he had no earthly idea what else to do with them. Time traveling, indeed! He thought not!

CHAPTER TWO

Despite his fatigue, Rory did not sleep a wink, the gentleman in him keeping an alert ear tuned for a soft knock on his door or the sound of distress in the next compartment such as he had heard earlier. Though he heard no untoward noise, he remained awake, his body tense in anticipation of rising to render aid.

Their individual beauty had not been lost on him even in the midst of their surreal meeting—Annie, petite with her lovely hair the color of autumn leaves, and Marie, taller with striking, gold-highlighted blonde hair. Banishing the vision of their lithe lower limbs from his mind, he forced himself to concentrate less on their physical appearance and more on their state of mind. It was possible that one of the sisters might be experiencing some sort of delusion, but that both women should fall victim to the same fantasy was indeed disturbing. A familial trait? An inherited mental disease? He contemplated contacting his physician to make inquiries into the matter but deferred a decision for the moment. Not only were the sisters likely to be confined to the psychiatric facility at Western State Hospital for observation, it was possible the good doctor would wish to extend an invitation for him to sojourn in the hospital awhile as well.

No, it would not do. He could not imagine the sisters in such a facility. He would do what he could to ensure their safety and comfort for as long as necessary, though he had only verbally committed to a week. How he could best handle the matter taxed him at the moment, but he knew he had no time to waste in devising a scheme. A survey of his pocket watch showed six o'clock. They would reach Seattle in approximately two hours. The first order of business, and the first test of his ingenuity, was breakfast. The Misses St. John certainly could not go to the dining room car dressed in their current attire.

Rory climbed out of bed and dressed quickly, suddenly concerned they might choose, in the light of day, to saunter through the adjoining sleeping car and into the dining room. He did not like to think what might happen to them there or whether they would even be waited upon.

He exited his compartment and tapped on their door.

Annie, her hair charmingly tousled, opened the door with a hesitant smile. Beyond her, he could see the shades had been raised, and soft early morning light filled the compartment. Marie, her head tucked against the wall, still slept on the bench.

"Good morning, Mr. O'Rourke," Annie said. The lilt in her voice suggested a more optimistic outlook than the previous night.

"Good morning, Miss St. John. I cannot help but notice that your sister sleeps on the bench. Please tell me that you and she did not sleep upright all night."

She turned to look at her sister before returning her attention to him with a look of surprise.

"Well, the benches aren't long enough to really lie down on, so we just sat up. It's not the first time I've slept sitting up, let me tell you—especially on road trips."

Rory cursed himself. "My apologies, Miss St. John. I didn't realize you were not aware that the benches fold down into a sleeper berth. Normally the porter attends to that, but I could have assisted you."

She studied at the bench again, and laughed. "Oh, really? We didn't even think to check on that. That's okay. We got some sleep. I have to admit, though, I'm starved."

"Ah, yes, I am sure you are, and that is why I hastened over to tap on your door this morning." He hesitated, keeping his eyes trained on her face and nowhere else. "With all due respect, Miss St. John, it would not be seemly for you or your sister to be seen in public in your current...em...costumes. I realize how discourteous my words may sound to you at the moment, and I apologize, but your attire is...unexpected...and would elicit comment. I am not at all certain you could be seated for breakfast. You say you have nothing with you? No baggage? No other clothing?"

Annie tilted her head to the side and regarded him with her lips pressed together, almost as if she were prepared to both laugh and cry at the same time.

"Nope, nothing."

"Miss St. John! Are you laughing? I can assure you I am very serious about this."

"I know you are, Mr. O'Rourke, but there's nothing I can do about it. If I don't laugh, I'm going to cry." She turned to look at her sister. "Is there a chance you could bring us back some food after you eat?"

Rory could not imagine how he might ask the waiter for extra food to bring back to the observation car. He checked his pocket watch again. Six-fifteen. The porter would arrive soon, and perhaps other passengers might visit the car, although the hour was still early for that.

"I will see what I can do, Miss St. John. In the meantime, I think it best if you and your sister remain in your compartment. If you need to freshen up, there is a women's lavatory just next to your compartment, but I would make haste before the porter arrives."

"Okay, we will. Thanks."

Rory gave her a small bow. "My pleasure, Miss St. John."

She shut the door, and he turned away and made his way through the sleeper car and to the dining car. Being one of the first passengers to arrive, he was seated promptly. A waiter handed him a menu and poured him a cup of coffee. Rory studied the menu, wondering how on earth he was going to enjoy a leisurely breakfast while the women went hungry and without food.

"I noted the porter in the compartment-observation car served coffee, tea, sandwiches and bullion yesterday," Rory said to the waiter upon his return. "Do you know if he will be serving again this morning, given our imminent arrival?"

The middle-aged waiter shook his head. "No, sir. There won't be any sandwiches or soup this morning in the observation car. You might still be able to get coffee or tea there, though."

Rory sighed. "Well, I wonder if I could make a request. My...sisters are not feeling well, and they do not wish to present themselves to the dining room. Could the cook prepare something for them to eat? Perhaps some sandwiches? I could take the food to them myself."

"Sure," the amiable waiter said. "We can have the porter take the food to them. No need to carry the food yourself, sir."

"Oh, no," Rory said. "No trouble at all." Rory closed his menu. He knew he could not do more than enjoy his coffee while he waited for the food. "In fact, could you ask the cook to prepare a sandwich for me as well? I think I will join my sisters. And put the whole in a small container of some sort. I do not wish to be seen carrying a tray through the length of two cars. Thank you."

The waiter nodded and moved away, and Rory sipped his coffee and contemplated the scenery from the window. Evergreen trees huddled near the tracks, forming a lush gauntlet. He knew they had reached the mountains but could not see the hills for the thickness of the dense forests.

So engrossed was he that he failed to note when two women and a man were seated at the table next to him. One of the women faced him, an attractive woman in a fetching beribboned hat who looked to be about twenty-five. The other woman, middle-aged, sat next to the man, and he assumed they were husband and wife. He was not at all certain he would have noticed the threesome except for the frequent glances the young redheaded woman directed toward him caught his eye. He was not immune to the admiration of a beautiful woman, and would normally have engaged in a flirtatious exchange with the lady, but at the moment he could think of little else but a pair of bewildered sisters wearing little more than bathing costumes who needed his help.

He favored the redhead with a brief smile, paid his bill and left the dining car, feeling not a little foolish carrying a basket resembling a picnic hamper, heavy with dishes and cutlery and covered with linen napkins.

When he returned to the compartment-observation car, the porter had indeed arrived. Rory cast a quick glance around to see that the sisters were not in sight. The porter ran forward to assist Rory with the basket, but Rory waved him away.

"Thank you, no. I have just picked up some food for my sisters who are not feeling well. Could you prepare some tea and coffee? I'll come and get the beverages and take them to my sisters."

The porter gave him a surprised look but nodded and moved away to the front of the car toward the small kitchen, not much larger than a closet.

Rory set the basket down and tapped lightly on the young women's compartment door. He listened carefully, but heard no response in answer to his knock. He cast a quick look toward the front of the car, but the porter was not in sight. He knocked again, this time harder. Still no response.

"Miss St. John," he called in a low voice. "It is Mr. O'Rourke. I have brought food. Are you there?"

No response. Rory wondered if they had gone to use the lavatory and had been trapped there by the porter's arrival. He ensured the porter was still out of sight, and he moved toward the lavatory and rapped on the door.

"Miss St. John! Are you in there?"

There was no response to his knock. Had they disappeared? Was it possible that they had indeed traveled in time and had vanished back to wherever they had come from? No, he refused to entertain such a theory.

Rory turned away from the door of the lavatory and surveyed the length of the observation room, lined on both sides with dark green plush chairs. The room was silent, empty, the seats vacant. He slumped against the wall, crossing his arms across his chest and stared unseeingly at the carpet. Weariness overcame him. Either Miss St. John and her sister had made their way to another compartment unseen by him, though that seemed unlikely, or they had vanished into thin air as rapidly as they had arrived.

Was he so tired that he had conjured them up? Had his mind played tricks on him? He rubbed his eyes and bent to retrieve the basket before the porter returned with the beverages. A flash of movement at the far end of the car caught his eye. A large plate-glass window looked out over the observation deck, but the window had been shuttered for the night. The smaller window in the door, however, was uncovered, and it was through that window that Rory had seen a spot of color—the turquoise color of Miss Annie St. John's blouse.

They were on the observation deck? In the open? What had possessed them? His anger at their disregard for his warnings warred with his relief that they had not somehow vanished.

Rory, picnic basket in hand, strode through the observation room and pushed open the door. Annie leaned over the side of the railing gazing at the ground flying past, her hair billowing in the wind. Marie reclined in a chair tucked up against the wall, appearing as if she felt ill. A red and white striped awning blocked the sun from her face.

"Good gravy, Miss St. John! I expressly directed you to stay in your compartment!" He addressed himself to Annie, almost shouting to be heard above the wind and the rumbling of the train on the tracks. "The porter is within, and he will soon see you given the brightness of your blouse."

Annie whipped around at his voice. She looked toward her sister with a look of concern before turning back to him with a raised brow and narrowed dark eyes.

"I beg your pardon," she said, also raising her voice against the elements. "I appreciate the help you're willing to give us, Mr. O'Rourke, but please don't think you have the right to talk to me like that. You don't get to *direct* me...or my sister." She added the last few words almost as an afterthought. "Marie was feeling nauseous, maybe from being enclosed on the train—there are a lot of strange smells—and I had to bring her outside. Otherwise, she was likely to puke in the compartment."

Rory cursed himself for his unusual heavy-handedness. "I am sorry, Miss St. John. Of course, you are right. I was out of line." Apologizing by bellowing—as he was forced to do by loud reverberations of the train on the rails—seemed as if it might add insult to injury, and he bowed his head. "Is there anything we can do for your sister? Perhaps some food?" He held out the basket as a peace offering and favored Annie with a bright smile, one that had successfully eased women's displeasure on occasion in the past. However, the dubious expression of the woman before him showed no sign she had succumbed to his smile.

"Thank you for the food, Mr. O'Rourke. That probably *will* help Marie feel better. She might just be hungry." Annie turned toward her sister but paused and looked over her shoulder. "Oh, and that smile of yours?" She shook her head with a twitch of her lips. "It's pretty effective but I'm not going to fall for it. I've seen a lot of smiling men in my time, and you look like you've practiced that smile quite a bit." She chuckled and moved forward to help her sister up.

Rory, taken aback at her frank comments, closed his mouth and jumped to open the door. He peered inside then stood back to allow the women to precede him, with a fervent hope that the porter was still ensconced in the small kitchen. He led the way toward their compartment and opened the door as Annie and Marie stepped inside. Following them inside, he set the basket down.

"I am afraid they have packed my breakfast in with yours, so if you have no objection, I shall have to dine with you." Rory, smarting just a little, pressed his lips together, unwilling to attempt a smile of any sort at the moment.

"Please do," Marie said. "Thank you so much for going to get the food."

Rory nodded. "You are welcome. I asked the porter to prepare tea and coffee as well. I hope that will suit you?"

"Yes, thank you," Annie said. She ran her fingers through her hair before tying it back into a ponytail again.

"I will go get the beverages and return. Please serve yourselves."

Rory made his way down the passage toward the front of the car. He paused outside the kitchen where the porter was setting a pot of coffee, a pot of water and four cups on a silver tray, along with a small creamer and sugar cubes. Rory eyed the tray with misgiving. Never in his life had he served tea or coffee, nor had he balanced a tray while making his way down the hallway of a moving tray.

"I think you had better carry that, my good man. I will surely make a mess of it." He smiled his usual smile, but dropped it quickly, the image of Annie's amused expression before him. The porter responded in kind with a grin.

"Yes, sir, I was hoping you would say that. I wasn't too keen on cleaning up the hallway when you dropped the tray."

Rory grinned. "Ah, I feel you must know me well." He patted the porter on the shoulder. "Shall we?"

Rory led the way, and the porter followed. He tapped on the women's compartment door, and turned to take the tray.

"Thank you, my good man. I shall take it from here. My sisters are not well and would not wish to have anyone enter the compartment."

The porter nodded, handed off the tray, and Rory turned as Annie opened the door. He juggled the tray inside the room and set it down on a side table. He noted with a small measure of delight that the Misses St. John had waited to begin eating until he returned.

"These sandwiches look wonderful," Marie said, her face pale. "Thank you again."

"Please eat," Rory said. He took the bench opposite. "I hope the food helps restore your good health."

"Oh, I'm sure it will," she said as she bit into her sandwich.

"Thanks again, Mr. O'Rourke," Annie said. She eyed him speculatively. "At the risk of telling you off one minute and then asking your advice the next—which is what I'm doing—do you have any idea what's going to happen when we get to Seattle? It's daytime, and we can't really hide our clothing."

Rory swallowed his food and gave his head a slight shake. "Not at the moment, Miss St. John, but it is not for lack of pondering the matter. The first thing we must do is ensure that you have proper clothing. Your attire, does it have a name?" He found himself distracted by their limbs once again.

Marie smiled, evidently feeling better. "Shorts and a T-shirt?" she asked almost as if she expected him to agree.

"I'm wearing black capri leggings," Annie said pointing to her legs. "They *are* tight, I know, especially for your time, but they're pretty normal where we come from."

"Shorts and leggings," Rory murmured. He took a deep breath. "No, these are not usual fashion for Seattle—not for women at any rate. And you say you wear these in Chicago? I have traveled to Chicago many times and would have noticed women dressed in this way."

"Not in 1906, you wouldn't," Annie said.

Rory eyed them sardonically. "Ladies, I cannot in all conscience join in your fantasy of time travel. It is not possible. If it were, we would know of it by now. At the risk of offending you even further," he directed a pointed look toward Annie, "I submit that you are both suffering from some sort of delusion...of time travel. I am concerned for you. I can assist you financially for a period and I can situate you in a comfortable hotel. I can even secure proper ladies' clothing for you, but I cannot protect you from the consequences if you continue to espouse this theory of time travel. I do not wish to alarm you but feel I must speak frankly. This sort of talk will only find you ensconced in the state asylum."

Annie set down her sandwich and turned to her sister. "He's right, Marie. Not about the delusion." She threw Rory a sharp look. "But about getting us locked up. I'm not sure what's happening, but we're going to have to keep our mouths shut about time travel—for as long as we're here."

"I just want to go on my cruise," Marie fussed. "What are we going to do? How do we get back?"

Annie shook her head. "I don't know."

Rory's heart melted at their obvious distress. "Finish eating, ladies. You must keep up your strength. Before we reach Seattle, I will devise a plan to get you safely to a hotel. From then on, we must decide what is to be done."

CHAPTER THREE

Annie studied the handsome, dark-haired man with startling cobalt blue eyes, who looked every bit as Irish as a man with the name O'Rourke ought to. His thick, well-groomed hair was parted on the side and trimmed evenly at the neck. He sported short sideburns, and he was clean-shaven, albeit with a bit of a dark stubble—no doubt from traveling. She had thought men at the turn of the century would look different in some way, but Rory could have passed for any regular American guy in her time, except for his more formal speech. Even his clothing—dark blue coat and trousers, white shirt and tie under a pale gray vest—could have passed for a retro look on any modern American male.

He looked troubled, with deep creases between his dark eyebrows. She felt guilty—for snapping at him and for putting him in this position. She didn't know anything about him—what his own worries were, what his life was like, how difficult it might be for him to help them, or even if he was married. She gulped on the last thought but put it out of her mind.

"Mr. O'Rourke," she began hesitantly, unsure of what she wanted to say. "I'm sorry to have put you into such a...an awkward position." She paused, and her heart skipped a beat as he looked up at her with his incredibly blue eyes. "Ummm...what was I saying? Oh, yes! I had no idea when I asked for your help that we would become such a burden. I don't know what I was thinking...maybe that you'd slip us a twenty-dollar bill and drop us off at the nearest...boarding house? Or something. But I can see that was a pretty simplistic plan." She shrugged her shoulders. "Marie and I *will* pay you back, you have to know that. Somehow." She looked to her sister, who nodded firmly.

"Yes, we will," Marie added. "We don't exactly have our wallets, but we'll figure something out."

"Please, ladies, do not add to your distress by feelings of obligation. I am happy to be of assistance."

He started to smile but stopped and sobered his expression, and Annie could have smacked herself. He really did have the most charming smile. Thanks to her smart-aleck comment, he was probably going to refuse to smile in her presence ever again.

With a sigh, she placed the dishes, unused cutlery and wax paper sandwich coverings back in the basket. Rory rose to set it outside the door.

"I have managed to give some thought to our arrival at the train station," he began as he returned to his seat. "I think it best if I leave the train first, find my carriage and make sure my driver maneuvers as close to the platform as possible. I will return for you, and we shall boldly descend from the train and make haste to the carriage. If you are seen, it is unavoidable. Once you are safely in the carriage, no one will know, and should you meet anyone in the future who might have seen you at the train, they will probably not recognize you. I have a great many acquaintances as my father is well known in Seattle, and it is likely that I shall be more easily recognized than you."

Annie opened her mouth to ask about his father, but Rory continued.

"The next obstacle I foresee will be getting you into the hotel. It would be best if you remained in the carriage while I register you and inquire about a back entrance to the hotel. I shall see you to your rooms and then leave to make arrangements at a women's clothing shop so they may attend you at the hotel. You will need to order sufficient clothing for your sojourn in Seattle."

Annie glanced at Marie, who stared at Rory with an open mouth.

"Gosh," Marie said, echoing Annie's thoughts.

"Umm...what if we order ball gowns?" Annie said with an attempt at a playful grin. His generosity to strangers seemed excessive and unnerving.

The right corner of Rory's lips twitched, but he held back a smile. "You will need several dinner gowns. If you wish to order ball gowns, you may do so. However, they will do you little good as daytime wear and will make you the center of attention at any event other than a ball. Do you wish to become the center of attention in Seattle in 1906?" He raised a sardonic eyebrow in her direction.

"Oh, heck no!" Marie exclaimed with a frown directed toward her sister. "Annie was just kidding, Rory."

"Yes, I suspected as much," Rory said.

"I'm sure Mr. O'Rourke knew I was kidding, Marie. I have to say that I'm a bit overwhelmed by your generosity—to complete strangers."

"No need," he said. He checked his pocket watch and rose to peer out the window. "We will arrive in Seattle soon. I shall leave you to rest." He opened the door, but stepped back quickly and eased the door shut.

"Ladies, it seems we are no longer alone in the compartment-observation car. Other travelers have seated themselves in the observation room and, I suspect, on the platform."

"Really? I want to see," Annie said as she jumped up and headed for the door. "Just let me take a quick peek!"

"Annie!" Marie exclaimed.

Rory stepped back for a moment, and Annie pulled open the door and stuck her head out. Marie, unable to contain her curiosity, joined her, peering over Annie's head.

Several of the previously empty chairs were now occupied by two women and a man. The women sported large straw hats festooned with a myriad of colorful silk flowers. Both wore long skirts in varying shades of beige. Black boots protruded from under the hems. The older of the two women wore a matching bolero-style jacket over her white shirtwaist, and the younger woman wore a broach at the high neck of her frilly white blouse. The man, a middle-aged gentleman dressed much like Rory did in a dark suit, tie and vest, sported a hat of white straw with a dark ribbon around the band. Unlike Rory though, he had a handlebar mustache that must have taken him hours to groom.

Beyond the threesome, through the window at the rear of the compartment, Annie could see several people standing on the observation platform. If ever she had a doubt that she and Marie had traveled in time, a survey of the new arrivals put that to rest. She looked up at her sister, who shook her head with widened eyes.

"This is really happening, isn't it?" Marie muttered as Annie closed the door.

"I'm afraid so," Annie murmured. She turned to Rory, who watched them curiously. She opened her mouth to speak but nothing came out. He didn't believe them, and from the look in his eyes, he thought they were slightly loony. Annie had a sudden vision of Marie and her settled in a little house somewhere, long skirts draped around their ankles as they drank tea, petting a few of the hundred or so cats that wandered the house. Maybe Rory, his wife and children might stop by on occasion and leave a casserole at their doorstep.

"Please do not leave your compartment until I return," Rory said. As the door closed, Annie slumped down onto the bench opposite Marie, who stared unseeingly out of the window.

"This is a nightmare," Marie said. "How are we going to get out of this?"

Annie looked out the window at evergreen-forested mountains as the train wound its way through a pass. "I have no idea. I doubt we're going to find a cruise ship at the end of this train trip, though."

"But what happened, Annie? How did we get here?"

Annie shook her head. "I don't know. I mean...time travel? Seriously? I don't blame Rory for not believing us. He must think we're crazy. And it's not like we have any proof or anything—no driver's licenses, no passports. Everything's gone!"

"I wonder what it will be like to wear those long dresses. Those hats!" Marie shook her head.

"Oh, gosh—don't even go there. I doubt they're going to be a lot of fun to wear, even if Rory really does help out in that way. Don't you think it's kind of strange that he offered to do all of that for us, Marie? Why would he?"

Marie shrugged. "I don't know. Chivalry?"

"Maybe. That's pretty chivalrous," Annie said dubiously. "Some ulterior motive? We don't know what people are like in 1906. We don't even know the laws, but I'm pretty sure there aren't many laws to protect women." Annie sighed. "Well, maybe some. It *is* the twentieth century, after all. Barely..."

"Well, all I know is that we can't stay here. At least, *I* can't. I've got stuff to do, and a fiancé who's going to want to know where I went. Even though you're grumpy right now, this is right up your alley, Miss Traveler. You're the one who always wants to go on trips, to travel. Well, here you are!" Marie crossed her arms and eyed Annie with her best this-is-your-fault look.

"*I* didn't do this!" Annie exclaimed, jabbing a thumb toward her chest. "It's not like I sat there in the observation car wishing I could travel back in time. And if I had, I wouldn't have picked 1906. I might have picked the year I met Sean, so I could make sure I never met him!"

"Oh, yes, your creep of an ex-boyfriend. That would have been nice."

"Yes, it would. I could start my whole life over again...fresh... innocent...believing in love again." Annie smiled weakly. Having broken up a year ago from her cheating long-time boyfriend, her heart was on the mend, but she thought she would never regain her faith in the honesty of men.

"I might have picked 2010," Marie mused, "before Mom and Dad passed away, just to talk to them again."

"Oh, yeah," Annie murmured. "That would be so wonderful." She sighed.

"Well, Miss Traveler, wishing and wanting are not going to get us out of this mess. Even if I don't have to worry about believing in love at the moment, I believe I love my TV, my computer, my cell phone, my fiancé and my job at the school too much to be staying here."

"I know," Annie sighed. "But I'm clueless. I got nothing. Nada. No ideas. Yet..." She grinned. "We'll just have to wait and see what Mr. O'Rourke has in store for us. It's two against one. We can take him if he tries any funny stuff—you know, like locking us in a warehouse and auctioning us off as sex slaves or something."

Marie rolled her eyes. "You are so weird!"

Annie wagged her finger playfully. "Just you keep an eye out, Sis. I'm not sure I trust Mr. Chivalrous all that much. No one with a smile like his can be trusted completely."

****

Annie woke from a doze to feel a change in the rhythm of the train. A look out the window revealed the train was slowing. An immense snow-capped mountain dominated the horizon in the distance, seeming to float on the clouds at its base.

"Marie! Wake up! Is that Mt. Rainier? That is one big mountain!"

Marie rubbed her eyes and glanced out the window. "I don't know. I'm so tired." She started to close her eyes again.

"Wake up, Marie. I think we're almost there."

Marie's eyes popped open, and she straightened.

"Look!" Annie pointed out the window toward the front of the train. "Buildings!" She clamped her mouth shut. Seattle's skyline looked nothing like it had in the photos she'd seen in making preparations for the cruise. The famous Space Needle was gone...or had never been there. In fact, there were no skyscrapers at all. Since she'd never been to Seattle before, she'd had no particular expectations of the city, but the panorama before her of a sprawling city hovering close to the hills, which led down to a bay, caught her by surprise.

"Are those tall ships?" she gasped. "Can you see them?" Though distant, the masts of the ships were unmistakable.

"Tall ships?" Marie asked vaguely. She pressed her nose against the window. "Where?"

"In the bay down there? Oh my gosh, Marie, where are we?" Annie whispered. "Look at them! They're beautiful. Can you see the tall masts?"

The train descended the hills and rumbled down toward the waterfront. Two large steamers docked at a long pier caught Annie's eye. Black smoke billowed from their stacks.

"Look at those," she breathed. A knock on the door startled her, and she rose to open it. Rory, carrying an umbrella in his hand, bowed, and she stepped back to let him in, peeking over his shoulder to see that the observation car now seemed to be vacant.

"As you can see, we have arrived in Seattle," Rory said. "Were you able to rest?"

"A little," Annie said. "Is the observation lounge empty?"

"Yes, fortunately for us, Mr. and Mrs. Washburn, and Miss Washburn, returned to their own cars."

"Did you know them? You didn't mention that," Annie said.

Rory almost smiled but seemed as if he stopped deliberately.

"I had not made their acquaintance before leaving your compartment, but only saw them at breakfast. However, Miss Washburn waylaid me with questions regarding the picnic, which she had seen me procure from the dining car, and I was forced to devise a story involving 'sisters not feeling well,' which I had previously mentioned to the porter. At that point, her parents wished to make themselves known to me, and we have been ensconced in the observation lounge sipping tea and discussing the merits of train travel on young fragile women such as 'my sisters' and Miss Washburn, who seems to be of a hardy sort and well used to traveling."

Anna watched his lips move in fascination, a necessary action because she wasn't sure she could follow his speech all the time. Reading the formal dialogue of an Edith Wharton novel in high school was one thing, but actually comprehending the rapidly spoken words was much more difficult.

"Miss St. John? Do not say that you have fulfilled the prophecy and actually become ill? You are staring at my chin."

Annie blinked. Yes, she had! A charming and boyish cleft in his chin.

"No, I'm fine. I think Marie is feeling better, too. We've been studying the view of Seattle...in *your* time."

Rory shook his head with a sigh but didn't argue.

"The train should arrive at the station within a few minutes. Are you prepared?"

"I don't think there's any way to prepare for this, Mr. O'Rourke." Just then, the train jerked and Annie caught the edge of the bench for balance. Rory reached for her, but he withdrew his hand when he saw her regain her footing

"Nope, no way to prepare," Marie agreed. "Are you sure we'll be all right between the train and your...ummm...carriage?"

"I think we will have to be. We have no other choice."

Marie grabbed Annie's hand, a gesture she'd left behind in childhood when she clung to her older sister. Annie squeezed her hand.

"We're going to be fine, Marie—aren't we, Mr. O'Rourke?" Annie willed him with her eyes to reassure Marie, and he rose to the challenge.

"Yes, of course. I do not foresee any complications. This is not the Dark Ages. We shall hold our heads up, make haste to the carriage, and all will be well."

Annie felt Marie's grip ease slightly, and she silently thanked Rory. He did not return her smile but nodded.

The train jerked again and slowed to a crawl. A shrill whistle announced their arrival at the station.

"We have arrived. Please wait here until I return," Rory said. He left the compartment, and Annie dashed to the window.

"Horses and carriages," Marie murmured, peering out the window. "Oh, wait! There are some cars over there...kind of."

The train station yard was filled with horse-drawn carriages and wagons, which lined in a row at the end of the platform. As Marie had said, several old-fashioned automobiles like the classic Ford models were parked nearby as well.

Annie strained to see the passengers who disembarked from the train. Not a single woman showed bare legs or wore capris as she and Marie did. Even the little girls and boys wore stockings that extended below their short dresses and pants. Mesmerized by the scene, she found herself holding her breath, and she released it.

"I can't believe this," she murmured. "Look at everybody. I'd say it's like we've dropped into a time warp, but I think we have. Look at those dresses...and those hats! Everyone is just so...beautiful!"

"I don't know, Annie," Marie muttered. "This really isn't my thing. I like jeans and T-shirts, shorts and tank tops. Gosh, even the men are dressed to the nines. Everyone's wearing a coat and vest and...what are those hats? The man in the observation lounge was wearing one. Like picnic hats? See?" Marie pointed. "Some of the women are wearing them too, but they're a bit fancier."

"I think they're called straw boaters, but I'm not sure. We'll ask Rory."

"Oh, I meant to ask you about that, Annie. Why do you keep calling him *Mr. O'Rourke* to his face?"

Annie shrugged, her eyes glued to the mass of people moving about on the platform. The women walked effortlessly without lifting their skirts, not something she thought she could do.

"Oh, I don't know. It seems to fit him somehow. Maybe because he keeps calling us Miss St. John."

"He does seem kind of formal, doesn't he?"

"I think it's the era, Marie. I don't think they used first names necessarily unless they were related or knew each other really well."

"Well, I can see I'm going to stay in trouble the whole time I'm here because I'm not going to be able to keep up with all these rules."

"We'll manage, Sis. At least we've got each other. If they lock us up, at least—" Annie clamped her lips shut.

"Lock us up?" Marie said shrilly. Her wide eyes flew to Annie's face.

"I'm just kidding, Marie. It was a stupid joke. I won't make them anymore. We're fine. As Rory said, this isn't the Dark Ages."

A knock on the door signaled Rory's arrival. "Come, ladies—my luggage is loaded and my driver awaits us." He stepped back to allow them to exit the compartment. "We will leave by the observation deck." He led the way to the door at the rear of the car. Annie, wishing she could at least pull her leggings down to her ankles, followed with Marie in tow.

Rory pulled open the door, and a myriad of smells hit Annie in the face—burning coal, smoke, manure and seawater. Marie hesitated at the door, peering outside as if she were stepping off the edge of the earth, and Annie gave her hand a tug.

"Come on, we can't stand here."

"My carriage is just over there. My driver, Joseph, stands by it." Rory climbed down the stairs and reached to help Annie down and then Marie. He strode across the densely packed dirt lot to the carriage, where a short man in a dark livery tipped his cap to them and held open the door of the carriage.

Annie couldn't resist patting the horses' noses before she followed Marie to the carriage.

"A lover of animals, Miss St. John?" Rory asked as he helped her into the enclosed carriage.

"Always," she said with a smile. "You hustled us over here so quickly, I don't think anyone saw anything but a flash."

A twinkle in his eyes gave him away, but he kept his lips firm.

"Just so," he said. He climbed in after her and settled himself on the opposite bench. "What do you think of our fair city thus far?" he asked them.

"It has a lot of strange smells," Marie said, her hand hovering near her nose.

At that, Rory laughed. Annie reddened and nudged her sister, but short of whispering "Be polite!" which Rory would surely hear, she could do nothing else.

The carriage moved forward with a jerk and Marie grabbed Annie's hand with a nervous laugh.

"Whoa!" Marie said. "I've never been in a carriage before."

"Never?" Rory tilted his head and regarded them with an incredulous expression.

Annie and Marie shook their heads.

"Why don't you have a car?" Marie asked. She nodded in the direction of the train station.

Annie had wondered the same thing when she'd seen the old-fashioned automobiles, but she didn't dare ask. What if he couldn't afford a car? That hardly seemed likely given his offer to set them up in a hotel...and clothe them. She averted her eyes from his face as she wondered again about the extraordinary offer. They'd be lucky if he didn't bundle them off on one of the steam ships she'd seen in the bay, bound for who knew where.

"I do have an automobile, Miss St. John—a Model N Ford, a delightfully small and nimble bit of nonsense, but it would not have been able to accommodate the four of us and my luggage." He eyed Annie. "And like your sister, I enjoy the horses."

"Oh..." Marie replied. She threw a sideways glance at Annie, who gave her a crooked smile.

"Are the streets all dirt?" Annie asked. Dust swirled from the horses' hooves and wheels of the carriage as they moved away from the train station.

"No, not all," Rory replied. "Many streets are cobblestoned and some are paved now. Soon, I think, most of the roads will be paved. That will help keep the dirt and mud to a minimum. Is the dust bothering you? We can close the windows if you like."

"Oh, no!" Annie said quickly. "I want to look out. I don't want to miss anything."

"As you can tell by the clattering of the horses' hooves and the rumbling of the carriage wheels, we have reached the paved streets of the downtown area."

Annie stuck her head out and looked down. They were, in fact, rattling along a cobblestone street—a wide one teeming with other carriages, pedestrians, a few cars and streetcars.

"Look, Marie! Streetcars!"

Marie leaned over to look past Annie's shoulder. "Oh, just like San Francisco!"

Annie threw Rory a quick look, wondering if he might complain about the indecorum of sticking her head out the window, but he only watched them with a slight smile on his face. His eyes were unreadable.

"Look at all those power lines!" Marie continued with rounded eyes.

"Surely they have power lines in Chicago, ladies, do they not?" Rory quirked an eyebrow.

"I know you don't want to hear it, Mr. O'Rourke, but not like this, and not downtown," Annie said. "Most of the power lines are buried now. You might find some on poles in the older neighborhoods."

Rory pressed his lips together with a slight shake of his head, but said nothing.

"Where exactly are we going, by the way?" Annie asked.

"I would have situated you at the Washington Hotel, but that fine edifice has sadly closed to be demolished and will be reborn again when regrading of the city's iconic hills has been concluded." Rory gave her an ironic smile, and she thought she heard unhappiness in his words. "But I think that I must seek rooms for you at the Hotel Seattle for now. I have eaten dinner there, but I have never stayed at the hotel. Of course, if you wish to stay in Seattle indefinitely, it would be prudent to find a boarding house for ladies. But if you intend to return to Chicago then that might not be necessary. I will not press you for your plans at this time but encourage you both to rest and orient yourselves to the city."

Marie looked at Annie, and Annie patted her sister's hand. "Thank you, Mr. O'Rourke. That sounds like a good plan. I don't think Marie and I would want to spend too much time...or money...in a hotel. I know I've said it before, but we do appreciate all you're doing for us. I'm not sure *why* you're helping us, but we *are* grateful."

"Annie!" Marie remonstrated. She turned to Rory. "Annie doesn't mean to sound suspicious, Rory." She chuckled nervously. "Well, maybe she does—but she's right, we are grateful."

"It is only natural that you are wary of strangers, especially those bearing gifts," Rory said with a twitch of his lips. "If I had a sister, I would wish her to be as guarded as you are."

"So you don't have a sister," Annie said. "Do you have other family? A wife?" Her cheeks burned. "Children?"

"I am not married, Miss St. John. If I were, I would most likely enlist my wife's aid in seeing you and your sister situated. My parents are alive and reside on Capitol Hill with my younger brother. He is just twenty and attends the university."

"What do you do for a living, Rory?" Marie asked the question on the tip of Annie's tongue.

"I am a photographer. I photograph essays for magazines. As a matter of fact, I just returned from photographing a lovely place in Montana called Lake McDonald near a glaciated wilderness. It was a memorable assignment."

Annie blinked. A photographer! She looked at Marie, but Marie was probably oblivious to the fact that photographers didn't make much money unless they were very famous or were independently wealthy. The hairs on her arm rose, and she promised herself that she and Marie would find their own "lodgings" as soon as possible. Mr. O'Rourke wasn't getting anything from either one of them other than a verbal thanks and maybe money when they managed to figure out how to get some.

"Miss St. John, you have narrowed your eyes as you regarded me, and not for the first time. I feel I have offended you in some way. Please tell me how."

Annie startled and her cheeks burned. "Really? Did I?" She rubbed her eyes. "I'm sorry. No, you haven't offended me. I'm just tired, I think." She had to watch her face carefully around him. He seemed very intuitive, as if he could read her mind. She turned to look out the window, resting her elbow on the edge of the window and nonchalantly covering her lower face with her hand.

The carriage slowed considerably as they negotiated their way through the downtown area, and came to a halt at an interesting intersection fed by three avenues which was as busy as any street she'd ever seen in downtown Chicago. Tall stone buildings peered down on the pedestrians, carriages, cars, wagons and streetcars from every corner of the intersection. The sight was busy, noisy, dusty and overwhelming, as was the smell of coal, smoke, horse manure and, oddly enough, a whiff of tantalizing food no doubt coming from one of the nearby awning-covered doorways at ground level.

"We have arrived, ladies. Please wait in the carriage while I check in at the front desk and obtain your key. When I return, Joseph will take us around to the back of the hotel, where we may enter with some degree of privacy." Rory rose and stepped down from the carriage to climb a small set of brick steps to the narrowed entrance of the Hotel Seattle—a five-story sandstone flatiron building which sat on a triangular-shaped island block.

Marie leaned over to follow his progress from the window.

"So, why the dirty looks, Annie? Do you think he's up to something? I'm so confused right now, I don't think I care."

"I don't mean to give him dirty looks, Marie. I'm just still worried about his motives for helping us out like this. No one would do something like this in our time."

"No, probably not, but I'm not sure he has any ulterior motives other than..." Marie stopped, and Annie turned from her study of the street to look at her.

"What?"

"Well, I think he might have a bit of a crush on you," Marie answered with a half-smile.

"What?" Annie narrowed her eyes and gave her head a quick shake. "Oh, I don't think so, Marie!"

"Well, *I* do," Marie said firmly. "I wouldn't mind if he had a crush on me, frankly, but I don't think he can see me when you're around."

"Marie! You must be more tired than I am. I get the distinct impression that Mr. O'Rourke can't wait to see the last of us."

"Well, if that's true, then he doesn't have any evil plans for us. Which is it?" Marie crossed her arms and eyed her sister with a raised brow.

Annie couldn't help but grin. "You're right. I'm making no sense at all. But I can't help it. I do think he wants to wash his hands of us, *and* I don't trust his motives." Marie opened her mouth but Annie forestalled her. "No, no crush. Not on *me*, anyway." She shrugged. "I know! He can't wait to hand us off to the slave traders." She chuckled and turned to look at Marie, whose face paled. "Marie! I'm just kidding! Don't take that seriously. I'm sure everything is going to be fine...at least regarding our knight in shining armor."

"You know the slave trade for women is alive and well in our time, and I'm sure it is in 1906," Marie said. "Especially for vulnerable women. That's us. I watched a TV program on it a couple of months ago."

"I know," Annie sighed. "I probably saw the same program and that's why I have it on my mind. I'm sorry, Marie. I shouldn't have said anything. Honestly, nothing seems to be very funny right now anyway."

"Any ideas how we're going to get home?" Marie asked.

"Not a clue, Sis. Not a clue."

Rory came out of the hotel and stopped to speak to Joseph before climbing into the carriage.

"I apologize for the delay, ladies. The hotel is very busy today, and the wait at the desk was long. I know you must be wishing for a cup of tea now."

Joseph maneuvered the carriage around the front end of the triangular building and down the street past a streetcar, where he pulled up to the sidewalk at the back of the hotel. Rory climbed down and paused at the carriage door.

"There is nothing for it, Misses St. John. We must simply stride forward as swiftly as possible to reach your rooms, which are on the third floor. I obtained two rooms for you, a bedroom and an adjoining sitting room. I hope that will be satisfactory."

Annie bit her lip. "Thank you, Mr. O'Rourke. We will pay you back. I promise."

Rory held his hand out, and she took it and climbed out of the carriage. "I understand the wish not to be beholden to someone. Do not concern yourselves at this time."

Annie cast a furtive glance at passersby on the street while Marie descended. The shocked looks on the faces of both women and men made her want to pull and stretch her capris down to her ankles, but that wasn't possible.

"They're staring at us," she murmured, keeping her head low.

"Yes, I know, Miss St. John. I am so sorry. Let us make haste." Rory led the way into the large wooden door at the back of the hotel. Marie and Annie hurried after him. They emerged into a long red-carpeted hallway.

"Now, where are those stairs?" he muttered. A well-dressed silver-haired couple came around the corner of the far end of the hallway, and Annie grabbed Marie and huddled behind Rory, who greeted them cordially while blithely ignoring their disapproving stares.

"Come, this way." He moved down the hallway and found the stairs at the end, looking over his shoulder to see that Annie and Marie followed.

"No elevator?" Marie mumbled breathlessly at the top of three flights of stairs.

"Not invented yet?" Annie guessed. She wasn't sure.

Luckily, they met no other people on the stairs, and Rory opened the door to the third-floor hallway. Annie peeked out and stepped into the hallway. Marie followed, and Rory came last.

"Which way?" Annie asked hurriedly, longing to be on the safe end of a locked door.

"This way, I think." Rory checked the number on the key and scanned the doors. "Aha! Here we are!"

He unlocked the door and ushered the sisters in, closing the door behind him. They paused to survey the sitting room. An elegant rose and beige-striped damask sofa with rolled arms faced a mahogany-trimmed fireplace with a marble mantle. Several occasional chairs in the same material flanked the sofa. Rose-patterned paper covered the walls, mirroring the flower-filled vases on the mantle and the cherry wood coffee table. Dark hardwood floors sported Oriental carpets in the same soft shades as the wallpaper.

Annie, her mouth hanging open in awe of the furnishings, watched Rory peek into the bedroom. She followed him to the door. Two single brass beds dominated one wall, their coverlets of white satin and lace. Ornate Victorian-globed lamps perched atop the gleaming cherry wood end tables between the beds and on either side. A large wardrobe propped up another wall opposite the large window. A gleaming dresser in the same cherry wood took up the final wall, the large mirror above it reflecting the lace curtains at the window. The colorful wallpaper and carpets were repeated in the bedroom. A bathroom adjoined the bedroom.

"Would you look at this?" Marie breathed. "It's beautiful."

"Then you approve of the accommodations?" Rory asked—rather deferentially, Annie thought.

"Oh, yes," she murmured. "This is stunning. It must be very expensive."

Rory clucked and frowned. "Let us not discuss money again so soon, Miss Marie. I am happy that you are pleased." He addressed himself to both of them. "I must leave now and procure some salesgirls to deliver clothing for you, or you will be trapped in this room indefinitely given your current attire. Do you require the services of a maid? I believe you will need to dress your hair, as most adult women in Seattle do not wear their hair down." His face reddened and he looked away. "Forgive me, ladies. It is not my intent to offend you. I realize the subject of a woman's clothing and hair are intensely personal matters, but I would be remiss if I did not make clear that you will continue to be an object of curiosity if you do not attempt to conform in some small way to the customs of Seattle. I understand that your manner of dress and hairstyle are different where you come from, but I feel certain you would feel happier if you blended in, so to speak. Am I incorrect in my assumptions?"

Annie shook her head. "No, you're right. We don't want to stand out, but I don't think we need a maid. I can put Marie's hair up and she can do mine." She thought she could do something with their hair and the elastic.

Rory bowed. "As you wish. On my way out, I will stop by the desk and ask them to deliver some tea and pastries for you." Rory turned and walked toward the door. Annie followed, strangely reluctant to let him out of her sight. Over her shoulder, she saw Marie head for the bathroom.

"Mr. O'Rourke," she called out as he moved down the hall. He stopped and turned. His vivid blue eyes watched her with a guarded expression.

"Yes, Miss St. John."

"I just wanted to thank you again." She couldn't think of anything else to say, but she didn't want him to go.

"And you wish to reassure me you will recompense me, is that correct, Miss St. John?" A twinkle in his eyes charmed her.

Annie grinned. "You betcha!"

Rory nodded and turned.

"Mr. O'Rourke!"

He turned again with patience.

"Yes, Miss St. John."

"Are you coming back?" Annie hadn't meant for her voice to sound so...desperate.

Finally, finally, Rory smiled—that beautiful, wide, bright smile she had fallen for on the train.

"But of course, Miss St. John. I had every intention of taking you and your sister to dinner in the hotel this evening."

CHAPTER FOUR

"I will see you at eight o'clock. The salesgirls will guide you in the proper clothing for evening." Rory relaxed into his smile, feeling not a little fatigued at having to control his features for the majority of the day. He couldn't even remember why he had felt the need. Oh, yes, Miss Annie St. John had scoffed at him and told him she would not "fall for" his smile. She had been right, of course. He had attempted to use his smile to advantage—a habit of long standing. It had seemed to have wondrous effects with his nanny, his governess, and later on as an adult, with women—but not with his mother, and apparently not with Miss Annie St. John.

He bowed again in her direction and turned away, wondering if she would call him back yet again. To his regret, though, he heard the door close behind him. Rory made his way down to the front desk and ordered tea and scones for the sisters before returning to the back of the building and the carriage. He directed Joseph to a nearby well-known women's clothing store—one that his mother frequented.

He entered the shop and asked for the manager. A tall, thin man approached.

"Mr. Becker," the man introduced himself. "How may we be of service today?"

Rory surveyed the shop. Several women, seated on velvet benches, watched him curiously. Presumably, they awaited other customers in fitting rooms? He could not say.

"Could we speak in private, Mr. Becker?"

Mr. Becker, appearing to be in his mid-forties, nodded, too professional to raise an eyebrow.

"Certainly, sir. This way, if you please." He led the way behind a curtain to a small, unassuming office and indicated a chair facing a desk. "Would you care for some tea, Mr...?"

"Harold O'Rourke. No, thank you, Mr. Becker. I am pressed for time, and so will you be if you can help me; therefore, I think it prudent I begin."

Mr. Becker sat down behind the desk and listened.

"I have two young cousins staying at the Hotel Seattle who are from...out of town. The railroad has apparently lost their luggage, and we are forced to find suitable clothing for them at short notice—preferably ready-to-wear. I hope you have some things in stock. They will need the usual women's clothing—day dresses, several evening dresses, hats, shoes and handbags, as well as whatever else you deem necessary for a modern, well-bred lady in Seattle. Perhaps a coat for the wet weather. Umbrellas. I leave that to you. I am not familiar with their measurements, so I think it best you have your staff deliver several sizes of clothing. Spare no expense. I would expect your salesgirls to assist them in dressing, as they are not familiar with our Seattle styles. Additionally, they will at least need dinner dresses for this evening." Rory pulled money from his wallet. Mr. Becker's eyes widened at the amount. "I am paying you, Mr. Becker, not only for your immediate and prompt service, but for your discretion. I do not wish to hear of my cousins' affairs discussed in public. I admit the situation is quite unusual, but I hope I can count on you."

Mr. Becker rose. "Certainly, sir. You may count on me. With your permission, I shall assemble some of my staff and send them on their way. If you could leave your cousins' address with me, we will gather whatever we have ready and hurry over there. That is, my salesgirls will. Do you have any idea as to their...em...figures, Mr. O'Rourke?"

Rory smiled at Mr. Becker's red cheeks. Oh, yes, he certainly had an idea.

"Miss Annie St. John, the smaller of the two, is petite and shapely. She is about five feet two inches tall. Her sister, Miss Marie St. John, is taller, about five feet eight inches, and more slender." Rory took the paper and pen offered and wrote down their address.

"Thank you, sir. That is a good beginning. We shall work miracles."

"Thank you, Mr. Becker. If I have not given you enough money, please send a bill to me at this address. Do not discuss payment with my cousins. This is my gift to them."

Mr. Becker eyed the address. "Oh, Mr. *O'Rourke*. You would be Mrs. O'Rourke's son. I apologize for not recognizing the name. Your mother is one of our favorite customers, most particular in her selections. She always knows exactly what she wants."

"Yes, I know of your service to her. That is why I chose your shop. However, my mother is not to know of this matter, Mr. Becker. My cousins' arrival will be a great surprise for her." Rory did not know when or how, but his mother would likely meet the Misses St. John.

"Certainly, sir."

Rory left the shop and directed Joseph home. They arrived at his residence on Queen Anne Hill, a large two-story brick home in the Queen Anne style with a large wraparound porch, which he had purchased some years ago in a moment of weakness. Though the house was far too large for an unmarried man, he determined he must have it though he'd had no staff and no family to fill it. In fact, he was hardly ever at home, traveling the world as he did on photographic assignments. The large inheritance from his maternal grandfather which subsidized his comfortable lifestyle had gone wanting for an investment, and when he had seen the house, he knew it to be a sound purchase, if a sentimental one. An image of a loving wife and several children had somehow tantalized him of late, but they had not been included in the house purchase, and had not, to date, materialized.

Not that he had pursued the option of marriage with any great degree of enthusiasm, he thought as he stepped down from the carriage and gave Joseph instructions for collecting him in the evening. Rory was not unaware that the catalyst for his home purchase should be the wedding of his university friend, Stephen Sadler, to the delightful, if unusual, Dani—but he preferred not to examine that theory with any great depth. Marriages such as that of Stephen and Dani were hardly usual, and he did not think he would be so fortunate to form such an attachment for any one woman. The image of his philandering father's face came to mind, but he banished it from his thoughts. His mother did not seem overly concerned, so why should he?

Rory traversed his walkway and entered the house, where his housekeeper held open the door with a greeting.

"Good day, Mrs. Sanford. Is all well?" He removed his hat and handed it to Mrs. Sanford, a tall, slender woman with graying hair, who nodded.

"Yes, sir. Welcome home."

"Thank you, Mrs. Sanford. I have an engagement this evening, so I will not have dinner at home. Is there any mail?" Rory lingered a moment in the foyer.

"On your desk in the library, Mr. O'Rourke." She shut the front door behind him. "Your mother sent a message around this morning asking that you visit her upon your return at your convenience. I have included the note with your mail."

Rory sighed. Although his mother seemed omniscient, she could not possibly know of the Misses St. John yet, could she?

"Thank you, Mrs. Sanford."

"Yes, sir." She moved to turn away.

"Mrs. Sanford?" Rory had not yet formed his thoughts or his words. He did not know Mrs. Sanford well, as he was rarely at home, but he suspected he should know more about her. His intent had always been to familiarize himself with her in a more friendly capacity, but it seemed he never had time.

"Yes, sir?" She turned hazel eyes on him.

"Is your employment here satisfactory?"

Her eyes widened for a minute before she relaxed her expression.

"Yes, sir, perfectly satisfactory. You are a very undemanding employer."

"Thank you," Rory said with a smile. "I will take that as a compliment."

Mrs. Sanford smiled, a warm smile he had heretofore not seen from her, as she normally kept her expression carefully neutral.

"You may, sir."

"I apologize that I have not inquired after your comfort. It seems that I run from one train to the next with my suitcase in hand with little time spent here in this big house. I wish you to know though that I value your services here and depend entirely upon you to run the house during my absences."

A dot of pink appeared in both of Mrs. Sanford's normally pale cheeks.

"Thank you, sir. I try to do my best."

"I can see that you do." Rory smile again and turned to see Joseph entering with his luggage. He turned to make his way to the library but hesitated.

"Mrs. Sanford? Do you have family?"

"A sister and several nieces who are grown up and at university now. But I do not have children of my own, and I never married."

"At university?" Rory raised an eyebrow. "You must be proud."

"I am, thank you. They are brilliant girls."

"Women have come so far today, have they not?" The image of Annie's face came unbidden.

"Only to a certain point, sir," Mrs. Sanford replied. "While my nieces may avail themselves of a college education, they are still destined to become teachers or nurses, and that is only before they marry. They are still expected to marry and have children."

"Is that not a goal of every woman?" Rory contemplated the numerous young ladies of his acquaintance who seemed perfectly happy—in fact, eager—to make marriages. So eager that he'd had to restrict himself to flirtations with mature women his own age who sought nothing more than delightful banter at an occasional dinner party. The younger women often misinterpreted his smile as one of encouragement, and more than once, he'd had to distance himself from figurative, if not literal, clutching fingers.

He was too well bred to toy with the vulnerable aspirations of young unmarried ladies hoping to make good marriages. At least, he was too well bred by his mother. His father was a reprehensible rake, in his opinion, who had only demonstrated his contempt for his marriage vows.

Mrs. Sanford shook her head decisively. "No, Mr. O'Rourke, marriage is most certainly *not* the goal of every young woman in today's society. Not for my nieces, at any rate, and not for many of their classmates. While marriage seems a desirable situation for many of the young women, some do not wish to give up careers to care for a husband and a home but would prefer to have both careers and marriage."

Rory blinked at the vehemence in Mrs. Sanford's voice. "A lofty goal, Mrs. Sanford, and a subject about which you seem very passionate."

The housekeeper smiled and smoothed her hands on her apron. "I'm sorry, Mr. O'Rourke. I do get on my soapbox occasionally. Forgive me."

Rory smiled. "No need for forgiveness. I appreciate your frankness. It has given me much to think about."

"Can I bring you some tea while you read your mail?"

"Yes, thank you, Mrs. Sanford. And thank you again for speaking with me."

She bowed her head and turned toward the back of the house.

Rory entered his library—a mahogany-paneled room of luxurious furnishings which made him feel at home. Brown plush chairs and a sofa fronted the fireplace, and from his desk in the corner, he could see out the floor-to-ceiling windows over the city and the waters of Lake Union. The view at night was especially delightful when the lights of the city twinkled on the water.

He shed his jacket and settled into the chair at his desk to read his mother's note.

Dear Rory,
I am so pleased that you are at last home for a few days. Please come to see me today before you busy yourself with engagements this evening. I have some news for you, though I am not certain how you shall feel once you hear it.
Mother

Rory wondered what news his mother had to impart. Hopefully, she had not found him an "eligible young lady" to marry, as she had often threatened to do. She mourned his frequent absences and had noted more than once that she believed he would settle down if he found a wife. Rory could not imagine such a fate.

"But if you marry, Rory, you must give up this hobby of yours," his mother had said more than once before.

Rory had shaken his head and responded patiently, as he always did. "My work is not a hobby, Mother. I enjoy documenting the world in photographs. The newspapers and magazines that carry my work need the photographs for their articles, and I love traveling. I cannot imagine meeting an 'eligible young lady' who would be content to stay at home while I traveled so extensively, nor could I imagine wanting to marry such a creature if she were indeed so content with my absence."

He would smile, and his mother would relent and forget the matter for the moment.

Mrs. Sanford entered with a tea tray and poured him a cup of tea.

"Mrs. Sanford, I wonder if I might discuss a matter of some sensitivity with you that requires discretion. Given our earlier discussion, I feel you might be just the person who could provide me with some advice in this matter."

"Of course, Mr. O'Rourke." She clasped her hands in front of her and waited.

"Could you sit for a moment?"

The housekeeper look at the brown velvet chair near the desk uncertainly and perched on the edge of the seat.

"On my journey back from Montana, I met two young women on the train who seemed to be in need of assistance—the kind of assistance neither a conductor nor a porter could render." He took a sip of tea while he contemplated his next words.

"They seemed to be confused about their origins. In fact, they seem to be lost. They state they are from Chicago, but not the Chicago that you and I might be familiar with."

Mrs. Sanford furrowed her brow and shook her head with apparent confusion. He did not blame her, as he was botching the matter.

"I am sorry. I am not explaining this well. The young women appeared with no luggage, no money and no personal possessions except the clothes on their backs. They seem to be well bred and well educated." He hesitated. "But they believe that they come from the future."

At Mrs. Sanford's expression of incredulity, he raised a hand. "I believe I understand your expression, Mrs. Sanford. I share your skepticism, I do, but the ladies were in dire straits, and I could not abandon them on the train."

"You did not bring them here, did you, Mr. O'Rourke? That would cause quite a scandal." Mrs. Sanford scanned the corners of the room as if he had hidden them behind the furniture.

Rory sighed. "It would, wouldn't it? I was certain of it, but I did want to verify that with you. I can state most emphatically that I have never contemplated bringing a woman home to my house, much less two women, but I could not leave them on the train. They are not from Seattle and do genuinely appear to be distressed at their circumstances."

"Are they...deranged, Mr. O'Rourke?"

Rory laughed out loud. "I admit I have often thought so over the past few hours, but no, they do not exhibit any qualities, other than their concept of time, which would lead me to believe they are not in possession of their faculties. They do, however, have strange mannerisms, forms of speech and clothing. They do not cover their lower limbs as ladies do in our time, nor do they seem interested in dressing their hair as adult women."

"Uncovered legs?" Mrs. Sanford shook her head. "I would not think that acceptable anywhere except at the beach. Where are they now, Mr. O'Rourke?"

"I have acquired rooms for them at the Hotel Seattle. I am having Mr. Becker from my mother's dress shop send his staff there to attend them this afternoon with some suitable clothing. I hope that given a few days' rest, they can reclaim their bearings and find their way home. I am prepared to assist them in that endeavor...perhaps train fare back to Chicago. Whatever they need."

"That is very generous of you, Mr. O'Rourke," Mrs. Sanford said with a dubious look. "And if they can't reclaim their...em...bearings? Will you have a physician attend them?"

Rory shook his head vehemently. "I cannot tolerate such a thought, Mrs. Sanford. He would certainly wish to admit them for observation. I really could not allow that."

Mrs. Sanford tilted her head and eyed him with curiosity.

"I see," she said. "How can I help?"

Rory, absentmindedly toying with his mother's note, returned his attention to his housekeeper.

"I am not certain, Mrs. Sanford. When you told me of your nieces, it was as if you described the two women, so progressive are their behaviors and mannerisms." He smiled crookedly. "I think I simply needed a confidante who might understand the young women in a way that I cannot. I do not believe I shall be discussing their origins with my mother, and most assuredly not with my father. I hope to consult with several ladies of my acquaintance, Mrs. Stephen Sadler and Mrs. Ellie Chamberlain, regarding the young women as they share some common mannerisms, but I just left Mrs. Sadler and Mrs. Chamberlain at the Sadlers' lakeside residence in Montana, and they are not expected back in town in the near future."

"I am not certain how I can be of assistance, Mr. O'Rourke, but if you wish me to supervise the clothing store's attendance upon the young women today, I would be happy to help. As a young woman, I worked as a ladies' maid." She hesitated. "I might also be able to give you my thoughts on the...em...soundness of the young ladies? Respectfully, of course."

Rory turned startled eyes on his housekeeper. "I had not thought of that. What a capital idea, Mrs. Sanford! Could you? I realize assisting the young women with their toilette is not within the purview of your employment and is better served by the housemaid, but I could not entrust a maid with this matter. I shall send you in the carriage at your convenience."

"It is my pleasure, Mr. O'Rourke. I'll just ensure that a small luncheon is set out for you and then I will leave."

Rory held the door open for her and returned to his desk to review the rest of his correspondence, though his thoughts were often on a pair of dark brown eyes. He reached for paper and pen and wrote a quick note to Miss Annie St. John with an introduction for Mrs. Sanford. When the housekeeper brought him a tray of food, he handed her the note.

"I cannot thank you enough, Mrs. Sanford. I look forward to your thoughts upon your return."

Following luncheon, Rory refreshed himself, changed his clothes and climbed into his Ford to make the three-and-a-half-mile journey to his mother's house on Capitol Hill. He would have much preferred to have Joseph maneuver the carriage through the congestion of downtown Seattle, preferring his larger automobile for drives in the country—not an activity he had indulged in more than twice, as he was too often away from home.

The streets widened into boulevards on Capitol Hill, and he parked his car in front of his parents' home on Residence Street. He climbed the steps of the large, ornate white house in the Italianate style, shaking his head as he always did at the ostentatious Doric columns fronting the house favored by his father.

"Rory!" His brother, Eddie, pulled open the door before Rory had a chance to ring the bell. Mr. Smith, the butler, greeted him from behind.

"Mr. Rory, it is good to see you," the short, rotund man said as he took Rory's hat.

"And you, Smith. I hope you are well?"

"Tolerably, sir. Thank you for asking."

"When did you get back?" Eddie asked.

"Just this morning," Rory said, wrapping an arm around his dark-haired, slender brother, who seemed to grow an inch every week. "I swear you have grown since I saw you only a few weeks ago."

Rory and Eddie followed the butler across the large marble foyer toward their mother's parlor.

"I know. Father keeps complaining about the cost of buying new trousers for me."

Rory looked down, and indeed, Eddie's trousers fell just a bit short of what was the standard.

"I am sure Mother will have you at the tailor's in no time once she sees that suit. Even your arms seem to have grown past your sleeves." Rory laughed.

Mr. Smith opened the door to the parlor, and Rory and Eddie stepped into a room softly lit by the natural sunlight which filtered in through a large picture window. Gilt-edged chairs in a delicate flower print and a matching sofa faced the marble fireplace. Their dainty mother, a picture in a peach dress, rose from a small cherry wood desk positioned in a corner of the room.

"Rory! You are home!" She moved forward to accept Rory's kiss on her cheek. Rory thought, irrelevantly, that his mother and Miss Annie St. John seemed to be similar in stature.

"I just arrived this morning, Mother. I hope nothing is amiss? You sent a note that you wished to see me?"

His mother tossed her still-dark hair and shot a quick look in Eddie's direction. "Did I, dear? I must have sent that some time ago, for I hardly remember it. And why should a mother not wish to see her son? Especially an errant son who is away for months on end."

She took a seat on the sofa. "Come! Sit down. Smith will bring us some tea. Eddie, I thought you were going to play tennis this afternoon."

Eddie, who had taken a seat in one of the chairs, rose quickly. "Oh, yes, I am! I do wish to stay and visit with Rory, but I am committed. I was just going to change when you arrived." He patted Rory on the shoulder as he passed.

"Tennis? I cannot imagine," Rory murmured with a smile. "Are you playing with the university?"

"Yes, I am," Eddie replied. "You must come photograph us some time."

"I will," Rory said. Eddie waved and left the room at the same time that Smith arrived with tea.

"Thank you, Smith. I will pour," Mrs. O'Rourke said. She poured a cup for herself and one for Rory. Rory studied his mother carefully, but she seemed to be in good health. Comforted that she remained so, he reverted to his earlier speculation that she was on a matchmaking scheme. Eddie, still considered young for marriage, had no idea how fortunate he was, but his time would soon come.

He accepted the tea and waited. His mother had clearly desired Eddie's absence, and now that he was gone, she had no further need to stall, but she appeared content to sip her tea and inquire about his recent trip to Montana. He chatted with her briefly regarding his stay.

"Well, Mother, Eddie has been gone these past fifteen minutes. Your note, which you so brazenly denied having sent, indicated you had news of importance to share with me. I am waiting."

His mother's cheeks took on a pink tinge, and she set her cup and saucer down with an unsteady hand.

"I am sure there is no other way to say this, so I will just blurt it out. I have asked your father for a divorce."

Rory drew in a sharp breath. A tear slipped down his mother's face, and then two. He rose swiftly and came to sit beside her on the sofa, taking her into his arms, and not for the first time on the subject of his father. At his touch, she started to cry in earnest, and he brought out his handkerchief.

"Thank you, dear," she sobbed as she pressed the cloth to her face. Within minutes, she managed to draw in a ragged breath and mopped her face.

"I must look a fright," she said, straightening and reaching for her hair.

"Not at all, Mother," Rory said gallantly. "Was it very bad? Your discussion with Father? I cannot imagine."

She shrugged. "Not as awful as I expected. He was more upset about having to remove to a hotel than he was about my demand, I think."

"So, you have asked him to leave." Rory felt no sympathy for his father. He had been an unfaithful husband for as long as Rory could remember.

"Yes. He has already packed some things and taken them to the hotel. Eddie does not know yet. I am not at all certain how he will take the news."

"Eddie will be fine. He may be shocked initially that you have requested a divorce, but he is not unaware of our father's...ways."

"I am humiliated that he should have known about your father's philandering. It is bad enough that I cried on your shoulder a time or two over the past few years, but I had hoped Eddie would not know."

"My father has made little secret of his activities, Mother. Eddie is not obtuse."

"No, of course not." She dabbed at her eyes again and took a sip of tea.

"Where has Father gone?"

"To the Hotel Seattle, I believe." Her face darkened. "I think he is not unfamiliar with the rooms there."

Rory gritted his teeth. Of all the hotels his father must remove to...

He pushed the thought aside and returned his attention to his mother's plight.

"How can I help, Mother?"

"There is nothing you can do, Rory, thank you. Your fidelity means a great deal to me. I needed to tell you of my decision, though."

"Do you have an attorney? Can I arrange that for you?"

"No, thank you. You would be surprised, but I have busied myself with the prospect of divorce for some time. I have managed to secure legal counsel and some money of my own lest your father cut me off, though I do not think he will. My attorney will sue for the house, maintenance and staff costs, Eddie's education and something for me to live on. I shall be right as rain."

Rory almost smiled at the faint Irish lilt in her last words—a legacy from her immigrant Irish parents, who had passed away only two years prior. She had once told him that his father's English-Irish family had always felt he married beneath him, which is why he had never met them. He had spent considerable time in Ireland on photographic assignments, often staying with his mother's extended family in the north while there.

"I do believe you will, Mother. At the risk of sounding like the most undutiful son, I must say that I am pleased with your decision, and I applaud your courage."

"Thank you, son. My parents would roll over in the graves if they knew. It is fortunate divorce is not prohibited in our family—otherwise, I should be stuck with the man forever."

Rory permitted himself a chuckle, and his mother's face lightened.

"When will you tell Eddie?"

"I suppose I must tell him soon. Could you be here when I do?"

"Certainly, Mother. If you like, I could tell him in advance—let him absorb the shock and any untoward reactions before you speak to him." Rory checked his pocket watch.

"Would you?" his mother asked hopefully. "I confess I wished that you would. I could not bear it if Eddie were angry with me."

"I shall take care of it the day after tomorrow, first thing." Rory checked his watch again. "I must return to the house now. Will you be all right?"

"Yes, of course. I have been alone here many times before. Your father's absence will hardly be noted."

Rory rose and planted a kiss on top of his mother's head.

"I *am* proud of you, Mother. Know that," he said.

His mother followed him to the parlor door. "Thank you, Rory. That is all I could have ever hoped for."

"I shall see you in two days. Advise Eddie I will visit him at ten o'clock in the morning." He checked his watch again, wondering how Mrs. Sanford was faring, wondering how Annie and her sister were faring.

"You have checked your pocket watch three times in the last five minutes, Rory. Are you late for an appointment?"

"Not exactly, Mother. Not exactly."

CHAPTER FIVE

Annie opened the door a crack to see a tall, slender, gray-haired woman in a dark dress and a nondescript hat.

"Yes?" she said. Marie hovered behind the door, still eating food from the lunch delivered by a young waiter.

"Miss St. John?" the woman asked. "I am Mrs. Sanford. Mr. O'Rourke sent me. Here is a message from him." She offered a folded piece of paper.

Annie took the paper and scanned it quickly, noting Rory's handwriting was large and elegant.

Miss St. John,

This is my housekeeper, Mrs. Sanford, who has kindly offered to look after you this afternoon while you are attended by the staff of Becker's Ladies Wear. Mrs. Sanford knows of our meeting, so you may speak freely with her, but I urge you to be more circumspect with the salesgirls from Becker's.

I shall be pleased to collect you and Miss Marie at eight o'clock for dinner in the hotel.

Yours,

Harold O'Rourke, Jr.

Annie pulled the door wide. "I apologize for leaving you standing out there, Mrs. Sanford. Come on in."

Mrs. Sanford entered and scanned the room. She turned and noted Marie behind the door as Annie shut it. Her eyes ran up and down their bodies without comment, almost as if she expected to see them dressed as they were. Annie wondered how much Rory had disclosed.

362

"Miss Annie St. John?" she asked, looking at her.

"Yes, I'm Annie, and this is my sister, Marie."

"I am Mr. O'Rourke's housekeeper. He was worried about you, and I offered to come and see after you while Mr. Becker's people attend to your clothing necessities." She appraised the room quickly. "I see you have eaten lunch. Do you require anything else from the restaurant? Was your meal satisfactory?"

"It was great!" Marie said with her mouth partially full of bread. "So, who are 'Mr. Becker's people?'"

"I think that's the clothing store that Rory is having come by," Annie said. "You can stop hiding by the door now, Marie. It's closed, so you're in full view now." She grinned as her sister slipped past Mrs. Sanford with a wary glance and took a seat on the sofa.

"Would you like to sit down, Mrs. Sanford? Can we offer you some tea? I think there's an extra cup here." Annie reached for the teapot.

"Yes, thank you, that would be lovely. I am not used to riding in the carriage that Mr. O'Rourke so kindly offered me, and I admit to feeling a bit jostled." She took a seat on the sofa near Marie.

"I know what you mean. I'd never been in a carriage before this morning," Annie murmured. "Mr. O'Rourke says he told you of our…meeting?"

Mrs. Sanford removed her hat and set it down on a side table, along with a small purse. She accepted a cup of tea.

"Yes, he did," she said, but offered nothing more.

Annie had the distinct impression she was assessing them, much like a psychiatrist would. She shot a warning glance to Marie but didn't get the impression her sister understood her message. She wasn't even sure what she was trying to say. *Be careful? Watch what you say? She'll tell Rory?*

"Let me guess," Annie said. "Mr. O'Rourke asked you to give him your impression of us? Whether we're a bit off our rockers?"

Mrs. Sanford colored, but her lips twitched. "I see why he finds you so fascinating."

Annie blinked. *Fascinating?*

"Yes, Mr. O'Rourke mentioned you two feel you have come from a different time, from the future. Is that correct? Or is Mr. O'Rourke the one who is 'off his rocker?'"

Annie and Marie laughed.

"No, he seems pretty sane to me," Marie piped in. "But I know he thinks we're bonkers. And maybe we are."

Annie took a seat on one of the damask-covered occasional chairs.

"Would you happen to know when these people are coming, Mrs. Sanford? I have to tell you, Marie and I have never worn anything like the clothes we've seen over the past few hours since our arrival. I'm worried that the clothing store people will suspect something."

"I understand, Miss St. John. I am not sure when they will arrive, but I will stay until they do. I have given the matter some thought, and I think the best approach would be for me to help you and Miss Marie dress in the other room, which appears to be a bedroom. The salesgirls can remain here in the sitting room, and I'll appoint myself a liaison to act between you."

"Call me Annie. Thank you, Mrs. Sanford. I feel like we're imposing."

"Not at all," Mrs. Sanford said. "Mr. O'Rourke wished to see you comfortable and at ease."

"Is he...is he at home now?" Annie asked, wishing in some strange way that he had stayed. What he was supposed to do while they dressed was beyond her.

"No, he had lunch and then went to visit with his mother."

"Oh!" Annie said.

"What's she like?" Marie said, snagging the last bread roll from the tray.

"Mrs. O'Rourke?" Mrs. Sanford hesitated, and Annie suspected Marie's question exceeded the housekeeper's comfort level. To her surprise, Mrs. Sanford answered.

"Mrs. O'Rourke is a lovely woman. I do not know her well, though. She is small, dainty and dark-haired like her sons. They favor her except in height, which they must have acquired from their father. She seems very lively, very kind. Her family is Irish, I believe as is Mr. O'Rourke's father."

"Aw, she sounds cute!" Marie said.

Mrs. Sanford quirked an eyebrow but smiled. "Yes, one might say that."

Annie eyed Mrs. Sanford speculatively. "Mrs. Sanford, I wonder if I could ask you a question."

"Yes?"

"You may or may not know, but Marie and I don't have any money. Our purses were...lost, and I'm not sure we'll ever find them. We can't possibly stay in this expensive hotel." Annie made an expansive gesture toward the room in general. "Mr. O'Rourke mentioned boarding houses or rooming houses? Where women could stay? I was wondering if you knew of any."

"I'm sure Mr. O'Rourke would wish to assist you with that himself, Miss St—Annie, especially if you cannot find a way to return home. Do you *wish* to stay in Seattle?"

"No!" Marie almost barked. "I mean, no, we don't. We have our lives in Chicago." Mrs. Sanford looked taken aback at the sharp note in Marie's voice.

Annie threw a pointed look at her sister. Maybe Marie had a life in Chicago, but Annie really didn't, and Marie knew it. Not that she really wanted to be stuck in the early twentieth century either.

"No, I know my sister really wants to…return, and I guess I do, too, but we don't know quite how that is supposed to happen, so just in case, I think we probably need to find a boarding house. I'd really rather we find one ourselves. We don't really know Mr. O'Rourke. He owes us nothing, and I don't feel comfortable taking his money, or letting his pay for us like this."

"Oh, Annie," Marie said. "Just relax."

"I have kept house for Mr. O'Rourke for several years now, Annie, and although he travels a great deal and is gone for great periods of time, I feel I know him fairly well. He is a generous man, and I feel certain that what he has done for you and Miss Marie comes without a price. He is a gentleman and would never think to impose himself on you in any way. However, I do understand your desire to be independent. I myself have lived independently all my life, beholden to no one, and I think I understand your concerns."

"He travels a lot?" Annie lost her train of thought. "Oh, he would, wouldn't he? He's a photojournalist or something, isn't he?"

"I've not heard the term photojournalist, but it makes sense. Yes, he's a very famous photographer, actually, with photographs in museums, private collections, libraries, magazines and newspapers."

"Really?" Marie said.

"I had no idea," Annie murmured.

"Is he…rich?" Marie asked as she surveyed the room.

"Marie!" Annie said with a shake of her head.

Mrs. Sanford coughed discreetly behind her hand, but Annie swore she saw the woman's lips twitch.

"Yes, Mr. O'Rourke is wealthy, Miss Marie, independent of his earnings as a photographer."

A knock sounded on the door. Annie jumped up, but Mrs. Sanford stayed her and went to the door herself. She opened it a crack, listened to the person on the other side, nodded and closed the door behind her.

"Hurry, ladies, into the bedroom, Mr. Becker's girls are here laden with bags and boxes."

Annie and Marie jumped up and scrambled into the bedroom. Annie left the door open a crack to see Mrs. Sanford open the door wide to two young women and an older woman who brought in multiple bags and boxes, which they set on every available chair and table, and the sofa.

"My ladies are on the shy side, Miss Simpson, so I will assist them with dressing. What sizes have you brought for them?"

Annie couldn't hear the response from the smallest of the salesgirls, a redhead, but Mrs. Sanford seemed satisfied.

"Yes, I think that is about right. If they need to be tailored, I presume your girls brought their sewing kits with them?"

Miss Simpson, a short, plump, gray-haired woman, nodded.

"Yes, Mrs. Sanford."

"Good! Let's start with some undergarments, then I will return for the evening dresses. That is our first priority as my ladies have an engagement this evening."

The other salesgirl, a taller blonde, lifted the covers off several boxes to peer in and selected three to hand to Mrs. Sanford. She murmured something Annie couldn't hear, and Mrs. Sanford nodded and turned toward the bedroom. Annie and Marie jumped back from the door, and she entered the room and shut the door behind her.

"I see you have been watching," she smiled. She set the boxes on the bed and rummaged through them to pull out several white garments, which she handed to Annie and Marie. "Here is your chemise and your unmentionables, ladies. Can I assist you in undressing?"

She moved toward Annie, who instinctively jumped back. "Oh, sorry! No, I'm sure we can undress ourselves. What are unmentionables?"

"What are unmentionables?" Marie asked almost at the same time.

Mrs. Sanford looked from one of the sisters to the other, looking as if she already wished she hadn't volunteered to help.

"Unmentionables? Your drawers?" Clearly, Mrs. Sanford didn't understand that Marie and Annie had no clue. She held up a garment that looked like more bloomers with frilly bits of material and lace attached to the bottom of the legs. "These are your drawers," Mrs. Sanford said, "and made of the finest lawn, I think. Very lovely."

Annie stared at the open flap between the legs. Oh, surely not!

Reluctantly, she stepped out of her capri pants and her underwear and slipped into the "unmentionables." Mrs. Sanford came around her to button the drawers at the back. Marie stared at Annie with rounded eyes before dropping her own skirt and panties to step into the drawers.

"How do you...?" Marie began as Mrs. Sanford came to button the back of her drawers.

"The flap," Mrs. Sanford said without elaborating. She handed out the chemises—lovely bits of silk material with narrow straps of lace and embroidery.

"You must remove that article of clothing," Mrs. Sanford said when Annie attempted to slip the chemise over her comfortable sports bra. "The straps of your garment will show with almost any evening gown."

Annie sighed and removed the bra, unable to remember the last time she'd gone without support. Marie was more relaxed and was, in fact, not wearing a bra.

"So, now the dresses?" Marie asked, biting her lips to keep her face straight as she met Annie's eyes. Over the years, she had teased Annie gleefully about her need to wear a supporting undergarment.

"No, not quite yet. You must put on your corsets next."

"Corsets?" Marie repeated weakly. "Oh, no, not a corset. Not for me, thanks." Annie agreed, but Mrs. Sanford dashed those ideas.

"You must wear corsets, ladies. The clothing will not fit without the corsets, nor is it at all proper for women to go about in public without proper undergarments."

Annie sobered. The housekeeper didn't look like she was taking no for an answer from either of them.

Annie took the white satin corset, which looked nothing like the corsets she'd seen. The shape was odd, and two suspender straps dangled from the front, presumably for stockings.

"How do you put it on?" she asked.

"Would you like me to show you?"

Annie nodded, and Mrs. Sanford wrapped the corset around her back and pulled it around to the front.

"Hold it in place, and I will hook it." Annie tugged at each side of the corset, pulling it toward her midriff and wondering how on earth Mrs. Sanford was going to get it closed.

"Are you sure this fits? Maybe I need a larger size?" She sucked in her stomach as Mrs. Sanford began hooking the corset over her breasts. She looked over the housekeeper's shoulder and rolled her eyes at Marie, who watched with amusement.

"Well, maybe this fits after all—" Annie began, but she was brought up short as air was forced from her lungs when Mrs. Sanford grabbed hold of the edges of the corset and pulled tightly, forcing Annie's body into the oddest posture.

"Wait! No! This can't be right!" she wheezed. "I'm bent over! I can't straighten up."

"It is the style, Miss St. John. I am so sorry. I personally do not like these new corsets and wear my old favorites that are sadly out of date, but that option is not open to you, I am afraid—not at your age."

"Annie, you look like a pigeon!" Marie laughed, clearly forgetting she was next. "Mrs. Sanford, are you sure her corset isn't broken or damaged in some way?

"No, Miss Marie. The corset is as it should be. It was designed to emphasize a woman's most...alluring features, I believe—or so the advertisements explain." Mrs. Sanford attached the last hook and stood back to survey Annie, who had grabbed the footboard of one of the beds to lean on.

"How am I supposed to walk in this?" Annie muttered as she attempted to pivot to stare at herself in the large cherry oval cheval mirror. She looked ridiculous. The odd S-shaped curve of the corset forced an arch in her back, pushing her chest forward and her backside to jut out. She really did look like a pigeon, just as Marie had said.

"I have seen ladies carry parasols or walking sticks to stay upright. I'm afraid we have neither of those." Mrs. Sanford shook her head in sympathy and turned toward Marie.

"May I assist you, Miss Marie?"

Marie backed away a few steps with one hand outstretched, bent over double with laughter.

"Oh, no, Mrs. Sanford. I can't wear that. I can't believe you actually got Annie into that thing."

Though her back had begun to ache, Annie chuckled. Mrs. Sanford's lips twitched as well.

"Miss Marie, the clothes will not fit if you do not wear the proper undergarments. I do not think you really have a choice unless you wish to stay in seclusion in this room during your...visit."

"Just put it on, Marie. There are people waiting in the other room for us," Annie said, bracing a hand on her back. "Besides, if *I* have to do it, *you* have to do it."

Marie straightened and wiped tears from her face. "She has a point, Mrs. Sanford. Better hook me up."

Mrs. Sanford assisted Marie into her corset. The entire process seemed to go much more smoothly than it had on Annie.

Marie preened in front of the floor mirror, looking quite elegant and more like a regal peacock than Annie's puffed-up bird.

"That wasn't so bad," Marie said, turning from side to side to survey herself. "This corset gives me the curves I've always wanted. I like it!"

"Now, your stockings. You do know how to put those on, don't you?" Mrs. Sanford said, handing each of them a pair of pale off-white stockings.

"I think I can figure it out," Annie said. She tottered over to a straight-back chair in the room and perched on the edge, separating one stocking from the other as she attempted to stick her foot into the silky stocking. The spare stocking fell to the red and gold Oriental carpet at her feet. For all that the corset kept her in a bent shape, it didn't allow her to actually bend forward to reach the stocking near her foot.

"Help," she moaned. "I can't even put a stocking on."

"Miss Marie, why don't you help your sister while I go get the rest of your undergarments?"

"There's more?" Annie gasped. "It's not possible." Marie, her corset clearly made of a fabric much more flexible than Annie's, drifted over and bent to help Annie with her stockings.

"But of course, Miss St. John. You must wear petticoats." Mrs. Sanford moved into the other room.

"And what are you smirking about?" Annie asked as Marie pulled one stocking up Annie's outstretched leg. "What is your corset made of? Elastic? Because I don't see how you can move."

"No, silly, it's made of the same stuff as yours. They look exactly alike. I think it doesn't feel as stiff as yours because I'm, um…thinner."

Annie looked down at her own fuller figure with a sigh. "I've got to go on a diet, and I think this thing will ensure that I do. Probably won't be able to eat a bite."

Marie pulled the other stocking up, and helped Annie stand while they fiddled with the two clasps dangling from the corset above each leg. Annie convulsed with laughter at the absurdity of their situation.

"I just can't imagine Mrs. Sanford doing this for me," she gurgled.

Marie, struggling to work the clasps, joined in. "You keep laughing, dear Sis, cuz you're going to have to help me in a minute. There!" she exclaimed as she straightened. "Did she say there are more undergarments?"

"Yes, she did," Annie said as she picked up Marie's stockings and dangled them. "Here you go!"

"I think I can manage," Marie said with a broad smile. Naturally, she had no trouble slipping into the stockings and hooking them to the straps of her corset.

The door opened and Mrs. Sanford entered with another armful of garments. "I see you have managed the stockings, ladies. Here are your petticoats." She held aloft two long champagne-colored skirts of rustling taffeta, the bottom half elaborately decorated with large flounces and ruffles of intricately embroidered eyelet lace and scallops.

"Beautiful," Annie murmured.

"Yes, they are," Mrs. Sanford agreed. "It would seem that Mr. O'Rourke has spared no expense."

Annie cringed when Mrs. Sanford dropped the skirt to the floor so she could step into it. It seemed far too beautiful to lay on the floor. Mrs. Sanford pulled it up over Annie's hips and buttoned it in back. "I trust you ladies will assist each other in undressing tonight, as this amount of clothing will be difficult to remove without help."

"You're not wearing all these undergarments, are you, Mrs. Sanford?" Annie eyed her slender form speculatively.

"I am," Mrs. Sanford replied with pink cheeks, "though not so fashionable as those which you now wear."

When Mrs. Sanford finished with the petticoats, she returned to the sitting room again and came back with another armful of clothing, this time in shades of rose and Wedgewood blue. She laid the gowns out on the beds.

"Would you look at those?" Marie said with a short whistle. Annie eyed the elegant dresses of silk overlaid with some sort of filmy gauze embroidered with gold thread on the rose dress and white thread on the blue dress.

"I'd be afraid to rip that," Annie murmured. The rose dress had obviously been ordained for her as it was the shorter of the two garments. "It looks so delicate."

"They *are* beautiful, aren't they?" Mrs. Sanford said admiringly, a small sigh escaping her lips. All three women gazed at the evening gowns for a moment before Mrs. Sanford checked the small watch pinned to her blouse. "We still have much to do, ladies, so we mustn't dawdle." She picked up the rose-colored dress.

"Much to do?" Annie whispered. "What else? We're just going to dinner, right?"

"We must dress your hair. That is not my forte, but I will endeavor to make you presentable. Come, lift your arms."

Annie complied, and Mrs. Sanford pulled the dress down over Annie's head and settled it into place. While she fastened the buttons in the back of the dress, Annie studied Marie's reactions. Marie, running a finger along the silk of her own dress as it lay on the bed, shook her head open-mouthed as if she were speechless. Annie grinned.

"Seems like a bit much for dinner, doesn't it?"

"I'll say," Marie murmured. "But it's absolutely gorgeous. It suits you. For all that you hate that corset, your curves really compliment the dress."

Annie blushed, certain her cheeks had turned as rosy as the gown. Mrs. Sanford moved to help Marie into her dress, and Annie turned to stare at the mirror. Marie was right. The dress did accentuate her curves...or the underlying corset did. Shoulder straps of silk resembling tiny puffed sleeves left her neck and upper chest bare, with a hint of cleavage. Annie hoped the shop girls had brought a shawl. The tight bodice of the dress narrowed to her waist, ending in a V-shape just below her stomach. The skirt, not as wide as she'd imagined, fell away from her hips in a tulip shape with the gauze floating loosely over it. She wondered what Rory would think when he saw her...when he saw *them*, she corrected herself.

In the mirror, she saw Marie, stunning in her blue dress, more regal than she'd ever seen her.

"Well, look at you, Queenie!" Annie turned and said. "Beautiful. If nothing else, this Edwardian thing is making us look good. I wish I had a camera."

Mrs. Sanford looked up from buttoning Marie's gown. "Mr. O'Rourke has cameras, of course, though I do not imagine he would bring one to dinner."

"Well, maybe we'll get him to take a picture of us sometime," Annie said.

"Then you'd better ask him soon, Annie, because I'm not staying, beautiful clothes or not," Marie said.

Mrs. Sanford gave her a startled look, but said nothing.

"Shoes, gloves, hair."

"A shawl?" Annie said, flattening her hand against her chest in an effort to cover her cleavage.

"Grow up," Marie said with a grin. Given the leaner proportions of her athletic body, Marie's dress accented her broad shoulders while revealing no extra curves above her breasts.

"You are suitably dressed now, ladies. Come into the sitting room and see what the girls have brought. I am sure they would like to know if their selections meet with your approval."

Annie and Marie followed her to the room in a rustle of taffeta silk petticoats. Annie clutched a handful of skirt.

The older woman, whom Annie had heard introduced as Miss Simpson, rose from one of the chairs.

"Lovely!" She clapped her hands together. "Do the dresses require any alterations?"

Mrs. Sanford tilted her head and regarded Annie and Marie for a moment. "No, I think not. You have chosen well, Miss Simpson."

"Oh, thank you! Sally, Jennifer, please get the shoes." The young redhead and blonde, standing by the stacks of bags and boxes, rummaged through them and brought forth several boxes.

"We asked the shoe store for several sizes, so I feel confident we can find the right sizes," Miss Simpson said.

Annie, feeling a bit like Cinderella at the ball, lowered herself with care to one of the straight-backed chairs and perched on the edge, hoping to try on the shoes herself as she might at home, but the young redhead named Sally approached her with two boxes, while Jennifer saw to Marie.

"Let's try these on, miss," Sally said as she knelt at Annie's feet. She pulled out a pair of shoes in a dark rose color, a good match for the dress, and slipped them on Annie's feet. The shoes were remarkably similar to those worn in the twenty-first century, with pointed toes, broad square heels and a decorative gold bow at the top.

"Could you stand, miss, to see how they fit?" Except for the dress and the audience waiting with seemingly bated breath, Annie almost felt as if she were in a modern shoe store trying on shoes.

Annie stood and put her weight on the shoes.

"They fit fine," she murmured.

"Excellent!" Miss Simpson pronounced. "And you, miss?" She turned toward Marie.

"Too small," Marie chuckled. "I have big feet. You said there was another size?"

Marie found the right size, and the sisters looked toward Mrs. Sanford for guidance.

"Gloves, Miss Simpson? And Miss St. John would like a shawl. Did you happen to bring any shawls?"

"Yes, Mrs. Sanford. We did." Miss Simpson produced a beautiful, gauzy shawl in a shade of gold that matched the embroidery on Annie's overskirt. "We have a shawl for the other young lady as well. And here are the gloves for their evening wear."

Mrs. Sanford checked her watch. "I think since these dresses fit well, we will not keep you any longer, Miss Simpson. The ladies will try on the rest of the clothing tomorrow. Should we need alterations, I hope you can send someone promptly?"

"Oh, yes, Mrs. Sanford. Sally and Jennifer will be happy to return here tomorrow to help the young ladies with their clothing. Shall I have them come just in case?"

"An excellent idea. Yes, please do. At about eleven o'clock, I should think."

"Come, girls, let's go. Thank you so much, Mrs. Sanford, Misses St. John. Thank you for shopping with us."

After the door had closed behind them, Annie attempted to slump into her chair but couldn't do more than sit erect, if not slightly forward given the curvature of the corset.

"I'm too exhausted to go to dinner. Mrs. Sanford. Women can't possibly go through this every night, can they?" Annie asked.

Mrs. Sanford smiled. "Fashionable ladies change clothing frequently throughout the day depending upon their social calendar, so yes, they do 'go through this' often." She held out a hand to help Annie up. "And now to your hair."

Annie and Marie followed Mrs. Sanford back into the bedroom, where Mrs. Sanford seated Annie at a lovely cherry wood vanity.

"Mr. O'Rourke mentioned you had no luggage, so I took the liberty of bringing my own brushes with me. I hope that is acceptable. It is a pity the clothing store didn't bring combs or ribbons for your hair, but that would have been too much for Mr. O'Rourke to have remarked upon when he visited with them."

"No, that's fine," Annie said. "I appreciate everything you're doing for us, Mrs. Sanford. We both do." She pulled the band from her bedraggled ponytail and looked at Marie through the mirror, who nodded agreement.

"So, we have to wear our hair up?" Marie asked, alternately admiring herself in the cheval mirror and turning to watch Mrs. Sanford brush out Annie's hair. "Is that mandatory?"

"Mandatory?" Mrs. Sanford repeated. "It is customary for adult woman to wear their hair up. Only children and young girls may wear it long."

Annie watched as Mrs. Sanford backcombed her hair, teased the front into a pile and smoothed the hair around her forehead over the height to form a pompadour. She then formed a loose bun at the crown and wove the rest of Annie's hair into it, dropping a few loose curls for effect.

"Just a minute," Mrs. Sanford said as Annie prepared to rise. She hurried over to the vase of flowers on the cherry dresser and retrieved two pink rosebuds, which she broke off and inserted into Annie's coif.

"Oh how cute!" Marie said. Annie couldn't see the back of her hair but trusted Marie's assessment.

"It is very common to wear flowers in one's hair," Mrs. Sanford said. "Now, if you please, Miss Marie."

Annie rose and swapped with Marie.

"I am fortunate you ladies have such lovely waves in your hair as the texture holds this style better. Otherwise, we would have needed a frame, and I do not have one."

"A frame?" Marie asked.

"Hair that is collected, saved and formed to a frame, over which the hair is combed."

"Ugh," Marie said with a wrinkled nose.

"I do not favor collecting my hair either." Mrs. Sanford smiled. She bound up Marie's hair and stuck baby's breath from the vase into the bun at her crown.

"They call these hairstyles Gibson's, don't they, Mrs. Sanford?"

"Yes, for the Gibson Girls, a creation of Charles Gibson."

"Hah! I knew it!" Marie said with a grin. She stood and tilted her head. "My head feels heavy."

Mrs. Sanford checked her watch. "Mr. O'Rourke will arrive to escort you downstairs at any minute. I had no idea so much time had passed. Your gloves!"

She handed them each a pair of long white gloves.

"Do we have to wear these?" Annie said. "Not through dinner, right?"

"No, you may take them off to dine," Mrs. Sanford answered patiently, "but you must at least wear them into dinner."

Annie pulled her gloves on and then helped Marie into hers. They stared at themselves side by side in the mirror, similar expressions of awe on each of their faces.

Mrs. Sanford brought the rest of the boxes into the bedroom and set them in a corner.

"I believe there must be some nightwear in here, and clothing for tomorrow. As you know, the shop girls, Sally and Jennifer, will come around to see if you need any help with the clothing. I must leave. Will you be all right?"

"Yes, Mrs. Sanford," they answered in unison, looking at each other and giggling.

"Good night, girls," Mrs. Sanford said as she grabbed her hat and gloves. She pulled open the door.

"Mrs. Sanford! Still here?" Rory said, dazzling in black coattails, white shirt and a bowtie, his hand raised as if to knock.

CHAPTER SIX

Rory beheld the visions just beyond Mrs. Sanford—Marie, elegant and statuesque in blue, and Annie, petite and adorable in rose, the same color as her cheeks. She dropped her eyes at his admiring glance, and he returned his attention to Mrs. Sanford.

"Yes, sir. I was just leaving." She stood back and allowed him to enter.

"You have outdone yourself, Mrs. Sanford. The ladies look lovely."

"Yes, they do," she agreed.

Annie felt as if she should drop a curtsey, but resisted. She nodded her head in greeting.

"Miss St. John was wondering if you might take a photograph of them, sir. I understand you probably do not have your equipment with you, but perhaps another day."

Rory blinked. "A wonderful idea. I actually do have a small camera in the trunk of the car, which I carry around with me. One never knows when the opportunity to photograph beauty might present itself, as it has now."

"Oh, you don't have to..." Annie began. If possible, her cheeks were an even brighter shade of red than before.

"Would you?" Marie asked. "That would be great! We might not get this chance again, Annie." She elbowed her sister, who winced and grabbed her side.

"I shall return momentarily with the camera," Rory said. "If you are finished, Mrs. Sanford, I could escort you down to the carriage. Joseph is waiting for you."

He closed the door behind her and walked down the hallway toward the stairs.

"I had no idea dressing the young ladies would take you so long, Mrs. Sanford. I apologize."

"Neither did I, Mr. O'Rourke," she chuckled. "It has been some years since I worked as a lady's maid, and even then, my employer knew her clothing. The Misses St. John do appear to be lost, as you stated earlier. They had no inkling as to the articles of clothing or how to put them on. I hoped to form my thoughts better before I spoke to you about young ladies, but since we are together, I suppose I can offer my first impression."

They reached the red-carpeted stairs and began to descend them.

"Yes?" Rory encouraged her.

Mrs. Sanford lowered her voice. "If I believed in such things as time travel, I would say these young women have traveled in time. I cannot imagine where else they might have come from. If they are from Chicago, it can only be surmised that they were raised in a convent or some other austere environment without exposure to fashion, society, or...education."

Rory opened his mouth to protest the last, but Mrs. Sanford rushed to speak.

"I do not mean they are uneducated or without schooling, Mr. O'Rourke—far from it, as they do sound intelligent—but the Misses St. John do appear to be remarkably uninformed and naïve—certainly when compared to other young women I have known."

Rory sighed as they rounded the last landing before reaching the lobby.

"Yes, I know. Thank you for confirming my impression. I thought I must be losing my mind. Did you arrive at any conclusions regarding their origin? I confess I cannot imagine where they could come from."

Mrs. Sanford kept her silence while they crossed the lobby and exited through the front door to descend the stone steps. Joseph awaited her with the carriage at the street level.

She stopped and turned toward him, keeping her voice hushed as strollers passed by.

"I cannot wonder if we should not give some credence to their story of...time travel." She ended on a whisper.

Rory reared his head back and stared hard at his housekeeper. Had she also fallen under the young women's spell—as he had himself? He shook his head vehemently then smiled broadly, reaching to hand Mrs. Sanford into the carriage.

"I think not, Mrs. Sanford. I would more likely believe they came from the jungles of Borneo."

"Then I am at a loss, Mr. O'Rourke. Enjoy your dinner. I will see you tomorrow."

Rory went around the corner to his car and retrieved his small box camera from the trunk. The camera was a new portable version he enjoyed toying with, suitable for quick photographs. He returned to the hotel, doing his best to put Mrs. Sanford's earnest whisper from his thoughts. Time travel, indeed! Hah!

Upon his knock, Annie opened the door, and Rory felt the breath escape from his lips yet again. Jungles of Borneo notwithstanding, she looked beautiful in her ethereal gown with her glossy hair piled atop the crown of her head, and he could only stare at her besottedly for a moment before she stepped back and allowed him to enter. He gave himself a shake.

"Forgive me for ogling, Miss St. John. You and Miss Marie look stunning. I shall be the envy of all eyes as I escort you to dinner." He flashed her a smile, forgetting for a moment that Annie seemed to dislike it.

Rather than challenge him or mock him as she had on the train, she blushed and lowered her eyes.

"Thank you," she murmured quietly.

The quiet miss before him startled Rory for a moment, so different from her usual vivacious character.

"Have I embarrassed you? I apologize," he said quickly.

"No, no," she said, turning away.

"Well, not me! I agree with you. I think we do look stunning," Marie said with a grin. "Are you ready to take our pictures?"

"Yes, of course," Rory said. "If I could just set my hat here on the table." He removed his hat and checked his camera. "Where would you like to pose? I'm not traditionally a portrait photographer, but I think a portrait by the fireplace might be nice."

Annie and Marie moved across the room to stand by the marble mantle of the fireplace.

"Excellent! Are you ready?"

Both women smiled, and it was all he could do to keep the camera steady, so dazzling were they in their finery. His heart skipped a beat, and he took the picture, promising himself a copy.

"That's it?" Annie said. "I thought we would have to pose for a few minutes without moving while the camera focused."

"No, that was long ago. This is a new camera with a quick focus. I enjoy it for smaller projects." He set it down on the table. "I'll collect the camera when we have finished with dinner.

"When can we see the pictures?" Marie asked.

"I can have a copy to you by tomorrow," he said. "I have a darkroom in the house."

"Great!" Marie said.

"Shall we?" Rory said, grabbing his hat and holding open the door. They descended to the lobby. Rory was acutely aware that both Marie and Annie moved awkwardly on the stairs, both leaning heavily on the banister. Marie hitched her skirts a little higher than was proper. It was not possible for Rory to offer both women his arms in the confines of the stairwell, but he was able to extend his arms when they reached the lobby. Marie took his arm willingly, but Annie seemed reluctant. Nevertheless, she tucked her hand under his arm. They passed a myriad of well-dressed people and made their way to the dining room, where the maître d', having taken Rory's hat, escorted them through the crowded dining room to a table for four.

"It is good to see you again, Mr. O'Rourke," the elderly, rotund man in coattails said, pulling out chairs for Annie and Marie.

"Thank you, Mr. Hopkins. May I introduce Miss Annie St. John and Miss Marie St. John? They will be guests of the hotel for a time, and I know that you will extend the same welcome to them as you do to me."

He bowed, flicking his tails away in an exaggerated fashion. "But of course! It is a pleasure to serve you, ladies." He flicked his finger for a waiter who appeared with menus.

"What would you like to drink?" Rory asked. "They have many different wines, champagne, tea, coffee, water." He noted the sisters pulled their gloves off as if unused to them and laid them upon their laps.

"Oh, let's have champagne!" Marie said.

"Marie!" Annie remonstrated.

"My favorite," Rory said with a grin. He placed the order and sat back to watch Annie and Marie study the menu with interest. They consulted with each other as if there were some items on the menu they had not seen before.

"If you need assistance with the menu, I am happy to be of service," Rory offered, momentarily distracted by the delicate roundness of Annie's shoulders. He blinked and looked up to meet her eyes regarding him with an expression he couldn't decipher. An unusual heat spread across his face, and he rubbed his chin and pretended to cough behind his hand.

"There are a lot of foods we don't recognize, but I'm sure we can figure out what they are with my high school French. Is this a French restaurant?" Annie looked around with an expression of fascination.

Rory shook his head with a wry smile. "I think not. The use of the French menu is probably a bit of pretension, but I do enjoy the food here."

The waiter returned to pour the champagne, and they ordered.

"Look at all these people!" Marie marveled. "And so dressed up!"

"It is customary in the finer restaurants."

"So, you come here a lot?" Annie asked.

"Yes, when I am in town. I live alone and am not fond of dining by myself." He cleared his throat, worrying that his response had held a note of pathos. "I usually dine with friends," he offered.

Annie tilted her head and regarded him quizzically. He plastered a beatific smile upon his face and took a sip of champagne. Gracious! It was as if the woman could see right through him. Not even to himself had he admitted how lonely his life seemed…until now.

"Mr. O'Rourke!"

They all looked up to see a young redheaded woman in a yellow satin gown stop before their table. Accompanying her were a middle-aged couple, the man in coattails and the woman in an emerald green silk gown.

Rory jumped up. "Miss Washburn, Mr. and Mrs. Washburn! How nice to see you again." He bowed his head, trying to ignore the white-gloved hand Miss Washburn laid upon his arm.

"May I introduce Miss Annie St. John and Miss Marie St. John?"

Annie and Marie looked up and nodded politely.

"Misses St. John," Miss Washburn acknowledged. She turned to Rory. "Are these the sisters you mentioned on the train, Mr. O'Rourke?"

Rory's eyes flew to Annie's face. Her eyes rounded but her lips twitched. Had he really mentioned them to the Washburns? He could not remember.

"Yes, yes, they are. Well, no. Did I say sisters? Silly of me. I meant my cousins," he said. "Annie and Marie are my cousins…from Chicago."

"What lovely young women, Mr. O'Rourke," Mrs. Washburn offered. "I hope you are feeling better now?" she addressed Annie and Marie. "Train travel can be so exhausting, I know."

Annie nodded with a wide-eyed expression, a suggestion of a twitch to her lips. She looked up at Rory from under her lashes, and he ignored her.

"Yes, indeed," Mr. Washburn agreed, twisting one end of his handlebar mustache.

"Father, do you have a card?" Miss Washburn said. He produced one, and Rory already knew Miss Washburn's next words as she handed the card to him.

"Please come to call on us, Mr. O'Rourke, and bring your cousins. I should so like to hear more about your photography."

"Yes, yes, of course, we shall. I cannot schedule anything just yet as my mother has need of me, but soon."

"Excellent!" Mr. Washburn said. "Let's go find our table, girls."

"Soon, Mr. O'Rourke," Miss Washburn said with a coy look. "Perhaps next week?"

Rory looked down to see Annie watching with interest, albeit with narrowed eyes.

"Yes, of course, next week."

They moved off and were seated at a nearby table—too close for Rory's comfort, though he didn't understand why. Miss Washburn was a lovely woman, and he had no qualms with calling on women before.

He seated himself and, keeping his eyes on his glass, took a rather large swallow of champagne.

"Sisters, Mr. O'Rourke? Cousins? How awkward for you," Annie chuckled. "I forget. What did you decide?"

Marie grinned hugely.

"Cousins, I think," Rory said faintly.

"I take it that's the family you met on the train this morning?" Annie asked. "I thought they looked familiar."

"Did you see them? I did not realize," Rory said, throwing a glance in the Washburns' direction. Miss Washburn faced him and kept an inviting smile on her face.

"Yes, I saw them through a crack in the door," Annie said.

He returned his attention to her and saw that she'd been following his gaze.

"So, you and this Miss Washburn, huh?" Marie said, with what could only be described as a smirk on her face.

"No, no!" Rory said, his cheeks bronzing slightly. "We just met. No, there is no 'Miss Washburn and I.'"

"Oh!" Marie grinned, quirking an eyebrow. "Annie's right, then. You are a chick magnet."

"I never said that, Marie. For goodness' sake!" Annie directed an exasperated look in her sister's direction.

Marie chuckled. "No, you didn't, but I'll bet you were thinking it."

Annie shook her head and turned away to survey the room.

Rory, his cheeks unusually heated again, queried, "A chick magnet? I do not want to know what that means, do I, Miss St. John?"

"She means women are attracted to you," Annie interjected, "as in attracted to a magnet, but that's really none of our business. You should probably call us Annie and Marie, by the way…since we're cousins. How exactly are we related?" She quirked an eyebrow much as her sister had done. For all the experience Rory felt he'd had with the fairer sex, he considered himself particularly ill-equipped to cope with the unusually forthright sisters.

"I had not thought that far ahead, Miss St. John…*Annie*, when I felt compelled to explain your presence on the train to the steward. In fact, I believe I told him you were my sisters. Cousins seemed so improbable. However, both of my parents live and would certainly know you are not family connections. I cannot say that either of you are distant relatives from Ireland, as neither of you speaks English with an Irish accent. At any rate, my mother would know as her parents were from Ireland. In polite society, it is quite permissible to explain that you are cousins but not specify the degree of kinship. If and when you meet my mother, we shall have to concoct another story."

"While I'd love to meet your mother, I hope we won't be here for long, so that might be moot anyway," Marie said.

Rory's eyes flew to Annie's face, but she looked away.

"Not that we don't appreciate your hospitality and all," Marie continued, "it's just I have a life in Chicago that I love, and I want to get back to it."

"And you, Annie? Are you also anxious to return?" Rory cleared his throat. Such a frog he had in his throat this evening.

Annie reached for her glass of champagne with an unsteady hand and took a large swallow.

"My life isn't quite like Marie's," she said. She didn't elaborate, nor did she answer the question. Rory knew he couldn't pursue it.

"And what do you love about your life in Chicago, Marie?" Rory asked in what he hoped was a conversational tone.

As they ate dinner, Marie described her life, her employment as a personal banker, which surprised him. She spoke of a fiancé named Matt, whom she adored and missed already though they had only been apart for two days. She described museums, parks, musical theater and her favorite hobby of riding bicycles—none of which seemed out of the ordinary for a modern woman in a large city like Chicago, with the exception of her prestigious employment. Most banking positions other than clerical were normally occupied by men. He gleaned little of Annie's life through Marie's descriptions, other than that their parents were both deceased of cancer, and that they had no other siblings.

Annie attended to her food and smiled at many of Marie's comments but offered no personal details of her own, much to Rory's disappointment.

Every now and then, Rory made the mistake of looking up and beyond Marie's shoulder, where he caught Miss Washburn's observant eyes and quick smile. Short of keeping his eyes fixed on Annie, which seemed to make her uncomfortable, he could do little else but stare at his glass or his food. He wondered if Annie thought him quite the glutton.

"Did you find the rest of the clothing to your satisfaction?" Rory asked.

"We didn't have time to try anything else on. Dressing in these outfits took most of the afternoon and early evening," Annie said.

"I had no idea," Rory said as he shook his head. "Perhaps I never paid attention to the time my mother expended on her toilette."

"Mrs. Sanford arranged to have the shop girls come back at eleven tomorrow morning in case we need alterations with the rest of the clothes. I have to say, Mr. O'Rourke, that they brought a lot of boxes. I'm not sure you are aware of how much you bought."

"I am certain they brought what I said you might need for a week or so as I directed them. In the event, you are here longer than that, we can certainly order more clothing."

"I can't do a full week," Marie chimed in.

"We don't know exactly how long we'll be here, Marie, not unless you've figured out a way back, so..." Annie didn't finish the sentence.

"We'll think of something," Marie said with some confidence.

Rory shamed himself by hoping they did not.

As dinner concluded, Rory asked them if they would like to take a walk.

"Is it safe? At this time of night?" Marie asked.

"Certainly," Rory replied. "You will find many people in the downtown area at this hour—some strolling after dinner, others after attending the opera or a musical performance."

"I'd like to," Annie surprised him by saying. "I'm not sure how far I'll get in this outfit, but I'm game."

"Me, too," Marie said. "Might as well see something while I'm here."

Rory winced but said nothing. He did not begrudge Marie the need to return to her home and her affianced, but he fervently wished that Annie did not have the same desire...or a similar suitor.

He nodded briefly toward the Washburns as he passed, guiding Annie and Marie quickly past them. Rory collected his hat from the coatroom, and they crossed the lobby, where the bellman opened the door for them.

Annie hesitated at the top of the stairs leading to the street, a series of ten wide concrete steps. "More stairs?" she breathed.

Rory wasn't quite clear what her fears were, but he valiantly hoped to allay them.

"Can I be of assistance? Will you take my arm?"

He held out his arms and felt Annie and Marie slip their hands into the crooks of his elbows. As they took the first step, he almost tipped over, so tightly did both women clutch at his arms. He paused to steady himself, heedless of the stares of another couple passing them on the way down.

"I cannot help but think that you ladies have never, ever worn long skirts in your time. Is this true?"

"Never," Annie asked. "Not to mention, I can hardly move in this corset."

"Miss St. John! Annie! I-I..." Rory convulsed with laughter. "I think Mrs. Sanford cannot have informed you that we do not...em...that is to say, we do not discuss unmentionables in public."

"I'm sure she said something like that, but that doesn't worry me. It won't always be that way."

"Is there anything I can do?" he said with sympathy. He turned to Marie.

"Don't worry about me. My corset fits fine. I'm just wondering how to maneuver these steps in these shoes. I usually wear flat shoes. I'll just grab a handful of skirt and skip on down." Marie did just that, raising her skirts above the ankle and hopping lightly down the stairs.

"And you, Annie? How can I help?"

"Unlike Marie, I'm having a hard time moving, so if you'll just let me hang onto you for dear life, I'll get through this. These steps seem steeper than the stairs inside the hotel, if that's possible."

They descended the steps without mishap, and joined Marie at street level. The lights of the hotel spilled onto the sidewalk, giving the area a warm ambience. Rory, keeping his pace slow, escorted them down the street, nodding to passersby. He felt Annie's hand relax in his arm. Marie preferred to keep her hands free to attend to her skirts. The night air was warm and pleasant. Traffic was light, with only a few carriages and even fewer cars passing as people attended or left various social activities.

"How do you find the city?" Rory asked.

"Weird," Marie said. "Different."

"Quiet," Annie responded. "I've never been to Seattle before, but this seems like it's much more quiet than it would normally be in our time."

Rory ignored the reference to "our time," noting he was becoming quite proficient at hearing only what he wanted to hear.

"I mean, it's busy," Annie continued. "There are cars and...horses and carriages, but still probably not as many cars as would normally be out at this time of night in a large city's downtown area. We don't really use horses and carriages anymore, especially in the middle of cities, except to drive tourists around. Well, that and the Amish."

Rory listened but hesitated to ask for clarification, though his innate curiosity longed to do so. His reluctance to hear any more of the references to a future continued, and he wondered if he might try to explain himself.

"As you ladies know, I find it difficult to believe in your tale of time travel. I do not dispute that *you* believe it to be true, but I cannot. And yet, I am most curious about some of the things you say. Imagine my dilemma. I want to know more about you, I want to ask more questions, but I am troubled by the references to the future." He struggled for words.

"I think that's something you're going to have to work out for yourself, Rory. Marie and I have no way of proving ourselves to you. We don't have any documents to show you our birthdates or the date when we boarded the train. I can't imagine what it's like for you to listen to us and not call a doctor in to examine us, but I appreciate that you don't. I honestly wouldn't believe you if you showed up in 'my time' claiming to be from the past, so I do sympathize."

"It's not like we ever believed in time travel either, Rory," Marie added. "There are books about it, and movies about it, but no one really believes it's possible."

"'Movies' is a reference to moving pictures," Rory murmured. "How fascinating."

"Well, listen, my feet are killing me in these shoes. I think I'm going to head back," Marie said.

They returned to the hotel, and Rory escorted them upstairs, where he collected his camera.

"I know you will be attended by the staff of the clothing store tomorrow morning. Would you like to go for a drive with me to see the city when you are finished?"

"Oh, yes," Marie answered. "Carriage or car?"

"Which would you prefer?" he asked, hoping Annie would answer.

"You said you still like the carriage, right? So, let's do the carriage," Annie said.

"Excellent! I'll have Mrs. Sanford prepare a picnic lunch for us. We can drive to Leschi Park. Does that sound agreeable to you?"

"Yes, it sounds wonderful," Annie replied. He paused at the door as she held it open, with an unexpected longing to raise her hand to his lips, but the sight of Marie watching them put that notion to rest. He left and returned to his car, vowing to stay awake all night if necessary to process the film.

CHAPTER SEVEN

Annie awoke early the next morning to the feel of soft sunlight on her face. A faint line of warmth slipped through the partially closed velvet curtains. She started to stretch but froze for a moment, trying to orient herself to the strange room. The brightly colored flower-patterned wallpaper reminded her she wasn't in her comparatively sterile bare-walled bedroom at home.

She turned to see Marie breathing deeply in the next bed, her blonde hair spread over the pillow like some sort of fairy tale princess…except that Marie had never really been into princesses as a child. It was Annie who once dreamed of twirling about in long, flowing ball gowns like those of her dolls. Marie had been more interested in sports—especially volleyball and basketball—so much so that she'd grown up to become a high school volleyball coach.

Annie slid out of bed and crossed the room to look out the window. Their room faced another large brick and stone building across the street, perhaps a hotel. She looked down to see a streetcar car moving up the street. Several horse-drawn carts hugged the curbs as drivers offloaded supplies to nearby shops and stores. Massive power poles lined the street, with innumerable lines crisscrossing the road in seemingly chaotic fashion.

She longed to be out on the street—investigating, observing, studying and memorizing—but a glance over her shoulder toward the boxes of clothing reminded her that she couldn't just jump into her T-shirt and capris and toodle down the road. She let the curtain fall and turned from the window. She shot a quick glance toward Marie before quietly lifting the cover of one of the boxes and peeking in.

A beautiful, high-necked satin blouse of peach and lace lay within, and she pulled it from the box and held it up. Large puffed sleeves tapered down to the elbow and ended in a small froth of lace. She set the blouse on the chair with reverence and looked into the next box to find a garment of darker peach, almost a soft orange. Annie assumed this was a matching skirt and pulled it from the box. A belt of satin fell to the floor, and she picked it up.

She looked toward Marie again, still sleeping soundly. Could she dress herself? Just a quick walk down the street to ease her restlessness? To see what she could see in this strange and fascinating time?

Annie picked up the blouse again. It buttoned down the back. How was she going to handle that? And the cast-off corset? Did she really have to wear the thing? She eyed the deceivingly delicate-looking satin and beribboned garment suspiciously where she'd left it on the chair the night before.

Determined, Annie stepped out of the soft lawn nightgown provided by the clothing store and tiptoed into the bathroom to grab the underwear she'd hand washed the night before. She returned to her discarded pile of undergarments in the chair and debated what she could do without and what she had to wear. The drawers could go—way too drafty and unnecessary as long as her underwear held out. A quick image of trying to sew some panties together out of material remnants in the eventuality of a long stay in 1906 flashed through her mind, but she pushed the picture aside with a roll of her eyes.

She slipped the chemise over her head and stepped into the petticoat, attempting to button it behind her back at the waist. Without the corset, it simply wouldn't close. With a sigh, she dropped the petticoat and picked up the corset. By sucking in her stomach and holding her breath, she managed to hook the corset down the front without Mrs. Sanford's help. She noted with pleasure it didn't feel as tight as it had the night before. She tried the petticoat again and managed to button it.

She eyed the skirt and almost put it on until she remembered she had to wear shoes…and with the shoes, she needed stockings. Annie eyed the boxes, bags and clothing strewn about chairs, and almost gave up on her idea of simply taking a quick walk outside. There was nothing simple about dressing in 1906.

Just short of breaking out into a sweat, she managed to pull the stockings up to the suspenders on her corset…the same corset that hadn't allowed her to bend over last night and barely allowed her to reach her feet this morning. She eyed a pair of dark half boots, clearly meant for her due to their smaller size, with something close to despair. How was she going to get into those? Surely not everyone in this era had a maid to help them dress? She turned her back on the shoes and picked up the beautiful blouse.

Huffing and puffing her way through the buttons at her back, she managed to button most of them before the burning in her shoulders forced her to lower her arms. She managed the skirt without trouble, tucked the blouse into the skirt and wrapped the satin belt around her waist to buckle in back.

Marie still slept, and Annie debated waking her for help with her shoes. But she resisted. She wanted to experience the city for herself, alone, with no outside thoughts or influences.

Despite the pain in her stomach, Annie forced her corset to give way as she bent to lace the boots. As she tied the last bow, she straightened and let out a gasp, her face flushed from holding her breath. A glance in the floor mirror revealed she looked fairly presentable, except for her hair. She returned to the bathroom, picked up the pins she'd dropped on the counter the night before and wrapped her hair into a chignon at the crown of her head. It would have to do. Besides, she'd have to wear some sort of hat, wouldn't she?

Feeling as if she had been dressing all morning, and fearful the shop girls would arrive before she had a chance to get outside, Annie hustled over to the round boxes and pulled out a small brown hat with orange silk roses adorning the top. She stuck the hatpin in as best she could and took a final look in the mirror. She had to be ready to go. It seemed as if an hour had passed since she'd started to dress. Surely, she had to be done! She skipped the gloves, thinking they were a bit too much.

With a last look over her shoulder toward Marie, she slipped out of the door and headed down to the lobby. She kept her head down as she passed through the lobby, hoping not to notice if someone stopped and stared at the ridiculous way she wore her hat or the two buttons undone in the middle of her back, or whatever other clothing faux pas she had committed.

The doorman held the door open for her with a greeting, and she mumbled and passed by quickly, hoping he wouldn't stop her and announce in shocked tones that she couldn't possibly go outside by herself. But nothing in his pleasant "Good morning, madam" made her believe he saw anything out of place.

Annie burst into the morning sunshine and paused at the top of the steep stairs, taken aback at the sights, sounds and smells. Traffic in the street had built since she'd looked out the window earlier. The ringing bell of the streetcar caught her attention, and she watched it busily maneuver the street in front. People perched on benches on the streetcar—women in their long skirts, men in suits. She looked down at her own skirt, thinking that she looked very similar to the ladies on the streetcar, except they all wore gloves and she didn't.

Wagons pulled by weary horses passed by, some very close to the streetcar, and Annie winced at the danger to the animals. The jingling of their livery added to the general noise. A single car moved down the road, attempting to pass the wagons without success. The air smelled of coal, dust and that odd smell of moisture in clay or brick, probably emanating from the tall buildings surrounding the square an all sides. A light haze hovered over the downtown area, evident as she scanned the length of the street beyond.

With great care, Annie clung to the concrete banister and made her way down the steps. Without a particular direction in mind, she turned to the right and moved down the street, trying her best to avoid grabbing at her skirt; however, her innate desire to keep her clothes clear of the dust on the sidewalk overrode her best efforts, and she clutched at her skirt and petticoat with one hand to raise them just a bit. She noted women passing by had no such trouble and simply walked on heedless of whether or not their skirts swept the road. What a nice way to keep the sidewalks clean, Annie thought with a twitch of her lips.

She walked along the side of the hotel and studied the doorways of various shops and business across the street with interest. Bold red and white striped awnings over many of the entrances broke the hard surface of the often linear five-story buildings. She wanted to peer into the shops. Unclear of the jaywalking laws, she watched several people cross the street as needed, and she hiked up her skirt a little higher, looked both ways and stepped into the street.

In the general chaotic noise of the road, she missed the clip-clop of a horse's hooves, and a white horse reared as she stepped off the curb and into the path of a wagon. Annie jumped back with a screech and caught the edge of her skirt with her heel. She fell onto her backside and rolled away from the horse, covering her head with her hands. She barely noticed that her hat had come loose and lay by her face.

"Whoa, whoa!" said a man nearby. She assumed it was the driver, and peeked through the veil of her now disheveled hair to see two men settling the startled horse—an older man in a dusty dark coat and trousers wearing a cap, and another man, tall and well dressed in a dark suit and a bowler. The horse settled, and the second man rushed over to her.

Annie noted a crowd had begun to build.

"Madam! Are you all right? That was certainly a close call." Also an older man, he bent to help her up and helped her back to the curb.

"I'm fine," she mumbled. "I'm fine." She turned to look at the horse. "Is he all right?" she called to the driver. "I'm sorry. I didn't see you coming."

"Yes, miss, he's fine. No need to worry about him. Are you all right?" the driver asked, his large mustache barely moving as he spoke.

"I'm okay," she called. She half turned to the crowd of about ten people or so on the sidewalk behind her. "I'm okay," she called out to the bystanders, and gave them a short wave. Thankfully, they started to disperse and move on. The driver walked his horse and cart carefully by and moved down the road.

Annie brushed off her skirts and looked at the gentleman who picked up her hat. She followed his gaze to her hair, now hanging over her shoulders.

"I must look a mess," she muttered, hoping that sounded appropriate for the time. "Could you just hold my hat for me for a minute?" she asked as she pulled out her pins and bundled her hair back up again. "Thanks," she said as she stuck the hat back on her head. "I'm not from around here, so I'm afraid I wasn't watching carefully enough," she offered.

"Where are you from, Miss...?" Something about him seemed familiar, but she couldn't place it. Gleaming silver hair peeped out from beneath his hat. His clothing looked expensive, though Annie had no idea whether it was. The silver buttons of his dark blue waistcoat gleamed, and somehow the dust of the road had spared his shoes.

"St. John," she replied. "Annie St. John." She looked toward the hotel, hoping to escape the street and retreat to the room, perhaps to try her solo jaunt another time.

"Harold O'Rourke, at your service. Please call me Hal." He bowed gallantly.

Annie swung her head back towards him. "Harold O'Rourke?" she repeated. He shared Rory's height and build.

Silver eyebrows shot up. "Yes, O'Rourke. Have we met, madam?"

Annie shook her head, and resisted her first instincts to say, *But I know your son.*

"No, no, we haven't."

"Perhaps you do business with my bank, Seattle Union Bank?"

Annie shook her head. "No. Well, thank you very much for your help. I'd better get back inside."

"Oh, are you staying at the hotel? I was just on my way in. I am staying there as well. Let me escort you." He held out a hand, and Annie had little choice but to take his arm. If he had a local bank, why was he staying at a hotel?

"And where are you from, Miss St. John?" he asked as they walked back toward the hotel. Mr. O'Rourke kept the pace at a leisurely stroll.

"Chicago." Could this be Rory's father? Rory had let slip that he didn't seem to like his father very much. If so, and it seemed likely given the name, then it was especially odd that he was staying at the same hotel. Rory hadn't said anything. She gave in to her curiosity.

"If you own a bank in Seattle, why are you staying at the hotel, Mr. O'Rourke?"

He broke his stride for a moment and looked down at her in surprise. Then he smiled and resumed the slow pace.

"Mrs. O'Rourke requested that I do so," he murmured. "I acceded to her wishes."

"Oh!" Annie said. She bit her lips. That was forthright. Did Rory know? "I'm sorry for prying."

"Not at all," he said, almost jovially. "The news will soon be all over town. There is no reason a stranger from Chicago should not be one of the first to know."

Annie suspected he wasn't as overjoyed as he appeared to be. They reached the foot of the steps, and Annie did her best to get up the stairs without hanging onto him as she had clung to Rory for support the night before.

The doorman opened the door and they entered the lobby.

"Father! What on earth are you doing?" Rory said, his dark brows narrowed in a stormy expression.

Annie was right. They were of the same height. She dropped her arm as the men stared at one another.

"I might ask you the same thing," his father said. "Why are you here? I did not tell your mother I was staying here."

"I am not here for you," Rory said darkly.

His father followed Rory's eyes to Annie. One eyebrow shot up.

"Miss St. John? And how do you know Miss St. John?"

Rory held out his arm to Annie, and with a dizziness reminiscent of being handed off in a square dance move, she slipped her hand under his arm.

"We are acquainted," Rory said shortly. "Good day to you, Father." He nodded his head sharply and moved away, seeming to forget that Annie's hand was clasped beneath his arm.

She allowed him to clear to the lobby and move down the hallway before she pulled her arm from his grasp.

"I can't keep up with you, Rory. You're walking too fast."

Rory paused to look at her. "How on earth did you meet my father?

Where have you been? Why did you leave without your sister...or without me?"

Annie held up her hands as if to stop the horse in the street. "Whoa! Just a minute there, pal! Remember, I get a little cranky when you get in that demanding way that you do. Ask me nicely." She moved past him and rounded the corner to take the stairs.

Rory caught up to her. "Forgive me, Miss St. John. I was just surprised, and a little taken aback. My relationship with my father is not the best, and I apologize for allowing that to color my words to you."

She paused on the first landing. "I understand. I met him in the street. I...uh...had a little accident when I was crossing the street, scared a horse more than it scared me, and I fell down. Your father helped me up, and decided to walk me back to the hotel. He seems nice," she offered tentatively.

"My father is a very pleasant sort of fellow, if you are not married to him. What sort of accident?" Rory said. He surveyed her. "Your skirt and shirtwaist are dusty. Are you injured in any way? I do wish you had waited for me to escort you. Our streets are very busy, very congested, even dangerous at times, as you have seen."

"I'm fine," she said for the third time. "I'm sorry I didn't wait. I just wanted to get out first thing and experience the town for myself, the sights, the sounds..."

He tilted his head and regarded her quizzically. "You seem... interested in our era, Miss St. John. Dare I hope?"

Annie blinked. "Hope for what?"

With bronzed cheeks, Rory rubbed a hand along his chin and shook his head. "Poor choice of words," he muttered. He held out his arm to her once again, and they climbed the stairs. "What I meant to say is that I hope that you will not find your time here too onerous, too burdensome. I do not wish unhappiness on either you or your sister."

"Thank you, Mr. O'Rourke," she said. "I'm doing okay, but I'm not sure how well Marie will do. As you may have guessed from last night's conversation, her life is much fuller than mine. I'm not sure what she'll do if she can't get back. She enjoys her life in Chicago very much."

"And you?" he asked.

"It's a life," Annie murmured with a smile. "Nothing to write home about."

"I see," he said briefly. Annie detected a strange note in his voice, but couldn't decipher it.

They arrived at the door and Annie pushed it open, peeping in to ensure that Marie wasn't hanging out in the sitting room in her underwear. She wasn't. Annie opened the door to let Rory in.

"By the way, aren't you here early?" she asked as they stepped inside.

"I awoke early, and after developing the photographs, I thought I would rush over here to deliver them. I am not known as a portrait photographer, but I think I did quite well. Perhaps the subject matter was most inspiring." He flashed that brilliant smile, and Annie clutched a chair back to steady her knees. Such a handsome man! She could see a small resemblance to his father but suspected his dark hair and bright blue eyes came from his mother. And that smile...

"You're smiling," Annie said inconsequentially, her eyes glued to his mouth.

Rory broadened his smile even further, and Annie sank into the chair, heedless of the dirt on her skirt.

"I am, Miss St. John. I cannot help it." He removed his hat and pulled a packet from the inside of his coat pocket. "Would you like to see the photographs?"

"Sure."

He unwrapped the packet and brought the photographs to her. Just like the pictures from the old-time touristy photography shops, she and Marie stood by the fireplace in black and white, their faces softer than she would have thought, their hair gleaming under the reflected light of the wall sconces and their clothes utterly gorgeous. Annie never imagined she could look so good in such stark colors.

"Wow! These *are* beautiful," she said. "If you ever decide to give up traveling, I'm sure you could make a nice living doing portraits." She looked up. Rory's face sobered. Had she said something wrong?

"I have thought of settling down," he said with an almost wistful note. "I do not particularly care to give up my travels, but life on the road is not always conducive to a happy family."

Annie drew in a sharp breath. Was he thinking of marrying? No!

"However, it is not impossible that my future wife might not travel with me."

"Are you getting mar—"

A knock on the door startled them, and Annie rose to get the door. The girls from the clothing shop entered and sank into little curtseys in front of Rory. Annie wasn't quite sure curtseying was still that common, but Rory had that Prince Charming look about him.

He checked his pocket watch. "I shall await you in the lobby. Please take your time, as I arrived early."

Rory left, and the vibrancy in the room seemed to leave with him.

"Hi girls, let me go see if my sister is awake yet."

Annie entered the bedroom to find Marie standing at the window.

"Oh, I didn't know you were awake. Did you just wake up?"

Marie yawned and turned to her. "No, I've been up long enough to hear your boy talk about a future wife. That's not good," she chuckled.

"He's not *my boy*, dear sister. Somehow the modern terminology doesn't suit him. Man, I've got a lot to tell you. In the last hour, I met his father, almost got run over by a horse, my corset isn't quite as tight as it was, but the girls are here, so they can help you dress. And believe me, you're going to need their help!"

Annie called Sally and Jennifer into the bedroom, and the four of them set about getting Marie dressed in a beautiful sky blue silk blouse, dark blue skirt and matching bolero jacket. Unlike Annie, Marie slipped into her drawers without question. Wishing for Mrs. Sanford's salon-style skills, Annie pulled Marie's hair up and wrapped it into a bun.

"Good enough," Marie said.

"Miss, your skirt and your shirtwaist are soiled," Sally cried out when Marie was dressed with hat and gloves. "Let me see if I can clean those for you." She ran to the bathroom and returned with a damp cloth, which miraculously removed the dust from Annie's skirt and blouse.

"Oh, so this is a shirtwaist?" Annie asked as she surveyed her frilly blouse. "Interesting name."

"Yes, miss." Sally gave her a curious look. She turned to rummage through the boxes and came up with a similarly styled jacket that matched Annie's skirt.

"Wait, miss, there are a few buttons undone." Sally adjusted those, and handed her a pair of gloves.

After seeing the shop girls out, Annie and Marie descended the stairs while Annie gave her sister a recap of the morning's events.

"Why did you go outside by yourself, Annie? Who knows what could have happened to you? We're not in Kansas anymore, Dorothy!"

Annie shrugged. "Because I wanted to. I just wanted to experience the town for myself."

"That and the underside of a horse's hooves!" Marie said with a lift of her eyebrow.

Annie responded with a flash of her eyes. "*You* try trotting across the street in between moving streetcars, horses, wagons, pedestrians and the occasional 'automobile' honking that *moogah* sound. It's hectic out there. And not a streetlight or road crossing in sight."

"I've got better sense. That's why I would wait for Rory to accompany us."

They neared the lobby, and Annie paused. "Well, he's not going to be here all the time, Sis! We're going to have to figure out how to get around on our own. Besides, I think he might be engaged, and if that's true, I doubt his fiancée is going to tolerate him babysitting two other women." Annie swallowed hard at the thought.

"Engaged? I didn't know that."

"I don't know for sure, but I thought something he said this morning about a 'future wife' sounded like he was engaged." Annie sighed heavily.

"Interesting," Marie murmured. She gave Annie a sharp look. "Well, I'm starved. Let's see what they serve for breakfast here."

When Rory saw them, he folded his newspaper and stood.

"I took the liberty of requesting a table for breakfast as I assumed you ladies had not eaten. Mrs. Sanford has packed a delightful picnic lunch for us, but I think it will be some time before we are able to eat—therefore, you must have something to sustain you until then."

His smile encompassed them both, and Annie wondered how Marie hadn't succumbed to his charm, fiancé or not. Marie greeted Rory cordially, but she appeared composed, lacking the bright red cheeks which Annie knew she now sported under the brilliance of Rory's smile.

"Sounds good!" Marie said. Rory led the way into the dining room, now quieter than it had been the night before. Annie noted the men, like Rory, wore suits similar to those modern day men wore, if a bit old-fashioned in appearance. Gone were the black and white coattails, the glittering jewels and off-shoulder gowns of the evening before. She and Marie appeared to be dressed appropriately if the similarly lacy shirtwaists, tulip-shaped skirts and matching jackets of the other women were anything to go by.

Annie's natural instinct was to remove her hat once seated, and in fact, Marie reached up to do so, but Annie shook her head.

"I think we're supposed to leave the hats on," she said in a low voice. "Look." With a nod of her head, she gestured toward the room in general where all the women wore variations of hats—small and large—festooned with ribbons, silk flowers, feathers and even entire birds. Annie winced at the sight of a robin on one woman's hat.

"Is that a real bird?" she leaned toward Rory to whisper.

Rory and Marie followed her gaze.

"Yes, I am afraid so. In fact, while I was photographing in Montana I met with a man named George Bird Grinnell who founded a small organization called the Audubon Society about twenty years ago in an attempt to halt the mass slaughter of wild birds for the fashion industry. Many such conservation organizations have since sprung up, and coalesced into a larger society called the National Association Societies for the Protection of Wild Birds and Animals."

"Yes, the Audubon Society," Annie murmured. She looked away from the women's hat, thinking it hideous.

"However, sadly, no laws for the protection of these birds have been enacted as of yet," Rory said with a sigh.

"Do you photograph wildlife?" Annie asked.

"Yes, I must admit that I have been known on occasion to place myself in some precarious situations in an attempt to capture the perfect photograph. I have had several encounters with bears in Alaska, as well as one very cross mother moose during my recent trip to Montana. I should have realized that she had calves, but they were hidden in the brush, and I did not see them until I found myself between them and their mother." Rory's grin belied the seriousness of his words.

"Sounds perilous, Pauline," Annie said, studying him with more interest than usual, if that were possible. She hadn't previously imagined him facing off with a grizzly bear, but now that she thought about it, he seemed just the sort of man to put himself in danger for the perfect shot. Annie herself avoided situations and pursuits that frightened her—heights, the gaping jaws of wild animals, bungee jumping, whitewater rafting, but Marie enjoyed a good scare…as often as possible.

"Now, that's my kind of photography," Marie said with interest. "I always wanted to take up wildlife photography, but my job at school keeps me pretty busy taming the female wildlife on the court."

"On the court?" Rory asked. He turned to Annie. "Pauline?"

Annie chuckled to see him trying to keep up with their obscure comments.

"Court. Volleyball. I coach girls' volleyball," Marie responded. "You guys have volleyball, don't you?"

"Guys as in men? Yes, men do play volleyball. I believe young ladies do as well, though only informally."

"Oh, really?" Marie said as the waiter arrived with the tea to take their order. "Well, that has to change."

They busied themselves with placing their orders, and pouring tea.

"And how might that change?" Rory asked with interest.

Annie watched the exchange between Rory and her sister, thinking how much they had in common in addition to their tall, elegant and athletic frames.

Marie sipped her tea and quirked an eyebrow. "Well, if I had to stay here, I'd certainly organize a professional girls' volleyball league."

Rory matched the lift of her eyebrow. "Indeed? That is most

progressive of you, Miss Marie. The ladies of our time do participate in some organized athletic endeavors, of course—tennis, lawn bowling, but not volleyball, I think."

"They will, though," she said with a smirk.

"Ah, the future," Rory said. "Yes." He pressed his lips together and didn't elaborate, and Annie knew he continued to have doubts.

"At any rate," Marie continued, "I don't plan on staying too much longer, so unfortunately, I won't have time to educate Seattle on organized volleyball for women."

Rory shot a quick look toward Annie, but she couldn't interpret his expression. She remained silent.

"You do not like it here," he stated flatly.

Had Marie not answered, Annie would have because she couldn't bear to hear the disappointment in his voice.

"No, no, I'm sure it's fine," Marie said. "It's just different, that's all. I'll be frank. I do like my own time better."

"And you, Miss St. John?"

"Me?" Annie said, stalling. "It's...um...interesting." She could have bopped herself for such an uninspired answer. It did little to return the smile to Rory's face.

"But do *you* prefer your own time, as your sister calls it?"

Annie opened her mouth to mutter something unintelligible, but fortunately, the waiter arrived with the food and she pretended she had forgotten the question. Coincidentally, she thought she was rapidly forgetting that she'd ever had a life before meeting Rory O'Rourke. How could she know if she preferred her own time...if Rory wasn't in it?

He didn't press for an answer, and Annie suspected he'd already forgotten the question. Marie engaged Rory in a discussion on the value of the various athletic disciplines open to females in 1906, and Annie was content to listen. Having never been a sportster but more into art, she really had no opinion on the matter other than knowing that it would soon change.

They were sipping their last cup of tea following breakfast when Rory's father entered the dining room. He stopped short when he saw Rory but made his way over to the table. Annie felt rather than saw Rory tense.

"We meet again, Miss St. John," Mr. O'Rourke said with a gallant, if exaggerated bow. "And who might this lovely young lady be?" He seemed to avoid Rory's eyes as he smiled at Marie.

"This is Miss Marie St. John, Miss St. John's sister. Miss Marie, this is my father, Harold O'Rourke Senior."

Marie sent Annie a dubious look as Mr. O'Rourke bent over her hand. Rory rose abruptly. "Are you ready, ladies?"

Startled, Annie downed her cup of tea and jumped up. Marie nodded and stood.

"My apologies, Father," Rory said. "We were just about to set out."

Mr. O'Rourke seemed to ignore Rory's haste. "So lovely to meet you, Miss Marie. And I hope you have recovered from your mishap this morning, Miss St. John?" he asked Annie.

"Yes, thank you."

"Good day, Father." Rory held out his arms in a peremptory fashion, and Annie and Marie attached themselves to him as if commanded. Annie looked back as they left the room to see Rory's father watching them, a look of curiosity on his face mingled with something else...pain? He smiled, and she gave him a quick smile in return.

"So, that was your father," Marie murmured. "He seems nice."

"Yes," Rory said shortly. "Joseph will be waiting with the carriage below."

They stepped outside to the hustle and bustle of the three streets converging in front of the hotel given its flatiron shape; much busier and more congested than when Annie had emerged from the hotel earlier. A mass of pedestrians virtually covered the sidewalks as they went about their business. The now familiar ringing of the streetcar bells seemed almost deafening as numerous cars butted up to one another in the congested square.

Marie maneuvered the stairs with more ease than the previous night, and Annie's morning practice paid off in growing comfort with the steep steps.

"Marie, look at all the streetcars!" Annie said. "I've never been on one," she confided to Rory.

"Would you like to take the streetcar to the park?" Rory said with enthusiasm. "Joseph can follow us in the carriage."

Annie saw the carriage waiting at curbside, the patient driver having jumped down to hold the door open for them.

"Really?" Annie almost squeaked.

"Don't encourage her, Rory," Marie said dryly. "Annie loves all things involving travel. Trains, planes, ships, and now apparently streetcars."

"A girl after my own heart," Rory responded with a grin.

Annie caught her breath at his words but scolded herself almost immediately. It was just an expression.

"Let me speak to Joseph and then we shall hop aboard." Rory stopped and addressed a few words to Joseph, who nodded and climbed back onto the carriage.

"Shall we?" Rory said. He held out a hand, and one of the slow-moving cars stopped. Rory helped them aboard, and Annie and Marie took the last remaining seats facing outward while he stood on the running board and hung onto a rail. Marie watched the commotion of the downtown streets with interest while Annie, self-conscious that Rory faced them, touched her hat to reassure herself it still sat straight on her head.

"That is a lovely hat, Miss St. John," Rory said with a nod of approval. "And yes, it is still on top of your head where it should be." Annie thought she saw a teasing light in his eyes, and she returned his smile. Given the close proximity necessitated by him standing on the platform, she didn't think they had more than a foot between them, and her heart jumped around irregularly.

"Thank you, Mr. O'Rourke. It's hard to tell. I don't usually wear hats, certainly not any that require a hatpin, so I'd never know if I was wearing it or not. That's a mighty sporty hat you have on today." She nodded toward his straw hat, a dark blue ribbon wrapped around the crown.

He tapped the edge of his hat and nodded his appreciation. "Ah! My boater! It is summer, and we are embarking on a picnic. It is only fitting."

Annie noted quite a few men on the streetcar and along the road wore the "boaters," though none so well as Rory, in her opinion. Something about his black hair set the jaunty hat off to perfection.

"Where do you get your dark hair, Mr. O'Rourke?"

Rory looked taken aback for a moment. "Well, I suppose my mother," he said. "My father's hair was more red before it silvered, but my mother's hair is still black, even now. I believe her grandmother's hair was black as well."

"Black Irish," Annie mused, still staring at the handsome lines of his clean-cut face and well-trimmed sideburns.

"As you say, Black Irish."

"So, why don't you wear a mustache?" Annie, having surveyed several other men on the streetcar, noted they all had facial hair. "They look fairly common in your era."

Rory's raised a hand to his mouth to clear his throat. "A mustache?" He shook his head. "I do not like them. I prefer to be smooth shaven, though my toilette might take less time if I did grow facial hair."

"So, it's not mandatory or anything? Growing a mustache or a beard?"

"No, it is the fashion, and although you may think me a slave to fashion given my boater, I am not." He grinned and tapped his hat again as he spoke.

The streetcar jerked just then, and Rory seemed to lose his footing. Annie cried out and half rose to grab at him, pulling him down onto her. He braced his arms on either side of her, and his face came perilously close to hers. She could have kissed him if she'd had the courage. Blue eyes stared into hers for a moment.

"Annie!" Marie laughed. "Good gravy! Let the poor man go!"

Annie colored, and let Rory go. He grinned and brushed his lips against her cheek before pushing himself up to a standing position.

"I'm sorry! I thought you were going to fall off." She turned to Marie. "He was falling!"

"I was, Miss St. John. Had it not been for you, I would have landed on the street below, no doubt to be run down by a grocer's wagon." Rory's eyes twinkled.

"Been there," Annie mumbled with a bemused smile. Had he really kissed her cheek or had she imagined it?

"Ah, yes, you were…only this morning. I had better pay attention and grip the pole more tightly if I wish to make it to the park in one piece."

Annie avoided his sparkling eyes and turned to watch the activity in the streets as the streetcar picked up speed once free of the downtown area. The car began to ascend a hill, and Annie kept a veiled eye on Rory to see that he didn't lose his footing again. For the next hour, Rory pointed out various points of interest, and Annie listened intently, loving the nuances of his voice and his obvious pride in the city of his birth.

"If you turn your heads, you can see the pavilion, which is the terminus for the streetcar at Leschi Park—a beautiful building, to be sure."

Annie looked to her right and saw the building, an immense brick building, about three stories high, topped with caps and turrets.

"They hold dances here in the summer. The pavilion is situated next to a delightful boathouse where visitors can rent canoes and drift about on Lake Washington."

"Canoes?" Annie asked.

"I told you, Rory," Marie interjected, "any form of transportation, and Annie is in!"

"Then we shall hire a canoe and satisfy her hunger for travel," Rory said with a chuckle.

"Oh, no, we don't have to," Annie said half-heartedly. Of course, she wanted to. A canoe? Oh, yes, please!

They descended from the streetcar and wandered around the pavilion for a while. Annie, mesmerized by the grandeur of the primarily open-air building, paused on the second floor wraparound balcony to survey the park. Lush trees and shrubs provided an emerald border for concrete walkways that meandered through the well-maintained gardens of the park. A rainbow of flowers bloomed, providing a colorful backdrop for the park goers who strolled the paths or rested on the benches dotted throughout—the women and children in their summer finery, many of the men sporting lighter-colored suits than she had seen downtown. Apparently, light colors were the order of the day for the park.

"This is Lake Washington," Rory said. Annie turned to the right to see a stunning lake of immense proportions. No small pond, she would not have wanted to attempt to swim to the heavily treed shores on the other side of the lake. The boathouse, a wonderfully Victorian-style single-story building crowned by a cupola, floated at the edge of the dock to the pavilion. Canoes and small boats were tied up alongside in a picturesque sight. As Rory had said, boaters drifted on the lake, seemingly in no hurry to row in any given direction. The occasional brightly colored parasol could be seen shading ladies in some of the boats.

"Would you like to go out on the lake first or are you hungry?" Rory asked.

"Lake," Annie chimed in.

"Lake," Marie echoed. "I'll row."

Rory laughed. "No, no, Miss Marie, rowing is a man's job—at least, it will be today."

Annie chuckled as he intercepted Marie's likely retort, which had appeared likely from the breath she sucked in at his words.

They made their way down to the boathouse, and Annie and Marie watched the boaters on the lake while Rory rented a canoe.

"This looks like fun, but how are we going to get into a canoe in these skirts?" Annie muttered.

"What I want to know is where's my umbrella?" Marie snickered.

"Parasol."

"Umbrella to me," Marie maintained. "What a chauvinist," she said in a dry voice with an eye on Rory.

"I know. Isn't he adorable? So turn of the century!" Annie said, turning to study his tall, trim form in light brown suit and boater. She would never be able to return to her own time and think a straw hat on a man was only suitable for a barbershop quartet. In fact, she wasn't quite sure how she would be able to return at all. There was something so special about this era, so relaxed, so peaceful. It wasn't that Seattle, or even the park, weren't crowded and didn't exhibit the usual hustle and bustle of a large city, but that people seemed to walk slower, drive slower, travel slower, eat slower. She sighed.

Marie clicked her fingers in Annie's face. "Snap out of it! You can't stay here. Don't go falling for him, Annie. That's just a pipe dream. We don't belong here. This fun little living history vacation is all well and good, but we're not staying. Besides, I thought you said he was engaged."

Annie averted her gaze from Rory to look at Marie. She shrugged helplessly.

"I know! He might be, I don't know. I hope not." She hurried on when Marie started to protest. "I know we can't stay, not if we can get back. I shouldn't be so lucky," she finished darkly.

"Lucky? To stay here? Have you forgotten how awful most of these historical periods were for women compared to our lives now? No vote? No rights? Lower-paying jobs? Not to mention how awful it was for minorities."

Annie nodded. "I know, I know. I'm not forgetting how difficult it was for lots of people in the past, but there's something about this particular era that makes me feel more comfortable than present-day Chicago ever did. Except for the corset, of course. That's still not comfortable."

Marie chuckled. "Well, lose a few pounds then."

"Marie!" Annie laughed. Marie's lifelong quips at Annie's fuller figure hadn't bothered her in years, not since her similarly framed mother had sat her down as a young teenager and told her that she wasn't fat, just curvy, and that rounded corners were softer and less painful than sharp edges. Her father had nodded in agreement, and the tender look in his eyes when he regarded her mother opened Annie's eyes to the notion that curvy girls were as desirable to some as lean girls were to others— eye of the beholder and all that.

"We are all set," Rory said behind them. They rounded the dock and followed a man toward a dark red-painted canoe tied up alongside the dock. The dockworker held the canoe steady while Rory helped Marie in and then Annie. Annie grabbed her skirts, heedless of propriety, and stepped in gingerly. With the canoe wobbling, she seated herself quickly in the remaining seat facing the rear of the canoe. Rory stepped in and took the paddle from the dockworker, who cast off the rope and pushed the canoe away from the dock. Annie hadn't quite thought about the seating position when she boarded, and now found herself facing Rory as he paddled. He seemed proficient at it, if a little incongruous rowing in a suit and tie. But then, so were all the other men on the lake. The day was pleasant, the lake calm, and the sun gentle and warm. A gentle breeze played on the back of Annie's neck, and she relaxed.

"Have you done this before?" she asked.

"Rented a canoe at the park? No, I don't think so. My friends and I rented canoes from the local Indians when we were young boys. And I've rowed on rivers and lakes in Montana, Alaska, Wyoming, California and several other places I have probably forgotten—all with a view to getting the best photograph."

"Lots of traveling," Annie said wistfully. His life sounded wonderfully adventurous, filled with travels, memories and stories. She had access to every modern form of travel—even a space shuttle if she were wealthy enough—but it seemed like she hadn't really gone anywhere. It had taken her a year of coaxing to get her sister on the Alaskan cruise—the one they hadn't quite made yet.

"You sound envious, my dear Miss St. John, and yet to hear you speak, you and your sister have traveled through time. Surely, a great journey."

"There *is* that," she smiled. "I'd forgotten."

"I hope that is a sign of your growing ease with Seattle?"

"Maybe," she said, "or just maybe with the turn of the century." Annie chuckled.

A sudden, unexpected breeze whipped over the lake and caught under the brim of Annie's hat, whisking it away.

"Catch it!" she called to Marie. Annie jumped up to try to catch it, and the boat teetered.

"Annie! Sit down!" Rory and Marie commanded in unison, but it was too late. Annie stepped on the edge of her skirt, lost her balance and tipped over the edge into the water.

CHAPTER EIGHT

Rory's heart stopped when he saw Annie fall into the water. Fortunately, she came up sputtering right away, and treading water. He ripped off his jacket and vest, tossed his hat into the boat and kicked off his shoes. The canoe rocked precariously as Marie, holding Annie's hat, leaned far over the edge to reach for her sister.

"Annie!" she called.

"Sit down before you fall in as well, Marie! I'll get her!" Rory barked.

"Help!" Annie yelled. "My skirts are wrapped around my legs, and I can't kick. Freezing. Can't catch my breath."

Rory dove into the water near Annie and came up behind her. He grabbed her by the waist and dragged her toward the boat. The water was freezing, but he had expected that. Annie tried to help by kicking, but the motion seemed to drag her deeper into the water.

"Don't kick, Annie! I've got you," he reassured her.

Her teeth chattered when she spoke. "I'm such a klutz. I'm sorry. You must be freezing!"

"Don't worry about me, dearest. Here, cling to the edge of the boat. Let's see how we shall get you aboard without capsizing it and tossing Marie into the drink."

"If I could just get out of these skirts," she said as she hung onto the canoe and shivered.

"Can't you take them off, Rory?" Marie asked. "It would be easier to pull her out." She grabbed Annie's hands as if to try to haul her aboard.

"I think that will not be necessary," Rory said, his own voice beginning to tremble from the cold. "Forgive me, Miss St. John, but I must push you out of the water by your nether regions. Marie, sit on the other side of the canoe so that it does not tip over."

Marie reluctantly let go of Annie's hands and slid over to the opposite side of the boat.

"Ready, Annie?" Rory said.

She nodded and shivered.

"One, two, three!" Rory grabbed Annie by her backside and pushed with all his might, half submerging himself. He kicked forcefully several times to keep himself above water. Annie hoisted herself over the edge of the canoe and onto the floor before immediately popping up to offer him her hands. Touched by the sweet but ineffective gesture, Rory pulled himself from the water and rolled into the canoe—not the first time he had ever done so.

"Are you all right?" he asked as he raised his head to look at Annie. "Your skin is so blue." Her wet, bedraggled hair hung down her back and around her face. Marie rubbed her sister's arms.

"I'm freezing, but I'll be all right. It's pretty warm today," Annie said with a shiver.

Rory pulled her to a sitting position and wrapped his jacket around her shoulders.

"Come, we must get back to shore and return you to the hotel so you can get out of your wet clothes."

"What about the picnic?" Annie said. "I don't want to spoil the picnic! I'll dry. Really! This isn't the first time I've gone swimming in my clothes."

Marie laughed. "That's true. There was this one time in high school that she fell into a friend's pool and stayed in there for the next hour, fully clothed. We all jumped in after her. Of course, the pool was heated."

Annie chuckled. "See? No problem. But I suppose you're miserable, aren't you?"

"I keep a change of clothes in the carriage as well as in the car. Always. I've been in too many wild and undeveloped areas during photography shoots not to have a change of clothes available in the event of a mishap."

"It's settled then," Annie said. "We're picnicking. I refuse to be the reason we have to leave the park so soon. But I *am* going to get rid of this petticoat and the jacket. My skirt and blouse will dry faster if I lighten the load."

"There is a lavatory in the boathouse where you can remove some of your clothing, if you wish," Rory said with a twitch of his lips.

"Perfect!" Annie said.

Rory rowed back to the dock house, and within a half-hour of their arrival, Annie and Marie emerged from the lavatory carrying the bag that

Rory had managed to procure for them from the boathouse owner. As Annie had predicted, her clothing appeared to be drying, as was his. He thought he may as well forgo the opportunity to change clothes in sympathy with Annie, opting only to loosen his tie and unbutton the collar of his shirt. It would not do for him to sit comfortably dry picnicking while Annie's clothes were still a bit damp.

A bit taken aback by her unconventionality, he could only admire the damp curls at the nape of her neck, remnants of an obvious attempt to redo her hair without benefit of a comb or brush. He opted not to offer his comb so as not to insult her efforts. Her hair looked charmingly disordered, much like her personality. She seemed to exhibit a remarkable proclivity for accidents.

"You didn't change!" Annie exclaimed when she saw him. "Why not? I would not have suggested we stay if I'd known you weren't going to get out of your damp clothes. Though they do look like they're drying well." She handed him his jacket.

He shook his head and chuckled. "As we discussed, this is not my first time in a canoe, therefore, not my first time in the water fully dressed either. I did not get so many of my clothes wet as you, and I will survive a damp shirt and trousers." He led them over to the picnic spot where he had directed Joseph to lay out their picnic lunch before they set out on the lake.

"Joseph, bring some blankets from the carriage, please. Miss St. John had a small mishap." He handed Joseph the bag of wet clothing and his vest and jacket. Joseph hurried away with the clothing and returned within moments carrying several brown woolen blankets.

"Let me wrap this around you," Rory said as he gently draped one of the blankets around Annie's shoulders. She looked up at him and smiled. "You should take one for yourself."

"I will be fine," he said. "As you say, it is a fine summer day. My shirt feels almost dry."

"This looks wonderful!" Annie said as she took Rory's offered hand to lower herself to the thick red and green plaid blanket. He handed her the other blanket and she laid it across her lap. Marie declined a third blanket for herself.

"If it's all the same to you, I think I'll just take my shoes off and let them dry out." Annie reached under the blanket as if to fidget with her boots.

Rory's lips twitched. "Certainly, Miss St. John. I had forgotten your shoes would not dry as easily. Are you certain you do not wish to return to the hotel? We can picnic another day."

"Oh, no! I'm fine. Just need to get this other boot undone." She scrunched her face as she labored under the blanket but beamed when she produced two small half boots, which she placed behind her.

"Well done," Rory murmured. "Are you comfortable?"

"Perfectly," Annie grinned.

Rory chuckled and turned to Marie to help her sit. She had been watching Joseph with interest.

"What does he do while we're eating? Seems like he waits around a lot."

Rory turned to see Joseph rummaging in the carriage to pull out a small basket.

"Joseph? Oh, he amuses himself. Give him time. He will be chatting with a woman before you know it, and offering to share his own lunch."

"Oh, he has food with him?" Marie asked as she allowed Rory to help her sit.

"Of course, he does, Miss Marie. What sort of employer do you imagine me to be?" He grinned. "Joseph acts as my valet and driver when I am in town, and as my camera assistant when we are traveling. I have known him for a very long time. He does not want for food."

Rory seated himself and peered into the wicker baskets, retrieving sandwiches, various small covered dishes, china, silverware, linen napkins, a bottle of wine and some glasses.

"Rory!"

Rory froze at the familiar young voice. Eddie! Rory stood as his brother approached. Eddie turned to wave at several companions as if to say goodbye, and Rory sighed. Apparently, Eddie meant to stay. He could already see the curiosity on his brother's face.

"Hello, how do you do?" Eddie bowed in front of Annie. "My name is Edward O'Rourke. I'm Rory's brother." Eddie exuded their father's charm. Rory had always hoped his young brother wouldn't additionally inherit his father's character flaws.

Annie took Eddie's proffered hand with a startled look in Rory's direction. Marie followed suit.

"Eddie, this is Miss Annie St. John and Miss Marie St. John." Rory did not elaborate. He still wasn't sure exactly how to explain the Misses St. John, even to himself.

"May I sit?" Eddie knew better than to ask Rory, and he directed his question to Annie. Annie smiled and nodded silently.

"I did not know you were coming to the park on a picnic today, Rory. You should have told me yesterday when I saw you. I would have liked to join you. I must say you are dressed very casually for the park today with your shirt unbuttoned and without vest or jacket. I should like to do without my tie, but Mother would not have it, I'm sure." He grinned, and began poking shamelessly about in the baskets. "Is there enough for me to eat?"

"Yes, of course there is, but what will your friends think?" Rory said. He sat down again and directed a warning glance to Annie and Marie.

"We just finished a meeting at the pavilion to discuss the new rowing program at the university. I'm going to crew a boat, Rory, can you imagine? Puttering about on the lake in a canoe with you has paid off." Edward piled a plate of food for himself while Rory served Annie and Marie. He clapped his brother on the back.

"Congratulations, Eddie! Great news! I shall have to take some photographs of your competitions."

"Yes, please do." He turned to Annie and Marie. "I do not think I have heard Rory mention you before, Miss St. John, Miss Marie. I am certain he could not have mentioned your names, and I forgot. He is not often in town."

"My brother has always been an affable sort of young man," Rory said with an even smile. "He understands, though, that it is not polite to quiz a guest."

Eddie beamed unrepentantly. "I do, but I thought I would try at any rate. I only meant to say that you must be new friends of my brother's, as I feel certain I have met most of his other acquaintances in Seattle."

Eddie grinned at the women, directing a particular look of admiration to Annie.

"That's enough, Eddie!" Rory said sharply. He could have sworn he saw the reflection of his father on Eddie's face, an unpleasant image that reminded him of his father's womanizing.

"You and your brother have the same smile," Annie said with a pointed look in Rory's direction. Rory jerked and stared hard at Annie. Was it true? Did they both share the trait with their father? Rory swallowed hard. No!

"Thank you, Miss St. John," said Eddie. "A high compliment indeed! Rory is well known about town for his smile. I believe I've heard it called 'charming,' 'delightful,' even 'captivating.'" Eddie winked, nodded and bit into a sandwich.

"That will do, Edward," Rory snapped. "You will give Miss St. John and Miss Marie the wrong impression about me, not that Miss St. John, at least, does not already believe I am anything other than a inveterate flirt."

"Well…" Annie said with a grin. "There *is* that."

Marie and Eddie laughed, and even Rory allowed himself a faint reserved, though genuine, smile. He vowed at that moment to change his ways, in the certain knowledge that Annie's good opinion mattered more to him than any other woman's opinion ever had. He promised himself never to favor her with a false smile designed to manipulate or charm her, as had been his habit of many years—a talent he had learned from his father as a youngster.

Rory returned his attention to the group where Eddie regaled them with information regarding his upcoming crewing activities while they ate. Although Eddie continued to attempt to elicit information regarding the Misses St. John's origins, neither of the women, to their credit, gave him any information, deferring instead to Rory, who ignored his brother's inquisitiveness. By the picnic's end, Eddie appeared to have a crush on Annie, and Rory didn't blame him. Not one little bit.

"Rory, you must bring Miss St. John and Miss Marie to the house for dinner one night to meet Mother. I know she would be pleased to make their acquaintance." Eddie smiled wistfully in Annie's direction.

"I don't think…" Rory began uncertainly. What a terrible idea! He never introduced acquaintances to his mother, certainly not women, but Eddie had put him in a difficult position with his innocent suggestion. To now deny Annie and Marie an introduction to his mother would be the height of discourtesy, yet surely the women would understand that his mother would ask more questions than he had answers for, and nor did he want the Misses St. John to attempt any explanations of their origins with rumors of time travel.

"That is…" Rory began again.

"Tomorrow! Come tomorrow evening. I know for a fact that Mother has no engagements. She said you wanted to speak to me anyway, though I cannot imagine what must be of such importance that you set an appointment to speak to your own brother." He bit into a piece of fruit. "Tomorrow!"

"Really, Eddie, I think we must consult with Mother before we descend upon her with guests. Forgive me, ladies. My brother would have you think my mother runs a boarding house such that she can whip up a meal in only a few hours. Eddie, Mother and Cook need to plan a meal before Cook can send a maid out to buy the food." He knew his tone was exasperated, but he felt backed into a corner.

"Oh, don't worry about us, Mr. O'Rourke," Annie said quickly, her cheeks bright red. "Marie and I will probably be busy looking for one of those boarding houses to stay in anyway. We'll catch a meal at the hotel or something. We'll be just fine. You've been so kind." She dropped her eyes to the apple in her hand.

Rory cursed his mishandling of the matter. Clearly, Annie was humiliated by his clumsy attempts to avoid introducing them to his mother. That his mother might look upon either of them with speculative interest as a possible future wife for her eldest son would only make a dinner more uncomfortable.

"A boarding house?" Eddie repeated. "So, you are not just visiting? You have come to live in Seattle? What wonderful news! I am certain my mother might know of some establishments that might be suitable. She seems to know everything."

"Eddie!" Rory remonstrated, but was intercepted by Annie.

"No, Eddie, we *are* just visiting, but we might be here for a while, so we think it best we move out of the hotel and into a boarding house. The expense, you know." Annie finished half-heartedly.

"I shall speak to my mother as soon as I get home."

Rory opened his mouth to forbid his brother to speak to their mother but pressed his lips together and clenched his jaw. That his brother was a good-hearted young man was not in doubt, but the idea of involving their mother in the lodging concerns of two strange young women without family would astonish their mother, and Eddie appeared not to realize that. Rory resolved to speak to Eddie privately before they left the park.

He caught Annie's look of alarm and turned a reassuring smile on her with a slight nod. Annie was a perceptive woman. He trusted she would understand his unspoken message. She returned the nod and turned away.

"I say, Miss St. John, are those your boots that I see behind you?" Eddie asked.

"Yes, they are," Annie responded before Rory could speak.

Had his mother taught the boy no manners? She would never have allowed Rory to be so intrusive as Eddie was behaving today.

"They were tight, so I took them off to rest my feet for a bit."

"Eddie, I trust you are quite finished interrogating Miss St. John on every possible aspect of her life," Rory said dryly. He shot Annie a quick conspiratorial wink. Annie's cheeks flamed, and Rory instantly regretted the casual gesture which no doubt served to reinforce Annie's opinion of him as an incorrigible flirt.

"Ladies, if you do not mind, I think my brother and I will take a short stroll to speak of some family matters. Please relax and finish your luncheon. Joseph is nearby if you need anything. I will return shortly." Rory rose and held out his hand to pull Eddie to his feet.

They moved away from the lawn and stepped onto the walkway.

"I think I must be in trouble," Eddie said with a nervous laugh.

"I think you must be," Rory said flatly. "I am surprised at you, Eddie! Since when has it been good manners to question strangers as you have done today?" Rory held up a hand as his brother opened his mouth to respond. "Never! You bandy about Mother's name, and yet I know she would never tolerate such bold inquisitiveness from you."

"I did not think I was being rude, Rory," Eddie said rather hotly. "I've heard Father quiz people, and people seem to like talking about themselves."

"Well, you're not Father, thank goodness!" Rory barked, his suspicions confirmed. He relented at the startled look on Eddie's face. "What I mean to say is that you must let your behavior in society be guided by Mother. Father is known to be...overly friendly."

"Well, how does one find anything out about anyone if one never asks?" Eddie said in frustration. "If you think I can't tell there's more to the Misses St. John than you're letting on, you're wrong. The way they speak, the way—"

"All you need to know about the Misses St. John is that they are visiting from Chicago. I met them on the train, and they seemed to be in need of some assistance as they are strangers to Seattle. They are currently staying in the Hotel Seattle for a few days, and as you have heard from Miss Annie St. John, she apparently intends to find lodgings. There is no other information that we need to know."

Eddie stopped and stared at him, before throwing a look over his shoulder toward the two women under the trees on the lawn.

"I don't know, Rory. I think you know more than you're saying. I didn't miss the looks exchanged between you and Annie."

"Miss St. John," Rory corrected. "There were no 'looks' exchanged between Miss St. John and myself."

"Well, I hope they stay. I think 'Miss St. John' is beautiful!" Rory turned to follow his eyes. The women had risen. Marie had crossed over to the carriage to talk to Joseph, and Annie watched Rory and his brother.

"Yes, she is," Rory murmured. "They both are, but that should not be your concern, Eddie. You are too young for both of them. And at any rate, as they said, they are only visiting. It would not do to give your heart to someone who cannot stay." Rory realized as soon as he spoke that the words applied to him as well. Regardless of where they came from, the Misses St. John had no intention of staying.

"But they are so delightfully unusual. Not at all like the other girls I know," Eddie said. "Perhaps we could convince them to extend their visit indefinitely." Rory understood his wistful note.

"They *are* unusual," Rory agreed, "almost as if they come from another time." Rory stiffened. Had he actually said it?

"Yes, that's it!" Eddie exclaimed. "I couldn't put my finger on it, but that is exactly it! It's as if they are from a less formal world than the one we live in. Is Chicago so very different from Seattle?"

"No, no, it is not," Rory said. He stared at Annie, who now bent over in the most unladylike fashion to lace one of her boots. "Come, I must help Miss St. John with her footwear."

Rory strode back to the picnic area just in time to seize Annie under her arm as she threatened to topple over in her quest to don her shoes.

"Allow me, Miss St. John," he said with a small grin.

She looked up at him with a reddened face from her exertions. "Oh, thanks. I guess I could have leaned on that tree over there." She stuck her foot into her other boot, and Rory bent on one knee.

"Let me tie them lest you fall over in an ignominious heap." He smiled broadly. "Place your hand upon my shoulder for balance." He pushed the edge of her skirt aside to lace up the small boots.

"There's that smile again, Rory. Now I know where you get it. Your brother has it, and your father has it, too."

Rory looked up at her with a suddenly sober face. "I do not mean to misuse it, Annie, not as my father does. Until today, I did not realize I shared that trait with him. I would change the nature of my smile if I could to present a more sincere expression."

"Don't change anything," Annie said. "Not a single thing," she said in a low voice. She cleared her throat. "So, did you tell Eddie everything?"

Rory, touched by her words, redirected his attention to the task at hand.

"No, certainly not. I love my brother, but he is a bit of a talker. I am not sure I could trust him to be discreet. I had forgotten though that I am meant to speak to him about our father. I may as well tell you that my mother announced yesterday morning that she has asked our father for a divorce. That is why you find him at the hotel. Mother wanted me to break the news to Eddie. Not expecting to see him at the park today, I forgot to speak to him. However, this does not seem the appropriate venue for such a discussion."

"Oh, gosh, I'm sorry, Rory." Rory felt the soft touch of Annie's fingers along his cheek. He turned his face into the palm of her hand and kissed it before jumping up.

Annie's cheeks flamed, and she looked away toward the carriage. He noted she rubbed her hands together.

"I should apologize but find I cannot," Rory said. He cleared his throat. "Come, let us return you to the hotel so that you may rest before dinner tonight."

"You don't have to keep babysitting us, Rory," Annie said in a husky voice. "Marie and I can fend for ourselves. Really."

"I do not 'babysit,' Miss St. John. It is my privilege to escort you to dinner. However, if you feel you wish to dispense with my company, I can oblige you. It is not my intention to force myself upon you and your sister."

"Oh, no! That's not it at all," Annie said. "I just think you must have some kind of life you might want to get back to. Eddie mentioned friends." She said no more.

"I am fortunate in that I do have friends here in Seattle, given that I travel so much, but I do not need to see them every time I am in town. My mother, however, is another story. She does insist on seeing me, and as soon as Eddie mentions you and Miss Marie, I am sure she will want to meet you. I apologize if I seemed reluctant for you to meet my mother. That was not my intention. I sought only to prevent further unanswerable questions. I will speak with her this afternoon but feel certain she would echo Eddie's invitation to dinner tomorrow night. Would that be agreeable to you? Should we ask Miss Marie?"

He looked toward Marie, still conversing with Joseph and Eddie. The younger Miss St. John appeared to have an ease with men, no doubt due to her athletic enterprises. Annie, on the other hand, though more reserved with men, seemed to elicit adoration. At least, she had drawn his.

Rory dropped the sisters off at their hotel and made his way home to wash before hurrying over to his mother's house. He did not care to have her stew about the strange new women in her son's life for overly long. Rory had no doubt his brother had already told his mother about the Misses St. John, and he was anxious to attempt some sort of explanation.

He hopped into his automobile and headed for his mother's house, arriving just as Eddie could be heard regaling his mother with news of Rory's "new friends."

"One is very tall, statuesque like a Grecian goddess," his brother waxed unexpectedly eloquent. "The other sister, Miss Annie St. John, is petite with chestnut hair and eyes of chocolate."

His mother, seated on a sofa in the parlor while Eddie paced in front of her, saw Rory enter and rose to kiss him on the cheek.

"Rory! I have just been hearing of your new friends from your brother, who appears to have become besotted with one of them. How did you meet these young women and where did they come from? Are they from a local family?"

Rory shot his brother a dark look and settled his mother back onto the sofa before taking a seat himself. She poured him a cup of tea.

"Do sit down, Eddie," Rory said. He accepted the tea from his mother. "You speak of the Misses St. John, I believe, Mother. Yes, Eddie is quite taken with them." He sipped his tea, still unsure what he wanted to tell his family.

"The Misses St. John are visiting from Chicago. That is really all I know. I met them on the train. Since we are here together though, perhaps now would be a good time for us to have that discussion you mentioned." He quirked an eyebrow in his mother's direction.

"Oh! Yes, of course, that makes sense," his mother said with a harried look at Eddie, who had taken a seat on the sofa. "Dear, I wanted to talk to you about your father."

Eddie turned to her with interest. "So, Father is to be the subject of the appointment Rory had set for me tomorrow. I am all ears."

"Eddie, Mother finds the subject difficult, and she wanted me to broach the subject first. Since you are neither ignorant nor obtuse, I think it would be best if I were straightforward with you. Mother informed me yesterday that she has asked Father for a divorce."

Rory's mother winced at his directness, and she turned an apprehensive look on her younger son.

Eddie nodded. "I suspected as much. I knew when Father moved to the hotel that he would not be able to come back. You have been less angry since he has been gone, Mother."

Rory smiled at his brother, who had apparently inherited their mother's compassion.

"Yes, you do appear to be more calm, Mother," Rory agreed. "Eddie took that quite well, I think, don't you?"

Mrs. O'Rourke looked from one of her sons to the other in bemusement. "Yes, he did," she murmured. "I thought you would be terribly upset, Eddie. There will be scandal, of course. People will talk."

Rory held back the retort, "Not more than they already do."

"It will blow over in no time at all, Mother. Don't fret," Eddie said. "Father will be fine. He always seems to land on his feet."

"Well, then," their mother said, looking down with pink cheeks and smoothing her skirt. "As long as my sons do not disapprove of me, I shall be fine."

"You know you have my blessing, Mother," Rory murmured.

"And mine," Eddie echoed. He leaned over to kiss her on the cheek. Mrs. O'Rourke cleared her throat.

"Well, tell us more about these young women then," she said. "What do you mean 'they are visiting?' Are they visiting relatives? Eddie mentioned they wished to procure lodgings in a boarding house? I sense a mystery, Rory."

Rory sighed.

"I really do not know much more than I have told you, Mother. They appear to be low on funds and do not wish to stay at the hotel for much longer. I do not know whom they came to visit. It is my understanding they do not have family here."

"Did you offer to assist them, Rory? You were never mean with money. I understand that they are strangers, but they are young ladies. I would think you would have helped them."

Rory's jaw tightened. "Of course I offered assistance, Mother, but they have declined any offer of financial help." Rory was not about to tell his mother of their apparent destitution. To do so would only raise further questions.

"But you will invite them to dinner tomorrow night, won't you, Mother?" Eddie said. He turned to Rory. "I already asked Mother to have them over."

"I do not see how I could not," she said with an affectionate smile at her youngest son. "I am more curious now than ever to meet them. Rory, instead of shedding any light on their origins, has made them sound even more mysterious than you did, Eddie."

"Mother, it is kind of you to invite them, but I would not wish them to be invited to dinner only to be gawked at. Promise me that the dinner will be a small affair, just the family. They are new to town and seem uncertain."

"Of course, dear. Will you take my invitation to them?" She rose to move toward her desk.

"I can take it, Mother," Eddie volunteered enthusiastically.

"No, I will deliver the invitation, Eddie," Rory said dryly. "You have done quite enough today."

Rory left his mother's house shortly thereafter and returned home to attend to some business affairs prior to bathing and dressing for dinner.

"And how are the young ladies today, Mr. O'Rourke?" Mrs. Sanford asked as she brought a cup of tea and a small snack into his office.

"Fine, Mrs. Sanford." Rory looked up with a smile. "I believe they enjoyed the picnic luncheon you prepared immensely—as did my brother, who happened to pop by the park."

"I'm so pleased," Mrs. Sanford responded. "Was there a mishap of some sort? Joseph brought in a bag of wet...em...women's under things and handed them to me with some mention of one of the young ladies falling into the lake? I picked up your clothing for laundering and noted that some of your garments were also slightly damp."

Rory gave her a wry smile. "Yes, as it happens, there was. At their request, I took the ladies out in a canoe, and Miss Annie St. John tried to stand in the canoe to catch her hat, as I recall, and toppled over into the water. I dove in after her."

"Mr. O'Rourke! Thank goodness you were there to save her!"

"Oh, I think she would have managed just fine without me. Her skirts hampered her, but she seemed proficient at treading water. I presume she knows how to swim."

Mrs. Sanford nodded. She bit her lip before speaking. "And the petticoat?" Her eyebrows lifted, and Rory thought he might laugh. Only someone who had been there could understand Annie's rationale.

"Yes, the petticoat. Well, Miss St. John did not wish to abandon plans for the picnic, wet clothing notwithstanding, and she divested herself of any garment she considered unnecessary at the moment so that her dress might dry faster." He looked up at Mrs. Sanford from under his lashes, knowing his cheeks had bronzed.

She stared at him pointedly for a moment but said nothing.

Rory chuckled and rubbed his jaw. He felt very much as if he had not one, but two mothers at the moment.

"Yes, I know, Mrs. Sanford. How could I allow such a thing? Why did I not have the good sense to wrap Miss St. John in a blanket and return her to the hotel for a hot bath and change of clothes? How could I allow her to picnic in damp clothing? Did I mention she removed her boots as well? And finally, why should I return her wet clothing to you for laundering?"

"Oh, no, Mr. Sanford, I would *never* ask the last question regarding laundering. It is my pleasure to wash and dry Miss St. John's clothing." She quirked an eyebrow and continued to regard him.

He sighed. "Thank you, Mrs. Sanford. Please do not regard me with that censuring expression. Had it been you there instead of me, I am not certain you could have resisted Miss St. John's pleas not to abandon the picnic either. I find it hard to deny Miss St. John or her sister anything, as it happens, not that they have asked for much. They are unique."

Mrs. Sanford softened her features and smiled. "Yes, they are indeed. Have you given any more thought to their origins? To their story of time travel?"

Rory nodded. "I almost convinced myself today that their story was true, but I find the notion of time travel fantastical, and I cannot truly believe that they have traveled through time. Yet everything about them would suggest that they have indeed come from the future, for there seems to be no other explanation for their descriptions of their lives, their mannerisms, language or unfamiliarity with this era." He shook his head with a sigh. "And if it were true? Will they stay? Miss Marie has stated most emphatically that she would return to wherever she came from immediately if she could. Miss Annie seems ambivalent. I am not always able to understand her thoughts or her emotions."

"And neither should you, Mr. O'Rourke, if you don't mind my saying so. She is entitled to her own secrets, her own innermost feelings. You sound quite taken with her, Mr. O'Rourke. Rarely, in my experience, do men wish to 'understand' a woman unless they have formed an attachment to her."

Rory looked up quickly, his cheeks heating.

"As Miss St. John said to me only today, there *is* that." He gave Mrs. Sanford a wry smile and nodded. "There *is* that."

"Oh, goodness, Mr. O'Rourke." Mrs. Sanford repeated his sigh. "I wish you the best. I had better leave you to your correspondence. You are dining with the Misses St. John tonight?"

"Yes, and we are all dining with my mother tomorrow night, thanks to my young scallywag of a brother. That is, if Miss St. John and Miss Marie agree. I admit to being nervous about the encounter."

"They will do well, Mr. O'Rourke. Do not worry. It was inevitable that your mother should hear about them." Mrs. Sanford chuckled and left his office.

Rory, no longer able to focus on his correspondence and uninterested in eating, leaned back in his chair and stared out the window onto the city below. He wondered what Annie was doing at that moment. Was she resting? Bathing? Perhaps conversing with her sister? He fervently hoped she hadn't set out on another adventure of wandering the busy streets of Seattle. Two mishaps in one day were more than enough for any one woman. He couldn't endure the thought of her being trampled under yet another oncoming cart, or worse yet— an automobile or a streetcar.

Rory opened his desk drawer and removed his copy of the photograph he had taken the night before. Smiling with wide lips, the expression in her dark eyes somewhat indecipherable, Annie glowed like a jewel in the photograph, like an opal—warm and soft, yet with sparkling depths if one looked closely.

Underneath the photograph laid his ticket on the SS Minnesota, scheduled to leave for the Orient in two weeks' time. He was to photograph Japan and China for the next few months. He had no earthly idea how he was going to board a ship and leave Annie behind, perhaps never to see her again if she disappeared as fast as she had come, and yet he couldn't very well cancel the shoot. The magazine relied upon him.

Rory replaced the photograph in the drawer, laying it on top of the ticket. His seemingly simple life—free of attachment—had become much, much more complicated, and he wasn't entirely unhappy with the situation. If only he could convince Annie to stay.

CHAPTER NINE

Annie closed the door softly, so as not to awaken Marie, and headed down the hall toward the stairs. She whipped through the lobby and down the hotel steps, shamelessly grabbing a handful of brown serge skirt to lift it above her ankles as she descended. Once at street level, she dropped her skirt and touched her small black and brown-ribboned hat to make sure it was firmly seated on her head before boldly crossing the street with the other pedestrians. It seemed likely that no one suspected she was from the future, nor was anyone about to haul her off to jail for modest dress gaffes, so she lifted her chin and returned the smiles of passersby.

Somehow, she'd gotten the impression that she shouldn't walk out alone, that it showed some sort of lack of decorum, but she'd seen women walking alone on the streets from her bedroom window, and had seen no reason why she shouldn't as well. She couldn't possibly stay cooped up in the room all afternoon—not when there was so much to see in the early twentieth century. Knowing Rory would be displeased, even worried if he knew she strolled the streets alone, she determined not to mention her outing to him.

Seattle in 1906 felt a good deal safer than Chicago in 2013. Annie peered into shop windows and even stepped into a few doorways, but retreated from those quickly when she discovered they were cigar stores. One small shop with a fanciful red and yellow striped awning and hardback books in the window caught her eye, and she entered. It appeared to be a small bookstore, and she nodded to the middle-aged woman on the other side of the counter. No coffee bar hissed as a barista steamed milk, no CDs perched on shelves, no oversized lounge chairs took up floor space. The store was lined with wooden shelves of books.

An occasional straight-back wooden chair rested against a wall.

"Do you have a local section?" she asked the saleswoman.

"Local?" the woman repeated.

"Yes, books on Seattle?" Annie said more hesitantly. Was she using the right terminology?

"Certainly. Right this way." The silver-haired woman bustled toward the back of the store and pointed to a shelf. "These are all our books on Seattle and Washington State. There are some picture books too, if you like those. I always do."

"Thank you," Annie said. She wished at the moment that she had money to buy a book, but the issue of money hadn't resolved itself yet. She reminded herself to take it slow. They'd only been in 1906 for a few days. She and Marie had plenty of marketable skills to be able to make a living in this era for however long they were here. Or so she hoped.

She pulled down a few books and looked at them. The covers were the old-fashioned cloth over a board, although many of the books appeared new. She leafed through a few of the books before replacing them and reaching for one of the larger "picture books," as the saleswoman called them. She opened the book and her attention was instantly caught by several pictures with stunning views of Mt. Rainier, seemingly hovering above the horizon on clouds—just as she had seen from the train when they approached the city. A name on the page sprung out. *Photography by Harold O'Rourke, Jr.*

Annie's heart raced as she closed the book and looked at the cover. *Dreams of Seattle* was the title of the book. Rory was listed as both photographer and author. Annie looked up and saw several more pictorial essays by Rory—another of Washington, one of Montana, one of Italy and another of Ireland. With a beaming smile and an inordinate sense of pride, she pulled down the book called *Dreams of Ireland* and leafed through it. Rory clearly loved Ireland and the Irish, as evidenced by the beautiful photographs of lush green landscape both with and without people.

The dedication in the book read simply *For my Irish mother.* Annie scanned the book quickly but didn't want to appear as if she were looking at all the photographs without buying it, so she replaced it and left the shop.

Rory was certainly industrious. She didn't know much about publishing, but it seemed likely that Rory had a contract with a publishing house to produce his pictorial essays. No wonder he traveled so much. She had a sudden vision of being stuck in 1906 with Rory gone for a year on one of his many adventures, and "stuck" it would be. She wasn't at all sure she could bear to stay in the early twentieth century if Rory were somehow not there.

She returned to the hotel and reentered the room, closing the door behind her softly.

"Did you go out by yourself again?" Marie asked as she wandered out of the bedroom in a lovely blue satin wrapper. "You know Rory doesn't want you doing that."

"Well, if I were married to him, I might think that was important, but since I'm not, I'm not overly concerned about what Rory does and doesn't want." Annie could have laughed at herself. Of course, she cared what Rory wanted, thought, said, dreamed, desired, ate or breathed. In fact, they all mattered a great deal to her.

Marie laughed for her. "Oh, please!" she said with a smirk as she dropped into a chair in the sitting room. "You are so hung up on that man, you can't even think straight. Like about how we're going to get home."

Annie pulled her hatpin and removed her hat and black gloves before dropping into the matching chair in an unladylike heap.

"Well, it's just an infatuation with a handsome turn-of-the-century, old-fashioned man with fabulous manners. I'm sure it will pass. As to how we're supposed to get home, I have no idea. I imagine we ought to jump aboard the train again and see if we can't reverse the spell."

"Spell?" Marie asked. "As in witchcraft?"

"No, just time travel," Annie sighed. "How soon do you want to go? Can't we stay awhile?"

"I think this is all very interesting, Annie, but if I don't know that I *can* get back, then I don't see how I can *visit* or stall in trying to return. If I knew we could get back, maybe I wouldn't stress about it so much."

"We don't even have money for train fare," Annie muttered. She avoided looking at her sister.

"Maybe Rory will lend it to us."

"Gosh, no! I don't want to ask him! You've heard him. He doesn't even think we've traveled through time. So, imagine—if we ask him for train fare so we can return in time, he's just going to think we're going to get lost on the train again, and he'll want to accompany us to make sure we're all right. Surely you know him well enough by now to know that's what he would do?"

"Yup, you're right. I'll bet that's exactly what he'd do," Marie groaned. "But if we could get back…if we disappeared on the train, then he would finally know, wouldn't he? And we'd be out of his hair."

Annie shook her head. "And leave him wondering forever what

happened to us? That would be awful. I can't imagine how long and how hard he would look for us if we just disappeared on the train. I don't want to do that to him."

"Annie! We have to do something. We can't stay here."

"I know," Annie said flatly. "I know." Annie really didn't understand why she couldn't stay, but she resisted saying so to Marie who might very well list a dozen practical reasons why they had to return.

Marie must have heard something in her tone.

"Annie? Please say you really understand. I can't leave you here. You don't have a job or money here. You can't mooch off Rory for the rest of your life. Didn't you say that you thought he was engaged?"

Annie drew in a sharp breath. "Oh, man, I'd forgotten. What if he is?"

"You should ask him at some point. I can't believe you didn't ask him today."

Annie shrugged. "I forgot, what with falling in the lake and all."

"So you did," Marie agreed. "Well, ask him at dinner tonight. If you don't, I will."

"I'll ask. Did you take a bath?"

"Yes, I washed my hair with their weird soap and everything."

"I know, I'd kill for some decent shampoo. My hair is still snarled from washing it when we got back. I think we'd better start getting dressed."

"You're really getting into this getting dressed thing, aren't you? Me? I'd just as soon have room service as pack all those clothes on again."

Annie grinned and went into the bedroom to rummage through the boxes for a dinner gown. The saleswoman had said there would be two for each of them.

An hour later, Annie and Marie were perched on the edge of the chairs when Rory arrived. He escorted them down to dinner, complimenting Annie on her peach-colored silk and lace evening gown and Marie on her lavender satin and gauze dress. They entered the dining room and were seated.

Annie stiffened when she saw Rory's father across the room dining with a woman not much older than herself, and she looked away quickly in case Rory noticed, but he had already caught the direction of her gaze. He frowned.

"It is not something I have not seen before, Miss St. John. Please do not trouble yourself."

"I'm so sorry, Rory. How awkward for you."

"At times," he murmured. "By the way, I am reminded that my mother did indeed invite you to dinner tomorrow night. Would that be convenient for you and Miss Marie? I specifically requested she limit the guests to family, just my brother and myself, and she agreed."

Annie looked at Marie who nodded. "Sure, that sounds lovely," Annie said. "Your brother was very determined. I'm sure she finds him hard to resist."

"She does," Rory affirmed with a smile. "Most women do. He is a charming young man."

"It appears to be a family trait," Annie said with a grin.

Rory's face colored, and he dropped his eyes to his menu.

"Rory!" a female voice said. "I thought you were off to the Japan and China as soon as you got back from Montana."

Rory looked up and rose quickly.

"Dani!" he said with enthusiasm as he took the hand of a small, but stunning woman with auburn hair. "I did not know you were coming to town. You said nothing when I left." He nodded toward a tall, blonde man who approached, as handsome as his wife was beautiful. "Stephen."

"We meet again, Rory," Stephen said in a pleasant voice.

"Stephen had to come to town for a few days to take care of some business, and I thought I'd come with him. I brought the kids. Mom is still at the cabin along with Ellie, Robert and their children."

Rory noted the couple looked expectantly at Annie and Marie.

"Mr. and Mrs. Stephen Sadler, may I introduce Miss Annie St. John and Miss Marie St. John."

"How do you do?" Annie enunciated, feeling a bit like Eliza Doolittle in *My Fair Lady*.

Marie was more casual in her greeting. "Hi!"

Dani blinked and looked toward Rory for a moment before returning her attention to Annie and her sister.

"I don't think we've met before," Dani said. "Where are you from, girls?" Annie was struck by Dani's casual lack of formality. It felt familiar in some way.

"Chicago," they said in unison.

Dani narrowed her eyes, and looked at her husband before addressing herself to Rory.

"Did you meet on the train, Rory? The one returning from Whitefish?"

"I did, Dani. How did you know?" Rory threw Annie a warning glance.

"Because I think these girls are from my neck of the woods." Dani grinned. "Am I right, ladies?"

Annie stiffened. "2013?"

Dani grinned. "Class of 2012. I'll bet you girls are very, very confused right now. How long have you been here?"

"A little over two days," Marie said with a broad smile. "I am *so* glad to meet you, Dani!"

"I think we should probably sit down with you, Rory. Do you mind? Stephen and I were planning to have a quick dinner before getting back to the kids at the house, but I think our plans have just changed."

"Yes, I think they have," Stephen agreed with an amused smile.

"Not at all, please do." In a state of confusion, Rory gestured toward the table. How could Dani possibly know of their story? He signaled the waiter, who placed two more settings at the table and another chair.

Stephen seated his wife next to Annie and took a seat by Rory.

"And I imagine you are very confused right now as well, my friend, aren't you?" He directed his comments to Rory.

Dani covered Annie's gloved hand with her own. "Look at you! Only here a few days and already wearing gloves and beautiful dinner gowns. I would never have known you just got here by looking at you. Is this your influence, Rory? Because unless they were wearing fanny packs, which no one does anymore, Annie and Marie arrived without a cent in their pockets, am I right?"

Annie nodded wordlessly, staring at the exquisitely beautiful turn-of-the-century woman who knew the word "fanny pack."

"You're right about that! Dani, tell me right away. Is there a way back?" Marie asked.

Dani beamed and nodded. "Yes, you can get back. In fact, up until a few years ago, I went back every year to visit my mother. Now, she's here with me so I don't try it. It's not foolproof, though." She turned to look at Rory. "Are you all right, Rory? How did you find them?"

Annie saw Rory swallow hard. His look of incredulity made her want to reach out and hug him to reassure him that the world hadn't gone crazy. He certainly looked as if he thought so.

"I met Miss St. John and Miss Marie on the train." His voice was low, uncertain.

Dani chuckled. "I'm sure there was more to it than that." Dani looked around and dropped her voice to a whisper. "Did they tell you they were time travelers?"

Annie breathed a sigh of relief. Yes, they were! Thank goodness someone believed them. Two someones, she thought from the continuing look of kindly amusement on Stephen's face.

Rory's eyes widened, and then he drew his brows together. He scanned the faces at the table as if they were all strangers to him. He had fought hard against the concept of time travel, and Annie worried that he was going to continue to resist the idea, even in the face of four people who confirmed the facts.

Rory's shoulders sagged, and he seemed to relent as he sat back in his seat. "Yes, they did, but I did not believe them." He looked to Stephen with a faint smile. "Please tell me that you did not come from the future as well, Stephen, before we attended college together?"

Stephen chuckled and patted Rory on the back. "No, no, Rory. I am like you. I was born in the nineteenth century. However, I *have* been to the future with Dani. Did you not wonder at my 'jeans' when you stayed with us?"

Rory grinned weakly. "Well, I assumed you preferred a tighter-fitting dungaree than I had seen in the past, that is all. I actually fancied a pair for myself, but I hated to say so." He turned his attention to Annie and Marie.

"I apologize for doubting you, ladies. How alone you must have felt when suddenly dropped into the past, and I not able to understand or help."

"But you did, Rory. You've helped us tremendously. The clothes, the hotel…" Annie gestured toward the dining room. She didn't miss the look of surprise Dani exchanged with her husband.

"From the sounds of it, Rory, you helped the girls a great deal, just like Stephen helped me." Dani gave her husband an affectionate smile, and his love for her showed on his face. Annie's heart fluttered. Was it possible? Dani seemed to be surviving in the past, and it sounded like she had figured out a way to go back and forth in time. Annie looked at Rory, who continued to study the group as if he'd never seen any of them before. She had the distinct impression he avoided her eyes in particular, though.

"It was nothing," Rory murmured. The table hushed as the waiter returned to take their orders. In the confusion, no one had scanned a menu, and there was a moment of chaos while everyone figured out what they wanted to eat.

"How do we get back?" Marie asked bluntly as soon as the waiter left.

Dani shot a quick look in Rory's direction before responding. "Well, I'm assuming you fell asleep and woke up in 1906, right? Just like I did in 1901. You just reverse the process. Get back on the train heading east, make sure you fall asleep again sometime before you get to Wenatchee, and you should wake up back in your time, 2013. I don't know what Wenatchee has to do with anything, but the area seems to be a catalyst for the time travel. I have a friend who also traveled back in time, and the same thing happened to her."

"How many of us are there?" Annie asked with wide eyes. She suddenly had visions of a multitude of time travelers from the future wandering the streets of Seattle in the early twentieth century.

"Just Ellie, me, and now you two. That's all I know of."

"Ellie?" Rory said in a sharp voice. "Ellie Chamberlain? No wonder you and she seem so much alike. I could not quite put my finger on it." He leaned his elbows on the table in an uncharacteristically ill-mannered gesture and pressed his face into his hands. "I am overwhelmed."

"You will get used to it, Rory," Stephen said. "We all have."

Rory looked up. "I cannot imagine that day." He looked at Dani. "And you and Ellie chose to stay. Did neither of you wish to return to your own time?"

"I was wondering the same thing," Marie said.

"I don't think Ellie ever did. I did, but only because my mother was sick. I didn't want to leave Stephen, but I had to go. He came with me for a bit but had to return to take care of Susan. Now that I have children I really don't want to travel back. Truthfully, you guys, although I've been lucky, there is always a possibility that you either can't get back or can't return here even if you want to."

"I think it's very interesting here, but I really want to get back," Marie chimed in. "The sooner, the better."

"And you, Annie?" Dani asked.

All eyes turned on Annie, and her face flamed. She avoided Rory's eyes. No, she didn't want to return. She wanted to stay where Rory was...with him. Her sister would never understand. Rory would probably be shocked and embarrassed. After all, she didn't know how he felt about her. He'd never shown her anything but kindness really, and a little flirtation.

"Well, I'm sure she wants to return, too," Marie said in answer to Annie's silence, "though I'm not sure she's in a particular hurry. Still, you're right, Dani. We didn't have a cent on us when we traveled, and neither of us can stay much longer mooching off Rory. It feels kind of weird."

Dani chuckled. "I do understand the feeling, Marie. So, you're ambivalent, Annie?"

"Yes," Annie said in a low voice. She kept her eyes on her glass as she took a sip of water. "That sounds about right."

"I don't blame you," Dani said. "Well, what is the plan? When I traveled back in time, Ellie came to my rescue with clothes, but I can see

Rory took care of that. I assume you have enough clothes for a while? That's a big thing here…the clothes."

Annie and Marie nodded.

"I know Rory is still probably digesting this, but when do you want to return? Marie said 'the sooner, the better.' Does that mean tomorrow?" Dani looked from Annie to Marie.

Annie's eyes widened, and her heart skipped several beats. She couldn't bear to look at Rory, unsure of what she might see on his face. Relief? Disappointment? That famous smile of his? No, this wouldn't be the right time for him to turn on the charm.

"We haven't really talked about it," Annie said. "We agreed to have dinner with Rory's mother tomorrow night?"

"Your mother wouldn't mind if we skipped that, would she, Rory?" Marie said. "I feel like I've been away forever."

"Marie! That's not nice. We can wait a day, can't we? We should talk about this in private, I think." Annie gave Rory, Dani and Stephen a wry smile. "Discovering you, Dani, and knowing there's a way back is almost as startling as finding ourselves in 1906."

Dani shot a warning glance over Annie's shoulder, and Annie turned to see the Rory's father approaching. The young woman with him waited at the doorway.

"Good evening, Rory. Miss St. John, Miss Marie. Stephen. Mrs. Sadler. You look very refreshed. I thought you were at your cabin in Montana?"

Everyone nodded, but an uncomfortable silence ensued. Stephen filled the void.

"Yes, we remain at our cabin on Lake McDonald but returned to town for a few days to take care of some business matters. Robert and Ellie Chamberlain are still there. You may know that Rory stayed with us for a few days while photographing the area for the *National and World Magazine*."

"Yes, I heard," Mr. O'Rourke said. He glanced at his son with a veiled expression.

"I hope you are well, Mr. O'Rourke?" Stephen offered. He sent Rory a pointed look, but Rory seemed to ignore him and sipped a glass of wine.

"Yes, thank you for asking. Well, it was good to see you, and you as well, ladies. Good night."

"Good night, Mr. O'Rourke," Annie, Stephen and Dani said in unison. They watched him walk toward the young woman but no one at the table spoke. Rory gulped his glass of wine and poured another.

The waiter brought their food, stalling further discussion for the moment.

"The news will be all over town soon, so I might as well tell you that my mother asked my father for a divorce. He is temporarily living at the hotel." Rory grimaced.

"Oh, Rory," Dani said. "I'm so sorry to hear that. I wish the best for both of them."

"Yes, of course," Stephen said on a gruff note, patting Rory on the back again.

"She is determined," he said. He looked up and directly at Annie. "So, you will return the day after tomorrow? Did I understand that correctly?"

"So soon," Annie murmured. She lowered her eyes, fearful that everyone at the table would know how madly in love with Rory she was. She couldn't stand the thought of leaving, and even the knowledge that she might be able to come back again failed to lessen her misery.

"Yes, it is soon," Rory said. "I had hoped to show you so much more of our time."

"Marie wants to go home," Annie said, as if she spoke only to him.

"I do!" Marie chirped. "I won't ask you to come with us, Dani, but please tell us every detail so we know what to expect."

"There's not much to tell really. Make sure you're asleep before you get to Wenatchee. If you want to take something or someone with you, make sure you're holding it. You'll wake up on the modern train, probably without a ticket, but you'll be all right. You'll wake up in the clothes from 1906, but that's okay, too. Everyone will think you're either really old-fashioned and eccentric or a re-enactor of some sort. And if you want to come back, just reverse the process, but make sure you have your ankle-length dress with you because people flip out when they see jeans or leggings or shorts."

Dani looked to Stephen. "Did I cover everything?"

"I think so, my dear. I understand your desire to return home to your loved ones, Miss St. John."

"Well, I've got one of those, but Annie's a free agent," Marie chuckled.

Stephen and Rory looked at each other in confusion, and Dani laughed. Annie rolled her eyes.

"She means single and unattached, dear," Dani said to Stephen.

"Hey, Rory, we never asked." Marie slid her eyes toward Annie, who stiffened at her sister's coy look. "Are you single and unattached? Annie thought you might be engaged?"

"Marie!" Annie protested.

Dani laughed. "And that's how we do it in the twenty-first century, gents. We just ask."

"Well, not all of us," Annie muttered.

Rory caught her eye and flashed his brilliant smile. "I cannot imagine why you thought I was engaged, Miss St. John. I am not. I am, as you say, 'single and unattached.'"

"There's your answer, girls," Dani said with a chuckle. "So, what happened to your trip to Japan and China, Rory?"

Rory's smile evaporated, and he cast a quick glance toward Annie. "That is still pending. The ship sails in two weeks."

"And you said you'd be gone for six months, right?"

"Approximately, yes. It could be longer."

Annie's heart shriveled. Six months? Without Rory? Single and unattached Rory? Even if she could find a place to stay and a job, what would be the point if Rory were gone?

"Oh!" she said with a catch in her breath. "I didn't know you were leaving," She knew she wasn't hiding anything from the perceptive Dani, or even her own sister, but she hoped she sounded nonchalant enough to keep Rory from discovering how devastated she was at the news.

"Yes," he sighed. "I thought to have your situation resolved by then. And now I find that you will have returned to your home long before I leave for the Orient; therefore, you will no longer need my assistance."

Annie wanted to shriek, *I'll always need you, Rory. Always!* But she pressed her lips together and toyed with her food. Her stomach tightened, and she tried to breathe as she fought against the tears that threatened to erupt.

"Ladies, if you decide to stay or even if you decide to go back and then return, I can help you out. I've been here long enough so I know the ropes." Dani's voice softened.

"Thank you, Dani," Annie said, turning to Dani. "I appreciate that."

"No problem," she responded with a sympathetic smile. Annie had the feeling that Dani saw right through her, saw how she felt about Rory.

Dani went on to ask about the details of their arrival in 1906, and Rory's experiences with them. At the end of their meal, Dani and Stephen rose, and Dani took Annie's hand in her own to pull her close and whisper in her ear.

"Do what you want, Annie. I know your sister wants to return, but you don't have to go if you don't want to. I meant what I said. I can help you here. You can even stay at my house for as long as you need, or you can come back to Montana with us."

"Thank you, Dani. I think Marie and I have to talk about it, though.

I'm not even sure this is right for me." She waved a vague hand around the room, unconsciously including Rory, who stood talking to Stephen and Marie, in her gesture.

"I'm sorry he's leaving so soon. I'll bet he is too," Dani said. "From the sounds of it, I don't think he can delay his trip, but I'll bet he wants to. I've known Rory for about five years, but I don't think I've ever seen that look on his face."

Annie turned a startled look on Dani. "What look?"

Dani surveyed Rory and turned back to Annie. "Well…" She paused. "You know that look men get when they're in love? That kind of vulnerable softening? Like a puppy rolling over on its back?"

Annie couldn't help grinning at the image of Rory exposing his underbelly. "I think so."

"Well, Rory's got it, and he only does it when he looks at you. I don't know what you did to him, but I think he's in love with you."

Annie's heart rolled over, and she leaned back to search Dani's face.

Dani nodded. "Yup!"

Annie looked toward Rory and chuckled nervously. "If that were really true, I'd be the happiest woman on earth."

"So, you're in love with him too? That was fast! I knew it though from the way you look at him." Dani beamed. "So, what are you going to do? Does Rory know how you feel?"

Annie shook her head. "No, and please don't tell him either, Dani. I don't want him to feel obligated or…" Annie wasn't sure of what she wanted, and she couldn't make sense of her chaotic thoughts. "He's going away for a long time, and I don't know what I'd do here without him, to tell you the truth. I can't live off of you, and I don't know how long it would take me to get a job. And honestly? I don't think I would stay if it weren't for Rory. You have to admit life is a bit harder here than in 2012 or 2013."

"They look ready to go. Let's talk about this tomorrow. I'll send a carriage for you tomorrow morning…about ten o'clock? You can come to my house and have tea. I hate to leave Marie out, though. That seems rude, and yet I don't think we can talk privately if she's there. She seems resistant to any thought of you staying here." Dani bit her lip and looked toward Marie, now walking with Stephen and Rory as they left the dining room.

Annie nodded. "Yes, I think that's true. She's a late riser, and doesn't really like to get out of bed before ten. I'll leave before she wakes up, with a note saying I've gone for a walk. She's getting used to my early morning forays into the city streets."

"It's a plan!" Dani said. "I'll see you in the morning."

Annie and Marie said good night to Dani, Stephen and Rory, and headed to their room.

"Well, thank heavens for Dani Sadler," Marie said as they walked down the hall. She looked around and spoke in a low voice. "I can't believe this has happened to other people. Makes you wonder how many people have traveled back here, or why?"

Annie shook her head. "I have no idea." To find love?

"Well, the 'why' question would be your thing anyway," Marie said, "since you inherited Mom's curiosity gene. I'm more interested in how we get back. It doesn't sound too complicated."

"No," Annie answered flatly. Her heart ached.

They reached the room and entered it.

"What's up, Annie?" Marie asked. "Oh, come on, you don't really want to stay here, do you?"

Annie removed her gloves and stepped out of her shoes before dropping into one of the chairs. She eyed her sister.

"And if I did?"

Marie stared hard at her then tossed her head. "Don't be silly. You can't stay here. It's ridiculous. I'm not going to let you. I'll drag you on that train kicking and screaming if I have to."

Annie jumped up to face her taller sister. "Don't talk to me like that, Marie! I'm not a child. You don't have the right to tell me what I can and cannot do."

Marie's eyes widened. They rarely argued. "What are you thinking, Annie? That I'll go back on the train and leave you here? How am I supposed to do that? Just leave you in the past? Gosh, Annie, if you stay here, you'll be dead when I get back. How am I supposed to live with that? And for what? Because you have a crush on Rory? He's leaving. How are you going to live? How are you going to make money? Can't you just accept that we had this little adventure and let it go? At least come back with me now just so we know we can jump through time again. Then you can decide what you want to do after you've been home for a while and things get back to normal."

Marie sank into a chair, and Annie crossed over to the mantle to stare into the cold fireplace.

"Yes, my desire to stay here probably *is* about Rory. I know he's leaving, and I hate the thought. Dani said I could stay with her as long as I needed to. What about if you go back day after tomorrow if you want, and I follow in two weeks after Rory leaves?"

"I think we should go together, Annie," Marie said. "I'm afraid if you don't, you might not be able to get back to 2013. You are the only family I have since Mom and Dad died. I don't want to lose you, too. I love you."

A tear slipped down Annie's face. "I love you, too, Marie...and I'm in love with Rory."

"But he's leaving, Annie." Marie's voice softened. "What good will that do you?"

"I just want to be with him until he leaves."

"Has he asked you to stay with him until he goes?"

Annie shook her head. "No, it never came up. I didn't even know he was leaving until today."

"What if you get stuck here and can't get back? Rory leaves. Then what?"

Annie shrugged. "I don't know. Get a job?"

"Doing what, Annie? What kind of graphic design do they have around here?"

Annie turned to look at her sister, defeat weighing heavy on her shoulders.

"None, I'm sure. Maybe I could paint billboards."

"Come back with me day after tomorrow. Please, Annie." Marie's face crumpled. She *never* cried.

Annie moved toward her sister and knelt beside her to cradle her hands.

"Please don't cry, Marie. I'll go. You're right. This has been fun, but it would be silly for me to stay. I have no job here and no money. Rory will be gone, and there's no use fantasizing about a relationship that might just be all in my head." Annie gave her a watery smile. "Stop crying. You haven't cried since Mom and Dad passed away. It's painful to see."

Marie rubbed her cheeks with the sleeve of her dress. "I know." She squeezed Annie's hand. "I know this is hard for you, Annie, but I think it's best. Maybe I haven't been spending enough time with you at home. I promise I'll leave Alex at home and do more with you."

Annie almost chuckled but didn't have the heart. "Hmmm...tall, dark and handsome Rory, or my tall, blonde and beautiful sister. What a choice."

"I'm not making you choose between us," Marie said. "You're just picking the most realistic thing."

"If you say so, Sis. Nothing, though, has felt more real to me in my life than Rory does."

"You're such a romantic," Marie said. "We'll find you a modern tall, dark and handsome guy."

"I never thought of myself as romantic," Annie murmured. "But no...no guys for me. I don't think I'm every going to feel like this again...about anyone."

CHAPTER TEN

Rory motored down to the hotel around ten o'clock the next morning. Though he had not planned any daytime activities with Annie and Marie the previous evening, he had an overwhelming desire to see Annie, to reassure himself that she was still there, that she had not jumped the morning train and returned to her own time just yet.

For all that he had scoffed at the notion of time travel, a part of him had known there could be no other explanation for the sisters' sudden appearance on the train. Discovering that Dani Sadler and Ellie Chamberlain were also from the twenty-first century made absolute sense. He remembered thinking that Annie and Marie shared similar dialects with Dani and Ellie.

Though Dani had reassured him she knew of no other time travelers, he searched the streets with curiosity. Were there others? Had any of the pedestrians strolling the sidewalks traveled through time? Did time travelers always travel to the early twentieth century? Dani said she had arrived in 1901. He remembered meeting her in the restaurant of the Hotel Seattle so many years ago. If so, what was it about their era that was so attractive to time travelers? Or did they have a choice? It did not appear as if Annie or Marie had a choice about where they traveled. And why had they traveled? What catalyst had brought Annie and Marie or Dani and Ellie to the 1900s? Dani and Ellie had fallen in love and married.

He determined to stop by and visit with Dani and Stephen that afternoon to ask them their thoughts on the matter.

Having arrived at the hotel, he knocked on Annie and Marie's door. There was no answer, and he returned to the lobby to look into the dining room. Annie and Marie were not at breakfast. Had they gone for a walk? He stopped by the desk.

"Have you seen Miss Annie St. John or Miss Marie St. John this morning? They were not expecting me, but there was no answer at their door."

"Yes, Mr. O'Rourke. I did see Miss Annie St. John leave about ten minutes ago, through the front door. I have not seen Miss Marie St. John this morning." The clerk smiled politely.

Rory's heart sank. Not again! Annie had not gone out by herself again. There was no telling what new accident might befall her.

"Thank you," he said hastily. He bolted from the lobby and ran down the front steps of the hotel to scan the street. Traffic moved slowly, streetcars taking the right of way while pedestrians and carriages waited for the cars to pass. He couldn't see Annie anywhere and did not know if he would recognize her as he had no idea what she wore that morning.

He returned to the hotel and hurried up the stairs. Where was Marie? He knocked on the door again.

Finally, the locked clicked, and the door opened. Marie stood inside in a blue wrapper rubbing her eyes.

"Where is Annie?" they asked in unison.

"She left a note saying she'd gone for a walk," Marie said.

"The front desk said she left over ten minutes ago, but I didn't see her in the street. Do you know which direction she might have gone? I really do not think it is wise for her to wander the streets alone."

"I don't either. Let me get dressed, and I'll go look for her."

"No, I will go, Miss St. John. I will make better time if I am able to search through the streets for her alone. It is much too congested to try to drive my car with any speed, and I must go on foot. You should wait here in case she returns and worries that you have gone out without a companion."

"Okay, I'll wait."

Rory hurried out of the hotel once again and made a more concerted effort to find Annie now that he was certain she was no longer in the hotel. For the next several hours, he roamed the streets, stopping often to peer into shop entrances. No Annie. He thought of waylaying a policeman but wondered if that act might be precipitous. Perhaps she had returned to the hotel while he was out, and he had missed her. His heart raced. Downtown Seattle during daylight hours was a relatively safe place for women, unlike the waterfront, but he worried about Annie and her predisposition for mishaps.

He almost ran back to the hotel. Just as he came around the front of the building, he saw Annie stepping down from a carriage. He strode up to her.

"Where on earth have you been?" he demanded.

Annie jumped, so startled was she, and he immediately regretted accosting her.

"You scared me, Rory! I've been to Dani's house if it's any of your business." Annie's eyes looked mutinous, and Rory regretted his hastiness even more.

"I apologize if I frightened you, Annie, it's just that I have been searching for you for hours. I was worried about you." Rory tapped on the carriage to signal the driver he could leave.

"Oh, really? Well, if I'm not mistaken, I told you on the train that you don't get to talk to me like that. You don't own me...or Marie! I appreciate all your help, Rory, I really do, but you're leaving and..." Annie suddenly broke down into tears and buried her face in her hands.

Rory cursed himself. What had he done? He ignored the curious stares of passersby, and took her hands.

"Annie, Annie, please don't cry, dear. I am so sorry I barked at you. You are right. It is not my place to tell you what to do. I can only defend myself by saying that I was concerned for your welfare." He pulled a handkerchief from his jacket and dabbed at her cheeks before pressing it into her hands.

"I'm sorry, too," she hiccupped. "I didn't mean to start blubbering in the street like this. Even in *my* time, people stare at folks crying in public." She dried her eyes and handed him the handkerchief with a sniff.

"Shall we go inside? Perhaps a cup of tea? I did not realize you were visiting with Dani this morning, nor do I think Marie knew. I hope you had a pleasant visit." He held his arm for her. "Of course, I am properly chastised and realize it is not my place to inquire after your whereabouts, but I cannot help myself. I have set myself up as your rescuer, it would seem. Such a lofty goal."

"For a few more weeks, anyway," Annie muttered.

"Or one more day," Rory returned. They climbed the stairs. "Are you unhappy that I am leaving, Annie?"

Annie stopped and looked at him. "What? Of course not! Well, I mean... No! What a great adventure for you!"

Rory eased out a sigh, and his shoulders slumped. "Oh! I thought you meant..."

"What?" Annie continued to climb the stairs. "No, I didn't mean anything. You know Marie wants to leave tomorrow. She's pretty insistent I go with her, so that's probably what we're going to do."

Rory, reaching for the door, froze. "So soon."

"Yes, soon," Annie said. "Could you...?" She nodded toward the door that he held, and he gave himself a shake and pulled it open. They stepped into the lobby.

"It is almost time for luncheon. Would you and Marie care to dine and then motor around the city for a bit?"

"Sure," Annie said without smiling. "I'll go get Marie. I'm sure she's starved. What time is dinner tonight?"

"Eight o'clock. I will pick you up in the carriage at quarter past seven."

"Okay, I'll see you in a few minutes. Hopefully, Marie is dressed for the day."

Following a pleasant lunch, Annie and Marie secured their hats with scarves and climbed into Rory's car. Marie opted to take the back seat, leaving Annie to sit in the front, which suited Rory admirably. Any time spent near Annie was precious to him. He was unclear what had transpired before lunch or why he had inferred that she mourned his upcoming departure, but no more had been said on the subject, and he assumed he had misinterpreted her words. Although she seemed subdued, her words before lunch suggested she wished to return to her own time. He could not stand in her way.

He drove them to the public market where they strolled among the horse-drawn wagons laden with goods, produce and fish. They drove to Green Lake Park and admired the ducks. At Annie's request, he took them down to the waterfront to view the tall ships, which she stated were no longer used for much more than tourist attractions in her time. Annie asked about the steamship in port.

"That is the SS Dakota, owned and operated by the Great Northern Railway, the company which runs the Oriental Limited. Normally, passengers would disembark from the Oriental Limited, rest a day or so, and then sail away to the Orient on either the SS Dakota or the SS Minnesota. In my case, I had a few business matters to attend to in Seattle, so I was not able to sail right away. I am booked on the SS Minnesota when it returns from the Orient."

At the moment, Rory regretted his imminent departure so much, he almost thought of canceling it, contract and commitments notwithstanding. And yet, if Annie were leaving, he knew he would not want to stay in Seattle without her. He hated to think of her imminent departure, but it seemed likely there was nothing he could say to make her stay. Even were he to declare himself, she might choose to leave, unable to bear the thought of spending her life in "the past." Clearly, things were much more modern and comfortable in the twenty-first century, and he could not ask her to give that up.

He gritted his teeth and stared at the steamship. Of course, there was an strong chance that she did not feel as he did, that the occasional soft light in her eyes when she looked at him was nothing more than gratitude or even friendship.

Had Stephen Sadler or Robert Chamberlain ever suffered so much angst for love of their time-traveling women? He regarded Annie, standing next to Marie on the docks and admiring the ships in the bay. How he longed to enfold her into his arms and never let her go, to sail the high seas with her at his side as he photographed the world, or even to sip a cup of tea with her on his porch while she spoke to him of the future.

As if she could read his thoughts, Annie looked over her shoulder and smiled at him, a wide smile that he knew he could not live without.

Rory returned them to the hotel an hour later to bathe and rest before dinner. As soon as he dropped them off, he drove up the hill to the house Stephen and Dani Sadler shared with his sister on their rare visits to Seattle.

On being admitted, he was directed to the sitting room, where Steven and Dani rose to greet him.

"Rory! I can't say I'm surprised to see you here today," Dani said. "Tea?"

"No, thank you," Rory said. He sat down on the sofa. "How are the children?"

"Fine, thank you," Dani said. "They've gone to the park with their nanny."

"And your sister, Susan, and her family?" He directed the question to Stephen.

"They are well. They remained behind in Montana at the cabin for the summer."

"Life seems so simple there. I envy you the cabin," Rory said with a sigh.

Dani gave him a sympathetic glance. "What's troubling you, Rory? Is it still the time traveling?"

He nodded and stared hard at Dani, enough to make Stephen restless.

"You may leave off ogling my wife, Rory. She is as you and I are, with all four limbs."

Dani looked at her husband and chuckled.

Rory blinked and gave his head a quick shake. "Forgive me for staring, Dani, but in light of your recent revelation, I cannot help but see you in a different light. I continue to be mystified, but you, Stephen, seem quite comfortable with this concept of time travel. I am just newly indoctrinated into this world."

"I understand, Rory," Stephen said kindly. "I do not forget how confused I was when I first met Dani." He favored his wife with an affectionate smile.

"I asked Annie to come here this morning, you know," Dani said.

"Yes, I do know. I went to the hotel, quite unannounced, which was my fault, and when I found her missing, I ran the streets like a madman looking for her." Rory noted Dani's look of interest. "That is to say, Miss St. John has a proclivity for accidents, and I worried that something had befallen her. Since I met her only a few short days ago, she has fallen...on me, she has been perilously close to being run over by a horse and wagon in the street, and she has fallen into Lake Washington...to date."

Dani laughed! "Oh my, you have your hands full, don't you?"

"Do I?" Rory said in a bemused tone.

"I would not normally presume to interfere in a fellow's private concerns, Rory, but you do realize that Miss St. John committed to her sister, Miss Marie, to return to the future with her tomorrow, don't you?" Stephen asked.

Rory lowered his head. "I did not know she had firmly decided to go, but I am not surprised. Marie is very eager to have her sister return home with her, and I do not blame her." He raised his head to look at Stephen and Dani. "I cannot stop her, and I do not have that right. As it is, I must leave for the Orient in a few weeks, and I could not stay to take care of Annie should she choose to remain here."

"I told her she could stay with me here or at the cabin in Montana, wherever we are," Dani said.

Rory gave her a grateful look. "What did she say?"

Dani shook her head. "She was polite, and I believe she wants to stay, but she said she has to go back with her sister." Dani covered Rory's clasped hands with one of her own. "Have you asked her to stay, Rory? Have you told her how you feel?"

"Is it so apparent?" Rory said. "I have spent my entire adult life in pursuit of my own pleasures without affinity for any one woman, save my mother," he said with a ragged voice. "And now, I am chained to a woman from the future by love. Yet I do not think the outcome will be as happy as that which you and Stephen have enjoyed. Her sister has a lifelong hold on her that I cannot compete with, and even were Annie to stay, I must leave." He narrowed his eyes. "But perhaps I could follow her to the future when I return from the Orient!" He looked up at Stephen. "You traveled to the future! So, it can be done."

"No, not on your own," Dani said with a shake of her head. "Once she goes, you can't follow her alone, Rory. The only people who can activate the travel seem to be the women who have traveled from the future. At least, that's what we've discovered so far. The only way Stephen could go with me was if I hung onto him. One time, we must have let go when we fell asleep, and I traveled to the future while he ended up on the train in Chicago in 1902. It's not a perfect system. I'd offer to take you, but Stephen and I agreed that I wouldn't travel anymore, especially because of my kids. I can't get stuck in the future with no way to get back to my husband and my kids. So I can't help you."

"No, no, of course not," Rory said. "I would never ask it of you. However, I am disheartened to find that I cannot travel forward on my own."

"There are other avenues, Rory," Stephen said. "I imagine you are not thinking clearly at the moment. You might try telling her how you feel about her. It cannot be easy for her to make a decision to go or stay if she feels there is no future for her here."

"Here in the past," Rory muttered. "A future for her in the past." He looked at Dani. "Do you have any regrets?"

Dani looked at Stephen, and Rory saw that she didn't. "Not a one," she said. "But Stephen let me know pretty early on that he loved me. As I mentioned last night, my mother was ill when I landed in 1901, and I needed to return to be with her. Stephen was going to let me go, but he decided to come with me. We weren't sure if it would work. You might remember. You were on the train that day."

"I do remember," Rory said. He had seen them on the train and then they seemed to disappear, but he had seen them again within a week and thought nothing of it. "That is the unfortunate day that Stephen felt I was taking advantage of you because I thought you were alone. I am still humbled by his anger."

"It is forgotten," Stephen said.

Dani chuckled. "You were such a flirt, Rory."

"Alas, Annie thinks so as well. I have changed, though." Rory smiled softly. "You were speaking of your decision to stay in our time."

"Oh, yes, where was I? Oh, my mother was sick, and I returned to my time, with Stephen, to see her. I made the decision to stay with her until she was well, and then to come back to marry Stephen. But my mother had plenty of support, and she encouraged me to return with Stephen right away. Fortunately, I've been able to see her over the years because I really would have struggled at the idea of never seeing her again. So, no regrets."

Rory rose. "I should return to my house. As you know, my brother finagled a way to invite the Misses St. John to my mother's house for dinner. Thank you for our frank discussion. I have much to think about."

"Good luck, Rory. Please keep us informed. I'll be so sad not to see Annie again, but if she wants to go, I guess there's nothing we can do to stop her. Right, Rory?" Dani gave Rory a pointed look, and he shrugged.

"I imagine not."

Rory returned to his house, defeated. Before entering his office, he directed Joseph to go to the train station and purchase two train tickets to Chicago on the following day for the Misses St. John. He pulled the picture of the sisters from his desk drawer and stared at it for a while before propping it against a lamp on his desktop.

He knew himself to be deeply in love with Annie, but he could find no solution to her imminent departure. Even if she felt a tiny sliver of the love he bore her, she seemed destined to return to the future with her sister—there to live out her life, marry and have children. He couldn't abide the thought.

****

"So, what's this about you going to Dani's house?" Marie said when they returned to the room. "Did you arrange that last night when you saw her?"

Annie knew better than to hope Marie had forgotten. "Well, yes, Dani wanted to talk to me about staying if I wanted to."

"Oh, gosh, not that again!" Marie grumbled as she washed. "You didn't change your mind, did you?"

"No," Annie said. "Last night, before you and I talked, Dani asked me to come by this morning. I told you I'd go back with you and that's what I'm doing."

Marie looked up. "Every time one of these 1900s sorts talks to you, you seem to waver. I wish they would stop trying to convince you that you'd be happy here. I really can't believe that you would."

Annie gave her sister a sharp look. "Dani is not a '1900s sort.' She's been through the same thing, frankly, and she just wanted to talk to me about it. Besides, she knows how I feel about Rory."

"Annie, look, just because she fell in love with someone from the past and chose to stay here doesn't necessarily mean it's right for you. I'll bet if Mom and Dad were alive, you wouldn't even consider this. It would break their heart if you disappeared."

"Marie! I can't believe you said that! That's not fair! They're not alive, so the point is moot. And I told you I'm returning, so can we please drop the subject?"

"All right, all right!" Marie held her hands up in surrender. "Don't bite! I'm sorry. I shouldn't have said that. Let's get ready to go meet Rory's mother. That young Eddie will be there. Such a cute kid. The men in that family clearly have their father's flirtatious ways, don't they?"

"Yes," Annie sighed. "They do." It felt like days since she had seen Rory's particularly brilliant smile, the one he turned on to charm. But she hadn't even known him for days.

"Well, I'm done. I'm going to lie down for a while. I swear I have jet lag or something. I've been sleepy every since I got here. Are you going to nap or...?"

"No," Annie replied. "I think I'll go down to the lobby and see if they have something to read. I'll be back." She went downstairs and scoured the lobby for a newspaper but could find nothing to read. No magazines rested on the occasional tables. If she'd had some money, she would have gone down the street to the bookstore to buy something to read, maybe even one of Rory's pictorial essays, but that wasn't possible.

She had turned to return upstairs when the front door opened, and Mr. O'Rourke and his female companion stepped in. Annie tried to scurry away, but he waylaid her.

"Miss St. John!" he called. Annie stopped and turned. "How have you been since your accident? I did not have an opportunity to speak to you at length last night."

"I'm fine, Mr. O'Rourke," she said. She studied the young woman at his side, who couldn't have been more than twenty-one, if that. Small and petite with dark hair, she smiled warmly.

"May I introduce my friend, Mrs. Letitia Cambridge?" he asked. "Letitia, this is Miss Annie St. John, a friend of my son's."

"How do you do, Miss St. John?" she said sweetly.

What was this girl doing with Rory's father? The answer soon became clear.

"Letitia is the daughter of a colleague of mine, Miss St. John. She was recently widowed. Her husband worked in Alaska, and I have been assisting her with arrangements for financing and housing for herself and her two children." He looked down at Letitia with genuine fondness. "Letitia is like the daughter I never had. I have known her since she was a child."

"Uncle Harold!" Letitia murmured with a blush. "Really! I cannot tell you how grateful I am for his assistance, Miss St. John. I had to move from my home quite unexpectedly as my husband's cousin inherited the house, and Uncle Harold has been so kind to me."

Annie did her best to keep her eyebrows from shooting up. Oh, goodness! This wasn't a romantic relationship at all!

"I'm so sorry to hear of your loss, Mrs. Cambrige."

"Thank you," Letitia said. She blinked rapidly and looked away for a moment.

"Why don't you go round up some tea in the dining room, dear? I'll be right along. Would you care to join us, Miss St. John?"

"Oh, no, I can't," Annie said automatically. "My sister is waiting for me."

"A pity," Mr. O'Rourke said. "I'll be right along, Letitia."

Letitia took the hint and moved away, and Annie turned to leave.

"Wait, Miss St. John, if I could speak with you for a moment?"

Annie turned back to face Mr. O'Rourke.

"I can tell from your expression that you suspected Letitia had another place in my life, but I can assure you, she does not. I know my son is angry with me. He had been for a long time, and perhaps rightly so. The difficulties his mother and I have undergone over the years have not been easy. I have not been a good husband, but despite all, I do still love my wife, and I wanted to ensure that you understood Letitia is not my 'paramour' but a young woman in need."

Annie swallowed hard. What was she supposed to say? Did he want her to pass the message to Rory?

"I understand," she said.

"You seem to have caught my son's attention, Miss St. John. I hardly dared hope any one woman would."

Annie shifted uncomfortable. "Well, I don't know—"

"I do. He appears to be entirely smitten by you. I watch him more carefully than he knows. Although I have my failings, I love my son. I want only the best for him. I do wish you and Rory the utmost happiness."

"Oh, no, we're not..." Annie began, but she let the words trail off.

"Not...?"

"We're not...together."

Mr. O'Rourke's eyebrows did shoot up. "Not 'together?' How is that possible? I have seen the way you look at each other. Whatever impediment is in your way, I hope that you can find resolution soon. I could not bear to see Rory's heart broken."

"I couldn't either," Annie whispered. "He's going away soon, you know."

"Yes, I do know. To the Orient. I do not imagine that he can cancel that journey, as he has been contracted to photograph for a magazine. But I suspect he now wishes he could cancel the trip."

"I wouldn't want him to do that. He loves traveling so much, doesn't he?"

"Yes, he does," Mr. O'Rourke agreed. "Almost as much as he loves photography. And perhaps almost as much as he seems to love you."

Annie smiled. "And you can tell all that from watching us at dinner?"

Mr. O'Rourke twitched his mustache. "I know my son. When I seem him smile without the flirtatious charm, I know that he must be sincere. I saw that last night." Mr. O'Rourke flashed his own charming smile, and Annie succumbed.

"Oh, goodness. He does get that from you, doesn't he?"

"It is an O'Rourke trait, I am afraid—one that has gotten the men in my family into trouble more than once."

"Yes, I can see that."

"I have kept Letitia waiting too long, I'm afraid. Please accept my best wishes, Miss St. John. I hope to see you soon."

Mr. O'Rourke tipped his hat and turned to walk into the dining room. Annie stared after him in bemusement. She didn't doubt that Rory's mother and father had their troubles, but he seemed to genuinely love his son.

****

Rory came for them in a few hours, and Joseph drove them in the carriage up to a residential area called Capitol Hill where his mother lived. Stately Victorian homes and mansions perched above small grassy rises, which bordered wide boulevards with sidewalks. Soft emerald green lawns fronted the homes and curbs. The residential area looked quite modern compared to some of the downtown buildings and landscaping.

"Miss St. John, Miss Marie!" Eddie said as he greeted them on the front steps of the gabled Victorian house. "I am so pleased to see you. My mother has been looking forward to meeting you." He escorted them up to the front door, where a butler took Rory's hat.

Annie, overwhelmed with emotion, smiled tightly. She dreaded their departure on the following day, and consequently dreaded this evening of polite conversation when all she wanted to do was beg Rory to...to what? Keep her? Stay with her? Put up with her? Come back with her? Throw his plans away for her? She didn't know what she wanted, or more to the point, she didn't know how she wanted things to turn out. She knew she wanted Rory, but wanting someone didn't make that person hers.

"Miss St. John, Miss Marie!" Mrs. O'Rourke came forward—a small, petite, dark-haired woman whose vibrancy was unmistakable. She wore a black satin dinner dress, which set her hair off to perfection. Annie herself wore her peach dinner gown and Marie wore her lavender gown from the night before. Rory looked splendid in coat and tails, as did Eddie. Although the men carried their father's height and smile, they had their mother's coloring.

"How delightful that you could come to dinner. Won't you come into the drawing room and have a glass of champagne?" Mrs. O'Rourke led the way to the drawing room, a beautiful, ivy-wallpapered room with soft moss-colored furniture and carpet.

"Rory, pour us a drink, will you?"

Rory poured champagne while his mother, Annie and Marie positioned themselves on the velvet sofa. Eddie perched on a matching chair just opposite, enthusiastically regarding Annie.

"Eddie, dear, could you please stop staring at the ladies?" his mother said in a dry tone. "They are beautiful indeed, but I am certain they are uncomfortable under your scrutiny."

Unabashed, Eddie laughed. "I will try, Mother, but it will not be easy."

Marie laughed, and even Annie managed a chuckle. The boy was irrepressible.

"Are you well, Annie?" Rory whispered as he bent to hand her a drink. "You are quiet this evening."

"I'm fine, thank you, Rory. Just tired, I think. Maybe stressed."

"Stressed?" Eddie caught part of the exchange. "What does that mean?"

Annie colored, and Marie nudged her in the ribs. "Oh, sorry, an old Chicago expression. Ummm…stressed, anxious."

"And what has made you anxious, Miss St. John?" Mrs. O'Rourke asked. Rory had taken a seat near his brother and awaited her answer. "I certainly hope not our invitation to dinner. We are all family here."

"No, no," Annie murmured. "Probably just about returning tomorrow…to Chicago."

"What?" Eddie said. "Returning to Chicago? Tomorrow? But you only just got here, didn't you?" He looked toward his brother. "Rory, you didn't say they were going back so soon. Can you not stay longer?"

"Eddie!" Rory remonstrated. "Do not harangue the ladies. They were only visiting Seattle for a few days and now they must return. I did not really know myself until today that they would leave so soon."

"I agree with Rory, dear. You must not implore them so. It isn't polite." She turned to Annie and Marie. "My youngest son is quite taken with you. He has talked of nothing all day except the beautiful Misses St. John, and his crewing team." She beamed at him with pride. "Though I am disappointed not to be able to see more of you as well, I can understand your desire to return home. I have not been to Chicago for many years. Tell us about the city. It must have changed so much."

Annie and Marie exchanged glances.

"Well..." Marie began.

"It has changed much, Mother, even I can assure you of that. It has grown large, crowded and busy, much like Seattle has. I am not sure you would like it."

"Oh, dear, Rory, you will give the ladies a poor opinion of me. I am not such a fuddy-duddy that I begrudge a city its vibrancy. Your father and I loved Chicago, especially the opera and the symphony. Tell me, do they still have the cabarets?" Mrs. O'Rourke pressed a hand to her throat, and her cheeks reddened. "I must say those were very risqué, but I so enjoyed those, and Rory's father indulged my every whim." Her face took on a wistful expression.

Annie noticed that Rory and Eddie regarded her with surprise.

"Mother, you surprise me," Rory said faintly. "Cabarets?"

"What are cabarets?" Eddie said.

"Nightclubs," Mrs. O'Rourke said. "With dancing and drinking and decadent shows—all very exciting for a young married couple. Not at all suitable for you, young man." She wagged a finger at her youngest son and rose. "I think dinner must be ready. Shall we?"

Annie looked at Marie and breathed a quiet sigh of relief. She supposed they still had a cabaret or two in Chicago, but she really had no idea. Marie might know that better, as her social life was more active than Annie's.

They made their way into the dining room—a massive, high-ceilinged room centered on a table for twenty or so guests. Annie surveyed the room with awe. Three large crystal chandeliers lit the room with brilliant light. Pale yellow and gold-patterned wallpaper adorned the walls, topped by various paintings with Northwest themes of evergreen trees and water. The place settings, silverware and crystal stemware were stunning. Rory's family was clearly very wealthy, but Annie had already known that.

They settled at one end of the table. Mrs. O'Rourke took the seat at the head of the table with Marie to her left and Annie to her right. She placed Rory next to Annie, and Eddie next to Marie.

Dinner was delightful. Luckily, Eddie and Mrs. O'Rourke kept up a lively banter because Annie and Marie were uncertain of what to say. Rory seemed quiet.

They had reached the dinner course when the butler entered the room and whispered in Mrs. O'Rourke's ear.

"Tell him I have guests and cannot see him," she spoke in a low voice, but Annie heard her and apparently so did Eddie.

"Who is it, Mother? Is it Father?" His mother nodded. "I'd like to see him." He jumped up and left the room. The butler followed him.

"Forgive my son's manners, ladies. His father has stopped by quite out of the blue, and he has not seen him in some days. I will just go see what he wants." She rose from the table but slipped back into her seat as Eddie dragged his father back into the dining room.

"Father, meet Miss Annie St. John and Miss Marie St. John."

"Eddie! What on earth—" Rory jumped up. "Sir, why would you come to this house unannounced at dinnertime?"

Mr. O'Rourke looked thoroughly confused. "I apologize. I did not know you had company, my dear. I was on the verge of leaving but Eddie brought me in here without, I might add, explaining that you had guests. I imagine that is what Smith was trying to tell me when Eddie grabbed my arm."

"We were almost done," Mrs. O'Rourke said. "Miss St. John, Miss Marie, this is my husband, Harold O'Rourke, Senior."

"We've met," Annie said with a warm smile and a nod in his direction.

"Yes, at the hotel," Mr. O'Rourke said. "So nice to see you again."

Annie noted that Rory gave her a strange look, but she ignored him. The man clearly only had eyes for his wife. Whatever womanizing he had done in the past didn't change the look of love on his face.

"I will meet you in the library, Hal. Rory, please take our guests back to the drawing room for coffee. Thank you."

Mrs. O'Rourke flounced out of the dining room, a tiny package of irate black satin and curls. Mr. O'Rourke sighed with a rueful expression and turned to follow her.

"My deepest apologies," Rory muttered. "My family has gone mad." He retook his seat and downed his glass of champagne.

"I would bet words are flying furiously right about now, especially from Mother," Eddie said with a certain amount of undutiful glee. Rory shot his brother a baleful glance.

"Your father still seems to be very much in love with your mother, Rory," Annie offered tentatively. "I think that whatever is going on between them isn't because they don't love each other."

"He did seem repentant," Marie offered. "I don't know what he's done, but he seems nice."

"Love?" Rory turned to Annie. "Love? My father doesn't know the meaning of the word. He has put my mother through years of grief. You saw him with that young woman at the restaurant…just last night."

"Letitia Cambridge," Annie said. "Yes, I met her this morning."

"My father had the gall to introduce his…" Rory searched for words.

Annie couldn't resist the imp on her shoulder. "Paramour?"

Rory gave her a narrow look. "Yes, that will do. Paramour. My father introduced her to you?"

Annie relented. Rory looked absolutely furious.

"Yes, but Rory, he says she's the daughter of a colleague, an old friend. Letitia is recently widowed, and he's been helping her getting settled. I think her husband worked in Alaska."

Rory stared hard at her. "Cambridge?" He looked at Eddie. "Mr. Cambridge from the bank? Didn't he have a daughter who moved to Alaska?"

Eddie nodded. "Yes, that sounds right."

"He assured me that it wasn't what it looked like, Rory. He loves you, you know. Both of you," Annie said. She downed her own glass of champagne with the feeling that she was way in over her head.

Rory drew in a deep breath. "I do not doubt that, Annie, and although perhaps this time, my father is not flaunting an affair, he has treated my mother abominably for many years."

"Maybe he's sorry. Maybe that's what he came here to say," Marie said.

Rory shook his head. "I do not think my mother would have him back. She was quite adamant about obtaining a divorce when I spoke to her only a few days ago."

"Would you be upset if they reconciled, Rory? I can't tell." Annie tilted her head to study his expression.

Rory regarded her for a moment, his eyes softening. "Perhaps a few days ago, I might have argued the matter, but for some reason, I feel more empathetic at the moment regarding matters of the heart."

Annie caught her breath. Her heart thumped loudly as she warmed under his gaze.

Chapter Eleven

"You? Empathetic? Since when?" Eddie hooted and broke the magical moment between Rory and Annie. Marie chuckled at Eddie's laughter.

At that moment, Rory's mother reentered the dining room, followed by his father. Rory's mother gave him a sheepish glance before she took the seat that his father pulled out.

"Our apologies for being away so long. Your father is going to have dessert and coffee with us."

Rory studied both his parents—as did everyone else in the room, he suspected. He caught Annie's eye, and she nodded with a smile. He could almost hear her thinking. Yes, it did appear as if his parents had some thought to reconcile. His mother had blushed when she was seated, and his father had laid her napkin solicitously in her lap before taking a seat across the table next to Marie.

He wished the best for his parents if that was indeed their plan. He had known them to treat each other with kind affection throughout his childhood, but something had changed over the past few years, bringing his mother to tears more times than he cared to say. Still, if his mother was prepared to forgive her husband, and his father did truly love her, as Annie had surmised, then perhaps their marriage could survive. He certainly hoped so.

At the moment, he had his own concerns—namely Annie. It had not yet been discussed, but he would pick them up and deliver them to the train tomorrow morning—a moment he dreaded with all his heart. How on earth was he going to say goodbye to Annie? It wasn't as if they might exchange a bit of correspondence once she left. How could he be assured they reached their destination safely? Unable to think clearly at the moment, he thought they might telegraph him when they arrived, but it seemed unlikely that a telegram would reach him from the future. There were so many unanswered questions, so many uncertainties.

Should he try to travel to the future with Annie as Stephen had done with Dani? No, again, he wasn't thinking clearly. Dani had said that one of the travelers from the future must accompany them to cross through time. If he saw Annie safely to her home in the future, she would only have to turn around and accompany him to ensure he was able to return. Such a conundrum. Of course, there was always the possibility that he might like the future and wish to stay there.

He looked across the table at his mother, his father and Eddie. His traveling had always been a source of grief for his mother. He could only imagine how she might feel if he were to travel to another century.

And Annie. How might Annie feel if he traveled with her? She had not invited him. She had given no hint that she wished him to travel to the future with her. On rare occasions, he thought he saw something in her eyes, a warmth, perhaps even an affection when she regarded him, but that was hardly enough for him to assume that she loved him.

"What do you think, Rory?" his mother asked.

"I apologize, Mother. I was distracted. What do I think about what?"

Rory's mother repeated the question, and Rory did his best to focus on the subject at hand, which was Eddie's crewing team.

On the way back to the hotel, Rory sat in silence, debating his options—of which there were almost none, but he could not let Annie go without telling her how he felt. When they reached the hotel, he asked if Annie and Marie cared to take a stroll in the warm evening air. Fortunately for him, Marie declined, stating she wished to return to the room, but Annie acquiesced.

He tucked her hand in his.

"You know that I wished to speak to you alone, I think," Rory began. He returned the polite nods of several passersby. His heart pounded, and his mouth had gone dry. He felt like a gangly young boy courting for the first time, and he missed the confidence he had once felt with women. Annie humbled him, and he felt uncertain with her.

He heard a sharp intake of breath from her, but her voice was nonchalant.

"No, really? Why didn't you just say so?"

"It would have been impolite for me to say, 'Excuse me, Marie, could you go to your room, so I could talk to Annie alone?'"

"Yes, I suppose so," she answered quietly. "What's up?"

"Up?"

"I'm sorry, I'm nervous, Rory. That means…what did you want to talk to me about, in this case?"

"Ah… What's up?" He repeated the words.

"Rory," Annie said in a warning tone.

"Yes, what's up. Well, what I wish to say is…" Rory swallowed hard. "You know, for all my flirtatious ways, which you have shown me are markedly similar to my father's, I feel as shy as a schoolboy at the moment." He paused and stopped to face her, taking her hands in his. "I love you, Annie. I know it seems premature to declare myself, and yet those are the words I want to say to you…*am* compelled to say to you. I love you."

Annie opened her mouth as if to protest.

"No, hear me out. I know you have committed to returning to your own time with your sister, and I understand you must go, but I wanted you to know how I felt about you before you leave."

"Oh, Rory," she sighed.

Rory's heart seemed to stop. Annie was about to tell him she regarded him kindly but did not return his feelings. He had never been in this position before, and had no earthly idea what to do, but he thought he could not bear to hear the words.

"No, say nothing, Annie," he said in a strangled voice. "I only wished to express my feelings for you, but in no way are you obligated to return those sentiments. And as I give the matter more thought, I realize that by declaring myself, I have put you in the most uncomfortable position. I know you are grateful for the assistance I have rendered you and your sister, which was minimal at best, and you must now struggle with expressing appreciation and yet disabusing me of any notions beyond gratitude and a measure of friendship. Please forgive me, Miss St. John. I only hope I can forgive myself for placing you in this untenable position."

He held out a rigid arm. "Come, let me return you to the hotel. I meant to tell you that I have your train tickets for tomorrow and will have Joseph pick you up in the morning at six-thirty. The train leaves at ten past seven. They will serve breakfast aboard the train. Joseph will be in possession of a small amount of currency to see you on your way."

They had only taken a few steps from the hotel stairs, and Rory was able to return Annie to the door of the hotel in the amount of time he took to speak. That she arrived out of breath due to his brisk pace troubled him, but he needed to leave so that she would not see his pain. His most fervent hope at the moment was that he had not caused her undue discomfort with his declaration.

He nodded. "Good night, Miss St. John." Rory ran down the stairs and jumped into the carriage, banging the side of it as he shut the door. The carriage moved forward with a jerk. He looked out to see Annie standing at the top of the stairs, seemingly stunned and staring after him. He resolutely turned his face away.

Rory leaned out of the carriage opposite the hotel and shouted, "Anywhere but home, Joseph!" He could not stomach returning to his silent house at the moment. Even the solitary pleasure of his dark room failed to entice him.

Joseph slowed the carriage several blocks away and came to a standstill in front of a club. A perceptive man, his driver understood that what Rory needed most at the moment was a stiff drink.

"Thank you, Joseph. I do not know how long I shall be."

"I'll wait, Mr. O'Rourke."

"If I am not out in an hour, come and get me. I shall have drunk myself quite under the table by that time, I would say."

Joseph tipped his cap. "Yes, sir."

Rory was admitted by the doorman into the building—a small supper and dancing club. He had been to the club on several occasions previously but always with friends. The maître d' recognized him.

"Mr. O'Rourke! It's good to see you. Are you accompanied?" The maître d' searched behind him as if to find his companions.

"No, I'm afraid I'm quite on my own this evening, Raymond. Do you have a private table? Something out of the way?"

"Yes, Mr. O'Rourke," the small, wiry man in coattails said. "Right this way." Raymond led him toward a series of small booths along the far edge of the wood-paneled walls. An orchestra played on the dais.

"Rory!" a female voice called out to him. "Mr. O'Rourke!"

Rory stopped and looked to his left. Miss Washburn called out to him and stood to wave, though he hardly recognized her. Her costume of bright red with a matching feather headdress seemed out of keeping with the proper young lady who had accompanied her parents. She sat with several other young women and men at a circular table near the dance floor.

"Come sit with us," she called.

Rory sighed. He was really in no mood for company—however, neither was he desirous of being alone.

"Thank you, Raymond. I shall join Miss Washburn's party." The maître d' nodded and faded away.

Rory approached the table and took the empty chair next to Miss Washburn.

"Rory! How delightful to see you. I had hoped to see you at the hotel at dinner tonight, but you weren't there." She pretended to pout, a typically flirtatious gesture that Rory had once enjoyed. It left him cold now.

He attempted to rally his old self, and forced a bright smile to his face.

"I am saddened that I was not able to see you then, Miss Washburn. I was having dinner with my mother. But here we are at night's end."

"Please call me Shirley," she said. "Your blue eyes, Rory. Goodness, they quite take my breath away." She placed a delicate hand to her heart. Rory had seen the motion many times, designed to pull a man's eyes toward a woman's neckline and beyond. He had appreciated the ploy in the past but was unmoved this time, and frustrated by his apathy.

"Thank you, Miss...Shirley. How do you come to be here tonight? Do you frequent the clubs often?"

Rory was interrupted by the waiter, who took his drink order and an order for a round for the table.

"Yes, I do," Shirley responded. "I love to go dancing. My parents are not aware, of course. They think I am staying with my friend, Sara. You wouldn't tell them if you saw them, would you?" She put a tempting finger to her lips.

Rory was not tempted. He hadn't thought about it before, but Annie never employed such tactics to draw attention to herself. No, Annie simply fell down often.

Rory downed his drink, and quickly signaled for another.

"Not at all, Shirley."

"I can't tell you how pleased I was to discover that the beautiful young ladies at your table the other night were your cousins, Rory. I lost hope when I saw your eyes sparkle as you regarded them, especially the smaller of the two. But my hopes were renewed when you reported they were family...whether they are cousins or sisters." She grinned coyly.

Rory smiled briefly and nodded. He seemed to have no words. Had he spent them all on Annie?

Several of Shirley's companions rose to dance, and she eyed him pointedly. When he failed to respond, she asked him point blank.

"Would you like to dance, Rory?"

Rory, staring at his glass, almost jumped. "Dance?" His drink was delivered, and he tossed it back.

He rose. "Do forgive me, Miss Washburn. I find I am not feeling well and must leave. It was a pleasure to see you again." He nodded and turned away, feeling like a cad at the look of disappointment on Miss Washburn's face.

Joseph, chatting with other drivers, turned and hurried to the carriage to open the door.

"I know, Joseph, that was quick. Drive around."

Over the next half-hour, Rory argued with himself about returning to the hotel to seek out Annie and press his case. It was the wrong thing to do, he knew it, and yet had he really tried hard enough? Had he put forth as much effort in convincing her of his love as he could have? He could not let her go without letting her know how much he loved her, and he was prepared to lay bare his soul and promise her anything. He would even go with her to the future if she would have him.

He pulled out his pocket watch. Half past ten. He leaned his head out of the window.

"Joseph! To the Hotel Seattle!"

****

"Are you asleep?" Annie whispered. She had been sitting in the window of the sitting room for the past half-hour watching the nightlife of the city. Pedestrians strolled, often arm in arm. A few automobiles drove by. The clopping of a horse's hooves as it pulled the occasional carriage could be heard.

Marie, in bed, turned over as Annie peeked in the door.

"Not really. I'm way too excited to go home. Well, nervous about the time travel part of it. What if we can't get back?"

Annie came to sit on the bed, and Marie reached for the bedside lamp.

"Dani said she's done it a lot. I don't think you have anything to worry about."

"Me? You mean us," Marie said.

"Us." Annie nodded. "He told me he loved me, Marie."

"What?" Marie pushed herself up in bed. "Oh, for goodness' sake! Why did he do that?"

"Well, maybe because he does," Annie said dryly.

"Don't tell me. Did he beg you to stay?"

"Actually, no," Annie said. "By the time he was done speaking, my head was spinning. He told me he loved me, and then almost right away said he was sorry he'd said anything—something about how I probably felt only gratitude and he shouldn't impose or something—and then he practically threw me into the hotel and took off in the carriage."

"Well, good!" Marie said. "He's right. He has done a lot for you, for us, and you'll never know if you feel just gratitude or real love."

Annie looked at her sister with a beatific smile. "You've got to be kidding, chickie. I *am* grateful, you betcha. And I'm in love for the first time in my life."

Marie pulled her legs up underneath her and crossed her arms over her knees.

"Don't do this, Annie. We've already talked about this."

"Well, that was before Rory told me he loved me. Of course, I didn't get a chance to say anything back to him because he kind of lost it, frankly."

"Annie, I really think you need to come back with me, even if it's only for a little while, just to get your head on straight. Remember, he's leaving. He'll be gone for what...six months? If you still feel the same way, you can come back then."

Annie eyed her sister thoughtfully. "That does sound sensible, doesn't it?"

"Well, yeah! I'm not the one with my head in the clouds...or the swirling black hole we fell into."

"Okay, I agree," Annie said. "But no fussing in six months when I come back...if I can come back."

"No fussing," Marie said. "Besides, I'll be married by then and have my hands full with my own love life. I won't have time to meddle in yours."

Annie chuckled. Knowing that Rory loved her made everything seem possible, warmer, brighter. She would miss him terribly, couldn't even think about it at the moment, but she would return in six months.

Annie awoke early the next morning and shook Marie.

"We have to get going. The train leaves early this morning. We'll have to eat breakfast on the train. Rory should be here soon."

Annie ran around the room stuffing clothing into bags and boxes.

"What should we do with the clothes? We can't take them with us. Maybe Rory can return them? No, they've been worn. What do we do with them?"

Marie crawled out of bed. "We'll carry the clothes out to the carriage and ask Rory to hang onto them, or donate them to charity or something. We still have to wear something today, though. Last day for the corset!" she chuckled.

"I hate to throw all this stuff back in his face. Maybe he'll hang onto the clothes until I come back?"

Marie stopped to stare. "Are you going to tell him you're coming back? Oh, gee, Annie, what if you don't? What if you can't? You might break the guy's heart."

Annie turned to look at her sister. "I thought I would," she murmured. "In fact, I'm sure I should tell him. I want him to know how I feel. I didn't get a chance to say a word last night."

"Do what you want," Marie shrugged. "He'll probably have Mrs. Sanford hang onto the stuff anyway." She slipped into her unmentionables and laced her corset with ease, pulling out a lavender skirt and bolo jacket to wear over her white shirtwaist.

Annie had struggled into her corset already, and retrieved a chocolate brown suit from a box to wear over a pale yellow shirtwaist. She threw her hair on top of her head, and turned to work on Marie's hair.

"I can't say I'll miss the hats," Annie muttered. "These things are huge. Maybe they get smaller in the next six months."

Marie gave her a pointed look in the mirror but said nothing.

"Okay, let's go," Annie said, grabbing boxes and bags. She checked the clock over the mantle. "I'm not sure why Rory isn't here yet, but we can be ready and waiting downstairs when he gets here. We're cutting it close."

They lugged their packages down the stairs to the sounds of giggles, and arrived in the lobby to find Joseph waiting, cap in hand. He ran forward to grab as many bags and boxes as he could.

"If you'll just follow me to the carriage, miss, I'll come back for the rest of your things. We are running a little bit late."

Annie froze and searched beyond him.

"Where is Mr. O'Rourke?" she asked, a feeling of dread robbing her of air.

"I'm not sure, ma'am. He left in the car early this morning. He told me to take you to the train station. I have your tickets and some money for you."

Marie turned wide eyes on Annie. "Oh, gee," she muttered.

Annie swallowed hard and almost bit through her lip. "I have to talk to him. I have to talk to him," she said. "Where did he go, Joseph?"

"You already asked him, Annie. He said he doesn't know."

Joseph nodded, and moved toward the door, his arms laden with packages.

Marie grabbed Annie's arm to pull her. "Come on!"

"Miss St. John, Miss Marie!" Mr. O'Rourke called out, stopping at the front desk to pick up a newspaper. "Do you leave this morning, then?"

"Yes, we're on our way to the train station," Marie said. Annie's throat seemed to have closed.

"You were here such a short time," he said with a voice of regret. "I know Rory will miss you, as will my youngest son, Eddie, I suppose." He smiled.

"Do you know where Rory is?" Annie managed to eke out. "I thought he'd see us off on the train."

"I do know where he is, Miss St. John, as I saw him here at the hotel late last night. I believe he had a few errands to run this morning and then had plans to visit with his mother this morning to discuss a matter of importance."

"Errands? His mother?" Annie said. She checked the clock behind the desk. "So, he didn't plan to see us off at the train station?" Tears welled up in her eyes, and she blinked them back. She couldn't break down.

"I am not sure about that, Miss St. John. May I take a message for him?"

Joseph ran back in and grabbed the rest of the bags. "Ladies, we must leave if we are to get to the train station on time!"

Marie pulled Annie's arm again. "We have to go, Annie. Goodbye, Mr. O'Rourke."

"Safe journey, Miss St. John." He raised his hand in a wave.

Annie opened her mouth to speak. What was she supposed to say? *Tell him I love him?* Marie had pulled her to the doorway. No time to write a note.

Annie turned. "Mr. O'Rourke!" she called. "Tell Rory I love him!" She thought she saw him nod and smile before Marie pulled her out of the building and down the stairs.

Joseph held open the door, and they climbed in. No sooner had they taken a seat than the carriage lurched forward. The ride was exciting, if nothing else. A few pedestrians jumped out of the way, and several carts hastily maneuvered over to the curb.

Annie heard the whistle of the train as they careened around the corner of the station. Joseph pulled up to the sidewalk with a flourish, and jumped off to open the carriage door. Marie and Annie stepped down, and Joseph handed them their tickets and an envelope.

"Hurry, you only have a few minutes before the train leaves. You still have to present your tickets."

Marie took off toward the station in an athletic jog, hanging onto her hat with one hand and clutching her skirts with the other.

"Thank you, Joseph! Say goodbye to Mr. O'Rourke for me." Annie ran after Marie, holding her own hat and skirts. A hiss of steam from the train startled her, and her ticket flew from her hand.

"Wait!" she called after Marie, who had already barreled through the door of the station. Annie ran after her ticket and missed the curb, falling to her hands and knees. Her hat flew off her head, pulling her hair along with it.

"Oh, my love, you are so clumsy," Rory said as he ran toward her from the station. Annie saw his car parked outside the front door. "Come, dearest!" He hauled her up and steadied her on her feet. Her hair hung about her shoulders, and passersby stared at her curiously, but she barely noticed them.

She threw herself in Rory's arms.

"I love you, Rory. I love you, I love you, I love you!" She pulled his head to hers and kissed him. His lips were warm, firm, soft, perfect! Rory slid his arms around her waist and pressed her against him.

"Annie, Annie! Come on!" Marie popped her head back out of the station door and waved. "Let's go!"

"Wait, Annie!" Rory said. "Please wait. I love you. I want to marry you. Now! Here is a marriage license, and here is a ticket to accompany me to the Orient. Please say you'll come with me. If you won't, I won't go. I will stay here, but please do not leave me. I do not think I can live without you!"

"Annie!" Marie shouted. "Come on!"

Annie turned in her sister's direction and waved her away. "Go! Go, Marie! I'm staying. I'm getting married! Just go! I love you, Sis. I'll see you soon!"

Marie hesitated and looked over her shoulder toward the train. "I love you too, Annie! Take care of her, Rory! Six months! I expect to see you all in six months! Bye!" She ran back through the door, and exited the building in seconds to hop onto the train with her skirts lifted to her knees. In the fashion of the great black and white movies, she clung to the railing, kissed her hand and waved it at them as the train pulled away.

Annie jumped up and down and waved back. "See you soon, Marie!" she shouted. The train's whistle drowned out her words, but she knew Marie saw her before the conductor pulled her inside.

Tears flowed down Annie's face as she watched the train move away. Black smoke billowed from the engine.

"I know how much you will miss your sister, Annie," Rory said. He pulled out her handkerchief and dabbed at her eyes as he had done once before.

"Ya know? I think I would miss you more, Rory. I love you. I was so terrified when you didn't come for us this morning. I wanted to tell you last night that I loved you, but you went off in a tizzy, and I didn't get a chance."

"Tizzy indeed," he murmured. "I consulted with my father last night, and he contacted his friend, the city clerk, to obtain the license early this morning, while I dashed off to the port to purchase your ticket—all with the fervent hope that you would stay. I am not sure what 'tizzy' means, but it sounds as if it accurately represents the chaos of the last eight hours."

He pressed his lips against hers again.

"Can we do this in public?" Annie pulled back and looked around, but they seemed to be alone on the walkway at the station's entrance.

"If not, we shall start a new fashion. I am sure that life with you will involve many new customs and fashions."

"Oh, you betcha it will." Annie grinned. "Where's my hat? That's going to be one of the first things to go," she said. Rory bent to pick it up for her. "And my skirts are getting hemmed above my ankles…just a bit, so I stop tripping over them."

"The first time I saw you trip, you wore only those very close-fitting black things you call capris. No skirt was to blame then."

"Oh, that's right," Annie said with a sly smile. "That's the first time you held me in your arms."

"Ah, yes, I remember now." He gave her a brilliant smile.

"Don't you think you can flash that smile at me, Mr. O'Rourke, and I just fall into your arms."

"But you have fallen into my arms, Miss St. John—more than once."

"Well, yes, I have, haven't I?" She pulled his head toward hers again. "You know, I really do love your smile. Don't ever stop, no matter how much I tease you."

"I cannot, Annie. Even my heart smiles for you."

EPILOGUE

Edward checked his watch. 7:20 a.m. His daughter looked around.

"Are you sure they said they'd be here at seven, Dad?

"Yes, I'm pretty sure they said they would meet me for breakfast." He shook his head. "I must be getting senile," he chuckled. "This isn't the first time I've lost young women on this train. Actually, I think it's the third time. There was one young lady...she was so nice. A teacher? I can't remember her name. Wait! Ellie...like my grandmother. That's right. And then, there was another young woman about five years ago. We were going to have coffee or something, I think?" He shook his head. "What was her name? Danielle? No, not Danielle. That was grandma's best friend. I can't remember." He shook his head. "And now the two girls. I just met them a few hours ago, and I only remember the little one's name. Annie."

"Well, Dad, you need to stop picking up these young girls." His daughter grinned at him.

"Very funny, dear," he said dryly. "We should go ahead and order breakfast. I have a feeling that I might not see either one of them again. Everyone seems to get off somewhere around Wenatchee. Must be an exciting town. Maybe I should get off the train one day when we're in the station and see why everyone disappears there. Kind of like a Bermuda Triangle, I think."

His daughter called the waiter over, and they placed their order.

"Annie," he said thoughtfully. "Didn't my grandmother have a friend called Annie? Married to some famous photographer. Seems they traveled a lot together, all over the world. Their kids always had wild stories about their travels. The parents took them everywhere, kind of an early home..." He paused. "What do you all call that nowadays?"

460

"Homeschooling, Dad."

"Yeah, homeschooling. Annie O'Rourke, that was her name. Boy, when Grandma Ellie, Dani and Annie got together, it was a hoot. Those women were kind of ahead of their time, you know? I guess you'd call it progressive these days." He smiled. "They sure loved trains, those women. Talked about them all the time. Trains, traveling and time. I never really understood what they were talking about."

ABOUT THE AUTHOR

BESS MCBRIDE is the best-selling author of over twenty time travel romances as well as contemporary, historical, romantic suspense and light paranormal romances. She loves to hear from readers, and you can contact her at bessmcbride@gmail.com or visit her website at www.bessmcbride.com, as well as connect with her on Facebook and Twitter. She also writes short cozy mysteries as Minnie Crockwell, and you can find her website at minniecrockwell@gmail.com.